9/17

means. The flow of his brilliant, scathingly funny and often controversial
journalism was undiminished.

Marcus Clarke died in 1881, aged only thirty-five. *For the Term of
His Natural Life* has been filmed numerous times and remains the great
nineteenth-century Australian novel, an unparalleled evocation of the
brutal penal

ROHAN WILSON is the author of two novels: *The Roving Party* (2011), which won the *Australian*/Vogel Literary Award, a New South Wales Premier's Literary Award and a Tasmanian Literary Prize; and *To Name Those Lost* (2014), which won a Victorian Premier's Literary Award and an Adelaide Festival Award for Literature. He grew up in Tasmania and lives in Queensland.

ALSO BY MARCUS CLARKE

FICTION

Long Odds

NON-FICTION

Old Tales of a Young Country
Australian Tales
The Marcus Clarke Memorial Volume

For the Term of His Natural Life
Marcus Clarke

Text Publishing Melbourne Australia

textclassics.com.au
textpublishing.com.au

The Text Publishing Company
Swann House
22 William Street
Melbourne Victoria 3000
Australia

First published 1874
This edition published by The Text Publishing Company 2016

Cover design by WH Chong
Page design by Text
Typeset by Jessica Horrocks

Printed in Australia by Griffin Press, an Accredited ISO AS/NZS 14001:2004 Environmental Management System printer

Primary print ISBN: 9781925355659
Ebook ISBN: 9781925410099
Creator: Clarke, Marcus, 1846–1881, author.
Title: For the term of his natural life / by Marcus Clarke ; introduced by Rohan Wilson.
Series: Text classics.
Dewey Number: A823.1

CONTENTS

The Unluckiest Man
Who Ever Lived
by Rohan Wilson

VISIT a gift shop in Tasmania. Beyond the plush tigers and devils, the Huon pine key rings, the wilderness postcards and the dried lavender, somewhere in a corner on a low bookshelf you'll find a copy of *For the Term of His Natural Life*. Marcus Clarke's fictional history, first published in book form in 1874, is the face Tasmania presents to the world. It's how we explain our idiosyncrasies. Read this, we say, and you'll understand. Read this, and see where we come from. You could be in Hobart, Strahan, Burnie or Bicheno. It doesn't matter. There's always a gift shop, always a copy of Clarke's great book.

I first encountered Clarke in a gift shop. My father, a peerless cray fisherman, docked his boat full of pots at the Port Arthur jetty and let us out to explore. It was the school holidays, sometime in the late 1980s. I was terrified. I knew all about Port Arthur. I knew it was haunted by ghosts and was the site of unspecified horrors. We had breakfast in the café— the same café where Martin Bryant would later commit his infamous massacre—and after we ate I went straight for the gifts. I remember holding Clarke's book and looking at the cover, which depicted men in chains and men in cells. Something about the expressions of those men told me that the real story of Port Arthur was not the ghosts. The real story was what had happened to the prisoners. To a young, easily scared boy, that story seemed too forbidding.

It would be another two decades before I finally read *For the Term of His Natural Life*: the tale of Rufus Dawes, the unluckiest man who ever lived, who is transported to Van Diemen's Land after being framed for the murder of his father. On being transported, he survives a series of ever more unlucky events—a mutiny, a failed suicide attempt, a gutsy rescue mission—before eventually arriving at Port Arthur, where the worst luck of all awaits. The only person who can save him, the forthright colonial girl Sylvia Vickers, has married his sworn enemy, the cruel overseer Maurice Frere. After suffering a bout of pneumonia, Sylvia forgets that it was Rufus who rescued her and Maurice from starvation at the Sarah Island prison settlement. This is the last arrow of outrageous fortune that poor Rufus can take. He descends into misery. But his suffering is not yet complete. Just when it appears things can get no worse for Rufus, the roguish John Rex arrives to steal his identity and his inheritance.

If all this sounds nightmarish, then that is more or less the point. Clarke wrote the original serialisation of *His*

Natural Life in the early 1870s, almost twenty years after transportation to the island had ceased and the colony had been renamed Tasmania. By then, convictism was already history. Like many people, Clarke found the period fascinating. He began a series of articles for the *Australasian* called 'Old Stories Retold', which looked at some of the nastiest aspects of convict life. He researched, he interviewed and he travelled. And soon the articles morphed into something much larger. In this regard, Clarke's novel is perhaps best understood as Australia's first major work of historical fiction, and it begins the nation-building project of capturing, in narrative form, the process of our becoming. That process in Tasmania, of course, was one of brutal penal servitude.

There is no more potent a symbol of transportation than Port Arthur. Nowadays, the Penitentiary has lost much of its Gothic power. The ruins of it stand peacefully in the forest of the Eaglehawk Peninsula, just as the remains of the Roman past stand in forests all over Europe. Perhaps its chief function is to remind us that we don't have access to the past, only to its mediated restorations. (The English artist John Glover used the imagery of Roman ruins in his paintings until he came to Van Diemen's Land in 1831, whereupon he started filling the holes in his landscapes with frolicking Aborigines, which served a similar thematic purpose.) It's easy to imagine the young English-born journalist Marcus Clarke visiting Port Arthur in 1870, while the prison was still in operation, and hearing the stories of how hard life had been in the early days. He was surely overwhelmed by the horror of what he heard and saw, or at least that's the impression you get from reading *For the Term of His Natural Life*. And in no small measure it was his writing which ensured that Port Arthur became the pre-eminent symbol of the humiliation and suffering visited upon the convict class.

This is reflected in the sensationalist nature of the novel. The bad luck that Rufus Dawes suffers often strains credulity—but, as incredible as much of the action appears, most of it has a basis in the historical records. The final ship to leave the Sarah Island settlement was in fact commandeered by its convict crew and sailed to South America, as Clarke portrays. A group of escaping prisoners, finding themselves lost in the wilderness, did in fact resort to cannibalism to survive, as Clarke portrays. Convicts were flogged to death. They were stretched on racks. They were locked in isolation. These stories are resituated, combined and tidied up, as is the way with historical fiction. This does not diminish their power. Rather, *For the Term of His Natural Life* reads like a distillation of the convict experience. It feels like the full breadth of the past brought down to five hundred pages.

*

Early in the novel, Clarke tries to probe how convict life may have felt to the men and women subjected to it. The narrator suggests that ordinary people, 'chained and degraded, fed like dogs, employed as beasts of burden, driven to...daily toil with threats and blows, and herded with wretches' in the manner of the Sarah Island convicts, would 'die, perhaps, or go mad'.

> No human creature could describe to what depth of personal abasement and self-loathing one week of such a life would plunge him...As one whom in

a desert, seeking for a face, should come to a pool of blood, and seeing his own reflection, fly—so would such a one hasten from the contemplation of his own degrading agony. Imagine such torment endured for six years!

That type of sublime suffering is beyond our comprehension. The passage is memorable not merely because it draws a distinction between the comfortable present of the narrator and the horrific past of which he speaks, but also because in the drawing of this distinction we see the task of the author laid bare. How could Clarke ever have hoped to capture what really happened? Could he ever have described those feelings and experiences accurately? We see Clarke confronting the past as something genuinely unknowable and unfathomable. It is the question that troubles all writers of history, but especially the writer of historical fiction, who has to mediate the human experience of the past for readers in the present and future. It is rare to see this question tackled as openly as Clarke does here.

In the years after his book first appeared, Marcus Clarke worked for the Public Library of Victoria, having been fired from various positions at newspapers around Melbourne. He spoke with a stammer, which was apparently not a hindrance. He drank. He socialised a little too much. He wrote in every form he could—short fiction, stage play, history, essay, even poetry. None of it amounted to much. He died, bankrupt, in 1881, leaving behind a wife and six children. He also left behind the foundation work of Australian fiction.

The last word on the book belongs to Martin Frobisher, the narrator of Michael Meehan's brilliant, innovative novel *Below the Styx* (2010). Meehan merges fiction with a biographical investigation into Clarke and the body of work he left behind. His character Frobisher, a publisher locked away for murdering his wife, takes it upon himself to write the definitive Clarke biography. In Frobisher's view, *For the Term of His Natural Life* is 'an excellent example for all of us in how not to go about putting a novel together. And with luck, just a few of us might show ourselves capable of making the same mistakes.' Marcus Clarke's novel, for all its faults, stands alone in the Australian literary canon as a monument to wild genius.

For the Term of His Natural Life

PREFACE

THE convict of fiction has been hitherto shown only at the beginning or at the end of his career. Either his exile has been the mysterious end to his misdeeds, or he has appeared upon the scene to claim interest by reason of an equally unintelligible love of crime acquired during his experience in a penal settlement. Charles Reade has drawn the interior of a house of correction in England, and Victor Hugo has shown how a French convict fares after the fulfilment of his sentence. But no writer—so far as I am aware—has attempted to depict the dismal condition of a felon during his term of transportation.

I have endeavoured in "His Natural Life" to set forth the working and results of an English system of transportation carefully considered and carried out under official supervision; and to illustrate in the manner best calculated, as I think, to attract general attention, the inexpediency of again allowing offenders against the law to be herded together in places remote from the wholesome influence of public opinion, and to be submitted to a discipline which must necessarily depend for its just administration upon the personal character and temper of their gaolers.

Some of the events narrated are doubtless tragic and terrible; but I hold it needful to my purpose to record them, for they are events which have actually occurred, and which, if the blunders which produce them be repeated, must infallibly occur again. It is true that the British Government have ceased to deport the criminals of England, but the method of punishment, of which that deportation was a part, is still in existence. Port Blair is a Port Arthur filled with Indian-men instead of Englishmen; and, within the last year, France has established, at New Caledonia, a penal settlement which will, in the natural course of things, repeat in its annals the history of Macquarie Harbour and of Norfolk Island.

M.C.
MELBOURNE, AUSTRALIA

PROLOGUE

ON the evening of May 3, 1827, the garden of a large red-brick bow-windowed mansion called North End House, which, enclosed in spacious grounds, stands on the eastern height of Hampstead Heath, between Finchley Road and the Chestnut Avenue, was the scene of a domestic tragedy.

Three persons were the actors in it. One was an old man, whose white hair and wrinkled face gave token that he was at least sixty years of age. He stood erect with his back to the wall, which separates the garden from the Heath, in the attitude of one surprised into sudden passion, and held uplifted the heavy ebon cane upon which he was ordinarily accustomed to lean. He was confronted by a man of two-and-twenty, unusually tall and athletic of figure, dressed in rough seafaring clothes, and who held in his arms, protecting her, a lady of middle age. The face of the young man wore an expression of horror-stricken astonishment, and the slight frame of the grey-haired woman was convulsed with sobs.

These three people were Sir Richard Devine, his wife, and his only son Richard, who had returned from abroad that morning.

"So, madam," said Sir Richard, in the high-strung accents which in crises of great mental agony are common to the most self-restrained of us, "you have been for twenty years a living lie! For twenty years you have cheated and mocked me. For twenty years—in company with a scoundrel whose name is a byword for all that is profligate and base—you have laughed at me for a credulous and hood-winked fool; and now, because I dared to raise my hand to that reckless boy, you confess your shame, and glory in the confession!"

"Mother, dear mother!" cried the young man, in a paroxysm of grief, "say that you did not mean those words; you said them but in anger! See, I am calm now, and he may strike me if he will."

Lady Devine shuddered, creeping close, as though to hide herself in the broad bosom of her son.

The old man continued: "I married you, Ellinor Wade, for your beauty; you married me for my fortune. I was a plebeian, a ship's carpenter; you were well born, your father was a man of fashion, a gambler, the friend of rakes and prodigals. I was rich. I had been knighted. I was in favour at Court. He wanted money, and he sold you. I paid the price he asked, but there was nothing of your cousin, my Lord Bellasis and Wotton, in the bond."

"Spare me, sir, spare me!" said Lady Ellinor faintly.

"Spare you! Ay, you have spared me, have you not? Look ye," he cried, in sudden fury, "I am not to be fooled so easily. Your family are proud. Colonel Wade has other daughters. Your lover, my Lord Bellasis, even now, thinks to retrieve his broken fortunes by marriage. You have confessed your shame. To-morrow your father, your sisters, all the world, shall know the story you have told me!"

"By Heaven, sir, you will not do this!" burst out the young man.

"Silence, *bastard*!" cried Sir Richard. "Ay, bite your lips; the word is of your precious mother's making!"

Lady Devine slipped through her son's arms and fell on her knees at her husband's feet.

"Do not do this, Richard. I have been faithful to you for two-and-twenty years. I have borne all the slights and insults you have heaped upon me. The shameful secret of my early love broke from me when in your rage, you threatened him. Let me go away; kill me; but do not shame me."

Sir Richard, who had turned to walk away, stopped suddenly, and his great white eyebrows came together in his red face with a savage scowl. He laughed, and in that laugh his fury seemed to congeal into a cold and cruel hate.

"You would preserve your good name then. You would conceal this disgrace from the world. You shall have your wish—upon one condition."

"What is it, sir?" she asked, rising, but trembling with terror, as she stood with drooping arms and widely opened eyes.

The old man looked at her for an instant, and then said slowly,—

"That this impostor, who so long has falsely borne my name, has wrongfully squandered my money, and unlawfully eaten my bread, shall pack! That he abandon for ever the name he has usurped, keep himself from my sight, and never set foot again in house of mine."

"You would not part me from my only son!" cried the wretched woman.

"Take him with you to his father then."

Richard Devine gently loosed the arms that again clung around his neck, kissed the pale face, and turned his own—scarcely less pale—towards the old man.

"I owe you no duty," he said. "You have always hated and reviled me. When by your violence you drove me from your house, you set spies to watch me in the life I had chosen. I have nothing in common with you. I have long felt it. Now when I learn for the first time whose son I really am, I rejoice to think that I have less to thank you for than I once believed. I accept the terms you offer. I will go. Nay, mother, think of your good name."

Sir Richard Devine laughed again. "I am glad to see you are so well disposed. Listen now. To-night I send for Quaid to alter my will. My sister's son, Maurice Frere, shall be my heir in your stead. I give you nothing. You leave this house in an hour. You change your name; you never by word or deed make claim on me or mine. No matter what strait or poverty you plead—if even your life should hang upon the issue—the instant I hear that there exists on earth one who calls himself Richard Devine, that instant shall your mother's shame become a public scandal. You know me. I keep my word. I return in an hour, madam; let me find him gone."

He passed them, upright, as if upborne by passion, strode down the garden with the vigour that anger lends, and took the road to London.

"Richard!" cried the poor mother. "Forgive me, my son! I have ruined you."

Richard Devine tossed his black hair from his brow in sudden passion of love and grief.

"Mother, dear mother, do not weep," he said. "I am not worthy of your tears. Forgive! It is I—impetuous and ungrateful during all your years of sorrow—who most need forgiveness. Let me share your burden that I may lighten it. He is just. It is fitting that I go. I can earn a name—a name that I need not blush to bear nor you to hear. I am strong. I can work. The world is wide. Farewell! my own mother!"

"Not yet, not yet! Ah! see he has taken the Belsize Road. Oh, Richard, pray Heaven they may not meet."

"Tush! They will not meet! You are pale, you faint!"

"A terror of I know not what coming evil overpowers me. I tremble for the future. Oh, Richard, Richard! forgive me! pray for me."

"Hush, dearest! Come, let me lead you in. I will write. I will send you news of me once at least, ere I depart. So—you are calmer, mother!"

*

Sir Richard Devine, knight, shipbuilder, naval contractor, and millionaire, was the son of a Harwich boat carpenter. Early left an orphan with a sister to support, he soon reduced his sole aim in life to the accumulation of money. In the Harwich boat-shed, nearly fifty years before, he had contracted—in defiance of prophesied failure—to build the *Hastings* sloop of war for His Majesty King George the Third's Lords of the Admiralty. This contract was the thin end of that wedge which eventually split the mighty oak block of Government patronage into three-deckers and ships of the line; which did good service under Pellew, Parker, Nelson, Hood; which exfoliated and ramified into huge dockyards at Plymouth, Portsmouth, and Sheerness, and bore, as its buds and flowers, countless barrels of measly pork and maggoty biscuit. The sole aim of the coarse, pushing and hard-headed son of Dick Devine was to make money. He had cringed and crawled and fluttered and blustered, had licked the dust off great men's shoes, and danced attendance in great men's ante-chambers. Nothing was too low, nothing too high for him. A shrewd man of business, a thorough master of his trade, troubled with no scruples of honour or of delicacy, he made money rapidly, and saved it when made. The first hint that the public received of his wealth was in 1796, when Mr. Devine, one of the shipwrights to the Government, and a comparatively young man of forty-four or thereabouts, subscribed five thousand pounds to the Loyalty Loan raised to prosecute the French war. In 1805, after doing good, and it was hinted not unprofitable, service in the trial of Lord Melville, the Treasurer of the Navy, he married his sister to a wealthy Bristol merchant, one Anthony Frere, and married himself to Ellinor Wade, the eldest daughter of Colonel Wotton Wade, a boon companion of the Regent, and uncle by marriage of a remarkable scamp and dandy, Lord Bellasis. At that time, what with lucky speculations in the Funds—assisted, it was whispered, by secret intelligence from France during the stormy years of '13, '14, and '15—and the legitimate profit on his Government contracts, he had accumulated a princely fortune, and could afford to live in princely magnificence. But the old-man-of-the-sea burden of parsimony and avarice which he had voluntarily taken upon him was not to be shaken off, and the only show he made of his wealth was by purchasing, on his knighthood, the rambling but comfortable house at Hampstead, and ostensibly retiring from active business.

His retirement was not a happy one. He was a stern father and a severe master. His servants hated, and his wife feared him. His only son Richard appeared to inherit his father's strong will and imperious manner. Under careful supervision and a just rule he might have been guided to good; but left to his own devices outside, and galled by the iron yoke of parental discipline at home, he became reckless and prodigal. The mother—poor, timid Ellinor, who had been rudely torn from the love of her youth, her cousin, Lord Bellasis—tried to restrain him, but the headstrong boy, though owning for his mother that strong love which is often a part of such violent natures, proved intractable, and after three years of parental feud, he went off to the Continent, to pursue there the same reckless life which in London had offended Sir Richard. Sir Richard, upon this, sent for Maurice Frere, his sister's son—the abolition of the slave trade had ruined the Bristol House of Frere—and bought for him a commission in a marching regiment, hinting darkly of special favours to come. His open preference for his nephew had galled to the quick his sensitive wife, who contrasted with some heart-pangs the gallant prodigality of her father with the niggardly economy of her husband. Between the houses of *parvenu* Devine and long-descended Wotton Wade there had long been little love. Sir Richard felt that the colonel despised him for a city knight, and had heard that over claret and cards Lord Bellasis and his friends had often lamented the hard fortune which gave the beauty, Ellinor, to so sordid a bridegroom. Armigell Esmé Wade, Viscount Bellasis and Wotton, was a product of his time. Of good family (his ancestor, Armigell, was reputed to have landed in America before Gilbert or Raleigh), he had inherited his manor of Bellasis, or Belsize, from one Sir Esmé Wade, ambassador from Queen Elizabeth to the King of Spain in the delicate matter of Mendoza, and afterwards counsellor to James I, and Lieutenant of the Tower. This Esmé was a man of dark devices. It was he who negotiated with Mary Stuart for Elizabeth; it was he who wormed out of Cobham the evidence against the great Raleigh. He became rich, and his sister (the widow of Henry de Kirkhaven, Lord of Hemfleet) marrying into the family of the Wottons, the wealth of the house was further increased by the union of her daughter Sybil with Marmaduke Wade. Marmaduke Wade was a Lord of the Admiralty, and a patron of Pepys, who in his diary (July 17, 1668) speaks of visiting him at Belsize. He was raised to the peerage in 1667 by the title of Baron Bellasis and Wotton, and married for his second wife Anne, daughter of Philip Stanhope, second Earl of Chesterfield. Allied to this powerful house, the family tree of Wotton Wade grew and flourished.

In 1784, Philip, third Baron, married the celebrated beauty, Miss Povey, and had issue Armigell Esmé, in whose person the family prudence seemed to have run itself out.

The fourth Lord Bellasis combined the daring of Armigell, the adventurer, with the evil disposition of Esmé, the Lieutenant of the Tower. No sooner had he become master of his fortune than he took to dice, drink, and debauchery with all the extravagance of the last century. He was foremost in every riot, most notorious of all the notorious "bloods" of the day.

Horace Walpole, in one of his letters to Selwyn in 1785, mentions a fact which may stand for a page of narrative. "Young Wade," he says, "is reported to have lost one thousand guineas last night to that vulgarest of all the Bourbons, the Duc de Chartres, and they say the fool is not yet nineteen." From a pigeon Armigell

Wade became a hawk, and at thirty years of age, having lost together with his estates all chance of winning the one woman who might have saved him—his cousin Ellinor—he became that most unhappy of all beings, a well-born blackleg. When he was told by thin-lipped, cool Colonel Wade that the rich shipbuilder, Sir Richard Devine, had proposed an alliance with fair-haired gentle Ellinor, he swore, with fierce knitting of his black brows, that no law of man nor Heaven should further restrain him in his selfish prodigality. "You have sold your daughter and ruined me," he said; "look to the consequences." Colonel Wade sneered at his fiery kinsman: "You will find Sir Richard's house a pleasant one to visit, Armigell; and he should be worth an income to so experienced a gambler as yourself." Lord Bellasis did visit at Sir Richard's house during the first year of his cousin's marriage; but upon the birth of the son who is the hero of this history, he affected a quarrel with the city knight, and cursing him to the Prince and Poins for a miserly curmudgeon, who neither diced nor drank like a gentleman, departed, more desperately at war with fortune than ever, for his old haunts. The year 1827 found him a hardened, hopeless old man of sixty, battered in health and ruined in pocket; but who, by dint of stays, hair-dye, and courage, yet faced the world with undaunted front, and dined as gaily in bailiff-haunted Belsize as he had dined at Carlton House. Of the possessions of the House of Wotton Wade, this old manor, timberless and bare, was all that remained, and its master rarely visited it.

On the evening of May 3, 1827, Lord Bellasis had been attending a pigeon match at Hornsey Wood, and having resisted the importunities of his companion, Mr. Lionel Crofton (a young gentleman-rake, whose position in the sporting world was not the most secure), who wanted him to go on into town, he had avowed his intention of striking across Hampstead to Belsize. "I have an appointment at the fir trees on the Heath," he said.

"With a woman?" asked Mr. Crofton.

"Not at all; with a parson."

"A parson!"

"You stare! Well, he is only just ordained. I met him last year at Bath on his vacation from Cambridge, and he was good enough to lose some money to me."

"And now waits to pay it out of his first curacy. I wish your lordship joy with all my soul. Then, we must push on, for it grows late."

"Thanks, my dear sir, for the 'we,' but I must go alone," said Lord Bellasis dryly. "To-morrow you can settle with me for the sitting of last week. Hark! the clock is striking nine. Good night."

*

At half-past nine Richard Devine quitted his mother's house to begin the new life he had chosen, and so, drawn together by that strange fate of circumstances which creates events, the father and son approached each other.

*

As the young man gained the middle of the path which led to the Heath, he met Sir Richard returning from the village. It was no part of his plan to seek an interview with the man whom his mother had so deeply wronged, and he would have slunk past in the gloom; but seeing him thus alone returning to a desolated home, the prodigal was tempted to utter some words of farewell and of regret. To his astonishment, however, Sir Richard passed swiftly on, with body bent forward as one in the act of falling, and with eyes unconscious of surroundings, staring straight into the distance. Half-terrified at this strange appearance, Richard hurried onward, and at a turn of the path stumbled upon something which horribly accounted for the curious action of the old man. A dead body lay upon its face in the heather; beside it was a heavy riding whip stained at the handle with blood, and an open pocket-book. Richard took up the book, and read, in gold letters on the cover, "Lord Bellasis."

The unhappy young man knelt down beside the body and raised it. The skull had been fractured by a blow, but it seemed that life yet lingered. Overcome with horror—for he could not doubt but that his mother's worst fears had been realized—Richard knelt there holding his murdered father in his arms, waiting until the murderer, whose name he bore, should have placed himself beyond pursuit. It seemed an hour to his excited fancy before he saw a light pass along the front of the house he had quitted, and knew that Sir Richard had safely reached his chamber. With some bewildered intention of summoning aid, he left the body and made towards the town. As he stepped out on the path he heard voices, and presently some dozen men, one of whom held a horse, burst out upon him, and, with sudden fury, seized and flung him to the ground.

At first the young man, so rudely assailed, did not comprehend his own danger. His mind, bent upon one hideous explanation of the crime, did not see another obvious one which had already occurred to the mind of the landlord of the Three Spaniards.

"God defend me!" cried Mr. Mogford, scanning by the pale light of the rising moon the features of the murdered man, "but it is Lord Bellasis!—oh, you bloody villain! Jem, bring him along here, p'r'aps his lordship can recognize him!"

"It was not I!" cried Richard Devine. "For God's sake, my lord, say—" then he stopped abruptly, and being forced on his knees by his captors, remained staring at the dying man, in sudden and ghastly fear. Those men in whom emotion has the effect of quickening circulation of the blood reason rapidly in moments of danger, and in the terrible instant when his eyes met those of Lord Bellasis, Richard Devine had summed up the chances of his future fortune, and realized to the full his personal peril. The runaway horse had given the alarm. The drinkers at the Spaniards' Inn had started to search the Heath, and had discovered a fellow in rough costume, whose person was unknown to them, hastily quitting a spot where, beside a rifled pocket-book and a blood-stained whip, lay a dying man. The web of circumstantial evidence had enmeshed him. An hour ago escape would have been easy. He would have had but to cry, "I am the son of Sir Richard Devine. Come with me to yonder house, and I will prove to you that I have but just quitted it,"—to place his innocence beyond immediate question. That course of action was impossible now. Knowing Sir Richard as he did, and believing, moreover, that in his raging passion the old man had himself met and murdered the destroyer of his honour, the son of Lord Bellasis and Lady Devine saw himself in a position which would compel him either to sacrifice himself, or to purchase a chance of safety at the price of his mother's dishonour and the death of the man whom his mother had deceived. If the outcast son were brought a prisoner to North End House, Sir Richard—now doubly oppressed of fate—would be certain to deny him; and he would be compelled, in self-defence, to reveal a story which would at once bring his mother to open infamy, and send to the gallows the man who had been for twenty years deceived—the man to whose kindness he owed education and former fortune. He knelt, stupefied, unable to speak or move.

"Come," cried Mogford again; "say, my lord, is this the villain?" Lord Bellasis rallied his failing senses, his glazing eyes stared into his son's face with horrible eagerness; he shook his head, raised a feeble arm as though to point elsewhere, and fell back dead.

"If you didn't murder him, you robbed him," growled Mogford, "and you shall sleep at Bow Street to-night. Tom, run on to meet the patrol, and leave word at the Gate-house that I've a passenger for the coach!—Bring him on, Jack!—What's your name, eh?"

He repeated the rough question twice before his prisoner answered, but at length Richard Devine raised a pale face which stern resolution had already hardened into defiant manhood, and said, "Dawes—Rufus Dawes."

*

His new life had begun already: for that night one, Rufus Dawes, charged with murder and robbery, lay awake in prison, waiting for the fortune of the morrow.

Two other men waited as eagerly. One, Mr. Lionel Crofton; the other, the horseman who had appointment with the murdered Lord Bellasis under the shadow of the fir trees on Hampstead Heath. As for Sir Richard Devine, he waited for no one, for upon reaching his room he had fallen senseless in a fit of apoplexy.

BOOK I
THE SEA   1827

CHAPTER I
THE PRISON SHIP

IN the breathless stillness of a tropical afternoon, when the air was hot and heavy, and the sky brazen and cloudless, the shadow of the *Malabar* lay solitary on the surface of the glittering sea.

The sun—who rose on the left hand every morning a blazing ball, to move slowly through the unbearable blue, until he sank fiery red in mingling glories of sky and ocean on the right hand—had just got low enough to peep beneath the awning that covered the poop-deck, and awaken a young man, in an undress military uniform, who was dozing on a coil of rope.

"Hang it!" said he, rising and stretching himself, with the weary sigh of a man who has nothing to do, "I must have been asleep"; and then, holding by a stay, he turned about and looked down into the waist of the ship.

Save for the man at the wheel and the guard at the quarter-railing, he was alone on the deck. A few birds flew round about the vessel, and seemed to pass under her stern windows only to appear again at her bows. A lazy albatross, with the white water flashing from his wings, rose with a dabbling sound to leeward, and in the place where he had been glided the hideous fin of a silently-swimming shark. The seams of the well-scrubbed deck were sticky with melted pitch, and the brass plate of the compass-case sparkled in the sun like a jewel. There was no breeze, and as the clumsy ship rolled and lurched on the heaving sea, her idle sails flapped against her masts with a regularly recurring noise, and her bowsprit would seem to rise higher with the water's swell, to dip again with a jerk that made each rope tremble and tauten. On the forecastle, some half-dozen soldiers, in all varieties of undress, were playing at cards, smoking, or watching the fishing-lines hanging over the catheads.

So far the appearance of the vessel differed in nowise from that of an ordinary transport. But in the waist a curious sight presented itself. It was as though one had built a cattle-pen there. At the foot of the foremast, and at the quarter-deck, a strong barricade, loop-holed and furnished with doors for ingress and egress, ran across the deck from bulwark to bulwark. Outside this cattle-pen an armed sentry stood on guard; inside, standing, sitting, or walking monotonously, within range of the shining barrels in the arm chest on the poop, were some sixty men and boys, dressed in uniform grey. The men and boys were prisoners of the Crown, and the cattle-pen was their exercise ground. Their prison was down the main hatchway, on the 'tween decks, and the barricade, continued down, made its side walls.

It was the fag end of the two hours' exercise graciously permitted each afternoon by His Majesty King George the Fourth to prisoners of the Crown, and the prisoners of the Crown were enjoying themselves. It was not, perhaps, so pleasant as under the awning on the poop-deck, but that sacred shade was only for such great men as the captain and his officers, Surgeon Pine, Lieutenant Maurice Frere, and, most important personages of all, Captain Vickers and his wife.

That the convict leaning against the bulwarks would like to have been able to get rid of his enemy the sun for a moment, was probable enough. His companions, sitting on the combings of the main-hatch, or crouched in careless fashion on the shady side of the barricade, were laughing and talking, with blasphemous and obscene merriment hideous to contemplate; but he, with cap pulled over his brows, and hands thrust into the pockets of his coarse grey garments, held aloof from their dismal joviality.

The sun poured his hottest rays on his head unheeded, and though every cranny and seam in the deck sweltered hot pitch under the fierce heat, the man stood there, motionless and morose, staring at the sleepy sea. He had stood thus, in one place or another, ever since the groaning vessel had escaped from the rollers of the Bay of Biscay, and the miserable hundred and eighty creatures among whom he was classed had been freed from their irons, and allowed to sniff fresh air twice a day.

The low-browed, coarse-featured ruffians grouped about the deck cast many a leer of contempt at the solitary figure, but their remarks were confined to gestures only. There are degrees in crime, and Rufus Dawes, the convicted felon, who had but escaped the gallows to toil for all his life in irons, was a man of mark. He had been tried for the robbery and murder of Lord Bellasis. The friendless vagabond's lame story of finding on the Heath a dying man would not have availed him, but for the curious fact sworn to by the landlord of the Spaniards' Inn, that the murdered nobleman had shaken his head when asked if the prisoner was his assassin. The vagabond was acquitted of the murder, but condemned to death for the robbery, and London, who took some interest in the trial, considered him fortunate when his sentence was commuted to transportation for life.

It was customary on board these floating prisons to keep each man's crime a secret from his fellows, so that if he chose, and the caprice of his gaolers allowed him, he could lead a new life in his adopted home, without being taunted with his former misdeeds. But, like other excellent devices, the expedient was only a nominal one, and few out of the doomed hundred and eighty were ignorant of the offence which their companions had committed. The more guilty boasted of their superiority in vice; the petty criminals swore that their guilt was blacker than it appeared. Moreover, a deed so bloodthirsty and a respite so unexpected, had invested the name of Rufus Dawes with a grim distinction, which his superior mental abilities, no less than his haughty temper and powerful frame, combined to support. A young man of two-and-twenty owning to no friends, and existing among them but by the fact of his criminality, he was respected and admired. The vilest of all the vile horde penned between decks, if they laughed at his "fine airs" behind his back, cringed and submitted when they met him face to face—for in a convict ship the greatest villain is the greatest hero, and the only nobility acknowledged by that hideous commonwealth is that Order of the Halter which is conferred by the hand of the hangman.

The young man on the poop caught sight of the tall figure leaning against the bulwarks, and it gave him an excuse to break the monotony of his employment.

"Here, you!" he called with an oath, "get out of the gangway!" Rufus Dawes was not in the gangway—was, in fact, a good two feet from it, but at the sound of Lieutenant Frere's voice he started, and went obediently towards the hatchway.

"Touch your hat, you dog!" cries Frere, coming to the quarter-railing. "Touch your damned hat! Do you hear?"

Rufus Dawes touched his cap, saluting in half military fashion.

"I'll make some of you fellows smart, if you don't have a care," went on the angry Frere, half to himself. "Insolent blackguards!"

And then the noise of the sentry, on the quarter-deck below him, grounding arms, turned the current of his thoughts. A thin, tall, soldier-like man, with a cold blue eye, and prim features, came out of the cuddy below, handing out a fair-haired, affected, mincing lady, of middle age. Captain Vickers, of Mr. Frere's regiment, ordered for service in Van Diemen's Land, was bringing his lady on deck to get an appetite for dinner.

Mrs. Vickers was forty-two (she owned to thirty-three), and had been a garrison-*belle* for eleven weary years before she married prim John Vickers. The marriage was not a happy one. Vickers found his wife extravagant, vain, and snappish, and she found him harsh, disenchanted, and commonplace. A daughter, born two years after their marriage, was the only link that bound the ill-assorted pair. Vickers idolized little Sylvia, and when the recommendation of a long sea-voyage for his failing health induced him to exchange into the—th, he insisted upon bringing the child with him, despite Mrs. Vickers's reiterated objections on the score of educational difficulties. "He could educate her himself, if need be," he said; "and she should not stay at home."

So Mrs. Vickers, after a hard struggle, gave up the point and her dreams of Bath together, and followed her husband with the best grace she could muster. When fairly out to sea she seemed reconciled to her fate, and employed the intervals between scolding her daughter and her maid, in fascinating the boorish young Lieutenant, Maurice Frere.

Fascination was an integral portion of Julia Vickers's nature; admiration was all she lived for: and even in a convict ship, with her husband at her elbow, she must flirt, or perish of mental inanition. There was no harm in the creature. She was simply a vain, middle-aged woman, and Frere took her attentions for what they were worth. Moreover, her good feeling towards him was useful, for reasons which will shortly appear.

Running down the ladder, cap in hand, he offered her his assistance.

"Thank you, Mr. Frere. These horrid ladders. I really—he, he!—quite tremble at them. Hot! Yes, dear me, most oppressive. John, the camp-stool. Pray, Mr. Frere—oh, *thank* you! Sylvia! Sylvia! John, have you my smelling salts? Still a calm, I suppose? These dreadful calms!"

This semi-fashionable slip-slop, within twenty yards of the wild beasts' den, on the other side of the barricade, sounded strange; but Mr. Frere thought nothing of it. Familiarity destroys terror, and the incurable flirt fluttered her muslins, and played off her second-rate graces, under the noses of the grinning convicts, with as much complacency as if she had been in a Chatham ball-room. Indeed, if there had been nobody else near, it is not unlikely that she would have disdainfully fascinated the 'tween-decks, and made eyes at the most presentable of the convicts there.

Vickers, with a bow to Frere, saw his wife up the ladder, and then turned for his daughter.

She was a delicate-looking child of six years old, with blue eyes and bright hair. Though indulged by her father, and spoiled by her mother, the natural sweetness of her disposition saved her from being disagreeable, and the effects of her education as yet only showed themselves in a thousand imperious prettinesses, which made her the darling of the ship. Little Miss Sylvia was privileged to go anywhere and do anything, and even convictism shut its foul mouth in her presence. Running to her father's side, the child chattered with all the volubility of flattered self-esteem. She ran hither and thither, asked questions, invented answers, laughed, sang, gambolled, peered into the compass-case, felt in the pockets of the man at the helm, put her tiny hand into the big palm of the officer of the watch, even ran down to the quarter-deck and pulled the coat-tails of the sentry on duty.

At last, tired of running about, she took a little striped leather ball from the bosom of her frock, and calling to her father, threw it up to him as he stood on the poop. He returned it, and, shouting with laughter, clapping her hands between each throw, the child kept up the game.

The convicts—whose slice of fresh air was nearly eaten—turned with eagerness to watch this new source of amusement. Innocent laughter and childish prattle were strange to them. Some smiled, and nodded with interest in the varying fortunes of the game. One young lad could hardly restrain himself from applauding. It was as though, out of the sultry heat which brooded over the ship, a cool breeze had suddenly arisen.

In the midst of this mirth, the officer of the watch, glancing round the fast crimsoning horizon, paused abruptly, and shading his eyes with his hand, looked out intently to the westward.

Frere, who found Mrs. Vickers's conversation a little tiresome, and had been glancing from time to time at the companion, as though in expectation of someone appearing, noticed the action.

"What is it, Mr. Best?"

"I don't know exactly. It looks to me like a cloud of smoke." And, taking the glass, he swept the horizon.

"Let me see," said Frere; and he looked also.

On the extreme horizon, just to the left of the sinking sun, rested, or seemed to rest, a tiny black cloud. The gold and crimson, splashed all about the sky, had overflowed around it, and rendered a clear view almost impossible.

"I can't quite make it out," says Frere, handing back the telescope. "We can see as soon as the sun goes down a little."

Then Mrs. Vickers must, of course, look also, and was prettily affected about the focus of the glass, applying herself to that instrument with much girlish giggling, and finally declaring, after shutting one eye with her fair hand, that positively she "could see nothing but sky, and believed that wicked Mr. Frere was doing it on purpose."

By and by, Captain Blunt appeared, and, taking the glass from his officer, looked through it long and carefully. Then the mizentop was appealed to, and declared that he could see nothing; and at last the sun went down with a jerk, as though it had slipped through a slit in the sea, and the black spot, swallowed up in the gathering haze, was seen no more.

As the sun sank, the relief guard came up the after hatchway, and the relieved guard prepared to superintend the descent of the convicts. At this moment Sylvia missed her ball, which, taking advantage of a sudden lurch of the vessel, hopped over the barricade, and rolled to the feet of Rufus Dawes, who was still leaning, apparently lost in thought, against the side.

The bright spot of colour rolling across the white deck caught his eye; stooping mechanically, he picked up the ball, and stepped forward to return it. The door of the barricade was open and the sentry—a young soldier, occupied in staring at the relief guard—did not notice the prisoner pass through it. In another instant he was on the sacred quarter-deck.

Heated with the game, her cheeks aglow, her eyes sparkling, her golden hair afloat, Sylvia had turned to leap after her plaything, but even as she turned, from under the shadow of the cuddy glided a rounded white arm; and a shapely hand caught the child by the sash and drew her back. The next moment the young man in grey had placed the toy in her hand.

Maurice Frere, descending the poop ladder, had not witnessed this little incident; on reaching the deck, he saw only the unexplained presence of the convict uniform.

"Thank you," said a voice, as Rufus Dawes stooped before the pouting Sylvia.

The convict raised his eyes and saw a young girl of eighteen or nineteen years of age, tall, and well developed, who, dressed in a loose-sleeved robe of some white material, was standing in the doorway. She had black hair, coiled around a narrow and flat head, a small foot, white skin, well-shaped hands, and large dark eyes, and as she smiled at him, her scarlet lips showed her white even teeth.

He knew her at once. She was Sarah Purfoy, Mrs. Vickers's maid, but he never had been so close to her before; and it seemed to him that he was in the presence of some strange tropical flower, which exhaled a heavy and intoxicating perfume.

For an instant the two looked at each other, and then Rufus Dawes was seized from behind by his collar, and flung with a shock upon the deck.

Leaping to his feet, his first impulse was to rush upon his assailant, but he saw the ready bayonet of the sentry gleam, and he checked himself with an effort, for his assailant was Mr. Maurice Frere.

"What the devil do you do here?" asked the gentleman with an oath. "You lazy, skulking hound, what brings you here? If I catch you putting your foot on the quarter-deck again, I'll give you a week in irons!"

Rufus Dawes, pale with rage and mortification, opened his mouth to justify himself, but he allowed the words to die on his lips. What was the use?

"Go down below, and remember what I've told you," cried Frere; and comprehending at once what had occurred, he made a mental minute of the name of the defaulting sentry.

The convict, wiping the blood from his face, turned on his heel without a word, and went back through the strong oak door into his den. Frere leant forward and took the girl's shapely hand with an easy gesture, but she drew it away, with a flash of her black eyes.

"You coward!" she said.

The stolid soldier close beside them heard it, and his eye twinkled. Frere bit his thick lips with mortification, as he followed the girl into the cuddy. Sarah Purfoy, however, taking the astonished Sylvia by the hand, glided into her mistress's cabin with a scornful laugh, and shut the door behind her.

CHAPTER II
SARAH PURFOY

CONVICTISM having been safely got under hatches, and put to bed in its Government allowance of sixteen inches of space per man, cut a little short by exigencies of shipboard, the cuddy was wont to pass some not unpleasant evenings. Mrs. Vickers, who was poetical and owned a guitar, was also musical and sang to it. Captain Blunt was a jovial, coarse fellow; Surgeon Pine had a mania for story-telling; while if Vickers was sometimes dull, Frere was always hearty. Moreover, the table was well served, and what with dinner, tobacco, whist, music, and brandy and water, the sultry evenings passed away with a rapidity of which the wild beasts 'tween decks, cooped by sixes in berths of a mere five feet square, had no conception.

On this particular evening, however, the cuddy was dull. Dinner fell flat, and conversation languished.

"No signs of a breeze, Mr. Best?" asked Blunt, as the first officer came in and took his seat.

"None, sir."

"These—he, he!—awful calms," says Mrs. Vickers. "A week, is it not, Captain Blunt?"

"Thirteen days, mum," growled Blunt.

"I remember, off the Coromandel coast," put in cheerful Pine, "when we had the plague in the *Rattlesnake*—"

"Captain Vickers, another glass of wine?" cried Blunt, hastening to cut the anecdote short.

"Thank you, no more. I have the headache."

"Headache—um—don't wonder at it, going down among those fellows. It is infamous the way they crowd these ships. Here we have over two hundred souls on board, and not boat room for half of 'em."

"Two hundred souls! Surely not," says Vickers. "By the King's Regulations—"

"One hundred and eighty convicts, fifty soldiers, thirty in ship's crew, all told, and—how many?—one, two three—seven in the cuddy. How many do you make that?"

"We *are* just a little crowded this time," says Best.

"It is very wrong," says Vickers, pompously. "Very wrong. By the King's Regulations—"

But the subject of the King's Regulations was even more distasteful to the cuddy than Pine's interminable anecdotes, and Mrs. Vickers hastened to change the subject.

"Are you not heartily tired of this dreadful life, Mr. Frere?"

"Well, it is not exactly the life I had hoped to lead," said Frere, rubbing a freckled hand over his stubborn red hair; "but I must make the best of it."

"Yes, indeed," said the lady, in that subdued manner with which one comments upon a well-known accident, "it must have been a great shock to you to be so suddenly deprived of so large a fortune."

"Not only that, but to find that the black sheep who got it all sailed for India within a week of my uncle's death! Lady Devine got a letter from him on the day of the funeral to say that he had taken his passage in the *Hydaspes* for Calcutta, and never meant to come back again!"

"Sir Richard Devine left no other children?"

"No, only this mysterious Dick, whom I never saw, but who must have hated me."

"Dear, dear! These family quarrels are dreadful things. Poor Lady Devine, to lose in one day a husband and a son!"

"And the next morning to hear of the murder of her cousin! You know that we are connected with the Bellasis family. My aunt's father married a sister of the second Lord Bellasis."

"Indeed. That was a horrible murder. So you think that the dreadful man you pointed out the other day did it?"

"The jury seemed to think not," said Mr. Frere, with a laugh; "but I don't know anybody else who could have a motive for it. However, I'll go on deck and have a smoke."

"I wonder what induced that old hunks of a shipbuilder to try to cut off his only son in favour of a cub of that sort," said Surgeon Pine to Captain Vickers as the broad back of Mr. Maurice Frere disappeared up the companion.

"Some boyish follies abroad, I believe; self-made men are always impatient of extravagance. But it is hard upon Frere. He is not a bad sort of fellow for all his roughness, and when a young man finds that an accident deprives him of a quarter of a million of money and leaves him without a sixpence beyond his commission in a marching regiment under orders for a convict settlement, he has some reason to rail against fate."

"How was it that the son came in for the money after all, then?"

"Why, it seems that when old Devine returned from sending for his lawyer to alter his will, he got a fit of apoplexy, the result of his rage, I suppose, and when they opened his room door in the morning they found him dead."

"And the son's away on the sea somewhere," said Mr. Vickers "and knows nothing of his good fortune. It is quite a romance."

"I am glad that Frere did not get the money," said Pine, grimly sticking to his prejudice; "I have seldom seen a face I liked less, even among my yellow jackets yonder."

"Oh dear, Dr. Pine! How can you?" interjected Mrs. Vickers.

"'Pon my soul, ma'am, some of them have mixed in good society, I can tell you. There's pickpockets and swindlers down below who have lived in the best company."

"Dreadful wretches!" cried Mrs. Vickers, shaking out her skirts. "John, I will go on deck."

At the signal, the party rose.

"Ecod, Pine," says Captain Blunt, as the two were left alone together, "you and I are always putting our foot into it!"

"Women are always in the way aboard ship," returned Pine.

"Ah! doctor, you don't mean that, I know," said a rich soft voice at his elbow.

It was Sarah Purfoy emerging from her cabin.

"Here *is* the wench!" cries Blunt. "We are talking of your eyes, my dear."

"Well, they'll bear talking about, captain, won't they?" asked she, turning them full upon him.

"By the Lord, they will!" says Blunt, smacking his hand on the table. "They're the finest eyes I've seen in my life, and they've got the reddest lips under'm that—"

"Let me pass, Captain Blunt, if you please. Thank you, doctor."

And before the admiring commander could prevent her, she modestly swept out of the cuddy.

"She's a fine piece of goods, eh?" asked Blunt, watching her. "A spice o' the devil in her, too."

Old Pine took a huge pinch of snuff.

"Devil! I tell you what it is, Blunt. I don't know where Vickers picked her up, but I'd rather trust my life with the worst of those ruffians 'tween decks, than in *her* keeping, if I'd done her an injury."

Blunt laughed.

"I don't believe she'd think much of sticking a man, either!" he said, rising. "But I must go on deck, doctor."

Pine followed him more slowly. "I don't pretend to know much about women," he said to himself, "but that girl's got a story of her own, or I'm much mistaken. What brings her on board this ship as lady's-maid is more than I can fathom." And as, sticking his pipe between his teeth, he walked down the now deserted deck to the main hatchway, and turned to watch the white figure gliding up and down the poop-deck, he saw it joined by another and a darker one, he muttered, "She's after no good, I'll swear."

At that moment his arm was touched by a soldier in undress uniform, who had come up the hatchway. "What is it?"

The man drew himself up and saluted.

"If you please, doctor, one of the prisoners is taken sick, and as the dinner's over, and he's pretty bad, I ventured to disturb your honour."

"You ass!" says Pine—who, like many gruff men, had a good heart under his rough shell—"why didn't you tell me before?" and knocking the ashes out of his barely-lighted pipe, he stopped that implement with a twist of paper and followed his summoner down the hatchway.

In the meantime the woman who was the object of the grim old fellow's suspicions was enjoying the comparative coolness of the night air. Her mistress and her mistress's daughter had not yet come out of their cabin, and the men had not yet finished their evening's tobacco. The awning had been removed, the stars were shining in the moonless sky, the poop guard had shifted itself to the quarter-deck, and Miss Sarah Purfoy was walking up and down the deserted poop, in close *tete-a-tete* with no less a person than Captain Blunt himself. She had passed and repassed him twice silently, and at the third turn the big fellow, peering into the twilight ahead somewhat uneasily, obeyed the glitter of her great eyes, and joined her.

"You weren't put out, my wench," he asked, "at what I said to you below?"

She affected surprise.

"What do you mean?"

"Why, at my—at what I—at my rudeness, there! For I was a bit rude, I admit."

"I? Oh dear, no. You were not rude."

"Glad you think so!" returned Phineas Blunt, a little ashamed at what looked like a confession of weakness on his part.

"You *would* have been—if I had let you."

"How do you know?"

"I saw it in your face. Do you think a woman can't see in a man's face when he's going to insult her?"

"Insult you, hey! Upon my word!"

"Yes, insult me. You're old enough to be my father, Captain Blunt, but you've no right to kiss me, unless I ask you."

"Haw, haw!" laughed Blunt. "I like that. Ask me! Egad, I wish you would, you black-eyed minx!"

"So would other people, I have no doubt."

"That soldier officer, for instance. Hey, Miss Modesty? I've seen him looking at you as though he'd like to try."

The girl flashed at him with a quick side glance.

"You mean Lieutenant Frere, I suppose. Are you jealous of him?"

"Jealous! Why, damme, the lad was only breeched the other day. Jealous!"

"I think you are—and you've no need to be. He is a stupid booby, though he is Lieutenant Frere."

"So he is. You are right there, by the Lord."

Sarah Purfoy laughed a low, full-toned laugh, whose sound made Blunt's pulse take a jump forward, and sent the blood tingling down to his fingers ends.

"Captain Blunt," said she, "you're going to do a very silly thing."

He came close to her and tried to take her hand.

"What?"

She answered by another question.

"How old are you?"

"Forty-two, if you must know."

"Oh! And you are going to fall in love with a girl of nineteen."

"Who is that?"

"Myself!" she said, giving him her hand and smiling at him with her rich red lips.

The mizen hid them from the man at the wheel, and the twilight of tropical stars held the main-deck. Blunt felt the breath of this strange woman warm on his cheek, her eyes seemed to wax and wane, and the hard, small hand he held burnt like fire.

"I believe you are right," he cried. "I *am* half in love with you already."

She gazed at him with a contemptuous sinking of her heavily fringed eyelids, and withdrew her hand.

"Then don't get to the other half, or you'll regret it."

"Shall I?" asked Blunt. "That's my affair. Come, you little vixen, give me that kiss you said I was going to ask you for below," and he caught her in his arms.

In an instant she had twisted herself free, and confronted him with flashing eyes.

"You dare!" she cried. "Kiss me by force! Pooh! you make love like a schoolboy. If you can make me like you, I'll kiss you as often as you will. If you can't, keep your distance, please."

Blunt did not know whether to laugh or be angry at this rebuff. He was conscious that he was in rather a ridiculous position, and so decided to laugh.

"You're a spitfire, too. What must I do to make you like me?"

She made him a curtsy.

"That is your affair," she said; and as the head of Mr. Frere appeared above the companion, Blunt walked aft, feeling considerably bewildered, and yet not displeased.

"She's a fine girl, by jingo," he said, cocking his cap, "and I'm hanged if she ain't sweet upon me."

And then the old fellow began to whistle softly to himself as he paced the deck, and to glance towards the man who had taken his place with no friendly eyes. But a sort of shame held him as yet, and he kept aloof.

Maurice Frere's greeting was short enough.

"Well, Sarah," he said, "have you got out of your temper?"

She frowned.

"What did you strike the man for? He did you no harm."

"He was out of his place. What business had he to come aft? One must keep these wretches down, my girl."

"Or they will be too much for you, eh? Do you think one man could capture a ship, Mr. Maurice?"

"No, but one hundred might."

"Nonsense! What could they do against the soldiers? There are fifty soldiers."

"So there are, but—"

"But what?"

"Well, never mind. It's against the rules, and I won't have it."

"'Not according to the King's Regulations,' as Captain Vickers would say."

Frere laughed at her imitation of his pompous captain.

"You are a strange girl; I can't make you out. Come," and he took her hand, "tell me what you are really."

"Will you promise not to tell?"

"Of course."

"Upon your word?"

"Upon my word."

"Well, then—but you'll tell?"

"Not I. Come, go on."

"Lady's-maid in the family of a gentleman going abroad."

"Sarah, you can't be serious?"

"I am serious. That was the advertisement I answered."

"But I mean what you *have* been. You were not a lady's-maid all your life?"

She pulled her shawl closer round her and shivered.

"People are not born ladies'-maids, I suppose?"

"Well, who are you, then? Have you no friends? What have you been?"

She looked up into the young man's face—a little less harsh at that moment than it was wont to be—and creeping closer to him, whispered—"Do you love me, Maurice?"

He raised one of the little hands that rested on the taffrail, and, under cover of the darkness, kissed it.

"You know I do," he said. "You may be a lady's-maid or what you like, but you are the loveliest woman I ever met."

She smiled at his vehemence.

"Then, if you love me, what does it matter?"

"If *you* loved me, you would tell me," said he, with a quickness which surprised himself.

"But I have nothing to tell, and I don't love you—yet."

He let her hand fall with an impatient gesture; and at that moment Blunt—who could restrain himself no longer—came up.

"Fine night, Mr. Frere?"

"Yes, fine enough."

"No signs of a breeze yet, though."

"No, not yet."

Just then, from out of the violet haze that hung over the horizon, a strange glow of light broke.

"Hallo," cries Frere, "did you see that?"

All had seen it, but they looked for its repetition in vain. Blunt rubbed his eyes.

"I saw it," he said, "distinctly. A flash of light." They strained their eyes to pierce through the obscurity.

"Best saw something like it before dinner. There must be thunder in the air."

At that instant a thin streak of light shot up and then sank again. There was no mistaking it this time, and a simultaneous exclamation burst from all on deck. From out the gloom which hung over the horizon rose a column of flame that lighted up the night for an instant, and then sunk, leaving a dull red spark upon the water.

"It's a ship on fire," cried Frere.

CHAPTER III

THE MONOTONY BREAKS

THEY looked again, the tiny spark still burned, and immediately over it there grew out of the darkness a crimson spot, that hung like a lurid star in the air. The soldiers and sailors on the forecastle had seen it also, and in a moment the whole vessel was astir. Mrs. Vickers, with little Sylvia clinging to her dress, came up to share the new sensation; and at the sight of her mistress, the modest maid withdrew discreetly from Frere's side. Not that there was any need to do so; no one heeded her. Blunt, in his professional excitement, had already forgotten her presence, and Frere was in earnest conversation with Vickers.

"Take a boat?" said that gentleman. "Certainly, my dear Frere, by all means. That is to say, if the captain does not object, and it is not contrary to the Regulations—"

"Captain, you'll lower a boat, eh? We may save some of the poor devils," cries Frere, his heartiness of body reviving at the prospect of excitement.

"Boat!" said Blunt, "why, she's twelve miles off and more, and there's not a breath o' wind!"

"But we can't let 'em roast like chestnuts!" cried the other, as the glow in the sky broadened and became more intense.

"What is the good of a boat?" said Pine. "The long-boat only holds thirty men, and that's a big ship yonder."

"Well, take two boats—three boats! By Heaven, you'll never let 'em burn alive without stirring a finger to save 'em!"

"They've got their own boats," says Blunt, whose coolness was in strong contrast to the young officer's impetuosity; "and if the fire gains, they'll take to 'em, you may depend. In the meantime, we'll show 'em that there's someone near 'em." And as he spoke, a blue light flared hissing into the night.

"There, they'll see that, I expect!" he said, as the ghastly flame rose, extinguishing the stars for a moment, only to let them appear again brighter in a darker heaven.

"Mr. Best—lower and man the quarter-boats! Mr. Frere—you can go in one, if you like, and take a volunteer or two from those grey jackets of yours amidships. I shall want as many hands as I can spare to man the long-boat and cutter, in case we want 'em. Steady there, lads! Easy!" and as the first eight men who could reach the deck parted to the larboard and starboard quarter-boats, Frere ran down on the main-deck.

Mrs. Vickers, of course, was in the way, and gave a genteel scream as Blunt rudely pushed past her with a scarce-muttered apology; but her maid was standing erect and motionless, by the quarter-railing, and as the captain paused for a moment to look round him, he saw her dark eyes fixed on him admiringly. He was, as he said, over forty-two, burly and grey-haired, but he blushed like a girl under her approving gaze. Nevertheless, he said only, "That wench is a trump!" and swore a little.

Meanwhile Maurice Frere had passed the sentry and leapt down into the 'tween decks. At his nod, the prison door was thrown open. The air was hot, and that strange, horrible odour peculiar to closely-packed human bodies filled the place. It was like coming into a full stable.

He ran his eye down the double tier of bunks which lined the side of the ship, and stopped at the one opposite him.

There seemed to have been some disturbance there lately, for instead of the six pair of feet which should have protruded therefrom, the gleam of the bull's-eye showed but four.

"What's the matter here, sentry?" he asked.

"Prisoner ill, sir. Doctor sent him to hospital."

"But there should be two."

The other came from behind the break of the berths. It was Rufus Dawes. He held by the side as he came, and saluted.

"I felt sick, sir, and was trying to get the scuttle open."

The heads were all raised along the silent line, and eyes and ears were eager to see and listen. The double tier of bunks looked terribly like a row of wild beast cages at that moment.

Maurice Frere stamped his foot indignantly.

"Sick! What are you sick about, you malingering dog? I'll give you something to sweat the sickness out of you. Stand on one side here!"

Rufus Dawes, wondering, obeyed. He seemed heavy and dejected, and passed his hand across his forehead, as though he would rub away a pain there.

"Which of you fellows can handle an oar?" Frere went on. "There, curse you, I don't want fifty! Three'll do. Come on now, make haste!"

The heavy door clashed again, and in another instant the four "volunteers" were on deck. The crimson glow was turning yellow now, and spreading over the sky.

"Two in each boat!" cries Blunt. "I'll burn a blue light every hour for you, Mr. Best; and take care they don't swamp you. Lower away, lads!" As the second prisoner took the oar of Frere's boat, he uttered a groan and fell forward, recovering himself instantly. Sarah Purfoy, leaning over the side, saw the occurrence.

"What is the matter with that man?" she said. "Is he ill?"

Pine was next to her, and looked out instantly. "It's that big fellow in No. 10," he cried. "Here, Frere!"

But Frere heard him not. He was intent on the beacon that gleamed ever brighter in the distance. "Give way, my lads!" he shouted. And amid a cheer from the ship, the two boats shot out of the bright circle of the blue light, and disappeared into the darkness.

Sarah Purfoy looked at Pine for an explanation, but he turned abruptly away. For a moment the girl paused, as if in doubt; and then, ere his retreating figure turned to retrace its steps, she cast a quick glance around, and slipping down the ladder, made her way to the 'tween decks.

The iron-studded oak barricade that, loop-holed for musketry, and perforated with plated trapdoor for sterner needs, separated soldiers from prisoners, was close to her left hand, and the sentry at its padlocked door looked at her inquiringly. She laid her little hand on his big rough one—a sentry is but mortal—and opened her brown eyes at him.

"The hospital," she said. "The doctor sent me"; and before he could answer, her white figure vanished down the hatch, and passed round the bulkhead, behind which lay the sick man.

CHAPTER IV

THE HOSPITAL

THE hospital was nothing more nor less than a partitioned portion of the lower deck, filched from the space allotted to the soldiers. It ran fore and aft, coming close to the stern windows, and was, in fact, a sort of artificial stern cabin. At a pinch, it might have held a dozen men.

Though not so hot as in the prison, the atmosphere of the lower deck was close and unhealthy, and the girl, pausing to listen to the subdued hum of conversation coming from the soldiers' berths, turned strangely sick and giddy. She drew herself up, however, and held out her hand to a man who came rapidly across the misshapen shadows, thrown by the sulkily swinging lantern, to meet her. It was the young soldier who had been that day sentry at the convict gangway.

"Well, miss," he said, "I am here, yer see, waiting for yer."

"You are a good boy, Miles; but don't you think I'm worth waiting for?"

Miles grinned from ear to ear.

"Indeed you be," said he.

Sarah Purfoy frowned, and then smiled.

"Come here, Miles; I've got something for you."

Miles came forward, grinning harder.

The girl produced a small object from the pocket of her dress. If Mrs. Vickers had seen it she would probably have been angry, for it was nothing less than the captain's brandy-flask.

"Drink," said she. "It's the same as they have upstairs, so it won't hurt you."

The fellow needed no pressing. He took off half the contents of the bottle at a gulp, and then, fetching a long breath, stood staring at her.

"That's prime!"

"Is it? I dare say it is." She had been looking at him with unaffected disgust as he drank. "Brandy is all you men understand." Miles—still sucking in his breath—came a pace closer.

"Not it," said he, with a twinkle in his little pig's eyes.

"I understand something else, miss, I can tell yer."

The tone of the sentence seemed to awaken and remind her of her errand in that place. She laughed as loudly and as merrily as she dared, and laid her hand on the speaker's arm. The boy—for he was but a boy, one of those many ill-reared country louts who leave the plough-tail for the musket, and, for a shilling a day, experience all the "pomp and circumstance of glorious war"—reddened to the roots of his closely-cropped hair.

"There, that's quite close enough. You're only a common soldier, Miles, and you mustn't make love to me."

"Not make love to yer!" says Miles. "What did yer tell me to meet yer here for then?"

She laughed again.

"What a practical animal you are! Suppose I had something to say to you?"

Miles devoured her with his eyes.

"It's hard to marry a soldier," he said, with a recruit's proud intonation of the word; "but yer might do worse, miss, and I'll work for yer like a slave, I will."

She looked at him with curiosity and pleasure. Though her time was evidently precious, she could not resist the temptation of listening to praises of herself.

"I know you're above me, Miss Sarah. You're a lady, but I love yer, I do, and you drives me wild with yer tricks."

"Do I?"

"Do yer? Yes, yer do. What did yer come an' make up to me for, and then go sweetheartin' with them others?"

"What others?"

"Why, the cuddy folk—the skipper, and the parson, and that Frere. I see yer walkin' the deck wi' un o' nights. Dom 'um, I'd put a bullet through his red head as soon as look at un."

"Hush! Miles dear—they'll hear you."

Her face was all aglow, and her expanded nostrils throbbed. Beautiful as the face was, it had a tigerish look about it at that moment.

Encouraged by the epithet, Miles put his arm round her slim

waist, just as Blunt had done, but she did not resent it so abruptly. Miles had promised more.

"Hush!" she whispered, with admirably-acted surprise—"I heard a noise!" and as the soldier started back, she smoothed her dress complacently.

"There is no one!" cried he.

"Isn't there? My mistake, then. Now come here, Miles."

Miles obeyed.

"Who is in the hospital?"

"I dunno."

"Well, I want to go in."

Miles scratched his head, and grinned.

"Yer carn't."

"Why not? You've let me in before."

"Against the doctor's orders. He told me special to let no one in but himself."

"Nonsense."

"It ain't nonsense. There was a convict brought in to-night, and nobody's to go near him."

"A convict!" She grew more interested. "What's the matter with him?"

"Dunno. But he's to be kep' quiet until old Pine comes down." She became authoritative.

"Come, Miles, let me go in."

"Don't ask me, miss. It's against orders, and—"

"Against orders? Why, you were blustering about shooting people just now."

The badgered Miles grew angry. "Was I? Bluster or no bluster, you don't go in." She turned away. "Oh, very well. If this is all the thanks I get for wasting my time down here, I shall go on deck again."

Miles became uneasy.

"There are plenty of agreeable people there."

Miles took a step after her.

"Mr. Frere will let me go in, I dare say, if I ask him."

Miles swore under his breath.

"Dom Mr. Frere! Go in if yer like," he said. "I won't stop yer, but remember what I'm doin' of."

She turned again at the foot of the ladder, and came quickly back. "That's a good lad. I knew you would not refuse me"; and smiling at the poor lad she was befooling, she passed into the cabin.

There was no lantern, and from the partially-blocked stern windows came only a dim, vaporous light. The dull ripple of the water as the ship rocked on the slow swell of the sea made a melancholy sound, and the sick man's heavy breathing seemed to fill the air. The slight noise made by the opening door roused him; he rose on his elbow and began to mutter. Sarah Purfoy paused in the doorway to listen, but she could make nothing of the low, uneasy murmuring. Raising her arm, conspicuous by its white sleeve in the gloom, she beckoned Miles.

"The lantern," she whispered, "bring me the lantern!"

He unhooked it from the rope where it swung, and brought it towards her. At that moment the man in the bunk sat up erect, and twisted himself towards the light. "Sarah!" he cried, in shrill sharp tones. "Sarah!" and swooped with a lean arm through the dusk, as though to seize her.

The girl leapt out of the cabin like a panther, struck the lantern out of her lover's hand, and was back at the bunk-head in a moment. The convict was a young man of about four-and-twenty. His hands—clutched convulsively now on the blankets—were small and well-shaped, and the unshaven chin bristled with promise of a strong beard. His wild black eyes glared with all the fire of delirium, and as he gasped for breath, the sweat stood in beads on his sallow forehead.

The aspect of the man was sufficiently ghastly, and Miles, drawing back with an oath, did not wonder at the terror which had seized Mrs. Vickers's maid. With open mouth and agonized face, she stood in the centre of the cabin, lantern in hand, like one turned to stone, gazing at the man on the bed.

"Ecod, he be a sight!" says Miles, at length. "Come away, miss, and shut the door. He's raving, I tell yer."

The sound of his voice recalled her.

She dropped the lantern, and rushed to the bed.

"You fool; he's choking, can't you see? Water! give me water!"

And wreathing her arms around the man's head, she pulled it down on her bosom, rocking it there, half savagely, to and fro.

Awed into obedience by her voice, Miles dipped a pannikin into a small puncheon, cleated in the corner of the cabin, and gave it her; and, without thanking him, she placed it to the sick prisoner's lips. He drank greedily, and closed his eyes with a grateful sigh.

Just then the quick ears of Miles heard the jingle of arms. "Here's the doctor coming, miss!" he cried. "I hear the sentry saluting. Come away! Quick!"

She seized the lantern, and, opening the horn slide, extinguished it.

"Say it went out," she said in a fierce whisper, "and hold your tongue. Leave me to manage."

She bent over the convict as if to arrange his pillow, and then glided out of the cabin, just as Pine descended the hatchway.

"Hallo!" cried he, stumbling, as he missed his footing; "where's the light?"

"Here, sir," says Miles, fumbling with the lantern. "It's all right, sir. It went out, sir."

"Went out! What did you let it go out for, you blockhead!" growled the unsuspecting Pine. "Just like you boobies! What is the use of a light if it 'goes out', eh?" As he groped his way, with outstretched arms, in the darkness, Sarah Purfoy slipped past him unnoticed, and gained the upper deck.

CHAPTER V
THE BARRACOON

IN the prison of the 'tween decks reigned a darkness pregnant with murmurs. The sentry at the entrance to the hatchway was supposed to "prevent the prisoners from making a noise," but he put a very liberal interpretation upon the clause, and so long as the prisoners refrained from shouting, yelling, and fighting—eccentricities in which they sometimes indulged—he did not disturb them. This course of conduct was dictated by prudence, no less than by convenience, for one sentry was but little over so many; and the convicts, if pressed too hard, would raise a sort of bestial boo-hoo, in which all voices were confounded, and which, while it made noise enough and to spare, utterly precluded individual punishment. One could not flog a hundred and eighty men, and it was impossible to distinguish any particular offender. So, in virtue of this last appeal, convictism had established a tacit right to converse in whispers, and to move about inside its oaken cage.

To one coming in from the upper air, the place would have seemed in pitchy darkness, but the convict eye, accustomed to the sinister twilight, was enabled to discern surrounding objects with tolerable distinctness. The prison was about fifty feet long and fifty feet wide, and ran the full height of the 'tween decks, viz., about five feet ten inches high. The barricade was loop-holed here and there, and the planks were in some places wide enough to admit a musket barrel. On the aft side, next the soldiers' berths, was a trap door, like the stoke-hole of a furnace. At first sight this appeared to be contrived for the humane purpose of ventilation, but a second glance dispelled this weak conclusion. The opening was just large enough to admit the muzzle of a small howitzer, secured on the deck below. In case of a mutiny, the soldiers could sweep the prison from end to end with grape shot. Such fresh air as there was, filtered through the loopholes, and came, in somewhat larger quantity, through a wind-sail passed into the prison from the hatchway. But the wind-sail, being necessarily at one end only of the place, the air it brought was pretty well absorbed by the twenty or thirty lucky fellows near it, and the other hundred and fifty did not come so well off. The scuttles were open, certainly, but as the row of bunks had been built against them, the air *they* brought was the peculiar property of such men as occupied the berths into which they penetrated. These berths were twenty-eight in number, each containing six men. They ran in a double tier round three sides of the prison, twenty at each side, and eight affixed to that portion of the forward barricade opposite the door. Each berth was presumed to be five feet six inches square, but the necessities of stowage had deprived them of six inches, and even under that pressure twelve men were compelled to sleep on the deck. Pine did not exaggerate when he spoke of the custom of overcrowding convict ships; and as he was entitled to half a guinea for every man he delivered alive at Hobart Town, he had some reason to complain.

When Frere had come down, an hour before, the prisoners were all snugly between their blankets. They were not so now; though, at the first clink of the bolts, they would be back again in their old positions, to all appearances sound asleep. As the eye became accustomed to the foetid duskiness of the prison, a strange picture presented itself. Groups of men, in all imaginable attitudes, were lying, standing, sitting, or pacing up and down. It was the scene on the poop-deck over again; only, here being no fear of restraining keepers, the wild beasts were a little more free in their movements. It is impossible to convey, in words, any idea of the hideous phantasmagoria of shifting limbs and faces which moved through the evil-smelling twilight of this terrible prison-house. Callot might have drawn it, Dante might have suggested it, but a minute attempt to describe its horrors would but disgust. There are depths in humanity which one cannot explore, as there are mephitic caverns into which one dare not penetrate.

Old men, young men, and boys, stalwart burglars and highway robbers, slept side by side with wizened pickpockets or cunning-featured area-sneaks. The forger occupied the same berth with the body-snatcher. The man of education learned strange secrets of house-breakers' craft, and the vulgar ruffian of St. Giles took lessons of self-control from the keener intellect of the professional swindler. The fraudulent clerk and the flash "cracksman" interchanged experiences. The smuggler's stories of lucky ventures and successful runs were capped by the footpad's reminiscences of foggy nights and stolen watches. The poacher, grimly thinking of his sick wife and orphaned children, would start as the night-house ruffian clapped him on the shoulder and bade him, with a curse, to take good heart and "be a man." The fast shopboy whose love of fine company and high living had brought him to this pass, had shaken off the first shame that was on him, and listened eagerly to the narratives of successful vice that fell so glibly from the lips of his older companions. To be transported seemed no such uncommon fate. The old fellows laughed, and wagged their grey heads with all the glee of past experience, and listening youth longed for the time when it might do likewise. Society was the common foe, and magistrates, gaolers, and parsons were the natural prey of all noteworthy mankind. Only fools were honest, only cowards kissed the rod, and failed to meditate revenge on that world of respectability which had wronged them. Each new-comer was one more recruit to the ranks of ruffianism, and not a man penned in that reeking den of infamy but became a sworn hater of law, order, and "free-men." What he might have been before mattered not. He was now a prisoner, and—thrust into a suffocating barracoon, herded with the foulest of mankind, with all imaginable depths of blasphemy and indecency sounded hourly in his sight and hearing—he lost his self-respect, and became what his gaolers took him to be—a wild beast to be locked under bolts and bars, lest he should break out and tear them.

The conversation ran upon the sudden departure of the four. What could they want with them at that hour?

"I tell you there's something up on deck," says one to the group nearest him. "Don't you hear all that rumbling and rolling?"

"What did they lower boats for? I heard the dip o' the oars."

"Don't know, mate. P'r'aps a burial job," hazarded a short, stout fellow, as a sort of happy suggestion.

"One of those coves in the parlour!" said another; and a laugh followed the speech.

"No such luck. You won't hang your jib for them yet awhile. More like the skipper agone fishin'."

"The skipper don't go fishin', yer fool. What would he do fishin'?—special in the middle o' the night."

"That 'ud be like old Dovery, eh?" says a fifth, alluding to an old grey-headed fellow, who—a returned convict—was again under sentence for body-snatching.

"Ay," put in a young man, who had the reputation of being the smartest "crow" in London—"'fishers of men,' as the parson says."

The snuffling imitation of a Methodist preacher was good, and there was another laugh.

Just then a miserable little cockney pickpocket, feeling his way to the door, fell into the party.

A volley of oaths and kicks received him.

"I beg your pardon, gen'l'men," cries the miserable wretch, "but I want h'air."

"Go to the barber's and buy a wig, then!" says the "Crow", elated at the success of his last sally.

"Oh, sir, my back!"

"Get up!" groaned someone in the darkness. "Oh, Lord, I'm smothering! Here, sentry!"

"Vater!" cried the little cockney. "Give us a drop o' vater, for mercy's sake. I haven't moist'ned my chaffer this blessed day."

"Half a gallon a day, bo', and no more," says a sailor next him.

"Yes, what have yer done with yer half-gallon, eh?" asked the Crow derisively. "Someone stole it," said the sufferer.

"He's been an' blued it," squealed someone. "Been an' blued it to buy a Sunday veskit with! Oh, ain't he a vicked young man?" And the speaker hid his head under the blankets, in humorous affectation of modesty.

All this time the miserable little cockney—he was a tailor by trade—had been grovelling under the feet of the Crow and his companions.

"Let me h'up, gents" he implored—"let me h'up. I feel as if I should die—I do."

"Let the gentleman up," says the humorist in the bunk. "Don't yer see his kerridge is avaitin' to take him to the Hopera?"

The conversation had got a little loud, and, from the topmost bunk on the near side, a bullet head protruded.

"Ain't a cove to get no sleep?" cried a gruff voice. "My blood, if I have to turn out, I'll knock some of your empty heads together."

It seemed that the speaker was a man of mark, for the noise ceased instantly; and, in the lull which ensued, a shrill scream broke from the wretched tailor.

"Help! they're killing me! Ah-h-h-!"

"Wot's the matter," roared the silencer of the riot, jumping from his berth, and scattering the Crow and his companions right and left. "Let him be, can't yer?"

"H'air!" cried the poor devil—"h'air; I'm fainting!"

Just then there came another groan from the man in the opposite bunk. "Well, I'm blessed!" said the giant, as he held the gasping tailor by the collar and glared round him. "Here's a pretty go! All the blessed chickens ha' got the croup!"

The groaning of the man in the bunk redoubled.

"Pass the word to the sentry," says someone more humane than the rest. "Ah," says the humorist, "pass him out; it'll be one the less. We'd rather have his room than his company."

"Sentry, here's a man sick."

But the sentry knew his duty better than to reply. He was a young soldier, but he had been well informed of the artfulness of convict stratagems; and, moreover, Captain Vickers had carefully apprised him *that by the King's Regulations, he was forbidden to reply to any question or communication addressed to him by a convict, but, in the event of being addressed, was to call the non-commissioned officer on duty.* Now, though he was within easy hailing distance of the guard on the quarter-deck, he felt a natural disinclination to disturb those gentlemen merely for the sake of a sick convict, and knowing that, in a few minutes, the third relief would come on duty, he decided to wait until then.

In the meantime the tailor grew worse, and began to moan dismally.

"Here! 'ullo!" called out his supporter, in dismay. "Hold up 'ere! Wot's wrong with yer? Don't come the drops 'ere. Pass him down, some of yer," and the wretch was hustled down to the doorway.

"Vater!" he whispered, beating feebly with his hand on the thick oak.

"Get us a drink, mister, for Gord's sake!"

But the prudent sentry answered never a word, until the ship's bell warned him of the approach of the relief guard; and then honest old Pine, coming with anxious face to inquire after his charge, received the intelligence that there was another prisoner sick. He had the door unlocked and the tailor outside in an instant. One look at the flushed, anxious face was enough.

"Who's that moaning in there?" he asked.

It was the man who had tried to call for the sentry an hour back, and Pine had him out also; convictism beginning to wonder a little.

"Take 'em both aft to the hospital," he said; "and, Jenkins, if there are any more men taken sick, let them pass the word for me at once. I shall be on deck."

The guard stared in each other's faces, with some alarm, but said nothing, thinking more of the burning ship, which now flamed furiously across the placid water, than of peril nearer home; but as Pine went up the hatchway he met Blunt.

"We've got the fever aboard!"

"Good God! Do you mean it, Pine?"

Pine shook his grizzled head sorrowfully.

"It's this cursed calm that's done it; though I expected it all along, with the ship crammed as she is. When I was in the *Hecuba*—"

"Who is it?"

Pine laughed a half-pitying, half-angry laugh.

"A convict, of course. Who else should it be? They are reeking like bullocks at Smithfield down there. A hundred and eighty men penned into a place fifty feet long, with the air like an oven—what could you expect?"

Poor Blunt stamped his foot.

"It isn't my fault," he cried. "The soldiers are berthed aft. If the Government will overload these ships, I can't help it."

"The Government! Ah! The Government! The Government don't sleep, sixty men a-side, in a cabin only six feet high. The Government don't get typhus fever in the tropics, does it?"

"No—but—"

"But what does the Government care, then?"

Blunt wiped his hot forehead.

"Who was the first down?"

"No. 97 berth; ten on the lower tier. John Rex he calls himself."

"Are you sure it's the fever?"

"As sure as I can be yet. Head like a fire-ball, and tongue like a strip of leather. Gad, don't I know it?" and Pine grinned mournfully. "I've got him moved into the hospital. Hospital! It is a hospital! As dark as a wolfs mouth. I've seen dog kennels I liked better."

Blunt nodded towards the volume of lurid smoke that rolled up out of the glow.—"Suppose there is a shipload of those poor devils? I can't refuse to take 'em in."

"No," says Pine gloomily, "I suppose you can't. If they come, I must stow 'em somewhere. We'll have to run for the Cape, with the first breeze, if they *do* come, that is all I can see for it," and he turned away to watch the burning vessel.

CHAPTER VI

THE FATE OF THE "HYDASPES"

IN the meanwhile the two boats made straight for the red column that uprose like a gigantic torch over the silent sea.

As Blunt had said, the burning ship lay a good twelve miles from the *Malabar,* and the pull was a long and a weary one. Once fairly away from the protecting sides of the vessel that had borne them thus far on their dismal journey, the adventurers seemed to have come into a new atmosphere. The immensity of the ocean over which they slowly moved revealed itself for the first time. On board the prison ship, surrounded with all the memories if not with the comforts of the shore they had quitted, they had not realized how far they were from that civilization which had given them birth. The well-lighted, well-furnished cuddy, the homely mirth of the forecastle, the setting of sentries and the changing of guards, even the gloom and terror of the closely-locked prison, combined to make the voyagers feel secure against the unknown dangers of the sea. That defiance of Nature which is born of contact with humanity, had hitherto sustained them, and they felt that, though alone on the vast expanse of waters, they were in companionship with others of their kind, and that the perils one man had passed might be successfully dared by another. But now—with one ship growing smaller behind them, and the other, containing they knew not what horror of human agony and human helplessness, lying a burning wreck in the black distance ahead of them—they began to feel their own littleness. The *Malabar,* that huge sea monster, in whose capacious belly so many human creatures lived and suffered, had dwindled to a walnut-shell, and yet beside her bulk how infinitely small had their own frail cockboat appeared as they shot out from under her towering stern! *Then* the black hull rising above them, had seemed a tower of strength, built to defy the utmost violence of wind and wave; *now* it was but a slip of wood floating—on an unknown depth of black, fathomless water. The blue light, which, at its first flashing over the ocean, had made the very stars pale their lustre, and lighted up with ghastly radiance the enormous vault of heaven, was now only a point, brilliant and distinct it is true, but which by its very brilliance dwarfed the ship into insignificance. The *Malabar* lay on the water like a glow-worm on a floating leaf, and the glare of the signal-fire made no more impression on the darkness than the candle carried by a solitary miner would have made on the abyss of a coal-pit.

And yet the *Malabar* held two hundred creatures like themselves!

The water over which the boats glided was black and smooth, rising into huge foamless billows, the more terrible because they were silent. When the sea hisses, it speaks, and speech breaks the spell of terror; when it is inert, heaving noiselessly, it is dumb, and seems to brood over mischief. The ocean in a calm is like a sulky giant; one dreads that it may be meditating evil. Moreover, an angry sea looks less vast in extent than a calm one. Its mounting waves bring the horizon nearer, and one does not discern how for many leagues the pitiless billows repeat themselves. To appreciate the hideous vastness of the ocean one must see it when it sleeps.

The great sky uprose from this silent sea without a cloud. The stars hung low in its expanse, burning in a violent mist of lower ether. The heavens were emptied of sound, and each dip of the oars was re-echoed in space by a succession of subtle harmonies. As the blades struck the dark water, it flashed fire, and the tracks of the boats resembled two sea-snakes writhing with silent undulations through a lake of quicksilver.

It had been a sort of race hitherto, and the rowers, with set teeth and compressed lips, had pulled stroke for stroke. At last the foremost boat came to a sudden pause. Best gave a cheery shout and passed her, steering straight into the broad track of crimson that already reeked on the sea ahead.

"What is it?" he cried.

But he heard only a smothered curse from Frere, and then his consort pulled hard to overtake him.

It was, in fact, nothing of consequence—only a prisoner "giving in".

"Curse it!" says Frere, "What's the matter with you? Oh, you, is it?—Dawes! Of course, Dawes. I never expected anything better from such a skulking hound. Come, this sort of nonsense won't do with me. It isn't as nice as lolloping about the hatchways, I dare say, but you'll have to go on, my fine fellow."

"He seems sick, sir," said compassionate bow.

"Sick! Not he. Shamming. Come, give way now! Put your backs into it!" and the convict having picked up his oar, the boat shot forward again.

But, for all Mr. Frere's urging, he could not recover the way he had lost, and Best was the first to run in under the black cloud that hung over the crimsoned water.

At his signal, the second boat came alongside.

"Keep wide," he said. "If there are many fellows yet aboard, they'll swamp us; and I think there must be, as we haven't met the boats," and then raising his voice, as the exhausted crew lay on their oars, he hailed the burning ship.

She was a huge, clumsily-built vessel, with great breadth of beam, and a lofty poop-deck. Strangely enough, though they had so lately seen the fire, she was already a wreck, and appeared to be completely deserted. The chief hold of the fire was amidships, and the lower deck was one mass of flame. Here and there were great charred rifts and gaps in her sides, and the red-hot fire glowed through these as through the bars of a grate. The mainmast had fallen on the starboard side, and trailed a blackened wreck in the water, causing the unwieldy vessel to lean over heavily. The fire roared like a cataract, and huge volumes of flame-flecked smoke poured up out of the hold, and rolled away in a low-lying black cloud over the sea.

As Frere's boat pulled slowly round her stem, he hailed the deck again and again.

Still there was no answer, and though the flood of light that dyed the water blood-red struck out every rope and spar distinct and clear, his straining eyes could see no living soul aboard. As they came nearer, they could distinguish the gilded letters of her name.

"What is it, men?" cried Frere, his voice almost drowned amid the roar of the flames. "Can you see?"

Rufus Dawes, impelled, it would seem, by some strong impulse of curiosity, stood erect, and shaded his eyes with his hand.

"Well—can't you speak? What is it?"

"The *Hydaspes*!"

Frere gasped.

The *Hydaspes*! The ship in which his cousin Richard Devine had sailed! The ship for which those in England might now look in vain! The *Hydaspes* which—something he had heard during the speculations as to this missing cousin flashed across him.

"Back water, men! Round with her! Pull for your lives!"

Best's boat glided alongside.

"Can you see her name?"

Frere, white with terror, shouted a reply.

"The *Hydaspes*! I know her. She is bound for Calcutta, and she has five tons of powder aboard!"

There was no need for more words. The single sentence explained the whole mystery of her desertion. The crew had taken to the boats on the first alarm, and had left their death-fraught vessel to her fate. They were miles off by this time, and unluckily for themselves, perhaps, had steered away from the side where rescue lay.

The boats tore through the water. Eager as the men had been to come, they were more eager to depart. The flames had even now reached the poop; in a few minutes it would be too late. For ten minutes or more not a word was spoken. With straining arms and labouring chests, the rowers tugged at the oars, their eyes fixed on the lurid mass they were leaving. Frere and Best, with their faces turned back to the terror they fled from, urged the men to greater efforts. Already the flames had lapped the flag, already the outlines of the stern carvings were blurred by the fire.

Another moment, and all would be over. Ah! it had come at last. A dull rumbling sound; the burning ship parted asunder; a pillar of fire, flecked with black masses that were beams and planks, rose up out of the ocean; there was a terrific crash, as though sea and sky were coming together; and then a mighty mountain of water rose, advanced, caught, and passed them, and they were alone—deafened, stunned, and breathless, in a sudden horror of thickest darkness, and a silence like that of the tomb.

The splashing of the falling fragments awoke them from their stupor, and then the blue light of the *Malabar* struck out a bright pathway across the sea, and they knew that they were safe.

*

On board the *Malabar* two men paced the deck, waiting for dawn.

It came at last. The sky lightened, the mist melted away, and then a long, low, far-off streak of pale yellow light floated on the eastern horizon. By and by the water sparkled, and the sea changed colour, turning from black to yellow, and from yellow to lucid green. The man at the masthead hailed the deck. The boats were in sight, and as they came towards the ship, the bright water flashing from the labouring oars, a crowd of spectators hanging over the bulwarks cheered and waved their hats.

"Not a soul!" cried Blunt. "No one but themselves. Well, I'm glad they're safe anyway."

The boats drew alongside, and in a few seconds Frere was upon deck.

"Well, Mr. Frere?"

"No use," cried Frere, shivering. "We only just had time to get away. The nearest thing in the world, sir."

"Didn't you see anyone?"

"Not a soul. They must have taken to the boats."

"Then they can't be far off," cried Blunt, sweeping the horizon with his glass. "They must have pulled all the way, for there hasn't been enough wind to fill a hollow tooth with."

"Perhaps they pulled in the wrong direction," said Frere. "They had a good four hours' start of us, you know."

Then Best came up, and told the story to a crowd of eager listeners. The sailors having hoisted and secured the boats, were hurried off to the forecastle, there to eat, and relate their experience between mouthfuls, and the four convicts were taken in charge and locked below again.

"You had better go and turn in, Frere," said Pine gruffly.

"It's no use whistling for a wind *here* all day."

Frere laughed—in his heartiest manner. "I think I will," he said. "I'm dog tired, and as sleepy as an owl," and he descended the poop ladder. Pine took a couple of turns up and down the deck, and then catching Blunt's eye, stopped in front of Vickers.

"You may think it a hard thing to say, Captain Vickers, but it's just as well if we don't find these poor devils. We have quite enough on our hands as it is."

"What do you mean, Mr. Pine?" says Vickers, his humane feelings getting the better of his pomposity. "You would not surely leave the unhappy men to their fate."

"Perhaps," returned the other, "they would not thank us for taking them aboard."

"I don't understand you."

"The fever has broken out."

Vickers raised his brows. He had no experience of such things; and though the intelligence was startling, the crowded condition of the prison rendered it easy to be understood, and he apprehended no danger to himself.

"It is a great misfortune; but, of course, you will take such steps—"

"It is only in the prison, as *yet*," says Pine, with a grim emphasis on the word; "but there is no saying how long it may stop there. I have got three men down as it is."

"Well, sir, all authority in the matter is in your hands. Any suggestions you make, I will, of course, do my best to carry out."

"Thank ye. I must have more room in the hospital to begin with. The soldiers must lie a little closer."

"I will see what can be done."

"And you had better keep your wife and the little girl as much on deck as possible."

Vickers turned pale at the mention of his child. "Good Heaven! do you think there is any danger?"

"There is, of course, danger to all of us; but with care we may escape it. There's that maid, too. Tell her to keep to herself a little more. She has a trick of roaming about the ship I don't like.

Infection is easily spread, and children always sicken sooner than grown-up people."

Vickers pressed his lips together. This old man, with his harsh, dissonant voice, and hideous practicality, seemed like a bird of ill omen.

Blunt, hitherto silently listening, put in a word for defence of the absent woman. "The wench is right enough, Pine," said he. "What's the matter with her?"

"Yes, *she's* all right, I've no doubt. She's less likely to take it than any of us. You can see her vitality in her face—as many lives as a cat. But she'd *bring* infection quicker than anybody."

"I'll—I'll go at once," cried poor Vickers, turning round. The woman of whom they were speaking met him on the ladder. Her face was paler than usual, and dark circles round her eyes gave evidence of a sleepless night. She opened her red lips to speak, and then, seeing Vickers, stopped abruptly.

"Well, what is it?"

She looked from one to the other. "I came for Dr. Pine."

Vickers, with the quick intelligence of affection, guessed her errand. "Someone is ill?"

"Miss Sylvia, sir. It is nothing to signify, I think. A little feverish and hot, and my mistress—"

Vickers was down the ladder in an instant, with scared face.

Pine caught the girl's round firm arm. "Where have you been?" Two great flakes of red came out in her white cheeks, and she shot an indignant glance at Blunt.

"Come, Pine, let the wench alone!"

"Were you with the child last night?" went on Pine, without turning his head.

"No; I have not been in the cabin since dinner yesterday. Mrs. Vickers only called me in just now. Let go my arm, sir, you hurt me."

Pine loosed his hold as if satisfied at the reply. "I beg your pardon, " he said gruffly. "I did not mean to hurt you. But the fever has broken out in the prison, and I think the child has caught it. You must be careful where you go." And then, with an anxious face, he went in pursuit of Vickers.

Sarah Purfoy stood motionless for an instant, in deadly terror.

Her lips parted, her eyes glittered, and she made a movement as though to retrace her steps.

"Poor soul!" thought honest Blunt, "how she feels for the child! D— that lubberly surgeon, he's hurt her!—Never mind, my lass," he said aloud. It was broad daylight, and he had not as much courage in love-making as at night. "Don't be afraid. I've been in ships with fever before now."

Awaking, as it were, at the sound of his voice, she came closer to him. "But ship fever! I have heard of it! Men have died like rotten sheep in crowded vessels like this."

"Tush! Not they. Don't be frightened; Miss Sylvia won't die, nor you neither." He took her hand. "It may knock off a few dozen prisoners or so. They are pretty close packed down there—"

She drew her hand away; and then, remembering herself, gave it him again.

"What is the matter?"

"Nothing—a pain. I did not sleep last night."

"There, there; you are upset, I dare say. Go and lie down."

She was staring away past him over the sea, as if in thought. So intently did she look that he involuntarily turned his head, and the action recalled her to herself. She brought her fine straight brows together for a moment, and then raised them with the action of a thinker who has decided on his course of conduct.

"I have a toothache," said she, putting her hand to her face.

"Take some laudanum," says Blunt, with dim recollections of his mother's treatment of such ailments. "Old Pine'll give you some."

To his astonishment she burst into tears.

"There—there! Don't cry, my dear. Hang it, don't cry. What are you crying about?"

She dashed away the bright drops, and raised her face with a rainy smile of trusting affection. "Nothing! I am lonely. So far from home; and—and Dr. Pine hurt my arm. Look!"

She bared that shapely member as she spoke, and sure enough there were three red marks on the white and shining flesh.

"The ruffian!" cried Blunt, "it's too bad." And after a hasty look around him, the infatuated fellow kissed the bruise. "I'll get the laudanum for you," he said. "You shan't ask that bear for it. Come into my cabin."

Blunt's cabin was in the starboard side of the ship, just under the poop awning, and possessed three windows—one looking out over the side, and two upon deck. The corresponding cabin on the other side was occupied by Mr. Maurice Frere. He closed the door, and took down a small medicine chest, cleated above the hooks where hung his signal-pictured telescope.

"Here," said he, opening it. "I've carried this little box for years, but it ain't often I want to use it, thank God. Now, then, put some o' this into your mouth, and hold it there."

"Good gracious, Captain Blunt, you'll poison me! Give me the bottle; I'll help myself."

"Don't take too much," says Blunt. "It's dangerous stuff, you know."

"You need not fear. I've used it before."

The door was shut, and as she put the bottle in her pocket, the amorous captain caught her in his arms.

"What do you say? Come, I think I deserve a kiss for that."

Her tears were all dry long ago, and had only given increased colour to her face. This agreeable woman never wept long enough to make herself distasteful. She raised her dark eyes to his for a moment, with a saucy smile. "By and by," said she, and escaping, gained her cabin. It was next to that of her mistress, and she could hear the sick child feebly moaning. Her eyes filled with tears—real ones this time.

"Poor little thing," she said; "I hope she won't die."

And then she threw herself on her bed, and buried her hot head in the pillow. The intelligence of the fever seemed to have terrified her. Had the news disarranged some well-concocted plan of hers? Being near the accomplishment of some cherished scheme long kept in view, had the sudden and unexpected presence of disease falsified her carefully-made calculations, and cast an almost insurmountable obstacle in her path?

"She die! and through me? How did I know that he had the fever? Perhaps I have taken it myself—I feel ill." She turned over on the bed, as if in pain, and then started to a sitting position, stung by a sudden thought. "Perhaps *he* might die! The fever spreads quickly, and if so, all this plotting will have been useless. It must be done at once. It will never do to break down *now,*" and taking the phial from her pocket, she held it up, to see how much it contained. It was three parts full. "Enough for both," she said, between her set teeth. The action of holding up the bottle reminded her of the amorous Blunt, and she smiled. "A strange way to show affection for a man," she said to herself, "and yet *he* doesn't care, and I suppose I shouldn't by this time. I'll go through with it, and, if the worst comes to the worst, I can fall back on Maurice." She loosened the cork of the phial, so that it would come out with as little noise as possible, and then placed it carefully in her bosom. "I will get a little sleep if I can," she said. "They have got the note, and it shall be done to-night."

CHAPTER VII

TYPHUS FEVER

THE felon Rufus Dawes had stretched himself in his bunk and tried to sleep. But though he was tired and sore, and his head felt like lead, he could not but keep broad awake. The long pull through the pure air, if it had tired him, had revived him, and he felt stronger; but for all that, the fatal sickness that was on him maintained its hold; his pulse beat thickly, and his brain throbbed with unnatural heat. Lying in his narrow space—in the semi-darkness—he tossed his limbs about, and closed his eyes in vain—he could not sleep. His utmost efforts induced only an oppressive stagnation of thought, through which he heard the voices of his fellow-convicts; while before his eyes was still the burning *Hydaspes*—that vessel whose destruction had destroyed for ever all trace of the unhappy Richard Devine.

It was fortunate for his comfort, perhaps, that the man who had been chosen to accompany him was of a talkative turn, for the prisoners insisted upon hearing the story of the explosion a dozen times over, and Rufus Dawes himself had been roused to give the name of the vessel with his own lips. Had it not been for the hideous respect in which he was held, it is possible that he might have been compelled to give his version also, and to join in the animated discussion which took place upon the possibility of the saving of the fugitive crew. As it was, however, he was left in peace, and lay unnoticed, trying to sleep.

The detachment of fifty being on deck—airing—the prison was not quite so hot as at night, and many of the convicts made up for their lack of rest by snatching a dog-sleep in the bared bunks. The four volunteer oarsmen were allowed to "take it out."

As yet there had been no alarm of fever. The three seizures had excited some comment, however, and had it not been for the counter-excitement of the burning ship, it is possible that Pine's precaution would have been thrown away. The "Old Hands"—who had been through the Passage before—suspected, but said nothing, save among themselves. It was likely that the weak and sickly would go first, and that there would be more room for those remaining. The Old Hands were satisfied.

Three of these Old Hands were conversing together just behind the partition of Dawes's bunk. As we have said, the berths were five feet square, and each contained six men. No. 10, the berth occupied by Dawes, was situated on the corner made by the joining of the starboard and centre lines, and behind it was a slight recess, in which the scuttle was fixed. His "mates" were at present but three in number, for John Rex and the cockney tailor had been removed to the hospital. The three that remained were now in deep conversation in the shelter of the recess. Of these, the giant—who had the previous night asserted his authority in the prison—seemed to be the chief. His name was Gabbett. He was a returned convict, now on his way to undergo a second sentence for burglary. The other two were a man named Sanders, known as the "Moocher", and Jemmy Vetch, the Crow. They were talking in whispers, but Rufus Dawes, lying with his head close to the partition, was enabled to catch much of what they said.

At first the conversation turned on the catastrophe of the burning ship and the likelihood of saving the crew. From this it grew to anecdote of wreck and adventure, and at last Gabbett said something which made the listener start from his indifferent efforts to slumber, into sudden broad wakefulness.

It was the mention of his own name, coupled with that of the woman he had met on the quarter-deck, that roused him.

"I saw her speaking to Dawes yesterday," said the giant, with an oath. "We don't want no more than we've got. I ain't goin' to risk my neck for Rex's woman's fancies, and so I'll tell her."

"It was something about the kid," says the Crow, in his elegant slang. "I don't believe she ever saw him before. Besides, she's nuts on Jack, and ain't likely to pick up with another man."

"If I thort she was agoin' to throw us over, I'd cut her throat as soon as look at her!" snorts Gabbett savagely.

"Jack ud have a word in that," snuffles the Moocher; "and he's a curious cove to quarrel with."

"Well, stow yer gaff," grumbled Mr. Gabbett, "and let's have no more chaff. If we're for bizness, let's come to bizness."

"What are we to do now?" asked the Moocher. "Jack's on the sick list, and the gal won't stir a'thout him."

"Ay," returned Gabbett, "that's it."

"My dear friends," said the Crow, "my keyind and keristian friends, it is to be regretted that when natur' gave you such tremendously thick skulls, she didn't put something inside of 'em. I say that now's the time. Jack's in the 'orspital; what of that? That don't make it no better for him, does it? Not a bit of it; and if he drops his knife and fork, why then, it's my opinion that the gal won't stir a peg. It's on *his* account, not ours, that she's been manoovering, ain't it?"

"Well!" says Mr. Gabbett, with the air of one who was but partly convinced, "I s'pose it is."

"All the more reason of getting it off quick. Another thing, when the boys know there's fever aboard, you'll see the rumpus there'll be. They'll be ready enough to join us then. Once get the snapper chest, and we're right as ninepenn'orth o' hapence."

This conversation, interspersed with oaths and slang as it was, had an intense interest for Rufus Dawes. Plunged into prison, hurriedly tried, and by reason of his surroundings ignorant of the death of his father and his own fortune, he had hitherto—in his agony and sullen gloom—held aloof from the scoundrels who surrounded him, and repelled their hideous advances of friendship. He now saw his error. He knew that the name he had once possessed was blotted out, that any shred of his old life which had clung to him hitherto, was shrivelled in the fire that consumed the *Hydaspes*. The secret, for the preservation of which Richard Devine had voluntarily flung away his name, and risked a terrible and disgraceful death, would be now for ever safe; for Richard Devine was dead—lost at sea with the crew of the ill-fated vessel in which, deluded by a skilfully-sent letter from the prison, his mother believed him to have sailed. Richard Devine was dead, and the secret of his birth would die with him. Rufus Dawes, his *alter ego,* alone should live. Rufus Dawes, the convicted felon, the suspected murderer, should live to claim his freedom, and work out his vengeance; or, rendered powerful by the terrible experience of the prison-sheds, should seize both, in defiance of gaol or gaoler.

With his head swimming, and his brain on fire, he eagerly listened for more. It seemed as if the fever which burnt in his veins had consumed the grosser part of his sense, and given him increased power of hearing. He was conscious that he was ill. His bones ached, his hands burned, his head throbbed, but he could hear distinctly, and, he thought, reason on what he heard profoundly.

"But we can't stir without the girl," Gabbett said. "She's got to stall off the sentry and give us the orfice."

The Crow's sallow features lighted up with a cunning smile.

"Dear old caper merchant! Hear him talk!" said he, "as if he had the wisdom of Solomon in all his glory? Look here!"

And he produced a dirty scrap of paper, over which his companions eagerly bent their heads.

"Where did yer get that?"

"Yesterday afternoon Sarah was standing on the poop throwing bits o' toke to the gulls, and I saw her a-looking at me very hard. At last she came down as near the barricade as she dared, and throwed crumbs and such like up in the air over the side. By and by a pretty big lump, doughed up round, fell close to my foot, and, watching a favourable opportunity, I pouched it. Inside was this bit o' rag-bag."

"Ah!" said Mr. Gabbett, "that's more like. Read it out, Jemmy." The writing, though feminine in character, was bold and distinct. Sarah had evidently been mindful of the education of her friends, and had desired to give them as little trouble as possible.

All is right. Watch me when I come up to-morrow evening at three bells. If I drop my handkerchief, get to work at the time agreed on. The sentry will be safe.

Rufus Dawes, though his eyelids would scarcely keep open, and a terrible lassitude almost paralysed his limbs, eagerly drank in the whispered sentence. There was a conspiracy to seize the ship. Sarah Purfoy was in league with the convicts—was herself the wife or mistress of one of them. She had come on board armed with a plot for his release, and this plot was about to be put in execution. He had heard of the atrocities perpetrated by successful mutineers.

Story after story of such nature had often made the prison resound with horrible mirth. He knew the characters of the three ruffians who, separated from him by but two inches of planking, jested and laughed over their plans of freedom and vengeance. Though he conversed but little with his companions, these men were his berth mates, and he could not but know how *they* would proceed to wreak their vengeance on their gaolers.

True, that the head of this formidable chimera—John Rex, the forger—was absent, but the two hands, or rather claws—the burglar and the prison-breaker—were present, and the slimly-made, effeminate Crow, if he had not the brains of the master, yet made up for his flaccid muscles and nerveless frame by a cat-like cunning, and a spirit of devilish volatility that nothing could subdue. With such a powerful ally outside as the mock maid-servant, the chance of success was enormously increased. There were one hundred and eighty convicts and but fifty soldiers. If the first rush proved successful—and the precautions taken by Sarah Purfoy rendered success possible—the vessel was theirs. Rufus Dawes thought of the little bright-haired child who had run so confidingly to meet him, and shuddered.

"There!" said the Crow, with a sneering laugh, "what do you think of that? Does the girl look like nosing us now?"

"No," says the giant, stretching his great arms with a grin of delight, as one stretches one's chest in the sun, "that's right, that is. That's more like bizness."

"England, home and beauty!" said Vetch, with a mock-heroic air, strangely out of tune with the subject under discussion. "You'd like to go home again, wouldn't you, old man?"

Gabbett turned on him fiercely, his low forehead wrinkled into a frown of ferocious recollection.

"*You!*" he said—"You think the chain's fine sport, don't yer? But I've been there, my young chicken, and I *knows what it means*."

There was silence for a minute or two. The giant was plunged in gloomy abstraction, and Vetch and the Moocher interchanged a significant glance. Gabbett had been ten years at the colonial penal settlement of Macquarie Harbour, and he had memories that he did not confide to his companions. When he indulged in one of these fits of recollection, his friends found it best to leave him to himself.

Rufus Dawes did not understand the sudden silence. With all his senses stretched to the utmost to listen, the cessation of the whispered colloquy affected him strangely. Old artillery-men have said that, after being at work for days in the trenches, accustomed to the continued roar of the guns, a sudden pause in the firing will cause them intense pain. Something of this feeling was experienced by Rufus Dawes. His faculties of hearing and thinking—both at their highest pitch—seemed to break down. It was as though some prop had been knocked from under him. No longer stimulated by outward sounds, his senses appeared to fail him. The blood rushed into his eyes and ears. He made a violent, vain effort to retain his consciousness, but with a faint cry fell back, striking his head against the edge of the bunk.

The noise roused the burglar in an instant. There was someone in the berth! The three looked into each other's eyes, in guilty alarm, and then Gabbett dashed round the partition.

"It's Dawes!" said the Moocher. "We had forgotten him!"

"He'll join us, mate—he'll join us!" cried Vetch, fearful of bloodshed.

Gabbett uttered a furious oath, and flinging himself on to the prostrate figure, dragged it, head foremost, to the floor. The sudden vertigo had saved Rufus Dawes's life. The robber twisted one brawny hand in his shirt, and pressing the knuckles down, prepared to deliver a blow that should for ever silence the listener, when Vetch caught his arm. "He's been asleep," he cried. "Don't hit him! See, he's not awake yet."

A crowd gathered round. The giant relaxed his grip, but the convict gave only a deep groan, and allowed his head to fall on his shoulder. "You've killed him!" cried someone.

Gabbett took another look at the purpling face and the bedewed forehead, and then sprang erect, rubbing at his right hand, as though he would rub off something sticking there.

"He's got the fever!" he roared, with a terror-stricken grimace.

"The what?" asked twenty voices.

"The fever, ye grinning fools!" cried Gabbett. "I've seen it before to-day. The typhus is aboard, and he's the fourth man down!"

The circle of beast-like faces, stretched forward to "see the fight," widened at the half-uncomprehended, ill-omened word. It was as though a bombshell had fallen into the group. Rufus Dawes lay on the deck motionless, breathing heavily. The savage circle glared at his prostrate body. The alarm ran round, and all the prison crowded down to stare at him. All at once he uttered a groan, and turning, propped his body on his two rigid arms, and made an effort to speak. But no sound issued from his convulsed jaws.

"He's done," said the Moocher brutally. "He didn't hear nuffin', I'll pound it."

The noise of the heavy bolts shooting back broke the spell. The first detachment were coming down from "exercise." The door was flung back, and the bayonets of the guard gleamed in a ray of sunshine that shot down the hatchway. This glimpse of sunlight—sparkling at the entrance of the foetid and stifling prison—seemed to mock their miseries. It was as though Heaven laughed at them. By one of those terrible and strange impulses which animate crowds, the mass, turning from the sick man, leapt towards the doorway. The interior of the prison flashed white with suddenly turned faces. The gloom scintillated with rapidly moving hands. "Air! air! Give us air!"

"That's it!" said Sanders to his companions. "I thought the news would rouse 'em."

Gabbett—all the savage in his blood stirred by the sight of flashing eyes and wrathful faces—would have thrown himself forward with the rest, but Vetch plucked him back.

"It'll be over in a moment," he said. "It's only a fit they've got." He spoke truly. Through the uproar was heard the rattle of iron on iron, as the guard "stood to their arms," and the wedge of grey cloth broke, in sudden terror of the levelled muskets.

There was an instant's pause, and then old Pine walked, unmolested, down the prison and knelt by the body of Rufus Dawes.

The sight of the familiar figure, so calmly performing its familiar duty, restored all that submission to recognized authority which strict discipline begets. The convicts slunk away into their berths, or officiously ran to help "the doctor," with affectation of intense obedience. The prison was like a schoolroom, into which the master had suddenly returned. "Stand back, my lads! Take him up, two of you, and carry him to the door. The poor fellow won't hurt you." His orders were obeyed, and the old man, waiting until his patient had been safely received outside, raised his hand to command attention. "I see you know what I have to tell. The fever has broken out. That man has got it. It is absurd to suppose that no one else will be seized. I might catch it myself. You are much crowded down here, I know; but, my lads, I can't help that; I didn't make the ship, you know."

"'Ear, 'ear!"

"It is a terrible thing, but you must keep orderly and quiet, and bear it like men. You know what the discipline is, and it is not in my power to alter it. I shall do my best for your comfort, and I look to you to help me."

Holding his grey head very erect indeed, the brave old fellow passed straight down the line, without looking to the right or left. He had said just enough, and he reached the door amid a chorus of "'Ear, 'ear!"

"Bravo!"

"True for you, docther!" and so on. But when he got fairly outside, he breathed more freely. He had performed a ticklish task, and he knew it.

"'Ark at 'em," growled the Moocher from his corner, "a-cheerin' at the bloody noos!"

"Wait a bit," said the acuter intelligence of Jemmy Vetch. "Give 'em time. There'll be three or four more down afore night, and *then* we'll see!"

CHAPTER VIII

A DANGEROUS CRISIS

IT was late in the afternoon when Sarah Purfoy awoke from her uneasy slumber. She had been dreaming of the deed she was about to do, and was flushed and feverish; but, mindful of the consequences which hung upon the success or failure of the enterprise, she rallied herself, bathed her face and hands, and ascended with as calm an air as she could assume to the poop-deck.

Nothing was changed since yesterday. The sentries' arms glittered in the pitiless sunshine, the ship rolled and creaked on the swell of the dreamy sea, and the prison-cage on the lower deck was crowded with the same cheerless figures, disposed in the attitudes of the day before. Even Mr. Maurice Frere, recovered from his midnight fatigues, was lounging on the same coil of rope, in precisely the same position.

Yet the eye of an acute observer would have detected some difference beneath this outward varnish of similarity. The man at the wheel looked round the horizon more eagerly, and spit into the swirling, unwholesome-looking water with a more dejected air than before. The fishing-lines still hung dangling over the catheads, but nobody touched them. The soldiers and sailors on the forecastle, collected in knots, had no heart even to smoke, but gloomily stared at each other. Vickers was in the cuddy writing; Blunt was in his cabin; and Pine, with two carpenters at work under his directions, was improvising increased hospital accommodation. The noise of mallet and hammer echoed in the soldiers' berth ominously; the workmen might have been making coffins. The prison was strangely silent, with the lowering silence which precedes a thunderstorm; and the convicts on deck no longer told stories, nor laughed at obscene jests, but sat together, moodily patient, as if waiting for something. Three men—two prisoners and a soldier—had succumbed since Rufus Dawes had been removed to the hospital; and though as yet there had been no complaint or symptom of panic, the face of each man, soldier, sailor, or prisoner, wore an expectant look, as though he wondered whose turn would come next. On the ship—rolling ceaselessly from side to side, like some wounded creature, on the opaque profundity of that stagnant ocean—a horrible shadow had fallen. The *Malabar* seemed to be enveloped in an electric cloud, whose sullen gloom a chance spark might flash into a blaze that should consume her.

The woman who held in her hands the two ends of the chain that would produce this spark, paused, came up upon deck, and, after a glance round, leant against the poop railing, and looked down into the barricade. As we have said, the prisoners were in knots of four and five, and to one group in particular her glance was directed. Three men, leaning carelessly against the bulwarks, watched her every motion.

"There she is, right enough," growled Mr. Gabbett, as if in continuation of a previous remark. "Flash as ever, and looking this way, too."

"I don't see no wipe," said the practical Moocher.

"Patience is a virtue, most noble knuckler!" says the Crow, with affected carelessness. "Give the young woman time."

"Blowed if I'm going to wait no longer," says the giant, licking his coarse blue lips. "'Ere we've been bluffed off day arter day, and kep' dancin' round the Dandy's wench like a parcel o' dogs. The fever's aboard, and we've got all ready. What's the use o' waitin'? Orfice, or no orfice, I'm for bizness at once!—"

"—There, look at that," he added, with an oath, as the figure of Maurice Frere appeared side by side with that of the waiting-maid, and the two turned away up the deck together.

"It's all right, you confounded muddlehead!" cried the Crow, losing patience with his perverse and stupid companion. "How can she give us the office with that cove at her elbow?"

Gabbett's only reply to this question was a ferocious grunt, and a sudden elevation of his clenched fist, which caused Mr. Vetch to retreat precipitately. The giant did not follow; and Mr. Vetch, folding his arms, and assuming an attitude of easy contempt, directed his attention to Sarah Purfoy. She seemed an object of general attraction, for at the same moment a young soldier ran up the ladder to the forecastle, and eagerly bent his gaze in her direction.

Maurice Frere had come behind her and touched her on the shoulder. Since their conversation the previous evening, he had made up his mind to be fooled no longer. The girl was evidently playing with him, and he would show her that he was not to be trifled with.

"Well, Sarah!"

"Well, Mr. Frere," dropping her hand, and turning round with a smile.

"How well you are looking to-day! Positively lovely!"

"You have told me that so often," says she, with a pout. "Have you nothing else to say?"

"Except that I love you." This in a most impassioned manner.

"That is no news. I know you do."

"Curse it, Sarah, what is a fellow to do?" His profligacy was failing him rapidly. "What is the use of playing fast and loose with a fellow this way?"

"A 'fellow' should be able to take care of himself, Mr. Frere. I didn't ask you to fall in love with me, did I? If you don't please me, it is not your fault, perhaps."

"What do you mean?"

"You soldiers have so many things to think of—your guards and sentries, and visits and things. You have no time to spare for a poor woman like me."

"Spare!" cries Frere, in amazement. "Why, damme, you won't let a fellow spare! I'd spare fast enough, if that was all." She cast her eyes down to the deck, and a modest flush rose in her cheeks. "I have so much to do," she said, in a half-whisper. "There are so many eyes upon me, I cannot stir without being seen."

She raised her head as she spoke, and to give effect to her words, looked round the deck. Her glance crossed that of the young soldier on the forecastle, and though the distance was too great for her to distinguish his features, she guessed who he was—Miles was jealous. Frere, smiling with delight at her change of manner, came close to her, and whispered in her ear. She affected to start, and took the opportunity of exchanging a signal with the Crow.

"I will come at eight o'clock," said she, with modestly averted face.

"They relieve the guard at eight," he said deprecatingly.

She tossed her head. "Very well, then, attend to your guard; *I* don't care."

"But, Sarah, consider—"

"As if a woman in love *ever* considers!" said she, turning upon him a burning glance, which in truth might have melted a more icy man than he.

She loved him then! What a fool he would be to refuse. To get her to come was the first object; how to make duty fit with pleasure would be considered afterwards. Besides, the guard could relieve itself for once without his supervision.

"Very well, at eight then, dearest."

"Hush!" said she. "Here comes that stupid captain."

And as Frere left her, she turned, and with her eyes fixed on the convict barricade, dropped the handkerchief she held in her hand over the poop railing. It fell at the feet of the amorous captain, and with a quick upward glance, that worthy fellow picked it up, and brought it to her.

"Oh, *thank* you, Captain Blunt," said she, and her eyes spoke more than her tongue.

"Did you take the laudanum?" whispered Blunt, with a twinkle in his eye.

"Some of it," said she. "I will bring you back the bottle to-night."

Blunt walked aft, humming cheerily, and saluted Frere with a slap on the back. The two men laughed, each at his own thoughts, but their laughter only made the surrounding gloom seem deeper than before.

Sarah Purfoy, casting her eyes toward the barricade, observed a change in the position of the three men. They were together once more, and the Crow, having taken off his prison cap, held it at arm's length with one hand, while he wiped his brow with the other. Her signal had been observed.

During all this, Rufus Dawes, removed to the hospital, was lying flat on his back, staring at the deck above him, trying to think of something he wanted to say.

When the sudden faintness, which was the prelude to his sickness, had overpowered him, he remembered being torn out of his bunk by fierce hands—remembered a vision of savage faces, and the presence of some danger that menaced him. He remembered that, while lying on his blankets, struggling with the coming fever, he had overheard a conversation of vital importance to himself and to the ship, but of the purport of that conversation he had not the least idea. In vain he strove to remember—in vain his will, struggling with delirium, brought back snatches and echoes of sense; they slipped from him again as fast as caught. He was oppressed with the weight of half-recollected thought. He knew that a terrible danger menaced him; that could he but force his brain to reason connectedly for ten consecutive minutes, he could give such information as would avert that danger, and save the ship. But, lying with hot head, parched lips, and enfeebled body, he was as one possessed—he could move nor hand nor foot.

The place where he lay was but dimly lighted. The ingenuity of Pine had constructed a canvas blind over the port, to prevent the sun striking into the cabin, and this blind absorbed much of the light. He could but just see the deck above his head, and distinguish the outlines of three other berths, apparently similar to his own. The only sounds that broke the silence were the gurgling of the water below him, and the *Tap tap, tap tap,* of Pine's hammers at work upon the new partition. By and by the noise of these hammers ceased, and then the sick man could hear gasps, and moans, and mutterings—the signs that his companions yet lived.

All at once a voice called out, "Of course his bills are worth four hundred pounds; but, my good sir, four hundred pounds to a man in my position is not worth the getting. Why, I've *given* four hundred pounds for a freak of my girl Sarah! Is it right, eh, Jezebel? She's a good girl, though, as girls go. Mrs. Lionel Crofton, of the Crofts, Sevenoaks, Kent—Sevenoaks, Kent—Seven—"

A gleam of light broke in on the darkness which wrapped Rufus Dawes's tortured brain. The man was John Rex, his berth mate. With an effort he spoke.

"Rex!"

"Yes, yes. I'm coming; don't be in a hurry. The sentry's safe, and the howitzer is but five paces from the door. A rush upon deck, lads, and she's ours! That is, mine. Mine and my wife's, Mrs. Lionel Crofton, of Seven Crofts, no oaks—Sarah Purfoy, lady's-maid and nurse—ha! ha!—lady's-maid and nurse!"

This last sentence contained the name-clue to the labyrinth in which Rufus Dawes's bewildered intellects were wandering. "Sarah Purfoy!" He remembered now each detail of the conversation he had so strangely overheard, and how imperative it was that he should, without delay, reveal the plot that threatened the ship. How that plot was to be carried out, he did not pause to consider; he was conscious that he was hanging over the brink of delirium, and that, unless he made himself understood before his senses utterly deserted him, all was lost.

He attempted to rise, but found that his fever-thralled limbs refused to obey the impulse of his will. He made an effort to speak, but his tongue clove to the roof of his mouth, and his jaws stuck together. He could not raise a finger nor utter a sound. The boards over his head waved like a shaken sheet, and the cabin whirled round, while the patch of light at his feet bobbed up and down like the reflection from a wavering candle. He closed his eyes with a terrible sigh of despair, and resigned himself to his fate. At that instant the sound of hammering ceased, and the door opened. It was six o'clock, and Pine had come to have a last look at his patients before dinner. It seemed that there was somebody with him, for a kind, though somewhat pompous, voice remarked upon the scantiness of accommodation, and the "necessity—the absolute necessity" of complying with the King's Regulations.

Honest Vickers, though agonized for the safety of his child, would not abate a jot of his duty, and had sternly come to visit the sick men, aware as he was that such a visit would necessitate his isolation from the cabin where his child lay. Mrs. Vickers—weeping and bewailing herself coquettishly at garrison parties—had often said that "poor dear John was *such* a disciplinarian, quite a *slave* to the service."

"Here they are," said Pine; "six of 'em. This fellow"—going to the side of Rex—"is the worst. If he had not a constitution like a horse, I don't think he could live out the night."

"Three, eighteen, seven, four," muttered Rex; "dot and carry one. Is that an occupation for a gentleman? No, sir. Good night, my lord, good night. Hark! The clock is striking nine; five, six, seven, eight! Well, you've had your day, and can't complain."

"A dangerous fellow," says Pine, with the light upraised. "A very dangerous fellow—that is, he was. This is the place, you see—a regular rat-hole; but what can one do?"

"Come, let us get on deck," said Vickers, with a shudder of disgust.

Rufus Dawes felt the sweat break out into beads on his forehead. They suspected nothing. They were going away. He *must* warn them. With a violent effort, in his agony he turned over in the bunk and thrust out his hand from the blankets.

"Hullo! what's this?" cried Pine, bringing the lantern to bear upon it. "Lie down, my man. Eh!—water, is it? There, steady with it now"; and he lifted a pannikin to the blackened, froth-fringed lips. The cool draught moistened his parched gullet, and the convict made a last effort to speak.

"Sarah Purfoy—to-night—the prison—MUTINY!"

The last word, almost shrieked out, in the sufferer's desperate efforts to articulate, recalled the wandering senses of John Rex.

"Hush!" he cried. "Is that you, Jemmy? Sarah's right. Wait till she gives the word."

"He's raving," said Vickers.

Pine caught the convict by the shoulder. "What do you say, my man? A mutiny of the prisoners!"

With his mouth agape and his hands clenched, Rufus Dawes, incapable of further speech, made a last effort to nod assent, but his head fell upon his breast; the next moment, the flickering light, the gloomy prison, the eager face of the doctor, and the astonished face of Vickers, vanished from before his straining eyes. He saw the two men stare at each other, in mingled incredulity and alarm, and then he was floating down the cool brown river of his boyhood, on his way—in company with Sarah Purfoy and Lieutenant Frere—to raise the mutiny of the *Hydaspes*, that lay on the stocks in the old house at Hampstead.

CHAPTER IX

WOMAN'S WEAPONS

THE two discoverers of this awkward secret held a council of war. Vickers was for at once calling the guard, and announcing to the prisoners that the plot—whatever it might be—had been discovered; but Pine, accustomed to convict ships, overruled this decision.

"You don't know these fellows as well as I do," said he. "In the first place there may be no mutiny at all. The whole thing is, perhaps, some absurdity of that fellow Dawes—and should we once put the notion of attacking us into the prisoners' heads, there is no telling what they might do."

"But the man seemed certain," said the other. "He mentioned my wife's maid, too!"

"Suppose he did?—and, begad, I dare say he's right—I never liked the look of the girl. To tell them that we have found them out this time won't prevent 'em trying it again. We don't know what their scheme is either. If it is a mutiny, half the ship's company may be in it. No, Captain Vickers, allow me, as surgeon-superintendent, to settle our course of action. You are aware that—"

"—That, by the King's Regulations, you are invested with full powers," interrupted Vickers, mindful of discipline in any extremity. "Of course, I merely suggested—and I know nothing about the girl, except that she brought a good character from her last mistress—a Mrs. Crofton I think the name was. We were glad to get *anybody* to make a voyage like this."

"Well," says Pine, "look here. Suppose we tell these scoundrels that their design, whatever it may be, is known. Very good. They will profess absolute ignorance, and try again on the next opportunity, when, perhaps, we may *not* know anything about it. At all events, we are completely ignorant of the nature of the plot and the names of the ringleaders. Let us double the sentries, and quietly get the men under arms. Let Miss Sarah do what she pleases, and *when* the mutiny breaks out, we will nip it in the bud; clap all the villains we get in irons, and hand them over to the authorities in Hobart Town.

I am not a cruel man, sir, but we have got a cargo of wild beasts aboard, and we must be careful."

"But surely, Mr. Pine, have you considered the probable loss of life? I—really—some more humane course perhaps? Prevention, you know—"

Pine turned round upon him with that grim practicality which was a part of his nature. "Have *you* considered the safety of the ship, Captain Vickers? You know, or have heard of, the sort of things that take place in these mutinies. Have you considered what will befall those half-dozen women in the soldiers' berths? Have you thought of the fate of your own wife and child?"

Vickers shuddered.

"Have it your way, Mr. Pine; you know best perhaps. But don't risk more lives than you can help."

"Be easy, sir," says old Pine; "I am acting for the best; upon my soul I am. You don't know what convicts are, or rather what the law has made 'em—*yet*—"

"Poor wretches!" says Vickers, who, like many martinets, was in reality tender-hearted. "Kindness might do much for them. After all, they are our fellow-creatures."

"Yes," returned the other, "they are. But if you use that argument to them when they have taken the vessel, it won't avail you much. Let me manage, sir; and for God's sake, say nothing to anybody. Our lives may hang upon a word."

Vickers promised, and kept his promise so far as to chat cheerily with Blunt and Frere at dinner, only writing a brief note to his wife to tell her that, whatever she heard, she was not to stir from her cabin until he came to her; he knew that, with all his wife's folly, she would obey unhesitatingly, when he couched an order in such terms.

According to the usual custom on board convict ships, the guards relieved each other every two hours, and at six p.m. the poop guard was removed to the quarter-deck, and the arms which, in the daytime, were disposed on the top of the arm-chest, were placed in an arm-rack constructed on the quarter-deck for that purpose. Trusting nothing to Frere—who, indeed, by Pine's advice, was, as we have seen, kept in ignorance of the whole matter—Vickers ordered all the men, save those who had been on guard during the day, to be under arms in the barrack, forbade communication with the upper deck, and placed as sentry at the barrack door his own servant, an old soldier, on whose fidelity he could thoroughly rely. He then doubled the guards, took the keys of the prison himself from the non-commissioned officer whose duty it was to keep them, and saw that the howitzer on the lower deck was loaded with grape. It was a quarter to seven when Pine and he took their station at the main hatchway, determined to watch until morning.

At a quarter past seven, any curious person looking through the window of Captain Blunt's cabin would have seen an unusual sight. That gallant commander was sitting on the bed-place, with a glass of rum and water in his hand, and the handsome waiting-maid of Mrs. Vickers was seated on a stool by his side. At a first glance it was perceptible that the captain was very drunk. His grey hair was matted all ways about his reddened face, and he was winking and blinking like an owl in the sunshine. He had drunk a larger quantity of wine than usual at dinner, in sheer delight at the approaching assignation, and having got out the rum bottle for a quiet "settler" just as the victim of his fascinations glided through the carefully-adjusted door, he had been persuaded to go on drinking.

"Cuc-come, Sarah," he hiccuped. "It's all very fine, my lass, but you needn't be so—hie—proud, you know. I'm a plain sailor—plain s'lor, Srr'h. Ph'n'as Bub—blunt, commander of the *Mal-Mal-Malabar*. Wors' 'sh good talkin'?"

Sarah allowed a laugh to escape her, and artfully protruded an ankle at the same time. The amorous Phineas lurched over, and made shift to take her hand.

"You lovsh me, and I—hie—lovsh you, Sarah. And a preshus tight little craft you—hie—are. Giv'sh—kiss, Sarah."

Sarah got up and went to the door.

"Wotsh this? Goin'! Sarah, don't go," and he staggered up; and with the grog swaying fearfully in one hand, made at her.

The ship's bell struck the half-hour. Now or never was the time. Blunt caught her round the waist with one arm, and hiccuping with love and rum, approached to take the kiss he coveted. She seized the moment, surrendered herself to his embrace, drew from her pocket the laudanum bottle, and passing her hand over his shoulder, poured half its contents into the glass.

"Think I'm—hie—drunk, do yer? Nun—not I, my wench."

"You will be if you drink much more. Come, finish that and be quiet, or I'll go away."

But she threw a provocation into her glance as she spoke, which belied her words, and which penetrated even the sodden intellect of poor Blunt. He balanced himself on his heels for a moment, and holding by the moulding of the cabin, stared at her with a fatuous smile of drunken admiration, then looked at the glass in his hand, hiccuped with much solemnity thrice, and, as though struck with a sudden sense of duty unfulfilled, swallowed the contents at a gulp. The effect was almost instantaneous. He dropped the tumbler, lurched towards the woman at the door, and then making a half-turn in accordance with the motion of the vessel, fell into his bunk, and snored like a grampus.

Sarah Purfoy watched him for a few minutes, and then having blown out the light, stepped out of the cabin, and closed the door behind her. The dusky gloom which had held the deck on the previous night enveloped all forward of the main-mast. A lantern swung in the forecastle, and swayed with the motion of the ship. The light at the prison door threw a glow through the open hatch, and in the cuddy, at her right hand, the usual row of oil-lamps burned. She looked mechanically for Vickers, who was ordinarily there at that hour, but the cuddy was empty. So much the better, she thought, as she drew her dark cloak around her, and tapped at Frere's door. As she did so, a strange pain shot through her temples, and her knees trembled. With a strong effort she dispelled the dizziness that had almost overpowered her, and held herself erect. It would never do to break down now.

The door opened, and Maurice Frere drew her into the cabin. "So you have come?" said he.

"You see I have. But, oh! if I should be seen!"

"Seen? Nonsense! Who is to see you?"

"Captain Vickers, Doctor Pine, anybody."

"Not they. Besides, they've gone off down to Pine's cabin since dinner. They're all right."

Gone off to Pine's cabin! The intelligence struck her with dismay. What was the cause of such an unusual proceeding? Surely they did not suspect! "What do they want there?" she asked.

Maurice Frere was not in the humour to argue questions of probability. "Who knows? I don't. Confound 'em," he added, "what does it matter to us? We don't want them, do we, Sarah?"

She seemed to be listening for something, and did not reply. Her nervous system was wound up to the highest pitch of excitement. The success of the plot depended on the next five minutes.

"What are you staring at? Look at me, can't you? What eyes you have! And what hair!"

At that instant the report of a musket-shot broke the silence. The mutiny had begun!

The sound awoke the soldier to a sense of his duty. He sprang to his feet, and disengaging the arms that clung about his neck, made for the door. The moment for which the convict's accomplice had waited approached. She hung upon him with all her weight. Her long hair swept across his face, her warm breath was on his cheek, her dress exposed her round, smooth shoulder. He, intoxicated, conquered, had half-turned back, when suddenly the rich crimson died away from her lips, leaving them an ashen grey colour. Her eyes closed in agony; loosing her hold of him, she staggered to her feet, pressed her hands upon her bosom, and uttered a sharp cry of pain.

The fever which had been on her two days, and which, by a strong exercise of will, she had struggled against—encouraged by the violent excitement of the occasion—had attacked her at this supreme moment. Deathly pale and sick, she reeled to the side of the cabin. There was another shot, and a violent clashing of arms; and Frere, leaving the miserable woman to her fate, leapt out on to the deck.

CHAPTER X

EIGHT BELLS

AT seven o'clock there had been also a commotion in the prison. The news of the fever had awoke in the convicts all that love of liberty which had but slumbered during the monotony of the earlier part of the voyage. Now that death menaced them, they longed fiercely for the chance of escape which seemed permitted to freemen. "Let us get out!" they said, each man speaking to his particular friend. "We are locked up here to die like sheep." Gloomy faces and desponding looks met the gaze of each, and sometimes across this gloom shot a fierce glance that lighted up its blackness, as a lightning-flash renders luridly luminous the indigo dullness of a thunder-cloud. By and by, in some inexplicable way, it came to be understood that there was a conspiracy afloat, that they were to be released from their shambles, that some amongst them had been plotting for freedom. The 'tween decks held its foul breath in wondering anxiety, afraid to breathe its suspicions. The influence of this predominant idea showed itself by a strange shifting of atoms. The mass of villainy, ignorance, and innocence began to be animated with something like a uniform movement. Natural affinities came together, and like allied itself to like, falling noiselessly into harmony, as the pieces of glass and coloured beads in a kaleidoscope assume mathematical forms. By seven bells it was found that the prison was divided into three parties—the desperate, the timid, and the cautious. These three parties had arranged themselves in natural sequence. The mutineers, headed by Gabbett, Vetch, and the Moocher, were nearest to the door; the timid—boys, old men, innocent poor wretches condemned on circumstantial evidence, or rustics condemned to be turned into thieves for pulling a turnip—were at the farther end, huddling together in alarm; and the prudent—that is to say, all the rest, ready to fight or fly, advance or retreat, assist the authorities or their companions, as the fortune of the day might direct—occupied the middle space. The mutineers proper numbered, perhaps, some thirty men, and of these thirty only half a dozen knew what was really about to be done.

The ship's bell strikes the half-hour, and as the cries of the three sentries passing the word to the quarter-deck die away, Gabbett, who has been leaning with his back against the door, nudges Jemmy Vetch.

"Now, Jemmy," says he in a whisper, "tell 'em!"

The whisper being heard by those nearest the giant, a silence ensues, which gradually spreads like a ripple over the surface of the crowd, reaching even the bunks at the further end.

"Gentlemen," says Mr. Vetch, politely sarcastic in his own hangdog fashion, "myself and my friends here are going to take the ship for you. Those who like to join us had better speak at once, for in about half an hour they will not have the opportunity."

He pauses, and looks round with such an impertinently confident air, that three waverers in the party amidships slip nearer to hear him.

"You needn't be afraid," Mr. Vetch continues, "we have arranged it all for you. There are friends waiting for us outside, and the door will be open directly. All we want, gentlemen, is your vote and interest—I mean your—"

"Gaffing agin!" interrupts the giant angrily. "Come to business, carn't yer? Tell 'em they may like it or lump it, but we mean to have the ship, and them as refuses to join us we mean to chuck overboard. That's about the plain English of it!"

This practical way of putting it produces a sensation, and the conservative party at the other end look in each other's faces with some alarm. A grim murmur runs round, and somebody near Mr. Gabbett laughs a laugh of mingled ferocity and amusement, not reassuring to timid people. "What about the sogers?" asked a voice from the ranks of the cautious.

"D— the sogers!" cries the Moocher, moved by a sudden inspiration. "They can but shoot yer, and that's as good as dyin' of typhus anyway!"

The right chord had been struck now, and with a stifled roar the prison admitted the truth of the sentiment. "Go on, old man!" cries Jemmy Vetch to the giant, rubbing his thin hands with eldritch glee. "They're all right!" And then, his quick ears catching the jingle of arms, he said, "Stand by now for the door—one rush'll do it."

It was eight o'clock and the relief guard was coming from the after deck. The crowd of prisoners round the door held their breath to listen. "It's all planned," says Gabbett, in a low growl. "W'en the door h'opens we rush, and we're in among the guard afore they know where they are. Drag 'em back into the prison, grab the h'arm-rack, and it's all over."

"They're very quiet about it," says the Crow suspiciously. "I hope it's all right."

"Stand from the door, Miles," says Pine's voice outside, in its usual calm accents.

The Crow was relieved. The tone was an ordinary one, and Miles was the soldier whom Sarah Purfoy had bribed not to fire. All had gone well.

The keys clashed and turned, and the bravest of the prudent party, who had been turning in his mind the notion of risking his life for a pardon, to be won by rushing forward at the right moment and alarming the guard, checked the cry that was in his throat as he saw the men round the door draw back a little for their rush, and caught a glimpse of the giant's bristling scalp and bared gums.

"NOW!" cries Jemmy Vetch, as the iron-plated oak swung back, and with the guttural snarl of a charging wild boar, Gabbett hurled himself out of the prison.

The red line of light which glowed for an instant through the doorway was blotted out by a mass of figures. All the prison surged forward, and before the eye could wink, five, ten, twenty, of the most desperate were outside. It was as though a sea, breaking against a stone wall, had found some breach through which to pour its waters. The contagion of battle spread. Caution was forgotten; and those at the back, seeing Jemmy Vetch raised upon the crest of that human billow which reared its black outline against an indistinct perspective of struggling figures, responded to his grin of encouragement by rushing furiously forward.

Suddenly a horrible roar like that of a trapped wild beast was heard. The rushing torrent choked in the doorway, and from out the lantern glow into which the giant had rushed, a flash broke, followed by a groan, as the perfidious sentry fell back shot through the breast.

The mass in the doorway hung irresolute, and then by sheer weight of pressure from behind burst forward, and as it so burst, the heavy door crashed into its jambs, and the bolts were shot into their places.

All this took place by one of those simultaneous movements which are so rapid in execution, so tedious to describe in detail. At one instant the prison door had opened, at the next it had closed. The picture which had presented itself to the eyes of the convicts was as momentary as are those of the thaumatoscope. The period of time that had elapsed between the opening and the shutting of the door could have been marked by the musket shot.

The report of another shot, and then a noise of confused cries, mingled with the clashing of arms, informed the imprisoned men that the ship had been alarmed. How would it go with their friends on deck? Would they succeed in overcoming the guards, or would they be beaten back? They would soon know; and in the hot dusk, straining their eyes to see each other, they waited for the issue Suddenly the noises ceased, and a strange rumbling sound fell upon the ears of the listeners.

*

What had taken place?

This—the men pouring out of the darkness into the sudden glare of the lanterns, rushed, bewildered, across the deck. Miles, true to his promise, did not fire, but the next instant Vickers had snatched the firelock from him, and leaping into the stream, turned about and fired down towards the prison. The attack was more sudden then he had expected, but he did not lose his presence of mind. The shot would serve a double purpose. It would warn the men in the barrack, and perhaps check the rush by stopping up the doorway with a corpse. Beaten back, struggling, and indignant, amid the storm of hideous faces, his humanity vanished, and he aimed deliberately at the head of Mr. James Vetch; the shot, however, missed its mark, and killed the unhappy Miles.

Gabbett and his companions had by this time reached the foot of the companion ladder, there to encounter the cutlasses of the doubled guard gleaming redly in the glow of the lanterns. A glance up the hatchway showed the giant that the arms he had planned to seize were defended by ten firelocks, and that, behind the open doors of the partition which ran abaft the mizenmast, the remainder of the detachment stood to their arms. Even his dull intellect comprehended that the desperate project had failed, and that he had been betrayed. With the roar of despair which had penetrated into the prison, he turned to fight his way back, just in time to see the crowd in the gangway recoil from the flash of the musket fired by Vickers. The next instant, Pine and two soldiers, taking advantage of the momentary cessation of the press, shot the bolts, and secured the prison.

The mutineers were caught in a trap.

The narrow space between the barracks and the barricade was choked with struggling figures. Some twenty convicts, and half as many soldiers, struck and stabbed at each other in the crowd. There was barely elbow-room, and attacked and attackers fought almost without knowing whom they struck. Gabbett tore a cutlass from a soldier, shook his huge head, and calling on the Moocher to follow, bounded up the ladder, desperately determined to brave the fire of the watch. The Moocher, close at the giant's heels, flung himself upon the nearest soldier, and grasping his wrist, struggled for the cutlass. A brawny, bull-necked fellow next him dashed his clenched fist in the soldier's face, and the man maddened by the blow, let go the cutlass, and drawing his pistol, shot his new assailant through the head. It was this second shot that had aroused Maurice Frere.

As the young lieutenant sprang out upon the deck, he saw by the position of the guard that others had been more mindful of the safety of the ship than he. There was, however, no time for explanation, for, as he reached the hatchway, he was met by the ascending giant, who uttered a hideous oath at the sight of this unexpected adversary, and, too close to strike him, locked him in his arms. The two men were drawn together. The guard on the quarter-deck dared not fire at the two bodies that, twined about each other, rolled across the deck, and for a moment Mr. Frere's cherished existence hung upon the slenderest thread imaginable.

The Moocher, spattered with the blood and brains of his unfortunate comrade, had already set his foot upon the lowest step of the ladder, when the cutlass was dashed from his hand by a blow from a clubbed firelock, and he was dragged roughly backwards. As he fell upon the deck, he saw the Crow spring out of the mass of prisoners who had been, an instant before, struggling with the guard, and, gaining the cleared space at the bottom of the ladder, hold up his hands, as though to shield himself from a blow. The confusion had now become suddenly stilled, and upon the group before the barricade had fallen that mysterious silence which had perplexed the inmates of the prison.

They were not perplexed for long. The two soldiers who, with the assistance of Pine, had forced-to the door of the prison, rapidly unbolted that trap-door in the barricade, of which mention has been made in a previous chapter, and, at a signal from Vickers, three men ran the loaded howitzer from its sinister shelter near the break of the barrack berths, and, training the deadly muzzle to a level with the opening in the barricade, stood ready to fire.

"Surrender!" cried Vickers, in a voice from which all "humanity" had vanished. "Surrender, and give up your ringleaders, or I'll blow you to pieces!"

There was no tremor in his voice, and though he stood, with Pine by his side, at the very mouth of the levelled cannon, the mutineers perceived, with that acuteness which imminent danger brings to the most stolid of brains, that, did they hesitate an instant, he would keep his word. There was an awful moment of silence, broken only by a skurrying noise in the prison, as though a family of rats, disturbed at a flour cask, were scampering to the ship's side for shelter.

This skurrying noise was made by the convicts rushing to their berths to escape the threatened shower of grape; to the twenty desperadoes cowering before the muzzle of the howitzer it spoke more eloquently than words. The charm was broken; their comrades would refuse to join them. The position of affairs at this crisis was a strange one. From the opened trap-door came a sort of subdued murmur, like that which sounds within the folds of a sea-shell, but, in the oblong block of darkness which it framed, nothing was visible. The trap-door might have been a window looking into a tunnel. On each side of this horrible window, almost pushed before it by the pressure of one upon the other, stood Pine, Vickers, and the guard. In front of the little group lay the corpse of the miserable boy whom Sarah Purfoy had led to ruin; and forced close upon, yet shrinking back from the trampled and bloody mass, crouched in mingled terror and rage, the twenty mutineers. Behind the mutineers, withdrawn from the patch of light thrown by the open hatchway, the mouth of the howitzer threatened destruction; and behind the howitzer, backed up by an array of brown musket barrels, suddenly glowed the tiny fire of the burning match in the hand of Vickers's trusty servant.

The entrapped men looked up the hatchway, but the guard had already closed in upon it, and some of the ship's crew—with that carelessness of danger characteristic of sailors—were peering down upon them. Escape was hopeless.

"One minute!" cried Vickers, confident that one second would be enough—"one minute to go quietly, or—"

"Surrender, mates, for God's sake!" shrieked some unknown wretch from out of the darkness of the prison. "Do you want to be the death of us?"

Jemmy Vetch, feeling, by that curious sympathy which nervous natures possess, that his comrades wished him to act as spokesman, raised his shrill tones. "We surrender," he said. "It's no use getting our brains blown out." And raising his hands, he obeyed the motion of Vickers's fingers, and led the way towards the barrack.

"Bring the irons forward, there!" shouted Vickers, hastening from his perilous position; and before the last man had filed past the still smoking match, the cling of hammers announced that the Crow had resumed those fetters which had been knocked off his dainty limbs a month previously in the Bay of Biscay.

In another moment the trap-door was closed, the howitzer rumbled back to its cleatings, and the prison breathed again.

*

In the meantime, a scene almost as exciting had taken place on the upper deck. Gabbett, with the blind fury which the consciousness of failure brings to such brute-like natures, had seized Frere by the throat, determined to put an end to at least one of his enemies. But desperate though he was, and with all the advantage of weight and strength upon his side, he found the young lieutenant a more formidable adversary than he had anticipated.

Maurice Frere was no coward. Brutal and selfish though he might be, his bitterest enemies had never accused him of lack of physical courage. Indeed, he had been—in the rollicking days of old that were gone—celebrated for the display of very opposite qualities. He was an amateur at manly sports. He rejoiced in his muscular strength, and, in many a tavern brawl and midnight riot of his own provoking, had proved the fallacy of the proverb which teaches that a bully is *always* a coward. He had the tenacity of a bulldog—once let him get his teeth in his adversary, and he would hold on till he died. In fact he was, as far as personal vigour went, a Gabbett with the education of a prize-fighter; and, in a personal encounter between two men of equal courage, science tells more than strength. In the struggle, however, that was now taking place, science seemed to be of little value. To the inexperienced eye, it would appear that the frenzied giant, gripping the throat of the man who had fallen beneath him, must rise from the struggle an easy victor. Brute force was all that was needed—there was neither room nor time for the display of any cunning of fence.

But knowledge, though it cannot give strength, gives coolness. Taken by surprise as he was, Maurice Frere did not lose his presence of mind. The convict was so close upon him that there was no time to strike; but, as he was forced backwards, he succeeded in crooking his knee round the thigh of his assailant, and thrust one hand into his collar. Over and over they rolled, the bewildered sentry not daring to fire, until the ship's side brought them up with a violent jerk, and Frere realized that Gabbett was below him. Pressing with all the might of his muscles, he strove to resist the leverage which the giant was applying to turn him over, but he might as well have pushed against a stone wall. With his eyes protruding, and every sinew strained to its uttermost, he was slowly forced round, and he felt Gabbett releasing his grasp, in order to draw back and aim at him an effectual blow. Disengaging his left hand, Frere suddenly allowed himself to sink, and then, drawing up his right knee, struck Gabbett beneath the jaw, and as the huge head was forced backwards by the blow, dashed his fist into the brawny throat. The giant reeled backwards, and, falling on his hands and knees, was in an instant surrounded by sailors.

Now began and ended, in less time than it takes to write it, one of those Homeric struggles of one man against twenty, which are none the less heroic because the Ajax is a convict, and the Trojans merely ordinary sailors. Shaking his assailants to the deck as easily as a wild boar shakes off the dogs which clamber upon his bristly sides, the convict sprang to his feet, and, whirling the snatched-up cutlass round his head, kept the circle at bay. Four times did the soldiers round the hatchway raise their muskets, and four times did the fear of wounding the men who had flung themselves upon the enraged giant compel them to restrain their fire. Gabbett, his stubbly hair on end, his bloodshot eyes glaring with fury, his great hand opening and shutting in air, as though it gasped for something to seize, turned himself about from side to side— now here, now there, bellowing like a wounded bull. His coarse shirt, rent from shoulder to flank, exposed the play of his huge muscles. He was bleeding from a cut on his forehead, and the blood, trickling down his face, mingled with the foam on his lips, and dropped sluggishly on his hairy breast. Each time that an assailant came within reach of the swinging cutlass, the ruffian's form dilated with a fresh access of passion. At one moment bunched with clinging adversaries—his arms, legs, and shoulders a hanging mass of human bodies—at the next, free, desperate, alone in the midst of his foes, his hideous countenance contorted with hate and rage, the giant seemed less a man than a demon, or one of those monstrous and savage apes which haunt the solitudes of the African forests. Spurning the mob who had rushed in at him, he strode towards his risen adversary, and aimed at him one final blow that should put an end to his tyranny for ever. A notion that Sarah Purfoy had betrayed him, and that the handsome soldier was the cause of the betrayal, had taken possession of his mind, and his rage had concentrated itself upon Maurice Frere. The aspect of the villain was so appalling, that, despite his natural courage, Frere, seeing the backward sweep of the cutlass, absolutely closed his eyes with terror, and surrendered himself to his fate.

As Gabbett balanced himself for the blow, the ship, which had been rocking gently on a dull and silent sea, suddenly lurched—the convict lost his balance, swayed, and fell. Ere he could rise he was pinioned by twenty hands.

Authority was almost instantaneously triumphant on the upper and lower decks. The mutiny was over.

CHAPTER XI

DISCOVERIES AND CONFESSIONS

THE shock was felt all through the vessel, and Pine, who had been watching the ironing of the last of the mutineers, at once divined its cause.

"Thank God!" he cried, "there's a breeze at last!" and as the overpowered Gabbett, bruised, bleeding, and bound, was dragged down the hatchway, the triumphant doctor hurried upon deck to find the *Malabar* plunging through the whitening water under the influence of a fifteen-knot breeze.

"Stand by to reef topsails! Away aloft, men, and furl the royals!" cries Best from the quarter-deck; and in the midst of the cheery confusion Maurice Frere briefly recapitulated what had taken place, taking care, however, to pass over his own dereliction of duty as rapidly as possible.

Pine knit his brows. "Do you think that she was in the plot?" he asked.

"Not she!" says Frere—eager to avert inquiry. "How should she be? Plot! She's sickening of fever, or I'm much mistaken."

Sure enough, on opening the door of the cabin, they found Sarah Purfoy lying where she had fallen a quarter of an hour before. The clashing of cutlasses and the firing of muskets had not roused her.

"We must make a sick-bay somewhere," says Pine, looking at the senseless figure with no kindly glance; "though I don't think she's likely to be very bad. Confound her! I believe that she's the cause of all this. I'll find out, too, before many hours are over; for I've told those fellows that unless they confess all about it before to-morrow morning, I'll get them six dozen 'a-piece the day after we anchor in Hobart Town. I've a great mind to do it before we get there. Take her head, Frere, and we'll get her out of this before Vickers comes up. What a fool you are, to be sure! I knew what it would be with women aboard ship. I wonder Mrs. V. hasn't been out before now. There—steady past the door. Why, man, one would think you never had your arm round a girl's waist before! Pooh!

don't look so scared—I won't tell. Make haste, now, before that little parson comes. Parsons are regular old women to chatter"; and thus muttering Pine assisted to carry Mrs. Vickers's maid into her cabin.

"By George, but she's a fine girl!" he said, viewing the inanimate body with the professional eye of a surgeon. "I don't wonder at you making a fool of yourself. Chances are, you've caught the fever, though this breeze will help to blow it out of us, please God. That old jackass, Blunt, too!—he ought to be ashamed of himself, at his age!"

"What do you mean?" asked Frere hastily, as he heard a step approach.

"What has Blunt to say about her?"

"Oh, I don't know," returned Pine. "He was smitten too, that's all. Like a good many more, in fact."

"A good many more!" repeated the other, with a pretence of carelessness.

"Yes!" laughed Pine. "Why, man, she was making eyes at every man in the ship! I caught her kissing a soldier once."

Maurice Frere's cheeks grew hot. The experienced profligate had been taken in, deceived, perhaps laughed at. All the time he had flattered himself that he was fascinating the black-eyed maid, the black-eyed maid had been twisting him round her finger, and perhaps imitating his love-making for the gratification of her soldier-lover. It was not a pleasant thought; and yet, strange to say, the idea of Sarah's treachery did not make him dislike her. There is a sort of love—if love it can be called—which thrives under ill-treatment. Nevertheless, he cursed with some appearance of disgust.

Vickers met them at the door. "Pine, Blunt has the fever. Mr. Best found him in his cabin groaning. Come and look at him."

The commander of the *Malabar* was lying on his bunk in the betwisted condition into which men who sleep in their clothes contrive to get themselves. The doctor shook him, bent down over him, and then loosened his collar. "He's not sick," he said; "he's drunk! Blunt! wake up! Blunt!"

But the mass refused to move.

"Hallo!" says Pine, smelling at the broken tumbler, "what's this? Smells queer. Rum? No. Eh! Laudanum! By George, he's been hocussed!"

"Nonsense!"

"I see it," slapping his thigh. "It's that infernal woman! She's drugged him, and meant to do the same for—"(Frere gave him an imploring look)—"for anybody else who would be fool enough to let her do it. Dawes was right, sir. She's in it; I'll swear she's in it."

"What! my wife's maid? Nonsense!" said Vickers.

"Nonsense!" echoed Frere.

"It's no nonsense. That soldier who was shot, what's his name?—Miles, he—but, however, it doesn't matter. It's all over now."

"The men will confess before morning," says Vickers, "and we'll see." And he went off to his wife's cabin.

His wife opened the door for him. She had been sitting by the child's bedside, listening to the firing, and waiting for her husband's return without a murmur. Flirt, fribble, and shrew as she was, Julia Vickers had displayed, in times of emergency, that glowing courage which women of her nature at times possess. Though she would yawn over any book above the level of a genteel love story; attempt to fascinate, with ludicrous assumption of girlishness, boys young enough to be her sons; shudder at a frog, and scream at a spider, she could sit throughout a quarter of an hour of such suspense as she had just undergone with as much courage as if she had been the strongest-minded woman that ever denied her sex. "Is it all over?" she asked.

"Yes, thank God!" said Vickers, pausing on the threshold. "All is safe now, though we had a narrow escape, I believe. How's Sylvia?" The child was lying on the bed with her fair hair scattered over the pillow, and her tiny hands moving restlessly to and fro.

"A little better, I think, though she has been talking a good deal."

The red lips parted, and the blue eyes, brighter than ever, stared vacantly around. The sound of her father's voice seemed to have roused her, for she began to speak a little prayer: "God bless papa and mamma, and God bless all on board this ship. God bless me, and make me a good girl, for Jesus Christ's sake, our Lord. Amen."

The sound of the unconscious child's simple prayer had something awesome in it, and John Vickers, who, not ten minutes before, would have sealed his own death-warrant unhesitatingly to preserve the safety of the vessel, felt his eyes fill with unwonted tears. The contrast was curious. From out the midst of that desolate ocean—in a fever-smitten prison ship, leagues from land, surrounded by ruffians, thieves, and murderers, the baby voice of an innocent child called confidently on Heaven.

*

Two hours afterwards—as the *Malabar,* escaped from the peril which had menaced her, plunged cheerily through the rippling water—the mutineers, by the spokesman, Mr. James Vetch, confessed.

"They were very sorry, and hoped that their breach of discipline would be forgiven. It was the fear of the typhus which had driven them to it. They had no accomplices either in the prison or out of it, but they felt it but right to say that the man who had planned the mutiny was Rufus Dawes."

The malignant cripple had guessed from whom the information which had led to the failure of the plot had been derived, and this was his characteristic revenge.

CHAPTER XII
A NEWSPAPER PARAGRAPH

EXTRACTED from the *Hobart Town Courier* of the 12th November, 1827:—

> "The examination of the prisoners who were concerned in the attempt upon the *Malabar* was concluded on Tuesday last. The four ringleaders, Dawes, Gabbett, Vetch, and Sanders, were condemned to death; but we understand that, by the clemency of his Excellency the Governor, their sentence has been commuted to six years at the penal settlement of Macquarie Harbour."

BOOK II
MACQUARIE HARBOUR 1833

CHAPTER I
THE TOPOGRAPHY OF
VAN DIEMEN'S LAND

THE south-east coast of Van Diemen's Land, from the solitary Mewstone to the basaltic cliffs of Tasman's Head, from Tasman's Head to Cape Pillar, and from Cape Pillar to the rugged grandeur of Pirates' Bay, resembles a biscuit at which rats have been nibbling. Eaten away by the continual action of the ocean which, pouring round by east and west, has divided the peninsula from the mainland of the Australasian continent—and done for Van Diemen's Land what it has done for the Isle of Wight—the shore line is broken and ragged.

Viewed upon the map, the fantastic fragments of island and promontory which lie scattered between the South-West Cape and the greater Swan Port, are like the curious forms assumed by melted lead spilt into water. If the supposition were not too extravagant, one might imagine that when the Australian continent was fused, a careless giant upset the crucible, and spilt Van Diemen's land in the ocean. The coast navigation is as dangerous as that of the Mediterranean. Passing from Cape Bougainville to the east of Maria Island, and between the numerous rocks and shoals which lie beneath the triple height of the Three Thumbs, the mariner is suddenly checked by Tasman's Peninsula, hanging, like a huge double-dropped earring, from the mainland. Getting round under the Pillar rock through Storm Bay to Storing Island, we sight the Italy of this miniature Adriatic. Between Hobart Town and Sorrell, Pittwater and the Derwent, a strangely-shaped point of land—the Italian boot with its toe bent upwards—projects into the bay, and, separated from this projection by a narrow channel, dotted with rocks, the long length of Bruny Island makes, between its western side and the cliffs of Mount Royal, the dangerous passage known as D'Entrecasteaux Channel. At the southern entrance of D'Entrecasteaux Channel, a line of sunken rocks, known by the generic name of the Actaeon reef, attests that Bruny Head was once joined with the shores of Recherche Bay; while, from the South Cape to the jaws of Macquarie Harbour, the white water caused by sunken reefs, or the jagged peaks of single rocks abruptly rising in mid sea, warn the mariner off shore.

It would seem as though nature, jealous of the beauties of her silver Derwent, had made the approach to it as dangerous as possible; but once through the archipelago of D'Entrecasteaux Channel, or the less dangerous eastern passage of Storm Bay, the voyage up the river is delightful. From the sentinel solitude of the Iron Pot to the smiling banks of New Norfolk, the river winds in a succession of reaches, narrowing to a deep channel cleft between rugged and towering cliffs. A line drawn due north from the source of the Derwent would strike another river winding out from the northern part of the island, as the Derwent winds out from the south. The force of the waves, expended, perhaps, in destroying the isthmus which, two thousand years ago, probably connected Van Diemen's Land with the continent has been here less violent. The rounding currents of the Southern Ocean, meeting at the mouth of the Tamar, have rushed upwards over the isthmus they have devoured, and pouring against the south coast of Victoria, have excavated there that inland sea called Port Philip Bay. If the waves have gnawed the south coast of Van Diemen's Land, they have bitten a mouthful out of the south coast of Victoria. The Bay is a millpool, having an area of nine hundred square miles, with a race between the heads two miles across.

About a hundred and seventy miles to the south of this mill-race lies Van Diemen's Land, fertile, fair, and rich, rained upon by the genial showers from the clouds which, attracted by the Frenchman's Cap, Wyld's Crag, or the lofty peaks of the Wellington and Dromedary range, pour down upon the sheltered valleys their fertilizing streams. No parching hot wind—the scavenger, if the torment, of the continent—blows upon her crops and corn. The cool south breeze ripples gently the blue waters of the Derwent, and fans the curtains of the open windows of the city which nestles in the broad shadow of Mount Wellington. The hot wind, born amid the burning sand of the interior of the vast Australian continent, sweeps over the scorched and cracking plains, to lick up their streams and wither the herbage in its path, until it meets the waters of the great south bay; but in its passage across the straits it is reft of its fire, and sinks, exhausted with its journey, at the feet of the terraced slopes of Launceston.

The climate of Van Diemen's Land is one of the loveliest in the world. Launceston is warm, sheltered, and moist; and Hobart Town, protected by Bruny Island and its archipelago of D'Entrecasteaux Channel and Storm Bay from the violence of the southern breakers, preserves the mean temperature of Smyrna; whilst the district between these two towns spreads in a succession of beautiful valleys, through which glide clear and sparkling streams. But on the western coast, from the steeple-rocks of Cape Grim to the scrub-encircled barrenness of Sandy Cape, and the frowning entrance to Macquarie Harbour, the nature of the country entirely changes. Along that iron-bound shore, from Pyramid Island and the forest-backed solitude of Rocky Point, to the great Ram Head, and the straggling harbour of Port Davey, all is bleak and cheerless. Upon that dreary beach the rollers of the southern sea complete their circuit of the globe, and the storm that has devastated the Cape, and united in its eastern course with the icy blasts which sweep northward from the unknown terrors of the southern pole, crashes unchecked upon the Huon pine forests, and lashes with rain the grim front of Mount Direction. Furious gales and sudden tempests affright the natives of the coast. Navigation is dangerous, and the entrance to the "Hell's Gates" of Macquarie Harbour—at the time of which we are writing (1833), in the height of its ill-fame as a convict settlement—is only to be attempted in calm weather. The sea-line is marked with wrecks. The sunken rocks are dismally named after the vessels they have destroyed. The air is chill and moist, the soil prolific only in prickly undergrowth and noxious weeds, while foetid exhalations from swamp and fen cling close to the humid, spongy ground. All around breathes desolation; on the face of nature is stamped a perpetual frown. The shipwrecked sailor, crawling painfully to the summit of basalt cliffs, or the ironed convict, dragging his tree trunk to the edge of some beetling *plateau*, looks down upon a sea of fog, through which rise mountain-tops like islands; or sees through the biting sleet a desert of scrub and crag rolling to the feet of Mount Heemskirk and Mount Zeehan—crouched like two sentinel lions keeping watch over the seaboard.

CHAPTER II

THE SOLITARY OF "HELL'S GATES"

"HELL'S Gates," formed by a rocky point, which runs abruptly northward, almost touches, on its eastern side, a projecting arm of land which guards the entrance to King's River. In the middle of the gates is a natural bolt-that is to say, an island—which, lying on a sandy bar in the very jaws of the current, creates a double whirlpool, impossible to pass in the smoothest weather. Once through the gates, the convict, chained on the deck of the inward-bound vessel, sees in front of him the bald cone of the Frenchman's Cap, piercing the moist air at a height of five thousand feet; while, gloomed by overhanging rocks, and shadowed by gigantic forests, the black sides of the basin narrow to the mouth of the Gordon. The turbulent stream is the colour of indigo, and, being fed by numerous rivulets, which ooze through masses of decaying vegetable matter, is of so poisonous a nature that it is not only undrinkable, but absolutely kills the fish, which in stormy weather are driven in from the sea. As may be imagined, the furious tempests which beat upon this exposed coast create a strong surf-line. After a few days of north-west wind the waters of the Gordon will be found salt for twelve miles up from the bar. The headquarters of the settlement were placed on an island not far from the mouth of this inhospitable river, called Sarah Island.

Though now the whole place is desolate, and a few rotting posts and logs alone remain—mute witnesses of scenes of agony never to be revived—in the year 1833 the buildings were numerous and extensive. On Philip's Island, on the north side of the harbour, was a small farm, where vegetables were grown for the use of the officers of the establishment; and, on Sarah Island, were sawpits, forges, dockyards, gaol, guard-house, barracks, and jetty. The military force numbered about sixty men, who, with convict-warders and constables, took charge of more than three hundred and fifty prisoners. These miserable wretches, deprived of every hope, were employed in the most degrading labour. No beast of burden was allowed on the settlement;

all the pulling and dragging was done by human beings. About one hundred "good-conduct" men were allowed the lighter toil of dragging timber to the wharf, to assist in shipbuilding; the others cut down the trees that fringed the mainland, and carried them on their shoulders to the water's edge. The denseness of the scrub and bush rendered it necessary for a "roadway," perhaps a quarter of a mile in length, to be first constructed; and the trunks of trees, stripped of their branches, were rolled together in this roadway, until a "slide" was made, down which the heavier logs could be shunted towards the harbour. The timber thus obtained was made into rafts, and floated to the sheds, or arranged for transportation to Hobart Town. The convicts were lodged on Sarah Island, in barracks flanked by a two-storied prison, whose "cells" were the terror of the most hardened. Each morning they received their breakfast of porridge, water, and salt, and then rowed, under the protection of their guard, to the wood-cutting stations, where they worked without food, until night. The launching and hewing of the timber compelled them to work up to their waists in water. Many of them were heavily ironed. Those who died were buried on a little plot of ground, called Halliday's Island (from the name of the first man buried there), and a plank stuck into the earth, and carved with the initials of the deceased, was the only monument vouchsafed him.

Sarah Island, situated at the south-east corner of the harbour, is long and low. The commandant's house was built in the centre, having the chaplain's house and barracks between it and the gaol. The hospital was on the west shore, and in a line with it lay the two penitentiaries. Lines of lofty palisades ran round the settlement, giving it the appearance of a fortified town. These palisades were built for the purpose of warding off the terrific blasts of wind, which, shrieking through the long and narrow bay as through the keyhole of a door, had in former times tore off roofs and levelled boat-sheds. The little town was set, as it were, in defiance of Nature, at the very extreme of civilization, and its inhabitants maintained perpetual warfare with the winds and waves.

But the gaol of Sarah Island was not the only prison in this desolate region.

At a little distance from the mainland is a rock, over the rude side of which the waves dash in rough weather. On the evening of the 3rd December, 1833, as the sun was sinking behind the tree-tops on the left side of the harbour, the figure of a man appeared on the top of this rock. He was clad in the coarse garb of a convict, and wore round his ankles two iron rings, connected by a short and heavy chain. To the middle of this chain a leathern strap was attached, which, splitting in the form of a T, buckled round his waist, and pulled the chain high enough to prevent him from stumbling over it as he walked. His head was bare, and his coarse, blue-striped shirt, open at the throat, displayed an embrowned and muscular neck. Emerging from out a sort of cell, or den, contrived by nature or art in the side of the cliff, he threw on a scanty lire, which burned between two hollowed rocks, a small log of pine wood, and then returning to his cave, and bringing from it an iron pot, which contained water, he scooped with his toil-hardened hands a resting-place for it in the ashes, and placed it on the embers. It was evident that the cave was at once his storehouse and larder, and that the two hollowed rocks formed his kitchen.

Having thus made preparations for supper, he ascended a pathway which led to the highest point of the rock. His fetters compelled him to take short steps, and, as he walked, he winced as though the iron bit him. A handkerchief or strip of cloth was twisted round his left ankle; on which the circlet had chafed a sore. Painfully and slowly, he gained his destination, and flinging himself on the ground, gazed around him. The afternoon had been stormy, and the rays of the setting sun shone redly on the turbid and rushing waters of the bay. On the right lay Sarah Island; on the left the bleak shore of the opposite and the tall peak of the Frenchman's Cap; while the storm hung sullenly over the barren hills to the eastward. Below him appeared the only sign of life. A brig was being towed up the harbour by two convict-manned boats. The sight of this brig seemed to rouse in the mind of the solitary of the rock a strain of reflection, for, sinking his chin upon his hand, he fixed his eyes on the incoming vessel, and immersed himself in moody thought. More than an hour had passed, yet he did not move. The ship anchored, the boats detached themselves from her sides, the sun sank, and the bay was plunged in gloom. Lights began to twinkle along the shore of the settlement. The little fire died, and the water in the iron pot grew cold; yet the watcher on the rock did not stir. With his eyes staring into the gloom, and fixed steadily on the vessel, he lay along the barren cliff of his lonely prison as motionless as the rock on which he had stretched himself.

This solitary man was Rufus Dawes.

CHAPTER III
A SOCIAL EVENING

IN the house of Major Vickers, Commandant of Macquarie Harbour, there was, on this evening of December 3rd, unusual gaiety.

Lieutenant Maurice Frere, late in command at Maria Island, had unexpectedly come down with news from head-quarters. The *Ladybird,* Government schooner, visited the settlement on ordinary occasions twice a year, and such visits were looked forward to with no little eagerness by the settlers. To the convicts the arrival of the *Ladybird* meant arrival of new faces, intelligence of old comrades, news of how the world, from which they were exiled, was progressing. When the *Ladybird* arrived, the chained and toil-worn felons felt that they were yet human, that the universe was not bounded by the gloomy forests which surrounded their prison, but that there was a world beyond, where men, like themselves, smoked, and drank, and laughed, and rested, and were Free. When the *Ladybird* arrived, they heard such news as interested them—that is to say, not mere foolish accounts of wars or ship arrivals, or city gossip, but matters appertaining to their own world—how Tom was with the road gangs, Dick on a ticket-of-leave, Harry taken to the bush, and Jack hung at the Hobart Town Gaol. Such items of intelligence were the only news they cared to hear, and the new-comers were well posted up in such matters. To the convicts the *Ladybird* was town talk, theatre, stock quotations, and latest telegrams. She was their newspaper and post-office, the one excitement of their dreary existence, the one link between their own misery and the happiness of their fellow-creatures. To the Commandant and the "free men" this messenger from the outer life was scarcely less welcome. There was not a man on the island who did not feel his heart grow heavier when her white sails disappeared behind the shoulder of the hill.

On the present occasion business of more than ordinary importance had procured for Major Vickers this pleasurable excitement. It had been resolved by Governor Arthur that the convict establishment should be broken up. A succession of murders and attempted escapes had called public attention to the place, and its distance from Hobart Town rendered it inconvenient and expensive. Arthur had fixed upon Tasman's Peninsula—the earring of which we have spoken—as a future convict depot, and naming it Port Arthur, in honour of himself, had sent down Lieutenant Maurice Frere with instructions for Vickers to convey the prisoners of Macquarie Harbour thither.

In order to understand the magnitude and meaning of such an order as that with which Lieutenant Frere was entrusted, we must glance at the social condition of the penal colony at this period of its history.

Nine years before, Colonel Arthur, late Governor of Honduras, had arrived at a most critical moment. The former Governor, Colonel Sorrell, was a man of genial temperament, but little strength of character. He was, moreover, profligate in his private life; and, encouraged by his example, his officers violated all rules of social decency. It was common for an officer to openly keep a female convict as his mistress. Not only would compliance purchase comforts, but strange stories were afloat concerning the persecution of women who dared to choose their own lovers. To put down this profligacy was the first care of Arthur; and in enforcing a severe attention to etiquette and outward respectability, he perhaps erred on the side of virtue. Honest, brave, and high-minded, he was also penurious and cold, and the ostentatious good humour of the colonists dashed itself in vain against his polite indifference. In opposition to this official society created by Governor Arthur was that of the free settlers and the ticket-of-leave men. The latter were more numerous than one would be apt to suppose. On the 2nd November, 1829, thirty-eight free pardons and fifty-six conditional pardons appeared on the books; and the number of persons holding tickets-of-leave, on the 26th of September the same year, was seven hundred and forty-five.

Of the social condition of these people at this time it is impossible to speak without astonishment. According to the recorded testimony of many respectable persons—Government officials, military officers, and free settlers—the profligacy of the settlers was notorious. Drunkenness was a prevailing vice. Even children were to be seen in the streets intoxicated. On Sundays, men and women might be observed standing round the public-house doors, waiting for the expiration of the hours of public worship, in order to continue their carousing. As for the condition of the prisoner population, that, indeed, is indescribable. Notwithstanding the severe punishment for sly grog-selling, it was carried on to a large extent. Men and women were found intoxicated together, and a bottle of brandy was considered to be cheaply bought at the price of twenty lashes. In the factory—a prison for females—the vilest abuses were committed, while the infamies current, as matters of course, in chain gangs and penal settlements, were of too horrible a nature to be more than hinted at here. All that the vilest and most bestial of human creatures could invent and practise, was in this unhappy country invented and practised without restraint and without shame.

Seven classes of criminals were established in 1826, when the new barracks for prisoners at Hobart Town were finished. The first class were allowed to sleep out of barracks, and to work for themselves on Saturday; the second had only the last-named indulgence; the third were only allowed Saturday afternoon; the fourth and fifth were "refractory and disorderly characters—to work in irons;" the sixth were "men of the most degraded and incorrigible character—to be worked in irons, and kept entirely separate from the other prisoners;" while the seventh were the refuse of this refuse—the murderers, bandits, and villains, whom neither chain nor lash could tame. They were regarded as socially dead, and shipped to Hell's Gates, or Maria Island. Hell's Gates was the most dreaded of all these houses of bondage. The discipline at the place was so severe, and the life so terrible, that prisoners would risk all to escape from it. In one year, of eighty-five deaths there, only thirty were from natural causes; of the remaining dead, twenty-seven were drowned, eight killed accidentally, three shot by the soldiers, and twelve murdered by their comrades. In 1822, one hundred and sixty-nine men out of one hundred and eighty-two were punished to the extent of two thousand lashes. During the ten years of its existence, one hundred and twelve men escaped, out of whom sixty-two only were found— dead. The prisoners killed themselves to avoid living any longer, and if so fortunate as to penetrate the desert of scrub, heath, and swamp, which lay between their prison and the settled districts, preferred death to recapture. Successfully to transport the remnant of this desperate band of doubly-convicted felons to Arthur's new prison, was the mission of Maurice Frere.

He was sitting by the empty fire-place, with one leg carelessly thrown over the other, entertaining the company with his usual indifferent air. The six years that had passed since his departure from England had given him a sturdier frame and a fuller face. His hair was coarser, his face redder, and his eye more hard, but in demeanour he was little changed. Sobered he might be, and his voice had acquired that decisive, insured tone which a voice exercised only in accents of command invariably acquires, but his bad qualities were as prominent as ever. His five years' residence at Maria Island had increased that brutality of thought, and overbearing confidence in his own importance, for which he had been always remarkable, but it had also given him an assured air of authority, which covered the more unpleasant features of his character. He was detested by the prisoners—as he said, "it was a word and a blow with him"—but, among his superiors, he passed for an officer, honest and painstaking, though somewhat bluff and severe.

"Well, Mrs. Vickers," he said, as he took a cup of tea from the hands of that lady, "I suppose you won't be sorry to get away from this place, eh? Trouble you for the toast, Vickers!"

"No indeed," says poor Mrs. Vickers, with the old girlishness shadowed by six years; "I shall be only too glad. A dreadful place! John's duties, however, are imperative. But the wind! My dear Mr. Frere, you've no idea of it; I wanted to send Sylvia to Hobart Town, but John would not let her go."

"By the way, how *is* Miss Sylvia?" asked Frere, with the patronising air which men of his stamp adopt when they speak of children.

"Not very well, I'm sorry to say," returned Vickers. "You see, it's lonely for her here. There are no children of her own age, with the exception of the pilot's little girl, and she cannot associate with her. But I did not like to leave her behind, and endeavoured to teach her myself."

"Hum! There was a—ha—governess, or something, was there not?" said Frere, staring into his tea-cup. "That maid, you know—what was her name?"

"Miss Purfoy," said Mrs. Vickers, a little gravely. "Yes, poor thing! A sad story, Mr. Frere."

Frere's eye twinkled.

"Indeed! I left, you know, shortly after the trial of the mutineers, and never heard the full particulars." He spoke carelessly, but he awaited the reply with keen curiosity.

"A sad story!" repeated Mrs. Vickers. "She was the wife of that wretched man, Rex, and came out as my maid in order to be near him. She would never tell me her history, poor thing, though all through the dreadful accusations made by that horrid doctor—I *always* disliked that man—I begged her almost on my knees. You know how she nursed Sylvia and poor John. Really a most superior creature. I think she must have been a governess."

Mr. Frere raised his eyebrows abruptly, as though he would say, *Governess! Of course. Happy suggestion. Wonder it never occurred to me before.* "However, her conduct was most exemplary—really *most* exemplary—and during the six months we were in Hobart Town she taught little Sylvia a great deal. Of course she could not help her wretched husband, you know. Could she?"

"Certainly not!" said Frere heartily. "I heard something about him too. Got into some scrape, did he not? Half a cup, please."

"Miss Purfoy, or Mrs. Rex, as she really was, though I don't suppose Rex is her real name either—sugar *and* milk, I think you said—came into a little legacy from an old aunt in England." Mr. Frere gave a little bluff nod, meaning thereby, *Old aunt! Exactly. Just what might have been expected.* "And left my service. She took a little cottage on the New Town road, and Rex was assigned to her as her servant."

"I see. The old dodge!" says Frere, flushing a little. "Well?"

"Well, the wretched man tried to escape, and she helped him. He was to get to Launceston, and so on board a vessel to Sydney; but they took the unhappy creature, and he was sent down here. She was only fined, but it ruined her."

"Ruined her?"

"Well, you see, only a few people knew of her relationship to Rex, and she was rather respected. Of course, when it became known, what with that dreadful trial and the horrible assertions of Dr. Pine—you will not believe me, I know, there was something about that man I never liked—she was quite left alone. She wanted me to bring her down here to teach Sylvia; but John thought that it was only to be near her husband, and wouldn't allow it."

"Of course it was," said Vickers, rising. "Frere, if you'd like to smoke, we'll go on the verandah.—She will never be satisfied until she gets that scoundrel free."

"He's a bad lot, then?" says Frere, opening the glass window, and leading the way to the sandy garden. "You will excuse my roughness, Mrs. Vickers, but I have become quite a slave to my pipe. Ha, ha, it's wife and child to me!"

"Oh, a very bad lot," returned Vickers; "quiet and silent, but ready for any villainy. I count him one of the worst men we have. With the exception of one or two more, I think he is the worst."

"Why don't you flog 'em?" says Frere, lighting his pipe in the gloom. "By George, sir, I cut the hides off my fellows if they show any nonsense!"

"Well," says Vickers, "I don't care about too much cat myself. Barton, who was here before me, flogged tremendously, but I don't think it did any good. They tried to kill him several times. You remember those twelve fellows who were hung? No! Ah, of course, you were away."

"What do you do with 'em?"

"Oh, flog the worst, you know; but I don't flog more than a man a week, as a rule, and never more than fifty lashes. They're getting quieter now. Then we iron, and dumb-cells, and maroon them."

"Do what?"

"Give them solitary confinement on Grummet Island. When a man gets very bad, we clap him into a boat with a week's provisions and pull him over to Grummet. There are cells cut in the rock, you see, and the fellow pulls up his commissariat after him, and lives there by himself for a month or so. It tames them wonderfully."

"Does it?" said Frere. "By Jove! it's a capital notion. I wish I had a place of that sort at Maria."

"I've a fellow there now," says Vickers; "Dawes. You remember him, of course—the ringleader of the mutiny in the *Malabar*. A dreadful ruffian.

He was most violent the first year I was here. Barton used to flog a good deal, and Dawes had a childish dread of the cat. When I came in—when was it?—in '29, he'd made a sort of petition to be sent back to the settlement. Said that he was innocent of the mutiny, and that the accusation against him was false."

"The old dodge," said Frere again. "A match? Thanks."

"Of course, I couldn't let him go; but I took him out of the chain-gang, and put him on the *Osprey*. You saw her in the dock as you came in. He worked for some time very well, and then tried to bolt again."

"The old trick. Ha! ha! don't I know it?" says Mr. Frere, emitting a streak of smoke in the air, expressive of preternatural wisdom.

"Well, we caught him, and gave him fifty. Then he was sent to the chain-gang, cutting timber. Then we put him into the boats, but he quarrelled with the coxswain, and then we took him back to the timber-rafts. About six weeks ago he made another attempt—together with Gabbett, the man who nearly killed you—but his leg was chafed with the irons, and we took him. Gabbett and three more, however, got away."

"Haven't you found 'em?" asked Frere, puffing at his pipe.

"No. But they'll come to the same fate as the rest," said Vickers, with a sort of dismal pride. "No man ever escaped from Macquarie Harbour."

Frere laughed. "By the Lord!" said he, "it will be rather hard for 'em if they don't come back before the end of the month, eh?"

"Oh," said Vickers, "they're sure to come—if they can come at all; but once lost in the scrub, a man hasn't much chance for his life."

"When do you think you will be ready to move?" asked Frere.

"As soon as you wish. I don't want to stop a moment longer than I can help. It is a terrible life, this."

"Do you think so?" asked his companion, in unaffected surprise.

"I like it. It's dull, certainly. When I first went to Maria I was dreadfully bored, but one soon gets used to it. There is a sort of satisfaction to me, by George, in keeping the scoundrels in order. I like to see the fellows' eyes glint at you as you walk past 'em. Gad, they'd tear me to pieces, if they dared, some of 'em!" and he laughed grimly, as though the hate he inspired was a thing to be proud of.

"How shall we go?" asked Vickers. "Have you got any instructions?"

"No," says Frere; "it's all left to you. Get 'em up the best way you can, Arthur said, and pack 'em off to the new peninsula. He thinks you too far off here, by George! He wants to have you within hail."

"It's dangerous taking so many at once," suggested Vickers.

"Not a bit. Batten 'em down and keep the sentries awake, and they won't do any harm."

"But Mrs. Vickers and the child?"

"I've thought of that. You take the *Ladybird* with the prisoners, and leave me to bring up Mrs. Vickers in the *Osprey*."

"We might do that. Indeed, it's the best way, I think. I don't like the notion of having Sylvia among those wretches, and yet I don't like to leave her."

"Well," says Frere, confident of his own ability to accomplish anything he might undertake, "*I'll* take the *Ladybird,* and *you* the *Osprey*. Bring up Mrs. Vickers yourself."

"No, no," said Vickers, with a touch of his old pomposity, "that won't do. By the King's Regulations—"

"All right," interjected Frere, "you needn't quote 'em. '*The officer commanding is obliged to place himself in charge*'—all right, my dear sir. I've no objection in life."

"It was Sylvia that I was thinking of," said Vickers.

"Well, then," cries the other, as the door of the room inside opened, and a little white figure came through into the broad verandah. "Here she is! Ask her yourself. Well, Miss Sylvia, will you come and shake hands with an old friend?"

The bright-haired baby of the *Malabar* had become a bright-haired child of some eleven years old, and as she stood in her simple white dress in the glow of the lamplight, even the unaesthetic mind of Mr. Frere was struck by her extreme beauty. Her bright blue eyes were as bright and as blue as ever. Her little figure was as upright and as supple as a willow rod; and her innocent, delicate face was framed in a nimbus of that fine golden hair—dry and electrical, each separate thread shining with a lustre of its own—with which the dreaming painters of the middle ages endowed and glorified their angels. "Come and give me a kiss, Miss Sylvia!" cries Frere. "You haven't forgotten me, have you?"

But the child, resting one hand on her father's knee, surveyed Mr. Frere from head to foot with the charming impertinence of childhood, and then, shaking her head, inquired: "Who is he, papa?"

"Mr. Frere, darling. Don't you remember Mr. Frere, who used to play ball with you on board the ship, and who was so kind to you when you were getting well? For shame, Sylvia!"

There was in the chiding accents such an undertone of tenderness, that the reproof fell harmless.

"I remember you," said Sylvia, tossing her head; "but you were nicer then than you are now. I don't like you at all."

"You don't remember me," said Frere, a little disconcerted, and affecting to be intensely at his ease. "I am sure you don't. What is my name?"

"Lieutenant Frere. You knocked down a prisoner who picked up my ball. I don't like you."

"You're a forward young lady, upon my word!" said Frere, with a great laugh. "Ha! ha! so I did, begad, I recollect now. What a memory you've got!"

"He's here now, isn't he, papa?" went on Sylvia, regardless of interruption. "Rufus Dawes is his name, and he's always in trouble. Poor fellow, I'm sorry for him. Danny says he's queer in his mind."

"And who's Danny?" asked Frere, with another laugh.

"The cook," replied Vickers. "An old man I took out of hospital. Sylvia, you talk too much with the prisoners. I have forbidden you once or twice before."

"But Danny is not a prisoner, papa—he's a cook," says Sylvia, nothing abashed, "and he's a clever man. He told me all about

London, where the Lord Mayor rides in a glass coach, and all the work is done by free men. He says you never hear chains there. I should like to see London, papa!"

"So would Mr. Danny, I have no doubt," said Frere.

"No—he didn't say that. But he wants to see his old mother, he says. Fancy Danny's mother! What an ugly old woman she must be! He says he'll see her in Heaven. Will he, papa?"

"I hope so, my dear."

"Papa!"

"Yes."

"Will Danny wear his yellow jacket in Heaven, or go as a free man?"

Frere burst into a roar at this.

"You're an impertinent fellow, sir!" cried Sylvia, her bright eyes flashing. "How dare you laugh at me? If I was papa, I'd give you half an hour at the triangles. *Oh*, you impertinent man!" and, crimson with rage, the spoilt little beauty ran out of the room.

Vickers looked grave, but Frere was constrained to get up to laugh at his ease.

"Good! 'Pon honour, that's good! The little vixen!—Half an hour at the triangles! Ha-ha! ha, ha, ha!"

"She is a strange child," said Vickers, "and talks strangely for her age; but you mustn't mind her. She is neither girl nor woman, you see; and her education has been neglected. Moreover, this gloomy place and its associations—what can you expect from a child bred in a convict settlement?"

"My dear sir," says the other, "she's delightful! Her innocence of the world is amazing!"

"She must have three or four years at a good finishing school at Sydney. Please God, I will give them to her when we go back—or send her to England if I can. She is a good-hearted girl, but she wants polishing sadly, I'm afraid."

Just then someone came up the garden path and saluted.

"What is it, Troke?"

"Prisoner given himself up, sir."

"Which of them?"

"Gabbett. He came back to-night."

"Alone?"

"Yes, sir. The rest have died—he says."

"What's that?" asked Frere, suddenly interested.

"The bolter I was telling you about—Gabbett, your old friend. He's returned."

"How long has he been out?"

"Nigh six weeks, sir," said the constable, touching his cap.

"Gad, he's had a narrow squeak for it, I'll be bound. I should like to see him."

"He's down at the sheds," said the ready Troke—a "good conduct" burglar.

"You can see him at once, gentlemen, if you like."

"What do you say, Vickers?"

"Oh, by all means."

CHAPTER IV
THE BOLTER

IT was not far to the sheds, and after a few minutes' walk through the wooden palisades they reached a long stone building, two storeys high, from which issued a horrible growling, pierced with shrilly screamed songs. At the sound of the musket butts clashing on the pine-wood flagging, the noises ceased, and a silence more sinister than sound fell on the place.

Passing between two rows of warders, the two officers reached a sort of ante-room to the gaol, containing a pine-log stretcher, on which a mass of something was lying. On a roughly-made stool, by the side of this stretcher, sat a man, in the grey dress (worn as a contrast to the yellow livery) of "good conduct" prisoners. This man held between his knees a basin containing gruel, and was apparently endeavouring to feed the mass on the pine logs.

"Won't he eat, Steve?" asked Vickers.

And at the sound of the Commandant's voice, Steve arose.

"Dunno what's wrong wi' 'un, sir," he said, jerking up a finger to his forehead. "He seems jest muggy-pated. I can't do nothin' wi' 'un."

"Gabbett!"

The intelligent Troke, considerately alive to the wishes of his superior officers, dragged the mass into a sitting posture.

Gabbett—for it was he—passed one great hand over his face, and leaning exactly in the position in which Troke placed him, scowled, bewildered, at his visitors.

"Well, Gabbett," says Vickers, "you've come back again, you see. When will you learn sense, eh? Where are your mates?"

The giant did not reply.

"Do you hear me? Where are your mates?"

"Where are your mates?" repeated Troke.

"Dead," says Gabbett.

"All three of them?"

"Ay."

"And how did you get back?"

Gabbett, in eloquent silence, held out a bleeding foot.

"We found him on the point, sir," said Troke, jauntily explaining, "and brought him across in the boat. He had a basin of gruel, but he didn't seem hungry."

"Are you hungry?"

"Yes."

"Why don't you eat your gruel?"

Gabbett curled his great lips.

"I *have* eaten it. Ain't yer got nuffin' better nor that to flog a man on? Ugh! yer a mean lot! Wot's it to be this time, Major? Fifty?"

And laughing, he rolled down again on the logs.

"A nice specimen!" said Vickers, with a hopeless smile. "What *can* one do with such a fellow?"

"I'd flog his soul out of his body," said Frere, "if he spoke to *me* like that!"

Troke and the others, hearing the statement, conceived an instant respect for the new-comer. He looked as if he would keep his word.

The giant raised his great head and looked at the speaker, but did not recognize him. He saw only a strange face—a visitor perhaps. "You may flog, and welcome, master," said he, "if you'll give me a fig o' tibbacky." Frere laughed. The brutal indifference of the rejoinder suited his humour, and, with a glance at Vickers, he took a small piece of cavendish from the pocket of his pea-jacket, and gave it to the recaptured convict. Gabbett snatched it as a cur snatches at a bone, and thrust it whole into his mouth.

"How many mates had he?" asked Maurice, watching the champing jaws as one looks at a strange animal, and asking the question as though a "mate" was something a convict was born with—like a mole, for instance.

"Three, sir."

"Three, eh? Well, give him thirty lashes, Vickers."

"And if I ha' had three more," growled Gabbett, mumbling at his tobacco, "you wouldn't ha' had the chance."

"What does he say?"

But Troke had not heard, and the "good-conduct" man, shrinking as it seemed, slightly from the prisoner, said he had not heard either. The wretch himself, munching hard at his tobacco, relapsed into his restless silence, and was as though he had never spoken.

As he sat there gloomily chewing, he was a spectacle to shudder at. Not so much on account of his natural hideousness, increased a thousand-fold by the tattered and filthy rags which barely covered him. Not so much on account of his unshaven jaws, his hare-lip, his torn and bleeding feet, his haggard cheeks, and his huge, wasted frame. Not only because, looking at the animal, as he crouched, with one foot curled round the other, and one hairy arm pendant between his knees, he was so horribly unhuman, that one shuddered to think that tender women and fair children must, of necessity, confess to fellowship of kind with such a monster. But also because, in his slavering mouth, his slowly grinding jaws, his restless fingers, and his bloodshot, wandering eyes, there lurked a hint of some terror more awful than the terror of starvation—a memory of a tragedy played out in the gloomy depths of that forest which had vomited him forth again; and the shadow of this unknown horror, clinging to him, repelled and disgusted, as though he bore about with him the reek of the shambles.

"Come," said Vickers, "Let us go back. I shall have to flog him again, I suppose. Oh, this place! No wonder they call it 'Hell's Gates'."

"You are too soft-hearted, my dear sir," said Frere, half-way up the palisaded path. "We must treat brutes like brutes."

Major Vickers, inured as he was to such sentiments, sighed. "It is not for me to find fault with the system," he said, hesitating, in his reverence for "discipline", to utter all the thought; "but I have sometimes wondered if kindness would not succeed better than the chain and the cat."

"Your old ideas!" laughed his companion. "Remember, they nearly cost us our lives on the *Malabar*. No, no. *I've* seen something of convicts—though, to be sure, my fellows were not so bad as yours—and there's only one way. Keep 'em down, sir. Make 'em *feel* what they are. They're there to work, sir. If they won't work, flog 'em until they will. If they work well—why a taste of the cat now and then keeps 'em in mind of what they may expect if they get lazy."

They had reached the verandah now. The rising moon shone softly on the bay beneath them, and touched with her white light the summit of the Grummet Rock.

"That is the general opinion, I know," returned Vickers. "But consider the life they lead. Good God!" he added, with sudden vehemence, as Frere paused to look at the bay. "I'm not a cruel man, and never, I believe, inflicted an unmerited punishment, but since I have been here ten prisoners have drowned themselves from yonder rock, rather than live on in their misery. Only three weeks ago, two men, with a wood-cutting party in the hills, having had some words with the overseer, shook hands with the gang, and then, hand in hand, flung themselves over the cliff. It's horrible to think of!"

"They shouldn't get sent here," said practical Frere. "They knew what they had to expect. Serve 'em right."

"But imagine an innocent man condemned to this place!"

"I can't," said Frere, with a laugh. "Innocent man be hanged! They're all innocent , if you'd believe their own stories. Hallo! what's that red light there?"

"Dawes's fire, on Grummet Rock," says Vickers, going in; "the man I told you about. Come in and have some brandy-and-water, and we'll shut the door in place."

"WELL," said Frere, as they went in, "you'll be out of it soon. You can get all ready to start by the end of the month, and I'll bring on Mrs. Vickers afterwards."

"What is that you say about me?" asked the sprightly Mrs. Vickers from within. "You wicked men, leaving me alone all this time!"

"Mr. Frere has kindly offered to bring you and Sylvia after us in the *Osprey*. I shall, of course, have to take the *Ladybird*."

"You are most kind, Mr. Frere, really you are," says Mrs. Vickers, a recollection of her flirtation with a certain young lieutenant, six years before, tinging her cheeks. "It is really most considerate of you. Won't it be nice, Sylvia, to go with Mr. Frere and mamma to Hobart Town?"

"Mr. Frere," says Sylvia, coming from out a corner of the room, "I am very sorry for what I said just now. Will you forgive me?"

She asked the question in such a prim, old-fashioned way, standing in front of him, with her golden locks streaming over her shoulders, and her hands clasped on her black silk apron (Julia Vickers had her own notions about dressing her daughter), that Frere was again inclined to laugh.

"Of course I'll forgive you, my dear," he said. "You didn't mean it, I know."

"Oh, but I *did* mean it, and that's why I'm sorry. I am a very naughty girl sometimes, though you wouldn't think so" (this with a charming consciousness of her own beauty), "especially with Roman history. I don't think the Romans were half as brave as the Carthaginians; do you, Mr. Frere?"

Maurice, somewhat staggered by this question, could only ask, "Why not?"

"Well, I don't like them half so well myself," says Sylvia, with feminine disdain of reasons. "They always had so many soldiers, though the others *were* so cruel when they conquered."

"Were they?" says Frere.

"Were they! Goodness gracious, yes! Didn't they cut poor Regulus's eyelids off, and roll him down hill in a barrel full of nails? What do you call that, I should like to know?" and Mr. Frere, shaking his red head with vast assumption of classical learning, could not but concede that *that* was not kind on the part of the Carthaginians.

"You are a great scholar, Miss Sylvia," he remarked, with a consciousness that this self-possessed girl was rapidly taking him out of his depth.

"Are you fond of reading?"

"Very."

"And what books do you read?"

"Oh, lots! 'Paul and Virginia", and 'Paradise Lost', and 'Shakespeare's Plays', and 'Robinson Crusoe', and 'Blair's Sermons', and 'The Tasmanian Almanack', and 'The Book of Beauty', and 'Tom Jones'."

"A somewhat miscellaneous collection, I fear," said Mrs. Vickers, with a sickly smile—*she*, like Gallio, cared for none of these things—"but our little library is necessarily limited, and I am not a great reader. John, my dear, Mr. Frere would like another glass of brandy-and-water. Oh, don't apologize; I am a soldier's wife, you know. Sylvia, my love, say good-night to Mr. Frere, and retire."

"Good-night, Miss Sylvia. Will you give me a kiss?"

"No!"

"Sylvia, don't be rude!"

"I'm not rude," cries Sylvia, indignant at the way in which her literary confidence had been received. "*He's* rude! I won't kiss you. *Kiss* you indeed! My goodness gracious!"

"Won't you, you little beauty?" cried Frere, suddenly leaning forward, and putting his arm round the child. "Then I must kiss you!"

To his astonishment, Sylvia, finding herself thus seized and kissed despite herself, flushed scarlet, and, lifting up her tiny fist, struck him on the cheek with all her force.

The blow was so sudden, and the momentary pain so sharp, that Maurice nearly slipped into his native coarseness, and rapped out an oath.

"My *dear* Sylvia!" cried Vickers, in tones of grave reproof.

But Frere laughed, caught both the child's hands in one of his own, and kissed her again and again, despite her struggles. "There!" he said, with a sort of triumph in his tone. "You got nothing by that, you see."

Vickers rose, with annoyance visible on his face, to draw the child away; and as he did so, she, gasping for breath, and sobbing with rage, wrenched her wrist free, and in a storm of childish passion struck her tormentor again and again. "Man!" she cried, with flaming eyes, "Let me go! I hate you! I hate you! I hate you!"

"I am very sorry for this, Frere," said Vickers, when the door was closed again. "I hope she did not hurt you."

"Not she! I like her spirit. Ha, ha! That's the way with women all the world over. Nothing like showing them that they've got a master."

Vickers hastened to turn the conversation, and, amid recollections of old days, and speculations as to future prospects, the little incident was forgotten. But when, an hour later, Mr. Frere traversed the passage that led to his bedroom, he found himself confronted by a little figure wrapped in a shawl. It was his childish enemy.

"I've waited for you, Mr. Frere," said she, "to beg pardon. I ought not to have struck you; I am a wicked girl. Don't say no, because I am; and if I don't grow better I shall never go to Heaven."

Thus addressing him, the child produced a piece of paper, folded like a letter, from beneath the shawl, and handed it to him.

"What's this?" he asked. "Go back to bed, my dear; you'll catch cold."

"It's a written apology; and I sha'n't catch cold, because I've got my stockings on. If you don't accept it," she added, with an arching of the brows, "it is not my fault. I have struck you, but I apologize. Being a woman, I can't offer you satisfaction in the usual way."

Mr. Frere stifled the impulse to laugh, and made his courteous adversary a low bow.

"I accept your apology, Miss Sylvia," said he.

"Then," returned Miss Sylvia, in a lofty manner, "there is nothing more to be said, and I have the honour to bid you good-night, sir."

The little maiden drew her shawl close around her with immense dignity, and marched down the passage as calmly as though she had been Amadis of Gaul himself.

Frere, gaining his room choking with laughter, opened the folded paper by the light of the tallow candle, and read, in a quaint, childish hand—

SIR,—I have struck you. I apologize in writing.
Your humble servant to command,
SYLVIA VICKERS.

"I wonder what book she took that out of?" he said. "'Pon my word she must be a little cracked. Gad, it's a queer life for a child in this place, and no mistake."

CHAPTER VI

A LEAP IN THE DARK

TWO or three mornings after the arrival of the *Ladybird*, the solitary prisoner of the Grummet Rock noticed mysterious movements along the shore of the island settlement. The prison boats, which had put off every morning at sunrise to the foot of the timbered ranges on the other side of the harbour, had not appeared for some days. The building of a pier, or breakwater, running from the western point of the settlement, was discontinued; and all hands appeared to be occupied with the newly-built *Osprey*, which was lying on the slips. Parties of soldiers also daily left the *Ladybird*, and assisted at the mysterious work in progress. Rufus Dawes, walking his little round each day, in vain wondered what this unusual commotion portended. Unfortunately, no one came to enlighten his ignorance.

A fortnight after this, about the 15th of December, he observed another curious fact. All the boats on the island put off one morning to the opposite side of the harbour, and in the course of the day a great smoke arose along the side of the hills. The next day the same was repeated; and on the fourth day the boats returned, towing behind them a huge raft. This raft, made fast to the side of the *Ladybird*, proved to be composed of planks, beams, and joists, all of which were duly hoisted up, and stowed in the hold of the brig.

This set Rufus Dawes thinking. Could it possibly be that the timber-cutting was to be abandoned, and that the Government had hit upon some other method of utilizing its convict labour? He had hewn timber and built boats, and tanned hides and made shoes. Was it possible that some new trade was to be initiated? Before he had settled this point to his satisfaction, he was startled by another boat expedition. Three boats' crews went down the bay, and returned, after a day's absence, with an addition to their number in the shape of four strangers and a quantity of stores and farming implements. Rufus Dawes, catching sight of these last, came to the conclusion that the boats had been to Philip's Island, where the "garden" was established, and had taken off the gardeners and garden produce. Rufus

Dawes decided that the *Ladybird* had brought a new commandant—his sight, trained by his half-savage life, had already distinguished Mr. Maurice Frere—and that these mysteries were "improvements" under the new rule. When he arrived at this point of reasoning, another conjecture, assuming his first to have been correct, followed as a natural consequence. Lieutenant Frere would be a more severe commandant than Major Vickers. Now, severity had already reached its height, so far as he was concerned; so the unhappy man took a final resolution—he would kill himself.

Before we exclaim against the sin of such a determination, let us endeavour to set before us what the sinner had suffered during the past six years.

We have already a notion of what life on a convict ship means; and we have seen through what a furnace Rufus Dawes had passed before he set foot on the barren shore of Hell's Gates. But to appreciate in its intensity the agony he suffered since that time, we must multiply the infamy of the 'tween decks of the *Malabar* a hundredfold. In that prison was at least some ray of light. All were not abominable; all were not utterly lost to shame and manhood. Stifling though the prison, infamous the companionship, terrible the memory of past happiness—there was yet ignorance of the future, there was yet hope. But at Macquarie Harbour was poured out the very dregs of this cup of desolation. The worst had come, and the worst must for ever remain. The pit of torment was so deep that one could not even see Heaven. There was no hope there so long as life remained. Death alone kept the keys of that island prison.

Is it possible to imagine, even for a moment, what an innocent man, gifted with ambition, endowed with power to love and to respect, must have suffered during one week of such punishment? We ordinary men, leading ordinary lives—walking, riding, laughing, marrying and giving in marriage—can form no notion of such misery as this. Some dim ideas we may have about the sweetness of liberty and the loathing that evil company inspires; but that is all. We know that were we chained and degraded, fed like dogs, employed as beasts of burden, driven to our daily toil with threats and blows, and herded with wretches among whom all that savours of decency and manliness is held in an open scorn, we should die, perhaps, or go mad. But we do not know, and can never know, how unutterably loathsome life must become when shared with such beings as those who dragged the tree-trunks to the banks of the Gordon, and toiled, blaspheming, in their irons, on the dismal sandpit of Sarah Island. No human creature could describe to what depth of personal abasement and self-loathing one week of such a life would plunge him. Even if he had the power to write, he dared not. As one whom in a desert, seeking for a face, should come to a pool of blood, and seeing his own reflection, fly—so would such a one hasten from the contemplation of his own degrading agony. Imagine such torment endured for six years!

Ignorant that the sights and sounds about him were symptoms of the final abandonment of the settlement, and that the *Ladybird* was sent down to bring away the prisoners, Rufus Dawes decided upon getting rid of that burden of life which pressed upon him so heavily. For six years he had hewn wood and drawn water; for six years he had hoped against hope; for six years he had lived in the valley of the shadow of Death. He dared not recapitulate to himself what he had suffered. Indeed, his senses were deadened and dulled by torture. He cared to remember only one thing—that he was a Prisoner for Life. In vain had been his first dream of freedom. He had done his best, by good conduct, to win release; but the villainy of Vetch and Rex had deprived him of the fruit of his labour. Instead of gaining credit by his exposure of the plot on board the *Malabar*, he was himself deemed guilty, and condemned, despite his asseverations of innocence. The knowledge of his "treachery"—for so it was deemed among his associates—while it gained for him no credit with the authorities, procured for him the detestation and ill-will of the monsters among whom he found himself. On his arrival at Hell's Gates he was a marked man—a Pariah among those beings who were Pariahs to all the world beside.

Thrice his life was attempted; but he was not then quite tired of living, and he defended it. This defence was construed by an overseer into a brawl, and the irons from which he had been relieved were replaced. His strength—brute attribute that alone could avail him—

made him respected after this, and he was left at peace. At first this treatment was congenial to his temperament; but by and by it became annoying, then painful, then almost unendurable. Tugging at his oar, digging up to his waist in slime, or bending beneath his burden of pine wood, he looked greedily for some excuse to be addressed. He would take double weight when forming part of the human caterpillar along whose back lay a pine tree, for a word of fellowship. He would work double tides to gain a kindly sentence from a comrade. In his utter desolation he agonized for the friendship of robbers and murderers. Then the reaction came, and he hated the very sound of their voices. He never spoke, and refused to answer when spoken to. He would even take his scanty supper alone, did his chain so permit him. He gained the reputation of a sullen, dangerous, half-crazy ruffian. Captain Barton, the superintendent, took pity on him, and made him his gardener. He accepted the pity for a week or so, and then Barton, coming down one morning, found the few shrubs pulled up by the roots, the flower-beds trampled into barrenness, and his gardener sitting on the ground among the fragments of his gardening tools. For this act of wanton mischief he was flogged. At the triangles his behaviour was considered curious. He wept and prayed to be released, fell on his knees to Barton, and implored pardon. Barton would not listen, and at the first blow the prisoner was silent. From that time he became more sullen than ever, only at times he was observed, when alone, to fling himself on the ground and cry like a child. It was generally thought that his brain was affected.

When Vickers came, Dawes sought an interview, and begged to be sent back to Hobart Town. This was refused, of course, but he was put to work on the *Osprey*. After working there for some time, and being released from his irons, he concealed himself on the slip, and in the evening swam across the harbour. He was pursued, retaken, and flogged. Then he ran the dismal round of punishment. He burnt lime, dragged timber, and tugged at the oar. The heaviest and most degrading tasks were always his. Shunned and hated by his companions, feared by the convict overseers, and regarded with unfriendly eyes by the authorities, Rufus Dawes was at the very bottom of that abyss of woe into which he had voluntarily cast himself. Goaded to desperation by his own thoughts, he had joined with Gabbett and the unlucky three in their desperate attempt to escape; but, as Vickers stated, he had been captured almost instantly. He was lamed by the heavy irons he wore, and though Gabbett—with a strange eagerness for which after events accounted—insisted that he could make good his flight, the unhappy man fell in the first hundred yards of the terrible race, and was seized by two volunteers before he could rise again. His capture helped to secure the brief freedom of his comrades; for Mr. Troke, content with one prisoner, checked a pursuit which the nature of the ground rendered dangerous, and triumphantly brought Dawes back to the settlement as his peace-offering for the negligence which had resulted in the loss of the other four. For this madness the refractory convict had been condemned to the solitude of the Grummet Rock.

In that dismal hermitage, his mind, preying on itself, had become disordered. He saw visions and dreamt dreams. He would lie for hours motionless, staring at the sun or the sea. He held converse with imaginary beings. He enacted the scene with his mother over again. He harangued the rocks, and called upon the stones about him to witness his innocence and his sacrifice. He was visited by the phantoms of his early friends, and sometimes thought his present life a dream. Whenever he awoke, however, he was commanded by a voice within himself to leap into the surges which washed the walls of his prison, and to dream these sad dreams no more.

In the midst of this lethargy of body and brain, the unusual occurrences along the shore of the settlement roused in him a still fiercer hatred of life. He saw in them something incomprehensible and terrible, and read in them threats of an increase of misery. Had he known that the *Ladybird* was preparing for sea, and that it had been already decided to fetch him from the Rock and iron him with the rest for safe passage to Hobart Town, he might have paused; but he knew nothing, save that the burden of life was insupportable, and that the time had come for him to be rid of it.

In the meantime, the settlement was in a fever of excitement. In less than three weeks from the announcement made by Vickers, all had been got ready. The Commandant had finally arranged with

Frere as to his course of action. He would himself accompany the *Ladybird* with the main body. His wife and daughter were to remain until the sailing of the *Osprey,* which Mr. Frere—charged with the task of final destruction—was to bring up as soon as possible. "I will leave you a corporal's guard, and ten prisoners as a crew," Vickers said. "You can work her easily with that number." To which Frere, smiling at Mrs. Vickers in a self-satisfied way, had replied that he could do with five prisoners if necessary, for he knew how to get double work out of the lazy dogs.

Among the incidents which took place during the breaking up was one which it is necessary to chronicle. Near Philip's Island, on the north side of the harbour, is situated Coal Head, where a party had been lately at work. This party, hastily withdrawn by Vickers to assist in the business of devastation, had left behind it some tools and timber, and at the eleventh hour a boat's crew was sent to bring away the *debris*. The tools were duly collected, and the pine logs—worth twenty-five shillings apiece in Hobart Town—duly rafted and chained. The timber was secured, and the convicts, towing it after them, pulled for the ship just as the sun sank. In the general relaxation of discipline and haste, the raft had not been made with as much care as usual, and the strong current against which the boat was labouring assisted the negligence of the convicts. The logs began to loosen, and although the onward motion of the boat kept the chain taut, when the rowers slackened their exertions the mass parted, and Mr. Troke, hooking himself on to the side of the *Ladybird,* saw a huge log slip out from its fellows and disappear into the darkness. Gazing after it with an indignant and disgusted stare, as though it had been a refractory prisoner who merited two days' "solitary", he thought he heard a cry from the direction in which it had been borne. He would have paused to listen, but all his attention was needed to save the timber, and to prevent the boat from being swamped by the struggling mass at her stern.

The cry had proceeded from Rufus Dawes. From his solitary rock he had watched the boat pass him and make for the *Ladybird* in the channel, and he had decided—with that curious childishness into which the mind relapses on such supreme occasions—that the moment when the gathering gloom swallowed her up, should be the moment when he would plunge into the surge below him. The heavily-labouring boat grew dimmer and dimmer, as each tug of the oars took her farther from him. Presently, only the figure of Mr. Troke in the stern sheets was visible; then that also disappeared, and as the nose of the timber raft rose on the swell of the next wave, Rufus Dawes flung himself into the sea.

He was heavily ironed, and he sank like a stone. He had resolved not to attempt to swim, and for the first moment kept his arms raised above his head, in order to sink the quicker. But, as the short, sharp agony of suffocation caught him, and the shock of the icy water dispelled the mental intoxication under which he was labouring, he desperately struck out, and, despite the weight of his irons, gained the surface for an instant. As he did so, all bewildered, and with the one savage instinct of self-preservation predominant over all other thoughts, be became conscious of a huge black mass surging upon him out of the darkness. An instant's buffet with the current, an ineffectual attempt to dive beneath it, a horrible sense that the weight at his feet was dragging him down,—and the huge log, loosened from the raft, was upon him, crushing him beneath its rough and ragged sides. All thoughts of self-murder vanished with the presence of actual peril, and uttering that despairing cry which had been faintly heard by Troke, he flung up his arms to clutch the monster that was pushing him down to death. The log passed completely over him, thrusting him beneath the water, but his hand, scraping along the splintered side, came in contact with the loop of hide rope that yet hung round the mass, and clutched it with the tenacity of a death grip. In another instant he got his head above water, and making good his hold, twisted himself, by a violent effort, across the log.

For a moment he saw the lights from the stern windows of the anchored vessels low in the distance, Grummet Rock disappeared on his left, then, exhausted, breathless, and bruised, he closed his eyes, and the drifting log bore him swiftly and silently away into the darkness.

*

At daylight the next morning, Mr. Troke, landing on the prison rock found it deserted. The prisoner's cap was lying on the edge of the little cliff, but the prisoner himself had disappeared. Pulling back to the *Ladybird*, the intelligent Troke pondered on the circumstance, and in delivering his report to Vickers mentioned the strange cry he had heard the night before. "It's my belief, sir, that he was trying to swim the bay," he said. "He must ha' gone to the bottom anyhow, for he couldn't swim five yards with them irons."

Vickers, busily engaged in getting under weigh, accepted this very natural supposition without question. The prisoner had met his death either by his own act, or by accident. It was either a suicide or an attempt to escape, and the former conduct of Rufus Dawes rendered the latter explanation a more probable one. In any case, he was dead. As Mr. Troke rightly surmised, no man could swim the bay in irons; and when the *Ladybird*, an hour later, passed the Grummet Rock, all on board her believed that the corpse of its late occupant was lying beneath the waves that seethed at its base.

CHAPTER VII

THE LAST OF MACQUARIE HARBOUR

RUFUS Dawes was believed to be dead by the party on board the *Ladybird*, and his strange escape was unknown to those still at Sarah Island. Maurice Frere, if he bestowed a thought upon the refractory prisoner of the Rock, believed him to be safely stowed in the hold of the schooner, and already half-way to Hobart Town; while not one of the eighteen persons on board the *Osprey* suspected that the boat which had put off for the marooned man had returned without him. Indeed the party had little leisure for thought; Mr. Frere, eager to prove his ability and energy, was making strenuous exertions to get away, and kept his unlucky ten so hard at work that within a week from the departure of the *Ladybird* the *Osprey* was ready for sea. Mrs. Vickers and the child, having watched with some excusable regret the process of demolishing their old home, had settled down in their small cabin in the brig, and on the evening of the 11th of January, Mr. Bates, the pilot, who acted as master, informed the crew that Lieutenant Frere had given orders to weigh anchor at daybreak.

At daybreak accordingly the brig set sail, with a light breeze from the south-west, and by three o'clock in the afternoon anchored safely outside the Gates. Unfortunately the wind shifted to the northwest, which caused a heavy swell on the bar, and prudent Mr. Bates, having consideration for Mrs. Vickers and the child, ran back ten miles into Wellington Bay, and anchored there again at seven o'clock in the morning. The tide was running strongly, and the brig rolled a good deal. Mrs. Vickers kept to her cabin, and sent Sylvia to entertain Lieutenant Frere. Sylvia went, but was not entertaining. She had conceived for Frere one of those violent antipathies which children sometimes own without reason, and since the memorable night of the apology had been barely civil to him. In vain did he pet her and compliment her, she was not to be flattered into liking him. "I do not like you, sir," she said in her stilted fashion, "but that need make no difference to you. You occupy yourself with your prisoners; I can amuse myself without you, thank you."

"Oh, all right," said Frere, "I don't want to interfere"; but he felt a little nettled nevertheless. On this particular evening the young lady relaxed her severity of demeanour. Her father away, and her mother sick, the little maiden felt lonely, and as a last resource accepted her mother's commands and went to Frere. He was walking up and down the deck, smoking.

"Mr. Frere, I am sent to talk to you."

"Are you? All right—go on."

"Oh dear, no. It is the gentleman's place to entertain. Be amusing!"

"Come and sit down then," said Frere, who was in good humour at the success of his arrangements. "What shall we talk about?"

"You stupid man! As if I knew! It is your place to talk. Tell me a fairy story."

"'Jack and the Beanstalk'?" suggested Frere.

"Jack and the grandmother! Nonsense. Make one up out of your head, you know."

Frere laughed.

"I can't," he said. "I never did such a thing in my life."

"Then why not begin? I shall go away if you don't begin."

Frere rubbed his brows. "Well, have you read—have you read 'Robinson Crusoe'?"—as if the idea was a brilliant one.

"Of *course* I have," returned Sylvia, pouting. "Read it?—yes. Everybody's read 'Robinson Crusoe'!"

"Oh, have they? Well, I didn't know; let me see now." And pulling hard at his pipe, he plunged into literary reflection.

Sylvia, sitting beside him, eagerly watching for the happy thought that never came, pouted and said, "What a stupid, stupid man you are! I shall be so glad to get back to papa again. He knows all sorts of stories, nearly as many as old Danny."

"Danny knows some, then?"

"Danny!"—with as much surprise as if she said "Walter Scott!"

"Of course he does. I suppose now," putting her head on one side, with an amusing expression of superiority, "you never heard the story of the 'Banshee'?"

"No, I never did."

"Nor the 'White Horse of the Peppers'?"

"No."

"No, I suppose not. Nor the 'Changeling'? nor the 'Leprechaun'?"

"No."

Sylvia got off the skylight on which she had been sitting, and surveyed the smoking animal beside her with profound contempt.

"Mr. Frere, you are really a most ignorant person. Excuse me if I hurt your feelings; I have no wish to do that; but really you are a *most* ignorant person—for your age, of course."

Maurice Frere grew a little angry. "You are very impertinent, Sylvia," said he.

"Miss Vickers is *my* name, Lieutenant Frere, and I shall go and talk to Mr. Bates."

Which threat she carried out on the spot; and Mr. Bates, who had filled the dangerous office of pilot, told her about divers and coral reefs, and some adventures of his—a little apocryphal—in the China Seas. Frere resumed his smoking, half angry with himself, and half angry with the provoking little fairy. This elfin creature had a fascination for him which he could not account for.

However, he saw no more of her that evening, and at breakfast the next morning she received him with quaint haughtiness.

"When shall we be ready to sail? Mr. Frere, I'll take some marmalade. Thank you."

"I don't know, missy," said Bates. "It's very rough on the Bar; me and Mr. Frere was a soundin' of it this marnin', and it ain't safe yet."

"Well," said Sylvia, "I do hope and trust we sha'n't be ship-wrecked, and have to swim miles and miles for our lives."

"Ho, ho!" laughed Frere; "don't be afraid. I'll take care of you."

"Can *you* swim, Mr. Bates?" asked Sylvia.

"Yes, miss, I can."

"Well, then, *you* shall take me; I like you. Mr. Frere can take mamma. We'll go and live on a desert island, Mr. Bates, won't we, and grow cocoa-nuts and bread-fruit, and—what nasty hard biscuits!—I'll be Robinson Crusoe, and you shall be Man Friday. I'd like to live on a desert island, if I was sure there were no savages, and plenty to eat and drink."

"That would be right enough, my dear, but you don't find

them sort of islands every day."

"*Then*," said Sylvia, with a decided nod, "we won't be ship-wrecked, will we?"

"I hope not, my dear."

"Put a biscuit in your pocket, Sylvia, in case of accidents," suggested Frere, with a grin.

"Oh! you know my opinion of *you*, sir. Don't speak; I don't want any argument".

"Don't you?—that's right."

"Mr. Frere," said Sylvia, gravely pausing at her mother's cabin door, "if I were Richard the Third, do you know what I should do with you?"

"No," says Frere, eating complacently; "what would you do?"

"Why, I'd make you stand at the door of St. Paul's Cathedral in a white sheet, with a lighted candle in your hand, until you gave up your wicked aggravating ways—you Man!"

The picture of Mr. Frere in a white sheet, with a lighted candle in his hand, at the door of St. Paul's Cathedral, was too much for Mr. Bates's gravity, and he roared with laughter. "She's a queer child, ain't she, sir? A born nateral, and a good-natered little soul."

"When shall we be able to get away, Mr. Bates?" asked Frere, whose dignity was wounded by the mirth of the pilot.

Bates felt the change of tone, and hastened to accommodate himself to his officer's humour. "I hopes by evening, sir," said he; "if the tide slackens then I'll risk it; but it's no use trying it now."

"The men were wanting to go ashore to wash their clothes," said Frere.

"If we are to stop here till evening, you had better let them go after dinner."

"All right, sir," said Bates.

The afternoon passed off auspiciously. The ten prisoners went ashore and washed their clothes. Their names were James Barker, James Lesly, John Lyon, Benjamin Riley, William Cheshire, Henry Shiers, William Russen, James Porter, John Fair, and John Rex.

This last scoundrel had come on board latest of all. He had behaved himself a little better recently, and during the work attendant upon the departure of the *Ladybird,* had been conspicuously useful. His intelligence and influence among his fellow-prisoners combined to make him a somewhat important personage, and Vickers had allowed him privileges from which he had been hitherto debarred. Mr. Frere, however, who superintended the shipment of some stores, seemed to be resolved to take advantage of Rex's evident willingness to work. He never ceased to hurry and find fault with him. He vowed that he was lazy, sulky, or impertinent. It was "Rex, come here! Do this! Do that!" As the prisoners declared among themselves, it was evident that Mr. Frere had a "down" on the "Dandy". The day before the *Ladybird* sailed, Rex—rejoicing in the hope of speedy departure—had suffered himself to reply to some more than usually galling remark and Mr. Frere had complained to Vickers. "The fellow's too ready to get away," said he. "Let him stop for the *Osprey,* it will be a lesson to him."

Vickers assented, and John Rex was informed that he was not to sail with the first party. His comrades vowed that this order was an act of tyranny; but he himself said nothing. He only redoubled his activity, and—despite all his wish to the contrary—Frere was unable to find fault.

He even took credit to himself for "taming" the convict's spirit, and pointed out Rex—silent and obedient—as a proof of the excellence of severe measures. To the convicts, however, who knew John Rex better, this silent activity was ominous. He returned with the rest, however, on the evening of the 13th, in apparently cheerful mood. Indeed Mr. Frere, who, wearied by the delay, had decided to take the whale-boat in which the prisoners had returned, and catch a few fish before dinner, observed him laughing with some of the others, and again congratulated himself.

The time wore on. Darkness was closing in, and Mr. Bates, walking the deck, kept a look-out for the boat, with the intention of weighing anchor and making for the Bar. All was secure. Mrs. Vickers and the child were safely below. The two remaining soldiers (two had gone with Frere) were upon deck, and the prisoners in the forecastle were singing. The wind was fair, and the sea had gone down. In less than an hour the *Osprey* would be safely outside the harbour.

CHAPTER VIII

THE POWER OF THE WILDERNESS

THE drifting log that had so strangely served as a means of saving Rufus Dawes swam with the current that was running out of the bay. For some time the burden that it bore was an insensible one. Exhausted with his desperate struggle for life, the convict lay along the rough back of this Heaven-sent raft without motion, almost without breath. At length a violent shock awoke him to consciousness, and he perceived that the log had become stranded on a sandy point, the extremity of which was lost in darkness. Painfully raising himself from his uncomfortable posture, he staggered to his feet, and crawling a few paces up the beach, flung himself upon the ground and slept.

When morning dawned, he recognized his position. The log had, in passing under the lee of Philip's Island, been cast upon the southern point of Coal Head; some three hundred yards from him were the mutilated sheds of the coal gang. For some time he lay still, basking in the warm rays of the rising sun, and scarcely caring to move his bruised and shattered limbs. The sensation of rest was so exquisite, that it overpowered all other considerations, and he did not even trouble himself to conjecture the reason for the apparent desertion of the huts close by him. If there was no one there—well and good. If the coal party had not gone, he would be discovered in a few moments, and brought back to his island prison. In his exhaustion and misery, he accepted the alternative and slept again.

As he laid down his aching head, Mr. Troke was reporting his death to Vickers, and while he still slept, the *Ladybird*, on her way out, passed him so closely that any one on board her might, with a good glass, have espied his slumbering figure as it lay upon the sand.

When he woke it was past midday, and the sun poured its full rays upon him. His clothes were dry in all places, save the side on which he had been lying, and he rose to his feet refreshed by his long sleep. He scarcely comprehended, as yet, his true position. He had escaped, it was true, but not for long. He was versed in the history of escapes, and knew that a man alone on that barren coast was face to face with starvation or recapture. Glancing up at the sun, he wondered indeed, how it was that he had been free so long. Then the coal sheds caught his eye, and he understood that they were untenanted. This astonished him, and he began to tremble with vague apprehension. Entering, he looked around, expecting every moment to see some lurking constable, or armed soldier. Suddenly his glance fell upon the food rations which lay in the corner where the departing convicts had flung them the night before. At such a moment, this discovery seemed like a direct revelation from Heaven. He would not have been surprised had they disappeared. Had he lived in another age, he would have looked round for the angel who had brought them.

By and by, having eaten of this miraculous provender, the poor creature began—reckoning by his convict experience—to understand what had taken place. The coal workings were abandoned; the new Commandant had probably other work for his beasts of burden to execute, and an absconder would be safe here for a few hours at least. But he must not stay. For him there was no rest. If he thought to escape, it behoved him to commence his journey at once. As he contemplated the meat and bread, something like a ray of hope entered his gloomy soul. Here was provision for his needs. The food before him represented the rations of six men. Was it not possible to cross the desert that lay between him and freedom on such fare? The very supposition made his heart beat faster. It surely *was* possible. He must husband his resources; walk much and eat little; spread out the food for one day into the food for three. Here was six men's food for one day, or one man's food for six days. He would live on a third of this, and he would have rations for eighteen days. Eighteen days! What could he not do in eighteen days? He could walk thirty miles a day—forty miles a day—that would be six hundred miles and more. Yet stay; he must not be too sanguine; the road was difficult; the scrub was in places impenetrable. He would have to make *detours,* and turn upon his tracks, to waste precious time. He would be moderate, and say twenty miles a day. Twenty miles a day was very easy walking. Taking a piece of stick from the ground, he made the calculation in the sand. Eighteen days, and twenty miles a day—three hundred and sixty miles. More than enough to take him to freedom. It could be done! With prudence, it could be done! He must be careful and abstemious! Abstemious! He had already eaten too much, and he hastily pulled a barely-tasted piece of meat from his mouth, and replaced it with the rest. The action which at any other time would have seemed disgusting, was, in the case of this poor creature, merely pitiable.

Having come to this resolution, the next thing was to disen-cumber himself of his irons. This was more easily done than he expected. He found in the shed an iron gad, and with that and a stone he drove out the rivets. The rings were too strong to be "ovalled", or he would have been free long ago. He packed the meat and bread together, and then pushing the gad into his belt—it might be needed as a weapon of defence—he set out on his journey.

His intention was to get round the settlement to the coast, reach the settled districts, and, by some tale of shipwreck or of wandering, procure assistance. As to what was particularly to be done *when* he found himself among free men, he did not pause to consider. At that point his difficulties seemed to him to end. Let him but traverse the desert that was before him, and he would trust to his own ingenuity, or the chance of fortune, to avert suspicion. The peril of immediate detection was so imminent that, beside it, all other fears were dwarfed into insignificance.

Before dawn next morning he had travelled ten miles, and by husbanding his food, he succeeded by the night of the fourth day in accomplishing forty more. Footsore and weary, he lay in a thicket of the thorny melaleuca, and felt at last that he was beyond pursuit. The next day he advanced more slowly. The bush was unpropitious. Dense scrub and savage jungle impeded his path; barren and stony mountain ranges arose before him. He was lost in gullies, entangled in thickets, bewildered in morasses. The sea that had hitherto gleamed, salt, glittering, and hungry upon his right hand, now shifted to his left. He had mistaken his course, and he must turn again. For two days did this bewilderment last, and on the third he came to a mighty cliff that pierced with its blunt pinnacle the clustering bush. He must go over or round this obstacle, and he decided to go round it. A natural pathway wound about its foot. Here and there branches were broken, and it seemed to the poor wretch, fainting under the weight of his lessening burden, that his were not the first footsteps which had trodden there. The path terminated in a glade, and at the bottom of this glade was something that fluttered. Rufus Dawes pressed forward, and stumbled over a corpse!

In the terrible stillness of that solitary place he felt suddenly as though a voice had called to him. All the hideous fantastic tales of murder which he had read or heard seemed to take visible shape in the person of the loathly carcase before him, clad in the yellow dress of a convict, and lying flung together on the ground as though struck down. Stooping over it, impelled by an irresistible impulse to know the worst, he found the body was mangled. One arm was missing, and the skull had been beaten in by some heavy instrument! The first thought—that this heap of rags and bones was a mute witness to the folly of his own undertaking, the corpse of some starved absconder—gave place to a second more horrible suspicion. He recognized the number imprinted on the coarse cloth as that which had designated the younger of the two men who had escaped with Gabbett. He was standing on the place where a murder had been committed! A murder!—and what else? Thank God the food *he* carried was not yet exhausted! He turned and fled, looking back fearfully as he went. He could not breathe in the shadow of that awful mountain.

Crashing through scrub and brake, torn, bleeding, and wild with terror, he reached a spur on the range, and looked around him. Above him rose the iron hills, below him lay the panorama of the bush. The white cone of the Frenchman's Cap was on his right hand, on his left a succession of ranges seemed to bar further progress. A gleam, as of a lake, streaked the eastward. Gigantic pine trees reared their graceful heads against the opal of the evening sky, and at their feet the dense scrub through which he had so painfully toiled, spread without break and without flaw. It seemed as though he could leap from where he stood upon a solid mass of tree-tops. He raised his eyes, and right against him, like a long dull sword, lay the narrow steel-blue reach of the harbour from which he had escaped. One darker speck moved on the dark water. It was the *Osprey* making for the Gates. It seemed that he could throw a stone upon her deck. A faint cry of rage escaped him. During the last three days in the bush he must have retraced his steps, and returned upon his own track to the settlement! More than half his allotted time had passed, and he was not yet thirty miles from his prison. Death had waited to overtake him in this barbarous wilderness. As a cat allows a mouse to escape her for a while, so had he been permitted to trifle with his fate, and lull himself into a false security. Escape was hopeless now. He never *could* escape; and as the unhappy man raised his despairing eyes, he saw that the sun, redly sinking behind a lofty pine which topped the opposite hill, shot a ray of crimson light into the glade below him. It was as though a bloody finger pointed at the corpse which lay there, and Rufus Dawes, shuddering at the dismal omen, averting his face, plunged again into the forest.

For four days he wandered aimlessly through the bush. He had given up all hopes of making the overland journey, and yet, as long as his scanty supply of food held out, he strove to keep away from the settlement. Unable to resist the pangs of hunger, he had increased his daily ration; and though the salted meat, exposed to rain and heat, had begun to turn putrid, he never looked at it but he was seized with a desire to eat his fill. The coarse lumps of carrion and the hard rye-loaves were to him delicious morsels fit for the table of an emperor. Once or twice he was constrained to pluck and eat the tops of tea-trees and peppermint shrubs. These had an aromatic taste, and sufficed to stay the cravings of hunger for a while, but they induced a raging thirst, which he slaked at the icy mountain springs. Had it not been for the frequency of these streams, he must have died in a few days. At last, on the twelfth day from his departure from the Coal Head, he found himself at the foot of Mount Direction, at the head of the peninsula which makes the western side of the harbour. His terrible wandering had but led him to make a complete circuit of the settlement, and the next night brought him round the shores of Birches Inlet to the landing-place opposite to Sarah Island. His stock of provisions had been exhausted for two days, and he was savage with hunger. He no longer thought of suicide. His dominant idea was now to get food. He would do as many others had done before him—give himself up to be flogged and fed. When he reached the landing-place, however, the guard-house was empty. He looked across at the island prison, and saw no sign of life. The settlement was deserted! The shock of this discovery almost deprived him of reason. For days, that had seemed centuries, he had kept life in his jaded and lacerated body solely by the strength of his fierce determination to reach the settlement; and now that he had reached it, after a journey of unparalleled horror, he found it deserted. He struck himself to see if he was not dreaming. He refused to believe his eyesight. He shouted, screamed, and waved his tattered garments in the air. Exhausted by these paroxysms, he said to himself, quite calmly, that the sun beating on his unprotected head had dazed his brain, and that in a few minutes he should see well-remembered boats pulling towards him. Then, when no boat came, he argued that he was mistaken in the place; the island yonder was not Sarah Island, but some other island like it, and that in a second or so he would be able to detect the difference. But the inexorable mountains, so hideously familiar for six weary years, made mute reply, and the sea, crawling at his feet, seemed to grin at him with a thin-lipped, hungry mouth. Yet the fact of the desertion seemed so inexplicable that he could not realize it. He felt as might have felt that wanderer in the enchanted mountains, who, returning in the morning to look for his companions, found them turned to stone.

At last the dreadful truth forced itself upon him; he retired a few paces, and then, with a horrible cry of furious despair, stumbled forward towards the edge of the little reef that fringed the shore. Just as he was about to fling himself for the second time into the dark water, his eyes, sweeping in a last long look around the bay, caught sight of a strange appearance on the left horn of the sea beach. A thin, blue streak, uprising from behind the western arm of the little inlet, hung in the still air. It was the smoke of a fire!

The dying wretch felt inspired with new hope. God had sent him a direct sign from Heaven. The tiny column of bluish vapour seemed to him as glorious as the Pillar of Fire that led the Israelites. There were yet human beings near him!—and turning his face from the hungry sea, he tottered with the last effort of his failing strength towards the blessed token of their presence.

CHAPTER IX
THE SEIZURE OF THE "OSPREY"

FRERE'S fishing expedition had been unsuccessful, and in consequence prolonged. The obstinacy of his character appeared in the most trifling circumstances, and though the fast deepening shades of an Australian evening urged him to return, yet he lingered, unwilling to come back empty-handed. At last a peremptory signal warned him. It was the sound of a musket fired on board the brig: Mr. Bates was getting impatient; and with a scowl, Frere drew up his lines, and ordered the two soldiers to pull for the vessel.

The *Osprey* yet sat motionless on the water, and her bare masts gave no sign of making sail. To the soldiers, pulling with their backs to her, the musket shot seemed the most ordinary occurrence in the world. Eager to quit the dismal prison-bay, they had viewed Mr Frere's persistent fishing with disgust, and had for the previous half hour longed to hear the signal of recall which had just startled them. Suddenly, however, they noticed a change of expression in the sullen face of their commander. Frere, sitting in the stern sheets, with his face to the *Osprey*, had observed a peculiar appearance on her decks. The bulwarks were every now and then topped by strange figures, who disappeared as suddenly as they came, and a faint murmur of voices floated across the intervening sea. Presently the report of another musket shot echoed among the hills, and something dark fell from the side of the vessel into the water. Frere, with an imprecation of mingled alarm and indignation, sprang to his feet, and shading his eyes with his hand, looked towards the brig. The soldiers, resting on their oars, imitated his gesture, and the whale-boat, thus thrown out of trim, rocked from side to side dangerously. A moment's anxious pause, and then another musket shot, followed by a woman's shrill scream, explained all. The prisoners had seized the brig. "Give way!" cried Frere, pale with rage and apprehension, and the soldiers, realizing at once the full terror of their position, forced the heavy whale-boat through the water as fast as the one miserable pair of oars could take her.

*

Mr. Bates, affected by the insidious influence of the hour, and lulled into a sense of false security, had gone below to tell his little playmate that she would soon be on her way to the Hobart Town of which she had heard so much; and, taking advantage of his absence, the soldier not on guard went to the forecastle to hear the prisoners singing. He found the ten together, in high good humour, listening to a "shanty" sung by three of their number.

The voices were melodious enough, and the words of the ditty— chanted by many stout fellows in many a forecastle before and since—of that character which pleases the soldier nature. Private Grimes forgot all about the unprotected state of the deck, and sat down to listen.

While he listened, absorbed in tender recollections, James Lesly, William Cheshire, William Russen, John Fair, and James Barker slipped to the hatchway and got upon the deck. Barker reached the aft hatchway as the soldier who was on guard turned to complete his walk, and passing his arm round his neck, pulled him down before he could utter a cry. In the confusion of the moment the man loosed his grip of the musket to grapple with his unseen antagonist, and Fair, snatching up the weapon, swore to blow out his brains if he raised a finger. Seeing the sentry thus secured, Cheshire, as if in pursuance of a preconcerted plan, leapt down the after hatchway, and passed up the muskets from the arm-racks to Lesly and Russen. There were three muskets in addition to the one taken from the sentry, and Barker, leaving his prisoner in charge of Fair, seized one of them, and ran to the companion ladder. Russen, left unarmed by this manoeuvre, appeared to know his own duty. He came back to the forecastle, and passing behind the listening soldier, touched the singer on the shoulder. This was the appointed signal, and John Rex, suddenly terminating his song with a laugh, presented his fist in the face of the gaping Grimes. "No noise!" he cried. "The brig's ours"; and ere Grimes could reply, he was seized by Lyon and Riley, and bound securely.

"Come on, lads!" says Rex, "and pass the prisoner down here. We've got her this time, I'll go bail!" In obedience to this order, the now gagged sentry was flung down the fore hatchway, and the hatch secured. "Stand on the hatchway, Porter," cries Rex again; "and if those fellows come up, knock 'em down with a handspoke. Lesly and Russen, forward to the companion ladder! Lyon, keep a look-out for the boat, and if she comes too near, fire!"

As he spoke the report of the first musket rang out. Barker had apparently fired up the companion hatchway.

*

When Mr. Bates had gone below, he found Sylvia curled upon the cushions of the state-room, reading. "Well, missy!" he said, "we'll soon be on our way to papa."

Sylvia answered by asking a question altogether foreign to the subject. "Mr. Bates," said she, pushing the hair out of her blue eyes, "what's a coracle?"

"A which?" asked Mr. Bates.

"A coracle. C-o-r-a-c-l-e," said she, spelling it slowly. "I want to know."

The bewildered Bates shook his head. "Never heard of one, missy," said he, bending over the book. "What does it say?"

"'The Ancient Britons,'" said Sylvia, reading gravely, "'were little better than Barbarians. They painted their bodies with Woad'— that's blue stuff, you know, Mr. Bates—'and, seated in their light coracles of skin stretched upon slender wooden frames, must have presented a wild and savage appearance.'"

"Hah," said Mr. Bates, when this remarkable passage was read to him, "that's very mysterious, that is. A corricle, a cory"—a bright light burst upon him. "A *curricle* you mean, missy! It's a carriage! I've seen 'em in Hy' Park, with young bloods a-drivin' of 'em."

"What are young bloods?" asked Sylvia, rushing at this "new opening".

"Oh, nobs! Swell coves, don't you know," returned poor Bates, thus again attacked. "Young men o' fortune that is, that's given to doing it grand."

"I see," said Sylvia, waving her little hand graciously. "Noblemen and Princes and that sort of people. Quite so. But what about coracle?"

"Well," said the humbled Bates, "*I* think it's a carriage, missy. A sort of Pheayton, as they call it."

Sylvia, hardly satisfied, returned to the book. It was a little mean-looking volume—a "Child's History of England"—and after perusing it awhile with knitted brows, she burst into a childish laugh.

"Why, my dear Mr. Bates!" she cried, waving the History above her head in triumph, "what a pair of geese we are! A *carriage*! Oh you silly man! It's a *boat*!"

"Is it?" said Mr. Bates, in admiration of the intelligence of his companion. "Who'd ha' thought that now? Why couldn't they call it a boat at once, then, and ha' done with it?" and he was about to laugh also, when, raising his eyes, he saw in the open doorway the figure of James Barker, with a musket in his hand.

"Hallo! What's this? What do you do here, sir?"

"Sorry to disturb yer," says the convict, with a grin, "but you must come along o' me, Mr. Bates."

Bates, at once comprehending that some terrible misfortune had occurred, did not lose his presence of mind. One of the cushions of the couch was under his right hand, and snatching it up he flung it across the little cabin full in the face of the escaped prisoner. The soft mass struck the man with force sufficient to blind him for an instant. The musket exploded harmlessly in the air, and ere the astonished Barker could recover his footing, Bates had hurled him out of the cabin, and crying "Mutiny!" locked the cabin door on the inside.

The noise brought out Mrs. Vickers from her berth, and the poor little student of English history ran into her arms.

"Good Heavens, Mr. Bates, what is it?"

Bates, furious with rage, so far forgot himself as to swear. "It's a mutiny, ma'am," said he. "Go back to your cabin and lock the door. Those bloody villains have risen on us!" Julia Vickers felt her heart grow sick. Was she never to escape out of this dreadful life? "Go into your cabin, ma'am," says Bates again, "and don't move a finger till I tell ye. Maybe it ain't so bad as it looks; I've got my pistols with me, thank God, and Mr. Frere'll hear the shot anyway. Mutiny? On deck there!" he cried at the full pitch of his voice, and his brow grew damp with dismay when a mocking laugh from above was the only response.

Thrusting the woman and child into the state berth, the bewildered pilot cocked a pistol, and snatching a cutlass from the arm stand fixed to the butt of the mast which penetrated the cabin, he burst open the door with his foot, and rushed to the companion ladder. Barker had retreated to the deck, and for an instant he thought the way was clear, but Lesly and Russen thrust him back with the muzzles of the loaded muskets. He struck at Russen with the cutlass, missed him, and, seeing the hopelessness of the attack, was fain to retreat.

In the meanwhile, Grimes and the other soldier had loosed themselves from their bonds, and, encouraged by the firing, which seemed to them a sign that all was not yet lost, made shift to force up the forehatch. Porter, whose courage was none of the fiercest, and who had been for years given over to that terror of discipline which servitude induces, made but a feeble attempt at resistance, and forcing the handspike from him, the sentry, Jones, rushed aft to help the pilot. As Jones reached the waist, Cheshire, a cold-blooded blue-eyed man, shot him dead. Grimes fell over the corpse, and Cheshire, clubbing the musket—had he another barrel he would have fired—coolly battered his head as he lay, and then, seizing the body of the unfortunate Jones in his arms, tossed it into the sea. "Porter, you lubber!" he cried, exhausted with the effort to lift the body, "come and bear a hand with this other one!" Porter advanced aghast, but just then another occurrence claimed the villain's attention, and poor Grimes's life was spared for that time.

Rex, inwardly raging at this unexpected resistance on the part of the pilot, flung himself on the skylight, and tore it up bodily. As he did so, Barker, who had reloaded his musket, fired down into the cabin. The ball passed through the state-room door, and splintering the wood, buried itself close to the golden curls of poor little Sylvia. It was this hair's-breadth escape which drew from the agonized mother that shriek which, pealing through the open stern window, had roused the soldiers in the boat.

Rex, who, by the virtue of his dandyism, yet possessed some

abhorrence of useless crime, imagined that the cry was one of pain, and that Barker's bullet had taken deadly effect. "You've killed the child, you villain!" he cried.

"What's the odds?" asked Barker sulkily. "She must die any way, sooner or later."

Rex put his head down the skylight, and called on Bates to surrender, but Bates only drew his other pistol. "Would you commit murder?" he asked, looking round with desperation in his glance.

"No, no," cried some of the men, willing to blink the death of poor Jones. "It's no use making things worse than they are. Bid him come up, and we'll do him no harm."

"Come up, Mr. Bates," says Rex, "and I give you my word you sha'n't be injured."

"Will you set the major's lady and child ashore, then?" asked Bates, sturdily facing the scowling brows above him.

"Yes."

"Without injury?" continued the other, bargaining, as it were, at the very muzzles of the muskets.

"Ay, ay! It's all right!" returned Russen. "It's our liberty we want, that's all."

Bates, hoping against hope for the return of the boat, endeavoured to gain time. "Shut down the skylight, then," said he, with the ghost of an authority in his voice, "until I ask the lady."

This, however, John Rex refused to do. "You can ask well enough where you are," he said.

But there was no need for Mr. Bates to put a question. The door of the state-room opened, and Mrs. Vickers appeared, trembling, with Sylvia by her side. "Accept, Mr. Bates," she said, "since it must be so. We should gain nothing by refusing. We are at their mercy—God help us!"

"Amen to that," says Bates under his breath, and then aloud, "We agree!"

"Put your pistols on the table, and come up, then," says Rex, covering the table with his musket as he spoke. "And nobody shall hurt you."

CHAPTER X

JOHN REX'S REVENGE

MRS. Vickers, pale and sick with terror, yet sustained by that strange courage of which we have before spoken, passed rapidly under the open skylight, and prepared to ascend. Sylvia—her romance crushed by too dreadful reality—clung to her mother with one hand, and with the other pressed close to her little bosom the "English History". In her all-absorbing fear she had forgotten to lay it down.

"Get a shawl, ma'am, or something," says Bates, "and a hat for missy."

Mrs. Vickers looked back across the space beneath the open skylight, and shuddering, shook her head. The men above swore impatiently at the delay, and the three hastened on deck.

"Who's to command the brig now?" asked undaunted Bates, as they came up.

"I am," says John Rex, "and, with these brave fellows, I'll take her round the world."

The touch of bombast was not out of place. It jumped so far with the humour of the convicts that they set up a feeble cheer, at which Sylvia frowned. Frightened as she was, the prison-bred child was as much astonished at hearing convicts cheer as a fashionable lady would be to hear her footman quote poetry. Bates, however—practical and calm—took quite another view of the case. The bold project, so boldly avowed, seemed to him a sheer absurdity. The "Dandy" and a crew of nine convicts navigate a brig round the world! Preposterous; why, not a man aboard could work a reckoning! His nautical fancy pictured the *Osprey* helplessly rolling on the swell of the Southern Ocean, or hopelessly locked in the ice of the Antarctic Seas, and he dimly guessed at the fate of the deluded ten. Even if they got safe to port, the chances of final escape were all against them, for what account could they give of themselves? Overpowered by these reflections, the honest fellow made one last effort to charm his captors back to their pristine bondage.

"Fools!" he cried, "do you know what you are about to do? You will never escape. Give up the brig, and I will declare, before my God, upon the Bible, that I will say nothing, but give all good characters."

Lesly and another burst into a laugh at this wild proposition, but Rex, who had weighed his chances well beforehand, felt the force of the pilot's speech, and answered seriously.

"It's no use talking," he said, shaking his still handsome head. "We have got the brig, and we mean to keep her. I can navigate her, though I am no seaman, so you needn't talk further about it, Mr. Bates. It's liberty we require."

"What are you going to do with us?" asked Bates.

"Leave you behind."

Bates's face blanched. "What, *here*?"

"Yes. It don't look a picturesque spot, does it? And yet I've lived here for some years"; and he grinned.

Bates was silent. The logic of that grin was unanswerable.

"Come!" cried the Dandy, shaking off his momentary melancholy, "look alive there! Lower away the jolly-boat. Mrs. Vickers, go down to your cabin and get anything you want. I am compelled to put you ashore, but I have no wish to leave you without clothes." Bates listened, in a sort of dismal admiration, at this courtly convict. *He* could not have spoken like that had life depended on it. "Now, my little lady," continued Rex, "run down with your mamma, and don't be frightened."

Sylvia flashed burning red at this indignity. "Frightened! If there had been anybody else here but women, you never would have taken the brig. Frightened! Let me pass, *prisoner*!"

The whole deck burst into a great laugh at this, and poor Mrs. Vickers paused, trembling for the consequences of the child's temerity. To thus taunt the desperate convict who held their lives in his hands seemed sheer madness. In the boldness of the speech however, lay its safeguard. Rex—whose politeness was mere bravado—was stung to the quick by the reflection upon his courage, and the bitter accent with which the child had pronounced the word *prisoner* (the generic name of convicts) made him bite his lips with rage. Had he had his will, he would have struck the little creature to the deck, but the hoarse laugh of his companions warned him to forbear. There is "public opinion" even among convicts, and Rex dared not vent his passion on so helpless an object. As men do in such cases, he veiled his anger beneath an affectation of amusement. In order to show that he was not moved by the taunt, he smiled upon the taunter more graciously than ever.

"Your daughter has her father's spirit, madam," said he to Mrs. Vickers, with a bow.

Bates opened his mouth to listen. His ears were not large enough to take in the words of this complimentary convict. He began to think that he was the victim of a nightmare. He absolutely felt that John Rex was a greater man at that moment than John Bates.

As Mrs. Vickers descended the hatchway, the boat with Frere and the soldiers came within musket range, and Lesly, according to orders, fired his musket over their heads, shouting to them to lay to But Frere, boiling with rage at the manner in which the tables had been turned on him, had determined not to resign his lost authority without a struggle. Disregarding the summons, he came straight on, with his eyes fixed on the vessel. It was now nearly dark, and the figures on the deck were indistinguishable. The indignant lieutenant could but guess at the condition of affairs. Suddenly, from out of the darkness a voice hailed him—

"Hold water! back water!" it cried, and was then seemingly choked in its owner's throat.

The voice was the property of Mr. Bates. Standing near the side, he had observed Rex and Fair bring up a great pig of iron, erst used as part of the ballast of the brig, and poise it on the rail. Their intention was but too evident; and honest Bates, like a faithful watch-dog, barked to warn his master. Bloodthirsty Cheshire caught him by the throat, and Frere, unheeding, ran the boat alongside, under the very nose of the revengeful Rex.

The mass of iron fell half in-board upon the now stayed boat, and gave her sternway, with a splintered plank.

"Villains!" cried Frere, "would you swamp us?"

"Aye," laughed Rex, "and a dozen such as ye! The brig's ours, can't ye see, and *we*'re your masters now!"

Frere, stifling an exclamation of rage, cried to the bow to hook on, but the bow had driven the boat backward, and she was already beyond arm's length of the brig. Looking up, he saw Cheshire's savage face, and heard the click of the lock as he cocked his piece. The two soldiers, exhausted by their long pull, made no effort to stay the progress of the boat, and almost before the swell caused by the plunge of the mass of iron had ceased to agitate the water, the deck of the *Osprey* had become invisible in the darkness.

Frere struck his fist upon the thwart in sheer impotence of rage. "The scoundrels!" he said, between his teeth, "they've mastered us. What do they mean to do next?"

The answer came pat to the question. From the dark hull of the brig broke a flash and a report, and a musket ball cut the water beside them with a chirping noise. Between the black indistinct mass which represented the brig, and the glimmering water, was visible a white speck, which gradually neared them.

"Come alongside with ye!" hailed a voice, "or it will be the worse for ye!"

"They want to murder us," says Frere. "Give way, men!"

But the two soldiers, exchanging glances one with the other, pulled the boat's head round, and made for the vessel. "It's no use, Mr. Frere," said the man nearest him; "we can do no good now, and they won't hurt us, I dare say."

"You dogs, you are in league with them," bursts out Frere, purple with indignation. "Do you mutiny?"

"Come, come, sir," returned the soldier, sulkily, "this ain't the time to bully; and, as for mutiny, why, one man's about as good as another just now."

This speech from the lips of a man who, but a few minutes before, would have risked his life to obey orders of his officer, did more than an hour's reasoning to convince Maurice Frere of the hopelessness of resistance. His authority—born of circumstance, and supported by adventitious aid—had left him. The musket shot had reduced him to the ranks. He was now no more than anyone else; indeed, he was less than many, for those who held the firearms were the ruling powers. With a groan he resigned himself to his fate, and looking at the sleeve of the undress uniform he wore, it seemed to him that virtue had gone out of it. When they reached the brig, they found that the jolly-boat had been lowered and laid alongside. In her were eleven persons; Bates with forehead gashed, and hands bound, the stunned Grimes, Russen and Fair pulling, Lyon, Riley, Cheshire, and Lesly with muskets, and John Rex in the stern sheets, with Bates's pistols in his trousers' belt, and a loaded musket across his knees. The white object which had been seen by the men in the whale-boat was a large white shawl which wrapped Mrs. Vickers and Sylvia.

Frere muttered an oath of relief when he saw this white bundle. He had feared that the child was injured. By the direction of Rex the whale-boat was brought alongside the jolly-boat, and Cheshire and Lesly boarded her. Lesly then gave his musket to Rex, and bound Frere's hands behind him, in the same manner as had been done for Bates. Frere attempted to resist this indignity, but Cheshire, clapping his musket to his ear, swore he would blow out his brains if he uttered another syllable; Frere, catching the malignant eye of John Rex, remembered how easily a twitch of the finger would pay off old scores, and was silent. "Step in here, sir, if you please," said Rex, with polite irony. "I am sorry to be compelled to tie you, but I must consult my own safety as well as your convenience." Frere scowled, and, stepping awkwardly into the jolly-boat, fell. Pinioned as he was, he could not rise without assistance, and Russen pulled him roughly to his feet with a coarse laugh. In his present frame of mind, that laugh galled him worse than his bonds.

Poor Mrs. Vickers, with a woman's quick instinct, saw this, and, even amid her own trouble, found leisure to console him. "The wretches!" she said, under her breath, as Frere was flung down beside her, "to subject you to such indignity!" Sylvia said nothing, and seemed to shrink from the lieutenant. Perhaps in her childish fancy she had pictured him as coming to her rescue, armed cap-a-pie, and clad in dazzling mail, or, at the very least, as a muscular hero, who would settle affairs out of hand by sheer personal prowess. If she had entertained any such notion, the reality must have struck coldly upon her senses. Mr. Frere, purple, clumsy, and bound, was not at all heroic.

"Now, my lads," says Rex—who seemed to have endued the cast-off authority of Frere—"we give you your choice. Stay at Hell's Gates, or come with us!"

The soldiers paused, irresolute. To join the mutineers meant a certainty of hard work, with a chance of ultimate hanging. Yet to stay with the prisoners was—as far as they could see—to incur the inevitable fate of starvation on a barren coast. As is often the case on such occasions, a trifle sufficed to turn the scale. The wounded Grimes, who was slowly recovering from his stupor, dimly caught the meaning of the sentence, and in his obfuscated condition of intellect must needs make comment upon it. "Go with him, ye beggars!;" said he, "and leave us honest men! Oh, ye'll get a tying-up for this."

The phrase "tying-up" brought with it recollection of the worst portion of military discipline, the cat, and revived in the minds of the pair already disposed to break the yoke that sat so heavily upon them, a train of dismal memories. The life of a soldier on a convict station was at that time a hard one. He was often stinted in rations, and of necessity deprived of all rational recreation, while punishment for offences was prompt and severe. The companies drafted to the penal settlements were not composed of the best material, and the pair had good precedent for the course they were about to take.

"Come," says Rex, "I can't wait here all night. The wind is freshening, and we must take the Bar. Which is it to be?"

"We'll go with *you*!" says the man who had pulled the stroke in the whale-boat, spitting into the water with averted face. Upon which utterance the convicts burst into joyous oaths, and the pair were received with much hand-shaking.

Then Rex, with Lyon and Riley as a guard, got into the whale-boat, and having loosed the two prisoners from their bonds, ordered them to take the place of Russen and Fair. The whale-boat was manned by the seven mutineers, Rex steering, Fair, Russen, and the two recruits pulling, and the other four standing up, with their muskets levelled at the jolly-boat. Their long slavery had begotten such a dread of authority in these men that they feared it even when it was bound and menaced by four muskets. "Keep your distance!"

shouted Cheshire, as Frere and Bates, in obedience to orders, began to pull the jolly-boat towards the shore; and in this fashion was the dismal little party conveyed to the mainland.

It was night when they reached it, but the clear sky began to thrill with a late moon as yet unrisen, and the waves, breaking gently upon the beach, glimmered with a radiance born of their own motion. Frere and Bates, jumping ashore, helped out Mrs. Vickers, Sylvia, and the wounded Grimes. This being done under the muzzles of the muskets, Rex commanded that Bates and Frere should push the jolly-boat as far as they could from the shore, and Riley catching her by a boat-hook as she came towards them, she was taken in tow.

"Now, boys," says Cheshire, with a savage delight, "three cheers for old England and Liberty!"

Upon which a great shout went up, echoed by the grim hills which had witnessed so many miseries.

To the wretched five, this exultant mirth sounded like a knell of death. "Great God!" cried Bates, running up to his knees in water after the departing boats, "would you leave us here to starve?"

The only answer was the jerk and dip of the retreating oars.

CHAPTER XI

LEFT AT "HELL'S GATES"

THERE is no need to dwell upon the mental agonies of that miserable night. Perhaps, of all the five, the one least qualified to endure it realized the prospect of suffering most acutely. Mrs. Vickers —lay-figure and noodle as she was—had the keen instinct of approaching danger, which is in her sex a sixth sense. She was a woman and a mother, and owned a double capacity for suffering. Her feminine imagination pictured all the horrors of death by famine, and having realized her own torments, her maternal love forced her to live them over again in the person of her child. Rejecting Bates's offer of a pea-jacket and Frere's vague tenders of assistance, the poor woman withdrew behind a rock that faced the sea, and, with her daughter in her arms, resigned herself to her torturing thoughts. Sylvia, recovered from her terror, was almost content, and, curled in her mother's shawl, slept. To her little soul this midnight mystery of boats and muskets had all the flavour of a romance. With Bates, Frere, and her mother so close to her, it was impossible to be afraid; besides, it was obvious that papa—the Supreme Being of the settlement—must at once return and severely punish the impertinent prisoners who had dared to insult his wife and child, and as Sylvia dropped off to sleep, she caught herself, with some indignation, pitying the mutineers for the tremendous scrape they had got themselves into. How they *would* be flogged when papa came back! In the meantime this sleeping in the open air was novel and rather pleasant.

Honest Bates produced a piece of biscuit, and, with all the generosity of his nature, suggested that this should be set aside for the sole use of the two females, but Mrs. Vickers would not hear of it. "We must all share alike," said she, with something of the spirit that she knew her husband would have displayed under like circumstance; and Frere wondered at her apparent strength of mind. Had he been gifted with more acuteness, he would not have wondered; for when a crisis comes to one of two persons who have lived much together, the influence of the nobler spirit makes itself felt. Frere had a tinder-box in his pocket, and he made a fire with some dry leaves and sticks. Grimes fell asleep, and the two men sitting at their fire discussed the chances of escape. Neither liked to openly broach the supposition that they had been finally deserted. It was concluded between them that unless the brig sailed in the night—and the now risen moon showed her yet lying at anchor—the convicts would return and bring them food. This supposition proved correct, for about an hour after daylight they saw the whale-boat pulling towards them.

A discussion had arisen amongst the mutineers as to the propriety of at once making sail, but Barker, who had been one of the pilot-boat crew, and knew the dangers of the Bar, vowed that he would not undertake to steer the brig through the Gates until morning; and so the boats being secured astern, a strict watch was set, lest the helpless Bates should attempt to rescue the vessel. During the evening—the excitement attendant upon the outbreak having passed away, and the magnitude of the task before them being more fully apparent to their minds—a feeling of pity for the unfortunate party on the mainland took possession of them. It was quite possible that the *Osprey* might be recaptured, in which case five useless murders would have been committed; and however callous in bloodshed were the majority of the ten, not one among them could contemplate in cold blood, without a twinge of remorse, the death of the harmless child of the Commandant.

John Rex, seeing how matters were going, made haste to take to himself the credit of mercy. He ruled, and had always ruled, his ruffians not so much by suggesting to them the course they should take, as by leading them on the way they had already chosen for themselves. "I propose," said he, "that we divide the provisions. There are five of them and twelve of us. Then nobody can blame us."

"Ay," said Porter, mindful of a similar exploit, "and if we're taken, they can tell what we have done. Don't let our affair be like that of the *Cypress*, to leave them to starve."

"Ay, ay," says Barker, "you're right! When Fergusson was topped at Hobart Town, I heard old Troke say that if he'd not refused to set the tucker ashore, he might ha' got off with a whole skin."

Thus urged, by self-interest, as well as sentiment, to mercy, the provision was got upon deck by daylight, and a division was made. The soldiers, with generosity born of remorse, were for giving half to the marooned men, but Barker exclaimed against this. "When the schooner finds they don't get to headquarters, she's bound to come back and look for 'em," said he; "and we'll want all the tucker we can get, maybe, afore we sights land."

This reasoning was admitted and acted upon. There was in the harness-cask about fifty pounds of salt meat, and a third of this quantity, together with half a small sack of flour, some tea and sugar mixed together in a bag, and an iron kettle and pannikin, was placed in the whale-boat. Rex, fearful of excesses among his crew, had also lowered down one of the two small puncheons of rum which the store-room contained. Cheshire disputed this, and stumbling over a goat that had been taken on board from Philip's Island, caught the creature by the leg, and threw it into the sea, bidding Rex take that with him also. Rex dragged the poor beast into the boat, and with this miscellaneous cargo pushed off to the shore. The poor goat, shivering, began to bleat piteously, and the men laughed. To a stranger it would have appeared that the boat contained a happy party of fishermen, or coast settlers, returning with the proceeds of a day's marketing.

Laying off as the water shallowed, Rex called to Bates to come for the cargo, and three men with muskets standing up as before, ready to resist any attempt at capture, the provisions, goat and all, were carried ashore. "There!" says Rex, "you can't say we've used you badly, for we've divided the provisions." The sight of this almost unexpected succour revived the courage of the five, and they felt grateful. After the horrible anxiety they had endured all that night, they were prepared to look with kindly eyes upon the men who had come to their assistance.

"Man," said Bates, with something like a sob in his voice, "I didn't expect this. You are good fellows, for there ain't much tucker aboard, I know."

"Yes," affirmed Frere, "you're good fellows."

Rex burst into a savage laugh. "Shut your mouth, you tyrant," said he, forgetting his dandyism in the recollection of his former suffering. "It ain't for your benefit. You may thank the lady and the child for it."

Julia Vickers hastened to propitiate the arbiter of her daughter's fate. "We are obliged to you," she said, with a touch of quiet dignity resembling her husband's; "and if I ever get back safely, I will take care that your kindness shall be known."

The swindler and forger took off his leather cap with quite an air. It was five years since a lady had spoken to him, and the old time when he was Mr. Lionel Crofton, a "gentleman sportsman", came back again for an instant. At that moment, with liberty in his hand, and fortune all before him, he felt his self-respect return, and he looked the lady in the face without flinching.

"I sincerely trust, madam," said he, "that you *will* get back safely. May I hope for your good wishes for myself and my companions?"

Listening, Bates burst into a roar of astonished enthusiasm. "What a dog it is!" he cried. "John Rex, John Rex, you were never made to be a convict, man!"

Rex smiled. "Good-bye, Mr. Bates, and God preserve you!"

"Good-bye," says Bates, rubbing his hat off his face, "and I—I—damme, I hope you'll get safe off—there! for liberty's sweet to every man."

"Good-bye, prisoners!" says Sylvia, waving her handkerchief; "and I hope they won't catch you, too."

So, with cheers and waving of handkerchiefs, the boat departed.

In the emotion which the apparently disinterested conduct of John Rex had occasioned the exiles, all earnest thought of their own position had vanished, and, strange to say, the prevailing feeling was that of anxiety for the ultimate fate of the mutineers. But as the boat grew smaller and smaller in the distance, so did their consciousness of their own situation grow more and more distinct; and when at last the boat had disappeared in the shadow of the brig, all started, as if from a dream, to the wakeful contemplation of their own case.

A council of war was held, with Mr. Frere at the head of it, and the possessions of the little party were thrown into common stock. The salt meat, flour, and tea were placed in a hollow rock at some distance from the beach, and Mr. Bates was appointed purser, to apportion to each, without fear or favour, his stated allowance. The goat was tethered with a piece of fishing line sufficiently long to allow her to browse. The cask of rum, by special agreement, was placed in the innermost recess of the rock, and it was resolved that its contents should not be touched except in case of sickness, or in last extremity. There was no lack of water, for a spring ran bubbling from the rocks within a hundred yards of the spot where the party had landed. They calculated that, with prudence, their provisions would last them for nearly four weeks.

It was found, upon a review of their possessions, that they had among them three pocket knives, a ball of string, two pipes, matches and a fig of tobacco, fishing lines with hooks, and a big jack-knife which Frere had taken to gut the fish he had expected to catch. But they saw with dismay that there was nothing which could be used axe-wise among the party. Mrs. Vickers had her shawl, and Bates a pea-jacket, but Frere and Grimes were without extra clothing. It was agreed that each should retain his own property, with the exception of the fishing lines, which were confiscated to the commonwealth.

Having made these arrangements, the kettle, filled with water from the spring, was slung from three green sticks over the fire, and a pannikin of weak tea, together with a biscuit, served out to each of the party, save Grimes, who declared himself unable to eat. Breakfast over, Bates made a damper, which was cooked in the ashes, and then another council was held as to future habitation.

It was clearly evident that they could not sleep in the open air. It was the middle of summer, and though no annoyance from rain was apprehended, the heat in the middle of the day was most oppressive. Moreover, it was absolutely necessary that Mrs. Vickers and the child should have some place to themselves. At a little distance from the beach was a sandy rise, that led up to the face of the cliff, and on the eastern side of this rise grew a forest of young trees. Frere proposed to cut down these trees, and make a sort of hut with them. It was soon discovered, however, that the pocket knives were insufficient for this purpose, but by dint of notching the young saplings and then breaking them down, they succeeded, in a couple of hours, in collecting wood enough to roof over a space between the hollow rock which contained the provisions and another rock, in shape like a hammer, which jutted out within five yards of it. Mrs. Vickers and Sylvia were to have this hut as a sleeping-place, and Frere and Bates, lying at the mouth of the larder, would at once act as a guard to it and them. Grimes was to make for himself another hut where the fire had been lighted on the previous night.

When they got back to dinner, inspirited by this resolution, they found poor Mrs. Vickers in great alarm. Grimes, who, by reason of the dint in his skull, had been left behind, was walking about the sea-beach, talking mysteriously, and shaking his fist at an imaginary foe. On going up to him, they discovered that the blow had affected his brain, for he was delirious. Frere endeavoured to soothe him, without effect; and at last, by Bates's advice, the poor fellow was rolled in the sea. The cold bath quelled his violence, and, being laid beneath the shade of a rock hard by, he fell into a condition of great muscular exhaustion, and slept.

The damper was then portioned out by Bates, and, together with a small piece of meat, it formed the dinner of the party. Mrs. Vickers reported that she had observed a great commotion on board the brig, and thought that the prisoners must be throwing overboard such portions of the cargo as were not absolutely necessary to them, in order to lighten her. This notion Bates declared to be correct, and further pointed out that the mutineers had got out a kedge-anchor, and by hauling on the kedge-line, were gradually warping the brig down the harbour. Before dinner was over a light breeze sprang up, and the *Osprey,* running up the union-jack reversed, fired a musket, either in farewell or triumph, and, spreading her sails, disappeared round the western horn of the harbour.

Mrs. Vickers, taking Sylvia with her, went away a few paces, and leaning against the rugged wall of her future home, wept bitterly. Bates and Frere affected cheerfulness, but each felt that he had hitherto regarded the presence of the brig as a sort of safeguard, and had never fully realized his own loneliness until now.

The necessity for work, however, admitted of no indulgence of vain sorrow, and Bates setting the example, the pair worked so hard that by nightfall they had torn down and dragged together sufficient brushwood to complete Mrs. Vickers's hut. During the progress of this work they were often interrupted by Grimes, who persisted in vague rushes at them, exclaiming loudly against their supposed treachery in leaving him at the mercy of the mutineers. Bates also complained of the pain caused by the wound in his forehead, and that he was afflicted with a giddiness which he knew not how to avert. By dint of frequently bathing his head at the spring, however, he succeeded in keeping on his legs, until the work of dragging together the boughs was completed, when he threw himself on the ground, and declared that he could rise no more.

Frere applied to him the remedy that had been so success-fully tried upon Grimes, but the salt water inflamed his wound and rendered his condition worse. Mrs. Vickers recommended that a little spirit and water should be used to wash the cut, and the cask was got out and broached for that purpose. Tea and damper formed their evening meal; and by the light of a blazing fire, their condition looked less desperate. Mrs. Vickers had set the pannikin on a flat stone, and dispensed the tea with an affectation of dignity which would have been absurd had it not been heart-rending. She had smoothed her hair and pinned the white shawl about her coquettishly; she even ventured to lament to Mr. Frere that she had not brought more clothes. Sylvia was in high spirits, and scorned to confess hunger. When the tea had been drunk, she fetched water from the spring in the kettle, and bathed Bates's head with it. It was resolved that, on the morrow, a search should be made for some place from which to cast the fishing line, and that one of the number should fish daily.

The condition of the unfortunate Grimes now gave cause for the greatest uneasiness. From maundering foolishly he had taken to absolute violence, and had to be watched by Frere. After much muttering and groaning, the poor fellow at last dropped off to sleep, and Frere, having assisted Bates to his sleeping-place in front of the rock, and laid him down on a heap of green brushwood, prepared to snatch a few hours' slumber. Wearied by excitement and the labours of the day, he slept heavily, but, towards morning, was awakened by a strange noise.

Grimes, whose delirium had apparently increased, had succeeded in forcing his way through the rude fence of brushwood, and had thrown himself upon Bates with the ferocity of insanity. Growling to himself, he had seized the unfortunate pilot by the throat, and the pair were struggling together. Bates, weakened by the sickness that had followed upon his wound in the head, was quite unable to cope with his desperate assailant, but calling feebly upon Frere for help, had made shift to lay hold upon the jack-knife of which we have before spoken. Frere, starting to his feet, rushed to the assistance of the pilot, but was too late. Grimes, enraged by the sight of the knife, tore it from Bates's grasp, and before Frere could catch his arm, plunged it twice into the unfortunate man's breast.

"I'm a dead man!" cried Bates faintly.

The sight of the blood, together with the exclamation of his victim, recalled Grimes to consciousness. He looked in bewilderment at the bloody weapon, and then, flinging it from him, rushed away towards the sea, into which he plunged headlong.

Frere, aghast at this sudden and terrible tragedy, gazed after him, and saw from out the placid water, sparkling in the bright beams of morning, a pair of arms, with outstretched hands, emerge; a black spot, that was a head, uprose between these stiffening arms, and then, with a horrible cry, the whole disappeared, and the bright water sparkled as placidly as before. The eyes of the terrified Frere, travelling back to the wounded man, saw, midway between this sparkling water and the knife that lay on the sand, an object that went far to explain the maniac's sudden burst of fury. The rum cask lay upon its side by the remnants of last night's fire, and close to it was a clout, with which the head of the wounded man had been bound. It was evident that the poor creature, wandering in his delirium, had come across the rum cask, drunk a quantity of its contents, and been maddened by the fiery spirit.

Frere hurried to the side of Bates, and lifting him up, strove to staunch the blood that flowed from his chest. It would seem that he had been resting himself on his left elbow, and that Grimes, snatching the knife from his right hand, had stabbed him twice in the right breast. He was pale and senseless, and Frere feared that the wound was mortal. Tearing off his neck-handkerchief, he endeavoured to bandage the wound, but found that the strip of silk was insufficient for the purpose. The noise had roused Mrs. Vickers, who, stifling her terror, made haste to tear off a portion of her dress, and with this a bandage of sufficient width was made. Frere went to the cask to see if, haply, he could obtain from it a little spirit with which to moisten the lips of the dying man, but it was empty. Grimes, after drinking his fill, had overturned the unheaded puncheon, and the greedy sand had absorbed every drop of liquor. Sylvia brought some water from the spring, and Mrs. Vickers bathing Bates's head with this, he revived a little. By-and-by Mrs. Vickers milked the goat—she had never done such a thing before in all her life—and the milk being given to Bates in a pannikin, he drank it eagerly, but vomited it almost instantly. It was evident that he was sinking from some internal injury.

None of the party had much appetite for breakfast, but Frere, whose sensibilities were less acute than those of the others, ate a piece of salt meat and damper. It struck him, with a curious feeling of pleasant selfishness, that now Grimes had gone, the allowance of provisions would be increased, and that if Bates went also, it would be increased still further.

He did not give utterance to his thoughts, however, but sat with the wounded man's head on his knees, and brushed the settling flies from his face. He hoped, after all, that the pilot would not die, for he should then be left alone to look after the women. Perhaps some such thought was agitating Mrs. Vickers also. As for Sylvia, she made no secret of her anxiety.

"Don't die, Mr. Bates—oh, don't die!" she said, standing piteously near, but afraid to touch him. "Don't leave mamma and me alone in this dreadful place!"

Poor Bates, of course, said nothing, but Frere frowned heavily, and Mrs. Vickers said reprovingly, "Sylvia!" just as if they had been in the old house on distant Sarah Island.

In the afternoon Frere went away to drag together some wood

for the fire, and when he returned he found the pilot near his end. Mrs. Vickers said that for an hour he had lain without motion, and almost without breath. The major's wife had seen more than one death-bed, and was calm enough; but poor little Sylvia, sitting on a stone hard by, shook with terror. She had a dim notion that death must be accompanied by violence. As the sun sank, Bates rallied; but the two watchers knew that it was but the final flicker of the expiring candle. "He's going!" said Frere at length, under his breath, as though fearful of awaking his half-slumbering soul. Mrs. Vickers, her eyes streaming with silent tears, lifted the honest head, and moistened the parched lips with her soaked handkerchief. A tremor shook the once stalwart limbs, and the dying man opened his eyes. For an instant he seemed bewildered, and then, looking from one to the other, intelligence returned to his glance, and it was evident that he remembered all. His gaze rested upon the pale face of the affrighted Sylvia, and then turned to Frere. There could be no mistaking the mute appeal of those eloquent eyes.

"Yes, I'll take care of her," said Frere.

Bates smiled, and then, observing that the blood from his wound had stained the white shawl of Mrs. Vickers, he made an effort to move his head. It was not fitting that a lady's shawl should be stained with the blood of a poor fellow like himself. The fashionable fribble, with quick instinct, understood the gesture, and gently drew the head back upon her bosom. In the presence of death the woman was womanly. For a moment all was silent, and they thought he had gone; but all at once he opened his eyes and looked round for the sea.

"Turn my face to it once more," he whispered; and as they raised him, he inclined his ear to listen. "It's calm enough here, God bless it," he said; "but I can hear the waves a-breaking hard upon the Bar!"

And so his head dropped, and he died.

As Frere relieved Mrs. Vickers from the weight of the corpse, Sylvia ran to her mother. "Oh, mamma, mamma," she cried, "why did God let him die when we wanted him so much?"

Before it grew dark, Frere made shift to carry the body to the shelter of some rocks at a little distance, and spreading the jacket over the face, he piled stones upon it to keep it steady. The march of events had been so rapid that he scarcely realized that since the previous evening two of the five human creatures left in this wilderness had escaped from it. As he did realize it, he began to wonder whose turn it would be next.

Mrs. Vickers, worn out by the fatigue and excitement of the day, retired to rest early; and Sylvia, refusing to speak to Frere, followed her mother. This manifestation of unaccountable dislike on the part of the child hurt Maurice more than he cared to own. He felt angry with her for not loving him, and yet he took no pains to conciliate her. It was with a curious pleasure that he remembered how she must soon look up to him as her chief protector. Had Sylvia been just a few years older, the young man would have thought himself in love with her.

The following day passed gloomily. It was hot and sultry, and a dull haze hung over the mountains. Frere spent the morning in scooping a grave in the sand, in which to inter poor Bates. Practically awake to his own necessities, he removed such portions of clothing from the body as would be useful to him, but hid them under a stone, not liking to let Mrs. Vickers see what he had done. Having completed the grave by midday, he placed the corpse therein, and rolled as many stones as possible to the sides of the mound. In the afternoon he cast the fishing line from the point of a rock he had marked the day before, but caught nothing. Passing by the grave, on his return, he noticed that Mrs. Vickers had placed at the head of it a rude cross, formed by tying two pieces of stick together.

After supper—the usual salt meat and damper—he lit an economical pipe, and tried to talk to Sylvia. "Why won't you be friends with me, missy?" he asked.

"I don't like you," said Sylvia. "You frighten me."

"Why?"

"You are not kind. I don't mean that you do cruel things; but you are—oh, I wish papa was here!"

"Wishing won't bring him!" says Frere, pressing his hoarded tobacco together with prudent forefinger.

"There! *That's* what I mean! Is that kind? 'Wishing won't bring him!' Oh, if it only would!"

"I didn't mean it unkindly," says Frere. "What a strange child you are."

"There are persons," says Sylvia, "who have no Affinity for each other. I read about it in a book papa had, and I suppose that's what it is. I have no Affinity for you. I can't help it, can I?"

"Rubbish!" Frere returned. "Come here, and I'll tell you a story."

Mrs. Vickers had gone back to her cave, and the two were alone by the fire, near which stood the kettle and the newly-made damper. The child, with some show of hesitation, came to him, and he caught and placed her on his knee. The moon had not yet risen, and the shadows cast by the flickering fire seemed weird and monstrous. The wicked wish to frighten this helpless creature came to Maurice Frere. "There was once," said he, "a Castle in an old wood, and in this Castle there lived an Ogre, with great goggle eyes."

"You silly man!" said Sylvia, struggling to be free. "You are trying to frighten me!"

"And this Ogre lived on the bones of little girls. One day a little girl was travelling the wood, and she heard the Ogre coming. 'Haw! haw! Haw! haw!'"

"Mr. Frere, let me down!"

"She was terribly frightened, and she ran, and ran, and ran, until all of a sudden she saw——"

A piercing scream burst from his companion. "Oh! oh! What's that?" she cried, and clung to her persecutor.

Beyond the fire stood the figure of a man. He staggered forward, and then, falling on his knees, stretched out his hands, and hoarsely articulated one word—"Food." It was Rufus Dawes.

The sound of a human voice broke the spell of terror that was on the child, and as the glow from the fire fell upon the tattered yellow garments, she guessed at once the whole story. Not so Maurice Frere. He saw before him a new danger, a new mouth to share the scanty provision, and snatching a brand from the fire he kept the convict at bay. But Rufus Dawes, glaring round with wolfish eyes, caught sight of the damper resting against the iron kettle, and made a clutch at it Frere dashed the brand in his face. "Stand back!" he cried.

"We have no food to spare!" The convict uttered a savage cry, and raising the iron gad, plunged forward desperately to attack this new enemy; but, quick as thought, the child glided past Frere, and, snatching the loaf, placed it in the hands of the starving man, with "Here, poor prisoner, eat!" and then, turning to Frere, she cast upon him a glance so full of horror, indignation, and surprise, that the man blushed and threw down the brand.

As for Rufus Dawes, the sudden apparition of this golden-haired girl seemed to have transformed him. Allowing the loaf to slip through his fingers, he gazed with haggard eyes at the retreating figure of the child, and as it vanished into the darkness outside the circle of firelight, the unhappy man sank his face upon his blackened, horny hands, and burst into tears.

CHAPTER XII
"MR." DAWES

THE coarse tones of Maurice Frere roused him. "What do you want?" he asked. Rufus Dawes, raising his head, contemplated the figure before him, and recognized it. "Is it *you*?" he said slowly.

"What do you mean? Do you know me?" asked Frere, drawing back. But the convict did not reply. His momentary emotion passed away, the pangs of hunger returned, and greedily seizing upon the piece of damper, he began to eat in silence.

"Do you hear, man?" repeated Frere, at length. "What are you?"

"An escaped prisoner. You can give me up in the morning. I've done my best, and I'm beat."

The sentence struck Frere with dismay. The man did not know that the settlement had been abandoned!

"I cannot give you up. There is no one but myself and a woman and child on the settlement." Rufus Dawes, pausing in his eating, stared at him in amazement. "The prisoners have gone away in the schooner. If you choose to remain free, you can do so as far as I am concerned. I am as helpless as you are."

"But how do *you* come here?"

Frere laughed bitterly. To give explanations to convicts was foreign to his experience, and he did not relish the task. In this case, however, there was no help for it. "The prisoners mutinied and seized the brig."

"What brig?"

"The *Osprey*."

A terrible light broke upon Rufus Dawes, and he began to understand how he had again missed his chance. "Who took her?"

"That double-dyed villain, John Rex," says Frere, giving vent to his passion. "May she sink, and burn, and—"

"Have they *gone*, then?" cried the miserable man, clutching at his hair with a gesture of hopeless rage.

"Yes; two days ago, and left us here to starve."

Rufus Dawes burst into a laugh so discordant that it made the other shudder. "We'll starve together, Maurice Frere," said he, "for while you've a crust, I'll share it. If I don't get liberty, at least I'll have revenge!"

The sinister aspect of this famished savage, sitting with his chin on his ragged knees, rocking himself to and fro in the light of the fire, gave Mr. Maurice Frere a new sensation. He felt as might have felt that African hunter who, returning to his camp fire, found a lion there. "Wretch!" said he, shrinking from him, "why should you wish to be revenged on *me*?"

The convict turned upon him with a snarl. "Take care what you say! I'll have no hard words. Wretch! If I am a wretch, who made me one? If I hate you and myself and the world, who made me hate it? I was born free—as free as you are. Why should I be sent to herd with beasts, and condemned to this slavery, worse than death? Tell me that, Maurice Frere—tell me that!"

"I didn't make the laws," says Frere, "why do you attack me?"

"Because you are what I *was*. You are FREE! You can do as you please. You can love, you can work, you can think. I can only *hate*!" He paused as if astonished at himself, and then continued, with a low laugh. "Fine words for a convict, eh! But, never mind, it's all right, Mr. Frere; we're equal now, and I sha'n't die an hour sooner than you, though you are a 'free man'!"

Frere began to think that he was dealing with another madman.

"Die! There's no need to talk of dying," he said, as soothingly as it was possible for him to say it. "Time enough for that by-and-by."

"There spoke the *free* man. We convicts have an advantage over you *gentlemen*. You are afraid of death; we pray for it. It is the best thing that can happen to us. Die! They were going to hang me once. I wish they had. My God, I wish they had!"

There was such a depth of agony in this terrible utterance that Maurice Frere was appalled at it. "There, go and sleep, my man," he said. "You are knocked up. We'll talk in the morning."

"Hold on a bit!" cried Rufus Dawes, with a coarseness of manner altogether foreign to that he had just assumed. "Who's with ye?"

"The wife and daughter of the Commandant," replied Frere, half afraid to refuse an answer to a question so fiercely put.

"No one else?"

"No."

"Poor souls!" said the convict, "I pity them." And then he stretched himself, like a dog, before the blaze, and went to sleep instantly. Maurice Frere, looking at the gaunt figure of this addition to the party, was completely puzzled how to act. Such a character had never before come within the range of his experience. He knew not what to make of this fierce, ragged, desperate man, who wept and threatened by turns—who was now snarling in the most repulsive bass of the convict gamut, and now calling upon Heaven in tones which were little less than eloquent. At first he thought of precipitating himself upon the sleeping wretch and pinioning him, but a second glance at the sinewy, though wasted, limbs forbade him to follow out the rash suggestion of his own fears. Then a horrible prompting—arising out of his former cowardice—made him feel for the jack-knife with which one murder had already been committed. Their stock of provisions was so scanty, and after all, the lives of the woman and child were worth more than that of this unknown desperado! But, to do him justice, the thought no sooner shaped itself than he crushed it out. "We'll wait till morning, and see how he shapes," said Frere to himself; and pausing at the brushwood barricade, behind which the mother and daughter were clinging to each other, he whispered that he was on guard outside, and that the absconder slept. But when morning dawned, he found that there was no need for alarm. The convict was lying in almost the same position as that in which he had left him, and his eyes were closed. His threatening outbreak of the previous night had been produced by the excitement of his sudden rescue, and he was now incapable of violence. Frere advanced, and shook him by the shoulder.

"Not alive!" cried the poor wretch, waking with a start, and raising his arm to strike. "Keep off!"

"It's all right," said Frere. "No one is going to harm you. Wake up."

Rufus Dawes glanced around him stupidly, and then remembering what had happened, with a great effort, he staggered to his feet. "I thought they'd got me!" he said, "but it's the other way, I see. Come, let's have breakfast, Mr. Frere. I'm hungry."

"You must wait," said Frere. "Do you think there is no one here but yourself?"

Rufus Dawes, swaying to and fro from weakness, passed his shred of a cuff over his eyes. "I don't know anything about it. I only know I'm hungry."

Frere stopped short. Now or never was the time to settle future relations. Lying awake in the night, with the jack-knife ready to his hand, he had decided on the course of action that must be adopted. The convict should share with the rest, but no more. If he rebelled at that, there must be a trial of strength between them. "Look you here," he said. "We have but barely enough food to serve us until help comes—if it does come. I have the care of that poor woman and child, and I will see fair play for their sakes. You shall share with us to our last bit and drop, but, by Heaven, you shall get no more."

The convict, stretching out his wasted arms, looked down upon them with the uncertain gaze of a drunken man. "I am weak now," he said. "You have the best of me"; and then he sank suddenly down upon the ground, exhausted. "Give me a drink," he moaned, feebly motioning with his hand. Frere got him water in the pannikin, and having drunk it, he smiled and lay down to sleep again. Mrs. Vickers and Sylvia, coming out while he still slept, recognized him as the desperado of the settlement.

"He was the most desperate man we had," said Mrs. Vickers, identifying herself with her husband. "Oh, what shall we do?"

"He won't do much harm," returned Frere, looking down at the notorious ruffian with curiosity. "He's as near dead as can be."

Sylvia looked up at him with her clear child's glance. "We mustn't let him die," said she. "That would be murder."

"No, no," returned Frere, hastily, "no one wants him to die. But what can we do?"

"I'll nurse him!" cried Sylvia.

Frere broke into one of his coarse laughs, the first one that he had indulged in since the mutiny. "You nurse him! By George, that's a good one!" The poor little child, weak and excitable, felt the contempt in the tone, and burst into a passion of sobs. "Why do you insult me, you wicked man? The poor fellow's ill, and he'll—he'll die, like Mr. Bates. Oh, mamma, mamma, Let's go away by ourselves."

Frere swore a great oath, and walked away. He went into the little wood under the cliff, and sat down. He was full of strange thoughts, which he could not express, and which he had never owned before. The dislike the child bore to him made him miserable, and yet he took delight in tormenting her. He was conscious that he had acted the part of a coward the night before in endeavouring to frighten her, and that the detestation she bore him was well earned; but he had fully determined to stake his life in her defence, should the savage who had thus come upon them out of the desert attempt violence, and he was unreasonably angry at the pity she had shown. It was not fair to be thus misinterpreted. But he had done wrong to swear, and more so in quitting them so abruptly. The consciousness of his wrong-doing, however, only made him more confirmed in it. His native obstinacy would not allow him to retract what he had said—even to himself. Walking along, he came to Bates's grave, and the cross upon it. Here was another evidence of ill-treatment. She had always preferred Bates. Now that Bates was gone, she must needs transfer her childish affections to a convict. "Oh," said Frere to himself, with pleasant recollections of many coarse triumphs in love-making, "if you were a woman, you little vixen, I'd make you love me!" When he had said this, he laughed at himself for his folly—he was turning romantic! When he got back, he found Dawes stretched upon the brushwood, with Sylvia sitting near him.

"He is better," said Mrs. Vickers, disdaining to refer to the scene of the morning. "Sit down and have something to eat, Mr. Frere."

"Are you better?" asked Frere, abruptly.

To his surprise, the convict answered quite civilly, "I shall be strong again in a day or two, and then I can help you, sir."

"Help me? How?"

"To build a hut here for the ladies. And we'll live here all our lives, and never go back to the sheds any more."

"He has been wandering a little," said Mrs. Vickers. "Poor fellow, he seems quite well behaved."

The convict began to sing a little German song, and to beat the refrain with his hand. Frere looked at him with curiosity. "I wonder what the story of that man's life has been," he said. "A queer one, I'll be bound."

Sylvia looked up at him with a forgiving smile. "I'll ask him when he gets well," she said, "and if you are good, I'll tell you, Mr. Frere."

Frere accepted the proffered friendship. "I am a great brute, Sylvia, sometimes, ain't I?" he said, "but I don't mean it."

"You are," returned Sylvia, frankly, "but let's shake hands, and be friends. It's no use quarrelling when there are only four of us, is it?" And in this way was Rufus Dawes admitted a member of the family circle.

Within a week from the night on which he had seen the smoke of Frere's fire, the convict had recovered his strength, and had become an important personage. The distrust with which he had been at first viewed had worn off, and he was no longer an outcast, to be shunned and pointed at, or to be referred to in whispers. He had abandoned his rough manner, and no longer threatened or complained, and though at times a profound melancholy would oppress him, his spirits were more even than those of Frere, who was often moody, sullen, and overbearing. Rufus Dawes was no longer the brutalized wretch who had plunged into the dark waters of the bay to escape a life he loathed, and had alternately cursed and wept in the solitudes of the forests. He was an active member of society—a society of four—and he began to regain an air of independence and authority. This change had been wrought by the influence of little Sylvia. Recovered from the weakness consequent upon this terrible journey, Rufus Dawes had experienced for the first time in six years the soothing power of kindness. He had now an object to live for beyond himself. He was of use to somebody, and had he died, he would have been regretted. To us this means little; to this unhappy man it meant everything. He found, to his astonishment, that he was not despised, and that, by the strange concurrence of circumstances, he had been brought into a position in which his convict experiences gave him authority. He was skilled in all the mysteries of the prison sheds. He knew how to sustain life on as little food as possible. He could fell trees without an axe, bake bread without an oven, build a weatherproof hut without bricks or mortar. From the patient he became the adviser; and from the adviser, the commander. In the semi-savage state to which these four human beings had been brought, he found that savage accomplishments were of most value. Might was Right, and Maurice Frere's authority of gentility soon succumbed to Rufus Dawes's authority of knowledge.

As the time wore on, and the scanty stock of provisions decreased, he found that his authority grew more and more powerful. Did a question arise as to the qualities of a strange plant, it was Rufus Dawes who could pronounce upon it. Were fish to be caught, it was Rufus Dawes who caught them. Did Mrs. Vickers complain of the instability of her brushwood hut, it was Rufus Dawes who worked a wicker shield, and plastering it with clay, produced a wall that defied the keenest wind. He made cups out of pine-knots, and plates out of bark-strips. He worked harder than any three men. Nothing daunted him, nothing discouraged him. When Mrs. Vickers fell sick, from anxiety and insufficient food, it was Rufus Dawes who gathered fresh leaves for her couch, who cheered her by hopeful words, who voluntarily gave up half his own allowance of meat that she might grow stronger on it. The poor woman and her child called him "Mr." Dawes.

Frere watched all this with dissatisfaction that amounted at times to positive hatred. Yet he could say nothing, for he could not but acknowledge that, beside Dawes, he was incapable. He even submitted to take orders from this escaped convict—it was so evident that the escaped convict knew better than he. Sylvia began to look upon Dawes as a second Bates. He was, moreover, all her own. She had an interest in him, for she had nursed and protected him. If it had not been for her, this prodigy would not have lived. He felt for her an absorbing affection that was almost a passion. She was his good angel, his protectress, his glimpse of Heaven. She had given him food when he was starving, and had believed in him when the world—the world of four—had looked coldly on him. He would have died for her, and, for love of her, hoped for the vessel which should take *her* back to freedom and give *him* again into bondage.

But the days stole on, and no vessel appeared. Each day they eagerly scanned the watery horizon; each day they longed to behold the bowsprit of the returning *Ladybird* glide past the jutting rock that shut out the view of the harbour—but in vain. Mrs. Vickers's illness increased, and the stock of provisions began to run short. Dawes talked of putting himself and Frere on half allowance. It was evident that, unless succour came in a few days, they must starve.

Frere mooted all sorts of wild plans for obtaining food. He would make a journey to the settlement, and, swimming the estuary, search if haply any casks of biscuit had been left behind in the hurry of departure. He would set springes for the seagulls, and snare the pigeons at Liberty Point. But all these proved impracticable, and with blank faces they watched their bag of flour grow smaller and smaller daily. Then the notion of escape was broached. Could they construct a raft? Impossible without nails or ropes. Could they build a boat? Equally impossible for the same reason. Could they raise a fire sufficient to signal a ship? Easily; but what ship would come within reach of that doubly-desolate spot? Nothing could be done but wait for a vessel, which was sure to come for them sooner or later; and, growing weaker day by day, they waited.

One morning Sylvia was sitting in the sun reading the "English History", which, by the accident of fright, she had brought with her on the night of the mutiny. "Mr. Frere," said she, suddenly, "what is an alchemist?"

"A man who makes gold," was Frere's not very accurate definition.

"Do you know one?"

"No."

"Do you, Mr. Dawes?"

"I knew a man once who thought himself one."

"What! A man who made gold?"

"After a fashion."

"But did he *make* gold?" persisted Sylvia.

"No, not absolutely *make* it. But he was, in his worship of money, an alchemist for all that."

"What became of him?"

"I don't know," said Dawes, with so much constraint in his tone that the child instinctively turned the subject.

"Then, alchemy is a very old art?"

"Oh, yes."

"Did the Ancient Britons know it?"

"No, not as old as that!"

Sylvia suddenly gave a little scream. The remembrance of the evening when she read about the Ancient Britons to poor Bates came vividly into her mind, and though she had since re-read the passage that had then attracted her attention a hundred times, it had never before presented itself to her in its full significance. Hurriedly turning the well-thumbed leaves, she read aloud the passage which had provoked remark:—

"'The Ancient Britons were little better than Barbarians. They painted their bodies with Woad, and, seated in their light coracles of skin stretched upon slender wooden frames, must have presented a wild and savage appearance.'"

"A coracle! That's a boat! Can't we make a coracle, Mr. Dawes?"

CHAPTER XIII

WHAT THE SEAWEED SUGGESTED

THE question gave the marooned party new hopes. Maurice Frere, with his usual impetuosity, declared that the project was a most feasible one, and wondered—as such men will wonder—that it had never occurred to him before. "It's the simplest thing in the world!" he cried. "Sylvia, you have saved us!" But upon taking the matter into more earnest consideration, it became apparent that they were as yet a long way from the realization of their hopes. To make a coracle of skins seemed sufficiently easy, but how to obtain the skins! The one miserable hide of the unlucky she-goat was utterly inadequate for the purpose. Sylvia—her face beaming with the hope of escape, and with delight at having been the means of suggesting it—watched narrowly the countenance of Rufus Dawes, but she marked no answering gleam of joy in those eyes. "Can't it be done, Mr. Dawes?" she asked, trembling for the reply.

The convict knitted his brows gloomily.

"Come, Dawes!" cried Frere, forgetting his enmity for an instant in the flash of new hope, "can't you suggest something?"

Rufus Dawes, thus appealed to as the acknowledged Head of the little society, felt a pleasant thrill of self-satisfaction. "I don't know," he said. "I must think of it. It looks easy, and yet—" He paused as something in the water caught his eye. It was a mass of bladdery seaweed that the returning tide was wafting slowly to the shore. This object, which would have passed unnoticed at any other time, suggested to Rufus Dawes a new idea. "Yes," he added slowly, with a change of tone, "it may be done. I think I can see my way."

The others preserved a respectful silence until he should speak again. "How far do you think it is across the bay?" he asked of Frere.

"What, to Sarah Island?"

"No, to the Pilot Station."

"About four miles."

The convict sighed. "Too far to swim now, though I might

have done it once. But this sort of life weakens a man. It must be done after all."

"What are you going to do?" asked Frere.

"To kill the goat."

Sylvia uttered a little cry; she had become fond of her dumb companion. "Kill Nanny! Oh, Mr. Dawes! What for?"

"I am going to make a boat for you," he said, "and I want hides, and thread, and tallow."

A few weeks back Maurice Frere would have laughed at such a sentence, but he had begun now to comprehend that this escaped convict was not a man to be laughed at, and though he detested him for his superiority, he could not but admit that he was superior.

"You can't get more than one hide off a goat, man?" he said, with an inquiring tone in his voice—as though it was just possible that such a marvellous being as Dawes *could* get a second hide, by virtue of some secret process known only to himself.

"I am going to catch other goats."

"Where?"

"At the Pilot Station."

"But how are you going to get there?"

"Float across. Come, there is not time for questioning! Go and cut down some saplings, and let us begin!"

The lieutenant-master looked at the convict prisoner with astonishment, and then gave way to the power of knowledge, and did as he was ordered. Before sundown that evening the carcase of poor Nanny, broken into various most unbutcherly fragments, was hanging on the nearest tree; and Frere, returning with as many young saplings as he could drag together, found Rufus Dawes engaged in a curious occupation. He had killed the goat, and having cut off its head close under the jaws, and its legs at the knee-joint, had extracted the carcase through a slit made in the lower portion of the belly, which slit he had now sewn together with string. This proceeding gave him a rough bag, and he was busily engaged in filling this bag with such coarse grass as he could collect. Frere observed, also, that the fat of the animal was carefully preserved, and the intestines had been placed in a pool of water to soak.

The convict, however, declined to give information as to what he intended to do. "It's my own notion," he said. "Let me alone. I may make a failure of it." Frere, on being pressed by Sylvia, affected to know all about the scheme, but to impose silence on himself. He was galled to think that a convict brain should contain a mystery which he might not share.

On the next day, by Rufus Dawes's direction, Frere cut down some rushes that grew about a mile from the camping ground, and brought them in on his back. This took him nearly half a day to accomplish. Short rations were beginning to tell upon his physical powers. The convict, on the other hand, trained by a woeful experience in the Boats to endurance of hardship, was slowly recovering his original strength.

"What are they for?" asked Frere, as he flung the bundles down. His master condescended to reply. "To make a float."

"Well?"

The other shrugged his broad shoulders. "You are very dull, Mr. Frere. I am going to swim over to the Pilot Station, and catch some of those goats. I can get across on the stuffed skin, but I must float *them* back on the reeds."

"How the doose do you mean to catch 'em?" asked Frere, wiping the sweat from his brow.

The convict motioned to him to approach. He did so, and saw that his companion was cleaning the intestines of the goat. The outer membrane having been peeled off, Rufus Dawes was turning the gut inside out. This he did by turning up a short piece of it, as though it were a coat-sleeve, and dipping the turned-up cuff into a pool of water. The weight of the water pressing between the cuff and the rest of the gut, bore down a further portion; and so, by repeated dippings, the whole length was turned inside out. The inner membrane having been scraped away, there remained a fine transparent tube, which was tightly twisted, and set to dry in the sun.

"There is the catgut for the noose," said Dawes. "I learnt *that* trick at the settlement. Now come here."

Frere, following, saw that a fire had been made between two

stones, and that the kettle was partly sunk in the ground near it. On approaching the kettle, he found it full of smooth pebbles.

"Take out those stones," said Dawes.

Frere obeyed, and saw at the bottom of the kettle a quantity of sparkling white powder, and the sides of the vessel crusted with the same material.

"What's that?" he asked.

"Salt."

"How did you get it?"

"I filled the kettle with sea-water, and then, heating those pebbles red-hot in the fire, dropped them into it. We could have caught the steam in a cloth and wrung out fresh water had we wished to do so. But, thank God, we have plenty."

Frere started. "Did you learn that at the settlement, too?" he asked.

Rufus Dawes laughed, with a sort of bitterness in his tones. "Do you think I have been at 'the settlement' all my life? The thing is very simple, it is merely evaporation."

Frere burst out in sudden, fretful admiration: "What a fellow you are, Dawes! What are you—I mean, what have you been?"

A triumphant light came into the other's face, and for the instant he seemed about to make some startling revelation. But the light faded, and he checked himself with a gesture of pain.

"I *am* a convict. Never mind what I *have* been. A sailor, a shipbuilder, prodigal, vagabond—what does it matter? It won't alter my fate, will it?"

"If we get safely back," says Frere, "I'll ask for a free pardon for you. You deserve it."

"Come," returned Dawes, with a discordant laugh. "Let us wait until we get back."

"You don't believe me?"

"I don't want favour at *your* hands," he said, with a return of the old fierceness. "Let us get to work. Bring up the rushes here, and tie them with a fishing line."

At this instant Sylvia came up. "Good afternoon, Mr. Dawes. Hard at work? Oh! what's this in the kettle?" The voice of the child acted like a charm upon Rufus Dawes. He smiled quite cheerfully.

"Salt, miss. I am going to catch the goats with that."

"Catch the goats! How? Put it on their tails?" she cried merrily.

"Goats are fond of salt, and when I get over to the Pilot Station I shall set traps for them baited with this salt. When they come to lick it, I shall have a noose of catgut ready to catch them—do you understand?"

"But how will you get across?"

"You will see to-morrow."

CHAPTER XIV
A WONDERFUL DAY'S WORK

THE next morning Rufus Dawes was stirring by daylight. He first got his catgut wound upon a piece of stick, and then, having moved his frail floats alongside the little rock that served as a pier, he took a fishing line and a larger piece of stick, and proceeded to draw a diagram on the sand. This diagram when completed represented a rude outline of a punt, eight feet long and three broad. At certain distances were eight points—four on each side—into which small willow rods were driven. He then awoke Frere and showed the diagram to him.

"Get eight stakes of celery-top pine," he said. "You can burn them where you cannot cut them, and drive a stake into the place of each of these willow wands. When you have done that, collect as many willows as you can get. I shall not be back until tonight. Now give me a hand with the floats."

Frere, coming to the pier, saw Dawes strip himself, and piling his clothes upon the stuffed goat-skin, stretch himself upon the reed bundles, and, paddling with his hands, push off from the shore. The clothes floated high and dry, but the reeds, depressed by the weight of the body, sank so that the head of the convict alone appeared above water. In this fashion he gained the middle of the current, and the out-going tide swept him down towards the mouth of the harbour.

Frere, sulkily admiring, went back to prepare the breakfast—they were on half rations now, Dawes having forbidden the slaughtered goat to be eaten, lest his expedition should prove unsuccessful—wondering at the chance which had thrown this convict in his way. "Parsons would call it 'a special providence,'" he said to himself. "For if it hadn't been for him, we should never have got thus far. If his 'boat' succeeds, we're all right, I suppose. He's a clever dog. I wonder who he is." His training as a master of convicts made him think how dangerous such a man would be on a convict station. It would be difficult to keep a fellow of such resources. "They'll have to look pretty sharp after him if they ever get him back," he thought. "I'll have a fine tale to tell of his ingenuity."

The conversation of the previous day occurred to him. "I promised to ask for a free pardon. He wouldn't have it, though. Too proud to accept it at *my* hands! Wait until we get back. I'll teach him his place; for, after all, it is his own liberty that he is working for as well as mine—I mean ours." Then a thought came into his head that was in every way worthy of him. "Suppose we took the boat, and left him behind!" The notion seemed so ludicrously wicked that he laughed involuntarily.

"What is it, Mr. Frere?"

"Oh, it's you, Sylvia, is it? Ha, ha, ha! I was thinking of something—something funny."

"Indeed," said Sylvia, "I am glad of that. Where's Mr. Dawes?"

Frere was displeased at the interest with which she asked the question.

"You are always thinking of that fellow. It's Dawes, Dawes, Dawes all day long. He has gone."

"Oh!" with a sorrowful accent. "Mamma wants to see him."

"What about?" says Frere roughly.

"Mamma is ill, Mr. Frere."

"Dawes isn't a doctor. What's the matter with her?"

"She is worse than she was yesterday. I don't know what is the matter."

Frere, somewhat alarmed, strode over to the little cavern.

The "lady of the Commandant" was in a strange plight. The cavern was lofty, but narrow. In shape it was three-cornered, having two sides open to the wind. The ingenuity of Rufus Dawes had closed these sides with wicker-work and clay, and a sort of door of interlaced brushwood hung at one of them. Frere pushed open this door and entered. The poor woman was lying on a bed of rushes strewn over young brushwood, and was moaning feebly. From the first she had felt the privation to which she was subjected most keenly, and the mental anxiety from which she suffered increased her physical debility. The exhaustion and lassitude to which she had partially succumbed soon after Dawes's arrival, had now completely overcome her, and she was unable to rise.

"Cheer up, ma'am," said Maurice, with an assumption of heartiness. "It will be all right in a day or two."

"Is it you? I sent for Mr. Dawes."

"He is away just now. I am making a boat. Did not Sylvia tell you?"

"She told me that *he* was making one."

"Well, I—that is, *we*—are making it. He will be back again tonight. Can I do anything for you?"

"No, thank you. I only wanted to know how he was getting on. I must go soon—if I am to go. Thank you, Mr. Frere. I am much obliged to you. This is a—he-he—a dreadful place to have visitors, isn't it?"

"Never mind," said Frere, again, "you will be back in Hobart Town in a few days now. We are sure to get picked up by a ship. But you must cheer up. Have some tea or something."

"No, thank you—I don't feel well enough to eat. I am tired." Sylvia began to cry.

"Don't cry, dear. I shall be better by-and-by. Oh, I wish Mr. Dawes was back."

Maurice Frere went out indignant. This "Mr." Dawes was everybody, it seemed, and he was nobody. Let them wait a little. All that day, working hard to carry out the convict's directions, he meditated a thousand plans by which he could turn the tables. He would accuse Dawes of violence. He would demand that he should be taken back as an "absconder". He would insist that the law should take its course, and that the "death" which was the doom of all who were caught in the act of escape from a penal settlement should be enforced. Yet if they got safe to land, the marvellous courage and ingenuity of the prisoner would tell strongly in his favour. The woman and child would bear witness to his tenderness and skill, and plead for him. As he had said, the convict deserved a pardon. The mean, bad man, burning with wounded vanity and undefined jealousy, waited for some method to suggest itself, by which he might claim the credit of the escape, and snatch from the prisoner, who had dared to rival him, the last hope of freedom.

Rufus Dawes, drifting with the current, had allowed himself to coast along the eastern side of the harbour until the Pilot Station appeared in view on the opposite shore. By this time it was nearly seven o'clock. He landed at a sandy cove, and drawing up his raft, proceeded to unpack from among his garments a piece of damper. Having eaten sparingly, and dried himself in the sun, he replaced the remains of his breakfast, and pushed his floats again into the water. The Pilot Station lay some distance below him, on the opposite shore. He had purposely made his second start from a point which would give him this advantage of position; for had he attempted to paddle across at right angles, the strength of the current would have swept him out to sea. Weak as he was, he several times nearly lost his hold on the reeds. The clumsy bundle presenting too great a broadside to the stream, whirled round and round, and was once or twice nearly sucked under. At length, however, breathless and exhausted, he gained the opposite bank, half a mile below the point he had attempted to make, and carrying his floats out of reach of the tide, made off across the hill to the Pilot Station.

Arrived there about midday, he set to work to lay his snares. The goats, with whose hides he hoped to cover the coracle, were sufficiently numerous and tame to encourage him to use every exertion. He carefully examined the tracks of the animals, and found that they converged to one point—the track to the nearest water. With much labour he cut down bushes, so as to mask the approach to the waterhole on all sides save where these tracks immediately conjoined. Close to the water, and at unequal distances along the various tracks, he scattered the salt he had obtained by his rude distillation of sea-water. Between this scattered salt and the points where he judged the animals would be likely to approach, he set his traps, made after the following manner. He took several pliant branches of young trees, and having stripped them of leaves and twigs, dug with his knife and the end of the rude paddle he had made for the voyage across the inlet, a succession of holes, about a foot deep. At the thicker end of these saplings he fastened, by a piece of fishing line, a small cross-bar, which swung loosely, like the stick handle which a schoolboy fastens to the string of his pegtop. Forcing the ends of the saplings thus prepared into the holes, he filled in and stamped down the earth all around them. The saplings, thus anchored as it were by the cross-pieces of stick, not only stood firm, but resisted all his efforts to withdraw them. To the thin ends of these saplings he bound tightly, into notches cut in the wood, and secured by a multiplicity of twisting, the catgut springes he had brought from the camping ground. The saplings were then bent double, and the gutted ends secured in the ground by the same means as that employed to fix the butts. This was the most difficult part of the business, for it was necessary to discover precisely the amount of pressure that would hold the bent rod without allowing it to escape by reason of this elasticity, and which would yet "give" to a slight pull on the gut. After many failures, however, this happy medium was discovered; and Rufus Dawes, concealing his springes by means of twigs, smoothed the disturbed sand with a branch and retired to watch the effect of his labours.

About two hours after he had gone, the goats came to drink. There were five goats and two kids, and they trotted calmly along the path to the water. The watcher soon saw that his precautions had been in a manner wasted. The leading goat marched gravely into the springe, which, catching him round his neck, released the bent rod, and sprang him off his legs into the air. He uttered a comical bleat, and then hung kicking. Rufus Dawes, though the success of the scheme was a matter of life and death, burst out laughing at the antics of the beast. The other goats bounded off at this sudden elevation of their leader, and three more were entrapped at a little distance. Rufus Dawes now thought it time to secure his prize, though three of the springes were as yet unsprung. He ran down to the old goat, knife in hand, but before he could reach him the barely-dried catgut gave way, and the old fellow, shaking his head with grotesque dismay, made off at full speed. The others, however, were secured and killed. The loss of the springe was not a serious one, for three traps remained unsprung, and before sundown Rufus Dawes had caught four more goats. Removing with care the catgut that had done such good service, he dragged the carcases to the shore, and proceeded to pack them upon his floats. He discovered, however, that the weight was too great, and that the water, entering through the loops of the stitching in the hide, had so soaked the rush-grass as to render the floats no longer buoyant. He was compelled, therefore, to spend two hours in re-stuffing the skin with such material as he could find. Some light and flock-like seaweed, which the action of the water had swathed after the fashion of haybands along the shore, formed an excellent substitute for grass, and, having bound his bundle of rushes lengthwise, with the goat-skin as a centre-piece, he succeeded in forming a sort of rude canoe, upon which the carcases floated securely.

He had eaten nothing since the morning, and the violence of his exertions had exhausted him. Still, sustained by the excitement of the task he had set himself, he dismissed with fierce impatience the thought of rest, and dragged his weary limbs along the sand, endeavouring to kill fatigue by further exertion. The tide was now running in, and he knew it was imperative that he should regain the further shore while the current was in his favour. To cross from the Pilot Station at low water was impossible. If he waited until the ebb, he must spend another day on the shore, and he could not afford to lose an hour. Cutting a long sapling, he fastened to one end of it the floating bundle, and thus guided it to a spot where the beach shelved abruptly into deep water. It was a clear night, and the risen moon large and low, flung a rippling streak of silver across the sea. On the other side of the bay all was bathed in a violet haze, which veiled the inlet from which he had started in the morning. The fire of the exiles, hidden behind a point of rock, cast a red glow into the air. The ocean breakers rolled in upon the cliffs outside the bar, with a hoarse and threatening murmur; and the rising tide rippled and lapped with treacherous melody along the sand. He touched the chill water and drew back. For an instant he determined to wait until the beams of morning should illumine that beautiful but treacherous sea, and then the thought of the helpless child, who was, without doubt, waiting and watching for him on the shore, gave new strength to his wearied frame; and fixing his eyes on the glow that, hovering above the dark tree-line, marked her presence, he pushed the raft before him out into the sea.

The reeds sustained him bravely, but the strength of the current sucked him underneath the water, and for several seconds he feared that he should be compelled to let go his hold. But his muscles, steeled in the slow fire of convict-labour, withstood this last strain upon them, and, half-suffocated, with bursting chest and paralysed fingers, he preserved his position, until the mass, getting out of the eddies along the shore-line, drifted steadily down the silvery track that led to the settlement. After a few moments' rest, he set his teeth, and urged his strange canoe towards the shore. Paddling and pushing, he gradually edged it towards the fire-light; and at last, just when his stiffened limbs refused to obey the impulse of his will, and he began to drift onwards with the onward tide, he felt his feet strike firm ground. Opening his eyes—closed in the desperation of his last efforts—he found himself safe under the lee of the rugged promontory which hid the fire. It seemed that the waves, tired of persecuting him, had, with disdainful pity, cast him ashore at the goal of his hopes. Looking back, he for the first time realized the frightful peril he had escaped, and shuddered. To this shudder succeeded a thrill of triumph. "Why had he stayed so long, when escape was so easy?" Dragging the carcases above high-water mark, he rounded the little promontory and made for the fire. The recollection of the night when he had first approached it came upon him, and increased his exultation. How different a man was he now from then! Passing up the sand, he saw the stakes which he had directed Frere to cut whiten in the moonshine. His officer worked for him! In his own brain alone lay the secret of escape! He—Rufus Dawes—the scarred, degraded "prisoner", could alone get these three beings back to civilization. Did he refuse to aid them, they would for ever remain in that prison, where he had so long suffered. The tables were turned—he had become a gaoler! He had gained the fire before the solitary watcher there heard his footsteps, and spread his hands to the blaze in silence. He felt as Frere would have felt, had their positions been reversed, disdainful of the man who had stopped at home.

Frere, starting, cried, "It is you! Have you succeeded?"

Rufus Dawes nodded.

"What! Did you catch them?"

"There are four carcases down by the rocks. You can have meat for breakfast to-morrow!"

The child, at the sound of the voice, came running down from the hut. "Oh, Mr. Dawes! I am so glad! We were beginning to despair—mamma and I."

Dawes snatched her from the ground, and bursting into a joyous laugh, swung her into the air. "Tell me," he cried, holding up the child with two dripping arms above him, "what you will do for me if I bring you and mamma safe home again?"

"Give you a free pardon," says Sylvia, "and papa shall make you his servant!" Frere burst out laughing at this reply, and Dawes, with a choking sensation in his throat, put the child upon the ground and walked away.

This was in truth all he could hope for. All his scheming, all his courage, all his peril, would but result in the patronage of a great man like Major Vickers. His heart, big with love, with self-denial, and with hopes of a fair future, would have this flattering unction laid to it. He had performed a prodigy of skill and daring, and for his reward he was to be made a servant to the creatures he had protected. Yet what more could a convict expect? Sylvia saw how deeply her unconscious hand had driven the iron, and ran up to the man she had wounded. "And, Mr. Dawes, remember that I shall love you always." The convict, however, his momentary excitement over, motioned her away; and she saw him stretch himself wearily under the shadow of a rock.

CHAPTER XV

THE CORACLE

IN the morning, however, Rufus Dawes was first at work, and made no allusion to the scene of the previous evening. He had already skinned one of the goats, and he directed Frere to set to work upon another. "Cut down the rump to the hock, and down the brisket to the knee," he said. "I want the hides as square as possible." By dint of hard work they got the four goats skinned, and the entrails cleaned ready for twisting, by breakfast time; and having broiled some of the flesh, made a hearty meal. Mrs. Vickers being no better, Dawes went to see her, and seemed to have made friends again with Sylvia, for he came out of the hut with the child's hand in his. Frere, who was cutting the meat in long strips to dry in the sun, saw this, and it added fresh fuel to the fire in his unreasonable envy and jealousy. However, he said nothing, for his enemy had not yet shown him how the boat was to be made. Before midday, however, he was a partner in the secret, which, after all, was a very simple one.

Rufus Dawes took two of the straightest and most tapered of the celery-top pines which Frere had cut on the previous day, and lashed them tightly together, with the butts outwards. He thus produced a spliced stick about twelve feet long. About two feet from either end he notched the young tree until he could bend the extremities upwards; and having so bent them, he secured the bent portions in their places by means of lashings of raw hide. The spliced trees now presented a rude outline of the section of a boat, having the stem, keel, and stern all in one piece. This having been placed lengthwise between the stakes, four other poles, notched in two places, were lashed from stake to stake, running crosswise to the keel, and forming the knees. Four saplings were now bent from end to end of the upturned portions of the keel that represented stem and stern. Two of these four were placed above, as gunwales; two below as bottom rails. At each intersection the sticks were lashed firmly with fishing line. The whole framework being complete, the stakes were drawn out, and there lay upon the ground the skeleton of a boat eight feet long by three broad.

Frere, whose hands were blistered and sore, would fain have rested; but the convict would not hear of it. "Let us finish," he said regardless of his own fatigue; "the skins will be dry if we stop."

"I can work no more," says Frere sulkily; "I can't stand. You've got muscles of iron, I suppose. I haven't."

"They made *me* work when I couldn't stand, Maurice Frere. It is wonderful what spirit the cat gives a man. There's nothing like work to get rid of aching muscles—so they used to tell me."

"Well, what's to be done now?"

"Cover the boat. There, you can set the fat to melt, and sew these hides together. Two and two, do you see? and then sew the pair at the necks. There is plenty of catgut yonder."

"Don't talk to me as if I was a dog!" says Frere suddenly. "Be civil, can't you."

But the other, busily trimming and cutting at the projecting pieces of sapling, made no reply. It is possible that he thought the fatigued lieutenant beneath his notice. About an hour before sundown the hides were ready, and Rufus Dawes, having in the meantime interlaced the ribs of the skeleton with wattles, stretched the skins over it, with the hairy side inwards. Along the edges of this covering he bored holes at intervals, and passing through these holes thongs of twisted skin, he drew the whole to the top rail of the boat. One last precaution remained. Dipping the pannikin into the melted tallow, he plentifully anointed the seams of the sewn skins. The boat, thus turned topsy-turvy, looked like a huge walnut shell covered with red and reeking hide, or the skull of some Titan who had been scalped. "There!" cried Rufus Dawes, triumphant. "Twelve hours in the sun to tighten the hides, and she'll swim like a duck."

The next day was spent in minor preparations. The jerked goat-meat was packed securely into as small a compass as possible. The rum barrel was filled with water, and water bags were improvised out of portions of the intestines of the goats. Rufus Dawes, having filled these last with water, ran a wooden skewer through their mouths, and twisted it tight, tourniquet fashion. He also stripped cylindrical pieces of bark, and having sewn each cylinder at the side, fitted to it a bottom of the same material, and caulked the seams with gum and pine-tree resin. Thus four tolerable buckets were obtained. One goatskin yet remained, and out of that it was determined to make a sail. "The currents are strong," said Rufus Dawes, "and we shall not be able to row far with such oars as we have got. If we get a breeze it may save our lives." It was impossible to "step" a mast in the frail basket structure, but this difficulty was overcome by a simple contrivance. From thwart to thwart two poles were bound, and the mast, lashed between these poles with thongs of raw hide, was secured by shrouds of twisted fishing line running fore and aft. Sheets of bark were placed at the bottom of the craft, and made a safe flooring. It was late in the afternoon on the fourth day when these preparations were completed, and it was decided that on the morrow they should adventure the journey. "We will coast down to the Bar," said Rufus Dawes, "and wait for the slack of the tide. I can do no more now."

Sylvia, who had seated herself on a rock at a little distance, called to them. Her strength was restored by the fresh meat, and her childish spirits had risen with the hope of safety. The mercurial little creature had wreathed seaweed about her head, and holding in her hand a long twig decorated with a tuft of leaves to represent a wand, she personified one of the heroines of her books.

"I am the Queen of the Island," she said merrily, "and you are my obedient subjects. Pray, Sir Eglamour, is the boat ready?"

"It is, your Majesty," said poor Dawes.

"Then we will see it. Come, walk in front of me. I won't ask you to rub your nose upon the ground, like Man Friday, because that would be uncomfortable. Mr. Frere, you don't play?"

"Oh, yes!" says Frere, unable to withstand the charming pout that accompanied the words. "I'll play. What am I to do?"

"You must walk on *this* side, and be respectful. Of course it is only Pretend, you know," she added, with a quick consciousness of Frere's conceit. "Now then, the Queen goes down to the Seashore surrounded by her Nymphs! There is no occasion to laugh, Mr. Frere. Of course, Nymphs are very different from *you,* but then we can't help that."

Marching in this pathetically ridiculous fashion across the sand, they halted at the coracle. "So that is the boat!" says the Queen, fairly surprised out of her assumption of dignity. "You are a Wonderful Man, Mr. Dawes!"

Rufus Dawes smiled sadly. "It is very simple."

"Do you call this simple?" says Frere, who in the general joy had shaken off a portion of his sulkiness. "By George, I don't! This is ship-building with a vengeance, this is. There's no scheming about this—it's all sheer hard work."

"Yes!" echoed Sylvia, "sheer hard work—sheer hard work by good Mr. Dawes!" And she began to sing a childish chant of triumph, drawing lines and letters in the sand the while, with the sceptre of the Queen.

"Good Mr. Dawes!
Good Mr. Dawes!
This is the work of Good Mr. Dawes!"

Maurice could not resist a sneer.

"See-saw, Margery Daw,
Sold her bed, and lay upon straw!"

said he.

"Good Mr. Dawes!" repeated Sylvia. "Good Mr. Dawes! Why shouldn't I say it? You are disagreeable, sir. I won't play with you any more," and she went off along the sand.

"Poor little child," said Rufus Dawes. "You speak too harshly to her."

Frere—now that the boat was made—had regained his self-confidence. Civilization seemed now brought sufficiently close to him to warrant his assuming the position of authority to which his social position entitled him. "One would think that a boat had never been built before to hear her talk," he said. "If this washing-basket had been one of my old uncle's three-deckers, she couldn't have said much more. By the Lord!" he added, with a coarse laugh, "I ought to have a natural talent for ship-building; for if the old villain hadn't died when he did, I should have been a ship-builder myself."

Rufus Dawes turned his back at the word "died", and busied

himself with the fastenings of the hides. Could the other have seen his face, he would have been struck by its sudden pallor.

"Ah!" continued Frere, half to himself, and half to his companion, "that's a sum of money to lose, isn't it?"

"What do you mean?" asked the convict, without turning his face.

"Mean! Why, my good fellow, I should have been left a quarter of a million of money, but the old hunks who was going to give it to me died before he could alter his will, and every shilling went to a scapegrace son, who hadn't been near the old man for years. That's the way of the world, isn't it?"

Rufus Dawes, still keeping his face away, caught his breath as if in astonishment, and then, recovering himself, he said in a harsh voice, "A fortunate fellow—that son!"

"Fortunate!" cries Frere, with another oath. "Oh yes, he was fortunate! He was burnt to death in the *Hydaspes,* and never heard of his luck. His mother has got the money, though. I never saw a shilling of it." And then, seemingly displeased with himself for having allowed his tongue to get the better of his dignity, he walked away to the fire, musing, doubtless, on the difference between Maurice Frere, with a quarter of a million, disporting himself in the best society that could be procured, with command of dogcarts, prize-fighters, and gamecocks galore; and Maurice Frere, a penniless lieutenant, marooned on the barren coast of Macquarie Harbour, and acting as boat-builder to a runaway convict.

Rufus Dawes was also lost in reverie. He leant upon the gunwale of the much-vaunted boat, and his eyes were fixed upon the sea, weltering golden in the sunset, but it was evident that he saw nothing of the scene before him. Struck dumb by the sudden intelligence of his fortune, his imagination escaped from his control, and fled away to those scenes which he had striven so vainly to forget. He was looking far away—across the glittering harbour and the wide sea beyond it—looking at the old house at Hampstead, with its well-remembered gloomy garden. He pictured himself escaped from this present peril, and freed from the sordid thraldom which so long had held him. He saw himself returning, with some plausible story of his wanderings, to take possession of the wealth which was his—saw himself living once more, rich, free, and respected, in the world from which he had been so long an exile. He saw his mother's sweet pale face, the light of a happy home circle. He saw himself—received with tears of joy and marvelling affection—entering into this home circle as one risen from the dead. A new life opened radiant before him, and he was lost in the contemplation of his own happiness.

So absorbed was he that he did not hear the light footstep of the child across the sand. Mrs. Vickers, having been told of the success which had crowned the convict's efforts, had overcome her weakness so far as to hobble down the beach to the boat, and now, heralded by Sylvia, approached, leaning on the arm of Maurice Frere.

"Mamma has come to see the boat, Mr. Dawes!" cries Sylvia, but Dawes did not hear.

The child reiterated her words, but still the silent figure did not reply.

"Mr. Dawes!" she cried again, and pulled him by the coat-sleeve.

The touch aroused him, and looking down, he saw the pretty, thin face upturned to his. Scarcely conscious of what he did, and still following out the imagining which made him free, wealthy, and respected, he caught the little creature in his arms—as he might have caught his own daughter—and kissed her. Sylvia said nothing; but Mr. Frere—arrived, by *his* chain of reasoning, at quite another conclusion as to the state of affairs—was astonished at the presumption of the man. The lieutenant regarded himself as already reinstated in his old position, and with Mrs. Vickers on his arm, reproved the apparent insolence of the convict as freely as he would have done had they both been at his own little kingdom of Maria Island. "You insolent beggar!" he cried. "Do you dare! Keep your place, sir!"

The sentence recalled Rufus Dawes to reality. His place was that of a convict. What business had he with tenderness for the daughter of his master? Yet, after all he had done, and proposed to do, this harsh judgment upon him seemed cruel. He saw the two looking at the boat he had built. He marked the flush of hope on the cheek of the poor lady, and the full-blown authority that already hardened the eye of Maurice Frere, and all at once he understood the result of what he had done. He had, by his own act, given himself again to bondage. As long as escape was impracticable, he had been useful, and even powerful. Now he had pointed out the way of escape, he had sunk into the beast of burden once again. In the desert he was "Mr." Dawes, the saviour; in civilized life he would become once more Rufus Dawes, the ruffian, the prisoner, the absconder. He stood mute, and let Frere point out the excellences of the craft in silence; and then, feeling that the few words of thanks uttered by the lady were chilled by her consciousness of the ill-advised freedom he had taken with the child, he turned on his heel, and strode up into the bush.

"A queer fellow," said Frere, as Mrs. Vickers followed the retreating figure with her eyes. "Always in an ill temper."

"Poor man! He has behaved very kindly to us," said Mrs. Vickers. Yet even she felt the change of circumstance, and knew that, without any reason she could name, her blind trust and hope in the convict who had saved their lives had been transformed into a patronizing kindliness which was quite foreign to esteem or affection.

"Come, let us have some supper," says Frere. "The last we shall eat here, I hope. He will come back when his fit of sulks is over."

But he did not come back, and, after a few expressions of wonder at his absence, Mrs. Vickers and her daughter, rapt in the hopes and fears of the morrow, almost forgot that he had left them. With marvellous credulity they looked upon the terrible stake they were about to play for as already won. The possession of the boat seemed to them so wonderful, that the perils of the voyage they were to make in it were altogether lost sight of. As for Maurice Frere, he was rejoiced that the convict was out of the way. He wished that he was out of the way altogether.

CHAPTER XVI

THE WRITING ON THE SAND

HAVING got out of eye-shot of the ungrateful creatures he had befriended, Rufus Dawes threw himself upon the ground in an agony of mingled rage and regret. For the first time for six years he had tasted the happiness of doing good, the delight of self-abnegation. For the first time for six years he had broken through the selfish misanthropy he had taught himself. And this was his reward! He had held his temper in check, in order that it might not offend others. He had banished the galling memory of his degradation, lest haply some shadow of it might seem to fall upon the fair child whose lot had been so strangely cast with his. He had stifled the agony he suffered, lest its expression should give pain to those who seemed to feel for him. He had forborne retaliation, when retaliation would have been most sweet. Having all these years waited and watched for a chance to strike his persecutors, he had held his hand now that an unlooked-for accident had placed the weapon of destruction in his grasp. He had risked his life, forgone his enmities, almost changed his nature—and his reward was cold looks and harsh words, so soon as his skill had paved the way to freedom. This knowledge coming upon him while the thrill of exultation at the astounding news of his riches yet vibrated in his brain, made him grind his teeth with rage at his own hard fate. Bound by the purest and holiest of ties—the affection of a son to his mother—he had condemned himself to social death, rather than buy his liberty and life by a revelation which would shame the gentle creature whom he loved. By a strange series of accidents, fortune had assisted him to maintain the deception he had practised. His cousin had not recognized him. The very ship in which he was believed to have sailed had been lost with every soul on board. His identity had been completely destroyed—no link remained which could connect Rufus Dawes, the convict, with Richard Devine, the vanished heir to the wealth of the dead ship-builder.

Oh, if he had only known! If, while in the gloomy prison, distracted by a thousand fears, and weighed down by crushing evidence of circumstance, he had but guessed that death had stepped between Sir Richard and his vengeance, he might have spared himself the sacrifice he had made. He had been tried and condemned as a nameless sailor, who could call no witnesses in his defence, and give no particulars as to his previous history. It was clear to him now that he might have adhered to his statement of ignorance concerning the murder, locked in his breast the name of the murderer, and have yet been free. Judges are just, but popular opinion is powerful, and it was not impossible that Richard Devine, the millionaire, would have escaped the fate which had overtaken Rufus Dawes, the sailor. Into his calculations in the prison—when, half-crazed with love, with terror, and despair, he had counted up his chances of life—the wild supposition that he had even then inherited the wealth of the father who had disowned him, had never entered. The knowledge of that fact would have altered the whole current of his life, and he learnt it for the first time now—too late. Now, lying prone upon the sand; now, wandering aimlessly up and down among the stunted trees that bristled white beneath the mist-barred moon; now, sitting—as he had sat in the prison long ago—with the head gripped hard between his hands, swaying his body to and fro, he thought out the frightful problem of his bitter life. Of little use was the heritage that he had gained. A convict-absconder, whose hands were hard with menial service, and whose back was scarred with the lash, could never be received among the gently nurtured. Let him lay claim to his name and rights, what then? He was a convicted felon, and his name and rights had been taken from him by the law. Let him go and tell Maurice Frere that he was his lost cousin. He would be laughed at. Let him proclaim aloud his birth and innocence, and the convict-sheds would grin, and the convict overseer set him to harder labour. Let him even, by dint of reiteration, get his wild story believed, what would happen? If it was heard in England—after the lapse of years, perhaps—that a convict in the chain-gang in Macquarie Harbour—a man held to be a murderer, and whose convict career was one long record of mutiny and punishment—claimed to be the heir to an English fortune, and to own the right to dispossess staid and worthy English folk of their rank and station, with what feeling would the announcement be received? Certainly not with a desire to redeem this ruffian from his bonds and place him in the honoured seat of his dead father. Such intelligence would be regarded as a calamity, an unhappy blot upon a fair reputation, a disgrace to an honoured and unsullied name. Let him succeed, let him return again to the mother who had by this time become reconciled, in a measure, to his loss; he would, at the best, be to her a living shame, scarcely less degrading than that which she had dreaded.

But success was almost impossible. He did not dare to retrace his steps through the hideous labyrinth into which he had plunged. Was he to show his scarred shoulders as a proof that he was a gentleman and an innocent man? Was he to relate the nameless infamies of Macquarie Harbour as a proof that he was entitled to receive the hospitalities of the generous, and to sit, a respected guest, at the tables of men of refinement? Was he to quote the horrible slang of the prison-ship, and retail the filthy jests of the chain-gang and the hulks, as a proof that he was a fit companion for pure-minded women and innocent children? Suppose even that he could conceal the name of the real criminal, and show himself guiltless of the crime for which he had been condemned, all the wealth in the world could not buy back that blissful ignorance of evil which had once been his. All the wealth in the world could not purchase the self-respect which had been cut out of him by the lash, or banish from his brain the memory of his degradation.

For hours this agony of thought racked him. He cried out as though with physical pain, and then lay in a stupor, exhausted with actual physical suffering. It was hopeless to think of freedom and of honour. Let him keep silence, and pursue the life fate had marked out for him. He would return to bondage. The law would claim him as an absconder, and would mete out to him such punishment as was fitting. Perhaps he might escape severest punishment, as a reward for his exertions in saving the child. He might consider himself fortunate if such was permitted to him. Fortunate! Suppose he did not go back at all, but wandered away into the wilderness and died? Better death than such a doom as his. Yet need he die? He had caught goats, he could catch fish. He could build a hut. In here was, perchance, at the deserted settlement some remnant of seed corn that, planted, would give him bread. He had built a boat, he had made an oven, he had fenced in a hut. Surely he could contrive to live alone savage and free. Alone! He had contrived all these marvels alone! Was not the boat he himself had built below upon the shore? Why not escape in her, and leave to their fate the miserable creatures who had treated him with such ingratitude?

The idea flashed into his brain, as though someone had spoken the words into his ear. Twenty strides would place him in possession of the boat, and half an hour's drifting with the current would take him beyond pursuit. Once outside the Bar, he would make for the westward, in the hopes of falling in with some whaler. He would doubtless meet with one before many days, and he was well supplied with provision and water in the meantime. A tale of shipwreck would satisfy the sailors, and—he paused—he had forgotten that the rags which he wore would betray him. With an exclamation of despair, he started from the posture in which he was lying. He thrust out his hands to raise himself, and his fingers came in contact with something soft. He had been lying at the foot of some loose stones that were piled cairnwise beside a low—growing bush; and the object that he had touched was protruding from beneath these stones. He caught it and dragged it forth. It was the shirt of poor Bates. With trembling hands he tore away the stones, and pulled forth the rest of the garments. They seemed as though they had been left purposely for him. Heaven had sent him the very disguise he needed.

The night had passed during his reverie, and the first faint streaks of dawn began to lighten in the sky. Haggard and pale, he rose to his feet, and scarcely daring to think about what he proposed to do, ran towards the boat. As he ran, however, the voice that he had heard encouraged him. "Your life is of more importance than theirs. They will die, but they have been ungrateful and deserve death. You will escape out of this Hell, and return to the loving heart who mourns you. You can do more good to mankind than by saving the lives of these people who despise you. Moreover, they may not die. They are sure to be sent for. Think of what awaits you when you return—an absconded convict!"

He was within three feet of the boat, when he suddenly checked himself, and stood motionless, staring at the sand with as much horror as though he saw there the Writing which foretold the doom of Belshazzar. He had come upon the sentence traced by Sylvia the evening before, and glittering in the low light of the red sun suddenly risen from out the sea, it seemed to him that the letters had shaped themselves at his very feet,

GOOD MR. DAWES.

"Good Mr. Dawes"! What a frightful reproach there was to him in that simple sentence! What a world of cowardice, baseness, and cruelty, had not those eleven letters opened to him! He heard the voice of the child who had nursed him, calling on him to save her. He saw her at that instant standing between him and the boat, as she had stood when she held out to him the loaf, on the night of his return to the settlement.

He staggered to the cavern, and, seizing the sleeping Frere by the arm, shook him violently. "Awake! awake!" he cried, "and let us leave this place!" Frere, starting to his feet, looked at the white face and bloodshot eyes of the wretched man before him with blunt astonishment. "What's the matter with you, man?" he said. "You look as if you'd seen a ghost!"

At the sound of his voice Rufus Dawes gave a long sigh, and drew his hand across his eyes.

"Come, Sylvia!" shouted Frere. "It's time to get up. I am ready to go!"

The sacrifice was complete. The convict turned away, and two great glistening tears rolled down his rugged face, and fell upon the sand.

CHAPTER XVII

AT SEA

AN hour after sunrise, the frail boat, which was the last hope of these four human beings, drifted with the outgoing current towards the mouth of the harbour. When first launched she had come nigh swamping, being overloaded, and it was found necessary to leave behind a great portion of the dried meat. With what pangs this was done can be easily imagined, for each atom of food seemed to represent an hour of life. Yet there was no help for it. As Frere said, it was "neck or nothing with them". They must get away at all hazards.

That evening they camped at the mouth of the Gates, Dawes being afraid to risk a passage until the slack of the tide, and about ten o'clock at night adventured to cross the Bar. The night was lovely, and the sea calm. It seemed as though Providence had taken pity on them; for, notwithstanding the insecurity of the craft and the violence of the breakers, the dreaded passage was made with safety. Once, indeed, when they had just entered the surf, a mighty wave, curling high above them, seemed about to overwhelm the frail structure of skins and wickerwork; but Rufus Dawes, keeping the nose of the boat to the sea, and Frere baling with his hat, they succeeded in reaching deep water. A great misfortune, however, occurred. Two of the bark buckets, left by some unpardonable oversight uncleated, were washed overboard, and with them nearly a fifth of their scanty store of water. In the face of the greater peril, the accident seemed trifling; and as, drenched and chilled, they gained the open sea, they could not but admit that fortune had almost miraculously befriended them.

They made tedious way with their rude oars; a light breeze from the north-west sprang up with the dawn, and, hoisting the goat-skin sail, they crept along the coast. It was resolved that the two men should keep watch and watch; and Frere for the second time enforced his authority by giving the first watch to Rufus Dawes. "I am tired," he said, "and shall sleep for a little while."

Rufus Dawes, who had not slept for two nights, and who had done all the harder work, said nothing. He had suffered so much during the last two days that his senses were dulled to pain.

Frere slept until late in the afternoon, and, when he woke, found the boat still tossing on the sea, and Sylvia and her mother both seasick. This seemed strange to him. Sea-sickness appeared to be a malady which belonged exclusively to civilization. Moodily watching the great green waves which curled incessantly between him and the horizon, he marvelled to think how curiously events had come about. A leaf had, as it were, been torn out of his autobiography. It seemed a lifetime since he had done anything but moodily scan the sea or shore. Yet, on the morning of leaving the settlement, he had counted the notches on a calendar-stick he carried, and had been astonished to find them but twenty-two in number. Taking out his knife, he cut two nicks in the wicker gunwale of the coracle. That brought him to twenty-four days. The mutiny had taken place on the 13th of January; it was now the 6th of February. "Surely," thought he, "the *Ladybird* might have returned by this time." There was no one to tell him that the *Ladybird* had been driven into Port Davey by stress of weather, and detained there for seventeen days.

That night the wind fell, and they had to take to their oars. Rowing all night, they made but little progress, and Rufus Dawes suggested that they should put in to the shore and wait until the breeze sprang up. But, upon getting under the lee of a long line of basaltic rocks which rose abruptly out of the sea, they found the waves breaking furiously upon a horseshoe reef, six or seven miles in length. There was nothing for it but to coast again. They coasted for two days, without a sign of a sail, and on the third day a great wind broke upon them from the south-east, and drove them back thirty miles. The coracle began to leak, and required constant bailing. What was almost as bad, the rum cask, that held the best part of their water, had leaked also, and was now half empty. They caulked it, by cutting out the leak, and then plugging the hole with linen.

"It's lucky we ain't in the tropics," said Frere. Poor Mrs. Vickers, lying in the bottom of the boat, wrapped in her wet shawl, and chilled to the bone with the bitter wind, had not the heart to speak.

Surely the stifling calm of the tropics could not be worse than this bleak and barren sea.

The position of the four poor creatures was now almost desperate. Mrs. Vickers, indeed, seemed completely prostrated; and it was evident that, unless some help came, she could not long survive the continued exposure to the weather. The child was in somewhat better case. Rufus Dawes had wrapped her in his woollen shirt, and, unknown to Frere, had divided with her daily his allowance of meat. She lay in his arms at night, and in the day crept by his side for shelter and protection. As long as she was near him she felt safe. They spoke little to each other, but when Rufus Dawes felt the pressure of her tiny hand in his, or sustained the weight of her head upon his shoulder, he almost forgot the cold that froze him, and the hunger that gnawed him.

So two more days passed, and yet no sail. On the tenth day after their departure from Macquarie Harbour they came to the end of their provisions. The salt water had spoiled the goat-meat, and soaked the bread into a nauseous paste. The sea was still running high, and the wind, having veered to the north, was blowing with increased violence. The long low line of coast that stretched upon their left hand was at times obscured by a blue mist. The water was the colour of mud, and the sky threatened rain. The wretched craft to which they had entrusted themselves was leaking in four places. If caught in one of the frequent storms which ravaged that iron-bound coast, she could not live an hour. The two men, wearied, hungry, and cold, almost hoped for the end to come quickly. To add to their distress, the child was seized with fever. She was hot and cold by turns, and in the intervals of moaning talked deliriously. Rufus Dawes, holding her in his arms, watched the suffering he was unable to alleviate with a savage despair at his heart. Was she to die after all?

So another day and night passed, and the eleventh morning saw the boat yet alive, rolling in the trough of the same deserted sea. The four exiles lay in her almost without breath.

All at once Dawes uttered a cry, and, seizing the sheet, put the clumsy craft about. "A sail! a sail!" he cried. "Do you not see her?"

Frere's hungry eyes ranged the dull water in vain.

"There is no sail, fool!" he said. "You mock us!"

The boat, no longer following the line of the coast, was running nearly due south, straight into the great Southern Ocean. Frere tried to wrest the thong from the hand of the convict, and bring the boat back to her course. "Are you mad?" he asked, in fretful terror, "to run us out to sea?"

"Sit down!" returned the other, with a menacing gesture, and staring across the grey water. "I tell you I see a sail!"

Frere, overawed by the strange light which gleamed in the eyes of his companion, shifted sulkily back to his place. "Have your own way," he said, "madman! It serves me right for putting off to sea in such a devil's craft as this!"

After all, what did it matter? As well be drowned in mid-ocean as in sight of land.

The long day wore out, and no sail appeared. The wind freshened towards evening, and the boat, plunging clumsily on the long brown waves, staggered as though drunk with the water she had swallowed, for at one place near the bows the water ran in and out as through a slit in a wine skin. The coast had altogether disappeared, and the huge ocean—vast, stormy, and threatening—heaved and hissed all around them. It seemed impossible that they should live until morning. But Rufus Dawes, with his eyes fixed on some object visible alone to him, hugged the child in his arms, and drove the quivering coracle into the black waste of night and sea. To Frere, sitting sullenly in the bows, the aspect of this grim immovable figure, with its back-blown hair and staring eyes, had in it something supernatural and horrible. He began to think that privation and anxiety had driven the unhappy convict mad.

Thinking and shuddering over his fate, he fell—as it seemed to him—into a momentary sleep, in the midst of which someone called to him. He started up, with shaking knees and bristling hair. The day had broken, and the dawn, in one long pale streak of sickly saffron, lay low on the left hand. Between this streak of saffron-coloured light and the bows of the boat gleamed for an instant a white speck.

"A sail! a sail!" cried Rufus Dawes, a wild light gleaming in his eyes, and a strange tone vibrating in his voice. "Did I not tell you that I saw a sail?"

Frere, utterly confounded, looked again, with his heart in his mouth, and again did the white speck glimmer. For an instant he felt almost safe, and then a blanker despair than before fell upon him. From the distance at which she was, it was impossible for the ship to sight the boat.

"They will never see us!" he cried. "Dawes—Dawes! Do you hear? They will never see us!"

Rufus Dawes started as if from a trance. Lashing the sheet to the pole which served as a gunwale, he laid the sleeping child by her mother, and tearing up the strip of bark on which he had been sitting, moved to the bows of the boat.

"They will see *this*! Tear up that board! So! Now, place it thus across the bows. Hack off that sapling end! Now that dry twist of osier! Never mind the boat, man; we can afford to leave her now. Tear off that outer strip of hide. See, the wood beneath is dry! Quick—you are so slow."

"What are you going to do?" cried Frere, aghast, as the convict tore up all the dry wood he could find, and heaped it on the sheet of bark placed on the bows.

"To make a fire! See!"

Frere began to comprehend. "I have three matches left," he said, fumbling, with trembling fingers, in his pocket. "I wrapped them in one of the leaves of the book to keep them dry."

The word "book" was a new inspiration. Rufus Dawes seized upon the *English History*, which had already done such service, tore out the drier leaves in the middle of the volume, and carefully added them to the little heap of touchwood.

"Now, steady!"

The match was struck and lighted. The paper, after a few obstinate curlings, caught fire, and Frere, blowing the young flame with his breath, the bark began to burn. He piled upon the fire all that was combustible, the hides began to shrivel, and a great column of black smoke rose up over the sea.

"Sylvia!" cried Rufus Dawes. "Sylvia! My darling! You are saved!"

She opened her blue eyes and looked at him, but gave no sign of recognition. Delirium had hold of her, and in the hour of safety the child had forgotten her preserver. Rufus Dawes, overcome by this last cruel stroke of fortune, sat down in the stern of the boat, with the child in his arms, speechless. Frere, feeding the fire, thought that the chance he had so longed for had come. With the mother at the point of death, and the child delirious, who could testify to this hated convict's skilfulness? No one but Mr. Maurice Frere, and Mr. Maurice Frere, as Commandant of convicts, could not but give up an "absconder" to justice.

The ship changed her course, and came towards this strange fire in the middle of the ocean. The boat, the fore part of her blazing like a pine torch, could not float above an hour. The little group of the convict and the child remained motionless. Mrs. Vickers was lying senseless, ignorant even of the approaching succour.

The ship—a brig, with American colours flying—came within hail of them. Frere could almost distinguish figures on her deck. He made his way aft to where Dawes was sitting, unconscious, with the child in his arms, and stirred him roughly with his foot.

"Go forward," he said, in tones of command, "and give the child to me."

Rufus Dawes raised his head, and, seeing the approaching vessel, awoke to the consciousness of his duty. With a low laugh, full of unutterable bitterness, he placed the burden he had borne so tenderly in the arms of the lieutenant, and moved to the blazing bows.

*

The brig was close upon them. Her canvas loomed large and dusky, shadowing the sea. Her wet decks shone in the morning sunlight. From her bulwarks peered bearded and eager faces, looking with astonishment at this burning boat and its haggard company, alone on that barren and stormy ocean.

Frere, with Sylvia in his arms, waited for her.

BOOK III
PORT ARTHUR 1838

CHAPTER I
A LABOURER IN THE VINEYARD

"SOCIETY in Hobart Town, in this year of grace 1838, is, my dear lord, composed of very curious elements." So ran a passage in the sparkling letter which the Rev. Mr. Meekin, newly-appointed chaplain, and seven-days' resident in Van Diemen's Land, was carrying to the post office, for the delectation of his patron in England. As the reverend gentleman tripped daintily down the summer street that lay between the blue river and the purple mountain, he cast his mild eyes hither and thither upon human nature, and the sentence he had just penned recurred to him with pleasurable appositeness. Elbowed by well-dressed officers of garrison, bowing sweetly to well-dressed ladies, shrinking from ill-dressed, ill-odoured ticket-of-leave men, or hastening across a street to avoid being run down by the hand-carts that, driven by little gangs of grey-clothed convicts, rattled and jangled at him unexpectedly from behind corners, he certainly felt that the society through which he moved was composed of curious elements. Now passed, with haughty nose in the air, a newly-imported government official, relaxing for an instant his rigidity of demeanour to smile languidly at the chaplain whom Governor Sir John Franklin delighted to honour; now swaggered, with coarse defiance of gentility and patronage, a wealthy ex-prisoner, grown fat on the profits of rum. The population that was abroad on that sunny December afternoon had certainly an incongruous appearance to a dapper clergyman lately arrived from London, and missing, for the first time in his sleek, easygoing life, those social screens which in London civilization decorously conceal the frailties and vices of human nature. Clad in glossy black, of the most fashionable clerical cut, with dandy boots, and gloves of lightest lavender—a white silk overcoat hinting that its wearer was not wholly free from sensitiveness to sun and heat—the Reverend Meekin tripped daintily to the post office, and deposited his letter. Two ladies met him as he turned.

"Mr. Meekin!"

Mr. Meekin's elegant hat was raised from his intellectual brow and hovered in the air, like some courteous black bird, for an instant. "Mrs. Jellicoe! Mrs. Protherick! My dear leddies, this is an unexpected pleasure! And where, pray, are you going on this lovely afternoon? To stay in the house is positively sinful. Ah! what a climate—but the Trail of the Serpent, my dear Mrs. Protherick—the Trail of the Serpent—" and he sighed.

"It must be a great trial to you to come to the colony," said Mrs. Jellicoe, sympathizing with the sigh.

Meekin smiled, as a gentlemanly martyr might have smiled. "The Lord's work, dear leddies—the Lord's work. I am but a poor labourer in the vineyard, toiling through the heat and burden of the day." The aspect of him, with his faultless tie, his airy coat, his natty boots, and his self-satisfied Christian smile, was so unlike a poor labourer toiling through the heat and burden of the day, that good Mrs. Jellicoe, the wife of an orthodox Comptroller of Convicts' Stores, felt a horrible thrill of momentary heresy. "I would rather have remained in England," continued Mr. Meekin, smoothing one lavender finger with the tip of another, and arching his elegant eyebrows in mild deprecation of any praise of his self-denial, "but I felt it my duty not to refuse the offer made me through the kindness of his lordship. Here is a field, leddies—a field for the Christian pastor. They appeal to me, leddies, these lambs of our Church—these lost and outcast lambs of our Church."

Mrs. Jellicoe shook her gay bonnet ribbons at Mr. Meekin, with a hearty smile. "You don't know our convicts," she said (from the tone of her jolly voice it might have been "our cattle"). "They are horrible creatures. And as for servants—my goodness, I have a fresh one every week. When you have been here a little longer, you will know them better, Mr. Meekin."

"They are quite unbearable at times." said Mrs. Protherick, the widow of a Superintendent of Convicts' Barracks, with a stately indignation mantling in her sallow cheeks. "I am ordinarily the most patient creature breathing, but I *do* confess that the stupid vicious wretches that one gets are enough to put a saint out of temper."

"We have all our crosses, dear leddies—all our crosses," said the Rev. Mr. Meekin piously. "Heaven send us strength to bear them! *Good*-morning."

"Why, you are going our way," said Mrs. Jellicoe. "We can walk together."

"Delighted! I am going to call on Major Vickers."

"And I live within a stone's throw," returned Mrs. Protherick.

"What a charming little creature she is, isn't she?"

"Who?" asked Mr. Meekin, as they walked.

"Sylvia. You don't know her! Oh, a dear little thing."

"I have only met Major Vickers at Government House," said Meekin.

"I haven't yet had the pleasure of seeing his daughter."

"A sad thing," said Mrs. Jellicoe. "Quite a romance, if it was not so sad, you know. His wife, poor Mrs. Vickers."

"Indeed! What of her?" asked Meekin, bestowing a condescending bow on a passer-by. "Is she an invalid?"

"She is dead, poor soul," returned jolly Mrs. Jellicoe, with a fat sigh.

"You don't mean to say you haven't heard the story, Mr. Meekin?"

"My dear leddies, I have only been in Hobart Town a week, and I have not heard the story."

"It's about the mutiny, you know, the mutiny at Macquarie Harbour. The prisoners took the ship, and put Mrs. Vickers and Sylvia ashore somewhere. Captain Frere was with them, too. The poor things had a dreadful time, and nearly died. Captain Frere made a boat at last, and they were picked up by a ship. Poor Mrs. Vickers only lived a few hours, and little Sylvia—she was only twelve years old then—was quite lightheaded. They thought she wouldn't recover."

"How dreadful! And has she recovered?"

"Oh, yes, she's quite strong now, but her memory's gone."

"Her memory?"

"Yes," struck in Mrs. Protherick, eager to have a share in the storytelling. "She doesn't remember anything about the three or four weeks they were ashore—at least, not distinctly."

"It's a great mercy!" interrupted Mrs. Jellicoe, determined to keep the post of honour. "Who wants her to remember these horrors? From Captain Frere's account, it was positively awful!"

"You don't say so!" said Mr. Meekin, dabbing his nose with a dainty handkerchief. "A 'bolter'—that's what we call an escaped prisoner, Mr. Meekin—happened to be left behind, and he found them out, and insisted on sharing the provisions—the wretch! Captain Frere was obliged to watch him constantly for fear he should murder them. Even in the boat he tried to run them out to sea and escape. He was one of the worst men in the Harbour, they say; but you should hear Captain Frere tell the story."

"And where is he now?" asked Mr. Meekin, with interest.

"Captain Frere?"

"No, the prisoner."

"Oh, goodness, I don't know—at Port Arthur, I think. I know that he was tried for bolting, and would have been hanged but for Captain Frere's exertions."

"Dear, dear! a strange story, indeed," said Mr. Meekin. "And so the young lady doesn't know anything about it?"

"Only what she has been told, of course, poor dear. She's engaged to Captain Frere."

"Really! To the man who saved her. How charming—quite a romance!"

"Isn't it? Everybody says so. And Captain Frere's so much older than she is."

"But her girlish love clings to her heroic protector," said Meekin, mildly poetical. "Remarkable and beautiful. Quite the—hem!—the ivy and the oak, dear leddies. Ah, in our fallen nature, what sweet spots—I think *this* is the gate."

A smart convict servant—he had been a pickpocket of note in days gone by—left the clergyman to repose in a handsomely furnished drawing-room, whose sun blinds revealed a wealth of bright garden flecked with shadows, while he went in search of Miss Vickers. The Major was out, it seemed, his duties as Superintendent of Convicts rendering such absences necessary; but Miss Vickers was in the garden, and could be called in at once. The Reverend Meekin, wiping his heated brow, and pulling down his spotless wristbands, laid himself back on the soft sofa, soothed by the elegant surroundings no less than by the coolness of the atmosphere. Having no better comparison at hand, he compared this luxurious room, with its soft couches, brilliant flowers, and opened piano, to the chamber in the house of a West India planter, where all was glare and heat and barbarism without, and all soft and cool and luxurious within. He was so charmed with this comparison—he had a knack of being easily pleased with his own thoughts—that he commenced to turn a fresh sentence for the Bishop, and to sketch out an elegant description of the oasis in his desert of a vineyard. While at this occupation, he was disturbed by the sound of voices in the garden, and it appeared to him that someone near at hand was sobbing and crying. Softly stepping on the broad verandah, he saw, on the grass-plot, two persons, an old man and a young girl. The sobbing proceeded from the old man.

"'Deed, miss, it's the truth, on my sowl. I've but jest come back to yez this morning. O my! but it's a cruel thrick to play an ould man."

He was a white-haired old fellow, in a grey suit of convict frieze, and stood leaning with one veiny hand upon the pedestal of a vase of roses.

"But it is your own fault, Danny; we all warned you against her," said the young girl softly.

"Sure ye did. But oh! how did I think it, miss? 'Tis the second time she served me so."

"How long was it this time, Danny?"

"Six months, miss. She said I was a drunkard, and beat her. Beat her, God help me!" stretching forth two trembling hands. "And they believed her, o' course. Now, when I kem back, there's me little place all thrampled by the boys, and she's away wid a ship's captain, saving your presence, miss, dhrinking in the 'George the Fourth'. O my, but it's hard on an old man!" and he fell to sobbing again.

The girl sighed. "I can do nothing for you, Danny. I dare say you can work about the garden as you did before. I'll speak to the Major when he comes home."

Danny, lifting his bleared eyes to thank her, caught sight of Mr. Meekin, and saluted abruptly. Miss Vickers turned, and Mr. Meekin, bowing his apologies, became conscious that the young lady was about seventeen years of age, that her eyes were large and soft, her hair plentiful and bright, and that the hand which held the little book she had been reading was white and small.

"Miss Vickers, I think. My name is Meekin—the Reverend Arthur Meekin."

"How do you do, Mr. Meekin?" said Sylvia, putting out one of her small hands, and looking straight at him. "Papa will be in directly."

"His daughter more than compensates for his absence, my dear Miss Vickers."

"I don't like flattery, Mr. Meekin, so don't use it. At least," she added, with a delicious frankness, that seemed born of her very brightness and beauty, "not *that* sort of flattery. Young girls *do* like flattery, of course. Don't you think so?"

This rapid attack quite disconcerted Mr. Meekin, and he could only bow and smile at the self-possessed young lady. "Go into the kitchen, Danny, and tell them to give you some tobacco. Say I sent you. Mr. Meekin, won't you come in?"

"A strange old gentleman, that, Miss Vickers. A faithful retainer, I presume?"

"An old convict servant of ours," said Sylvia. "He was with papa many years ago. He has got into trouble lately, though, poor old man."

"Into trouble?" asked Mr. Meekin, as Sylvia took off her hat.

"On the roads, you know. That's what they call it here. He married a free woman much younger than himself, and she makes him drink, and then gives him in charge for insubordination."

"For insubordination! Pardon me, my dear young lady, did I understand you rightly?"

"Yes, insubordination. He is her assigned servant, you know," said Sylvia, as if such a condition of things was the most ordinary in the world, "and if he misbehaves himself, she sends him back to the road-gang."

The Reverend Mr. Meekin opened his mild eyes very wide indeed. "What an extraordinary anomaly! I am beginning, my dear Miss Vickers, to find myself indeed at the antipodes."

"Society here is different from society in England, I believe. Most new arrivals say so," returned Sylvia quietly.

"But for a wife to imprison her husband, my dear young lady!"

"She can have him flogged if she likes. Danny has been flogged. But then his wife is a bad woman. He was very silly to marry her; but you can't reason with an old man in love, Mr. Meekin."

Mr. Meekin's Christian brow had grown crimson, and his decorous blood tingled to his finger-tips. To hear a young lady talk in such an open way was terrible. Why, in reading the Decalogue from the altar, Mr. Meekin was accustomed to soften one indecent prohibition, lest its uncompromising plainness of speech might offend the delicate sensibilities of his female souls! He turned from the dangerous theme without an instant's pause, for wonder at the strange power accorded to Hobart Town "free" wives. "You have been reading?"

"'Paul et Virginie'. I have read it before in English."

"Ah, you read French, then, my dear young lady?"

"Not very well. I had a master for some months, but papa had to send him back to the gaol again. He stole a silver tankard out of the dining-room."

"A French master! Stole——"

"He was a prisoner, you know. A clever man. He wrote for the *London Magazine*. I have read his writings. Some of them are quite above the average."

"And how did he come to be transported?" asked Mr. Meekin, feeling that his vineyard was getting larger than he had anticipated.

"Poisoning his niece, I think, but I forget the particulars. He was a gentlemanly man, but, oh, such a drunkard!"

Mr. Meekin, more astonished than ever at this strange country, where beautiful young ladies talked of poisoning and flogging as matters of little moment, where wives imprisoned their husbands, and murderers taught French, perfumed the air with his cambric handkerchief in silence.

"You have not been here long, Mr. Meekin," said Sylvia, after a pause.

"No, only a week; and I confess I am surprised. A lovely climate, but, as I said just now to Mrs. Jellicoe, the Trail of the Serpent—the Trail of the Serpent—my dear young lady."

"If you send all the wretches in England here, you must expect the Trail of the Serpent," said Sylvia. "It isn't the fault of the colony."

"Oh, no; certainly not," returned Meekin, hastening to apologize. "But it is very shocking."

"Well, you gentlemen should make it better. I don't know what the penal settlements are like, but the prisoners in the town have not much inducement to become good men."

"They have the beautiful Liturgy of our Holy Church read to them twice every week, my dear young lady," said Mr. Meekin, as though he should solemnly say, "if that doesn't reform them, what will?"

"Oh, yes," returned Sylvia, "they have that, certainly; but that is only on Sundays. But don't let us talk about this, Mr. Meekin," she added, pushing back a stray curl of golden hair. "Papa says that I am not to talk about these things, because they are all done according to the Rules of the Service, as he calls it."

"An admirable notion of papa's," said Meekin, much relieved as the door opened, and Vickers and Frere entered.

Vickers's hair had grown white, but Frere carried his thirty years as easily as some men carry two-and-twenty.

"My dear Sylvia," began Vickers, "here's an extraordinary thing!" and then, becoming conscious of the presence of the agitated Meekin, he paused.

"You know Mr. Meekin, papa?" said Sylvia. "Mr. Meekin, Captain Frere."

"I have that pleasure," said Vickers. "Glad to see you, sir. Pray sit down." Upon which, Mr. Meekin beheld Sylvia unaffectedly kiss both gentlemen; but became strangely aware that the kiss bestowed upon her father was warmer than that which greeted her affianced husband.

"Warm weather, Mr. Meekin," said Frere. "Sylvia, my darling, I hope you have not been out in the heat. You have! My dear, I've begged you!"

"It's not hot at all," said Sylvia pettishly. "Nonsense! I'm not made of butter—I sha'n't melt. Thank you, dear, you needn't pull the blind down." And then, as though angry with herself for her anger, she added, "You are always thinking of me, Maurice," and gave him her hand affectionately.

"It's very oppressive, Captain Frere," said Meekin; "and to a stranger, quite enervating."

"Have a glass of wine," said Frere, as if the house was his own. "One wants bucking up a bit on a day like this."

"Ay, to be sure," repeated Vickers. "A glass of wine. Sylvia, dear, some sherry. I hope she has not been attacking you with her strange theories, Mr. Meekin."

"Oh, dear, no; not at all," returned Meekin, feeling that this charming young lady was regarded as a creature who was not to be judged by ordinary rules. "We got on famously, my dear Major."

"That's right," said Vickers. "She is very plain-spoken, is my little girl, and strangers can't understand her sometimes. Can they, Poppet?"

Poppet tossed her head saucily. "I don't know," she said. "Why shouldn't they? But you were going to say something extraordinary when you came in. What is it, dear?"

"Ah," said Vickers with grave face. "Yes, a most extraordinary thing. They've caught those villains."

"What, you don't mean ? No, papa!" said Sylvia, turning round with alarmed face.

In that little family there were, for conversational purposes, but one set of villains in the world—the mutineers of the *Osprey*.

"They've got four of them in the bay at this moment—Rex, Barker, Shiers, and Lesly. They are on board the *Lady Jane*. The most extraordinary story I ever heard in my life. The fellows got to China and passed themselves off as shipwrecked sailors. The merchants in Canton got up a subscription, and sent them to London.

They were recognized there by old Pine, who had been surgeon on board the ship they came out in."

Sylvia sat down on the nearest chair, with heightened colour. "And where are the others?"

"Two were executed in England; the other six have not been taken. These fellows have been sent out for trial."

"To what are you alluding, dear sir?" asked Meekin, eyeing the sherry with the gaze of a fasting saint.

"The piracy of a convict brig five years ago," replied Vickers. "The scoundrels put my poor wife and child ashore, and left them to starve. If it hadn't been for Frere—God bless him!—they would have died. They shot the pilot and a soldier—and—but it's a long story."

"I have heard of it already," said Meekin, sipping the sherry, which another convict servant had brought for him; "and of your gallant conduct, Captain Frere."

"Oh, that's nothing," said Frere, reddening. "We were all in the same boat. Poppet, have a glass of wine?"

"No," said Sylvia, "I don't want any."

She was staring at the strip of sunshine between the verandah and the blind, as though the bright light might enable her to remember something. "What's the matter?" asked Frere, bending over her. "I was trying to recollect, but I can't, Maurice. It is all confused. I only remember a great shore and a great sea, and two men, one of whom—that's you, dear—carried me in his arms."

"Dear, dear," said Mr. Meekin.

"She was quite a baby," said Vickers, hastily, as though unwilling to admit that her illness had been the cause of her forgetfulness.

"Oh, no; I was twelve years old," said Sylvia; "that's not a baby, you know. But I think the fever made me stupid."

Frere, looking at her uneasily, shifted in his seat. "There, don't think about it now," he said.

"Maurice," asked she suddenly, "what became of the other man?"

"Which other man?"

"The man who was with us; the other one, you know."

"Poor Bates?"

"No, not Bates. The prisoner. What was his name?"

"Oh, ah—the prisoner," said Frere, as if he, too, had forgotten.

"Why, you know, darling, he was sent to Port Arthur."

"Ah!" said Sylvia, with a shudder. "And is he there still?"

"I believe so," said Frere, with a frown.

"By the by," said Vickers, "I suppose we shall have to get that fellow up for the trial. We have to identify the villains."

"Can't you and I do that?" asked Frere uneasily.

"I am afraid not. I wouldn't like to swear to a man after five years."

"By George," said Frere, "*I'd* swear to him! When once I see a man's face—that's enough for me."

"We had better get up a few prisoners who were at the Harbour at the time," said Vickers, as if wishing to terminate the discussion. "I wouldn't let the villains slip through my fingers for anything."

"And are the men at Port Arthur old men?" asked Meekin.

"Old convicts," returned Vickers. "It's our place for 'colonial sentence' men. The worst we have are there. It has taken the place of Macquarie Harbour. What excitement there will be among them when the schooner goes down on Monday!"

"Excitement! Indeed? How charming! Why?" asked Meekin.

"To bring up the witnesses, my dear sir. Most of the prisoners are Lifers, you see, and a trip to Hobart Town is like a holiday for them."

"And do they never leave the place when sentenced for life?" said Meekin, nibbling a biscuit. "How distressing!"

"Never, except when they die," answered Frere, with a laugh; "and then they are buried on an island. Oh, it's a fine place! You should come down with me and have a look at it, Mr. Meekin. Picturesque, I can assure you."

"My dear Maurice," says Sylvia, going to the piano, as if in protest to the turn the conversation was taking, "how can you talk like that?"

"I should much like to see it," said Meekin, still nibbling, "for Sir John was saying something about a chaplaincy there, and I understand that the climate is quite endurable."

The convict servant, who had entered with some official papers for the Major, stared at the dainty clergyman, and rough Maurice laughed again.

"Oh, it's a stunning climate," he said; "and nothing to do. Just the place for you. There's a regular little colony there. All the scandals in Van Diemen's Land are hatched at Port Arthur."

This agreeable chatter about scandal and climate seemed a strange contrast to the grave-yard island and the men who were prisoners for life. Perhaps Sylvia thought so, for she struck a few chords, which, compelling the party, out of sheer politeness, to cease talking for the moment, caused the conversation to flag, and hinted to Mr. Meekin that it was time for him to depart.

"Good afternoon, dear Miss Vickers," he said, rising with his sweetest smile. "Thank you for your delightful music. That piece is an old, old favourite of mine. It was quite a favourite of dear Lady Jane's, and the Bishop's. Pray excuse me, my dear Captain Frere, but this strange occurrence—of the capture of the wreckers, you know—must be my apology for touching on a delicate subject. How charming to contemplate! Yourself and your dear young lady! The preserved and preserver, dear Major. 'None but the brave, you know, none *but* the brave, none but the *brave*, deserve the fair!' You remember glorious John, of course. Well, good afternoon."

"It's rather a long invitation," said Vickers, always well disposed to anyone who praised his daughter, "but if you've nothing better to do, come and dine with us on Christmas Day, Mr. Meekin. We usually have a little gathering then."

"Charmed," said Meekin—"charmed, I am sure. It *is* so refreshing to meet with persons of one's own tastes in this delightful colony. 'Kindred souls together knit,' you know, dear Miss Vickers. Indeed yes. Once more—*good* afternoon."

Sylvia burst into laughter as the door closed. "What a ridiculous creature!" said she. "Bless the man, with his gloves and his umbrella, and his hair and his scent! Fancy that mincing noodle showing me the way to Heaven! I'd rather have old Mr. Bowes, papa, though he is as blind as a beetle, and makes you so angry by bottling up his trumps as you call it."

"My dear Sylvia," said Vickers, seriously, "Mr. Meekin is a clergyman, you know,"

"Oh, I know," said Sylvia, "but then, a clergyman can talk like a man, can't he? Why do they send such people here? I am sure they could do much better at home. Oh, by the way, papa dear, poor old Danny's come back again. I told him he might go into the kitchen. May he, dear?"

"You'll have the house full of these vagabonds, you little puss," said Vickers, kissing her. "I suppose I must let him stay. What has he been doing now?"

"His wife," said Sylvia, "locked him up, you know, for being drunk. Wife! What do people want with wives, I wonder?"

"Ask Maurice," said her father, smiling.

Sylvia moved away, and tossed her head.

"What does he know about it? Maurice, you are a great bear; and if you hadn't saved my life, you know, I shouldn't love you a bit. There, you may kiss me" (her voice grew softer). "This convict business has brought it all back; and I *should* be ungrateful if I didn't love you, dear."

Maurice Frere, with suddenly crimsoned face, accepted the proffered caress, and then turned to the window. A grey-clothed man was working in the garden, and whistling as he worked. "They're not so badly off," said Frere, under his breath.

"What's that, sir?" asked Sylvia.

"That I am not half good enough for you," cried Frere, with sudden vehemence. "I—"

"It's *my* happiness you've got to think of, Captain Bruin," said the girl. "You've saved my life, haven't you, and I should be wicked if I didn't love you! No, no more kisses," she added, putting out her hand. "Come, papa, it's cool now; let's walk in the garden, and leave Maurice to think of his own unworthiness."

Maurice watched the retreating pair with a puzzled expression. "She always leaves me for her father," he said to himself. "I wonder if she really *loves* me, or if it's only gratitude, after all?"

He had often asked himself the same question during the five years of his wooing, but he had never satisfactorily answered it.

CHAPTER II
SARAH PURFOY'S REQUEST

THE evening passed as it had passed a hundred times before; and having smoked a pipe at the barracks, Captain Frere returned home. His home was a cottage on the New Town Road—a cottage which he had occupied since his appointment as Assistant Police Magistrate, an appointment given to him as a reward for his exertions in connection with the *Osprey* mutiny. Captain Maurice Frere had risen in life. Quartered in Hobart Town, he had assumed a position in society, and had held several of those excellent appointments which in the year 1834 were bestowed upon officers of garrison. He had been Superintendent of Works at Bridgewater, and when he got his captaincy, Assistant Police Magistrate at Bothwell. The affair of the *Osprey* made a noise; and it was tacitly resolved that the first "good thing" that fell vacant should be given to the gallant preserver of Major Vickers's child.

Major Vickers also prospered. He had always been a careful man, and having saved some money, had purchased land on favourable terms. The "assignment system" enabled him to cultivate portions of it at a small expense, and, following the usual custom, he stocked his run with cattle and sheep. He had sold his commission, and was now a comparatively wealthy man. He owned a fine estate; the house he lived in was purchased property. He was in good odour at Government House, and his office of Superintendent of Convicts caused him to take an active part in that local government which keeps a man constantly before the public. Major Vickers, a colonist against his will, had become, by force of circumstances, one of the leading men in Van Diemen's Land. His daughter was a good match for any man; and many ensigns and lieutenants, cursing their hard lot in "country quarters", many sons of settlers living on their father's station among the mountains, and many dapper clerks on the civil establishment envied Maurice Frere his good fortune. Some went so far as to say that the beautiful daughter of "Regulation Vickers" was too good for the coarse red-faced Frere, who was noted for his fondness for low society, and overbearing, almost brutal demeanour. No one denied, however, that Captain Frere was a valuable officer. It was said that, in consequence of his tastes, he knew more about the tricks of convicts than any man on the island. It was said, even, that he was wont to disguise himself, and mix with the pass-holders and convict servants, in order to learn their signs and mysteries. When in charge at Bridgewater it had been his delight to rate the chain-gangs in their own hideous jargon, and to astound a new-comer by his knowledge of his previous history. The convict population hated and cringed to him, for, with his brutality, and violence, he mingled a ferocious good humour, that resulted sometimes in tacit permission to go without the letter of the law. Yet, as the convicts themselves said, "a man was never safe with the Captain"; for, after drinking and joking with them, as the Sir Oracle of some public-house whose hostess he delighted to honour, he would disappear through a side door just as the constables burst in at the back, and show himself as remorseless, in his next morning's sentence of the captured, as if he had never entered a tap-room in all his life. His superiors called this "zeal"; his inferiors "treachery". For himself, he laughed. "Everything is fair to those wretches," he was accustomed to say.

As the time for his marriage approached, however, he had in a measure given up these exploits, and strove, by his demeanour, to make his acquaintances forget several remarkable scandals concerning his private life, for the promulgation of which he once cared little. When Commandant at the Maria Island, and for the first two years after his return from the unlucky expedition to Macquarie Harbour, he had not suffered any fear of society's opinion to restrain his vices, but, as the affection for the pure young girl, who looked upon him as her saviour from a dreadful death, increased in honest strength, he had resolved to shut up those dark pages in his colonial experience, and to read therein no more. He was not remorseful, he was not even disgusted. He merely came to the conclusion that, when a man married, he was to consider certain extravagances common to all bachelors as at an end. He had "had his fling, like all young men", perhaps he had been foolish like most young men, but no reproachful ghost of past misdeeds haunted him. His nature was too prosaic to admit the existence of such phantoms. Sylvia, in her purity and excellence, was so far above him, that in raising his eyes to her, he lost sight of all the sordid creatures to whose level he had once debased himself, and had come in part to regard the sins he had committed, before his redemption by the love of this bright young creature, as evil done by him under a past condition of existence, and for the consequences of which he was not responsible. One of the consequences, however, was very close to him at this moment. His convict servant had, according to his instructions, sat up for him, and as he entered, the man handed him a letter, bearing a superscription in a female hand.

"Who brought this?" asked Frere, hastily tearing it open to read. "The groom, sir. He said that there was a gentleman at the 'George the Fourth' who wished to see you."

Frere smiled, in admiration of the intelligence which had dictated such a message, and then frowned in anger at the contents of the letter. "You needn't wait," he said to the man. "I shall have to go back again, I suppose."

Changing his forage cap for a soft hat, and selecting a stick from a miscellaneous collection in a corner, he prepared to retrace his steps. "What does she want now?" he asked himself fiercely, as he strode down the moonlit road; but beneath the fierceness there was an under-current of petulance, which implied that, whatever "she" did want, she had a right to expect.

The "George the Fourth" was a long low house, situated in Elizabeth Street. Its front was painted a dull red, and the narrow panes of glass in its windows, and the ostentatious affectation of red curtains and homely comfort, gave to it a spurious appearance of old English jollity. A knot of men round the door melted into air as Captain Frere approached, for it was now past eleven o'clock, and all persons found in the streets after eight could be compelled to "show their pass" or explain their business. The convict constables were not scrupulous in the exercise of their duty, and the bluff figure of Frere, clad in the blue serge which he affected as a summer costume, looked not unlike that of a convict constable.

Pushing open the side door with the confident manner of one

well acquainted with the house, Frere entered, and made his way along a narrow passage to a glass door at the further end. A tap upon this door brought a white-faced, pock-pitted Irish girl, who curtsied with servile recognition of the visitor, and ushered him upstairs. The room into which he was shown was a large one. It had three windows looking into the street, and was handsomely furnished. The carpet was soft, the candles were bright, and the supper tray gleamed invitingly from a table between the windows. As Frere entered, a little terrier ran barking to his feet. It was evident that he was not a constant visitor. The rustle of a silk dress behind the terrier betrayed the presence of a woman; and Frere, rounding the promontory of an ottoman, found himself face to face with Sarah Purfoy.

"Thank you for coming," she said. "Pray, sit down."

This was the only greeting that passed between them, and Frere sat down, in obedience to a motion of a plump hand that twinkled with rings.

The eleven years that had passed since we last saw this woman had dealt gently with her. Her foot was as small and her hand as white as of yore. Her hair, bound close about her head, was plentiful and glossy, and her eyes had lost none of their dangerous brightness. Her figure was coarser, and the white arm that gleamed through a muslin sleeve showed an outline that a fastidious artist might wish to modify. The most noticeable change was in her face. The cheeks owned no longer that delicate purity which they once boasted, but had become thicker, while here and there showed those faint red streaks—as though the rich blood throbbed too painfully in the veins—which are the first signs of the decay of "fine" women. With middle age and the fullness of figure to which most women of her temperament are prone, had come also that indescribable vulgarity of speech and manner which habitual absence of moral restraint never fails to produce.

Maurice Frere spoke first; he was anxious to bring his visit to as speedy a termination as possible. "What do you want of me?" he asked. Sarah Purfoy laughed; a forced laugh, that sounded so unnatural, that Frere turned to look at her. "I want you to do me a favour—a very great favour; that is if it will not put you out of the way."

"What do you mean?" asked Frere roughly, pursing his lips with a sullen air. "Favour! What do you call *this*?" striking the sofa on which he sat. "Isn't *this* a favour? What do you call your precious house and all that's in it? Isn't *that* a favour? What do you mean?"

To his utter astonishment the woman replied by shedding tears. For some time he regarded her in silence, as if unwilling to be softened by such shallow device, but eventually felt constrained to say something. "Have you been drinking again?" he asked, "or what's the matter with you? Tell me what it is you want, and have done with it. I don't know what possessed me to come here at all."

Sarah sat upright, and dashed away her tears with one passionate hand.

"I am ill, can't you see, you fool!" said she. "The news has unnerved me. If I have been drinking, what then? It's nothing to you, is it?"

"Oh, no," returned the other, "it's nothing to me. You are the principal party concerned. If you choose to bloat yourself with brandy, do it by all means."

"*You* don't pay for it, at any rate!" said she, with quickness of retaliation which showed that this was not the only occasion on which they had quarrelled.

"Come," said Frere, impatiently brutal, "get on. I can't stop here all night."

She suddenly rose, and crossed to where he was standing.

"Maurice, you were very fond of me once."

"Once," said Maurice.

"Not so very many years ago."

"Hang it!" said he, shifting his arm from beneath her hand, "don't let us have all that stuff over again. It was before you took to drinking and swearing, and going raving mad with passion, any way."

"Well, dear," said she, with her great glittering eyes belying the soft tones of her voice, "I suffered for it, didn't I? Didn't you turn me out into the streets? Didn't you lash me with your whip like a dog? Didn't you put me in gaol for it, eh? It's hard to struggle against you, Maurice."

The compliment to his obstinacy seemed to please him—perhaps the crafty woman intended that it should—and he smiled.

"Well, there; let old times be old times, Sarah. You haven't done badly, after all," and he looked round the well-furnished room. "What do you want?"

"There was a transport came in this morning."

"Well?"

"*You* know who was on board her, Maurice!"

Maurice brought one hand into the palm of the other with a rough laugh.

"Oh, that's it, is it! 'Gad, what a flat I was not to think of it before! You want to see him, I suppose?" She came close to him, and, in her earnestness, took his hand. "I want to save his life!"

"Oh, that be hanged, you know! Save his life! It can't be done."

"You can do it, Maurice."

"I save John Rex's life?" cried Frere. "Why, you must be mad!"

"He is the only creature that loves me, Maurice—the only man who cares for me. He has done no harm. He only wanted to be free—was it not natural? You can save him if you like. I only ask for his life. What does it matter to you? A miserable prisoner—his death would be of no use. Let him live, Maurice."

Maurice laughed. "What have I to do with it?"

"You are the principal witness against him. If you say that he behaved well—and he *did* behave well, you know: many men would have left you to starve—they won't hang him."

"Oh, won't they! That won't make much difference."

"Ah, Maurice, be merciful!" She bent towards him, and tried to retain his hand, but he withdrew it.

"You're a nice sort of woman to ask me to help your lover—a man who left me on that cursed coast to die, for all he cared," he said, with a galling recollection of his humiliation of five years back. "Save him! Confound him, not I!"

"Ah, Maurice, you will." She spoke with a suppressed sob in her voice. "What is it to you? You don't care for me now. You beat me, and turned me out of doors, though I never did you wrong. This man was a husband to me—long, long before I met you.

He never did you any harm; he never will. He will bless you if you save him, Maurice."

Frere jerked his head impatiently. "*Bless* me!" he said. "I don't want his blessings. Let him swing. Who cares?"

Still she persisted, with tears streaming from her eyes, with white arms upraised, on her knees even, catching at his coat, and beseeching him in broken accents. In her wild, fierce beauty and passionate abandonment she might have been a deserted Ariadne—a suppliant Medea. Anything rather than what she was—a dissolute, half-maddened woman, praying for the pardon of her convict husband.

Maurice Frere flung her off with an oath. "Get up!" he cried brutally, "and stop that nonsense. I tell you the man's as good as dead for all I shall do to save him."

At this repulse, her pent-up passion broke forth. She sprang to her feet, and, pushing back the hair that in her frenzied pleading had fallen about her face, poured out upon him a torrent of abuse. "You! Who are you, that you dare to speak to me like that? His little finger is worth your whole body. He is a man, a brave man, not a coward, like you. A coward! Yes, a coward! a coward! A coward! You are very brave with defenceless men and weak women. You have beaten me until I was bruised black, you cur; but who ever saw you attack a man unless he was chained or bound? Do not I know you? I have seen you taunt a man at the triangles, until I wished the screaming wretch could get loose, and murder you as you deserve! You will be murdered one of these days, Maurice Frere—take my word for it. Men are flesh and blood, and flesh and blood won't endure the torments you lay on it!"

"There, that'll do," says Frere, growing paler. "Don't excite yourself."

"I know you, you brutal coward. I have not been your mistress—God forgive me!—without learning you by heart. I've seen your ignorance and your conceit. I've seen the men who ate your food and drank your wine laugh at you. I've heard what your friends say; I've heard the comparisons they make. One of your dogs has more brains than you, and twice as much heart. And these are the men they send to *rule* us! Oh, Heaven! And such an animal as this has life and death in his hand! He may hang, may he? I'll hang with him, then, and God will forgive me for murder, for I will kill *you*!"

Frere had cowered before this frightful torrent of rage, but, at the scream which accompanied the last words, he stepped forward as though to seize her. In her desperate courage, she flung herself before him. "Strike me! You daren't! I defy you! Bring up the wretched creatures who learn the way to Hell in this cursed house, and let them see you do it. Call them! They are old friends of yours. They all know Captain Maurice Frere."

"Sarah!"

"You remember Lucy Barnes—poor little Lucy Barnes that stole sixpennyworth of calico. She is downstairs now. Would you know her if you saw her? She isn't the bright-faced baby she was when they sent her here to 'reform', and when Lieutenant Frere wanted a new housemaid from the Factory! Call for her!—call! do you hear? Ask any one of those beasts whom you lash and chain for Lucy Barnes. He'll tell you all about her—ay, and about many more—many more poor souls that are at the bidding of any drunken brute that has stolen a pound note to fee the Devil with! Oh, you good God in Heaven, will You not judge this man?" Frere trembled. He had often witnessed this creature's whirlwinds of passion, but never had he seen her so violent as this. Her frenzy frightened him. "For Heaven's sake, Sarah, be quiet. What is it you want? What would you do?"

"I'll go to this girl you want to marry, and tell her all I know of you. I have seen her in the streets—have seen her look the other way when I passed her—have seen her gather up her muslin skirts when my silks touched her—I that nursed her, that heard her say her baby-prayers (O Jesus, pity me!)—and I know what she thinks of women like me. She is good—and virtuous—and cold. She would shudder at you if she knew what I know. Shudder! She would hate you! And I will tell her! Ay, I will! You will be *respectable*, will you? A model husband! Wait till I tell her my story—till I send some of these poor women to tell theirs. You kill my love; I'll blight and ruin yours!" Frere caught her by both wrists, and with all his strength forced her to her knees. "Don't speak *her* name," he said in a hoarse voice, "or I'll do you a mischief. I know all you mean to do. I'm not such a fool as not to see that. Be quiet! Men have murdered women like you, and now I know how they came to do it."

For a few minutes a silence fell upon the pair, and at last Frere, releasing her hands, fell back from her.

"I'll do what you want, on one condition."

"What?"

"That you leave this place."

"Where for?"

"Anywhere—the farther the better. I'll pay your passage to Sydney, and you go or stay there as you please."

She had grown calmer, hearing him thus relenting. "But this house, Maurice?"

"You are not in debt?"

"No."

"Well, leave it. It's your own affair, not mine. If I help you, you must go."

"May I see *him*?"

"No."

"Ah, Maurice!"

"You can see him in the dock if you like," says Frere, with a laugh, cut short by a flash of her eyes. "There, I didn't mean to offend you."

"Offend me! Go on."

"Listen here," said he doggedly. "If you will go away, and promise never to interfere with me by word or deed, I'll do what you want."

"What will you do?" she asked, unable to suppress a smile at the victory she had won.

"I will not say all I know about this man. I will say he befriended me. I will do my best to save his life."

"You *can* save it if you like."

"Well, I will try. On my honour, I will try."

"I must believe you, I suppose?" said she doubtfully; and then, with a sudden pitiful pleading, in strange contrast to her former violence, "You are not deceiving me, Maurice?"

"No. Why should I? You keep your promise, and I'll keep mine. Is it a bargain?"

"Yes."

He eyed her steadfastly for some seconds, and then turned on his heel. As he reached the door she called him back. Knowing him as she did, she felt that he would keep his word, and her feminine nature could not resist a parting sneer.

"There is nothing in the bargain to prevent me helping him to escape!" she said with a smile.

"Escape! He won't escape again, I'll go bail. Once get him in double irons at Port Arthur, and he's safe enough."

The smile on her face seemed infectious, for his own sullen features relaxed. "Good night, Sarah," he said.

She put out her hand, as if nothing had happened. "Good night, Captain Frere. It's a bargain, then?"

"A bargain."

"You have a long walk home. Will you have some brandy?"

"I don't care if I do," he said, advancing to the table, and filling his glass. "Here's a good voyage to you!"

Sarah Purfoy, watching him, burst into a laugh. "Human beings are queer creatures," she said. "Who would have thought that we had been calling each other names just now? I say, I'm a vixen when I'm roused, ain't I, Maurice?"

"Remember what you've promised," said he, with a threat in his voice, as he moved to the door. "You must be out of this by the next ship that leaves."

"Never fear, I'll go."

Getting into the cool street directly, and seeing the calm stars shining, and the placid water sleeping with a peace in which he had no share, he strove to cast off the nervous fear that was on him. That interview had frightened him, for it had made him think. It was hard that, just as he had turned over a new leaf, this old blot should come through to the clean page. It was cruel that, having comfortably forgotten the past, he should be thus rudely reminded of it.

CHAPTER III

THE STORY OF TWO BIRDS OF PREY

THE reader of the foregoing pages has doubtless asked himself, "what is the link which binds together John Rex and Sarah Purfoy?"

In the year 1825 there lived at St. Heliers, Jersey, an old watch-maker, named Urban Purfoy. He was a hard-working man, and had amassed a little money—sufficient to give his grand-daughter an education above the common in those days. At sixteen, Sarah Purfoy was an empty-headed, strong-willed, precocious girl, with big brown eyes. She had a bad opinion of her own sex, and an immense admiration for the young and handsome members of the other. The neighbours said that she was too high and mighty for her rank in life. Her grandfather said she was a "beauty", and like her poor dear mother. She herself thought rather meanly of her personal attractions, and rather highly of her mental ones. She was brimful of vitality, with strong passions, and little religious sentiment. She had not much respect for moral courage, for she did not understand it; but she was a profound admirer of personal prowess. Her distaste for the humdrum life she was leading found expression in a rebellion against social usages. She courted notoriety by eccentricities of dress, and was never so happy as when she was misunderstood. She was the sort of girl of whom women say—"It is a pity she has no mother"; and men, "It is a pity she does not get a husband"; and who say to themselves, "When shall I have a lover?"

There was no lack of beings of this latter class among the officers quartered in Fort Royal and Fort Henry; but the female population of the island was free and numerous, and in the embar-rassment of riches, Sarah was overlooked. Though she adored the soldiery, her first lover was a civilian. Walking one day on the cliff, she met a young man. He was tall, well-looking, and well-dressed. His name was Lemoine; he was the son of a somewhat wealthy resident of the island, and had come down from London to recruit his health and to see his friends. Sarah was struck by his appearance, and looked back at him. He had been struck by hers, and looked back also. He followed her, and spoke to her—some remark about the wind or the weather—and she thought his voice divine. They got into conversation—about scenery, lonely walks, and the dullness of St. Heliers. "Did she often walk there?" "Sometimes." "Would she be there to-morrow?" "She might." Mr. Lemoine lifted his hat, and went back to dinner, rather pleased with himself.

They met the next day, and the day after that. Lemoine was not a gentleman, but he had lived among gentlemen, and had caught something of their manner. He said that, after all, virtue was a mere name, and that when people were powerful and rich, the world respected them more than if they had been honest and poor. Sarah agreed with this sentiment. Her grandfather was honest and poor, and yet nobody respected him—at least, not with such respect as she cared to acknowledge. In addition to his talent for argument, Lemoine was handsome and had money—he showed her quite a handful of bank-notes one day. He told her of London and the great ladies there, and hinting that *they* were not always virtuous, drew himself up with a moody air, as though *he* had been unhappily the cause of their fatal lapse into wickedness. Sarah did not wonder at this in the least. Had she been a great lady, she would have done the same. She began to coquet with this seductive fellow, and to hint to him that she had too much knowledge of the world to set a fictitious value upon virtue. He mistook her artfulness for innocence, and thought he had made a conquest. Moreover, the girl was pretty, and when dressed properly, would look well. Only one obstacle stood in the way of their loves—the dashing profligate was poor. He had been living in London above his means, and his father was not inclined to increase his allowance.

Sarah liked him better than anybody else she had seen, but there are two sides to every bargain. Sarah Purfoy must go to London. In vain her lover sighed and swore. Unless he would promise to take her away with him, Diana was not more chaste. The more virtuous she grew, the more vicious did Lemoine feel. His desire to possess her increased in proportionate ratio to her resistance, and at last he borrowed two hundred pounds from his father's confidential clerk (the Lemoines were merchants by profession), and acceded to her wishes. There was no love on either side—vanity was the mainspring of the whole transaction. Lemoine did not like to be beaten; Sarah sold herself for a passage to England and an introduction into the "great world".

We need not describe her career at this epoch. Suffice it to say that she discovered that vice is not always conducive to happiness, and is not, even in this world, so well rewarded as its earnest practice might merit. Sated, and disappointed, she soon grew tired of her life, and longed to escape from its wearying dissipations. At this juncture she fell in love.

The object of her affections was one Mr. Lionel Crofton. Crofton was tall, well made, and with an insinuating address. His features were too strongly marked for beauty. His eyes were the best part of his face, and, like his hair, they were jet black. He had broad shoulders, sinewy limbs, and small hands and feet. His head was round, and well-shaped, but it bulged a little over the ears which were singularly small and lay close to his head. With this man, barely four years older than herself, Sarah, at seventeen, fell violently in love. This was the more strange as, though fond of her, he would tolerate no caprices, and possessed an ungovernable temper, which found vent in curses, and even blows. He seemed to have no profession or business, and though he owned a good address, he was even less of a gentleman than Lemoine. Yet Sarah, attracted by one of the strange sympathies which constitute the romance of such women's lives, was devoted to him. Touched by her affection, and rating her intelligence and unscrupulousness at their true value, he told her who he was. He was a swindler, a forger, and a thief, and his name was John Rex. When she heard this she experienced a sinister delight. He told her of his plots, his tricks, his escapes, his villainies; and seeing how for years this young man had preyed upon the world which had deceived and disowned her, her heart went out to him. "I am glad you found me," she said. "Two heads are better than one. We will work together."

John Rex, known among his intimate associates as Dandy Jack, was the putative son of a man who had been for many years valet to Lord Bellasis, and who retired from the service of that profligate nobleman with a sum of money and a wife. John Rex was sent to as good a school as could be procured for him, and at sixteen was given, by the interest of his mother with his father's former master, a clerkship in an old-established city banking-house. Mrs. Rex was intensely fond of her son, and imbued him with a desire to shine in aristocratic circles. He was a clever lad, without any principle; he would lie unblushingly, and steal deliberately, if he thought he could do so with impunity. He was cautious, acquisitive, imaginative, self-conceited, and destructive. He had strong perceptive faculties, and much invention and versatility, but his "moral sense" was almost entirely wanting. He found that his fellow clerks were not of that "gentlemanly" stamp which his mother thought so admirable, and therefore he despised them. He thought he should like to go into the army, for he was athletic, and rejoiced in feats of muscular strength. To be tied all day to a desk was beyond endurance. But John Rex, senior, told him to "wait and see what came of it." He did so, and in the meantime kept late hours, got into bad company, and forged the name of a customer of the bank to a cheque for twenty pounds. The fraud was a clumsy one, and was detected in twenty-four hours. Forgeries by clerks, however easily detected, are unfortunately not considered to add to the attractions of a banking-house, and the old-established firm decided not to prosecute, but dismissed Mr. John Rex from their service. The ex-valet, who never liked his legalized son, was at first for turning him out of doors, but by the entreaties of his wife, was at last induced to place the promising boy in a draper's shop, in the City Road.

This employment was not a congenial one, and John Rex planned to leave it. He lived at home, and had his salary—about thirty shillings a week—for pocket money. Though he displayed considerable skill with the cue, and not infrequently won considerable sums for one in his position, his expenses averaged more than his income; and having borrowed all he could, he found himself again in difficulties. His narrow escape, however, had taught him a lesson, and he resolved to confess all to his indulgent mother, and be more economical for the future. Just then one of those "lucky chances" which blight so many lives occurred. The "shop-walker" died, and

Messrs. Baffaty & Co. made the gentlemanly Rex act as his substitute for a few days. Shop-walkers have opportunities not accorded to other folks, and on the evening of the third day Mr. Rex went home with a bundle of lace in his pocket. Unfortunately, he owed more than the worth of this petty theft, and was compelled to steal again. This time he was detected. One of his fellow-shopmen caught him in the very act of concealing a roll of silk, ready for future abstraction, and, to his astonishment, cried "Halves!" Rex pretended to be virtuously indignant, but soon saw that such pretence was useless; his companion was too wily to be fooled with such affectation of innocence. "I saw you take it," said he, "and if you won't share I'll tell old Baffaty." This argument was irresistible, and they shared. Having become good friends, the self-made partner lent Rex a helping hand in the disposal of the booty, and introduced him to a purchaser. The purchaser violated all rules of romance by being—not a Jew, but a very orthodox Christian. He kept a second-hand clothes warehouse in the City Road, and was supposed to have branch establishments all over London.

Mr. Blicks purchased the stolen goods for about a third of their value, and seemed struck by Mr. Rex's appearance. "I thort you was a swell mobsman," said he. This, from one so experienced, was a high compliment. Encouraged by success, Rex and his companion took more articles of value. John Rex paid off his debts, and began to feel himself quite a "gentleman" again. Just as Rex had arrived at this pleasing state of mind, Baffaty discovered the robbery. Not having heard about the bank business, he did not suspect Rex—he was such a gentlemanly young man—but having had his eye for some time upon Rex's partner, who was vulgar, and squinted, he sent for him. Rex's partner stoutly denied the accusation, and old Baffaty, who was a man of merciful tendencies, and could well afford to lose fifty pounds, gave him until the next morning to confess, and state where the goods had gone, hinting at the persuasive powers of a constable at the end of that time. The shopman, with tears in his eyes, came in a hurry to Rex, and informed him that all was lost. He did not want to confess, because he must implicate his friend Rex, but if he did not confess he would be given in charge. Flight was impossible, for neither had money. In this dilemma John Rex remembered Blicks's compliment, and burned to deserve it. If he must retreat, he would lay waste the enemy's country. His exodus should be like that of the Israelites—he would spoil the Egyptians. The shop-walker was allowed half an hour in the middle of the day for lunch. John Rex took advantage of this half-hour to hire a cab and drive to Blicks. That worthy man received him cordially, for he saw that he was bent upon great deeds. John Rex rapidly unfolded his plan of operations. The warehouse doors were fastened with a spring. He would remain behind after they were locked, and open them at a given signal. A light cart or cab could be stationed in the lane at the back, three men could fill it with valuables in as many hours. Did Blicks know of three such men? Blicks's one eye glistened. He thought he did know. At half-past eleven they should be there. Was that all? No. Mr. John Rex was not going to "put up" such a splendid thing for nothing. The booty was worth at least £5,000 if it was worth a shilling—he must have £100 cash when the cart stopped at Blicks's door. Blicks at first refused point blank. Let there be a division, but he would not buy a pig in a poke. Rex was firm, however; it was his only chance, and at last he got a promise of £80. That night the glorious achievement known in the annals of Bow Street as "The Great Silk Robbery" took place, and two days afterwards John Rex and his partner, dining comfortably at Birmingham, read an account of the transaction—not in the least like it—in a London paper.

John Rex, who had now fairly broken with dull respectability, bid adieu to his home, and began to realize his mother's wishes. He was, after his fashion, a "gentleman". As long as the £80 lasted, he lived in luxury, and by the time it was spent he had established himself in his profession. This profession was a lucrative one. It was that of a swindler. Gifted with a handsome person, facile manner, and ready wit, he had added to these natural advantages some skill at billiards, some knowledge of gambler's legerdemain, and the useful consciousness that he must prey or be preyed on. John Rex was no common swindler; his natural as well as his acquired abilities saved him from vulgar errors. He saw that to successfully swindle mankind, one must not aim at comparative, but superlative, ingenuity. He who is contented with being only cleverer than the majority must infallibly be outwitted at last, and to be once outwitted is—for a swindler—to be ruined. Examining, moreover, into the history of detected crime, John Rex discovered one thing. At the bottom of all these robberies, deceptions, and swindles, was some lucky fellow who profited by the folly of his confederates. This gave him an idea. Suppose he could not only make use of his own talents to rob mankind, but utilize those of others also? Crime runs through infinite grades. He proposed to himself to be at the top; but why should he despise those good fellows beneath him? His speciality was swindling, billiard-playing, card-playing, borrowing money, obtaining goods, never risking more than two or three *coups* in a year. But others plundered houses, stole bracelets, watches, diamonds—made as much in a night as he did in six months—only their occupation was more dangerous. Now came the question—why more dangerous? Because these men were mere clods, bold enough and clever enough in their own rude way, but no match for the law, with its Argus eyes and its Briarean hands. They did the rougher business well enough; they broke locks, and burst doors, and "neddied" constables, but in the finer arts of plan, attack, and escape, they were sadly deficient. Good. These men should be the hands; he would be the head. He would plan the robberies; they should execute them.

Working through many channels, and never omitting to assist a fellow-worker when in distress, John Rex, in a few years, and in a most prosaic business way, became the head of a society of ruffians. Mixing with fast clerks and unsuspecting middle-class profligates, he found out particulars of houses ill guarded, and shops insecurely fastened, and "put up" Blicks's ready ruffians to the more dangerous work. In his various disguises, and under his many names, he found his way into those upper circles of "fast" society, where animals turn into birds, where a wolf becomes a rook, and a lamb a pigeon. Rich spendthrifts who affected male society asked him to their houses, and Mr. Anthony Croftonbury, Captain James Craven, and Mr. Lionel Crofton were names remembered, sometimes with pleasure, oftener with regret, by many a broken man of fortune. He had one quality which, to a man of his profession, was invaluable—he was cautious, and master of himself. Having made a success, wrung commission from Blicks, rooked a gambling ninny like Lemoine, or secured an assortment of jewellery sent down to his "wife" in Gloucestershire, he would disappear for a time. He liked comfort, and revelled in the sense of security and respectability. Thus he had lived for three years when he met Sarah Purfoy, and thus he proposed to live for many more. With this woman as a coadjutor, he thought he could defy the law. She was the net spread to catch his "pigeons"; she was the well-dressed lady who ordered goods in London for her husband at Canterbury, and *paid* half the price down, "which was all this letter authorized her to do," and where a less beautiful or clever woman might have failed, she succeeded. Her husband saw fortune before him, and believed that, with common prudence, he might carry on his most lucrative employment of "gentleman" until he chose to relinquish it. Alas for human weakness! He one day did a foolish thing, and the law he had so successfully defied got him in the simplest way imaginable.

Under the names of Mr. and Mrs. Skinner, John Rex and Sarah Purfoy were living in quiet lodgings in the neighbourhood of Blooms-bury. Their landlady was a respectable poor woman, and had a son who was a constable. This son was given to talking, and, coming in to supper one night, he told his mother that on the following evening an attack was to be made on a gang of coiners in the Old Street Road. The mother, dreaming all sorts of horrors during the night, came the next day to Mrs. Skinner, in the parlour, and, under a pledge of profound secrecy, told her of the dreadful expedition in which her son was engaged. John Rex was out at a pigeon match with Lord Bellasis, and when he returned, at nine o'clock, Sarah told him what she had heard.

Now, 4, Bank Place, Old Street Road, was the residence of a man named Green, who had for some time carried on the lucrative but dangerous trade of "counterfeiting". This man was one of the most daring of that army of ruffians whose treasure chest and master of the mint was Blicks, and his liberty was valuable. John Rex, eating his dinner more nervously than usual, ruminated on the intelligence, and thought it would be but wise to warn Green of his danger. Not that he cared much for Green personally, but it was bad policy to miss doing a good turn to a comrade, and, moreover, Green, if captured might wag his tongue too freely. But how to do it? If he went to Blicks, it might be too late; he would go himself. He went out—and was captured. When Sarah heard of the calamity she set to work to help him. She collected all her money and jewels, paid Mrs. Skinner's rent, went to see Rex, and arranged his defence. Blicks was hopeful, but Green—who came very near hanging—admitted that the man was an associate of his, and the Recorder, being in a severe mood, transported him for seven years.

Sarah Purfoy vowed that she would follow him. She was going as passenger, as emigrant, anything, when she saw Mrs. Vickers's advertisement for a "lady's-maid," and answered it. It chanced that Rex was shipped in the *Malabar*, and Sarah, discovering this before the vessel had been a week at sea, conceived the bold project of inciting a mutiny for the rescue of her lover. We know the result of that scheme, and the story of the scoundrel's subsequent escape from Macquarie Harbour.

CHAPTER IV

"THE NOTORIOUS DAWES"

THE mutineers of the *Osprey* had been long since given up as dead, and the story of their desperate escape had become indistinct to the general public mind. Now that they had been recaptured in a remarkable manner, popular belief invested them with all sorts of strange surroundings. They had been—according to report—kings over savage islanders, chiefs of lawless and ferocious pirates, respectable married men in Java, merchants in Singapore, and swindlers in Hong Kong. Their adventures had been dramatized at a London theatre, and the popular novelist of that day was engaged in a work descriptive of their wondrous fortunes.

John Rex, the ringleader, was related, it was said, to a noble family, and a special message had come out to Sir John Franklin concerning him. He had every prospect of being satisfactorily hung, however, for even the most outspoken admirers of his skill and courage could not but admit that he had committed an offence which was death by the law. The Crown would leave nothing undone to convict him, and the already crowded prison was re-crammed with half a dozen life sentence men, brought up from Port Arthur to identify the prisoners. Amongst this number was stated to be "the notorious Dawes".

This statement gave fresh food for recollection and invention. It was remembered that "the notorious Dawes" was the absconder who had been brought away by Captain Frere, and who owed such fettered life as he possessed to the fact that he had assisted Captain Frere to make the wonderful boat in which the marooned party escaped. It was remembered, also, how sullen and morose he had been on his trial five years before, and how he had laughed when the commutation of his death sentence was announced to him. The *Hobart Town Gazette* published a short biography of this horrible villain—a biography setting forth how he had been engaged in a mutiny on board the convict ship, how he had twice escaped from the Macquarie Harbour, how he had been repeatedly flogged for violence and insubordination, and how he was now double-ironed at Port Arthur, after two more ineffectual attempts to regain his freedom. Indeed, the *Gazette*, discovering that the wretch had been originally transported for highway robbery, argued very ably it would be far better to hang such wild beasts in the first instance than suffer them to cumber the ground, and grow confirmed in villainy. "Of what use to society," asked the *Gazette*, quite pathetically, "has this scoundrel been during the last eleven years?" And everybody agreed that he had been of no use whatever.

Miss Sylvia Vickers also received an additional share of public attention. Her romantic rescue by the heroic Frere, who was shortly to reap the reward of his devotion in the good old fashion, made her almost as famous as the villain Dawes, or his confederate monster John Rex. It was reported that she was to give evidence on the trial, together with her affianced husband, they being the only two living witnesses who could speak to the facts of the mutiny. It was reported also that her lover was naturally most anxious that she should not give evidence, as she was—an additional point of romantic interest—affected deeply by the illness consequent on the suffering she had undergone, and in a state of pitiable mental confusion as to the whole business. These reports caused the Court, on the day of the trial, to be crowded with spectators; and as the various particulars of the marvellous history of this double escape were detailed, the excitement grew more intense. The aspect of the four heavily-ironed prisoners caused a sensation which, in that city of the ironed, was quite novel, and bets were offered and taken as to the line of defence which they would adopt. At first it was thought that they would throw themselves on the mercy of the Crown, seeking, in the very extravagance of their story, to excite public sympathy; but a little study of the demeanour of the chief prisoner, John Rex, dispelled that conjecture. Calm, placid, and defiant, he seemed prepared to accept his fate, or to meet his accusers with some plea which should be sufficient to secure his acquittal on the capital charge. Only when he heard the indictment, setting forth that he had "feloniously pirated the brig *Osprey*," he smiled a little.

Mr. Meekin, sitting in the body of the Court, felt his religious prejudices sadly shocked by that smile. "A perfect wild beast, my dear Miss Vickers," he said, returning, in a pause during the examination of the convicts who had been brought to identify the prisoner, to the little room where Sylvia and her father were waiting. "He has quite a tigerish look about him."

"Poor man!" said Sylvia, with a shudder.

"Poor! My *dear* young lady, you do not pity him?"

"I do," said Sylvia, twisting her hands together as if in pain. "I pity them all, poor creatures."

"Charming sensibility!" says Meekin, with a glance at Vickers. "The true woman's heart, my dear Major."

The Major tapped his fingers impatiently at this ill-timed twaddle. Sylvia was too nervous just then for sentiment. "Come here, Poppet," he said, "and look through this door. You can see them from here, and if you do not recognize any of them, I can't see what is the use of putting you in the box; though, of course, if it is necessary, you must go."

The raised dock was just opposite to the door of the room in which they were sitting, and the four manacled men, each with an armed warder behind him, were visible above the heads of the crowd. The girl had never before seen the ceremony of trying a man for his life, and the silent and antique solemnities of the business affected her, as it affects all who see it for the first time. The atmosphere was heavy and distressing. The chains of the prisoners clanked ominously. The crushing force of judge, gaolers, warders, and constables assembled to punish the four men, appeared cruel. The familiar faces, that in her momentary glance, she recognized, seemed to her evilly transfigured. Even the countenance of her promised husband, bent eagerly forward towards the witness-box, showed tyrannous and bloodthirsty. Her eyes hastily followed the pointing finger of her father, and sought the men in the dock. Two of them lounged, sullen and inattentive; one nervously chewed a straw, or piece of twig, pawing the dock with restless hand; the fourth scowled across the Court at the witness-box, which she could not see. The four faces were all strange to her.

"No, papa," she said, with a sigh of relief, "I can't recognize them at all."

As she was turning from the door, a voice from the witness-box behind her made her suddenly pale and pause to look again. The Court itself appeared, at that moment, affected, for a murmur ran through it, and some official cried, "Silence!"

The notorious criminal, Rufus Dawes, the desperado of Port Arthur, the wild beast whom the *Gazette* had judged not fit to live, had just entered the witness-box. He was a man of thirty, in the prime of life, with a torso whose muscular grandeur not even the ill-fitting yellow jacket could altogether conceal, with strong, embrowned, and nervous hands, an upright carriage, and a pair of fierce, black eyes that roamed over the Court hungrily.

Not all the weight of the double irons swaying from the leathern thong around his massive loins, could mar that elegance of attitude which comes only from perfect muscular development. Not all the frowning faces bent upon him could frown an accent of respect into the contemptuous tones in which he answered to his name, "Rufus Dawes, prisoner of the Crown".

"Come away, my darling," said Vickers, alarmed at his daughter's blanched face and eager eyes.

"Wait," she said impatiently, listening for the voice whose owner she could not see. "Rufus Dawes! Oh, I have heard that name before!"

"You are a prisoner of the Crown at the penal settlement of Port Arthur?"

"Yes."

"For life?"

"For life."

Sylvia turned to her father with breathless inquiry in her eyes. "Oh, papa! who is that speaking? I know the name! the voice!"

"That is the man who was with you in the boat, dear," says Vickers gravely. "The prisoner."

The eager light died out of her eyes, and in its place came a look of disappointment and pain. "I thought it was a good man," she said, holding by the edge of the doorway. "It sounded like a good voice."

And then she pressed her hands over her eyes and shuddered. "There, there," says Vickers soothingly, "don't be afraid, Poppet; he can't hurt you now."

"No, ha! ha!" says Meekin, with great display of off-hand courage, "the villain's safe enough now."

The colloquy in the Court went on. "Do you know the prisoners in the dock?"

"Yes."

"Who are they?"

"John Rex, Henry Shiers, James Lesly, and, and—I'm not sure about the last man."

"You are not sure about the last man. Will you swear to the three others?"

"Yes."

"You remember them well?"

"I was in the chain-gang at Macquarie Harbour with them for three years." Sylvia, hearing this hideous reason for acquaintance, gave a low cry, and fell into her father's arms.

"Oh, papa, take me away! I feel as if I was going to remember something terrible!"

Amid the deep silence that prevailed, the cry of the poor girl was distinctly audible in the Court, and all heads turned to the door. In the general wonder no one noticed the change that passed over Rufus Dawes. His face flushed scarlet, great drops of sweat stood on his forehead, and his black eyes glared in the direction from whence the sound came, as though they would pierce the envious wood that separated him from the woman whose voice he had heard. Maurice Frere sprang up and pushed his way through the crowd under the bench.

"What's this?" he said to Vickers, almost brutally. "What did you bring her here for? She is not wanted. I told you that."

"I considered it my duty, sir," says Vickers, with stately rebuke.

"What has frightened her? What has she heard? What has she seen?" asked Frere, with a strangely white face. "Sylvia, Sylvia!"

She opened her eyes at the sound of his voice. "Take me home, papa; I'm ill. Oh, what thoughts!"

"What does she mean?" cried Frere, looking in alarm from one to the other.

"That ruffian Dawes frightened her," said Meekin. "A gush of recollection, poor child. There, there, calm yourself, Miss Vickers. He is quite safe."

"Frightened her, eh?"

"Yes," said Sylvia faintly, "he frightened me, Maurice. I needn't stop any longer, dear, need I?"

"No," says Frere, the cloud passing from his face. "Major, I beg your pardon, but I was hasty. Take her home at once. This sort of thing is too much for her." And so he went back to his place, wiping his brow, and breathing hard, as one who had just escaped from some near peril.

Rufus Dawes had remained in the same attitude until the figure of Frere, passing through the doorway, roused him. "Who is she?" he said, in a low, hoarse voice, to the constable behind him.

"Miss Vickers," said the man shortly, flinging the information at him as one might fling a bone to a dangerous dog.

"Miss Vickers," repeated the convict, still staring in a sort of bewildered agony. "They told me she was dead!"

The constable sniffed contemptuously at this preposterous conclusion, as who should say, "If you know all about it, animal, why did you ask?" and then, feeling that the fixed gaze of his inter-rogator demanded some reply, added, "You thort she was, I've no doubt. You did your best to make her so, I've heard."

The convict raised both his hands with sudden action of wrathful despair, as though he would seize the other, despite the loaded muskets; but, checking himself with sudden impulse, wheeled round to the Court. "Your Honour!—Gentlemen! I want to speak."

The change in the tone of his voice, no less than the sudden loudness of the exclamation, made the faces, hitherto bent upon the door through which Mr. Frere had passed, turn round again. To many there it seemed that the "notorious Dawes" was no longer in the box, for, in place of the upright and defiant villain who stood there an instant back, was a white-faced, nervous, agitated creature, bending forward in an attitude almost of supplication, one hand grasping the rail, as though to save himself from falling, the other outstretched towards the bench. "Your Honour, there has been some dreadful mistake made. I want to explain about myself. I explained before, when first I was sent to Port Arthur, but the letters were never forwarded by the Commandant; of course, that's the rule, and I can't complain. I've been sent there unjustly, your Honour. *I* made that boat, your Honour. *I* saved the Major's wife and daughter. *I* was the man; I did it all myself, and my liberty was sworn away by a villain who hated me. I thought, until now, that no one knew the truth, for they told me that she was dead." His rapid utterance took the Court so much by surprise that no one interrupted him. "I was sentenced to death for bolting, sir, and they reprieved me because I helped them in the boat. Helped them! Why, I *made* it! She will tell you so. I nursed her! I carried her in my arms! I starved myself for her! She was fond of me, sir. She was indeed. She called me 'Good Mr. Dawes'."

At this, a coarse laugh broke out, which was instantly checked. The judge bent over to ask, "Does he mean Miss Vickers?" and in this interval Rufus Dawes, looking down into the Court, saw Maurice Frere staring up at him with terror in his eyes. "I see you, Captain Frere, coward and liar! Put him in the box, gentlemen, and make him tell his story. *She'll* contradict him, never fear. Oh, and I thought she was dead all this while!"

The judge had got his answer from the clerk by this time. "Miss Vickers had been seriously ill, had fainted just now in the Court. Her only memories of the convict who had been with her in the boat were those of terror and disgust. The sight of him just now had most seriously affected her. The convict himself was an inveterate liar and schemer, and his story had been already disproved by Captain Frere."

The judge, a man inclining by nature to humanity, but forced by experience to receive all statements of prisoners with caution, said all he could say, and the tragedy of five years was disposed of in the following dialogue:—

JUDGE: This is not the place for an accusation against Captain Frere, nor the place to argue upon your alleged wrongs. If you have suffered injustice, the authorities will hear your complaint, and redress it.

RUFUS DAWES: I have complained, your Honour. I wrote letter after letter to the Government, but they were never sent. Then

I heard she was dead, and they sent me to the Coal Mines after that, and we never hear anything there.

JUDGE: I can't listen to you. Mr. Mangles, have you any more questions to ask the witness?

But Mr. Mangles not having any more, someone called, "Matthew Gabbett," and Rufus Dawes, still endeavouring to speak, was clanked away with, amid a buzz of remark and surmise.

*

The trial progressed without further incident. Sylvia was not called, and, to the astonishment of many of his enemies, Captain Frere went into the witness-box and generously spoke in favour of John Rex. "He might have left us to starve," Frere said; "he might have murdered us; we were completely in his power. The stock of provisions on board the brig was not a large one, and I consider that, in dividing it with us, he showed great generosity for one in his situation." This piece of evidence told strongly in favour of the prisoners, for Captain Frere was known to be such an uncompromising foe to all rebellious convicts that it was understood that only the sternest sense of justice and truth could lead him to speak in such terms. The defence set up by Rex, moreover, was most ingenious. He was guilty of absconding, but his moderation might plead an excuse for that. His only object was his freedom, and, having gained it, he had lived honestly for nearly three years, as he could prove. He was charged with piratically seizing the brig *Osprey*, and he urged that the brig *Osprey*, having been built by convicts at Macquarie Harbour, and never entered in any shipping list, could not be said to be "piratically seized", in the strict meaning of the term. The Court admitted the force of this objection, and, influenced doubtless by Captain Frere's evidence, the fact that five years had passed since the mutiny, and that the two men most guilty (Cheshire and Barker) had been executed in England, sentenced Rex and his three companions to transportation for life to the penal settlements of the colony.

CHAPTER V

MAURICE FRERE'S GOOD ANGEL

AT this happy conclusion to his labours, Frere went down to comfort the girl for whose sake he had suffered Rex to escape the gallows. On his way he was met by a man who touched his hat, and asked to speak with him an instant. This man was past middle age, owned a red brandy-beaten face, and had in his gait and manner that nameless something that denotes the seaman.

"Well, Blunt," says Frere, pausing with the impatient air of a man who expects to hear bad news, "what is it now?"

"Only to tell you that it is all right, sir," says Blunt. "She's come aboard again this morning."

"Come aboard again!" ejaculated Frere. "Why, I didn't know that she had been ashore. Where did she go?" He spoke with an air of confident authority, and Blunt—no longer the bluff tyrant of old—seemed to quail before him. The trial of the mutineers of the *Malabar* had ruined Phineas Blunt. Make what excuses he might, there was no concealing the fact that Pine found him drunk in his cabin when he ought to have been attending to his duties on deck, and the "authorities" could not, or would not, pass over such a heinous breach of discipline. Captain Blunt—who, of course, had his own version of the story—thus deprived of the honour of bringing His Majesty's prisoners to His Majesty's colonies of New South Wales and Van Diemen's Land, went on a whaling cruise to the South Seas. The influence which Sarah Purfoy had acquired over him had, however, irretrievably injured him. It was as though she had poisoned his moral nature by the influence of a clever and wicked woman over a sensual and dull-witted man. Blunt gradually sank lower and lower. He became a drunkard, and was known as a man with a "grievance against the Government". Captain Frere, having had occasion for him in some capacity, had become in a manner his patron, and had got him the command of a schooner trading from Sydney. On getting this command—not without some wry faces on the part of the owner resident in Hobart Town—Blunt had taken the temperance pledge for the space of twelve months, and was a miserable dog in consequence. He was, however, a faithful henchman, for he hoped by Frere's means to get some "Government billet"—the grand object of all colonial sea captains of that epoch.

"Well, sir, she went ashore to see a friend," says Blunt, looking at the sky and then at the earth.

"What friend?"

"The—the prisoner, sir."

"And she saw him, I suppose?"

"Yes, but I thought I'd better tell you, sir," says Blunt.

"Of course; quite right," returned the other; "you had better start at once. It's no use waiting."

"As you wish, sir. I can sail to-morrow morning—or this evening, if you like."

"This evening," says Frere, turning away; "as soon as possible."

"There's a situation in Sydney I've been looking after," said the other, uneasily, "if you could help me to it."

"What is it?"

"The command of one of the Government vessels, sir."

"Well, keep sober, then," says Frere, "and I'll see what I can do. And keep that woman's tongue still if you can."

The pair looked at each other, and Blunt grinned slavishly.

"I'll do my best."

"Take care you do," returned his patron, leaving him without further ceremony.

Frere found Vickers in the garden, and at once begged him not to talk about the "business" to his daughter.

"You saw how bad she was to-day, Vickers. For goodness sake don't make her ill again."

"My dear sir," says poor Vickers, "*I* won't refer to the subject. She's been very unwell ever since. Nervous and unstrung. Go in and see her."

So Frere went in and soothed the excited girl, with real sorrow at her suffering.

"It's all right now, Poppet," he said to her. "Don't think of it any more. Put it out of your mind, dear."

"It was foolish of me, Maurice, I know, but I could not help it. The sound of—of—that man's voice seemed to bring back to me some great pity for something or someone. I don't explain what I mean, I know, but I felt that I was on the verge of remembering a story of some great wrong, just about to hear some dreadful revelation that should make me turn from all the people whom I ought most to love. Do you understand?"

"I think I know what you mean," says Frere, with averted face. "But that's all nonsense, you know."

"Of course," returned she, with a touch of her old childish manner of disposing of questions out of hand. "Everybody knows it's all nonsense. But then we *do* think such things. It seems to me that I am double, that I have lived somewhere before, and have had another life—a dream-life."

"What a romantic girl you are," said the other, dimly comprehending her meaning. "How could you have a dream-life?"

"Of course, not really, stupid! But in thought, you know. I dream such strange things now and then. I am always falling down precipices and into cataracts, and being pushed into great caverns in enormous rocks. Horrible dreams!"

"Indigestion," returned Frere. "You don't take exercise enough. You shouldn't read so much. Have a good five-mile walk."

"And in these dreams," continued Sylvia, not heeding his interruption, "there is one strange thing. You are always there, Maurice."

"Come, that's all right," says Maurice.

"Ah, but not kind and good as you *are*, Captain Bruin, but scowling, and threatening, and angry, so that I am afraid of you."

"But that is only a dream, darling."

"Yes, but—" playing with the button of his coat.

"But what?"

"But you looked just so to-day in the Court, Maurice, and I think that's what made me so silly."

"My darling! There; hush—don't cry!"

But she had burst into a passion of sobs and tears, that shook her slight figure in his arms.

"Oh, Maurice, I am a wicked girl! I don't know my own mind.

I think sometimes I don't love you as I ought—you who have saved me and nursed me."

"There, never mind about that," muttered Maurice Frere, with a sort of choking in his throat.

She grew more composed presently, and said, after a while, lifting her face, "Tell me, Maurice, did you ever, in those days of which you have spoken to me—when you nursed me as a little child in your arms, and fed me, and starved for me—did you ever think we should be married?"

"I don't know," says Maurice. "Why?"

"I think you must have thought so, because—it's not vanity, dear—you would not else have been so kind, and gentle, and devoted."

"Nonsense, Poppet," he said, with his eyes resolutely averted.

"No, but you have been, and I am very pettish, sometimes. Papa has spoiled me. You are always affectionate, and those worrying ways of yours, which I get angry at, all come from love for me, don't they?"

"I hope so," said Maurice, with an unwonted moisture in his eyes.

"Well, you see, that is the reason why I am angry with myself for not loving you as I ought. I want you to like the things I like, and to love the books and the music and the pictures and the—the World *I* love; and I forget that you are a man, you know, and I am only a girl; and I forget how nobly you behaved, Maurice, and how unselfishly you risked your life for mine. Why, what is the matter, dear?"

He had put her away from him suddenly, and gone to the window, gazing across the sloping garden at the bay below, sleeping in the soft evening light. The schooner which had brought the witnesses from Port Arthur lay off the shore, and the yellow flag at her mast fluttered gently in the cool evening breeze. The sight of this flag appeared to anger him, for, as his eyes fell on it, he uttered an impatient exclamation, and turned round again.

"Maurice!" she cried, "I have wounded you!"

"No, no. It is nothing," said he, with the air of a man surprised in a moment of weakness. "I—I did not like to hear you talk in this way—about not loving me."

"Oh, forgive me, dear; I did not mean to hurt you. It is my silly way of saying more than I mean. How could I do otherwise than love you—after all you have done?"

Some sudden desperate whim caused him to exclaim, "But suppose I had not done all you think, would you not love me still?"

Her eyes, raised to his face with anxious tenderness for the pain she had believed herself to have inflicted, fell at this speech.

"What a question! I don't know. I suppose I should; yet—but what is the use, Maurice, of *supposing*? I know you *have* done it, and that is enough. How can I say what I might have done if something else had happened? Why, you might not have loved *me*."

If there had been for a moment any sentiment of remorse in his selfish heart, the hesitation of her answer went far to dispel it.

"To be sure, that's true," and he placed his arm round her.

She lifted her face again with a bright laugh.

"We are a pair of geese—supposing! How can we help what has past? We have the Future, darling—the Future, in which I am to be your little wife, and we are to love each other all our lives, like the people in the story-books."

Temptation to evil had often come to Maurice Frere, and his selfish nature had succumbed to it when in far less witching shape than this fair and innocent child luring him with wistful eyes to win her. What hopes had he not built upon her love; what good resolutions had he not made by reason of the purity and goodness she was to bring to him? As she said, the past was beyond recall; the future—in which she was to love him all her life—was before them With the hypocrisy of selfishness which deceives even itself, he laid the little head upon his heart with a sensible glow of virtue.

"God bless you, darling! You are my Good Angel."

The girl sighed. "I *will* be your Good Angel, dear, if you will let me."

CHAPTER VI

MR. MEEKIN ADMINISTERS CONSOLATION

REX told Mr. Meekin, who, the next day, did him the honour to visit him, that, "under Providence, he owed his escape from death to the kind manner in which Captain Frere had spoken of him."

"I hope your escape will be a warning to you, my man," said Mr. Meekin, "and that you will endeavour to make the rest of your life, thus spared by the mercy of Providence, an atonement for your early errors."

"Indeed I will, sir," said John Rex, who had taken Mr. Meekin's measure very accurately, "and it is very kind of you to condescend to speak so to a wretch like me."

"Not at all," said Meekin, with affability; "it is my duty. I am a Minister of the Gospel."

"Ah! sir, I wish I had attended to the Gospel's teachings when I was younger. I might have been saved from all this."

"You might, indeed, poor man; but the Divine Mercy is infinite —quite infinite, and will be extended to all of us—to you as well as to me." (This with the air of saying, "What do you think of *that*!") "Remember the penitent thief, Rex—the—penitent thief."

"Indeed I do, sir."

"And read your Bible, Rex, and pray for strength to bear your punishment."

"I will, Mr. Meekin. I need it sorely, sir—physical as well as spiritual strength, sir—for the Government allowance is sadly insufficient."

"I will speak to the authorities about a change in your dietary scale," returned Meekin, patronizingly. "In the meantime, just collect together in your mind those particulars of your adventures of which you spoke, and have them ready for me when next I call. Such a remarkable history ought not to be lost."

"Thank you kindly, sir. I will, sir. Ah! I little thought when I occupied the position of a gentleman, Mr. Meekin"—the cunning scoundrel had been piously grandiloquent concerning his past career—"that I should be reduced to this. But it is only just, sir."

"The mysterious workings of Providence are always just, Rex," returned Meekin, who preferred to speak of the Almighty with well-bred vagueness.

"I am glad to see you so conscious of your errors. Good morning."

"Good morning, and Heaven bless you, sir," said Rex, with his tongue in his cheek for the benefit of his yard mates; and so Mr. Meekin tripped gracefully away, convinced that he was labouring most successfully in the Vineyard, and that the convict Rex was really a superior person.

"I will send his narrative to the Bishop," said he to himself. "It will amuse him. There must be many strange histories here, if one could but find them out."

As the thought passed through his brain, his eye fell upon the "notorious Dawes", who, while waiting for the schooner to take him back to Port Arthur, had been permitted to amuse himself by breaking stones. The prison-shed which Mr. Meekin was visiting was long and low, roofed with iron, and terminating at each end in the stone wall of the gaol. At one side rose the cells, at the other the outer wall of the prison. From the outer wall projected a weather-board under-roof, and beneath this were seated forty heavily-ironed convicts. Two constables, with loaded carbines, walked up and down the clear space in the middle, and another watched from a sort of sentry-box built against the main wall. Every half-hour a third constable went down the line and examined the irons. The admirable system of solitary confinement—which in average cases produces insanity in the space of twelve months—was as yet unknown in Hobart Town, and the forty heavily-ironed men had the pleasure of seeing each other's faces every day for six hours.

The other inmates of the prison were at work on the roads, or otherwise bestowed in the day time, but the forty were judged too desperate to be let loose. They sat, three feet apart, in two long lines, each man with a heap of stones between his outstretched legs, and cracked the pebbles in leisurely fashion. The double row of dismal woodpeckers tapping at this terribly hollow beech-tree of penal discipline had a semi-ludicrous appearance.

It seemed so painfully absurd that forty muscular men should be ironed and guarded for no better purpose than the cracking of a cartload of quartz-pebbles. In the meantime the air was heavy with angry glances shot from one to the other, and the passage of the parson was hailed by a grumbling undertone of blasphemy. It was considered fashionable to grunt when the hammer came in contact with the stone, and under cover of this mock exclamation of fatigue, it was convenient to launch an oath. A fanciful visitor, seeing the irregularly rising hammers along the line, might have likened the shed to the interior of some vast piano, whose notes an unseen hand was erratically fingering. Rufus Dawes was seated last on the line—his back to the cells, his face to the gaol wall. This was the place nearest the watching constable, and was allotted on that account to the most ill-favoured. Some of his companions envied him that melancholy distinction.

"Well, Dawes," says Mr. Meekin, measuring with his eye the distance between the prisoner and himself, as one might measure the chain of some ferocious dog. "How are you this morning, Dawes?"

Dawes, scowling in a parenthesis between the cracking of two stones, was understood to say that he was very well.

"I am afraid, Dawes," said Mr. Meekin reproachfully, "that you have done yourself no good by your outburst in court on Monday. I understand that public opinion is quite incensed against you."

Dawes, slowly arranging one large fragment of bluestone in a comfortable basin of smaller fragments, made no reply.

"I am afraid you lack patience, Dawes. You do not repent of your offences against the law, I fear."

The only answer vouchsafed by the ironed man—if answer it could be called—was a savage blow, which split the stone into sudden fragments, and made the clergyman skip a step backward.

"You are a hardened ruffian, sir! Do you not hear me speak to you?"

"I hear you," said Dawes, picking up another stone.

"Then listen respectfully, sir," said Meekin, roseate with celestial anger. "You have all day to break those stones."

"Yes, I have all day," returned Rufus Dawes, with a dogged

look upward, "and all next day, for that matter. Ugh!" and again the hammer descended.

"I came to console you, man—to console you," says Meekin, indignant at the contempt with which his well-meant overtures had been received. "I wanted to give you some good advice!"

The self-important annoyance of the tone seemed to appeal to whatever vestige of appreciation for the humorous, chains and degradation had suffered to linger in the convict's brain, for a faint smile crossed his features.

"I beg your pardon, sir," he said. "Pray, go on."

"I was going to say, my good fellow, that you have done yourself a great deal of injury by your ill-advised accusation of Captain Frere, and the use you made of Miss Vickers's name."

A frown, as of pain, contracted the prisoner's brows, and he seemed with difficulty to put a restraint upon his speech. "Is there to be no inquiry, Mr. Meekin?" he asked, at length. "What I stated was the truth—the truth, so help me God!"

"No blasphemy, sir," said Meekin, solemnly. "No blasphemy, wretched man. Do not add to the sin of lying the greater sin of taking the name of the Lord thy God in vain. He will not hold him guiltless, Dawes. He will not hold him guiltless, remember. No, there is to be no inquiry."

"Are they not going to ask her for her story?" asked Dawes, with a pitiful change of manner. "They told me that she was to be asked. Surely they will ask her."

"I am not, perhaps, at liberty," said Meekin, placidly unconscious of the agony of despair and rage that made the voice of the strong man before him quiver, "to state the intentions of the authorities, but I can tell you that Miss Vickers will not be asked anything about you. You are to go back to Port Arthur on the 24th, and to remain there."

A groan burst from Rufus Dawes; a groan so full of torture that even the comfortable Meekin was thrilled by it.

"It is the Law, you know, my good man. I can't help it," he said. "You shouldn't break the Law, you know."

"Curse the Law!" cries Dawes. "It's a Bloody Law; it's—there,

I beg your pardon," and he fell to cracking his stones again, with a laugh that was more terrible in its bitter hopelessness of winning attention or sympathy, than any outburst of passion could have been.

"Come," says Meekin, feeling uneasily constrained to bring forth some of his London-learnt platitudes. "You can't complain. You have broken the Law, and you must suffer. Civilized Society says you sha'n't do certain things, and if you do them you must suffer the penalty Civilized Society imposes. You are not wanting in intelligence, Dawes, more's the pity—and you can't deny the justice of that."

Rufus Dawes, as if disdaining to answer in words, cast his eyes round the yard with a glance that seemed to ask grimly if Civilized Society was progressing quite in accordance with justice, when its civilization created such places as that stone-walled, carbine-guarded prison-shed, and filled it with such creatures as those forty human beasts, doomed to spend the best years of their manhood cracking pebbles in it.

"You don't deny that?" asked the smug parson, "do you, Dawes?"

"It's not my place to argue with you, sir," said Dawes, in a tone of indifference, born of lengthened suffering, so nicely balanced between contempt and respect, that the inexperienced Meekin could not tell whether he had made a convert or subjected himself to an impertinence; "but I'm a prisoner for life, and don't look at it in the same way that you do."

This view of the question did not seem to have occurred to Mr. Meekin, for his mild cheek flushed. Certainly, the fact of being a prisoner for life did make some difference. The sound of the noonday bell, however, warned him to cease argument, and to take his consolations out of the way of the mustering prisoners.

With a great clanking and clashing of irons, the forty rose and stood each by his stone-heap. The third constable came round, rapping the leg-irons of each man with easy nonchalance, and roughly pulling up the coarse trousers (made with buttoned flaps at the sides, like Mexican *calzoneros,* in order to give free play to the ankle fetters), so that he might assure himself that no tricks had been played since his last visit. As each man passed this ordeal he saluted, and clanked, with wide-spread legs, to the place in the double line. Mr. Meekin, though not a patron of field sports, found something in the scene that reminded him of a blacksmith picking up horses' feet to examine the soundness of their shoes.

"Upon my word," he said to himself, with a momentary pang of genuine compassion, "it *is* a dreadful way to treat human beings. I don't wonder at that wretched creature groaning under it. But, bless me, it is near one o'clock, and I promised to lunch with Major Vickers at two. How time flies, to be sure!"

CHAPTER VII

RUFUS DAWES'S IDYLL

THAT afternoon, while Mr. Meekin was digesting his lunch, and chatting airily with Sylvia, Rufus Dawes began to brood over a desperate scheme. The intelligence that the investigation he had hoped for was not to be granted to him had rendered doubly bitter those galling fetters of self restraint which he had laid upon himself. For five years of desolation he had waited and hoped for a chance which might bring him to Hobart Town, and enable him to denounce the treachery of Maurice Frere. He had, by an almost miraculous accident, obtained that chance of open speech, and, having obtained it, he found that he was not allowed to speak. All the hopes he had formed were dashed to earth. All the calmness with which he had forced himself to bear his fate was now turned into bitterest rage and fury. Instead of one enemy he had twenty. All—judge, jury, gaoler, and parson—were banded together to work him evil and deny him right. The whole world was his foe: there was no honesty or truth in any living creature—save one.

During the dull misery of his convict life at Port Arthur one bright memory shone upon him like a star. In the depth of his degradation, at the height of his despair, he cherished one pure and ennobling thought—the thought of the child whom he had saved, and who loved him. When, on board the whaler that had rescued him from the burning boat, he had felt that the sailors, believing in Frere's bluff lies, shrunk from the moody felon, he had gained strength to be silent by thinking of the suffering child. When poor Mrs. Vickers died, making no sign, and thus the chief witness to his heroism perished before his eyes, the thought that the child was left had restrained his selfish regrets. When Frere, handing him over to the authorities as an absconder, ingeniously twisted the details of the boat-building to his own glorification, the knowledge that Sylvia would assign to these pretensions their true value had given him courage to keep silence. So strong was his belief in her gratitude, that he scorned to *beg* for the pardon he had taught himself to believe that she would ask for him. So utter was his contempt for the coward and boaster who, dressed in brief authority, bore insidious false witness against him, that, when he heard his sentence of life banishment, he disdained to make known the true part he had played in the matter, preferring to wait for the more exquisite revenge, the more complete justification which would follow upon the recovery of the child from her illness. But when, at Port Arthur, day after day passed over, and brought no word of pity or justification, he began, with a sickening feeling of despair, to comprehend that something strange had happened. He was told by newcomers that the child of the Commandant lay still and near to death. Then he heard that she and her father had left the colony, and that all prospect of her righting him by her evidence was at an end. This news gave him a terrible pang; and at first he was inclined to break out into upbraidings of her selfishness. But, with that depth of love which was in him, albeit crusted over and concealed by the sullenness of speech and manner which his sufferings had produced, he found excuses for her even then. She was ill. She was in the hands of friends who loved *her*, and disregarded *him*; perhaps, even her entreaties and explanations were put aside as childish babblings. She would free him if she had the power. Then he wrote "Statements", agonized to see the Commandant, pestered the gaolers and warders with the story of his wrongs, and inundated the Government with letters, which, containing, as they did always, denunciations of Maurice Frere, were never suffered to reach their destination. The authorities, willing at the first to look kindly upon him in consideration of his strange experience, grew weary of this perpetual iteration of what they believed to be malicious falsehoods, and ordered him heavier tasks and more continuous labour. They mistook his gloom for treachery, his impatient outbursts of passion at his fate for ferocity, his silent endurance for dangerous cunning. As he had been at Macquarie Harbour, so did he become at Port Arthur—a marked man. Despairing of winning his coveted liberty by fair means, and horrified at the hideous prospect of a life in chains, he twice attempted to escape, but escape was even more hopeless than it had been at Hell's Gates. The peninsula of Port Arthur was admirably guarded, signal stations drew a chain round the prison, an armed boat's crew watched each bay, and across the narrow isthmus which connected it with the mainland was a cordon of watch-dogs, in addition to the soldier guard. He was retaken, of course, flogged, and weighted with heavier irons. The second time, they sent him to the Coal Mines, where the prisoners lived underground, worked half-naked, and dragged their inspecting gaolers in wagons upon iron tramways, when such great people condescended to visit them. The day on which he started for this place he heard that Sylvia was dead, and his last hope went from him.

Then began with him a new religion. He worshipped the dead. For the living, he had but hatred and evil words; for the dead, he had love and tender thoughts. Instead of the phantoms of his vanished youth which were wont to visit him, he saw now but one vision—the vision of the child who had loved him. Instead of conjuring up for himself pictures of that home circle in which he had once moved, and those creatures who in the past years had thought him worthy of esteem and affection, he placed before himself but one idea, one embodiment of happiness, one being who was without sin and without stain, among all the monsters of that pit into which he had fallen. Around the figure of the innocent child who had lain in his breast, and laughed at him with her red young mouth, he grouped every image of happiness and love. Having banished from his thoughts all hope of resuming his name and place, he pictured to himself some quiet nook at the world's end—a deep-gardened house in a German country town, or remote cottage by the English seashore, where he and his dream-child might have lived together, happier in a purer affection than the love of man for woman. He bethought him how he could have taught her out of the strange store of learning which his roving life had won for him, how he could have confided to her his real name, and perhaps purchased for her wealth and honour by reason of it. Yet, he thought, she would not care for wealth and honour; she would prefer a quiet life—a life of unassuming usefulness, a life devoted to good deeds, to charity and love. He could see her—in his visions—reading by a cheery fireside, wandering in summer woods, or lingering by the marge of the slumbering mid-day sea. He could feel—in his dreams—her soft arms about his neck, her innocent kisses on his lips; he could hear her light laugh, and see her sunny ringlets float, back-blown, as she ran to meet him. Conscious that she was dead, and that he did to her gentle memory no disrespect by linking her fortunes to those of a wretch who had seen so much of evil as himself, he loved to think of her as still living, and to plot out for her and for himself impossible plans for future happiness. In the noisome darkness of the mine, in the glaring light of the noonday—dragging at his loaded wagon, he could see her ever with him, her calm eyes gazing lovingly on his, as they had gazed in the boat so long ago. She never seemed to grow older, she never seemed to wish to leave him. It was only when his misery became too great for him to bear, and he cursed and blasphemed, mingling for a time in the hideous mirth of his companions, that the little figure fled away. Thus dreaming, he had shaped out for himself a sorrowful comfort, and in his dream-world found a compensation for the terrible affliction of living. Indifference to his present suffer-ings took possession of him; only at the bottom of this indifference lurked a fixed hatred of the man who had brought these sufferings upon him, and a determination to demand at the first opportunity a reconsideration of that man's claims to be esteemed a hero. It was in this mood that he had intended to make the revelation which he had made in Court, but the intelligence that Sylvia lived unmanned him, and his prepared speech had been usurped by a passionate torrent of complaint and invective, which convinced no one, and gave Frere the very argument he needed. It was decided that the prisoner Dawes was a malicious and artful scoundrel, whose only object was to gain a brief respite of the punishment which he had so justly earned. Against this injustice he had resolved to rebel. It was monstrous, he thought, that they should refuse to hear the witness who was so ready to speak in his favour, infamous that they should send him back to his doom without allowing her to say a word in his defence. But he would defeat that scheme. He had planned a method of escape, and he would break from his bonds, fling himself at her feet, and pray her to speak the truth for him, and so save him. Strong in his faith in her, and with his love for her brightened by the love he had borne to her dream-image, he felt sure of her power to rescue him now, as he had rescued her before. "If she knew I was alive, she would come to me," he said. "I am sure she would. Perhaps they told her that I was dead."

Meditating that night in the solitude of his cell—his evil character had gained him the poor luxury of loneliness—he almost wept to think of the cruel deception that had doubtless been practised on her. "They have told her that I was dead, in order that she might learn to forget me; but she could not do that. I have thought of her so often during these weary years that she must sometimes have thought of me. Five years! She must be a woman now. My little child a woman! Yet she is sure to be childlike, sweet, and gentle. How she will grieve when she hears of my sufferings. Oh! my darling, my darling, you are not dead!" And then, looking hastily about him in the darkness, as though fearful even there of being seen, he pulled from out his breast a little packet, and felt it lovingly with his coarse, toil-worn fingers, reverently raising it to his lips, and dreaming over it, with a smile on his face, as though it were a sacred talisman that should open to him the doors of freedom.

A FEW days after this—on the 23rd of December—Maurice Frere was alarmed by a piece of startling intelligence. The notorious Dawes had escaped from gaol!

Captain Frere had inspected the prison that very afternoon, and it had seemed to him that the hammers had never fallen so briskly, nor the chains clanked so gaily, as on the occasion of his visit. "Thinking of their Christmas holiday, the dogs!" he had said to the patrolling warder. "Thinking about their Christmas pudding, the luxurious scoundrels!" and the convict nearest him had laughed appreciatively, as convicts and schoolboys do laugh at the jests of the man in authority. All seemed contentment. Moreover, he had—by way of a pleasant stroke of wit—tormented Rufus Dawes with his ill-fortune. "The schooner sails to-morrow, my man," he had said; "you'll spend *your* Christmas at the mines." And congratulated himself upon the fact that Rufus Dawes merely touched his cap, and went on with his stone-cracking in silence. Certainly double irons and hard labour were fine things to break a man's spirit. So that, when in the afternoon of that same day he heard the astounding news that Rufus Dawes had freed himself from his fetters, climbed the gaol wall in broad daylight, run the gauntlet of Macquarie Street, and was now supposed to be safely hidden in the mountains, he was dumbfounded.

"How the deuce did he do it, Jenkins?" he asked, as soon as he reached the yard.

"Well, I'm blessed if I rightly know, your honour," says Jenkins. "He was over the wall before you could say 'knife'. Scott fired and missed him, and then I heard the sentry's musket, but he missed him, too."

"Missed him!" cries Frere. "Pretty fellows you are, all of you! I suppose you couldn't hit a haystack at twenty yards? Why, the man wasn't three feet from the end of your carbine!"

The unlucky Scott, standing in melancholy attitude by the empty irons, muttered something about the sun having been in his eyes. "I don't know how it was, sir. I ought to have hit him, for certain. I think I did touch him, too, as he went up the wall."

A stranger to the customs of the place might have imagined that he was listening to a conversation about a pigeon match.

"Tell me all about it," says Frere, with an angry curse. "I was just turning, your honour, when I hears Scott sing out 'Hullo!' and when I turned round, I saw Dawes's irons on the ground, and him a-scrambling up the heap o' stones yonder. The two men on my right jumped up, and I thought it was a made-up thing among 'em, so I covered 'em with my carbine, according to instructions, and called out that I'd shoot the first that stepped out. Then I heard Scott's piece, and the men gave a shout like. When I looked round, he was gone."

"Nobody else moved?"

"No, sir. I was confused at first, and thought they were all in it, but Parton and Haines they runs in and gets between me and the wall, and then Mr. Short he come, and we examined their irons."

"All right?"

"All right, your honour; and they all swore they knowed nothing of it. I know Dawes's irons was all right when he went to dinner."

Frere stopped and examined the empty fetters. "All right be hanged," he said. "If you don't know your duty better than this, the sooner you go somewhere else the better, my man. Look here!"

The two ankle fetters were severed. One had been evidently filed through, and the other broken transversely. The latter was bent, as from a violent blow.

"Don't know where he got the file from," said Warder Short.

"Know! Of course you don't know. You men never do know anything until the mischiefs done. You want me here for a month or so. I'd teach you your duty! Don't know—with things like *this* lying about? I wonder the whole yard isn't loose and dining with the Governor."

"*This*" was a fragment of delft pottery which Frere's quick eye had detected among the broken metal.

"I'd cut the biggest iron you've got with this; and so would he and plenty more, I'll go bail. You ought to have lived with me at Sarah Island, Mr. Short. Don't know!"

"Well, Captain Frere, it's an accident," says Short, "and can't be helped now."

"An accident!" roared Frere. "What business have you with *accidents*? How, in the devil's name, you let the man get over the wall, I don't know."

"He ran up that stone heap," says Scott, "and seemed to me to jump at the roof of the shed. I fired at him, and he swung his legs over the top of the wall and dropped."

Frere measured the distance from his eye, and an irrepressible feeling of admiration, rising out of his own skill in athletics, took possession of him for an instant.

"By the Lord Harry, but it's a big jump!" he said; and then the instinctive fear with which the consciousness of the hideous wrong he had done the now escaped convict inspired him, made him add: "A desperate villain like that wouldn't stick at a murder if you pressed him hard. Which way did he go?"

"Right up Macquarie Street, and then made for the mountain. There were few people about, but Mr. Mays, of the Star Hotel, tried to stop him, and was knocked head over heels. He says the fellow runs like a deer."

"We'll have the reward out if we don't get him to-night," says Frere, turning away; "and you'd better put on an extra warder. This sort of game is catching." And he strode away to the Barracks.

From right to left, from east to west, through the prison city flew the signal of alarm, and the patrol, clattering out along the road to New Norfolk, made hot haste to strike the trail of the fugitive. But night came and found him yet at large, and the patrol returning, weary and disheartened, protested that he must be lying hid in some gorge of the purple mountain that overshadowed the town, and would have to be starved into submission. Meanwhile the usual message ran through the island, and so admirable were the arrangements which Arthur the reformer had initiated, that, before noon of the next day, not a signal station on the coast but knew that No. 8942, etc., etc., prisoner for life, was illegally at large. This intelligence, further aided by a paragraph in the *Gazette* anent the "Daring Escape", once noised abroad, the world cared little that the *Mary Jane*, Government schooner, had sailed for Port Arthur without Rufus Dawes.

But two or three persons cared a good deal. Major Vickers, for one, was indignant that his boasted security of bolts and bars should have been so easily defied, and in proportion to his indignation was the grief of Messieurs Jenkins, Scott, and Co., suspended from office, and threatened with absolute dismissal. Mr. Meekin was terribly frightened at the fact that so dangerous a monster should be roaming at large within reach of his own saintly person. Sylvia had shown symptoms of nervous terror, none the less injurious because carefully repressed; and Captain Maurice Frere was a prey to the most cruel anxiety. He had ridden off at a hand-gallop within ten minutes after he had reached the Barracks, and had spent the few hours of remaining daylight in scouring the country along the road to the North. At dawn the next day he was away to the mountain, and with a black-tracker at his heels, explored as much of that wilderness of gully and chasm as nature permitted to him. He had offered to double the reward, and had examined a number of suspicious persons. It was known that he had been inspecting the prison a few hours before the escape took place, and his efforts were therefore attributed to zeal, not unmixed with chagrin. "Our dear friend feels his reputation at stake," the future chaplain of Port Arthur said to Sylvia at the Christmas dinner. "He is so proud of his knowledge of these unhappy men that he dislikes to be outwitted by any of them."

Notwithstanding all this, however, Dawes had disappeared. The fat landlord of the Star Hotel was the last person who saw him, and the flying yellow figure seemed to have been as completely swallowed up by the warm summer's afternoon as if it had run headlong into the blackest night that ever hung above the earth.

CHAPTER IX

JOHN REX'S LETTER HOME

THE "little gathering" of which Major Vickers had spoken to Mr. Meekin, had grown into something larger than he had anticipated. Instead of a quiet dinner at which his own household, his daughter's betrothed, and the stranger clergyman only should be present, the Major found himself entangled with Mesdames Protherick and Jellicoe, Mr. McNab of the garrison, and Mr. Pounce of the civil list. His quiet Christmas dinner had grown into an evening party.

The conversation was on the usual topic.

"Heard anything about that fellow Dawes?" asked Mr. Pounce.

"Not yet," says Frere, sulkily, "but he won't be out long. I've got a dozen men up the mountain."

"I suppose it is not easy for a prisoner to make good his escape?" says Meekin.

"Oh, he needn't be caught," says Frere, "if that's what you mean; but he'll starve instead. The bushranging days are over now, and it's a precious poor look-out for any man to live upon luck in the bush."

"Indeed, yes," says Mr. Pounce, lapping his soup. "This island seems specially adapted by Providence for a convict settlement; for with an admirable climate, it carries little indigenous vegetation which will support human life."

"Wull," said McNab to Sylvia, "I don't think Prauvidence had any thocht o' caunveect deesiplin whun He created the cauleny o' Van Deemen's Lan'."

"Neither do I," said Sylvia.

"I don't know," says Mrs. Protherick. "Poor Protherick used say that it seemed as if some Almighty Hand had planned the Penal Settlements round the coast, the country is so delightfully barren."

"Ay, Port Arthur couldn't have been better if it had been made on purpose," says Frere; "and all up the coast from Tenby to St. Helen's there isn't a scrap for human being to make a meal on. The West Coast is worse. By George, sir, in the old days, I remember—"

"By the way," says Meekin, "I've got something to show you. Rex's confession. I brought it down on purpose."

"Rex's confession!"

"His account of his adventures after he left Macquarie Harbour. I am going to send it to the Bishop."

"Oh, I should like to see it," said Sylvia, with heightened colour. "The story of these unhappy men has a personal interest for me."

"A forbidden subject, Poppet."

"No, papa, not altogether forbidden; for it does not affect me now as it used to do. You must let me read it, Mr. Meekin."

"A pack of lies, I expect," said Frere, with a scowl. "That scoundrel Rex couldn't tell the truth to save his life."

"You misjudge him, Captain Frere," said Meekin. "All the prisoners are not hardened in iniquity like Rufus Dawes. Rex is, I believe, truly penitent, and has written a most touching letter to his father."

"A letter!" said Vickers. "You know that, by the King's—no, the Queen's Regulations, no letters are allowed to be sent to the friends of prisoners without first passing through the hands of the authorities."

"I am aware of that, Major, and for that reason have brought it with me, that you may read it for yourself. It seems to me to breathe a spirit of true piety."

"Let's have a look at it," said Frere.

"Here it is," returned Meekin, producing a packet; "and when the cloth is removed, I will ask permission of the ladies to read it aloud. It is most interesting."

A glance of surprise passed between the ladies Protherick and Jellicoe. The idea of a convict's letter proving interesting! Mr. Meekin was new to the ways of the place.

Frere, turning the packet between his finger, read the address:

John Rex, sen.,
Care of Mr. Blicks,
38, Bishopsgate Street Within,
London.

"Why can't he write to his father direct?" said he. "Who's Blick?"

"A worthy merchant, I am told, in whose counting-house the fortunate Rex passed his younger days. He had a tolerable education, as you are aware."

"Educated prisoners are always the worst," said Vickers. "James, some more wine. We don't drink toasts here, but as this is Christmas Eve, 'Her Majesty the Queen'!"

"Hear, hear, hear!" says Maurice. "'Her Majesty the Queen'!" Having drunk this loyal toast with due fervour, Vickers proposed, "His Excellency Sir John Franklin", which toast was likewise duly honoured.

"Here's a Merry Christmas and a Happy New Year to you, sir," said Frere, with the letter still in his hand. "God bless us all."

"Amen!" says Meekin piously. "Let us hope He will; and now, leddies, the letter. I will read you the Confession afterwards." Opening the packet with the satisfaction of a Gospel vineyard labourer who sees his first vine sprouting, the good creature began to read aloud:

"'Hobart Town,

"'December 27, 1838.

"'MY DEAR FATHER,—Through all the chances, changes, and vicissitudes of my chequered life, I never had a task so painful to my mangled feelings as the present one, of addressing you from this doleful spot—my sea-girt prison, on the beach of which I stand a monument of destruction, driven by the adverse winds of fate to the confines of black despair, and into the vortex of galling misery.'"

"Poetical!" said Frere.

"'I am just like a gigantic tree of the forest which has stood many a wintry blast, and stormy tempest, but now, alas! I am become a withered trunk, with all my greenest and tenderest branches lopped off. Though fast attaining middle age, I am not filling an envied and honoured post with credit and respect. No—I shall be soon wearing the garb of degradation, and the badge and brand of infamy at P.A., which is, being interpreted, Port Arthur, the 'Villain's Home'.'"

"Poor fellow!" said Sylvia.

"Touching, is it not?" assented Meekin, continuing—

"'I am, with heartrending sorrow and anguish of soul, ranged and mingled with the Outcasts of Society. My present circumstances and pictures you will find well and truly drawn in the 102nd Psalm, commencing with the 4th verse to the 12th inclusive, which, my dear father, I request you will read attentively before you proceed any further.'"

"Hullo!" said Frere, pulling out his pocket-book, "what's that? Read those numbers again."

Mr. Meekin complied, and Frere grinned.

"Go on," he said. "I'll show you something in that letter directly."

"'Oh, my dear father, avoid, I beg of you, the reading of profane books. Let your mind dwell upon holy things, and assiduously study to grow in grace. Psalm lxxiii 2. Yet I have hope even in this, my desolate condition. Psalm xxxv 18. "For the Lord our God is merciful, and inclineth His ear unto pity".'"

"Blasphemous dog!" said Vickers. "You don't believe all that, Meekin, do you?"

The parson reproved him gently. "Wait a moment, sir, until I have finished."

"'Party spirit runs very high, even in prison in Van Diemen's Land. I am sorry to say that a licentious press invariably evinces a very great degree of contumely, while the authorities are held in respect by all well-disposed persons, though it is often endeavoured by some to bring on them the hatred and contempt of prisoners. But I am glad to tell you that all their efforts are without avail; but, nevertheless, do not read in any colonial newspaper. There is so much scurrility and vituperation in their productions.'"

"That's for your benefit, Frere," said Vickers, with a smile. "You remember what was said about your presence at the race meetings?"

"Of course," said Frere. "Artful scoundrel! Go on, Mr. Meekin, pray."

> "'I am aware that you will hear accounts of cruelty and tyranny, said, by the malicious and the evil-minded haters of the Government and Government officials, to have been inflicted by gaolers on convicts. To be candid, this is not the dreadful place it has been represented to be by vindictive writers. Severe flogging and heavy chaining is sometimes used, no doubt, but only in rare cases; and nominal punishments are marked out by law for slight breaches of discipline. So far as I have an opportunity of judging, the lash is never bestowed unless merited.'"

"As far as he is concerned, I don't doubt it!" said Frere, cracking a walnut.

> "'The texts of Scripture quoted by our chaplain have comforted me much, and I have much to be grateful for; for after the rash attempt I made to secure my freedom, I have reason to be thankful for the mercy shown to me. Death—dreadful death of soul and body—would have been my portion; but, by the mercy of Omnipotence, I have been spared to repentance—John iii. I have now come to bitterness. The chaplain, a pious gentleman, says it never really pays to steal. "Lay up for yourselves treasures in Heaven, where neither moth nor rust doth corrupt." Honesty is the best policy, I am convinced, and I would not for £1,000 repeat my evil courses—Psalm xxxviii 14. When I think of the happy days I once passed with good Mr. Blicks, in the old house in Blue Anchor Yard, and reflect that since that happy time I have recklessly plunged in sin, and stolen goods and watches, studs, rings, and jewellery, become, indeed, a common thief, I tremble with remorse, and fly to prayer—Psalm v. Oh what sinners we are! Let me hope that now I, by God's blessing placed beyond temptation, will live safely, and that some day I even may, by the will of the Lord Jesus, find mercy for my sins. Some kind of madness has method in it, but madness of sin holds us without escape. Such is, dear father, then, my hope and trust for my remaining

life here—Psalm c 74. I owe my bodily well-being to Captain Maurice Frere, who was good enough to speak of my conduct in reference to the *Osprey*, when, with Shiers, Barker, and others, we captured that vessel. Pray for Captain Frere, my dear father. He is a good man, and though his public duty is painful and trying to his feelings, yet, as a public functionary, he could not allow his private feelings, whether of mercy or revenge, to step between him and his duty.'"

"Confound the rascal!" said Frere, growing crimson.

"'Remember me most affectionately to Sarah and little William, and all friends who yet cherish the recollection of me, and bid them take warning by my fate, and keep from evil courses. A good conscience is better than gold, and no amount can compensate for the misery incident to a return to crime. Whether I shall ever see you again, dear father, is more than uncertain; for my doom is life, unless the Government alter their plans concerning me, and allow me an opportunity to earn my freedom by hard work.

"'The blessing of God rest with you, my dear father, and that you may be washed white in the blood of the Lamb is the prayer of your

"'Unfortunate Son,
"'JOHN REX.
"'P.S.—Though your sins be as scarlet they shall be whiter than snow.'"

"Is that all?" said Frere.

"That is all, sir, and a very touching letter it is."

"So it is," said Frere. "Now let me have it a moment, Mr. Meekin."

He took the paper, and referring to the numbers of the texts which he had written in his pocket-book, began to knit his brows over Mr. John Rex's impious and hypocritical production. "I thought so," he said, at length. "Those texts were never written for nothing. It's an old trick, but cleverly done."

"What do you mean?" said Meekin.

"Mean!" cries Frere, with a smile at his own acuteness. "This precious composition contains a very gratifying piece of intelligence for Mr. Blicks, whoever he is. Some receiver, I've no doubt. Look here, Mr. Meekin. Take the letter and this pencil, and begin at the first text. The 102nd Psalm, from the 4th verse to the 12th inclusive, doesn't he say? Very good; that's nine verses, isn't it? Well, now, underscore nine consecutive words from the second word immediately following the next text quoted, 'I have hope,' etc. Have you got it?"

"Yes," says Meekin, astonished, while all heads bent over the table.

"Well, now, his text is the eighteenth verse of the thirty-fifth Psalm, isn't it? Count eighteen words on, then underscore five consecutive ones. You've done that?"

"A moment—sixteen—seventeen—eighteen, 'authorities'."

"Count and score in the same way until you come to the word 'Texts' somewhere. Vickers, I'll trouble you for the claret."

"Yes," said Meekin, after a pause. "Here it is—'the texts of Scripture quoted by our chaplain'. But surely Mr. Frere—"

"Hold on a bit now," cries Frere. "What's the next quotation?—John iii. That's every third word. Score every third word beginning with 'I' immediately following the text, now, until you come to a quotation. Got it? How many words in it?"

"'Lay up for yourselves treasures in Heaven, where neither moth nor rust doth corrupt'," said Meekin, a little scandalized. "Fourteen words."

"Count fourteen words on, then, and score the fourteenth. I'm up to this text-quoting business."

"The word '£1000'," said Meekin. "Yes."

"Then there's another text. Thirty-eighth—isn't it?—Psalm and the fourteenth verse. Do that the same way as the other—count fourteen words, and then score eight in succession. Where does that bring you?"

"The fifth Psalm."

"Every fifth word then. Go on, my dear sir—go on. 'Method' of 'escape', yes. The hundredth Psalm means a full stop. What verse? Seventy-four. Count seventy-four words and score."

There was a pause for a few minutes while Mr. Meekin counted. The letter had really turned out interesting.

"Read out your marked words now, Meekin. Let's see if I'm right." Mr. Meekin read with gradually crimsoning face:—

"'I have hope even in this my desolate condition...in prison Van Diemen's Land...the authorities are held in...hatred and contempt of prisoners...read in any colonial newspaper...accounts of cruelty and tyranny...inflicted by gaolers on convicts...severe flogging and heavy chaining...for slight breaches of discipline...I...come...the pious... it...pays...in the old house in Blue Anchor Yard...stolen goods and watches studs rings and jewellery...are...now...placed...safely...I... will...find...some...method of escape...then...for revenge.'"

"Well," said Maurice, looking round with a grin, "what do you think of that?"

"Most remarkable!" said Mr. Pounce.

"How did you find it out, Frere?"

"Oh, it's nothing," says Frere; meaning that it was a great deal. "I've studied a good many of these things, and this one is clumsy to some I've seen. But it's pious, isn't it, Meekin?"

Mr. Meekin arose in wrath.

"It's very ungracious on your part, Captain Frere. A capital joke, I have no doubt; but permit me to say I do not like jesting on such matters. This poor fellow's letter to his aged father to be made the subject of heartless merriment, I confess I do not understand. It was confided to me in my sacred character as a Christian pastor."

"That's just it. The fellows play upon the parsons, don't you know, and under cover of your 'sacred character' play all kinds of pranks. How the dog must have chuckled when he gave you that!"

"Captain Frere," said Mr. Meekin, changing colour like a chameleon with indignation and rage, "your interpretation is, I am convinced, an incorrect one. How could the poor man compose such an ingenious piece of cryptography?"

"If you mean, fake up that paper," returned Frere, unconsciously dropping into prison slang, "I'll tell you. He had a Bible, I suppose, while he was writing?"

"I certainly permitted him the use of the Sacred Volume, Captain

Frere. I should have judged it inconsistent with the character of my Office to have refused it to him."

"Of course. And that's just where you parsons are always putting your foot into it. If you'd put your 'Office' into your pocket and open your eyes a bit—"

"Maurice! My dear Maurice!"

"I beg your pardon, Meekin," says Maurice, with clumsy apology; "but I *know* these fellows. I've lived among 'em, I came out in a ship with 'em, I've talked with 'em, and drank with 'em, and I'm down to all their moves, don't you see. The Bible is the only book they get hold of, and texts are the only bits of learning ever taught'm, and being chockfull of villainy and plots and conspiracies, what other book should they make use of to aid their infernal schemes *but* the one that the chaplain has made a text book for 'em?" And Maurice rose in disgust, not unmixed with self-laudation.

"Dear me, it is really very terrible," says Meekin, who was not ill-meaning, but only self-complacent—"very terrible indeed."

"But unhappily true," said Mr. Pounce. "An olive? Thanks."

"Upon me soul!" burst out honest McNab, "the hail seestem seems to be maist ill-calculated tae advance the wark o' reeformation."

"Mr. McNab, I'll trouble you for the port," said equally honest Vickers, bound hand and foot in the chains of the rules of the services. And so, what seemed likely to become a dangerous discussion upon convict discipline, was stifled judiciously at the birth. But Sylvia, prompted, perhaps, by curiosity, perhaps by a desire to modify the parson's chagrin, in passing Mr. Meekin, took up the "confession," that lay unopened beside his wine glass, and bore it off.

"Come, Mr. Meekin," said Vickers, when the door closed behind the ladies, "help yourself. I am sorry the letter turned out so strangely, but you may rely on Frere, I assure you. He knows more about convicts than any man on the island."

"I see, Captain Frere, that you have studied the criminal classes."

"So I have, my dear sir, and know every turn and twist among 'em. I tell you my maxim. It's some French fellow's, too, I believe, but that don't matter—*divide to conquer*. Set all the dogs spying on each other."

"Oh!" said Meekin. "It's the only way. Why, my dear sir, if the prisoners were as faithful to each other as we are, we couldn't hold the island a week. It's just because no man can trust his neighbour that every mutiny falls to the ground."

"I suppose it must be so," said poor Meekin.

"It is so; and, by George, sir, if I had my way, I'd have it so that no prisoner should say a word to his right hand man, but his left hand man should tell me of it. I'd promote the men that peached, and make the beggars their own warders. Ha, ha!"

"But such a course, Captain Frere, though perhaps useful in a certain way, would surely produce harm. It would excite the worst passions of our fallen nature, and lead to endless lying and tyranny. I'm sure it would."

"Wait a bit," cries Frere. "Perhaps one of these days I'll get a chance, and then I'll try it. Convicts! By the Lord Harry, sir, there's only one way to treat 'em; give 'em tobacco when they behave 'emselves, and flog 'em when they don't."

"Terrible!" says the clergyman with a shudder. "You speak of them as if they were wild beasts."

"So they are," said Maurice Frere, calmly.

CHAPTER X

WHAT BECAME OF THE
MUTINEERS OF THE "OSPREY"

AT the bottom of the long luxuriant garden-ground was a rustic seat
abutting upon the low wall that topped the lane. The branches of
the English trees (planted long ago) hung above it, and between their
rustling boughs one could see the reach of the silver river. Sitting
with her face to the bay and her back to the house, Sylvia opened
the manuscript she had carried off from Meekin, and began to read.
It was written in a firm, large hand, and headed—

> "A NARRATIVE
> "OF THE SUFFERINGS AND ADVENTURES OF
> CERTAIN OF THE TEN CONVICTS WHO SEIZED THE
> BRIG *OSPREY*, AT MACQUARIE HARBOUR, IN VAN
> DIEMEN'S LAND, RELATED BY ONE OF THE SAID
> CONVICTS WHILE LYING UNDER SENTENCE FOR
> THIS OFFENCE IN THE GAOL AT HOBART TOWN."

Sylvia, having read this grandiloquent sentence, paused for a moment.
The story of the mutiny, which had been the chief event of her
childhood, lay before her, and it seemed to her that, were it related
truly, she would comprehend something strange and terrible, which
had been for many years a shadow upon her memory. Longing, and
yet fearing, to proceed, she held the paper, half unfolded, in her
hand, as, in her childhood, she had held ajar the door of some dark
room, into which she longed and yet feared to enter. Her timidity
lasted but an instant.

*

> "When orders arrived from head-quarters to break up the
> penal settlement of Macquarie Harbour, the Commandant
> (Major Vickers, —th Regiment) and most of the prisoners
> embarked on board a colonial vessel, and set sail for Hobart
> Town, leaving behind them a brig that had been built at

Macquarie Harbour, to be brought round after them, and placing Captain Maurice Frere in command. Left aboard her was Mr. Bates, who had acted as pilot at the settlement, also four soldiers, and ten prisoners, as a crew to work the vessel. The Commandant's wife and child were also aboard."

*

"How strangely it reads," thought the girl.

*

"On the 12th of January, 1834, we set sail, and in the afternoon anchored safely outside the Gates; but a breeze setting in from the north-west caused a swell on the Bar, and Mr. Bates ran back to Wellington Bay. We remained there all next day; and in the afternoon Captain Frere took two soldiers and a boat, and went a-fishing. There were then only Mr. Bates and the other two soldiers aboard, and it was proposed by William Cheshire to seize the vessel. I was at first unwilling, thinking that loss of life might ensue; but Cheshire and the others, knowing that I was acquainted with navigation—having in happier days lived much on the sea—threatened me if I refused to join. A song was started in the folksle, and one of the soldiers, coming to listen to it, was seized, and Lyon and Riley then made prisoner of the sentry. Forced thus into a project with which I had at first but little sympathy, I felt my heart leap at the prospect of freedom, and would have sacrificed all to obtain it. Maddened by the desperate hopes that inspired me, I from that moment assumed the command of my wretched companions; and honestly think that, however culpable I may have been in the eyes of the law, I prevented them from the display of a violence to which their savage life had unhappily made them but too accustomed."

*

"Poor fellow," said Sylvia, beguiled by Master Rex's specious paragraphs, "I think he was not to blame."

*

"Mr. Bates was below in the cabin, and on being summoned by Cheshire to surrender, with great courage attempted a defence. Barker fired at him through the skylight, but fearful of the lives of the Commandant's wife and child, I struck up his musket, and the ball passed through the mouldings of the stern windows. At the same time, the soldiers whom we had bound in the folksle forced up the hatch and came on deck. Cheshire shot the first one, and struck the other with his clubbed musket. The wounded man lost his footing, and the brig lurching with the rising tide, he fell into the sea. This was—by the blessing of God—the only life lost in the whole affair.

"Mr. Bates, seeing now that we had possession of the deck, surrendered, upon promise that the Commandant's wife and child should be put ashore in safety. I directed him to take such matters as he needed, and prepared to lower the jolly-boat. As she swung off the davits, Captain Frere came alongside in the whale-boat, and gallantly endeavoured to board us, but the boat drifted past the vessel. I was now determined to be free—indeed, the minds of all on board were made up to carry through the business—and hailing the whale-boat, swore to fire into her unless she surrendered. Captain Frere refused, and was for boarding us again, but the two soldiers joined with us, and prevented his intention. Having now got the prisoners into the jolly-boat, we transferred Captain Frere into her, and being ourselves in the whale-boat, compelled Captain Frere and Mr. Bates to row ashore. We then took the jolly-boat in tow, and returned to the brig, a strict watch being kept for fear that they should rescue the vessel from us.

"At break of day every man was upon deck, and a consultation took place concerning the parting of the provisions. Cheshire was for leaving them to starve, but Lesly, Shiers, and I held out for an equal division. After a long and violent controversy, Humanity gained the day, and the provisions were put into the whale-boat, and taken ashore. Upon the receipt of the provisions, Mr. Bates thus expressed himself: 'Men, I did not for one moment expect such kind treatment from you, regarding the provisions you have now brought ashore for us, out of so little which there was on board. When I consider your present undertaking, without a competent navigator, and in a leaky vessel, your situation seems most perilous; therefore I hope God will prove kind to you, and preserve you from the manifold dangers you may have to encounter on the stormy ocean.' Mrs. Vickers also was pleased to say that I had behaved kindly to her, that she wished me well, and that when she returned to Hobart Town she would speak in my favour. They then cheered us on our departure, wishing we might be prosperous on account of our humanity in sharing the provisions with them.

"Having had breakfast, we commenced throwing overboard the light cargo which was in the hold, which employed us until dinnertime. After dinner we ran out a small kedge-anchor with about one hundred fathoms of line, and having weighed anchor, and the tide being slack, we hauled on the kedge-line, and succeeded in this manner by kedging along, and we came to two islands, called the Cap and Bonnet. The whole of us then commenced heaving the brig short, sending the whale-boat to take her in tow, after we had tripped the anchor. By this means we got her safe across the Bar. Scarcely was this done when a light breeze sprang up from the south-west, and firing a musket to apprize the party we had left of our safety, we made sail and put out to sea."

Having read thus far, Sylvia paused in an agony of recollection. She remembered the firing of the musket, and that her mother had wept over her. But beyond this all was uncertainty. Memories slipped across her mind like shadows—she caught at them, and they were gone. Yet the reading of this strange story made her nerves thrill. Despite the hypocritical grandiloquence and affected piety of the narrative, it was easy to see that, save some warping of facts to make for himself a better case, and to extol the courage of the gaolers who had him at their mercy, the narrator had not attempted to better his tale by the invention of perils. The history of the desperate project that had been planned and carried out five years before was related with grim simplicity which (because it at once bears the stamp of truth, and forces the imagination of the reader to supply the omitted details of horror), is more effective to inspire sympathy than elaborate description. The very barrenness of the narration was hideously suggestive, and the girl felt her heart beat quicker as her poetic intellect rushed to complete the terrible picture sketched by the convict. She saw it all—the blue sea, the burning sun, the slowly moving ship, the wretched company on the shore; she heard Was that a rustling in the bushes below her? A bird! How nervous she was growing!

"Being thus fairly rid—as we thought—of our prison life, we cheerfully held consultation as to our future course. It was my intention to get among the islands in the South Seas, and scuttling the brig, to pass ourselves off among the natives as shipwrecked seamen, trusting to God's mercy that some homeward bound vessel might at length rescue us. With this view, I made James Lesly first mate, he being an experienced mariner, and prepared myself, with what few instruments we had, to take our departure from Birches Rock. Having hauled the whale-boat alongside, we stove her, together with the jolly-boat, and cast her adrift. This done, I parted the landsmen with the seamen, and, steering east south-east, at eight p.m. we set our first watch. In little more than an hour after this came on a heavy gale from the southwest. I, and others of the landsmen, were violently sea-sick, and Lesly had some difficulty in handling the brig, as the boisterous weather called for two men at the helm. In the morning, getting upon deck with difficulty, I found that the wind had abated, but upon sounding the well discovered much water in the hold. Lesly rigged the pumps, but the starboard one only could be made to work. From that time there were but two businesses aboard—from the pump to the helm. The gale lasted two days and a night, the brig running under close-reefed topsails, we being afraid to shorten sail lest we might be overtaken by some pursuing vessel, so strong was the terror of our prison upon us.

"On the 16th, at noon, I again forced myself on deck, and taking a meridian observation, altered the course of the brig to east and by south, wishing to run to the southward of New Zealand, out of the usual track of shipping; and having a notion that, should our provisions hold out, we might make the South American coast, and fall into Christian hands. This done, I was compelled to retire below, and for a week lay in my berth as one at the last gasp. At times I repented my resolution, Fair urging me to bestir myself, as the men were not satisfied with our course. On the 21st a mutiny occurred, led by Lyons, who asserted we were heading into the Pacific, and must infallibly perish. This disaffected man, though ignorant of navigation, insisted upon steering to the south, believing that we had run to the northward of the Friendly Islands, and was for running the ship ashore and beseeching the protection of the natives. Lesly in vain protested that a southward course would bring us into icefields. Barker, who had served on board a whaler, strove to convince the mutineers that the temperature of such latitudes was too warm for such an error to escape us. After much noise, Lyons rushed to the helm, and Russen, drawing one of the pistols taken from Mr. Bates, shot him dead, upon which the others returned to their duty. This dreadful deed was, I fear, necessary to the safety of the brig; and had it occurred on board a vessel manned by free-men, would have been applauded as a stern but needful measure.

"Forced by these tumults upon deck, I made a short speech to the crew, and convinced them that I was competent to perform what I had promised to do, though at the time my heart inwardly failed me, and I longed for some sign of land. Supported at each arm by Lesly and Barker, I took an observation, and altered our course to north by east, the brig running eleven knots an hour under single-reefed topsails, and the pumps hard at work. So we ran until the 31st of January, when a white squall took us, and nearly proved fatal to all aboard.

"Lesly now committed a great error, for, upon the brig righting (she was thrown upon her beam ends, and her spanker boom carried away), he commanded to furl the fore-top sail, strike top-gallant yards, furl the main course, and take a reef in the maintopsail, leaving her to scud under single-reefed maintopsail and fore-sail. This caused the vessel to leak to that degree that I despaired of reaching land in her, and prayed to the Almighty to send us speedy assistance. For nine days and nights the storm continued, the men being utterly exhausted. One of the two soldiers whom we had employed to fish the two pieces of the spanker boom, with some quartering that we had, was washed overboard and drowned. Our provision was now nearly done, but the gale abating on the ninth day, we hastened to put provisions on the launch. The sea was heavy, and we were compelled to put a purchase on the fore and main yards, with preventers to windward, to ease the launch in going over the side. We got her fairly afloat at last, the others battening down the hatches in the brig. Having dressed ourselves in the clothes of Captain Frere and the pilot, we left the brig at sundown, lying with her channel plates nearly under water.

"The wind freshening during the night, our launch, which might, indeed, be termed a long-boat, having been fitted with mast, bowsprit, and main boom, began to be very uneasy, shipping two seas one after the other. The plan we could devise was to sit, four of us about, in the stern sheets, with our backs to the sea, to prevent the water pooping us. This itself was enough to exhaust the strongest men. The day, however, made us some amends for the dreadful night. Land was not more than ten miles from us; approaching as nearly as we could with safety, we hauled our wind, and ran along in, trusting to find some harbour. At half-past two we sighted a bay of very curious appearance, having two large rocks at the entrance, resembling pyramids. Shiers, Russen, and Fair landed, in hopes of discovering fresh water, of which we stood much in need. Before long they returned, stating that they had found an Indian hut, inside of which were some rude earthenware vessels. Fearful of surprise, we lay off the shore all that night, and putting into the bay very early in the morning, killed a seal. This was the first fresh meat I had tasted for four years. It seemed strange to eat it under such circumstances. We cooked the flippers, heart, and liver for breakfast, giving some to a cat which we had taken with us out of the brig, for I would not, willingly, allow even that animal to perish. After breakfast, we got under weigh; and we had scarcely been out half an hour when we had a fresh breeze, which carried us along at the rate of seven knots an hour, running from bay to bay to find inhabitants. Steering along the shore, as the sun went down, we suddenly heard the bellowing of a bullock, and James Barker, whom, from his violent conduct, I thought incapable of such sentiment, burst into tears.

"In about two hours we perceived great fires on the beach and let go anchor in nineteen fathoms of water. We lay awake all that night. In the morning, we rowed further inshore, and moored the boat to some seaweed. As soon as the inhabitants caught sight of us, they came down to the beach. I distributed needles and thread among the Indians, and on my saying 'Valdivia,' a woman instantly pointed towards a tongue of land to the southward, holding up three fingers, and crying *'leaghos!'* which I conjectured to be three leagues; the distance we afterwards found it to be.

"About three o'clock in the afternoon, we weathered the point pointed out by the woman, and perceived a flagstaff and a twelve-gun battery under our lee. I now divided among the men the sum of six pounds ten shillings that I had found in Captain Frere's cabin, and made another and more equal distribution of the clothing. There were also two watches, one of which I gave to Lesly, and kept the other for myself. It was resolved among us to say that we were part crew of the brig *Julia*, bound for China and wrecked in the South Seas. Upon landing at the battery, we were heartily entertained, though we did not understand one word of what they said. Next morning it was agreed that Lesly, Barker, Shiers, and Russen should pay for a canoe to convey them to the town, which was nine miles up the river; and on the morning of the 6th March they took their departure. On the 9th March, a boat, commanded by a lieutenant, came down with orders that the rest of us should be conveyed to town; and we accordingly launched the boat under convoy of the soldiers, and reached the town the same evening, in some trepidation. I feared lest the Spaniards had obtained a clue as to our real character, and was not deceived—the surviving soldier having betrayed us. This fellow was thus doubly a traitor—first, in deserting his officer, and then in betraying his comrades.

"We were immediately escorted to prison, where we found our four companions. Some of them were for brazening out the story of shipwreck, but knowing how confused must necessarily be our accounts, were we examined separately, I persuaded them that open confession would be our best chance of safety. On the 14th we were taken before the Intendente or Governor, who informed us that we were free, on condition that we chose to live within the limits of the town. At this intelligence I felt my heart grow light, and only begged in the name of my companions that we might not be given up to the British Government; 'rather than which,' said I, 'I would beg to be shot dead in the palace square.' The Governor regarded us with tears in his eyes, and spoke as follows: 'My poor men, do not think that I would take that advantage over you. Do not make an attempt to escape, and I will be your friend, and should a vessel come to-morrow to demand you, you shall find I will be as good as my word. All I have to impress upon you is, to beware of intemperance, which is very prevalent in this country, and when you find it convenient, to pay Government the money that was allowed you for subsistence while in prison.'

"The following day we all procured employment in launching a vessel of three hundred tons burden, and my men showed themselves so active that the owner said he would rather have us than thirty of his own countrymen; which saying pleased the Governor, who was there with almost the whole of the inhabitants and a whole band of music, this vessel having been nearly three years on the stocks. After she was launched, the seamen amongst us helped to fit her out, being paid fifteen dollars a month, with provisions on board. As for myself, I speedily obtained employment in the shipbuilder's yard, and subsisted by honest industry, almost forgetting, in the unwonted pleasures of freedom, the sad reverse of fortune which had befallen me. To think that I, who had mingled among gentlemen and scholars, should be thankful to labour in a shipwright's yard by day, and sleep on a bundle of hides by night! But this is personal matter, and need not be obtruded.

"In the same yard with me worked the soldier who had betrayed us, and I could not but regard it as a special judgment of Heaven when he one day fell from a great height and was taken up for dead, dying in much torment in a few hours. The days thus passed on in comparative happiness until the 20th of May, 1836, when the old Governor took his departure, regretted by all the inhabitants of Valdivia, and the *Achilles,* a one-and-twenty-gun brig of war, arrived with the new Governor. One of the first acts of this gentleman was to sell our boat, which was moored at the back of Government-house. This proceeding looked to my mind indicative of ill-will; and, fearful lest the Governor should deliver us again into bondage, I resolved to make my escape from the place. Having communicated my plans to Barker, Lesly, Riley, Shiers, and Russen, I offered the Governor to get built for him a handsome whale-boat, making the iron work myself. The Governor consented, and in a little more than a fortnight we had completed a four-oared whale-boat, capable of weathering either sea or storm. We fitted her with sails and provisions in the Governor's name, and on the 4th of July, being a Saturday night, we took our departure from Valdivia, dropping down the river shortly after sunset. Whether the Governor, disgusted at the trick we had played him, decided not to pursue us, or whether—as I rather think—our absence was not discovered until the Monday morning, when we were beyond reach of capture, I know not, but we got out to sea without hazard, and, taking accurate bearings, ran for the Friendly Islands, as had been agreed upon amongst us.

"But it now seemed that the good fortune which had hitherto attended us had deserted us, for after crawling for four days in sultry weather, there fell a dead calm, and we lay like a log upon the sea for forty-eight hours. For three days we remained in the midst of the ocean, exposed to the burning rays of the sun, in a boat without water or provisions. On the fourth day, just as we had resolved to draw lots to determine who should die for the sustenance of the others, we were picked up by an opium clipper returning to Canton. The captain, an American, was most kind to us, and on our arrival at Canton, a subscription was got up for us by the British merchants of that city, and a free passage to England obtained for us. Russen, however, getting in drink, made statements which brought suspicion upon us. I had imposed upon the Consul with a fictitious story of a wreck, but had stated that my name was Wilson, forgetting that the sextant which had been preserved in the boat had Captain Bates's name engraved upon it. These circumstances together caused sufficient doubts in the Consul's mind to cause him to give directions that, on our arrival in London, we were to be brought before the Thames Police Court. There being no evidence against us, we should have escaped, had not a Dr. Pine, who had been surgeon on board the *Malabar* transport, being in the Court, recognized me and swore to my identity. We were remanded, and, to complete the chain of evidence, Mr. Capon, the Hobart Town gaoler, was, strangely enough, in London at the time, and identified us all. Our story was then made public, and Barker and Lesly, turning Queen's evidence against Russen, he was convicted of the murder of Lyons, and executed. We were then placed on board the *Leviathan* hulk, and remained there until shipped in the *Lady Jane*, which was chartered, with convicts, for Van Diemen's Land, in order to be tried in the colony, where the offence was committed, for piratically seizing the brig *Osprey*, and arrived here on the 15th December, 1838."

*

Coming, breathless, to the conclusion of this wonderful relation, Sylvia suffered her hand to fall into her lap, and sat meditative. The history of this desperate struggle for liberty was to her full of vague horror. She had never before realized among what manner of men she had lived. The sullen creatures who worked in the chain-gangs, or pulled in the boats—their faces brutalized into a uniform blankness—must be very different men from John Rex and his companions. Her imagination pictured the voyage in the leaky brig, the South American slavery, the midnight escape, the desperate rowing, the long, slow agony of starvation, and the heart-sickness that must have followed upon recapture and imprisonment. Surely the punishment of "penal servitude" must have been made very terrible for men to dare such hideous perils to escape from it. Surely John Rex, the convict, who, alone, and prostrated by sickness, quelled a mutiny and navigated a vessel through a storm-ravaged ocean, must possess qualities which could be put to better use than stone-quarrying. Was the opinion of Maurice Frere the correct one after all, and were these convict monsters gifted with unnatural powers of endurance, only to be subdued and tamed by unnatural and inhuman punishments of lash and chain? Her fancies growing amid the fast gathering gloom, she shuddered as she guessed to what extremities of evil might such men proceed did an opportunity ever come to them to retaliate upon their gaolers. Perhaps beneath each mask of servility and sullen fear that was the ordinary prison face, lay hid a courage and a despair as mighty as that which sustained those ten poor wanderers over the Pacific Ocean. Maurice had told her that these people had their secret signs, their secret language. She had just seen a specimen of the skill with which this very Rex—still bent upon escape—could send a hidden message to his friends beneath the eyes of his gaolers. What if the whole island was but one smouldering volcano of revolt and murder—the whole convict population but one incarnated conspiracy, bound together by crime and suffering! Terrible to think of—yet not impossible.

Oh, how strangely must the world have been civilized, that this most lovely corner of it must needs be set apart as a place of banishment for the monsters that civilization had brought forth and bred! She cast her eyes around, and all beauty seemed blotted out from the scene before her. The graceful foliage melting into indistinctness in the gathering twilight, appeared to her horrible and treacherous. The river seemed to flow sluggishly, as though thickened with blood and tears. The shadow of the trees seemed to hold lurking shapes of cruelty and danger. Even the whispering breeze bore with it sighs, and threats, and mutterings of revenge. Oppressed by a terror of loneliness, she hastily caught up the manuscript, and turned to seek the house, when, as if summoned from the earth by the power of her own fears, a ragged figure barred her passage.

To the excited girl this apparition seemed the embodiment of the unknown evil she had dreaded. She recognized the yellow clothing, and marked the eager hands outstretched to seize her. Instantly upon her flashed the story that three days since had set the prison-town agog. The desperado of Port Arthur, the escaped mutineer and murderer, was before her, with unchained arms, free to wreak his will of her. "Sylvia! It is you! Oh, at last! I have escaped, and come to ask—What? Do you not know me?"

Pressing both hands to her bosom, she stepped back a pace, speechless with terror.

"I am Rufus Dawes," he said, looking in her face for the grateful smile of recognition that did not come—"Rufus Dawes."

The party at the house had finished their wine, and, sitting on the broad verandah, were listening to some gentle dullness of the clergyman, when there broke upon their ears a cry.

"What's that?" said Vickers.

Frere sprang up, and looked down the garden. He saw two figures that seemed to struggle together. One glance was enough, and, with a shout, he leapt the flower-beds, and made straight at the escaped prisoner.

Rufus Dawes saw him coming, but, secure in the protection of the girl who owed to him so much, he advanced a step nearer, and loosing his respectful clasp of her hand, caught her dress.

"Oh, help, Maurice, help!" cried Sylvia again.

Into the face of Rufus Dawes came an expression of horror-stricken bewilderment. For three days the unhappy man had contrived to keep life and freedom, in order to get speech with the one being who, he thought, cherished for him some affection. Having made an unparalleled escape from the midst of his warders, he had crept to the place where lived the idol of his dreams, braving recapture, that he might hear from her two words of justice and gratitude. Not only did she refuse to listen to him, and shrink from him as from one accursed, but, at the sound of his name, she summoned his deadliest foe to capture him. Such monstrous ingratitude was almost beyond belief. *She*, too,—the child he had nursed and fed, the child for whom he had given up his hard-earned chance of freedom and fortune, the child of whom he had dreamed, the child whose image he had worshipped—she, too, against him! Then there was no justice, no Heaven, no God! He loosed his hold of her dress, and, regardless of the approaching footsteps, stood speechless, shaking from head to foot. In another instant Frere and McNab flung themselves upon him, and he was borne to the ground. Though weakened by starvation, he shook them off with scarce an effort, and, despite the servants who came hurrying from the alarmed house, might even then have turned and made good his escape. But he seemed unable to fly. His chest heaved convulsively, great drops of sweat beaded his white face, and from his eyes tears seemed about to break. For an instant his features worked convulsively, as if he would fain invoke upon the girl, weeping on her father's shoulder, some hideous curse. But no words came—only thrusting his hand into his breast, with a supreme gesture of horror and aversion, he flung something from him. Then a profound sigh escaped him, and he held out his hands to be bound.

There was something so pitiable about this silent grief that, as they led him away, the little group instinctively averted their faces, lest they should seem to triumph over him.

CHAPTER XI

A RELIC OF MACQUARIE HARBOUR

"YOU must try and save him from further punishment," said Sylvia next day to Frere. "I did not mean to betray the poor creature, but I had made myself nervous by reading that convict's story."

"You shouldn't read such rubbish," said Frere. "What's the use? I don't suppose a word of it's true."

"It must be true. I am sure it's true. Oh, Maurice, these are dreadful men. I thought I knew all about convicts, but I had no idea that such men as these were among them."

"Thank God, you know very little," said Maurice. "The servants you have here are very different sort of fellows from Rex and Company."

"Oh, Maurice, I am so tired of this place. It's wrong, perhaps, with poor papa and all, but I do wish I was somewhere out of the sight of chains. I don't know what has made me feel as I do."

"Come to Sydney," said Frere. "There are not so many convicts there. It was arranged that we should go to Sydney, you know."

"For our honeymoon? Yes," said Sylvia, simply. "I know it was. But we are not married yet."

"That's easily done," said Maurice.

"Oh, nonsense, sir! But I want to speak to you about this poor Dawes. I don't think he meant any harm. It seems to me now that he was rather going to ask for food or something, only I was so nervous. They won't hang him, Maurice, will they?"

"No," said Maurice. "I spoke to your father this morning. If the fellow is tried for his life, you may have to give evidence, and so we came to the conclusion that Port Arthur again, and heavy irons, will meet the case. We gave him another life sentence this morning. That will make the third he has had."

"What did he say?"

"Nothing. I sent him down aboard the schooner at once. He ought to be out of the river by this time."

"Maurice, I have a strange feeling about that man."

"Eh?" said Maurice.

"I seem to fear him, as if I knew some story about him, and yet didn't know it."

"That's not very clear," said Maurice, forcing a laugh, "but don't let's talk about him any more. We'll soon be far from Port Arthur and everybody in it."

"Maurice," said she, caressingly, "I love you, dear. You'll always protect me against these men, won't you?"

Maurice kissed her. "You have not got over your fright, Sylvia," he said. "I see I shall have to take a great deal of care of my wife."

"Of course," replied Sylvia.

And then the pair began to make love, or, rather, Maurice made it, and Sylvia suffered him.

Suddenly her eye caught something. "What's that—there, on the ground by the fountain?" They were near the spot where Dawes had been seized the night before. A little stream ran through the garden, and a Triton—of convict manufacture—blew his horn in the middle of a—convict built—rockery. Under the lip of the fountain lay a small packet. Frere picked it up. It was made of soiled yellow cloth, and stitched evidently by a man's fingers. "It looks like a needle-case," said he.

"Let me see. What a strange-looking thing! Yellow cloth, too. Why, it must belong to a prisoner. Oh, Maurice, the man who was here last night!"

"Ay," says Maurice, turning over the packet, "it might have been his, sure enough."

"He seemed to fling something from him, I thought. Perhaps this is it!" said she, peering over his arm, in delicate curiosity. Frere, with something of a scowl on his brow, tore off the outer covering of the mysterious packet, and displayed a second envelope, of grey cloth—the "good-conduct" uniform. Beneath this was a piece, some three inches square, of stained and discoloured merino, that had once been blue.

"Hullo!" says Frere. "Why, what's this?"

"It is a piece of a dress," says Sylvia.

It was Rufus Dawes's talisman—a portion of the frock she had worn at Macquarie Harbour, and which the unhappy convict had cherished as a sacred relic for five weary years.

Frere flung it into the water. The running stream whirled it away. "Why did you do that?" cried the girl, with a sudden pang of remorse for which she could not account. The shred of cloth, caught by a weed, lingered for an instant on the surface of the water. Almost at the same moment, the pair, raising their eyes, saw the schooner which bore Rufus Dawes back to bondage glide past the opening of the trees and disappear. When they looked again for the strange relic of the desperado of Port Arthur, it also had vanished.

CHAPTER XII

AT PORT ARTHUR

THE usual clanking and hammering was prevalent upon the stone jetty of Port Arthur when the schooner bearing the returned convict, Rufus Dawes, ran alongside. On the heights above the esplanade rose the grim front of the soldiers' barracks; beneath the soldiers' barracks was the long range of prison buildings with their workshops and tan-pits; to the left lay the Commandant's house, authoritative by reason of its embrasured terrace and guardian sentry; while the jetty, that faced the purple length of the "Island of the Dead," swarmed with parti-coloured figures, clanking about their enforced business, under the muskets of their gaolers.

Rufus Dawes had seen this prospect before, had learnt by heart each beauty of rising sun, sparkling water, and wooded hill. From the hideously clean jetty at his feet, to the distant signal station, that, embowered in bloom, reared its slender arms upwards into the cloudless sky, he knew it all. There was no charm for him in the exquisite blue of the sea, the soft shadows of the hills, or the soothing ripple of the waves that crept voluptuously to the white breast of the shining shore. He sat with his head bowed down, and his hands clasped about his knees, disdaining to look until they roused him.

"Hallo, Dawes!" says Warder Troke, halting his train of ironed yellow-jackets. "So you've come back again! Glad to see yer, Dawes! It seems an age since we had the pleasure of your company, Dawes!" At this pleasantry the train laughed, so that their irons clanked more than ever. They found it often inconvenient not to laugh at Mr. Troke's humour. "Step down here, Dawes, and let me introduce you to your h'old friends. They'll be glad to see yer, won't yer, boys? Why, bless me, Dawes, we thort we'd lost yer! We thort yer'd given us the slip altogether, Dawes. They didn't take care of yer in Hobart Town, I expect, eh, boys? We'll look after yer here, Dawes, though. You won't bolt any more."

"Take care, Mr. Troke," said a warning voice, "you're at it again! Let the man alone!"

By virtue of an order transmitted from Hobart Town, they had begun to attach the dangerous prisoner to the last man of the gang, riveting the leg-irons of the pair by means of an extra link, which could be removed when necessary, but Dawes had given no sign of consciousness. At the sound of the friendly tones, however, he looked up, and saw a tall, gaunt man, dressed in a shabby pepper-and-salt raiment, and wearing a black handkerchief knotted round his throat. He was a stranger to him.

"I beg your pardon, Mr. North," said Troke, sinking at once the bully in the sneak. "I didn't see yer reverence."

"A parson!" thought Dawes with disappointment, and dropped his eyes.

"I know that," returned Mr. North, coolly. "If you had, you would have been all butter and honey. Don't trouble yourself to tell a lie; it's quite unnecessary."

Dawes looked up again. This was a strange parson.

"What's your name, my man?" said Mr. North, suddenly, catching his eye.

Rufus Dawes had intended to scowl, but the tone, sharply authoritative, roused his automatic convict second nature, and he answered, almost despite himself, "Rufus Dawes."

"Oh," said Mr. North, eyeing him with a curious air of expectation that had something pitying in it. "This is the man, is it? I thought he was to go to the Coal Mines."

"So he is," said Troke, "but we hain't a goin' to send there for a fortnit, and in the meantime I'm to work him on the chain."

"Oh!" said Mr. North again. "Lend me your knife, Troke."

And then, before them all, this curious parson took a piece of tobacco out of his ragged pocket, and cut off a "chaw" with Mr. Troke's knife. Rufus Dawes felt what he had not felt for three days—an interest in something. He stared at the parson in unaffected astonishment. Mr. North perhaps mistook the meaning of his fixed stare, for he held out the remnant of tobacco to him.

The chain line vibrated at this, and bent forward to enjoy the vicarious delight of seeing another man chew tobacco. Troke grinned with a silent mirth that betokened retribution for the favoured convict. "Here," said Mr. North, holding out the dainty morsel upon which so many eyes were fixed. Rufus Dawes took the tobacco; looked at it hungrily for an instant, and then—to the astonishment of everybody—flung it away with a curse.

"I don't want your tobacco," he said; "keep it."

From convict mouths went out a respectful roar of amazement, and Mr. Troke's eyes snapped with pride of outraged janitorship. "You ungrateful dog!" he cried, raising his stick.

Mr. North put up a hand. "That will do, Troke," he said; "I know your respect for the cloth. Move the men on again."

"Get on!" said Troke, rumbling oaths beneath his breath, and Dawes felt his newly-riveted chain tug. It was some time since he had been in a chain-gang, and the sudden jerk nearly overbalanced him. He caught at his neighbour, and looking up, met a pair of black eyes which gleamed recognition. His neighbour was John Rex. Mr. North, watching them, was struck by the resemblance the two men bore to each other. Their height, eyes, hair, and complexion were similar. Despite the difference in name they might be related. "They might be brothers," thought he. "Poor devils! I never knew a prisoner refuse tobacco before." And he looked on the ground for the despised portion. But in vain. John Rex, oppressed by no foolish sentiment, had picked it up and put it in his mouth.

So Rufus Dawes was relegated to his old life again, and came back to his prison with the hatred of his kind, that his prison had bred in him, increased a hundred-fold. It seemed to him that the sudden awakening had dazed him, that the flood of light so suddenly let in upon his slumbering soul had blinded his eyes, used so long to the sweetly-cheating twilight. He was at first unable to apprehend the details of his misery. He knew only that his dream-child was alive and shuddered at him, that the only thing he loved and trusted had betrayed him, that all hope of justice and mercy had gone from him for ever, that the beauty had gone from earth, the brightness from Heaven, and that he was doomed still to live. He went about his work, unheedful of the jests of Troke, ungalled by his irons, unmindful of the groans and laughter about him. His magnificent muscles saved him from the lash; for the amiable Troke tried to break him down in vain. He did not complain, he did not laugh, he did not weep. His "mate" Rex tried to converse with him, but did not succeed. In the midst of one of Rex's excellent tales of London dissipation, Rufus Dawes would sigh wearily. "There's something on that fellow's mind," thought Rex, prone to watch the signs by which the soul is read. "He has some secret which weighs upon him."

It was in vain that Rex attempted to discover what this secret might be. To all questions concerning his past life—however artfully put—Rufus Dawes was dumb. In vain Rex practised all his arts, called up all his graces of manner and speech—and these were not few—to fascinate the silent man and win his confidence. Rufus Dawes met his advances with a cynical carelessness that revealed nothing; and, when not addressed, held a gloomy silence. Galled by this indifference, John Rex had attempted to practise those ingenious arts of torment by which Gabbett, Vetch, or other leading spirits of the gang asserted their superiority over their quieter comrades. But he soon ceased. "I have been longer in this hell than you," said Rufus Dawes, "and I know more of the devil's tricks than you can show me. You had best be quiet." Rex neglected the warning, and Rufus Dawes took him by the throat one day, and would have strangled him, but that Troke beat off the angered man with a favourite bludgeon. Rex had a wholesome respect for personal prowess, and had the grace to admit the provocation to Troke. Even this instance of self-denial did not move the stubborn Dawes. He only laughed. Then Rex came to a conclusion. His mate was plotting an escape. He himself cherished a notion of the kind, as did Gabbett and Vetch, but by common distrust no one ever gave utterance to thoughts of this nature. It would be too dangerous. "He would be a good comrade for a rush," thought Rex, and resolved more firmly than ever to ally himself to this dangerous and silent companion.

One question Dawes had asked which Rex had been able to answer: "Who is that North?"

"A chaplain. He is only here for a week or so. There is a new one coming. North goes to Sydney. He is not in favour with the Bishop."

"How do you know?"

"By deduction," says Rex, with a smile peculiar to him. "He wears coloured clothes, and smokes, and doesn't patter Scripture. The Bishop dresses in black, detests tobacco, and quotes the Bible like a concordance. North is sent here for a month, as a warming-pan for that ass Meekin. *Ergo*, the Bishop don't care about North."

Jemmy Vetch, who was next to Rex, let the full weight of his portion of tree-trunk rest upon Gabbett, in order to express his unrestrained admiration of Mr. Rex's sarcasm. "Ain't the Dandy a one'er?" said he.

"Are you thinking of coming the pious?" asked Rex. "It's no good with North. Wait until the highly-intelligent Meekin comes. You can twist that worthy successor of the Apostles round your little finger!"

"Silence there!" cries the overseer. "Do you want me to report yer?"

Amid such diversions the days rolled on, and Rufus Dawes almost longed for the Coal Mines. To be sent from the settlement to the Coal Mines, and from the Coal Mines to the settlement, was to these unhappy men a "trip". At Port Arthur one went to an out-station, as more fortunate people go to Queenscliff or the Ocean Beach now-a-days for "change of air."

CHAPTER XIII

THE COMMANDANT'S BUTLER

RUFUS Dawes had been a fortnight at the settlement when a new-comer appeared on the chain-gang. This was a young man of about twenty years of age, thin, fair, and delicate. His name was Kirkland, and he belonged to what were known as the "educated" prisoners. He had been a clerk in a banking house, and was transported for embezzlement, though, by some, grave doubts as to his guilt were entertained. The Commandant, Captain Burgess, had employed him as butler in his own house, and his fate was considered a "lucky" one. So, doubtless, it was, and might have been, had not an untoward accident occurred. Captain Burgess, who was a bachelor of the "old school", confessed to an amiable weakness for blasphemy, and was given to condemning the convicts' eyes and limbs with indiscriminate violence. Kirkland belonged to a Methodist family and owned a piety utterly out of place in that region. The language of Burgess made him shudder, and one day he so far forgot himself and his place as to raise his hands to his ears. "My blank!" cried Burgess. "You blank blank, is that your blank game? I'll blank soon cure you of that!" and forthwith ordered him to the chain-gang for "insubordination".

He was received with suspicion by the gang, who did not like white-handed prisoners. Troke, by way of experiment in human nature, perhaps, placed him next to Gabbett. The day was got through in the usual way, and Kirkland felt his heart revive.

The toil was severe, and the companionship uncouth, but despite his blistered hands and aching back, he had not experienced anything so very terrible after all. When the muster bell rang, and the gang broke up, Rufus Dawes, on his silent way to his separate cell, observed a notable change of custom in the disposition of the new convict. Instead of placing him in a cell by himself, Troke was turning him into the yard with the others.

"I'm not to go in there?" says the ex-bank clerk, drawing back in dismay from the cloud of foul faces which lowered upon him.

"By the Lord, but you are, then!" says Troke. "The Governor says a night in there'll take the starch out of ye. Come, in yer go."

"But, Mr. Troke—"

"Stow your gaff," says Troke, with another oath, and impatiently striking the lad with his thong—"I can't argue here all night. Get in." So Kirkland, aged twenty-two, and the son of Methodist parents, went in.

Rufus Dawes, among whose sinister memories this yard was numbered, sighed. So fierce was the glamour of the place, however, that when locked into his cell, he felt ashamed for that sigh, and strove to erase the memory of it. "What is he more than anybody else?" said the wretched man to himself, as he hugged his misery close.

About dawn the next morning, Mr. North—who, amongst other vagaries not approved of by his bishop, had a habit of prowling about the prison at unofficial hours—was attracted by a dispute at the door of the dormitory.

"What's the matter here?" he asked.

"A prisoner refractory, your reverence," said the watchman. "Wants to come out."

"Mr. North! Mr. North!" cried a voice, "for the love of God, let me out of this place!"

Kirkland, ghastly pale, bleeding, with his woollen shirt torn, and his blue eyes wide open with terror, was clinging to the bars.

"Oh, Mr. North! Mr. North! Oh, Mr. North! Oh, for God's sake, Mr. North!"

"What, Kirkland!" cried North, who was ignorant of the vengeance of the Commandant. "What do *you* do here?"

But Kirkland could do nothing but cry,—"Oh, Mr. North! For God's sake, Mr. North!" and beat on the bars with white and sweating hands.

"Let him out, watchman!" said North.

"Can't sir, without an order from the Commandant."

"I order you, sir!" North cried, indignant.

"Very sorry, your reverence; but your reverence knows that I daren't do such a thing."

"Mr. North!" screamed Kirkland. "Would you see me perish,

body and soul, in this place? Mr. North! Oh, you ministers of Christ—wolves in sheep's clothing—you shall be judged for this!"

"Let him out!" cried North again, stamping his foot.

"It's no good," returned the gaoler. "I *can't*. If he was dying, I can't."

North rushed away to the Commandant, and the instant his back was turned, Hailes, the watchman, flung open the door, and darted into the dormitory.

"Take that!" he cried, dealing Kirkland a blow on the head with his keys, that stretched him senseless. "There's more trouble with you bloody aristocrats than enough. Lie quiet!"

The Commandant, roused from slumber, told Mr. North that Kirkland might stop where he was, and that he'd thank the chaplain not to wake him up in the middle of the night because a blank prisoner set up a blank howling.

"But, my good sir," protested North, restraining his impulse to overstep the bounds of modesty in his language to his superior officer, "you know the character of the men in that ward. You can guess what that unhappy boy has suffered."

"Impertinent young beggar!" said Burgess. "Do him good, curse him! Mr. North, I'm sorry you should have had the trouble to come here, but *will* you let me go to sleep?"

North returned to the prison disconsolately, found the dutiful Hailes at his post, and all quiet.

"What's become of Kirkland?" he asked.

"Fretted hisself to sleep, yer reverence," said Hailes, in accents of parental concern. "Poor young chap! It's hard for such young 'uns."

In the morning, Rufus Dawes, coming to his place on the chain-gang, was struck by the altered appearance of Kirkland. His face was of a greenish tint, and wore an expression of bewildered horror.

"Cheer up, man!" said Dawes, touched with momentary pity. "It's no good being in the mopes, you know."

"What do they do if you try to bolt?" whispered Kirkland.

"Kill you," returned Dawes, in a tone of surprise at so preposterous a question.

"Thank God!" said Kirkland.

"Now then, Miss Nancy," said one of the men, "what's the matter with *you*!" Kirkland shuddered, and his pale face grew crimson.

"Oh," he said, "that such a wretch as I should live!"

"Silence!" cried Troke. "No. 44, if you can't hold your tongue I'll give you something to talk about. March!"

The work of the gang that afternoon was the carrying of some heavy logs to the water-side, and Rufus Dawes observed that Kirkland was exhausted long before the task was accomplished. "They'll kill you, you little beggar!" said he, not unkindly. "What have you been doing to get into this scrape?"

"Have you ever been in that—that place I was in last night?" asked Kirkland.

Rufus Dawes nodded.

"Does the Commandant know what goes on there?"

"I suppose so. What does he care?"

"Care! Man, do you believe in a God?"

"No," said Dawes, "not here. Hold up, my lad. If you fall, we must fall over you, and then you're done for."

He had hardly uttered the words, when the boy flung himself beneath the log. In another instant the train would have been scrambling over his crushed body, had not Gabbett stretched out an iron hand, and plucked the would-be suicide from death.

"Hold on to me, Miss Nancy," said the giant, "I'm big enough to carry double."

Something in the tone or manner of the speaker affected Kirkland to disgust, for, spurning the offered hand, he uttered a cry and then, holding up his irons with his hands, he started to run for the water.

"Halt! you young fool," roared Troke, raising his carbine. But Kirkland kept steadily on for the river. Just as he reached it, however, the figure of Mr. North rose from behind a pile of stones. Kirkland jumped for the jetty, missed his footing, and fell into the arms of the chaplain.

"You young vermin—you shall pay for this," cries Troke. "You'll see if you won't remember this day."

"Oh, Mr. North," says Kirkland, "why did you stop me? I'd better be dead than stay another night in that place."

"You'll get it, my lad," said Gabbett, when the runaway was brought back. "Your blessed hide'll feel for this, see if it don't."

Kirkland only breathed harder, and looked round for Mr. North, but Mr. North had gone. The new chaplain was to arrive that afternoon, and it was incumbent on him to be at the reception. Troke reported the ex-bank clerk that night to Burgess, and Burgess, who was about to go to dinner with the new chaplain, disposed of his case out of hand. "Tried to bolt, eh! Must stop that. Fifty lashes, Troke. Tell Macklewain to be ready—or stay, I'll tell him myself—I'll break the young devil's spirit, blank him."

"Yes, sir," said Troke. "Good evening, sir."

"Troke—pick out some likely man, will you? That last fellow you had ought to have been tied up himself. His flogging wouldn't have killed a flea."

"You can't get 'em to *warm* one another, your honour," says Troke.

"They *won't* do it."

"Oh, yes, they will, though," says Burgess, "or I'll know the reason why. I won't have my men knocked up with flogging these rascals. If the scourger won't do his duty, tie him up, and give him five-and-twenty for himself. I'll be down in the morning myself if I can."

"Very good, your honour," says Troke.

Kirkland was put into a separate cell that night; and Troke, by way of assuring him a good night's rest, told him that he was to have "fifty" in the morning. "And Dawes'll lay it on," he added. "He's one of the smartest men I've got, and he won't spare yer, yer may take your oath of that."

CHAPTER XIV

MR. NORTH'S DISPOSITION

"YOU will find this a terrible place, Mr. Meekin," said North to his supplanter, as they walked across to the Commandant's to dinner. "It has made me heartsick."

"I thought it was a little paradise," said Meekin. "Captain Frere says that the scenery is delightful."

"So it is," returned North, looking askance, "but the prisoners are not delightful."

"Poor, abandoned wretches," says Meekin, "I suppose not. How sweet the moonlight sleeps upon that bank! Eh!"

"Abandoned, indeed, by God and man—almost."

"Mr. North, Providence never abandons the most unworthy of His servants. Never have I seen the righteous forsaken, nor His seed begging their bread. In the valley of the shadow of death He is with us. His staff, you know, Mr. North. Really, the Commandant's house is charmingly situated!"

Mr. North sighed again. "You have not been long in the colony, Mr. Meekin. I doubt—forgive me for expressing myself so freely—if you quite know of our convict system."

"An admirable one! A most admirable one!" said Meekin. "There were a few matters I noticed in Hobart Town that did not quite please me—the frequent use of profane language for instance—but on the whole I was delighted with the scheme. It is so complete."

North pursed up his lips. "Yes, it is very complete," he said; "almost too complete. But I am always in a minority when I discuss the question, so we will drop it, if you please."

"If you please," said Meekin gravely. He had heard from the Bishop that Mr. North was an ill-conditioned sort of person, who smoked clay pipes, had been detected in drinking beer out of a pewter pot, and had been heard to state that white neck-cloths were of no consequence. The dinner went off successfully. Burgess—desirous, perhaps, of favourably impressing the chaplain whom the Bishop delighted to honour—shut off his blasphemy for a while, and was urbane enough. "You'll find us rough, Mr. Meekin," he said, "but you'll find us 'all there' when we're wanted. This is a little kingdom in itself."

"Like Beranger's?" asked Meekin, with a smile. Captain Burgess had never heard of Beranger, but he smiled as if he had learnt his words by heart.

"Or like Sancho Panza's island," said North. "You remember how justice was administered there?"

"Not at this moment, sir," said Burgess, with dignity. He had been often oppressed by the notion that the Reverend Mr. North "chaffed" him. "Pray help yourself to wine."

"Thank you, none," said North, filling a tumbler with water. "I have a headache." His manner of speech and action was so awkward that a silence fell upon the party, caused by each one wondering why Mr. North should grow confused, and drum his fingers on the table, and stare everywhere but at the decanter. Meekin—ever softly at his ease—was the first to speak. "Have you many visitors, Captain Burgess?"

"Very few. Sometimes a party comes over with a recommendation from the Governor, and I show them over the place; but, as a rule, we see no one but ourselves."

"I asked," said Meekin, "because some friends of mine were thinking of coming."

"And who may they be?"

"Do you know Captain Frere?"

"Frere! I should say so!" returned Burgess, with a laugh, modelled upon Maurice Frere's own. "I was quartered with him at Sarah Island. So he's a friend of yours, eh?"

"I had the pleasure of meeting him in society. He is just married, you know."

"Is he?" said Burgess. "The devil he is! I heard something about it, too."

"Miss Vickers, a charming young person. They are going to Sydney, where Captain Frere has some interest, and Frere thinks of taking Port Arthur on his way down."

"A strange fancy for a honeymoon trip," said North.

"Captain Frere takes a deep interest in all relating to convict discipline," went on Meekin, unheeding the interruption, "and is anxious that Mrs. Frere should see this place."

"Yes, one oughtn't to leave the colony without seeing it," says Burgess; "it's worth seeing."

"So Captain Frere thinks. A romantic story, Captain Burgess. He saved her life, you know."

"Ah! that was a queer thing, that mutiny," said Burgess. "We've got the fellows here, you know."

"I saw them tried at Hobart Town," said Meekin. "In fact, the ringleader, John Rex, gave me his confession, and I sent it to the Bishop."

"A great rascal," put in North. "A dangerous, scheming, cold-blooded villain."

"Well now!" said Meekin, with asperity, "I don't agree with you. Everybody seems to be against that poor fellow—Captain Frere tried to make me think that his letters contained a hidden meaning, but I don't believe they did. He seems to me to be truly penitent for his offences—a misguided, but not a hypocritical man, if my knowledge of human nature goes for anything."

"I hope he is," said North. "I wouldn't trust him."

"Oh! there's no fear of him," said Burgess cheerily; "if he grows uproarious, we'll soon give him a touch of the cat."

"I suppose severity is necessary," returned Meekin; "though to my ears a flogging sounds a little distasteful. It is a brutal punishment."

"It's a punishment for brutes," said Burgess, and laughed, pleased with the nearest approach to an epigram he ever made in his life.

Here attention was called by the strange behaviour of Mr. North. He had risen, and, without apology, flung wide the window, as though he gasped for air. "Hullo, North! what's the matter?"

"Nothing," said North, recovering himself with an effort. "A spasm. I have these attacks at times."

"Have some brandy," said Burgess.

"No, no, it will pass. *No*, I say. Well, if you insist." And seizing the tumbler offered to him, he half-filled it with raw spirit, and swallowed the fiery draught at a gulp.

The Reverend Meekin eyed his clerical brother with horror. The Reverend Meekin was not accustomed to clergymen who wore black neckties, smoked clay pipes, chewed tobacco, and drank neat brandy out of tumblers.

"Ha!" said North, looking wildly round upon them. "That's better."

"Let us go on to the verandah," said Burgess. "It's cooler than in the house."

So they went on to the verandah, and looked down upon the lights of the prison, and listened to the sea lapping the shore. The Reverend Mr. North, in this cool atmosphere, seemed to recover himself, and conversation progressed with some sprightliness.

By and by, a short figure, smoking a cheroot, came up out of the dark, and proved to be Dr. Macklewain, who had been prevented from attending the dinner by reason of an accident to a constable at Norfolk Bay, which had claimed his professional attention.

"Well, how's Forrest?" cried Burgess. "Mr. Meekin—Dr. Macklewain."

"Dead," said Dr. Macklewain. "Delighted to see you, Mr. Meekin."

"Confound it—another of my best men," grumbled Burgess. "Macklewain, have a glass of wine." But Macklewain was tired, and wanted to get home.

"I must also be thinking of repose," said Meekin; "the journey—though most enjoyable—has fatigued me."

"Come on, then," said North. "Our roads lie together, doctor."

"You *won't* have a nip of brandy before you start?" asked Burgess.

"No? Then I shall send round for you in the morning, Mr. Meekin. Good night. Macklewain, I want to speak with you a moment."

Before the two clergymen had got half-way down the steep path that led from the Commandant's house to the flat on which the cottages of the doctor and chaplain were built, Macklewain rejoined them. "Another flogging to-morrow," said he grumblingly. "Up at daylight, I suppose, again."

"Whom is he going to flog now?"

"That young butler-fellow of his."

"What, Kirkland?" cried North. "You don't mean to say he's going to flog Kirkland?"

"Insubordination," says Macklewain. "Fifty lashes."

"Oh, this must be stopped," cried North, in great alarm. "He can't stand it. I tell you, he'll die, Macklewain."

"Perhaps you'll have the goodness to allow me to be the best judge of that," returned Macklewain, drawing up his little body to its least insignificant stature.

"My dear sir," replied North, alive to the importance of conciliating the surgeon, "you haven't seen him lately. He tried to drown himself this morning."

Mr. Meekin expressed some alarm; but Dr. Macklewain re-assured him. "*That* sort of nonsense must be stopped," said he. "A nice example to set. I wonder Burgess didn't give him a hundred."

"He was put into the long dormitory," said North; "you know what sort of a place that is. I declare to Heaven his agony and shame terrified me."

"Well, he'll be put into the hospital for a week or so to-morrow," said Macklewain, "and that'll give him a spell."

"If Burgess flogs him I'll report it to the Governor," cries North, in great heat. "The condition of those dormitories is infamous."

"If the boy has anything to complain of, why don't he complain? We can't do anything without evidence."

"Complain! Would his life be safe if he did? Besides, he's not the sort of creature to complain. He'd rather kill himself."

"That's all nonsense," says Macklewain. "We can't flog a whole dormitory on suspicion. *I* can't help it. The boy's made his bed, and he must lie on it."

"I'll go back and see Burgess," said North. "Mr. Meekin, here's the gate, and your room is on the right hand. I'll be back shortly."

"Pray, don't hurry," said Meekin politely. "You are on an errand of mercy, you know. Everything must give way to that. I shall find my portmanteau in my room, you said."

"Yes, yes. Call the servant if you want anything. He sleeps at the back," and North hurried off.

"An impulsive gentleman," said Meekin to Macklewain, as the sound of Mr. North's footsteps died away in the distance. Macklewain shook his head seriously.

"There is something wrong about him, but I can't make out what it is. He has the strangest fits at times. Unless it's a cancer in the stomach, I don't know what it can be."

"Cancer in the stomach! dear me, how dreadful!" says Meekin. "Ah! Doctor, we all have our crosses, have we not? How delightful the grass smells! This seems a very pleasant place, and I think I shall enjoy myself very much. Good-night."

"Good-night, sir. I hope you will be comfortable."

"And let us hope poor Mr. North will succeed in his labour of love," said Meekin, shutting the little gate, "and save the unfortunate Kirkland. Goodnight, once more."

Captain Burgess was shutting his verandah-window when North hurried up.

"Captain Burgess, Macklewain tells me you are going to flog Kirkland."

"Well, sir, what of that?" said Burgess.

"I have come to beg you not to do so, sir. The lad has been cruelly punished already. He attempted suicide to-day—unhappy creature."

"Well, that's just what I'm flogging him for. I'll teach my prisoners to attempt suicide!"

"But he can't stand it, sir. He's too weak."

"That's Macklewain's business."

"Captain Burgess," protested North, "I assure you that he does not deserve punishment. I have seen him, and his condition of mind is pitiable."

"Look here, Mr. North, I don't interfere with what you do to the prisoner's souls; don't you interfere with what I do to their bodies."

"Captain Burgess, you have no right to mock at my office."

"Then don't you interfere with me, sir."

"Do you persist in having this boy flogged?"

"I've given my orders, sir."

"Then, Captain Burgess," cried North, his pale face flushing, "I tell you the boy's blood will be on your head. I am a minister of God, sir, and I forbid you to commit this crime."

"Damn your impertinence, sir!" burst out Burgess. "You're a dismissed officer of the Government, sir. You've no authority here in any way; and, by God, sir, if you interfere with my discipline, sir, I'll have you put in irons until you're shipped out of the island."

This, of course, was mere bravado on the part of the Commandant. North knew well that he would never dare to attempt any such act of violence, but the insult stung him like the cut of a whip. He made a stride towards the Commandant, as though to seize him by the throat, but, checking himself in time, stood still, with clenched hands, flashing eyes, and beard that bristled.

The two men looked at each other, and presently Burgess's eyes fell before those of the chaplain.

"Miserable blasphemer," says North, "I tell you that you shall not flog the boy."

Burgess, white with rage, rang the bell that summoned his convict servant.

"Show Mr. North out," he said, "and go down to the Barracks, and tell Troke that Kirkland is to have a *hundred* lashes to-morrow. I'll show you who's master here, my good sir."

"I'll report this to the Government," said North, aghast. "This is murderous."

"The Government may go to —, and you, too!" roared Burgess. "Get out!" And God's viceregent at Port Arthur slammed the door.

North returned home in great agitation. "They shall not flog that boy," he said. "I'll shield him with my own body if necessary. I'll report this to the Government. I'll see Sir John Franklin myself. I'll have the light of day let into this den of horrors." He reached his cottage, and lighted the lamp in the little sitting-room. All was silent, save that from the adjoining chamber came the sound of Meekin's gentlemanly snore. North took down a book from the shelf and tried to read, but the letters ran together. "I wish I hadn't taken that brandy," he said. "Fool that I am."

Then he began to walk up and down, to fling himself on the sofa, to read, to pray. "Oh, God, give me strength! Aid me! Help me! I struggle, but I am weak. O, Lord, look down upon me!"

To see him rolling on the sofa in agony, to see his white face, his parched lips, and his contracted brow, to hear his moans and muttered prayers, one would have thought him suffering from the pangs of some terrible disease. He opened the book again, and forced himself to read, but his eyes wandered to the cupboard. There lurked something that fascinated him. He got up at length, went into the kitchen, and found a packet of red pepper. He mixed a teaspoonful of this in a pannikin of water and drank it. It relieved him for a while.

"I *must* keep my wits for to-morrow. The life of that lad depends upon it. Meekin, too, will suspect. I will lie down."

He went into his bedroom and flung himself on the bed, but only to toss from side to side. In vain he repeated texts of Scripture and scraps of verse; in vain counted imaginary sheep, or listened to imaginary clock-tickings. Sleep would not come to him. It was as though he had reached the crisis of a disease which had been for days gathering force. "I *must* have a teaspoonful," he said, "to allay the craving."

Twice he paused on the way to the sitting-room, and twice was he driven on by a power stronger than his will. He reached it at length, and opening the cupboard, pulled out what he sought. A bottle of brandy. With this in his hand, all moderation vanished. He raised it to his lips and eagerly drank. Then, ashamed of what he had done, he thrust the bottle back, and made for his room. Still he could not sleep. The taste of the liquor maddened him for more. He saw in the darkness the brandy bottle—vulgar and terrible apparition! He saw its amber fluid sparkle. He heard it gurgle as he poured it out. He smelt the nutty aroma of the spirit. He pictured it standing in the corner of the cupboard, and imagined himself seizing it and quenching the fire that burned within him. He wept, he prayed, he fought with his desire as with a madness. He told himself that another's life depended on his exertions, that to give way to his fatal passion was unworthy of an educated man and a reasoning being, that it was degrading, disgusting, and bestial. That, at all times debasing, at this particular time it was infamous; that a vice, unworthy of any man, was doubly sinful in a man of education and a minister of God. In vain. In the midst of his arguments he found himself at the cupboard, with the bottle at his lips, in an attitude that was at once ludicrous and horrible.

He had no cancer. His disease was a more terrible one. The Reverend James North—gentleman, scholar, and Christian priest— was what the world calls "a confirmed drunkard".

CHAPTER XV

ONE HUNDRED LASHES

THE morning sun, bright and fierce, looked down upon a curious sight. In a stone-yard was a little group of persons—Troke, Burgess, Macklewain, Kirkland, and Rufus Dawes.

Three wooden staves, seven feet high, were fastened together in the form of a triangle. The structure looked not unlike that made by gipsies to boil their kettles. To this structure Kirkland was bound. His feet were fastened with thongs to the base of the triangle; his wrists, bound above his head, at the apex. His body was then extended to its fullest length, and his white back shone in the sunlight. During his tying up he had said nothing—only when Troke pulled off his shirt he shivered.

"Now, prisoner," said Troke to Dawes, "do your duty."

Rufus Dawes looked from the three stern faces to Kirkland's white back, and his face grew purple. In all his experience he had never been asked to flog before. He had been flogged often enough.

"You don't want me to flog him, sir?" he said to the Commandant.

"Pick up the cat, sir!" said Burgess, astonished; "what is the meaning of this?"

Rufus Dawes picked up the heavy cat, and drew its knotted lashes between his fingers.

"Go on, Dawes," whispered Kirkland, without turning his head. "You are no more than another man."

"What does he say?" asked Burgess.

"Telling him to cut light, sir," said Troke, eagerly lying; "they all do it."

"Cut light, eh! We'll see about that. Get on, my man, and look sharp, or I'll tie you up and give you fifty for yourself, as sure as God made little apples."

"Go on, Dawes," whispered Kirkland again. "I don't mind."

Rufus Dawes lifted the cat, swung it round his head, and brought its knotted cords down upon the white back.

"Wonn!" cried Troke.

The white back was instantly striped with six crimson bars. Kirkland stifled a cry. It seemed to him that he had been cut in half.

"Now then, you scoundrel!" roared Burgess; "separate your cats! What do you mean by flogging a man that fashion?"

Rufus Dawes drew his crooked fingers through the entangled cords, and struck again. This time the blow was more effective, and the blood beaded on the skin.

The boy did not cry; but Macklewain saw his hands clutch the staves tightly, and the muscles of his naked arms quiver.

"Tew!"

"That's better," said Burgess.

The third blow sounded as though it had been struck upon a piece of raw beef, and the crimson turned purple.

"My God!" said Kirkland, faintly, and bit his lips.

The flogging proceeded in silence for ten strikes, and then Kirkland gave a screech like a wounded horse.

"Oh!...Captain Burgess!...Dawes!...Mr. Troke!...Oh, my God!...Oh! oh!...Mercy!...Oh, Doctor!...Mr. North!...Oh! Oh! Oh!"

"Ten!" cried Troke, impassively counting to the end of the first twenty.

The lad's back, swollen into a lump, now presented the appearance of a ripe peach which a wilful child had scored with a pin. Dawes, turning away from his bloody handiwork, drew the cats through his fingers twice. They were beginning to get clogged a little.

"Go on," said Burgess, with a nod; and Troke cried "Wonn!" again.

Roused by the morning sun streaming in upon him, Mr. North opened his bloodshot eyes, rubbed his forehead with hands that trembled, and suddenly awakening to a consciousness of his promised errand, rolled off the bed and rose to his feet. He saw the empty brandy bottle on his wooden dressing-table, and remembered what had passed. With shaking hands he dashed water over his aching head, and smoothed his garments. The debauch of the previous night had left the usual effects behind it. His brain seemed on fire, his hands were hot and dry, his tongue clove to the roof of his mouth.

He shuddered as he viewed his pale face and red eyes in the little looking-glass, and hastily tried the door. He had retained sufficient sense in his madness to lock it, and his condition had been unobserved. Stealing into the sitting-room, he saw that the clock pointed to half-past six. The flogging was to have taken place at half-past five. Unless accident had favoured him he was already too late. Fevered with remorse and anxiety, he hurried past the room where Meekin yet slumbered, and made his way to the prison. As he entered the yard, Troke called "Ten!" Kirkland had just got his fiftieth lash.

"Stop!" cried North. "Captain Burgess, I call upon you to stop."

"You're rather late, Mr. North," retorted Burgess. "The punishment is nearly over."

"Wonn!" cried Troke again; and North stood by, biting his nails and grinding his teeth, during six more lashes.

Kirkland ceased to yell now, and merely moaned. His back was like a bloody sponge, while in the interval between lashes the swollen flesh twitched like that of a new-killed bullock. Suddenly, Macklewain saw his head droop on his shoulder. "Throw him off! Throw him off!" he cried, and Troke hurried to loosen the thongs.

"Fling some water over him!" said Burgess; "he's shamming."

A bucket of water made Kirkland open his eyes. "I thought so," said Burgess. "Tie him up again."

"No. Not if you are Christians!" cried North.

He met with an ally where he least expected one. Rufus Dawes flung down the dripping cat. "I'll flog no more," said he.

"What?" roared Burgess, furious at this gross insolence.

"I'll flog no more. Get someone else to do your blood work for you. I won't."

"Tie him up!" cried Burgess, foaming. "Tie him up. Here, constable, fetch a man here with a fresh cat. I'll give you that beggar's fifty, and fifty more on the top of 'em; and he shall look on while his back cools."

Rufus Dawes, with a glance at North, pulled off his shirt without a word, and stretched himself at the triangles. His back was not white and smooth, like Kirkland's had been, but hard and seamed. He had been flogged before. Troke appeared with Gabbett—

grinning. Gabbett liked flogging. It was his boast that he could flog a man to death on a place no bigger than the palm of his hand. He could use his left hand equally with his right, and if he got hold of a "favourite", would "cross the cuts".

Rufus Dawes planted his feet firmly on the ground, took fierce grasp on the staves, and drew in his breath. Macklewain spread the garments of the two men upon the ground, and, placing Kirkland upon them, turned to watch this new phase in the morning's amusement. He grumbled a little below his breath, for he wanted his breakfast, and when the Commandant once began to flog there was no telling where he would stop. Rufus Dawes took five-and-twenty lashes without a murmur, and then Gabbett "crossed the cuts". This went on up to fifty lashes, and North felt himself stricken with admiration at the courage of the man. "If it had not been for that cursed brandy," thought he, with bitterness of self-reproach, "I might have saved all this." At the hundredth lash, the giant paused, expecting the order to throw off, but Burgess was determined to "break the man's spirit".

"I'll make you speak, you dog, if I cut your heart out!" he cried. "Go on, prisoner."

For twenty lashes more Dawes was mute, and then the agony forced from his labouring breast a hideous cry. But it was not a cry for mercy, as that of Kirkland's had been. Having found his tongue, the wretched man gave vent to his boiling passion in a torrent of curses. He shrieked imprecation upon Burgess, Troke, and North. He cursed all soldiers for tyrants, all parsons for hypocrites. He blasphemed his God and his Saviour. With a frightful outpouring of obscenity and blasphemy, he called on the earth to gape and swallow his persecutors, for Heaven to open and rain fire upon them, for hell to yawn and engulf them quick. It was as though each blow of the cat forced out of him a fresh burst of beast-like rage. He seemed to have abandoned his humanity. He foamed, he raved, he tugged at his bonds until the strong staves shook again; he writhed himself round upon the triangles and spat impotently at Burgess, who jeered at his torments. North, with his hands to his ears, crouched against the corner of the wall, palsied with horror. It seemed to him that the passions of hell raged around him. He would fain have fled, but a horrible fascination held him back.

In the midst of this—when the cat was hissing its loudest—Burgess laughing his hardest, and the wretch on the triangles filling the air with his cries, North saw Kirkland look at him with what he thought a smile. Was it a smile? He leapt forward, and uttered a cry of dismay so loud that all turned.

"Hullo!" says Troke, running to the heap of clothes, "the young 'un's slipped his wind!"

Kirkland was dead.

"Throw him off!" says Burgess, aghast at the unfortunate accident; and Gabbett reluctantly untied the thongs that bound Rufus Dawes. Two constables were alongside him in an instant, for sometimes newly tortured men grew desperate. This one, however, was silent with the last lash; only in taking his shirt from under the body of the boy, he muttered, "Dead!" and in his tone there seemed to be a touch of envy. Then, flinging his shirt over his bleeding shoulders, he walked out—defiant to the last.

"Game, ain't he?" said one constable to the other, as they pushed him, not ungently, into an empty cell, there to wait for the hospital guard. The body of Kirkland was taken away in silence, and Burgess turned rather pale when he saw North's threatening face.

"It isn't my fault, Mr. North," he said. "I didn't know that the lad was chicken-hearted." But North turned away in disgust, and Macklewain and Burgess pursued their homeward route together.

"Strange that he should drop like that," said the Commandant.

"Yes, unless he had any internal disease," said the surgeon.

"Disease of the heart, for instance," said Burgess.

"I'll *post-mortem* him and see."

"Come in and have a nip, Macklewain. I feel quite qualmish," said Burgess. And the two went into the house amid respectful salutes from either side. Mr. North, in agony of mind at what he considered the consequence of his neglect, slowly, and with head bowed down, as one bent on a painful errand, went to see the prisoner who had survived. He found him kneeling on the ground, prostrated.

"Rufus Dawes."

At the low tone Rufus Dawes looked up, and, seeing who it was, waved him off.

"Don't speak to me," he said, with an imprecation that made North's flesh creep. "I've told you what I think of you—a hypocrite, who stands by while a man is cut to pieces, and then comes and whines religion to him."

North stood in the centre of the cell, with his arms hanging down, and his head bent.

"You are right," he said, in a low tone. "I must seem to you a hypocrite. *I* a servant of Christ? A besotted beast rather! I am not come to whine religion to you. I am come to—to ask your pardon. I might have saved you from punishment—saved that poor boy from death. I wanted to save him, God knows! But I have a vice; I am a drunkard. I yielded to my temptation, and—I was too late. I come to you as one sinful man to another, to ask you to forgive me." And North suddenly flung himself down beside the convict, and, catching his blood-bespotted hands in his own, cried, "Forgive me, brother!"

Rufus Dawes, too much astonished to speak, bent his black eyes upon the man who crouched at his feet, and a ray of divine pity penetrated his gloomy soul. He seemed to catch a glimpse of misery more profound than his own, and his stubborn heart felt human sympathy with this erring brother. "Then in this hell there is yet a man," said he; and a hand-grasp passed between these two unhappy beings. North arose, and, with averted face, passed quickly from the cell. Rufus Dawes looked at his hand which his strange visitor had taken, and something glittered there. It was a tear. He broke down at the sight of it, and when the guard came to fetch the tameless convict, they found him on his knees in a corner, sobbing like a child.

CHAPTER XVI

KICKING AGAINST THE PRICKS

THE morning after this, the Rev. Mr. North departed in the schooner for Hobart Town. Between the officious chaplain and the Commandant the events of the previous day had fixed a great gulf. Burgess knew that North meant to report the death of Kirkland, and guessed that he would not be backward in relating the story to such persons in Hobart Town as would most readily repeat it. "Blank awkward the fellow's dying," he confessed to himself. "If he hadn't died, nobody would have bothered about him." A sinister truth. North, on the other hand, comforted himself with the belief that the fact of the convict's death under the lash would cause indignation and subsequent inquiry. "The truth must come out if they only *ask*," thought he. Self-deceiving North! Four years a Government chaplain, and not yet attained to a knowledge of a Government's method of "asking" about such matters! Kirkland's mangled flesh would have fed the worms before the ink on the last "minute" from deliberating Authority was dry.

Burgess, however, touched with selfish regrets, determined to baulk the parson at the outset. He would send down an official "return" of the unfortunate occurrence by the same vessel that carried his enemy, and thus get the ear of the Office. Meekin, walking on the evening of the flogging past the wooden shed where the body lay, saw Troke bearing buckets filled with dark-coloured water, and heard a great splashing and sluicing going on inside the hut. "What is the matter?" he asked.

"Doctor's bin post-morticing the prisoner what was flogged this morning, sir," said Troke, "and we're cleanin' up."

Meekin sickened, and walked on. He had heard that unhappy Kirkland possessed unknown disease of the heart, and had unhappily died before receiving his allotted punishment. His duty was to comfort Kirkland's soul; he had nothing to do with Kirkland's slovenly unhandsome body, and so he went for a walk on the pier, that the breeze might blow his momentary sickness away from him.

On the pier he saw North talking to Father Flaherty, the Roman Catholic chaplain. Meekin had been taught to look upon a priest as a shepherd might look upon a wolf, and passed with a distant bow. The pair were apparently talking on the occurrence of the morning, for he heard Father Flaherty say, with a shrug of his round shoulders, "He woas not one of moi people, Mr. North, and the Govermint would not suffer me to interfere with matters relating to Prhotestint prisoners."

"The wretched creature was a Protestant," thought Meekin. "At least then his immortal soul was not endangered by belief in the damnable heresies of the Church of Rome." So he passed on, giving good-humoured Denis Flaherty, the son of the butter-merchant of Kildrum, a wide berth and sea-room, lest he should pounce down upon him unawares, and with Jesuitical argument and silken softness of speech, convert him by force to his own state of error—as was the well-known custom of those intellectual gladiators, the Priests of the Catholic Faith. North, on his side, left Flaherty with regret. He had spent many a pleasant hour with him, and knew him for a narrow-minded, conscientious, yet laughter-loving creature, whose God was neither his belly nor his breviary, but sometimes in one place and sometimes in the other, according to the hour of the day, and the fasts appointed for due mortification of the flesh. "A man who would do Christian work in a jog-trot parish, or where men lived too easily to sin harshly, but utterly unfit to cope with Satan, as the British Government had transported him," was North's sadly satirical reflection upon Father Flaherty, as Port Arthur faded into indistinct beauty behind the swift-sailing schooner. "God help those poor villains, for neither parson nor priest can."

He was right. North, the drunkard and self-tormented, had a power for good, of which Meekin and the other knew nothing. Not merely were the men incompetent and self-indulgent, but they understood nothing of that frightful capacity for agony which is deep in the soul of every evil-doer. They might strike the rock as they chose with sharpest-pointed machine-made pick of warranted Gospel manufacture, stamped with the approval of eminent divines of all ages, but the water of repentance and remorse would not gush for them. They possessed not the frail rod which alone was powerful to charm. They had no sympathy, no knowledge, no experience. He who would touch the hearts of men must have had his own heart seared. The missionaries of mankind have ever been great sinners before they earned the divine right to heal and bless. Their weakness was made their strength, and out of their own agony of repentance came the knowledge which made them masters and saviours of their kind. It was the agony of the Garden and the Cross that gave to the world's Preacher His kingdom in the hearts of men. The crown of divinity is a crown of thorns.

North, on his arrival, went straight to the house of Major Vickers. "I have a complaint to make, sir," he said. "I wish to lodge it formally with you. A prisoner has been flogged to death at Port Arthur. I saw it done."

Vickers bent his brow. "A serious accusation, Mr. North. I must, of course, receive it with respect, coming from you, but I trust that you have fully considered the circumstances of the case. I always understood Captain Burgess was a most humane man."

North shook his head. He would not accuse Burgess. He would let the events speak for themselves. "I only ask for an inquiry," said he.

"Yes, my dear sir, I know. Very proper indeed on your part, if you think any injustice has been done; but have you considered the expense, the delay, the immense trouble and dissatisfaction all this will give?"

"No trouble, no expense, no dissatisfaction, should stand in the way of humanity and justice," cried North.

"Of course not. But will justice be done? Are you sure you can prove your case? Mind, I admit nothing against Captain Burgess, whom I have always considered a most worthy and zealous officer; but, supposing your charge to be true, can you prove it?"

"Yes. If the witnesses speak the truth."

"Who are they?"

"Myself, Dr. Macklewain, the constable, and two prisoners, one of whom was flogged himself. *He* will speak the truth, I believe.

The other man I have not much faith in."

"Very well; then there is only a prisoner and Dr. Macklewain; for if there has been foul play the convict-constable will not accuse the authorities. Moreover, the doctor does not agree with you."

"No?" cried North, amazed.

"No. You see, then, my dear sir, how necessary it is not to be hasty in matters of this kind. I really think—pardon me for my plainness—that your goodness of heart has misled you. Captain Burgess sends a report of the case. He says the man was sentenced to a hundred lashes for gross insolence and disobedience of orders, that the doctor was present during the punishment, and that the man was thrown off by his directions after he had received fifty-six lashes. That, after a short interval, he was found to be dead, and that the doctor made a *post-mortem* examination and found disease of the heart."

North started. "A *post-mortem*? I never knew there had been one held."

"Here is the medical certificate," said Vickers, holding it out, "accompanied by the copies of the evidence of the constable and a letter from the Commandant."

Poor North took the papers and read them slowly. They were apparently straightforward enough. Aneurism of the ascending aorta was given as the cause of death; and the doctor frankly admitted that had he known the deceased to be suffering from that complaint he would not have permitted him to receive more than twenty-five lashes. "I think Macklewain is an honest man," said North, doubtfully. "He would not dare to return a false certificate. Yet the circumstances of the case—the horrible condition of the prisoners—the frightful story of that boy—"

"I cannot enter into these questions, Mr. North. My position here is to administer the law to the best of my ability, not to question it."

North bowed his head to the reproof. In some sort of justly unjust way, he felt that he deserved it. "I can say no more, sir. I am afraid I am helpless in this matter—as I have been in others. I see that the evidence is against me; but it is my duty to carry my efforts as far as I can, and I will do so." Vickers bowed stiffly and wished him good morning. Authority, however well-meaning in private life, has in its official capacity a natural dislike to those dissatisfied persons who persist in pushing inquiries to extremities.

North, going out with saddened spirits, met in the passage a beautiful young girl. It was Sylvia, coming to visit her father. He lifted his hat and looked after her. He guessed that she was the daughter of the man he had left—the wife of the Captain Frere concerning whom he had heard so much. North was a man whose morbidly excited brain was prone to strange fancies; and it seemed to him that beneath the clear blue eyes that flashed upon him for a moment, lay a hint of future sadness, in which, in some strange way, he himself was to bear part. He stared after her figure until it disappeared; and long after the dainty presence of the young bride—trimly booted, tight-waisted, and neatly-gloved—had faded, with all its sunshine of gaiety and health, from out of his mental vision, he still saw those blue eyes and that cloud of golden hair.

CHAPTER XVII

CAPTAIN AND MRS. FRERE

SYLVIA had become the wife of Maurice Frere. The wedding created excitement in the convict settlement, for Maurice Frere, though oppressed by the secret shame at open matrimony which affects men of his character, could not in decency—seeing how "good a thing for him" was this wealthy alliance—demand unceremonious nuptials. So, after the fashion of the town—there being no "continent" or "Scotland" adjacent as a hiding place for bridal blushes—the alliance was entered into with due pomp of ball and supper; bride and bridegroom departing through the golden afternoon to the nearest of Major Vickers's stations. Thence it had been arranged they should return after a fortnight, and take ship for Sydney.

Major Vickers, affectionate though he was to the man whom he believed to be the saviour of his child, had no notion of allowing him to live on Sylvia's fortune. He had settled his daughter's portion—ten thousand pounds—upon herself and children, and had informed Frere that he expected him to live upon an income of his own earning. After many consultations between the pair, it had been arranged that a civil appointment in Sydney would best suit the bridegroom, who was to sell out of the service. This notion was Frere's own. He never cared for military duty, and had, moreover, private debts to no inconsiderable amount. By selling his commission he would be enabled at once to pay these debts, and render himself eligible for any well-paid post under the Colonial Government that the interest of his father-in-law, and his own reputation as a convict disciplinarian, might procure. Vickers would fain have kept his daughter with him, but he unselfishly acquiesced in the scheme, admitting that Frere's plea as to the comforts she would derive from the society to be found in Sydney was a valid one.

"You can come over and see us when we get settled, papa," said Sylvia, with a young matron's pride of place, "and we can come and see you. Hobart Town is very pretty, but I want to see the world."

"You should go to London, Poppet," said Maurice, "that's the place. Isn't it, sir?"

"Oh, London!" cries Sylvia, clapping her hands. "And Westminster Abbey, and the Tower, and St. James's Palace, and Hyde Park, and Fleet-street!"

"'Sir,' said Dr. Johnson, 'let us take a walk down Fleet-street.' Do you remember, in Mr. Croker's book, Maurice? No, you don't I know, because you only looked at the pictures, and then read Pierce Egan's account of the Topping Fight between Bob Gaynor and Ned Neal, or some such person."

"Little girls should be seen and not heard," said Maurice, between a laugh and a blush. "You have no business to read my books."

"Why not?" she asked, with a gaiety which already seemed a little strained; "husband and wife should have no secrets from each other, sir. Besides, I want you to read my books. I am going to read Shelley to you."

"Don't, my dear," said Maurice simply. "I can't understand him."

This little scene took place at the dinner-table of Frere's cottage, in New Town, to which Major Vickers had been invited, in order that future plans might be discussed.

"I don't want to go to Port Arthur," said the bride, later in the evening. "Maurice, there can be no necessity to go there."

"Well," said Maurice. "I want to have a look at the place. I ought to be familiar with all phases of convict discipline, you know."

"There is likely to be a report ordered upon the death of a prisoner," said Vickers. "The chaplain, a fussy but well-meaning person, has been memorializing about it. You may as well do it as anybody else, Maurice."

"Ay. And save the expenses of the trip," said Maurice.

"But it is so melancholy," cried Sylvia.

"The most delightful place in the island, my dear. I was there for a few days once, and I really was charmed."

It was remarkable—so Vickers thought—how each of these newly-mated ones had caught something of the other's manner of speech. Sylvia was less choice in her mode of utterance; Frere more so. He caught himself wondering which of the two methods both would finally adopt.

"But those dogs, and sharks, and things. Oh, Maurice, haven't we had enough of convicts?"

"Enough! Why, I'm going to make my living out of 'em," said Maurice, with his most natural manner.

Sylvia sighed.

"Play something, darling," said her father; and so the girl, sitting down to the piano, trilled and warbled in her pure young voice, until the Port Arthur question floated itself away upon waves of melody, and was heard of no more for that time. But upon pursuing the subject, Sylvia found her husband firm. He wanted to go, and he would go. Having once assured himself that it was advantageous to him to do a certain thing, the native obstinacy of the animal urged him to do it despite all opposition from others, and Sylvia, having had her first "cry" over the question of the visit, gave up the point. This was the first difference of their short married life, and she hastened to condone it. In the sunshine of Love and Marriage—for Maurice at first really loved her; and love, curbing the worst part of him, brought to him, as it brings to all of us, that gentleness and abnegation of self which is the only token and assurance of a love aught but animal—Sylvia's fears and doubts melted away, as the mists melt in the beams of morning. A young girl, with passionate fancy, with honest and noble aspiration, but with the dark shadow of her early mental sickness brooding upon her childlike nature, Marriage made her a woman, by developing in her a woman's trust and pride in the man to whom she had voluntarily given herself. Yet by-and-by out of this sentiment arose a new and strange source of anxiety. Having accepted her position as a wife, and put away from her all doubts as to her own capacity for loving the man to whom she had allied herself, she began to be haunted by a dread lest *he* might do something which would lessen the affection she bore him. On one or two occasions she had been forced to confess that her husband was more of an egotist than she cared to think. He demanded of her no great sacrifices—had he done so she would have found, in making them, the pleasure that women of her nature always find in such self-mortification—but he now and then intruded on her that disregard for the feeling of others which was part of his character. He was fond of her—almost too passionately fond, for her staider liking—but he was unused to thwart his own will in anything, least of all in those seeming trifles, for the consideration of which true selfishness bethinks itself. Did she want to read when he wanted to walk, he good-humouredly put aside her book, with an assumption that a walk with him must, of necessity, be the most pleasing thing in the world. Did she want to walk when he wanted to rest, he laughingly set up his laziness as an all-sufficient plea for her remaining within doors. He was at no pains to conceal his weariness when she read her favourite books to him. If he felt sleepy when she sang or played, he slept without apology. If she talked about a subject in which he took no interest, he turned the conversation remorselessly. He would not have wittingly offended her, but it seemed to him natural to yawn when he was weary, to sleep when he was fatigued, and to talk only about those subjects which interested him. Had anybody told him that he was selfish, he would have been astonished. Thus it came about that Sylvia one day discovered that she led two lives—one in the body, and one in the spirit—and that with her spiritual existence her husband had no share. This discovery alarmed her, but then she smiled at it. "As if Maurice could be expected to take interest in all my silly fancies," said she; and, despite a harassing thought that these same fancies were not foolish, but were the best and brightest portion of her, she succeeded in overcoming her uneasiness. "A man's thoughts are different from a woman's," she said; "he has his business and his worldly cares, of which a woman knows nothing. I must comfort him, and not worry him with my follies."

As for Maurice, he grew sometimes rather troubled in his mind. He could not understand his wife. Her nature was an enigma to him; her mind was a puzzle which would not be pieced together with the rectangular correctness of ordinary life. He had known her from a child, had loved her from a child, and had committed a mean and cruel crime to obtain her; but having got her, he was no nearer to the mystery of her than before. She was all his own, he thought. Her golden hair was for his lingers, her lips were for his caress, her eyes looked love upon him alone. Yet there were times when her lips were cold to his kisses, and her eyes looked disdainfully upon his coarser passion. He would catch her musing when he spoke to her, much as she would catch him sleeping when she read to him—but she awoke with a start and a blush at her forgetfulness, which he never did. He was not a man to brood over these things; and, after some reflective pipes and ineffectual rubbings of his head, he "gave it up". How was it possible, indeed, for him to solve the mental enigma when the woman herself was to him a physical riddle? It was extraordinary that the child he had seen growing up by his side day by day should be a young woman with little secrets, now to be revealed to him for the first time. He found that she had a mole on her neck, and remembered that he had noticed it when she was a child. Then it was a thing of no moment, now it was a marvellous discovery. He was in daily wonderment at the treasure he had obtained. He marvelled at her feminine devices of dress and adornment. Her dainty garments seemed to him perfumed with the odour of sanctity.

The fact was that the patron of Sarah Purfoy had not met with many virtuous women, and had but just discovered what a dainty morsel Modesty was.

THE hospital of Port Arthur was not a cheerful place, but to the tortured and unnerved Rufus Dawes it seemed a paradise. There at least—despite the roughness and contempt with which his gaolers ministered to him—he felt that he was *considered*. There at least he was free from the enforced companionship of the men whom he loathed, and to whose level he felt, with mental agony unspeakable, that he was daily sinking. Throughout his long term of degradation he had, as yet, aided by the memory of his sacrifice and his love, preserved something of his self-respect, but he felt that he could not preserve it long. Little by little he had come to regard himself as one out of the pale of love and mercy, as one tormented of fortune, plunged into a deep into which the eye of Heaven did not penetrate. Since his capture in the garden of Hobart Town, he had given loose rein to his rage and his despair. "I am forgotten or despised; I have no name in the world; what matter if I become like one of these?" It was under the influence of this feeling that he had picked up the cat at the command of Captain Burgess. As the unhappy Kirkland had said, "As well you as another"; and truly, what was he that he should cherish sentiments of honour or humanity? But he had miscalculated his own capacity for evil. As he flogged, he blushed; and when he flung down the cat and stripped his own back for punishment, he felt a fierce joy in the thought that his baseness would be atoned for in his own blood. Even when, unnerved and faint from the hideous ordeal, he flung himself upon his knees in the cell, he regretted only the impotent ravings that the torture had forced from him. He could have bitten out his tongue for his blasphemous utterings—not because they were blasphemous, but because their utterance, by revealing his agony, gave their triumph to his tormentors. When North found him, he was in the very depth of this abasement, and he repulsed his comforter—not so much because he had seen him flogged, as because he had heard him cry. The self-reliance and force of will which had hitherto sustained him through his self-imposed trial had failed him—he felt—at the moment when he needed it most; and the man who had with unflinched front faced the gallows, the desert, and the sea, confessed his debased humanity beneath the physical torture of the lash. He had been flogged before, and had wept in secret at his degradation, but he now for the first time comprehended how terrible that degradation might be made, for he realized how the agony of the wretched body can force the soul to quit its last poor refuge of assumed indifference, and *confess itself conquered*.

Not many months before, one of the companions of the chain, suffering under Burgess's tender mercies, had killed his mate when at work with him, and, carrying the body on his back to the nearest gang, had surrendered himself—going to his death thanking God he had at last found a way of escape from his miseries, which no one would envy him—save his comrades. The heart of Dawes had been filled with horror at a deed so bloody, and he had, with others, commented on the cowardice of the man that would thus shirk the responsibility of that state of life in which it had pleased man and the devil to place him. Now he understood how and why the crime had been committed, and felt only pity. Lying awake with back that burned beneath its lotioned rags, when lights were low, in the breathful silence of the hospital, he registered in his heart a terrible oath that he would die ere he would again be made such hideous sport for his enemies. In this frame of mind, with such shreds of honour and worth as had formerly clung to him blown away in the whirlwind of his passion, he bethought him of the strange man who had deigned to clasp his hand and call him "brother". He had wept no unmanly tears at this sudden flow of tenderness in one whom he had thought as callous as the rest. He had been touched with wondrous sympathy at the confession of weakness made to him, in a moment when his own weakness had overcome him to his shame. Soothed by the brief rest that his fortnight of hospital seclusion had afforded him, he had begun, in a languid and speculative way, to turn his thoughts to religion. He had read of martyrs who had borne agonies unspeakable, upheld by their confidence in Heaven and God. In his old wild youth he had scoffed at prayers and priests; in the hate to his kind that had grown upon him with his later years he had despised a creed that told men to love one another. "God is love, my brethren," said the chaplain on Sundays, and all the week the thongs of the overseer cracked, and the cat hissed and swung. Of what practical value was a piety that preached but did not practise? It was admirable for the "religious instructor" to tell a prisoner that he must not give way to evil passions, but must bear his punishment with meekness. It was only right that he should advise him to "put his trust in God". But as a hardened prisoner, convicted of getting drunk in an unlicensed house of entertainment, had said, "God's terrible far from Port Arthur."

Rufus Dawes had smiled at the spectacle of priests admonishing men, who knew what *he* knew and had seen what *he* had seen, for the trivialities of lying and stealing. He had believed all priests impostors or fools, all religion a mockery and a lie. But now, finding how utterly his own strength had failed him when tried by the rude test of physical pain, he began to think that this Religion which was talked of so largely was not a mere bundle of legend and formulae, but must have in it something vital and sustaining. Broken in spirit and weakened in body, with faith in his own will shaken, he longed for something to lean upon, and turned—as all men turn when in such case—to the Unknown. Had now there been at hand some Christian priest, some Christian-spirited man even, no matter of what faith, to pour into the ears of this poor wretch words of comfort and grace; to rend away from him the garment of sullenness and despair in which he had wrapped himself; to drag from him a confession of his unworthiness, his obstinacy, and his hasty judgment, and to cheer his fainting soul with promise of immortality and justice, he might have been saved from his after fate; but there was no such man. He asked for the chaplain. North was fighting the Convict Department, seeking vengeance for Kirkland, and (victim of "clerks with the cold spurt of the pen") was pushed hither and thither, referred here, snubbed there, bowed out in another place. Rufus Dawes, half ashamed of himself for his request, waited a long morning, and then saw, respectfully ushered into his cell as his soul's physician—Meekin.

CHAPTER XIX

THE CONSOLATIONS OF RELIGION

"WELL, my good man," said Meekin, soothingly, "so you wanted to see me."

"I asked for the chaplain," said Rufus Dawes, his anger with himself growing apace. "I am the chaplain," returned Meekin, with dignity, as who should say—"none of your brandy-drinking, pea-jacketed Norths, but a Respectable chaplain who is the friend of a Bishop!"

"I thought that Mr. North was—"

"Mr. North has left, sir," said Meekin, dryly, "but I will hear what you have to say. There is no occasion to go, constable; wait outside the door."

Rufus Dawes shifted himself on the wooden bench, and resting his scarcely-healed back against the wall, smiled bitterly. "Don't be afraid, sir; I am not going to harm you," he said. "I only wanted to talk a little."

"Do you read your Bible, Dawes?" asked Meekin, by way of reply. "It would be better to read your Bible than to talk, I think. You must humble yourself in prayer, Dawes."

"I have read it," said Dawes, still lying back and watching him.

"But is your mind softened by its teachings? Do you realize the Infinite Mercy of God, Who has compassion, Dawes, upon the greatest sinners?" The convict made a move of impatience. The old, sickening, barren cant of piety was to be recommended then. He came asking for bread, and they gave him the usual stone.

"Do you believe that there is a God, Mr. Meekin?"

"Abandoned sinner! Do you insult a clergyman by such a question?"

"Because I think sometimes that if there is, He must often be dissatisfied at the way things are done here," said Dawes, half to himself.

"I can listen to no mutinous observations, prisoner," said Meekin. "Do not add blasphemy to your other crimes. I fear that all conversation with you, in your present frame of mind, would be worse than useless. I will mark a few passages in your Bible, that seem to me appropriate to your condition, and beg you to commit them to memory. Hailes, the door, if you please."

So, with a bow, the "consoler" departed.

Rufus Dawes felt his heart grow sick. North had gone, then. The only man who had seemed to have a heart in his bosom had gone. The only man who had dared to clasp his horny and blood-stained hand, and call him "brother", had gone. Turning his head, he saw through the window—wide open and unbarred, for Nature, at Port Arthur, had no need of bars—the lovely bay, smooth as glass, glittering in the afternoon sun, the long quay, spotted with groups of parti-coloured chain-gangs, and heard, mingling with the soft murmur of the waves, and the gentle rustling of the trees, the never-ceasing clashing of irons, and the eternal click of hammer. Was he to be for ever buried in this whitened sepulchre, shut out from the face of Heaven and mankind!

The appearance of Hailes broke his reverie. "Here's a book for you," said he, with a grin. "Parson sent it."

Rufus Dawes took the Bible, and, placing it on his knees, turned to the places indicated by slips of paper, embracing some twenty marked texts.

"Parson says he'll come and hear you to-morrer, and you're to keep the book clean."

"Keep the book clean!" and "hear him!" Did Meekin think that he was a charity school boy? The utter incapacity of the chaplain to understand his wants was so sublime that it was nearly ridiculous enough to make him laugh. He turned his eyes downwards to the texts. Good Meekin, in the fullness of his stupidity, had selected the fiercest denunciations of bard and priest. The most notable of the Psalmist's curses upon his enemies, the most furious of Isaiah's ravings anent the forgetfulness of the national worship, the most terrible thunderings of apostle and evangelist against idolatry and unbelief, were grouped together and presented to Dawes to soothe him. All the material horrors of Meekin's faith—stripped, by force of dissociation from the context, of all poetic feeling and local colouring—were launched at the suffering sinner by Meekin's ignorant hand. The miserable man, seeking for consolation and peace, turned over the leaves of the Bible only to find himself threatened with "the pains of Hell", "the never-dying worm", "the unquenchable fire", "the bubbling brimstone", the "bottomless pit", from out of which the "smoke of his torment" should ascend for ever and ever. Before his eyes was held no image of a tender Saviour (with hands soft to soothe, and eyes brimming with ineffable pity) dying crucified that he and other malefactors might have hope, by thinking on such marvellous humanity. The worthy Pharisee who was sent to him to teach him how mankind is to be redeemed with Love, preached only that harsh Law whose barbarous power died with the gentle Nazarene on Calvary.

Repelled by this unlooked-for ending to his hopes, he let the book fall to the ground. "Is there, then, nothing but torment for me in this world or the next?" he groaned, shuddering. Presently his eyes sought his right hand, resting upon it as though it were not his own, or had some secret virtue which made it different from the other. "*He* would not have done this? *He* would not have thrust upon me these savage judgments, these dreadful threats of Hell and Death. He called me 'Brother'!" And filled with a strange wild pity for himself, and yearning love towards the man who befriended him, he fell to nursing the hand on which North's tears had fallen, moaning and rocking himself to and fro.

Meekin, in the morning, found his pupil more sullen than ever.

"Have you learned these texts, my man?" said he, cheerfully, willing not to be angered with his uncouth and unpromising convert.

Rufus Dawes pointed with his foot to the Bible, which still lay on the floor as he had left it the night before. "No!"

"No! Why not?"

"I would learn no such words as those. I would rather forget them."

"Forget them! My good man, I—"

Rufus Dawes sprang up in sudden wrath, and pointing to his cell door with a gesture that—chained and degraded as he was—had something of dignity in it, cried, "What do you know about the feelings of such as I? Take your book and yourself away. When

I asked for a priest, I had no thought of *you*. Begone!"

Meekin, despite the halo of sanctity which he felt should surround him, found his gentility melt all of a sudden. Adventitious distinctions had disappeared for the instant. The pair had become simply man and man, and the sleek priest-master quailing before the outraged manhood of the convict-penitent, picked up his Bible and backed out.

"That man Dawes is very insolent," said the insulted chaplain to Burgess. "He was brutal to me to-day—quite brutal."

"Was he?" said Burgess. "Had too long a spell, I expect. I'll send him back to work to-morrow."

"It would be well," said Meekin, "if he had some employment."

CHAPTER XX

"A NATURAL PENITENTIARY"

THE "employment" at Port Arthur consisted chiefly of agriculture, shipbuilding, and tanning. Dawes, who was in the chain-gang, was put to chain-gang labour; that is to say, bringing down logs from the forest, or "lumbering" timber on the wharf. This work was not light. An ingenious calculator had discovered that the pressure of the log upon the shoulder was wont to average 125 lbs. Members of the chain-gang were dressed in yellow, and—by way of encouraging the others—had the word "Felon" stamped upon conspicuous parts of their raiment.

This was the sort of life Rufus Dawes led. In the summer-time he rose at half-past five in the morning, and worked until six in the evening, getting three-quarters of an hour for breakfast, and one hour for dinner. Once a week he had a clean shirt, and once a fortnight clean socks. If he felt sick, he was permitted to "report his case to the medical officer". If he wanted to write a letter he could ask permission of the Commandant, and send the letter, open, through that Almighty Officer, who could stop it if he thought necessary. If he felt himself aggrieved by any order, he was "to obey it instantly, but might complain afterwards, if he thought fit, to the Commandant". In making any complaint against an officer or constable it was strictly ordered that a prisoner "must be most respectful in his manner and language, when speaking of or to such officer or constable". He was held responsible only for the safety of his chains, and for the rest was at the mercy of his gaoler. These gaolers—owning right of search, entry into cells at all hours, and other *droits* of seigneury—were responsible only to the Commandant, who was responsible only to the Governor, that is to say, to nobody but God and his own conscience. The jurisdiction of the Commandant included the whole of Tasman's Peninsula, with the islands and waters within three miles thereof; and save the making of certain returns to head-quarters, his power was unlimited.

A word as to the position and appearance of this place of punishment. Tasman's Peninsula is, as we have said before, in the form of an earring with a double drop. The lower drop is the larger, and is ornamented, so to speak, with bays. At its southern extremity is a deep indentation called Maingon Bay, bounded east and west by the organ-pipe rocks of Cape Raoul, and the giant form of Cape Pillar. From Maingon Bay an arm of the ocean cleaves the rocky walls in a northerly direction. On the western coast of this sea-arm was the settlement; in front of it was a little island where the dead were buried, called The Island of the Dead. Ere the in-coming convict passed the purple beauty of this convict Golgotha, his eyes were attracted by a point of grey rock covered with white buildings, and swarming with life. This was Point Puer, the place of confinement for boys from eight to twenty years of age. It was astonishing—many honest folks averred—how ungrateful were these juvenile convicts for the goods the Government had provided for them. From the extremity of Long Bay, as the extension of the sea-arm was named, a convict-made tramroad ran due north, through the nearly impenetrable thicket to Norfolk Bay. In the mouth of Norfolk Bay was Woody Island. This was used as a signal station, and an armed boat's crew was stationed there. To the north of Woody Island lay One-tree Point—the southernmost projection of the drop of the earring; and the sea that ran between narrowed to the eastward until it struck on the sandy bar of Eaglehawk Neck. Eaglehawk Neck was the link that connected the two drops of the earring. It was a strip of sand four hundred and fifty yards across. On its eastern side the blue waters of Pirates' Bay, that is to say, of the Southern Ocean, poured their unchecked force. The isthmus emerged from a wild and terrible coast-line, into whose bowels the ravenous sea had bored strange caverns, resonant with perpetual roar of tortured billows. At one spot in this wilderness the ocean had penetrated the wall of rock for two hundred feet, and in stormy weather the salt spray rose through a perpendicular shaft more than five hundred feet deep. This place was called the Devil's Blow-hole. The upper drop of the earring was named Forrestier's Peninsula, and was joined to the mainland by another isthmus called East Bay Neck. Forrestier's Peninsula was an almost impenetrable thicket, growing to the brink of a perpendicular cliff of basalt.

Eaglehawk Neck was the door to the prison, and it was kept bolted. On the narrow strip of land was built a guard-house, where soldiers from the barrack on the mainland relieved each other night and day; and on stages, set out in the water in either side, watch-dogs were chained. The station officer was charged "to pay special attention to the feeding and care" of these useful beasts, being ordered "to report to the Commandant whenever any one of them became useless". It may be added that the bay was not innocent of sharks. Westward from Eaglehawk Neck and Woody Island lay the dreaded Coal Mines. Sixty of the "marked men" were stationed here under a strong guard. At the Coal Mines was the northernmost of that ingenious series of semaphores which rendered escape almost impossible. The wild and mountainous character of the peninsula offered peculiar advantages to the signalmen. On the summit of the hill which overlooked the guard-towers of the settlement was a gigantic gum-tree stump, upon the top of which was placed a semaphore. This semaphore communicated with the two wings of the prison— Eaglehawk Neck and the Coal Mines—by sending a line of signals right across the peninsula. Thus, the settlement communicated with Mount Arthur, Mount Arthur with One-tree Hill, One-tree Hill with Mount Communication, and Mount Communication with the Coal Mines. On the other side, the signals would run thus—the settlement to Signal Hill, Signal Hill to Woody Island, Woody Island to Eaglehawk. Did a prisoner escape from the Coal Mines, the guard at Eaglehawk Neck could be aroused, and the whole island informed of the "bolt" in less than twenty minutes. With these advantages of nature and art, the prison was held to be the most secure in the world. Colonel Arthur reported to the Home Government that the spot which bore his name was a "natural penitentiary". The worthy disciplinarian probably took as a personal compliment the polite forethought of the Almighty in thus considerately providing for the carrying out of the celebrated "Regulations for Convict Discipline".

CHAPTER XXI

A VISIT OF INSPECTION

ONE afternoon ever-active semaphores transmitted a piece of intelligence which set the peninsula agog. Captain Frere, having arrived
from head-quarters, with orders to hold an inquiry into the death of
Kirkland, was not unlikely to make a progress through the stations,
and it behoved the keepers of the Natural Penitentiary to produce
their Penitents in good case. Burgess was in high spirits at finding so
congenial a soul selected for the task of reporting upon him.

"It's only a nominal thing, old man," Frere said to his former
comrade, when they met. "That parson has made meddling, and they
want to close his mouth."

"I am glad to have the opportunity of showing you and Mrs.
Frere the place," returned Burgess. "I must try and make your stay
as pleasant as I can, though I'm afraid that Mrs. Frere will not find
much to amuse her."

"Frankly, Captain Burgess," said Sylvia, "I would rather have
gone straight to Sydney. My husband, however, was obliged to come,
and of course I accompanied him."

"You will not have much society," said Meekin, who was of the
welcoming party. "Mrs. Datchett, the wife of one of our stipendi-
aries, is the only lady here, and I hope to have the pleasure of making
you acquainted with her this evening at the Commandant's. Mr.
McNab, whom you know, is in command at the Neck, and cannot
leave, or you would have seen him."

"I have planned a little party," said Burgess, "but I fear that it
will not be so successful as I could wish."

"You wretched old bachelor," said Frere; "you should get
married, like me."

"Ah!" said Burgess, with a bow, "that would be difficult."

Sylvia was compelled to smile at the compliment, made in the
presence of some twenty prisoners, who were carrying the various
trunks and packages up the hill, and she remarked that the said
prisoners grinned at the Commandant's clumsy courtesy. "I don't like

Captain Burgess, Maurice," she said, in the interval before dinner. "I dare say he did flog that poor fellow to death. He looks as if he could do it."

"Nonsense!" said Maurice, pettishly; "he's a good fellow enough. Besides, I've seen the doctor's certificate. It's a trumped-up story. I can't understand your absurd sympathy with prisoners."

"Don't they sometimes deserve sympathy?"

"No, certainly not—a set of lying scoundrels. You are always whining over them, Sylvia. I don't like it, and I've told you before about it."

Sylvia said nothing. Maurice was often guilty of these small brutalities, and she had learnt that the best way to meet them was by silence. Unfortunately, silence did not mean indifference, for the reproof was unjust, and nothing stings a woman's fine sense like an injustice. Burgess had prepared a feast, and the "Society" of Port Arthur was present. Father Flaherty, Meekin, Doctor Macklewain, and Mr. and Mrs. Datchett had been invited, and the dining-room was resplendent with glass and flowers.

"I've a fellow who was a professional gardener," said Burgess to Sylvia during the dinner, "and I make use of his talents."

"We have a professional artist also," said Macklewain, with a sort of pride. "That picture of the 'Prisoner of Chillon' yonder was painted by him. A very meritorious production, is it not?"

"I've got the place full of curiosities," said Burgess; "quite a collection. I'll show them to you to-morrow. Those napkin rings were made by a prisoner."

"Ah!" cried Frere, taking up the daintily-carved bone, "very neat!"

"That is some of Rex's handiwork," said Meekin. "He is very clever at these trifles. He made me a paper-cutter that was really a work of art."

"We will go down to the Neck to-morrow or next day, Mrs. Frere," said Burgess, "and you shall see the Blow-hole. It is a curious place."

"Is it far?" asked Sylvia.

"Oh no! We shall go in the train."

"The train!"

"Yes—don't look so astonished. You'll see it to-morrow. Oh, you Hobart Town ladies don't know what we can do here."

"What about this Kirkland business?" Frere asked. "I suppose I can have half an hour with you in the morning, and take the depositions?"

"Any time you like, my dear fellow," said Burgess. "It's all the same to me."

"*I* don't want to make more fuss than I can help," Frere said apologetically—the dinner had been good—"but I must send these people up a 'full, true and particular', don't you know."

"Of course," cried Burgess, with friendly *nonchalance*. "That's all right. I want Mrs. Frere to see Point Puer."

"Where the boys are?" asked Sylvia.

"Exactly. Nearly three hundred of 'em. We'll go down to-morrow, and you shall be my witness, Mrs. Frere, as to the way they are treated."

"Indeed," said Sylvia, protesting, "I would rather not. I—I don't take the interest in these things that I ought, perhaps. They are very dreadful to me."

"Nonsense!" said Frere, with a scowl. "We'll come, Burgess, of course."

The next two days were devoted to sight-seeing. Sylvia was taken through the hospital and the workshops, shown the semaphores, and shut up by Maurice in a "dark cell". Her husband and Burgess seemed to treat the prison like a tame animal, whom they could handle at their leisure, and whose natural ferocity was kept in check by their superior intelligence. This bringing of a young and pretty woman into immediate contact with bolts and bars had about it an incongruity which pleased them. Maurice penetrated everywhere, questioned the prisoners, jested with the gaolers, even, in the munificence of his heart, bestowed tobacco on the sick.

With such graceful rattlings of dry bones, they got by and by to Point Puer, where a luncheon had been provided.

An unlucky accident had occurred at Point Puer that morning, however, and the place was in a suppressed ferment. A refractory little thief named Peter Brown, aged twelve years, had jumped off the high rock and drowned himself in full view of the constables. These "jumpings off" had become rather frequent lately, and Burgess was enraged at one happening on this particular day. If he could by any possibility have brought the corpse of poor little Peter Brown to life again, he would have soundly whipped it for its impertinence.

"It is most unfortunate," he said to Frere, as they stood in the cell where the little body was laid, "that it should have happened to-day."

"Oh," says Frere, frowning down upon the young face that seemed to smile up at him. "It can't be helped. I know those young devils. They'd do it out of spite. What sort of a character had he?"

"Very bad—Johnson, the book."

Johnson bringing it, the two saw Peter Brown's iniquities set down in the neatest of running hand, and the record of his punishments ornamented in quite an artistic way with flourishes of red ink.

"20th November, disorderly conduct, 12 lashes. 24th November, insolence to hospital attendant, diet reduced. 4th December, stealing cap from another prisoner, 12 lashes. 15th December, absenting himself at roll call, two days' cells. 23rd December, insolence and insubordination, two days' cells. 8th January, insolence and insubordination, 12 lashes. 20th January, insolence and insubordination, 12 lashes. 22nd February, insolence and insubordination, 12 lashes and one week's solitary. 6th March, insolence and insubordination, 20 lashes."

"That was the last?" asked Frere.

"Yes, sir," says Johnson.

"And then he—hum—did it?"

"Just so, sir. That was the way of it."

Just so! The magnificent system starved and tortured a child of twelve until he killed himself. That was the way of it.

After luncheon the party made a progress. Everything was most admirable. There was a long schoolroom, where such men as Meekin taught how Christ loved little children; and behind the schoolroom were the cells and the constables and the little yard where they gave their "twenty lashes". Sylvia shuddered at the array of faces. From the stolid nineteen years old booby of the Kentish hop-fields, to the wizened, shrewd, ten years old Bohemian of the London streets, all degrees and grades of juvenile vice grinned, in untamable wickedness, or snuffed in affected piety. "Suffer little children to come unto Me, and forbid them not, for of such is the Kingdom of Heaven," said, or is reported to have said, the Founder of our Established Religion. Of such it seemed that a large number of Honourable Gentlemen, together with Her Majesty's faithful commons in Parliament assembled, had done their best to create a Kingdom of Hell.

After the farce had been played again, and the children had stood up and sat down, and sung a hymn, and told how many twice five were, and repeated their belief in "One God the Father Almighty, maker of Heaven and Earth", the party reviewed the workshops, and saw the church, and went everywhere but into the room where the body of Peter Brown, aged twelve, lay starkly on its wooden bench, staring at the gaol roof which was between it and Heaven.

Just outside this room, Sylvia met with a little adventure. Meekin had stopped behind, and Burgess, being suddenly summoned for some official duty, Frere had gone with him, leaving his wife to rest on a bench that, placed at the summit of the cliff, overlooked the sea. While resting thus, she became aware of another presence, and, turning her head, beheld a small boy, with his cap in one hand and a hammer in the other. The appearance of the little creature, clad in a uniform of grey cloth that was too large for him, and holding in his withered little hand a hammer that was too heavy for him, had something pathetic about it.

"What is it, you mite?" asked Sylvia.

"We thought you might have seen him, mum," said the little figure, opening its blue eyes with wonder at the kindness of the tone. "Him! Whom?"

"Cranky Brown, mum," returned the child; "him as did it this morning. Me and Billy knowed him, mum; he was a mate of ours, and we wanted to know if he looked happy."

"What do you mean, child?" said she, with a strange terror at her heart; and then, filled with pity at the aspect of the little being, she drew him to her, with sudden womanly instinct, and kissed him. He looked up at her with joyful surprise. "Oh!" he said.

Sylvia kissed him again.

"Does nobody ever kiss you, poor little man?" said she.

"Mother used to," was the reply, "but she's at home. Oh, mum," with a sudden crimsoning of the little face, "may I fetch Billy?"

And taking courage from the bright young face, he gravely marched to an angle of the rock, and brought out another little creature, with another grey uniform and another hammer.

"This is Billy, mum," he said. "Billy never had no mother. Kiss Billy."

The young wife felt the tears rush to her eyes. "You two poor babies!" she cried. And then, forgetting that she was a lady, dressed in silk and lace, she fell on her knees in the dust, and, folding the friendless pair in her arms, wept over them.

"What is the matter, Sylvia?" said Frere, when he came up. "You've been crying."

"Nothing, Maurice; at least, I will tell you by and by."

When they were alone that evening, she told him of the two little boys, and he laughed. "Artful little humbugs," he said, and supported his argument by so many illustrations of the precocious wickedness of juvenile felons, that his wife was half convinced against her will.

* ˎ

Unfortunately, when Sylvia went away, Tommy and Billy put into execution a plan which they had carried in their poor little heads for some weeks.

"I can do it now," said Tommy. "I feel strong."

"Will it hurt much, Tommy?" said Billy, who was not so courageous.

"Not so much as a whipping."

"I'm afraid! Oh, Tom, it's so deep! Don't leave me, Tom!"

The bigger boy took his little handkerchief from his neck, and with it bound his own left hand to his companion's right.

"Now I *can't* leave you."

"What was it the lady that kissed us said, Tommy?"

"Lord, have pity on them two fatherless children!" repeated Tommy. "Let's say it together."

And so the two babies knelt on the brink of the cliff, and, raising the bound hands together, looked up at the sky, and ungrammatically said, "Lord have pity on we two fatherless children!" And then they kissed each other, and "did it".

*

The intelligence, transmitted by the ever-active semaphore, reached the Commandant in the midst of dinner, and in his agitation he blurted it out.

"These are the two poor things I saw in the morning," cried Sylvia. "Oh, Maurice, these two poor babies driven to suicide!"

"Condemning their young souls to everlasting fire," said Meekin, piously.

"Mr. Meekin! How can you talk like that? Poor little creatures! Oh, it's horrible! Maurice, take me away." And she burst into a passion of weeping.

"*I* can't help it, ma'am," says Burgess, rudely, ashamed. "It ain't my fault."

"She's nervous," says Frere, leading her away. "You must excuse her. Come and lie down, dearest."

"I will not stay here longer," said she. "Let us go to-morrow."

"We can't," said Frere.

"Oh, yes, we can. I insist. Maurice, if you love me, take me away."

"Well," said Maurice, moved by her evident grief, "I'll try."

He spoke to Burgess. "Burgess, this matter has unsettled my wife, so that she wants to leave at once. I must visit the Neck, you know. How can we do it?"

"Well," says Burgess, "if the wind only holds, the brig could go round to Pirates' Bay and pick you up. You'll only be a night at the barracks."

"I think that would be best," said Frere. "We'll start to-morrow, please, and if you'll give me a pen and ink I'll be obliged."

"I hope you are satisfied," said Burgess.

"Oh yes, quite," said Frere. "I must recommend more careful supervision at Point Puer, though. It will never do to have these young blackguards slipping through our fingers in this way."

So a neatly written statement of the occurrence was appended to the ledgers in which the names of William Tomkins and Thomas Grove were entered. Macklewain held an inquest, and nobody troubled about them any more. Why should they? The prisons of London were full of such Tommys and Billys.

*

Sylvia passed through the rest of her journey in a dream of terror. The incident of the children had shaken her nerves, and she longed to be away from the place and its associations. Even Eaglehawk Neck with its curious dog stages and its "natural pavement", did not interest her. McNab's blandishments were wearisome. She shuddered as she gazed into the boiling abyss of the Blow-hole, and shook with fear as the Commandant's "train" rattled over the dangerous tramway that wound across the precipice to Long Bay. The "train" was composed of a number of low wagons pushed and dragged up the steep inclines by convicts, who drew themselves up in the wagons when the trucks dashed down the slope, and acted as drags. Sylvia felt degraded at being thus drawn by human beings, and trembled when the lash cracked, and the convicts answered to the sting—like cattle. Moreover, there was among the foremost of these beasts of burden a face that had dimly haunted her girlhood, and only lately vanished from her dreams. This face looked on her—she thought—with bitterest loathing and scorn, and she felt relieved when at the midday halt its owner was ordered to fall out from the rest, and was with four others re-chained for the homeward journey. Frere, struck with the appearance of the five, said, "By Jove, Poppet, there are our old friends Rex and Dawes, and the others. They won't let 'em come all the way, because they are such a desperate lot, they might make a rush for it." Sylvia comprehended now the face was the face of Dawes; and as she looked after him, she saw him suddenly raise his hands above his head with a motion that terrified her. She felt for an instant a great shock of pitiful recollection. Staring at the group, she strove to recall when and how Rufus Dawes, the wretch from whose clutches her husband had saved her, had ever merited her pity, but her clouded memory could not complete the picture, and as the wagons swept round a curve, and the group disappeared, she awoke from her reverie with a sigh.

"Maurice," she whispered, "how is it that the sight of that man always makes me sad?"

Her husband frowned, and then, caressing her, bade her forget the man and the place and her fears. "I was wrong to have insisted on your coming," he said. They stood on the deck of the Sydney-bound vessel the next morning, and watched the "Natural Penitentiary" grow dim in the distance. "You were not strong enough."

*

"Dawes," said John Rex, "you love that girl! Now that you've seen her another man's wife, and have been harnessed like a beast to drag him along the road, while he held her in his arms!—now that you've seen and suffered that, perhaps you'll join us."

Rufus Dawes made a movement of agonized impatience.

"You'd better. You'll never get out of this place any other way. Come, be a man; join us!"

"No!"

"It is your only chance. Why refuse it? Do you want to live here all your life?"

"I want no sympathy from you or any other. I will not join you."

Rex shrugged his shoulders and walked away. "If you think to get any good out of that 'inquiry', you are mightily mistaken," said he, as he went. "Frere has put a stopper upon that, you'll find." He spoke truly. Nothing more was heard of it, only that, some six months afterwards, Mr. North, when at Parramatta, received an official letter (in which the expenditure of wax and printing and paper was as large as it could be made) which informed him that the "Comptroller-General of the Convict Department had decided that further inquiry concerning the death of the prisoner named in the margin was unnecessary", and that some gentleman with an utterly illegible signature "had the honour to be his most obedient servant".

CHAPTER XXII

GATHERING IN THE THREADS

MAURICE found his favourable expectations of Sydney fully realized. His notable escape from death at Macquarie Harbour, his alliance with the daughter of so respected a colonist as Major Vickers, and his reputation as a convict disciplinarian rendered him a man of note. He received a vacant magistracy, and became even more noted for hardness of heart and artfulness of prison knowledge than before. The convict population spoke of him as "that—Frere," and registered vows of vengeance against him, which he laughed—in his bluff-ness—to scorn.

One anecdote concerning the method by which he shepherded his flock will suffice to show his character and his value. It was his custom to visit the prison-yard at Hyde Park Barracks twice a week. Visitors to convicts were, of course, armed, and the two pistol-butts that peeped from Frere's waistcoat attracted many a longing eye. How easy would it be for some fellow to pluck one forth and shatter the smiling, hateful face of the noted disciplinarian! Frere, however, brave to rashness, never would bestow his weapons more safely, but lounged through the yard with his hands in the pockets of his shooting-coat, and the deadly butts ready to the hand of anyone bold enough to take them.

One day a man named Kavanagh, a captured absconder, who had openly sworn in the dock the death of the magistrate, walked quickly up to him as he was passing through the yard, and snatched a pistol from his belt. The yard caught its breath, and the attendant warder, hearing the click of the lock, instinctively turned his head away, so that he might not be blinded by the flash. But Kavanagh did not fire. At the instant when his hand was on the pistol, he looked up and met the magnetic glance of Frere's imperious eyes. An effort, and the spell would have been broken. A twitch of the finger, and his enemy would have fallen dead. There was an instant when that twitch of the finger could have been given, but Kavanagh let that instant pass. The dauntless eye fascinated him. He played with the pistol nervously, while all remained stupefied. Frere stood, without withdrawing his hands from the pockets into which they were plunged.

"That's a fine pistol, Jack," he said at last.

Kavanagh, down whose white face the sweat was pouring, burst into a hideous laugh of relieved terror, and thrust the weapon, cocked as it was, back again into the magistrate's belt.

Frere slowly drew one hand from his pocket, took the cocked pistol and levelled it at his recent assailant. "That's the best chance *you'll* ever get, Jack," said he.

Kavanagh fell on his knees. "For God's sake, Captain Frere!" Frere looked down on the trembling wretch, and then uncocked the pistol, with a laugh of ferocious contempt. "Get up, you dog," he said. "It takes a better man than you to best me. Bring him up in the morning, Hawkins, and we'll give him five-and-twenty."

As he went out—so great is the admiration for Power—the poor devils in the yard cheered him.

One of the first things that this useful officer did upon his arrival in Sydney was to inquire for Sarah Purfoy. To his astonishment, he discovered that she was the proprietor of large export warehouses in Pitt-street, owned a neat cottage on one of the points of land which jutted into the bay, and was reputed to possess a banking account of no inconsiderable magnitude. He in vain applied his brains to solve this mystery. His cast-off mistress had not been rich when she left Van Diemen's Land—at least, so she had assured him, and appearances bore out her assurance. How had she accumulated this sudden wealth? Above all, why had she thus invested it? He made inquiries at the banks, but was snubbed for his pains. Sydney banks in those days did some queer business. Mrs. Purfoy had come to them "fully accredited," said the manager with a smile.

"But where did she get the money?" asked the magistrate. "I am suspicious of these sudden fortunes. The woman was a notorious character in Hobart Town, and when she left hadn't a penny."

"My dear Captain Frere," said the acute banker—his father had been one of the builders of the "Rum Hospital"—"it is not the custom of our bank to make inquiries into the previous history of its customers. The bills were good, you may depend, or we should not have honoured them. Good morning!"

"The bills!" Frere saw but one explanation. Sarah had received the proceeds of some of Rex's rogueries. Rex's letter to his father and the mention of the sum of money "in the old house in Blue Anchor Yard" flashed across his memory. Perhaps Sarah had got the money from the receiver and appropriated it. But why invest it in an oil and tallow warehouse? He had always been suspicious of the woman, because he had never understood her, and his suspicions redoubled. Convinced that there was some plot hatching, he determined to use all the advantages that his position gave him to discover the secret and bring it to light. The name of the man to whom Rex's letters had been addressed was "Blicks". He would find out if any of the convicts under his care had heard of Blicks. Prosecuting his inquiries in the proper direction, he soon obtained a reply. Blicks was a London receiver of stolen goods, known to at least a dozen of the black sheep of the Sydney fold. He was reputed to be enormously wealthy, had often been tried, but never convicted. Frere was thus not much nearer enlightenment than before, and an incident occurred a few months afterwards which increased his bewilderment.

He had not been long established in his magistracy, when Blunt came to claim payment for the voyage of Sarah Purfoy. "There's that schooner going begging, one may say, sir," said Blunt, when the office door was shut.

"What schooner?"

"The *Franklin*."

Now the *Franklin* was a vessel of three hundred and twenty tons which plied between Norfolk Island and Sydney, as the *Osprey* had plied in the old days between Macquarie Harbour and Hobart Town. "I am afraid that is rather stiff, Blunt," said Frere. "That's one of the best billets going, you know. I doubt if I have enough interest to get it for you. Besides," he added, eyeing the sailor critically, "you are getting oldish for that sort of thing, ain't you?"

Phineas Blunt stretched his arms wide, and opened his mouth, full of sound white teeth. "I am good for twenty years more yet, sir," he said. "My father was trading to the Indies at seventy-five years of age.

I'm hearty enough, thank God; for, barring a drop of rum now and then, I've no vices to speak of. However, I ain't in a hurry, Captain, for a month or so; only I thought I'd jog your memory a bit, d'ye see."

"Oh, you're not in a hurry; where are you going then?"

"Well," said Blunt, shifting on his seat, uneasy under Frere's convict-disciplined eye, "I've got a job on hand."

"Glad of it, I'm sure. What sort of a job?"

"A job of whaling," said Blunt, more uneasy than before.

"Oh, that's it, is it? Your old line of business. And who employs you now?" There was no suspicion in the tone, and had Blunt chosen to evade the question, he might have done so without difficulty, but he replied as one who had anticipated such questioning, and had been advised how to answer it.

"Mrs. Purfoy."

"What!" cried Frere, scarcely able to believe his ears.

"She's got a couple of ships now, Captain, and she made me skipper of one of 'em. We look for beshdellamare, and take a turn at harpooning sometimes."

Frere stared at Blunt, who stared at the window. There was—so the instinct of the magistrate told him—some strange project afoot. Yet that common sense which so often misleads us, urged that it was quite natural Sarah should employ whaling vessels to increase her trade. Granted that there was nothing wrong about her obtaining the business, there was nothing strange about her owning a couple of whaling vessels. There were people in Sydney, of no better origin, who owned half-a-dozen. "Oh," said he. "And when do you start?"

"I'm expecting to get the word every day," returned Blunt, apparently relieved, "and I thought I'd just come and see you first, in *case* of anything falling in." Frere played with a pen-knife on the table in silence for a while, allowing it to fall through his fingers with a series of sharp clicks, and then he said, "Where does she get the money from?"

"Blest if I know!" said Blunt, in unaffected simplicity. "That's beyond me. She says she saved it. But that's all my eye, you know."

"*You* don't know anything about it, then?" cried Frere, suddenly fierce.

"No, not I."

"Because, if there's any game on, she'd better take care," he cried, relapsing, in his excitement, into the convict vernacular. "She knows me. Tell her that I've got my eyes on her. Let her remember her bargain. If she runs any rigs on me, let her take care." In his suspicious wrath he so savagely and unwarily struck downwards with the open pen-knife that it shut upon his fingers, and cut him to the bone.

"I'll tell her," said Blunt, wiping his brow. "I'm sure she wouldn't go to sell you. But I'll look in when I come back, sir." When he got outside he drew a long breath. "By the Lord Harry, but it's a ticklish game to play," he said to himself, with a lively recollection of the dreaded Frere's vehemence; "and there's only one woman in the world I'd be fool enough to play it for."

Maurice Frere, oppressed with suspicions, ordered his horse that afternoon, and rode down to see the cottage which the owner of "Purfoy Stores" had purchased. He found it a low white building, situated four miles from the city, at the extreme end of a tongue of land which ran into the deep waters of the harbour. A garden carefully cultivated, stood between the roadway and the house, and in this garden he saw a man digging.

"Does Mrs. Purfoy live here?" he asked, pushing open one of the iron gates.

The man replied in the affirmative, staring at the visitor with some suspicion.

"Is she at home?"

"No."

"You are sure?"

"If you don't believe me, ask at the house," was the reply, given in the uncourteous tone of a free man.

Frere pushed his horse through the gate, and walked up the broad and well-kept carriage drive. A man-servant in livery, answering his ring, told him that Mrs. Purfoy had gone to town, and then shut the door in his face. Frere, more astonished than ever at these outward and visible signs of independence, paused, indignant, feeling half inclined to enter despite opposition. As he looked through the break of the trees, he saw the masts of a brig lying at anchor off the extremity of the point on which the house was built, and understood that the cottage commanded communication by water as well as by land. Could there be a special motive in choosing such a situation, or was it mere chance? He was uneasy, but strove to dismiss his alarm.

Sarah had kept faith with him so far. She had entered upon a new and more reputable life, and why should he seek to imagine evil where perhaps no evil was? Blunt was evidently honest. Women like Sarah Purfoy often emerged into a condition of comparative riches and domestic virtue. It was likely that, after all, some wealthy merchant was the real owner of the house and garden, pleasure yacht, and tallow warehouse, and that he had no cause for fear.

The experienced convict disciplinarian did not rate the ability of John Rex high enough.

From the instant the convict had heard his sentence of life banishment, he had determined upon escaping, and had brought all the powers of his acute and unscrupulous intellect to the consideration of the best method of achieving his purpose. His first care was to procure money. This he thought to do by writing to Blick, but when informed by Meekin of the fate of his letter, he adopted the—to him—less pleasant alternative of procuring it through Sarah Purfoy.

It was peculiar to the man's hard and ungrateful nature that, despite the attachment of the woman who had followed him to his place of durance, and had made it the object of her life to set him free, he had cherished for her no affection. It was her beauty that had attracted him, when, as Mr. Lionel Crofton, he swaggered in the night-society of London. Her talents and her devotion were secondary considerations—useful to him as attributes of a creature he owned, but not to be thought of when his fancy wearied of its choice. During the twelve years which had passed since his rashness had delivered him into the hands of the law at the house of Green, the coiner, he had been oppressed with no regrets for her fate. He had, indeed, seen and suffered so much that the old life had been put away from him. When, on his return, he heard that Sarah Purfoy was still in Hobart Town, he was glad, for he knew that he had an ally who would do her utmost to help him—she had shown that on board the *Malabar*.

But he was also sorry, for he remembered that the price she would demand for her services was his affection, and that had cooled long ago. However, he would make use of her. There might be a way to discard her if she proved troublesome.

His pretended piety had accomplished the end he had assumed it for. Despite Frere's exposure of his cryptograph, he had won the confidence of Meekin; and into that worthy creature's ear he poured a strange and sad story. He was the son, he said, of a clergyman of the Church of England, whose real name, such was his reverence for the cloth, should never pass his lips. He was transported for a forgery which he did not commit. Sarah Purfoy was his wife—his erring, lost and yet loved wife. She, an innocent and trusting girl, had determined—strong in the remembrance of that promise she had made at the altar—to follow her husband to his place of doom, and had hired herself as lady's-maid to Mrs. Vickers. Alas! fever prostrated that husband on a bed of sickness, and Maurice Frere, the profligate and the villain, had taken advantage of the wife's unprotected state to ruin her! Rex darkly hinted how the seducer made his power over the sick and helpless husband a weapon against the virtue of the wife and so terrified poor Meekin that, had it not "happened so long ago", he would have thought it necessary to look with some disfavour upon the boisterous son-in-law of Major Vickers.

"I bear him no ill-will, sir," said Rex. "I did at first. There was a time when I could have killed him, but when I had him in my power, I—as you know—forbore to strike. No, sir, I could not commit murder!"

"Very proper," says Meekin, "very proper indeed."

"God will punish him in His own way, and His own time," continued Rex.

"My great sorrow is for the poor woman. She is in Sydney, I have heard, living respectably, sir; and my heart bleeds for her." Here Rex heaved a sigh that would have made his fortune on the boards.

"My poor fellow," said Meekin. "Do you know where she is?"

"I do, sir."

"You might write to her."

John Rex appeared to hesitate, to struggle with himself, and finally to take a deep resolve. "No, Mr. Meekin, I will not write."

"Why not?"

"You know the orders, sir—the Commandant *reads* all the letters sent. Could I write to my poor Sarah what other eyes were to read?" and he watched the parson slyly.

"N—no, you could not," said Meekin, at last.

"It is true, sir," said Rex, letting his head sink on his breast. The next day, Meekin, blushing with the consciousness that what he was about to do was wrong, said to his penitent, "If you will promise to write nothing that the Commandant *might* not see, Rex, I will send your letter to your wife."

"Heaven bless you, sir,", said Rex, and took two days to compose an epistle which should tell Sarah Purfoy how to act. The letter was a model of composition in one way. It stated everything clearly and succinctly. Not a detail that could assist was omitted—not a line that could embarrass was suffered to remain. John Rex's scheme of six months' deliberation was set down in the clearest possible manner. He brought his letter unsealed to Meekin. Meekin looked at it with an interest that was half suspicion. "Have I your word that there is nothing in this that might not be read by the Commandant?"

John Rex was a bold man, but at the sight of the deadly thing fluttering open in the clergyman's hand, his knees knocked together. Strong in his knowledge of human nature, however, he pursued his desperate plan. "Read it, sir," he said turning away his face reproachfully. "You are a gentleman. I can trust *you*."

"No, Rex," said Meekin, walking loftily into the pitfall; "I do not read private letters." It was sealed, and John Rex felt as if somebody had withdrawn a match from a powder barrel.

In a month Mr. Meekin received a letter, beautifully written, from "Sarah Rex", stating briefly that she had heard of his goodness, that the enclosed letter was for her husband, and that if it was against the rules to give it him, she begged it might be returned to her unread. Of course Meekin gave it to Rex, who next morning handed to Meekin a most touching pious production, begging him to read it. Meekin did so, and any suspicions he may have had were at once disarmed. He was ignorant of the fact that the pious letter contained a private one intended for John Rex only, which letter John Rex thought so highly of, that, having read it twice through most attentively, he *ate* it.

The plan of escape was after all a simple one. Sarah Purfoy was to obtain from Blicks the moneys he held in trust, and to embark the sum thus obtained in any business which would suffer her to keep a vessel hovering round the southern coast of Van Diemen's Land without exciting suspicion. The escape was to be made in the winter months, if possible, in June or July. The watchful vessel was to be commanded by some trustworthy person, who was to frequently land on the south-eastern side, and keep a look-out for any extraordinary appearance along the coast. Rex himself must be left to run the gauntlet of the dogs and guards unaided. "This seems a desperate scheme," wrote Rex, "but it is not so wild as it looks. I have thought over a dozen others, and rejected them all. This is the only way. Consider it well. I have my own plan for escape, which is easy if rescue be at hand. All depends upon placing a trustworthy man in charge of the vessel. You ought to know a dozen such. I will wait eighteen months to give you time to make all arrangements." The eighteen months had now nearly passed over, and the time for the desperate attempt drew near. Faithful to his cruel philosophy, John Rex had provided scape-goats, who, by their vicarious agonies, should assist him to his salvation.

He had discovered that of the twenty men in his gang eight had already determined on an effort for freedom. The names of these eight were Gabbett, Vetch, Bodenham, Cornelius, Greenhill, Sanders, called the "Moocher", Cox, and Travers. The leading spirits were Vetch and Gabbett, who, with profound reverence, requested the "Dandy" to join. John Rex, ever suspicious, and feeling repelled by the giant's strange eagerness, at first refused, but by degrees allowed himself to appear to be drawn into the scheme. He would urge these men to their fate, and take advantage of the excitement attendant on their absence to effect his own escape. "While all the island is looking for these eight boobies, I shall have a good chance to slip away unmissed." He wished, however, to have a companion. Some strong man, who, if pressed hard, would turn and keep the pursuers at bay, would be useful without doubt; and this comrade-victim he sought in Rufus Dawes.

Beginning, as we have seen, from a purely selfish motive, to urge his fellow-prisoner to abscond with him, John Rex gradually found himself attracted into something like friendliness by the sternness with which his overtures were repelled. Always a keen student of human nature, the scoundrel saw beneath the roughness with which it had pleased the unfortunate man to shroud his agony, how faithful a friend and how ardent and undaunted a spirit was concealed. There was, moreover, a mystery about Rufus Dawes which Rex, the reader of hearts, longed to fathom.

"Have you *no* friends whom you would wish to see?" he asked, one evening, when Rufus Dawes had proved more than usually deaf to his arguments.

"No," said Dawes gloomily. "My friends are all dead to me."

"What, all?" asked the other. "Most men have *some one* whom they wish to see."

Rufus Dawes laughed a slow, heavy laugh. "I am better here."

"Then are you content to live this dog's life?"

"Enough, enough," said Dawes. "I am resolved."

"Pooh! Pluck up a spirit," cried Rex. "It can't fail. I've been thinking of it for eighteen months, and it *can't* fail."

"Who are going?" asked the other, his eyes fixed on the ground. John Rex enumerated the eight, and Dawes raised his head. "I won't go. I have had two trials at it; I don't want another. I would advise you not to attempt it either."

"Why not?"

"Gabbett bolted twice before," said Rufus Dawes, shuddering at the remembrance of the ghastly object he had seen in the sunlit glen at Hell's Gates. "Others went with him, but each time he returned *alone*."

"What do you mean?" asked Rex, struck by the tone of his companion.

"What became of the others?"

"Died, I suppose," said the Dandy, with a forced laugh.

"Yes; but how? They were all without food. How came the surviving monster to live six weeks?"

John Rex grew a shade paler, and did not reply. He recollected the sanguinary legend that pertained to Gabbett's rescue. But he did not intend to make the journey in his company, so, after all, he had no cause for fear. "Come with me then," he said, at length. "We will try our luck together."

"No. I have resolved. I stay here."

"And leave your innocence unproved."

"How can I prove it?" cried Rufus Dawes, roughly impatient. "There are crimes committed which are never brought to light, and this is one of them."

"Well," said Rex, rising, as if weary of the discussion, "have it your own way, then. You know best. The private detective game is hard work. I, myself, have gone on a wild-goose chase before now. There's a mystery about a certain ship-builder's son which took me four months to unravel, and *then* I lost the thread."

"A ship-builder's son! Who was he?"

John Rex paused in wonderment at the eager interest with which the question was put, and then hastened to take advantage of this new opening for conversation. "A queer story. A well-known character in my time—Sir Richard Devine. A miserly old curmudgeon, with a scapegrace son."

Rufus Dawes bit his lips to avoid showing his emotion. This was the second time that the name of his dead father had been spoken in his hearing. "I think I remember something of him," he said, with a voice that sounded strangely calm in his own ears.

"A curious story," said Rex, plunging into past memories. "Amongst other matters, I dabbled a little in the Private Inquiry line of business, and the old man came to me. He had a son who had gone abroad—a wild young dog, by all accounts—and he wanted particulars of him."

"Did you get them?"

"To a certain extent. I hunted him through Paris into Brussels, from Brussels to Antwerp, from Antwerp back to Paris. I lost him there. A miserable end to a long and expensive search. I got nothing but a portmanteau with a lot of letters from his mother. I sent the particulars to the ship-builder, and by all accounts the news killed him, for he died not long after."

"And the son?"

"Came to the queerest end of all. The old man had left him his fortune—a large one, I believe—but he'd left Europe, it seems, for India, and was lost in the *Hydaspes*. Frere was his cousin."

"Ah!"

"By Gad, it annoys me when I think of it," continued Rex, feeling, by force of memory, once more the adventurer of fashion. "With the resources I had, too. Oh, a miserable failure! The days and nights I've spent walking about looking for Richard Devine, and never catching a glimpse of him. The old man gave me his son's portrait, with full particulars of his early life, and I suppose I carried that ivory gimcrack in my breast for nearly three months, pulling it out to refresh my memory every half-hour. By Gad, if the young gentleman was anything like his picture, I could have sworn to him if I'd met him in Timbuctoo."

"Do you think you'd know him again?" asked Rufus Dawes in a low voice, turning away his head.

There may have been something in the attitude in which the speaker had put himself that awakened memory, or perhaps the subdued eagerness of the tone, contrasting so strangely with the comparative inconsequence of the theme, that caused John Rex's brain to perform one of those feats of automatic synthesis at which we afterwards wonder. The profligate son—the likeness to the portrait—the mystery of Dawes's life! These were the links of a galvanic chain. He closed the circuit, and a vivid flash revealed to him—THE MAN.

Warder Troke, coming up, put his hand on Rex's shoulder. "Dawes," he said, "you're wanted at the yard"; and then, seeing his mistake, added with a grin, "Curse you two; you're so much alike one can't tell t'other from which."

Rufus Dawes walked off moodily; but John Rex's evil face turned pale, and a strange hope made his heart leap.

"Gad, Troke's right; we are alike. *I'll not press him to escape any more.*"

CHAPTER XXIII

RUNNING THE GAUNTLET

THE *Pretty Mary*—as ugly and evil-smelling a tub as ever pitched under a southerly burster—had been lying on and off Cape Surville for nearly three weeks. Captain Blunt was getting wearied. He made strenuous efforts to find the oyster-beds of which he was ostensibly in search, but no success attended his efforts. In vain did he take boat and pull into every cove and nook between the Hippolyte Reef and Schouten's Island. In vain did he run the *Pretty Mary* as near to the rugged cliffs as he dared to take her, and make perpetual expeditions to the shore. In vain did he—in his eagerness for the interests of Mrs. Purfoy—clamber up the rocks, and spend hours in solitary soundings in Blackman's Bay. He never found an oyster. "If I don't find something in three or four days more," said he to his mate, "I shall go back again. It's too dangerous cruising here."

*

On the same evening that Captain Blunt made this resolution, the watchman at Signal Hill saw the arms of the semaphore at the settlement make three motions, thus:

The semaphore was furnished with three revolving arms, fixed one above the other. The upper one denoted units, and had six motions, indicating ONE to SIX. The middle one denoted tens, TEN to SIXTY. The lower one marked hundreds, from ONE HUNDRED to SIX HUNDRED.

The lower and upper arms whirled out. That meant THREE HUNDRED AND SIX. A ball ran up to the top of the post. That meant ONE THOUSAND.

Number 1306, or, being interpreted, "PRISONERS ABSCONDED".

"By George, Harry," said Jones, the signalman, "there's a bolt!"

The semaphore signalled again: "Number 1411".

"WITH ARMS!" Jones said, translating as he read. "Come here, Harry! here's a go!"

But Harry did not reply, and, looking down, the watchman saw a dark figure suddenly fill the doorway. The boasted semaphore had failed *this* time, at all events. The "bolters" had arrived as soon as the signal! The man sprang at his carbine, but the intruder had already possessed himself of it. "It's no use making a fuss, Jones! There are eight of us. Oblige me by attending to your signals."

Jones knew the voice. It was that of John Rex. "Reply, can't you?" said Rex coolly. "Captain Burgess is in a hurry." The arms of the semaphore at the settlement were, in fact, gesticulating with comical vehemence. Jones took the strings in his hands, and, with his signal-book open before him, was about to acknowledge the message, when Rex stopped him. "Send this message," he said. "NOT SEEN! SIGNAL SENT TO EAGLEHAWK!" Jones paused irresolutely. He was himself a convict, and dreaded the inevitable cat that he knew would follow this false message. "If they finds me out—" he said. Rex cocked the carbine with so decided a meaning in his black eyes that Jones—who could be brave enough on occasions—banished his hesitation at once, and began to signal eagerly. There came up a clinking of metal, and a murmur from below. "What's keepin' yer, Dandy?"

"All right. Get those irons off, and then we'll talk, boys. I'm putting salt on old Burgess's tail." The rough jest was received with a roar, and Jones, looking momentarily down from his window on the staging, saw, in the waning light, a group of men freeing themselves from their irons with a hammer taken from the guard-house; while two, already freed, were casting buckets of water on the beacon wood-pile. The sentry was lying bound at a little distance.

"Now," said the leader of this surprise party, "signal to Woody Island." Jones perforce obeyed. "Say, 'AN ESCAPE AT THE MINES! WATCH ONE-TREE POINT! SEND ON TO EAGLEHAWK!' Quick now!"

Jones—comprehending at once the force of this manoeuvre, which would have the effect of distracting attention from the Neck— executed the order with a grin. "You're a knowing one, Dandy," said he. John Rex acknowledged the compliment by uncocking the carbine. "Hold out your hands!—Jemmy Vetch!"

"Ay, ay," replied the Crow, from beneath. "Come up and tie our friend Jones. Gabbett, have you got the axes?"

"There's only one," said Gabbett, with an oath. "Then bring that, and any tucker you can lay your hands on. Have you tied him? On we go then." And in the space of five minutes from the time when unsuspecting Harry had been silently clutched by two forms, who rushed upon him out of the shadows of the huts, the Signal Hill Station was deserted.

At the settlement Burgess was foaming. Nine men to seize the Long Bay boat, and get half an hour's start of the alarm signal, was an unprecedented achievement! What could Warder Troke have been about! Warder Troke, however, found eight hours afterwards, disarmed, gagged, and bound in the scrub, had been guilty of no negligence. How could he tell that, at a certain signal from Dandy Jack, the nine men he had taken to Stewart's Bay would "rush" him; and, before he could draw a pistol, truss him like a chicken? The worst of the gang, Rufus Dawes, had volunteered for the hated duties of pile-driving, and Troke had felt himself secure. How could he possibly guess that there was a plot, in which Rufus Dawes, of all men, had refused to join?

Constables, mounted and on foot, were despatched to scour the bush round the settlement. Burgess, confident from the reply of the Signal Hill semaphore, that the alarm had been given at Eaglehawk Isthmus, promised himself the re-capture of the gang before many hours; and, giving orders to keep the communications going, retired to dinner. His convict servants had barely removed the soup when the result of John Rex's ingenuity became manifest.

The semaphore at Signal Hill had stopped working.

"Perhaps the fools can't see," said Burgess. "Fire the beacon— and saddle my horse." The beacon was fired. All right at Mount Arthur, Mount Communication, and the Coal Mines. To the westward the line was clear. But at Signal Hill was no answering light. Burgess stamped with rage. "Get me my boat's crew ready; and tell the Mines to signal to Woody Island." As he stood on the jetty, a breathless messenger brought the reply. "A BOAT'S CREW GONE TO ONE-TREE POINT! FIVE MEN SENT FROM EAGLEHAWK

IN OBEDIENCE TO ORDERS!" Burgess understood it at once. The fellows had decoyed the Eaglehawk guard. "Give way, men!" And the boat, shooting into the darkness, made for Long Bay. "I won't be far behind 'em," said the Commandant, "at any rate."

Between Eaglehawk and Signal Hill were, for the absconders, other dangers. Along the indented coast of Port Bunche were four constables' stations. These stations—mere huts within signalling distance of each other—fringed the shore, and to avoid them it would be necessary to make a circuit into the scrub. Unwilling as he was to lose time, John Rex saw that to attempt to run the gauntlet of these four stations would be destruction. The safety of the party depended upon the reaching of the Neck while the guard was weakened by the absence of some of the men along the southern shore, and before the alarm could be given from the eastern arm of the peninsula. With this view, he ranged his men in single file; and, quitting the road near Norfolk Bay, made straight for the Neck. The night had set in with a high westerly wind, and threatened rain. It was pitch dark; and the fugitives were guided only by the dull roar of the sea as it beat upon Descent Beach. Had it not been for the accident of a westerly gale, they would not have had even so much assistance.

The Crow walked first, as guide, carrying a musket taken from Harry. Then came Gabbett, with an axe; followed by the other six, sharing between them such provisions as they had obtained at Signal Hill. John Rex, with the carbine, and Troke's pistols, walked last. It had been agreed that if attacked they were to run each one his own way. In their desperate case, disunion was strength. At intervals, on their left, gleamed the lights of the constables' stations, and as they stumbled onward they heard plainer and more plainly the hoarse murmur of the sea, beyond which was liberty or death.

After nearly two hours of painful progress, Jemmy Vetch stopped, and whispered them to approach. They were on a sandy rise. To the left was a black object—a constable's hut; to the right was a dim white line—the ocean; in front was a row of lamps, and between every two lamps leapt and ran a dusky, indistinct body. Jemmy Vetch pointed with his lean forefinger.

"The dogs!"

Instinctively they crouched down, lest even at that distance the two sentries, so plainly visible in the red light of the guard-house fire, should see them.

"Well, bo's," said Gabbett, "what's to be done now?"

As he spoke, a long low howl broke from one of the chained hounds, and the whole kennel burst into hideous outcry. John Rex, who perhaps was the bravest of the party, shuddered. "They have smelt us," he said. "We must go on."

Gabbett spat in his palm, and took firmer hold of the axe-handle.

"Right you are," he said. "I'll leave my mark on some of them before this night's out!"

On the opposite shore lights began to move, and the fugitives could hear the hurrying tramp of feet.

"Make for the right-hand side of the jetty," said Rex in a fierce whisper. "I think I see a boat there. It is our only chance now. We can never break through the station. Are we ready? Now! All together!"

Gabbett was fast outstripping the others by some three feet of distance. There were eleven dogs, two of whom were placed on stages set out in the water, and they were so chained that their muzzles nearly touched. The giant leapt into the line, and with a blow of his axe split the skull of the beast on his right hand. This action unluckily took him within reach of the other dog, which seized him by the thigh.

"Fire!" cried McNab from the other side of the lamps.

The giant uttered a cry of rage and pain, and fell with the dog under him. It was, however, the dog who had pulled him down, and the musket-ball intended for him struck Travers in the jaw. The unhappy villain fell—like Virgil's Dares—"spitting blood, teeth, and curses."

Gabbett clutched the mastiffs throat with iron hand, and forced him to loose his hold; then, bellowing with fury, seized his axe and sprang forward, mangled as he was, upon the nearest soldier. Jemmy Vetch had been beforehand with him. Uttering a low snarl of hate, he fired, and shot the sentry through the breast. The others rushed through the now broken cordon, and made headlong for the boat.

"Fools!" cried Rex behind them. "You have wasted a shot! LOOK TO YOUR LEFT!"

Burgess, hurried down the tramroad by his men, had tarried at Signal Hill only long enough to loose the surprised guard from their bonds, and taking the Woody Island boat was pulling with a fresh crew to the Neck. The reinforcement was not ten yards from the jetty.

The Crow saw the danger, and, flinging himself into the water, desperately seized McNab's boat.

"In with you for your lives!" he cried. Another volley from the guard spattered the water around the fugitives, but in the darkness the ill-aimed bullets fell harmless. Gabbett swung himself over the sheets, and seized an oar.

"Cox, Bodenham, Greenhill! Now, push her off! Jump, Tom, jump!" and as Burgess leapt to land, Cornelius was dragged over the stern, and the whale-boat floated into deep water.

McNab, seeing this, ran down to the water-side to aid the Commandant.

"Lift her over the Bar, men!" he shouted. "With a will—So!" And, raised in twelve strong arms, the pursuing craft slid across the isthmus.

"We've five minutes' start," said Vetch coolly, as he saw the Commandant take his place in the stem sheets. "Pull away, my jolly boys, and we'll best 'em yet."

The soldiers on the Neck fired again almost at random, but the blaze of their pieces only served to show the Commandant's boat a hundred yards astern of that of the mutineers, which had already gained the deep water of Pirates' Bay.

Then, for the first time, the six prisoners became aware that John Rex was not among them.

JOHN Rex had put into execution the first part of his scheme.

At the moment when, seeing Burgess's boat near the sand-spit, he had uttered the warning cry heard by Vetch, he turned back into the darkness, and made for the water's edge at a point some distance from the Neck. His desperate hope was that, the attention of the guard being concentrated on the escaping boat, he might, favoured by the darkness and the confusion—*swim* to the peninsula. It was not a very marvellous feat to accomplish, and he had confidence in his own powers. Once safe on the peninsula, his plans were formed. But, owing to the strong westerly wind, which caused an incoming tide upon the isthmus, it was necessary for him to attain some point sufficiently far to the southward to enable him, on taking the water, to be assisted, not impeded, by the current. With this view, he hurried over the sandy hummocks at the entrance to the Neck, and ran backwards towards the sea. In a few strides he had gained the hard and sandy shore, and, pausing to listen, heard behind him the sound of footsteps. He was pursued. The footsteps stopped, and then a voice cried—

"Surrender!"

It was McNab, who, seeing Rex's retreat, had daringly followed him. John Rex drew from his breast Troke's pistol and waited.

"Surrender!" cried the voice again, and the footsteps advanced two paces.

At the instant that Rex raised the weapon to fire, a vivid flash of lightning showed him, on his right hand, on the ghastly and pallid ocean, two boats, the hindermost one apparently within a few yards of him. The men looked like corpses. In the distance rose Cape Surville, and beneath Cape Surville was the hungry sea. The scene vanished in an instant—swallowed up almost before he had realized it. But the shock it gave him made him miss his aim, and, flinging away the pistol with a curse, he turned down the path and fled. McNab followed. The path had been made by frequent passage from the station, and

Rex found it tolerably easy running. He had acquired—like most men who live much in the dark—that cat-like perception of obstacles which is due rather to increased sensitiveness of touch than increased acuteness of vision. His feet accommodated themselves to the inequalities of the ground; his hands instinctively outstretched themselves towards the overhanging boughs; his head ducked of its own accord to any obtrusive sapling which bent to obstruct his progress. His pursuer was not so fortunate. Twice did John Rex laugh mentally, at a crash and scramble that told of a fall, and once—in a valley where trickled a little stream that he had cleared almost without an effort—he heard a splash that made him laugh outright. The track now began to go uphill, and Rex redoubled his efforts, trusting to his superior muscular energy to shake off his pursuer. He breasted the rise, and paused to listen. The crashing of branches behind him had ceased, and it seemed that he was alone.

He had gained the summit of the cliff. The lights of the Neck were invisible. Below him lay the sea. Out of the black emptiness came puffs of sharp salt wind. The tops of the rollers that broke below were blown off and whirled away into the night—white patches, swallowed up immediately in the increasing darkness. From the north side of the bay was borne the hoarse roar of the breakers as they dashed against the perpendicular cliffs which guarded Forrestier's Peninsula. At his feet arose a frightful shrieking and whistling, broken at intervals by reports like claps of thunder. Where was he? Exhausted and breathless, he sank down into the rough scrub and listened. All at once, on the track over which he had passed, he heard a sound that made him bound to his feet in deadly fear—the bay of a dog!

He thrust his hand to his breast for the remaining pistol, and uttered a cry of alarm. He had dropped it. He felt round about him in the darkness for some stick or stone that might serve as a weapon. In vain. His fingers clutched nothing but prickly scrub and coarse grass. The sweat ran down his face. With staring eyeballs, and bristling hair, he stared into the darkness, as if he would dissipate it by the very intensity of his gaze. The noise was repeated, and, piercing through the roar of wind and water, above and below him, seemed to be close at hand. He heard a man's voice cheering the dog in accents that the gale blew away from him before he could recognize them. It was probable that some of the soldiers had been sent to the assistance of McNab. Capture, then, was certain. In his agony, the wretched man almost promised himself repentance, should he escape this peril. The dog, crashing through the underwood, gave one short, sharp howl, and then ran mute.

The darkness had increased the gale. The wind, ravaging the hollow heaven, had spread between the lightnings and the sea an impenetrable curtain of black cloud. It seemed possible to seize upon this curtain and draw its edge yet closer, so dense was it. The white and raging waters were blotted out, and even the lightning seemed unable to penetrate that intense blackness. A large, warm drop of rain fell upon Rex's outstretched hand, and far overhead rumbled a wrathful peal of thunder. The shrieking which he had heard a few moments ago had ceased, but every now and then dull but immense shocks, as of some mighty bird flapping the cliff with monstrous wings, reverberated around him, and shook the ground where he stood. He looked towards the ocean, and a tall misty Form—white against the all-pervading blackness—beckoned and bowed to him. He saw it distinctly for an instant, and then, with an awful shriek, as of wrathful despair, it sank and vanished. Maddened with a terror he could not define, the hunted man turned to meet the material peril that was so close at hand.

With a ferocious gasp, the dog flung himself upon him. John Rex was borne backwards, but, in his desperation, he clutched the beast by the throat and belly, and, exerting all his strength, flung him off. The brute uttered one howl, and seemed to lie where he had fallen; while above his carcase again hovered that white and vaporous column. It was strange that McNab and the soldier did not follow up the advantage they had gained. Courage—perhaps he should defeat them yet! He had been lucky to dispose of the dog so easily. With a fierce thrill of renewed hope, he ran forward; when at his feet, in his face, arose that misty Form, breathing chill warning, as though to wave him back. The terror at his heels drove him on. A few steps more, and he should gain the summit of the cliff. He could *feel* the sea roaring in front of him in the gloom. The column disappeared; and in a lull of wind, uprose from the place where it had been such a hideous medley of shrieks, laughter, and exultant wrath, that John Rex paused in horror. Too late. The ground gave way—it seemed—beneath his feet. He was falling—clutching, in vain, at rocks, shrubs, and grass. The cloud-curtain lifted, and by the lightning that leaped and played about the ocean, John Rex found an explanation of his terrors, more terrible than they themselves had been. The track he had followed led to that portion of the cliff in which the sea had excavated the tunnel-spout known as the Devil's Blow-hole.

Clinging to a tree that, growing half-way down the precipice, had arrested his course, he stared into the abyss. Before him—already high above his head—was a gigantic arch of cliff. Through this arch he saw, at an immense distance below him, the raging and pallid ocean. Beneath him was an abyss splintered with black rocks, turbid and raucous with tortured water. Suddenly the bottom of this abyss seemed to advance to meet him; or, rather, the black throat of the chasm belched a volume of leaping, curling water, which mounted to drown him. Was it fancy that showed him, on the surface of the rising column, the mangled carcase of the dog?

The chasm into which John Rex had fallen was shaped like a huge funnel set up on its narrow end. The sides of this funnel were rugged rock, and in the banks of earth lodged here and there upon projections, a scrubby vegetation grew. The scanty growth paused abruptly half-way down the gulf, and the rock below was perpetually damp from the upthrown spray. Accident—had the convict been a Meekin, we might term it Providence—had lodged him on the lowest of these banks of earth. In calm weather he would have been out of danger, but the lightning flash revealed to his terror-sharpened sense a black patch of dripping rock on the side of the chasm some ten feet above his head. It was evident that upon the next rising of the water-spout the place where he stood would be covered with water.

The roaring column mounted with hideous swiftness. Rex felt it rush at him and swing him upward. With both arms round the tree, he clutched the sleeves of his jacket with either hand. Perhaps if he could maintain his hold he might outlive the shock of that suffocating torrent. He felt his feet rudely seized, as though by the hand of a giant, and plucked upwards. Water gurgled in his ears. His arms seemed about to be torn from their sockets. Had the strain lasted another instant, he must have loosed his hold; but, with a wild hoarse shriek, as though it was some sea-monster baffled of its prey, the column sank, and left him gasping, bleeding, half-drowned, but alive. It was impossible that he could survive another shock, and in his agony he unclasped his stiffened fingers, determined to resign himself to his fate. At that instant, however, he saw on the wall of rock that hollowed on his right hand, a red and lurid light, in the midst of which fantastically bobbed hither and thither the gigantic shadow of a man. He cast his eyes upwards and saw, slowly descending into the gulf, a blazing bush tied to a rope. McNab was taking advantage of the pause in the spouting to examine the sides of the Blow-hole.

A despairing hope seized John Rex. In another instant the light would reveal his figure, clinging like a limpet to the rock, to those above. He must be detected in any case; but if they could lower the rope sufficiently, he might clutch it and be saved. His dread of the horrible death that was beneath him overcame his resolution to avoid recapture. The long-drawn agony of the retreating water as it was sucked back again into the throat of the chasm had ceased, and he knew that the next tremendous pulsation of the sea below would hurl the spuming destruction up upon him. The gigantic torch slowly descended, and he had already drawn in his breath for a shout which should make itself heard above the roar of the wind and water, when a strange appearance on the face of the cliff made him pause. About six feet from him—glowing like molten gold in the gusty glow of the burning tree—a round sleek stream of water slipped from the rock into the darkness, like a serpent from its hole. Above this stream a dark spot defied the torchlight, and John Rex felt his heart leap with one last desperate hope as he comprehended that close to him was one of those tortuous drives which the worm-like action of the sea bores in such caverns as that in which he found himself. The drive, opened first to the light of the day by the natural convulsion which had raised the mountain itself above ocean level, probably extended into the bowels of the cliff. The stream ceased to let itself out of the crevice; it was then likely that the rising column of water did not penetrate far into this wonderful hiding-place.

Endowed with a wisdom, which in one placed in less desperate position would have been madness, John Rex shouted to his pursuers. "The rope! the rope!" The words, projected against the sides of the enormous funnel, were pitched high above the blast, and, reduplicated by a thousand echoes, reached the ears of those above.

"He's alive!" cried McNab, peering into the abyss. "I see him. Look!"

The soldier whipped the end of the bullock-hide lariat round the tree to which he held, and began to oscillate it, so that the blazing bush might reach the ledge on which the daring convict sustained himself. The groan which preceded the fierce belching forth of the torrent was cast up to them from below.

"God be gude to the puir felly!" said the pious young Scotchman, catching his breath.

A white spume was visible at the bottom of the gulf, and the groan changed into a rapidly increasing bellow. John Rex, eyeing the blazing pendulum, that with longer and longer swing momentarily neared him, looked up to the black heaven for the last time with a muttered prayer. The bush—the flame fanned by the motion—flung a crimson glow upon his frowning features which, as he caught the rope, had a sneer of triumph on them. "Slack out! slack out!" he cried; and then, drawing the burning bush towards him, attempted to stamp out the fire with his feet.

The soldier set his body against the tree trunk, and gripped the rope hard, turning his head away from the fiery pit below him. "Hold tight, your honour," he muttered to McNab. "She's coming!"

The bellow changed into a roar, the roar into a shriek, and with a gust of wind and spray, the seething sea leapt up out of the gulf. John Rex, unable to extinguish the flame, twisted his arm about the rope, and the instant before the surface of the rising water made a momentary floor to the mouth of the cavern, he spurned the cliff desperately with his feet, and flung himself across the chasm. He had already clutched the rock, and thrust himself forward, when the tremendous volume of water struck him. McNab and the soldier felt the sudden pluck of the rope and saw the light swing across the abyss. Then the fury of the waterspout burst with a triumphant scream, the tension ceased, the light was blotted out, and when the column sank, there dangled at the end of the lariat nothing but the drenched and blackened skeleton of the she-oak bough. Amid a terrific peal of thunder, the long pent-up rain descended, and a sudden ghastly rending asunder of the clouds showed far below them the heaving ocean, high above them the jagged and glistening rocks, and at their feet the black and murderous abyss of the Blow-hole—empty.

They pulled up the useless rope in silence; and another dead tree lighted and lowered showed them nothing.

"God rest his puir soul," said McNab, shuddering. "He's out o' our han's now."

CHAPTER XXV

THE FLIGHT

GABBETT, guided by the Crow, had determined to beach the captured boat on the southern point of Cape Surville. It will be seen by those who have followed the description of the topography of Colonel Arthur's Penitentiary, that nothing but the desperate nature of the attempt could have justified so desperate a measure. The perpendicular cliffs seemed to render such an attempt certain destruction; but Vetch, who had been employed in building the pier at the Neck, knew that on the southern point of the promontory was a strip of beach, upon which the company might, by good fortune, land in safety. With something of the decision of his leader, Rex, the Crow determined at once that in their desperate plight this was the only measure, and setting his teeth as he seized the oar that served as a rudder, he put the boat's head straight for the huge rock that formed the northern horn of Pirates' Bay.

Save for the faint phosphorescent radiance of the foaming waves, the darkness was intense, and Burgess for some minutes pulled almost at random in pursuit. The same tremendous flash of lightning which had saved the life of McNab, by causing Rex to miss his aim, showed to the Commandant the whale-boat balanced on the summit of an enormous wave, and apparently about to be flung against the wall of rock which—magnified in the flash—seemed frightfully near to them. The next instant Burgess himself—his boat lifted by the swiftly advancing billow—saw a wild waste of raging seas scooped into abysmal troughs, in which the bulk of a leviathan might wallow. At the bottom of one of these valleys of water lay the mutineers' boat, looking, with its outspread oars, like some six-legged insect floating in a pool of ink. The great cliff, whose every scar and crag was as distinct as though its huge bulk was but a yard distant, seemed to shoot out from its base towards the struggling insect, a broad, flat straw, that was a strip of dry land. The next instant the rushing water, carrying the six-legged atom with it, creamed up over this strip of beach; the giant crag, amid the thunder-crash which followed upon the lightning, appeared to stoop down over the ocean, and as it stooped, the billow rolled onwards, the boat glided down into the depths, and the whole phantasmagoria was swallowed up in the tumultuous darkness of the tempest.

Burgess—his hair bristling with terror—shouted to put the boat about, but he might with as much reason have shouted at an avalanche. The wind blew his voice away, and emptied it violently into the air. A snarling billow jerked the oar from his hand. Despite the desperate efforts of the soldiers, the boat was whirled up the mountain of water like a leaf on a water-spout, and a second flash of lightning showed them what seemed a group of dolls struggling in the surf, and a walnut-shell bottom upwards was driven by the recoil of the waves towards them. For an instant all thought that they must share the fate which had overtaken the unlucky convicts; but Burgess succeeded in trimming the boat, and, awed by the peril he had so narrowly escaped, gave the order to return. As the men set the boat's head to the welcome line of lights that marked the Neck, a black spot balanced upon a black line was swept under their stern and carried out to sea. As it passed them, this black spot emitted a cry, and they knew that it was one of the shattered boat's crew clinging to an oar.

"He was the only one of 'em alive," said Burgess, bandaging his sprained wrist two hours afterwards at the Neck, "and he's food for the fishes by this time!"

He was mistaken, however. Fate had in reserve for the crew of villains a less merciful death than that of drowning. Aided by the lightning, and that wonderful "good luck" which urges villainy to its destruction, Vetch beached the boat, and the party, bruised and bleeding, reached the upper portion of the shore in safety. Of all this number only Cox was lost. He was pulling stroke-oar, and, being something of a laggard, stood in the way of the Crow, who, seeing the importance of haste in preserving his own skin, plucked the man backwards by the collar, and passed over his sprawling body to the shore. Cox, grasping at anything to save himself, clutched an oar, and the next moment found himself borne out with the overturned whale-boat by the under-tow. He was drifted past his only hope of rescue—the guard-boat—with a velocity that forbade all attempts at rescue, and almost before the poor scoundrel had time to realize his condition, he was in the best possible way of escaping the hanging that his comrades had so often humorously prophesied for him. Being a strong and vigorous villain, however, he clung tenaciously to his oar, and even unbuckling his leather belt, passed it round the slip of wood that was his salvation, girding himself to it as firmly as he was able. In this condition, *plus* a swoon from exhaustion, he was descried by the helmsman of the *Pretty Mary,* a few miles from Cape Surville, at daylight next morning. Blunt, with a wild hope that this waif and stray might be the lover of Sarah Purfoy, *dead,* lowered a boat and picked him up. Nearly bisected by the belt, gorged with salt water, frozen with cold, and having two ribs broken, the victim of Vetch's murderous quickness retained sufficient life to survive Blunt's remedies for nearly two hours. During that time he stated that his name was Cox, that he had escaped from Port Arthur with eight others, that John Rex was the leader of the expedition, that the others were all drowned, and that he believed John Rex had been retaken. Having placed Blunt in possession of these particulars, he further said that it pricked him to breathe, cursed Jemmy Vetch, the settlement, and the sea, and so impenitently died. Blunt smoked three pipes, and then altered the course of the *Pretty Mary* two points to the eastward, and ran for the coast. It was possible that the man for whom he was searching had not been retaken, and was even now awaiting his arrival. It was clearly his duty—hearing of the planned escape having been actually attempted—not to give up the expedition while hope remained.

"I'll take one more look along," said he to himself.

The *Pretty Mary,* hugging the coast as closely as she dared, crawled in the thin breeze all day, and saw nothing. It would be madness to land at Cape Surville, for the whole station would be on the alert; so Blunt, as night was falling, stood off a little across the mouth of Pirates' Bay. He was walking the deck, groaning at the folly of the expedition, when a strange appearance on the southern horn of the bay made him come to a sudden halt. There was a furnace blazing in the bowels of the mountain! Blunt rubbed his eyes and stared. He looked at the man at the helm. "Do you see anything yonder, Jem?"

Jem—a Sydney man, who had never been round that coast before—briefly remarked, "Lighthouse."

Blunt stumped into the cabin and got out his charts. No lighthouse was laid down there, only a mark like an anchor, and a note, "Remarkable Hole at this Point." A remarkable hole indeed; a remarkable "lime kiln" would have been more to the purpose!

Blunt called up his mate, William Staples, a fellow whom Sarah Purfoy's gold had bought body and soul. William Staples looked at the waxing and waning glow for a while, and then said, in tones trembling with greed, "It's a fire. Lie to, and lower away the jolly-boat. Old man, that's our bird for a thousand pounds!"

The *Pretty Mary* shortened sail, and Blunt and Staples got into the jolly-boat.

"Goin' a-hoysterin', sir?" said one of the crew, with a grin, as Blunt threw a bundle into the stern-sheets.

Staples thrust his tongue into his cheek. The object of the voyage was now pretty well understood among the carefully picked crew. Blunt had not chosen men who were likely to betray him, though, for that matter, Rex had suggested a precaution which rendered betrayal almost impossible.

"What's in the bundle, old man?" asked Will Staples, after they had got clear of the ship.

"Clothes," returned Blunt. "We can't bring him off, if it *is* him, in his canaries. He puts on these duds, d'ye see, sinks Her Majesty's livery, and comes aboard, a 'shipwrecked mariner'."

"That's well thought of. Whose notion's that? The Madam's, I'll be bound."

"Ay."

"She's a knowing one."

And the sinister laughter of the pair floated across the violet water.

"Go easy, man," said Blunt, as they neared the shore. "They're all awake at Eaglehawk; and if those cursed dogs give tongue there'll be a boat out in a twinkling. It's lucky the wind's off shore."

Staples lay on his oar and listened. The night was moonless, and the ship had already disappeared from view. They were approaching the promontory from the south-east, and this isthmus of the guarded Neck was hidden by the outlying cliff. In the south-western angle of this cliff, about midway between the summit and the sea, was an arch, which vomited a red and flickering light, that faintly shone upon the sea in the track of the boat. The light was lambent and uncertain, now sinking almost into insignificance, and now leaping up with a fierceness that caused a deep glow to throb in the very heart of the mountain. Sometimes a black figure would pass across this gigantic furnace-mouth, stooping and rising, as though feeding the fire. One might have imagined that a door in Vulcan's Smithy had been left inadvertently open, and that the old hero was forging arms for a demigod.

Blunt turned pale. "It's no mortal," he whispered. "Let's go back."

"And what will Madam say?" returned dare-devil Will Staples who would have plunged into Mount Erebus had he been paid for it. Thus appealed to in the name of his ruling passion, Blunt turned his head, and the boat sped onward.

CHAPTER XXVI

THE WORK OF THE SEA

THE lift of the water-spout had saved John Rex's life. At the moment when it struck him he was on his hands and knees at the entrance of the cavern. The wave, gushing upwards, at the same time expanded, laterally, and this lateral force drove the convict into the mouth of the subterranean passage. The passage trended downwards, and for some seconds he was rolled over and over, the rush of water wedging him at length into a crevice between two enormous stones, which overhung a still more formidable abyss. Fortunately for the preservation of his hard-fought-for life, this very fury of incoming water prevented him from being washed out again with the recoil of the wave. He could hear the water dashing with frightful echoes far down into the depths beyond him, but it was evident that the two stones against which he had been thrust acted as breakwaters to the torrent poured in from the outside, and repelled the main body of the stream in the fashion he had observed from his position on the ledge. In a few seconds the cavern was empty.

Painfully extricating himself, and feeling as yet doubtful of his safety, John Rex essayed to climb the twin-blocks that barred the unknown depths below him. The first movement he made caused him to shriek aloud. His left arm—with which he clung to the rope—hung powerless. Ground against the ragged entrance, it was momentarily paralysed. For an instant the unfortunate wretch sank despairingly on the wet and rugged floor of the cave; then a terrible gurgling beneath his feet warned him of the approaching torrent, and, collecting all his energies, he scrambled up the incline. Though nigh fainting with pain and exhaustion, he pressed desperately higher and higher. He heard the hideous shriek of the whirlpool which was beneath him grow louder and louder. He saw the darkness grow darker as the rising water-spout covered the mouth of the cave. He felt the salt spray sting his face, and the wrathful tide lick the hand that hung over the shelf on which he fell. But that was all. He was out of danger at last! And as the thought blessed his senses, his eyes closed, and the wonderful courage and strength which had sustained the villain so long exhaled in stupor.

When he awoke the cavern was filled with the soft light of dawn. Raising his eyes, he beheld, high above his head, a roof of rock, on which the reflection of the sunbeams, playing upwards through a pool of water, cast flickering colours. On his right hand was the mouth of the cave, on his left a terrific abyss, at the bottom of which he could hear the sea faintly lapping and washing. He raised himself and stretched his stiffened limbs. Despite his injured shoulder, it was imperative that he should bestir himself. He knew not if his escape had been noticed, or if the cavern had another inlet, by which McNab, returning, might penetrate. Moreover, he was wet and famished. To preserve the life which he had torn from the sea, he must have fire and food. First he examined the crevice by which he had entered. It was shaped like an irregular triangle, hollowed at the base by the action of the water which in such storms as that of the preceding night was forced into it by the rising of the sea. John Rex dared not crawl too near the edge, lest he should slide out of the damp and slippery orifice, and be dashed upon the rocks at the bottom of the Blow-hole. Craning his neck, he could see, a hundred feet below him, the sullenly frothing water, gurgling, spouting, and creaming, in huge turbid eddies, occasionally leaping upwards as though it longed for another storm to send it raging up to the man who had escaped its fury. It was impossible to get down that way. He turned back into the cavern, and began to explore in that direction. The twin-rocks against which he had been hurled were, in fact, pillars which supported the roof of the water-drive. Beyond them lay a great grey shadow which was emptiness, faintly illumined by the sea-light cast up through the bottom of the gulf. Midway across the grey shadow fell a strange beam of dusky brilliance, which cast its flickering light upon a wilderness of waving sea-weeds. Even in the desperate position in which he found himself, there survived in the vagabond's nature sufficient poetry to make him value the natural marvel upon which he had so strangely stumbled. The immense promontory, which, viewed from the outside, seemed as solid as a mountain, was in reality but a hollow cone, reft and split into a thousand fissures by the unsuspected action of the sea for centuries. The Blow-hole was but an insignificant cranny compared with this enormous chasm. Descending with difficulty the steep incline, he found himself on the brink of a gallery of rock, which, jutting out over the pool, bore on its moist and weed-bearded edges signs of frequent submersion. It must be low tide without the rock. Clinging to the rough and root-like algae that fringed the ever-moist walls, John Rex crept round the projection of the gallery, and passed at once from dimness to daylight. There was a broad loop-hole in the side of the honey-combed and wave-perforated cliff. The cloudless heaven expanded above him; a fresh breeze kissed his cheek and, sixty feet below him, the sea wrinkled all its lazy length, sparkling in myriad wavelets beneath the bright beams of morning. Not a sign of the recent tempest marred the exquisite harmony of the picture. Not a sign of human life gave evidence of the grim neighbourhood of the prison. From the recess out of which he peered nothing was visible but a sky of turquoise smiling upon a sea of sapphire.

The placidity of Nature was, however, to the hunted convict a new source of alarm. It was a reason why the Blow-hole and its neighbourhood should be thoroughly searched. He guessed that the favourable weather would be an additional inducement to McNab and Burgess to satisfy themselves as to the fate of their late prisoner. He turned from the opening, and prepared to descend still farther into the rock pathway. The sunshine had revived and cheered him, and a sort of instinct told him that the cliff, so honey-combed above, could not be without some gully or chink at its base, which at low tide would give upon the rocky shore. It grew darker as he descended, and twice he almost turned back in dread of the gulfs on either side of him. It seemed to him, also, that the gullet of weed-clad rock through which he was crawling doubled upon itself, and led only into the bowels of the mountain. Gnawed by hunger, and conscious that in a few hours at most the rising tide would fill the subterranean passage and cut off his retreat, he pushed desperately onwards. He had descended some ninety feet, and had lost, in the devious windings of his downward path, all but the reflection of the light from the gallery, when he was rewarded by a glimpse of sunshine striking upwards. He parted two enormous masses of seaweed, whose bubble-headed fronds hung curtainwise across his path, and found himself in the very middle of the narrow cleft of rock through which the sea was driven to the Blow-hole. At an immense distance above him was the arch of cliff. Beyond that arch appeared a segment of the ragged edge of the circular opening, down which he had fallen. He looked in vain for the funnel-mouth whose friendly shelter had received him. It was now indistinguishable. At his feet was a long rift in the solid rock, so narrow that he could almost have leapt across it. This rift was the channel of a swift black current which ran from the sea for fifty yards under an arch eight feet high, until it broke upon the jagged rocks that lay blistering in the sunshine at the bottom of the circular opening in the upper cliff. A shudder shook the limbs of the adventurous convict. He comprehended that at high tide the place where he stood was under water, and that the narrow cavern became a subaqueous pipe of solid rock forty feet long, through which were spouted the league-long rollers of the Southern Sea.

The narrow strip of rock at the base of the cliff was as flat as a table. Here and there were enormous hollows like pans, which the retreating tide had left full of clear, still water. The crannies of the rock were inhabited by small white crabs, and John Rex found to his delight that there was on this little shelf abundance of mussels, which, though lean and acrid, were sufficiently grateful to his famished stomach. Attached to the flat surfaces of the numerous stones, moreover, were coarse limpets. These, however, John Rex found too salt to be palatable, and was compelled to reject them. A larger variety, however, having a succulent body as thick as a man's thumb, contained in long razor-shaped shells, were in some degree free from this objection, and he soon collected the materials for a meal. Having eaten and sunned himself, he began to examine the enormous rock, to the base of which he had so strangely penetrated. Rugged and worn, it raised its huge breast against wind and wave, secure upon a broad pedestal, which probably extended as far beneath the sea as the massive column itself rose above it.

Rising thus, with its shaggy drapery of seaweed clinging about its knees, it seemed to be a motionless but sentient being—some monster of the deep, a Titan of the ocean condemned ever to front in silence the fury of that illimitable and rarely-travelled sea. Yet—silent and motionless as he was—the hoary ancient gave hint of the mysteries of his revenge. Standing upon the broad and sea-girt platform where surely no human foot but his had ever stood in life, the convict saw, many feet above him, pitched into a cavity of the huge sun-blistered boulders, an object which his sailor eye told him at once was part of the top hamper of some large ship. Crusted with shells, and its ruin so overrun with the ivy of the ocean that its ropes could barely be distinguished from the weeds with which they were encumbered, this relic of human labour attested the triumph of nature over human ingenuity. Perforated below by the relentless sea, exposed above to the full fury of the tempest; set in solitary defiance to the waves, that rolling from the ice-volcano of the Southern Pole, hurled their gathered might unchecked upon its iron front, the great rock drew from its lonely warfare the materials of its own silent vengeance. Clasped in iron arms, it held its prey, snatched from the jaws of the all-devouring sea. One might imagine that, when the doomed ship, with her crew of shrieking souls, had splintered and gone down, the deaf, blind giant had clutched this fragment, upheaved from the seething waters, with a thrill of savage and terrible joy.

John Rex, gazing up at this memento of a forgotten agony, felt a sensation of the most vulgar pleasure. "There's wood for my fire!" thought he; and mounting to the spot, he essayed to fling down the splinters of timber upon the platform. Long exposed to the sun, and flung high above the water-mark of recent storms, the timber had dried to the condition of touchwood, and would burn fiercely. It was precisely what he required. Strange accident that had for years stored, upon a desolate rock, this fragment of a vanished and long-forgotten vessel, that it might aid at last to warm the limbs of a villain escaping from justice!

Striking the disintegrated mass with his iron-shod heel, John Rex broke off convenient portions; and making a bag of his shirt by tying the sleeves and neck, he was speedily staggering into the cavern with a supply of fuel. He made two trips, flinging down the wood on the floor of the gallery that overlooked the sea, and was returning for a third, when his quick ear caught the dip of oars. He had barely time to lift the seaweed curtain that veiled the entrance to the chasm, when the Eaglehawk boat rounded the promontory. Burgess was in the stern-sheets, and seemed to be making signals to someone on the top of the cliff. Rex, grinning behind his veil, divined the manoeuvre. McNab and his party were to search above, while the Commandant examined the gulf below. The boat headed direct for the passage, and for an instant John Rex's undaunted soul shivered at the thought that, perhaps, after all, his pursuers might be aware of the existence of the cavern. Yet that was unlikely. He kept his ground, and the boat passed within a foot of him, gliding silently into the gulf. He observed that Burgess's usually florid face was pale, and that his left sleeve was cut open, showing a bandage on the arm. There had been some fighting, then, and it was not unlikely that all his fellow-desperadoes had been captured! He chuckled at his own ingenuity and good sense. The boat, emerging from the archway, entered the pool of the Blow-hole, and, held with the full strength of the party, remained stationary. John Rex watched Burgess scan the rocks and eddies, saw him signal to McNab, and then, with much relief, beheld the boat's head brought round to the sea-board.

He was so intent upon watching this dangerous and difficult operation that he was oblivious of an extraordinary change which had taken place in the interior of the cavern. The water which, an hour ago, had left exposed a long reef of black hummock-rocks, was now spread in one foam-flecked sheet over the ragged bottom of the rude staircase by which he had descended. The tide had turned, and the sea, apparently sucked in through some deeper tunnel in the portion of the cliff which was below water, was being forced into the vault with a rapidity which bid fair to shortly submerge the mouth of the cave. The convict's feet were already wetted by the incoming waves, and as he turned for one last look at the boat he saw a green billow heave up against the entrance to the chasm, and, almost blotting out the daylight, roll majestically through the arch. It was high time for Burgess to take his departure if he did not wish his whale-boat to be cracked like a nut against the roof of the tunnel. Alive to his danger, the Commandant abandoned the search after his late prisoner's corpse, and he hastened to gain the open sea. The boat, carried backwards and upwards on the bosom of a monstrous wave, narrowly escaped destruction, and John Rex, climbing to the gallery, saw with much satisfaction the broad back of his out-witted gaoler disappear round the sheltering promontory. The last efforts of his pursuers had failed, and in another hour the only accessible entrance to the convict's retreat was hidden under three feet of furious seawater.

His gaolers were convinced of his death, and would search for him no more. So far, so good. Now for the last desperate venture—the escape from the wonderful cavern which was at once his shelter and his prison. Piling his wood together, and succeeding after many efforts, by the aid of a flint and the ring which yet clung to his ankle, in lighting a fire, and warming his chilled limbs in its cheering blaze, he set himself to meditate upon his course of action. He was safe for the present, and the supply of food that the rock afforded was amply sufficient to sustain life in him for many days, but it was impossible that he could remain for many days concealed. He had no fresh water, and though, by reason of the soaking he had received, he had hitherto felt little inconvenience from this cause, the salt and acrid mussels speedily induced a raging thirst, which he could not alleviate. It was imperative that within forty-eight hours at farthest he should be on his way to the peninsula. He remembered the little stream into which—in his flight of the previous night—he had so nearly fallen, and hoped to be able, under cover of the darkness, to steal round the reef and reach it unobserved. His desperate scheme was then to commence. He had to run the gauntlet of the dogs and guards, gain the peninsula, and await the rescuing vessel. He confessed to himself that the chances were terribly against him. If Gabbett and the others had been recaptured—as he devoutly trusted—the coast would be comparatively clear; but if they had escaped, he knew Burgess too well to think that he would give up the chase while hope of re-taking the absconders remained to him. If indeed all fell out as he had wished, he had still to sustain life until Blunt found him—if haply Blunt had not returned, wearied with useless and dangerous waiting.

As night came on, and the firelight showed strange shadows waving from the corners of the enormous vault, while the dismal abysses beneath him murmured and muttered with uncouth and ghastly utterance, there fell upon the lonely man the terror of Solitude. Was this marvellous hiding-place that he had discovered to be his sepulchre? Was he—a monster amongst his fellow-men—to die some monstrous death, entombed in this mysterious and terrible cavern of the sea? He had tried to drive away these gloomy thoughts by sketching out for himself a plan of action—but in vain. In vain he strove to picture in its completeness that—as yet vague—design by which he promised himself to wrest from the vanished son of the wealthy ship-builder his name and heritage. His mind, filled with forebodings of shadowy horror, could not give the subject the calm consideration which it needed. In the midst of his schemes for the baffling of the jealous love of the woman who was to save him, and the getting to England, in shipwrecked and foreign guise, as the long-lost heir to the fortune of Sir Richard Devine, there arose ghastly and awesome shapes of death and horror, with whose terrible unsubstantiality he must grapple in the lonely recesses of that dismal cavern. He heaped fresh wood upon his fire, that the bright light might drive out the gruesome things that lurked above, below, and around him. He became afraid to look behind him, lest some shapeless mass of mid-sea birth—some voracious polype, with far-reaching arms and jellied mouth ever open to devour— might slide up over the edge of the dripping caves below, and fasten upon him in the darkness. His imagination—always sufficiently vivid, and spurred to an unnatural effect by the exciting scenes of the previous night—painted each patch of shadow, clinging bat-like to the humid wall, as some globular sea-spider ready to drop upon him with its viscid and clay-cold body, and drain out his chilled blood, enfolding him in rough and hairy arms. Each splash in the water beneath him, each sigh of the multitudinous and melancholy sea, seemed to prelude the laborious advent of some misshapen and ungainly abortion of the ooze. All the sensations induced by lapping water and regurgitating waves took material shape and surrounded him. All creatures that could be engendered by slime and salt crept forth into the firelight to stare at him. Red dabs and splashes that were living beings, having a strange phosphoric light of their own, glowed upon the floor. The livid encrustations of a hundred years of humidity slipped from off the walls and painfully heaved their mushroom surfaces to the blaze. The red glow of the unwonted fire, crimsoning the wet sides of the cavern, seemed to attract countless blisterous and transparent shapelessnesses, which elongated themselves towards him. Bloodless and bladdery things ran hither and thither noiselessly. Strange carapaces crawled from out of the rocks. All the horrible unseen life of the ocean seemed to be rising up and surrounding him. He retreated to the brink of the gulf, and the glare of the upheld brand fell upon a rounded hummock, whose coronal of silky weed out-floating in the water looked like the head of a drowned man. He rushed to the entrance of the gallery, and his shadow, thrown into the opening, took the shape of an avenging phantom, with arms upraised to warn him back. The naturalist, the explorer, or the shipwrecked seaman would have found nothing frightful in this exhibition of the harmless life of the Australian ocean. But the convict's guilty conscience, long suppressed and derided, asserted itself in this hour when it was alone with Nature and Night. The bitter intellectual power which had so long supported him succumbed beneath imagination—the unconscious religion of the soul. If ever he was nigh repentance it was then. Phantoms of his past crimes gibbered at him, and covering his eyes with his hands, he fell shuddering upon his knees. The brand, loosening from his grasp, dropped into the gulf, and was extinguished with a hissing noise. As if the sound had called up some spirit that lurked below, a whisper ran through the cavern.

"John Rex!" The hair on the convict's flesh stood up, and he cowered to the earth.

"John Rex?"

It was a *human* voice! Whether of friend or enemy he did not pause to think. His terror over-mastered all other considerations.

"Here! here!" he cried, and sprang to the opening of the vault.

Arrived at the foot of the cliff, Blunt and Staples found themselves in almost complete darkness, for the light of the mysterious fire, which had hitherto guided them, had necessarily disappeared. Calm as was the night, and still as was the ocean, the sea yet ran with silent but dangerous strength through the channel which led to the Blow-hole; and Blunt, instinctively feeling the boat drawn towards some unknown peril, held off the shelf of rocks out of reach of the current. A sudden flash of fire, as from a flourished brand, burst out above them, and floating downwards through the darkness, in erratic circles, came an atom of burning wood. Surely no one but a hunted man would lurk in such a savage retreat.

Blunt, in desperate anxiety, determined to risk all upon one venture. "John Rex!" he shouted up through his rounded hands. The light flashed again at the eye-hole of the mountain, and on the point above them appeared a wild figure, holding in its hands a burning log, whose fierce glow illumined a face so contorted by deadly fear and agony of expectation that it was scarce human.

"Here! here!"

"The poor devil seems half-crazy," said Will Staples, under his breath; and then aloud, "We're FRIENDS!"

A few moments sufficed to explain matters. The terrors which had oppressed John Rex disappeared in human presence, and the villain's coolness returned. Kneeling on the rock platform, he held parley.

"It is impossible for me to come down now," he said. "The tide covers the only way out of the cavern."

"Can't you dive through it?" said Will Staples.

"No, nor you neither," said Rex, shuddering at the thought of trusting himself to that horrible whirlpool.

"What's to be done? You can't come down that wall."

"Wait until morning," returned Rex coolly. "It will be dead low tide at seven o'clock. You must send a boat at six, or there-abouts. It will be low enough for me to get out, I dare say, by that time."

"But the Guard?"

"Won't come here, my man. They've got their work to do in watching the Neck and exploring after my mates. They won't come here. Besides, I'm dead."

"Dead!"

"Thought to be so, which is as well—better for me, perhaps. If they don't see your ship, or your boat, you're safe enough."

"I don't like to risk it," said Blunt. "It's Life if we're caught."

"It's Death if *I'm* caught!" returned the other, with a sinister laugh. "But there's no danger if you are cautious. No one looks for rats in a terrier's kennel, and there's not a station along the beach from here to Cape Pillar. Take your vessel out of eye-shot of the Neck, bring the boat up Descent Beach, and the thing's done."

"Well," says Blunt, "I'll try it."

"You wouldn't like to stop here till morning? It is rather lonely," suggested Rex, absolutely making a jest of his late terrors.

Will Staples laughed. "You're a bold boy!" said he. "We'll come at daybreak."

"Have you got the clothes as I directed?"

"Yes."

"Then good night. I'll put my fire out, in case somebody else might see it, who wouldn't be as kind as you are."

"Good night."

"Not a word for the Madam," said Staples, when they reached the vessel.

"Not a word, the ungrateful dog," asserted Blunt, adding, with some heat, "That's the way with women. They'll go through fire and water for a man that doesn't care a snap of his fingers for 'em; but for any poor fellow who risks his neck to pleasure 'em they've nothing but sneers! I wish I'd never meddled in the business."

"There are no fools like old fools," thought Will Staples, looking back through the darkness at the place where the fire had been, but he did not utter his thoughts aloud.

At eight o'clock the next morning the *Pretty Mary* stood out to sea with every stitch of canvas set, alow and aloft. The skipper's fishing had come to an end. He had caught a shipwrecked seaman, who had been brought on board at daylight, and was then at breakfast in the cabin. The crew winked at each other when the haggard mariner, attired in garments that seemed remarkably well preserved, mounted the side. But they, none of them, were in a position to controvert the skipper's statement.

"Where are we bound for?" asked John Rex, smoking Staples's pipe in lingering puffs of delight. "I'm entirely in your hands, Blunt."

"My orders are to cruise about the whaling grounds until I meet my consort," returned Blunt sullenly, "and put you aboard her. She'll take you back to Sydney. I'm victualled for a twelve-months' trip."

"Right!" cried Rex, clapping his preserver on the back. "I'm bound to get to Sydney somehow; but, as the Philistines are abroad, I may as well tarry in Jericho till my beard be grown. Don't stare at my Scriptural quotation, Mr. Staples," he added, inspirited by creature comforts, and secure amid his purchased friends. "I assure you that I've had the very best religious instruction. Indeed, it is chiefly owing to my worthy spiritual pastor and master that I am enabled to smoke this very villainous tobacco of yours at the present moment!"

CHAPTER XXVII

THE VALLEY OF THE SHADOW OF DEATH

IT was not until they had scrambled up the beach to safety that the absconders became fully aware of the loss of another of their companions. As they stood on the break of the beach, wringing the water from their clothes, Gabbett's small eye, counting their number, missed the stroke oar.

"Where's Cox?"

"The fool fell overboard," said Jemmy Vetch shortly. "He never had as much sense in that skull of his as would keep it sound on his shoulders." Gabbett scowled. "That's three of us gone," he said, in the tones of a man suffering some personal injury.

They summed up their means of defence against attack. Sanders and Greenhill had knives. Gabbett still retained the axe in his belt. Vetch had dropped his musket at the Neck, and Bodenham and Cornelius were unarmed.

"Let's have a look at the tucker," said Vetch.

There was but one bag of provisions. It contained a piece of salt pork, two loaves, and some uncooked potatoes. Signal Hill station was not rich in edibles.

"That ain't much," said the Crow, with rueful face. "Is it, Gabbett?"

"It must do, any way," returned the giant carelessly.

The inspection over, the six proceeded up the shore, and encamped under the lee of a rock. Bodenham was for lighting a fire, but Vetch, who, by tacit consent, had been chosen leader of the expedition, forbade it, saying that the light might betray them. "They'll think we're drowned, and won't pursue us," he said. So all that night the miserable wretches crouched Tireless together.

Morning breaks clear and bright, and—free for the first time in ten years—they comprehend that their terrible journey has begun. "Where are we to go? How are we to live?" asked Bodenham, scanning the barren bush that stretches to the barren sea. "Gabbett, you've been out before—how's it done?"

"We'll make the shepherds' huts, and live on their tucker till we get a change o' clothes," said Gabbett evading the main question. "We can follow the coast-line."

"Steady, lads," said prudent Vetch; "we must sneak round yon sandhills, and so creep into the scrub. If they've a good glass at the Neck, they can see us."

"It does seem close," said Bodenham; "I could pitch a stone on to the guard-house. Good-bye, you Bloody Spot!" he adds, with sudden rage, shaking his fist vindictively at the Penitentiary; "I don't want to see you no more till the Day o' Judgment."

Vetch divides the provisions, and they travel all that day until dark night. The scrub is prickly and dense. Their clothes are torn, their hands and feet bleeding. Already they feel out-wearied. No one pursuing, they light a fire, and sleep. The second day they come to a sandy spit that runs out into the sea, and find that they have got too far to the eastward, and must follow the shore line to East Bay Neck. Back through the scrub they drag their heavy feet. That night they eat the last crumb of the loaf. The third day at high noon—after some toilsome walking—they reach a big hill, now called Collins' Mount, and see the upper link of the earring, the isthmus of East Bay Neck, at their feet. A few rocks are on their right hand, and blue in the lovely distance lies hated Maria Island. "We must keep well to the eastward," said Greenhill, "or we shall fall in with the settlers and get taken." So, passing the isthmus, they strike into the bush along the shore, and tightening their belts over their gnawing bellies, camp under some low-lying hills.

The fourth day is notable for the indisposition of Bodenham, who is a bad walker, and, falling behind, delays the party by frequent cooees. Gabbett threatens him with a worse fate than sore feet if he lingers. Luckily, that evening Greenhill espies a hut, but, not trusting to the friendship of the occupant, they wait until he quits it in the morning, and then send Vetch to forage. Vetch, secretly congratulating himself on having by his counsel prevented violence, returns bending under half a bag of flour. "You'd better carry the flour," said he to Gabbett, "and give me the axe."

Gabbett eyes him for a while, as if struck by his puny form, but finally gives the axe to his mate Sanders. That day they creep along cautiously between the sea and the hills, camping at a creek. Vetch, after much search, finds a handful of berries, and adds them to the main stock. Half of this handful is eaten at once, the other half reserved for "to-morrow". The next day they come to an arm of the sea, and as they struggle northward, Maria Island disappears, and with it all danger from telescopes. That evening they reach the camping ground by twos and threes; and each wonders between the paroxysms of hunger if his face is as haggard, and his eyes as bloodshot, as those of his neighbour.

On the seventh day, Bodenham says his feet are so bad he can't walk, and Greenhill, with a greedy look at the berries, bids him stay behind. Being in a very weak condition, he takes his companion at his word, and drops off about noon the next day. Gabbett, discovering this defection, however, goes back, and in an hour or so appears, driving the wretched creature before him with blows, as a sheep is driven to the shambles. Greenhill remonstrates at another mouth being thus forced upon the party, but the giant silences him with a hideous glance. Jemmy Vetch remembers that Greenhill accompanied Gabbett once before, and feels uncomfortable. He gives hint of his suspicions to Sanders, but Sanders only laughs. It is horribly evident that there is an understanding among the three.

The ninth sun of their freedom, rising upon sandy and barren hillocks, bristling thick with cruel scrub, sees the six famine-stricken wretches cursing their God, and yet afraid to die. All around is the fruitless, shadeless, shelterless bush. Above, the pitiless heaven. In the distance, the remorseless sea. Something terrible must happen. That grey wilderness, arched by grey heaven stooping to grey sea, is a fitting keeper of hideous secrets. Vetch suggests that Oyster Bay cannot be far to the eastward—the line of ocean is deceitfully close—and though such a proceeding will take them out of their course, they resolve to make for it. After hobbling five miles, they seem no nearer than before, and, nigh dead with fatigue and starvation, sink despairingly upon the ground. Vetch thinks Gabbett's eyes have a wolfish glare in them, and instinctively draws off from him.

Said Greenhill, in the course of a dismal conversation, "I am so weak that I could eat a piece of a man."

On the tenth day Bodenham refuses to stir, and the others, being scarce able to drag along their limbs, sit on the ground about him. Greenhill, eyeing the prostrate man, said slowly, "I have seen the same done before, boys, and it tasted like pork."

Vetch, hearing his savage comrade give utterance to a thought all had secretly cherished, speaks out, crying, "It would be murder to do it, and then, perhaps we couldn't eat it."

"Oh," said Gabbett, with a grin, "I'll warrant you that, but you must all have a hand in it."

Gabbett, Sanders and Greenhill then go aside, and presently Sanders, coming to the Crow, said, "He consented to act as flogger. He deserves it."

"So did Gabbett, for that matter," shudders Vetch.

"Ay, but Bodenham's feet are sore," said Sanders, "and 'tis a pity to leave him."

Having no fire, they make a little breakwind; and Vetch, half-dozing behind this at about three in the morning, hears someone cry out "Christ!" and awakes, sweating ice.

No one but Gabbett and Greenhill would eat that night. That savage pair, however, make a fire, fling ghastly fragments on the embers, and eat the broil before it is right warm. In the morning the frightful carcase is divided.

That day's march takes place in silence, and at midday halt Cornelius volunteers to carry the billy, affecting great restoration from the food. Vetch gives it to him, and in half an hour afterwards Cornelius is missing. Gabbett and Greenhill pursue him in vain, and return with curses. "He'll die like a dog," said Greenhill, "alone in the bush." Jemmy Vetch, with his intellect acute as ever, thinks that Cornelius may prefer such a death, but says nothing.

The twelfth morning dawns wet and misty, but Vetch, seeing the provision running short, strives to be cheerful, telling stories of men who have escaped greater peril. Vetch feels with dismay that he is the weakest of the party, but has some sort of ludicro-horrible consolation in remembering that he is also the leanest. They come to a creek that afternoon, and look, until nightfall, in vain for a crossing-place. The next day Gabbett and Vetch swim across, and Vetch directs Gabbett to cut a long sapling, which, being stretched across the water, is seized by Greenhill and the Moocher, who are dragged over.

"What would you do without me?" said the Crow with a ghastly grin.

They cannot kindle a fire, for Greenhill, who carries the tinder, has allowed it to get wet. The giant swings his axe in savage anger at enforced cold, and Vetch takes an opportunity to remark privately to him what a big man Greenhill is.

On the fourteenth day they can scarcely crawl, and their limbs pain them. Greenhill, who is the weakest, sees Gabbett and the Moocher go aside to consult, and crawling to the Crow, whimpers: "For God's sake, Jemmy, don't let 'em murder me!"

"I can't help you," says Vetch, looking about in terror. "Think of poor Tom Bodenham."

"But he was no murderer. If they kill me, I shall go to hell with Tom's blood on my soul." He writhes on the ground in sickening terror, and Gabbett arriving, bids Vetch bring wood for the fire. Vetch, going, sees Greenhill clinging to wolfish Gabbett's knees, and Sanders calls after him, "You will hear it presently, Jem."

The nervous Crow puts his hand to his ears, but is conscious of a dull crash and a groan. When he comes back, Gabbett is putting on the dead man's shoes, which are better than his own.

"We'll stop here a day or so and rest," said he, "now we've got provisions."

Two more days pass, and the three, eyeing each other suspiciously, resume their march. The third day—the sixteenth of their awful journey—such portions of the carcase as they have with them prove unfit to eat.

They look into each other's famine-sharpened faces, and wonder "who's next?"

"We must all die together," said Sanders quickly, "before anything else must happen."

Vetch marks the terror concealed in the words, and when the dreaded giant is out of earshot, says, "For God's sake, let's go on alone, Alick. You see what sort of a cove that Gabbett is—he'd kill his father before he'd fast one day."

They made for the bush, but the giant turned and strode towards them. Vetch skipped nimbly on one side, but Gabbett struck the Moocher on the forehead with the axe. "Help! Jem, help!" cried the victim, cut, but not fatally, and in the strength of his desperation tore the axe from the monster who bore it, and flung it to Vetch. "Keep it, Jemmy," he cried; "let's have no more murder done!"

They fare again through the horrible bush until nightfall, when Vetch, in a strange voice, called the giant to him.

"He must die."

"Either you or he," laughs Gabbett. "Give me the axe."

"No, no," said the Crow, his thin, malignant face distorted by a horrible resolution. "*I'll* keep the axe. Stand back! You shall hold him, and I'll do the job."

Sanders, seeing them approach, knew his end was come, and submitted, crying, "Give me half an hour to pray for myself." They consent, and the bewildered wretch knelt down and folded his hands like a child. His big, stupid face worked with emotion. His great cracked lips moved in desperate agony. He wagged his head from side to side, in pitiful confusion of his brutalized senses. "I can't think o' the words, Jem!"

"Pah," snarled the cripple, swinging the axe, "we can't starve here all night."

Four days had passed, and the two survivors of this awful journey sat watching each other. The gaunt giant, his eyes gleaming with hate and hunger, sat sentinel over the dwarf. The dwarf, chuckling at his superior sagacity, clutched the fatal axe. For two days they had not spoken to each other. For two days each had promised himself that on the next his companion must *sleep*—and die. Vetch comprehended the devilish scheme of the monster who had entrapped five of his fellow-beings to aid him by their deaths to his own safety, and held aloof. Gabbett watched to snatch the weapon from his companion, and make the odds even once and for ever. In the day-time they travelled on, seeking each a pretext to creep behind the other. In the night-time when they feigned slumber, each stealthily raising a head caught the wakeful glance of his companion.

Vetch felt his strength deserting him, and his brain overpowered by fatigue. Surely the giant, muttering, gesticulating, and slavering at the mouth, was on the road to madness. Would the monster find opportunity to rush at him, and, braving the blood-stained axe, kill him by main force? or would he sleep, and be himself a victim? Unhappy Vetch! It is the terrible privilege of insanity to be sleepless.

On the fifth day, Vetch, creeping behind a tree, takes off his belt, and makes a noose. He will hang himself. He gets one end of the belt over a bough, and then his cowardice bids him pause. Gabbett approaches; he tries to evade him, and steal away into the bush. In vain. The insatiable giant, ravenous with famine, and sustained by madness, is not to be shaken off. Vetch tries to run, but his legs bend under him. The axe that has tried to drink so much blood feels heavy as lead. He will fling it away. No—he dares not. Night falls again. He must rest, or go mad. His limbs are powerless. His eyelids are glued together. He sleeps as he stands. This horrible thing must be a dream. He is at Port Arthur, or will wake on his pallet in the penny lodging-house he slept at when a boy. Is that the Deputy come to wake him to the torment of living? It is not time—surely not time yet. He sleeps—and the giant, grinning with ferocious joy, approaches on clumsy tiptoe and seizes the coveted axe.

On the north coast of Van Diemen's Land is a place called St Helen's Point, and a certain skipper, being in want of fresh water; landing there with a boat's crew, found on the banks of the creek a gaunt and bloodstained man, clad in tattered yellow, who carried on his back an axe and a bundle. When the sailors came within sight of him, he made signs to them to approach, and, opening his bundle with much ceremony, offered them some of its contents. Filled with horror at what the maniac displayed, they seized and bound him. At Hobart Town he was recognized as the only survivor of the nine desperadoes who had escaped from Colonel Arthur's "Natural Penitentiary".

BOOK IV
NORFOLK ISLAND 1846

CHAPTER I

EXTRACTED FROM THE DIARY
OF THE REV. JAMES NORTH

BATHURST, *February* 11*th*, 1846.

In turning over the pages of my journal, to note the good fortune that has just happened to me, I am struck by the utter desolation of my life for the last seven years.

Can it be possible that I, James North, the college-hero, the poet, the prizeman, the Heaven knows what else, have been content to live on at this dreary spot—an animal, eating and drinking, for to-morrow I die? Yet it has been so. My world, that world of which I once dreamt so much, has been—here. My fame—which was to reach the ends of the earth—has penetrated to the neighbouring stations. I am considered a "good preacher" by my sheep-feeding friends. It is kind of them.

Yet, on the eve of leaving it, I confess that this solitary life has not been without its charms. I have had my books and my thoughts—though at times the latter were but grim companions, I have striven with my familiar sin, and have not always been worsted. Melancholy reflection. "Not always!"

"But yet" is as a gaoler to bring forth some monstrous malefactor. I vowed, however, that I would not cheat myself in this diary of mine, and I will not. No evasions, no glossings over of my own sins. This journal is my confessor, and I bare my heart to it.

It is curious the pleasure I feel in setting down here in black and white these agonies and secret cravings of which I dare not speak. It is for the same reason, I suppose, that murderers make confession to dogs and cats, that people with something "on their mind" are given to thinking aloud, that the queen of Midas must needs whisper to the sedges the secret of her husband's infirmity. Outwardly I am a man of God, pious and grave and softly spoken. Inwardly—what? The mean, cowardly, weak sinner that this book knows me...Imp! I could tear you in pieces!...One of these days I will. In the meantime, I will keep you under lock and key, and you shall hug my secrets close. No, old friend, with whom I have communed so long, forgive me, forgive me. You are to me instead of wife or priest. I tell to your cold blue pages—how much was it I bought you for in Parramatta, rascal?—these stories, longings, remorses, which I would fain tell to human ear could I find a human being as discreet as thou. It has been said that a man dare not *write* all his thoughts and deeds; the words would blister the paper. Yet your sheets are smooth enough, you fat rogue! Our neighbours of Rome know human nature. A man *must* confess. One reads of wretches who have carried secrets in their bosoms for years, and blurted them forth at last. I, shut up here without companionship, without sympathy, without letters, cannot lock up my soul, and feed on my own thoughts. They will out, and so I whisper them to thee.

> What art thou, thou tremendous power
> Who dost inhabit us without our leave,
> And art, within ourselves, another self,
> A master self that loves to domineer?

What? Conscience? That is a word to frighten children. The conscience of each man is of his own making. My friend the shark-toothed cannibal whom Staples brought in his whaler to Sydney would have found his conscience reproach him sorely did he refuse to partake of the feasts made sacred by the customs of his ancestors A spark of divinity? The divinity that, according to received doctrine; Sits apart, enthroned amid sweet music, and leaves poor humanity to earn its condemnation as it may? I'll have none of that—though I preach it. One must soothe the vulgar senses of the people Priesthood has its "pious frauds". The Master spoke in parables. Wit? The wit that sees how ill-balanced are our actions and our aspirations? The devilish wit born of our own brain, that sneers at us for our own failings? Perhaps madness? More likely, for there are few men who are not mad one hour of the waking twelve. If differing from the judgment of the majority of mankind in regard to familiar things be madness, I suppose *I* am mad—or too wise. The speculation draws near to hair-splitting. James North, recall your early recklessness, your ruin, and your redemption; bring your mind back to earth. Circumstances have made you what you are, and will shape your destiny for you without your interference. That's comfortably settled!

Now supposing—to take another canter on my night-mare— that man *is* the slave of circumstances (a doctrine which I am inclined to believe, though unwilling to confess); what circumstance can have brought about the sudden awakening of the powers that be to James North's fitness for duty?

"HOBART TOWN, *Jan. 12th.*

"DEAR NORTH,—I have much pleasure in informing you that you can be appointed Protestant chaplain at Norfolk Island, if you like. It seems that they did not get on well with the last man, and when my advice was asked, I at once recommended you for the office. The pay is small, but you have a house and so on. It is certainly better than Bathurst, and indeed is considered rather a prize in the clerical lottery.

"There is to be an investigation into affairs down there. Poor old Pratt—who went down, as you know, at the earnest solicitation of the Government—seems to have become absurdly lenient with the prisoners, and it is reported that the island is in a frightful state. Sir Eardley is looking out for some disciplinarian to take the place in hand.

"In the meantime, the chaplaincy is vacant, and I thought of you."

I must consider this seeming good fortune further.

February 19th.—I accept. There is work to be done among those unhappy men that may be my purgation. The authorities shall hear me yet—though inquiry was stifled at Port Arthur. By the way, a

Pharaoh had arisen who knows not Joseph. It is evident that the meddlesome parson, who complained of men being flogged to death, is forgotten, as the men are! How many ghosts must haunt the dismal loneliness of that prison shore! Poor Burgess is gone the way of all flesh. I wonder if *his* spirit revisits the scenes of its violences? I have written "poor" Burgess.

It is strange how we pity a man gone out of this life. Enmity is extinguished when one can but *remember* injuries. If a man had injured me, the fact of his living at all would be sufficient grounds for me to hate him; if I had injured *him*, I should hate him still more. Is that the reason I hate myself at times—my greatest enemy, and one whom I have injured beyond forgiveness? There are offences against one's own nature that are not to be forgiven. Isn't it Tacitus who says "the hatred of those most nearly related is most inveterate"? But—I am taking flight again.

February 27th, 11.30 p.m.—Nine Creeks Station. I do like to be accurate in names, dates, etc. Accuracy is a virtue. To exercise it, then. Station ninety miles from Bathurst. I should say about 4,000 head of cattle. Luxury without refinement. Plenty to eat, drink, and read. Hostess's name—Carr. She is a well-preserved creature, about thirty-four years of age, and a clever woman—not in a poetical sense, but in the widest worldly acceptation of the term. At the same time, I should be sorry to be her husband. Women have no business with a brain like hers—that is, if they wish to be women and not sexual monsters. Mrs. Carr is not a lady, though she might have been one. I don't think she is a good woman either. It is possible, indeed, that she has known the factory before now. There is a mystery about her, for I was informed that she was a Mrs. Purfoy, the widow of a whaling captain, and had married one of her assigned servants, who had deserted her five years ago, as soon as he obtained his freedom. A word or two at dinner set me thinking. She had received some English papers, and, accounting for her pre-occupied manner, grimly said, "I think I have news of my husband." I should not like to be in Carr's shoes if she *has* news of him! I don't think she would suffer indignity calmly. After all, what business is it of mine? I was beguiled into taking more wine at dinner than I needed. Confessor, do you hear me? But I will not allow myself to be carried away. You grin, you fat Familiar! So may I, but I shall be eaten with remorse to-morrow.

March 3rd.—A place called Jerrilang, where I have a head and heartache. "One that hath let go himself from the hold and stay of reason, and lies open to the mercy of all temptations."

March 20th.—Sydney. At Captain Frere's.—Seventeen days since I have opened you, beloved and detested companion of mine. I have more than half a mind to never open you again! To read you is to recall to myself all I would most willingly forget; yet not to read you would be to forget all that which I should for my sins remember.

The last week has made a new man of me. I am no longer morose, despairing, and bitter, but genial, and on good terms with fortune. It is strange that accident should have induced me to stay a week under the same roof with that vision of brightness which has haunted me so long. A meeting in the street, an introduction, an invitation—the thing is done.

The circumstances which form our fortunes are certainly curious things. I had thought never again to meet the bright young face to which I felt so strange an attraction—and lo! here it is smiling on me daily. Captain Frere should be a happy man. Yet there is a skeleton in this house also. That young wife, by nature so lovable and so mirthful, ought not to have the sadness on her face that twice to-day has clouded it. He seems a passionate and boorish creature, this wonderful convict disciplinarian. His convicts—poor devils—are doubtless disciplined enough. Charming little Sylvia, with your quaint wit and weird beauty, he is not good enough for you—and yet it was a love match.

March 21st.—I have read family prayers every night since I have been here—my black coat and white tie gave me the natural pre-eminence in such matters—and I feel guilty every time I read. I wonder what the little lady of the devotional eyes would say if she knew that I am a miserable hypocrite, preaching that which I do not practise, exhorting others to believe those marvels which I do not believe? I am a coward not to throw off the saintly mask, and appear as a Freethinker. Yet, am I a coward? I urge upon myself that it is for the glory of God I hold my peace. The scandal of a priest turned infidel would do more harm than the reign of reason would do good. Imagine this trustful woman for instance—she would suffer anguish at the thoughts of such a sin, though another were the sinner. "If anyone offend one of these little ones it were better for him that a millstone be hanged about his neck and that he be cast into the sea." Yet truth is truth, and should be spoken—should it not, malignant monitor, who remindest me how often I fail to speak it? Surely among all his army of black-coats our worthy Bishop must have some men like me, who cannot bring their reason to believe in things contrary to the experience of mankind and the laws of nature.

March 22nd.—This unromantic Captain Frere had had some romantic incidents in his life, and he is fond of dilating upon them. It seems that in early life he expected to have been left a large fortune by an uncle who had quarrelled with his heir. But the uncle dies on the day fixed for the altering of the will, the son disappears, and is thought to be drowned. The widow, however, steadfastly refuses to believe in any report of the young man's death, and having a life-interest in the property, holds it against all comers. My poor host in consequence comes out here on his pay, and, three years ago, just as he is hoping that the death of his aunt may give him opportunity to enforce a claim as next of kin to some portion of the property, the long-lost son returns, is recognized by his mother and the trustees, and installed in due heirship! The other romantic story is connected with Frere's marriage. He told me after dinner to-night how his wife had been wrecked when a child, and how he had saved her life, and defended her from the rude hands of an escaped convict—one of the monsters our monstrous system breeds. "That was how we fell in love," said he, tossing off his wine complacently.

"An auspicious opportunity," said I. To which he nodded. He is not overburdened with brains, I fancy. Let me see if I can set down some account of this lovely place and its people.

A long low white house, surrounded by a blooming garden. Wide windows opening on a lawn. The ever glorious, ever changing sea beneath. It is evening. I am talking with Mrs. Frere, of theories of social reform, of picture galleries, of sunsets, and new books. There comes a sound of wheels on the gravel. It is the magistrate returned from his convict-discipline. We hear him come briskly up the steps, but we go on talking. (I fancy there was a time when the lady would have run to meet him.) He enters, coldly kisses his wife, and disturbs at once the current of our thoughts. "It has been hot to-day. What, still no letter from head-quarters, Mr. North! I saw Mrs. Golightly in town, Sylvia, and she asked for you. There is to be a ball at Government House. We must go." Then he departs, and is heard in the distance indistinctly cursing because the water is not hot enough, or because Dawkins, his convict servant, has not brushed his trousers sufficiently. We resume our chat, but he returns all hungry, and bluff, and whisker-brushed. "Dinner. Ha-ha! I'm ready for it. North take Mrs. Frere." By and by it is, "North, some sherry? Sylvia, the soup is spoilt again. Did you go out to-day? No?" His eyebrows contract here, and I know he says inwardly, "Reading some trashy novel, I suppose." However, he grins, and obligingly relates how the police have captured Cockatoo Bill, the noted bushranger.

After dinner the disciplinarian and I converse—of dogs and horses, gamecocks, convicts, and moving accidents by flood and field. I remember old college feats, and strive to keep pace with him in the relation of athletics. What hypocrites we are!—for all the time I am longing to get to the drawing-room, and finish my criticism of the new poet, Mr. Tennyson, to Mrs. Frere. Frere does not read Tennyson—nor anybody else. Adjourned to the drawing-room, we chat—Mrs. Frere and I—until supper. (He eats supper.) She is a charming companion, and when I talk my best—I *can* talk, you must admit, O Familiar—her face lightens up with an interest I rarely see upon it at other times. I feel cooled and soothed by this companionship. The quiet refinement of this house, after bullocks and Bathurst, is like the shadow of a great rock in a weary land.

Mrs. Frere is about five-and-twenty. She is rather beneath the middle height, with a slight, girlish figure. This girlish appearance is enhanced by the fact that she has bright fair hair and blue eyes. Upon conversation with her, however, one sees that her face has lost much of the delicate plumpness which it probably owned in youth. She has had one child, born only to die. Her cheeks are thin, and her eyes have a tinge of sadness, which speak of physical pain or mental grief. This thinness of face makes the eyes appear larger and the brow broader than they really are. Her hands are white and painfully thin. They must have been plump and pretty once. Her lips are red with perpetual fever.

Captain Frere seems to have absorbed all his wife's vitality. (Who quotes the story of Lucius Claudius Hermippus, who lived to a great age by being constantly breathed on by young girls? I suppose Burton—who quotes everything.) In proportion as she has lost her vigour and youth, he has gained strength and heartiness. Though he is at least forty years of age, he does not look more than thirty. His face is ruddy, his eyes bright, his voice firm and ringing. He must be a man of considerable strength and—I should say—of more than ordinary animal courage and animal appetite. There is not a nerve in his body which does not twang like a piano wire. In appearance, he is tall, broad, and bluff, with red whiskers and reddish hair slightly touched with grey. His manner is loud, coarse, and imperious; his talk of dogs, horses, and convicts. What a strangely-mated pair!

March 30th.—A letter from Van Diemen's Land. "There is a row in the pantry," said Frere, with his accustomed slang. It seems that the Comptroller-General of Convicts has appointed a Mr. Pounce to go down and make a report on the state of Norfolk Island. I am to go down with him, and shall receive instructions to that effect from the Comptroller-General. I have informed Frere of this, and he has written to Pounce to come and stay on his way down. There has been nothing but convict discipline talked since. Frere is great upon this point, and wearies me with his explanations of convict tricks and wickedness. He is celebrated for his knowledge of such matters. Detestable wisdom! His servants hate him, but they obey him without a murmur. I have observed that habitual criminals—like all savage beasts—cower before the man who has once mastered them. I should not be surprised if the Van Diemen's Land Government selected Frere as their "disciplinarian". I hope they won't and yet I hope they will.

April 4th.—Nothing worth recording until to-day. Eating, drinking, and sleeping. Despite my forty-seven years, I begin to feel almost like the James North who fought the bargee and took the gold medal. What a drink water is! The *fons Bandusiœ splendidior vitreo* was better than all the Massic, Master Horace! I doubt if your celebrated liquor, bottled when Manlius was consul, could compare with it.

But to my notable facts. I have found out to-night two things which surprise me. One is that the convict who attempted the life of Mrs. Frere is none other than the unhappy man whom my fatal weakness caused to be flogged at Port Arthur, and whose face comes before me to reproach me even now. The other that Mrs. Carr is an old acquaintance of Frere's. The latter piece of information I obtained in a curious way. One night, while Mrs. Frere was not there, we were talking of clever women. I broached my theory, that strong intellect in women went far to destroy their womanly nature.

"Desire in man," said I, "should be Volition in women: Reason, Intuition; Reverence, Devotion; Passion, Love. The woman should strike a lower key-note, but a sharper sound. Man has vigour of reason, woman quickness of feeling. The woman who possesses masculine force of intellect is abnormal." He did not half comprehend me, I could see, but he agreed with the broad view of the case. "I only knew one woman who was really 'strong-minded', as they call it," he said, "and she was a regular bad one."

"It does not follow that she should be *bad*," said I.

"This one was, though—stock, lock, and barrel. But as sharp as a needle, sir, and as immovable as a rock. A fine woman, too." I saw by the expression of the man's face that he owned ugly memories, and pressed him further. "She's up country somewhere," he said. "Married her assigned servant, I was told, a fellow named Carr. I haven't seen her for years, and don't know what she may be like now, but in the days when I knew her she was just what you describe." (Let it be noted that I had described nothing.) "She came out in the ship with me as maid to my wife's mother."

It was on the tip of my tongue to say that I had met her, but I don't know what induced me to be silent. There are passages in the lives of men of Captain Frere's complexion, which don't bear descanting on. I expect there have been in this case, for he changed the subject abruptly, as his wife came in. Is it possible that these two creatures—the notable disciplinarian and the wife of the assigned servant—could have been more than friends in youth? Quite possible. He is the sort of man for gross amours. (A pretty way I am abusing my host!) And the supple woman with the dark eyes would have been just the creature to enthral him. Perhaps some such story as this may account in part for Mrs. Frere's sad looks. Why do I speculate on such things? I seem to do violence to myself and to insult *her* by writing such suspicions. If I was a Flagellant now, I would don hairshirt and up flail. "For this sort cometh not out but by prayer and fasting."

April 7th.—Mr. Pounce has arrived—full of the importance of his mission. He walks with the air of a minister of state on the eve of a vacant garter, hoping, wondering, fearing, and dignified even in his dubitancy. I am as flippant as a school-girl concerning this fatuous official, and yet—Heaven knows—I feel deeply enough the importance of the task he has before him. One relieves one's brain by these whirlings of one's mental limbs. I remember that a prisoner at Hobart Town, twice condemned and twice reprieved, jumped and shouted with frenzied vehemence when he heard his sentence of death was finally pronounced. He told me, if he had not so shouted, he believed he would have gone mad.

April 10th.—We had a state dinner last night. The conversation was about nothing in the world but convicts. I never saw Mrs. Frere to less advantage. Silent, *distraite,* and sad. She told me after dinner that she disliked the very name of "convict" from early associations. "I have lived among them all my life," she said, "but that does not make it the better for me. I have terrible fancies at times, Mr. North, that seem half-memories. I dread to be brought in contact with prisoners again. I am sure that some evil awaits me at their hands."

I laughed, of course, but it would not do. She holds to her own opinion, and looks at me with horror in her eyes. This terror in her face is perplexing.

"You are nervous," I said. "You want rest."

"I *am* nervous," she replied, with that candour of voice and manner I have before remarked in her, "and I have presentiments of evil."

We sat silent for a while, and then she suddenly turned her large eyes on me, and said calmly, "Mr. North, what death shall I die?" The question was an echo of my own thoughts—I have some foolish (?) fancies as to physiognomy—and it made me start. What death, indeed? What sort of death would one meet with widely-opened eyes, parted lips, and brows bent as though to rally fast-flying courage? Not a peaceful death surely. I brought my black coat to my aid. "My dear lady, you must not think of such things. Death is but a sleep, you know. Why anticipate a nightmare?"

She sighed, slowly awaking as though from some momentary trance. Checking herself on the verge of tears, she rallied, turned the conversation, and finding an excuse for going to the piano, dashed into a waltz. This unnatural gaiety ended, I fancy, in an hysterical fit. I heard her husband afterwards recommending sal volatile. He is the sort of man who would recommend sal volatile to the Pythoness if she consulted him.

April 26th.—All has been arranged, and we start to-morrow. Mr. Pounce is in a condition of painful dignity. He seems afraid to move lest motion should thaw his official ice. Having found out that I am the "chaplain", he has refrained from familiarity. My self-love is wounded, but my patience relieved. *Query.* Would not the majority of mankind rather be bored by people in authority than not noticed by them? James North declines to answer for his part. I have made my farewells to my friends, and on looking back on the pleasant hours I have spent, felt saddened. It is not likely that I shall have many such pleasant hours. I feel like a vagabond who, having been allowed to sit by a cheerful fireside for a while, is turned out into the wet and windy streets, and finds them colder than ever. What were the lines I wrote in her album?

"As some poor tavern-haunter drenched in wine
With staggering footsteps through the streets returning,
Seeing through blinding rain a beacon shine
From household lamp in happy window burning,—

"Pauses an instant at the reddened pane
To gaze on that sweet scene of love and duty,
Then turns into the wild wet night again,
Lest his sad presence mar its homely beauty."

Yes, those were the lines. With more of truth in them than she expected; and yet what business have I sentimentalizing. My socius thinks "what a puling fool this North is!"

So, that's over! Now for Norfolk Island and my purgation.

CHAPTER II

THE LOST HEIR

THE lost son of Sir Richard Devine had returned to England, and made claim to his name and fortune. In other words, John Rex had successfully carried out the scheme by which he had usurped the rights of his old convict-comrade.

Smoking his cigar in his bachelor lodgings, or pausing in a calculation concerning a race, John Rex often wondered at the strange ease with which he had carried out so monstrous and seemingly difficult an imposture. After he was landed in Sydney, by the vessel which Sarah Purfoy had sent to save him, he found himself a slave to a bondage scarcely less galling than that from which he had escaped—the bondage of enforced companionship with an unloved woman. The opportune death of one of her assigned servants enabled Sarah Purfoy to instal the escaped convict in his room. In the strange state of society which prevailed of necessity in New South Wales at that period, it was not unusual for assigned servants to marry among the free settlers, and when it was heard that Mrs. Purfoy, the widow of a whaling captain, had married John Carr, her storekeeper, transported for embezzlement, and with two years of his sentence yet to run, no one expressed surprise. Indeed, when the year after, John Carr blossomed into an "expiree", master of a fine wife and a fine fortune, there were many about him who would have made his existence in Australia pleasant enough. But John Rex had no notion of remaining longer than he could help, and ceaselessly sought means of escape from this second prison-house. For a long time his search was unsuccessful. Much as she loved the scoundrel, Sarah Purfoy did not scruple to tell him that she had bought him and regarded him as her property. He knew that if he made any attempt to escape from his marriage-bonds, the woman who had risked so much to save him would not hesitate to deliver him over to the authorities, and state how the opportune death of John Carr had enabled her to give name and employment to John Rex, the absconder. He had thought once that the fact of her being his wife would prevent her from giving evidence against him, and that he could thus defy her. But she reminded him that a word to Blunt would be all sufficient.

"I know you don't care for me now, John," she said, with grim complacency; "but your life is in my hands, and if you desert me I will bring you to the gallows."

In vain, in his secret eagerness to be rid of her, he raged and chafed. He was tied hand and foot. She held his money, and her shrewd wit had more than doubled it. She was all-powerful, and he could but wait until her death or some lucky accident should rid him of her, and leave him free to follow out the scheme he had matured. "Once rid of her," he thought, in his solitary rides over the station of which he was the nominal owner, "the rest is easy. I shall return to England with a plausible story of shipwreck, and shall doubtless be received with open arms by the dear mother from whom I have been so long parted. Richard Devine shall have his own again."

To be rid of her was not so easy. Twice he tried to escape from his thraldom, and was twice brought back. "I have bought you, John," his partner had laughed, "and you don't get away from me. Surely you can be content with these comforts. You were content with less once. I am not so ugly and repulsive, am I?"

"I am home-sick," John Carr retorted. "Let us go to England, Sarah."

She tapped her strong white fingers sharply on the table. "Go to England? No, no. That is what you would like to do. You would be master there. You would take my money, and leave me to starve. I know you, Jack. We stop here, dear. Here, where I can hand you over to the first trooper as an escaped convict if you are not kind to me."

"She-devil!"

"Oh, I don't mind your abuse. Abuse me if you like, Jack. Beat me if you will, but don't leave me, or it will be worse for you."

"You are a strange woman!" he cried, in sudden petulant admiration.

"To love such a villain? I don't know that. I love you because you are a villain. A better man would be wearisome to such as I am."

"I wish to Heaven I'd never left Port Arthur. Better there than this dog's life."

"Go back, then. You have only to say the word!" And so they would wrangle, she glorying in her power over the man who had so long triumphed over her, and he consoling himself with the hope that the day was not far distant which should bring him at once freedom and fortune. One day the chance came to him. His wife was ill, and the ungrateful scoundrel stole five hundred pounds, and taking two horses reached Sydney, and obtained passage in a vessel bound for Rio.

Having escaped thraldom, John Rex proceeded to play for the great stake of his life with the utmost caution. He went to the Continent, and lived for weeks together in the towns where Richard Devine might possibly have resided, familiarizing himself with streets, making the acquaintance of old inhabitants, drawing into his own hands all loose ends of information which could help to knit the meshes of his net the closer. Such loose ends were not numerous; the prodigal had been too poor, too insignificant, to leave strong memories behind him. Yet Rex knew well by what strange accidents the deceit of an assumed identity is often penetrated. Some old comrade or companion of the lost heir might suddenly appear with keen questions as to trifles which could cut his flimsy web to shreds, as easily as the sword of Saladin divided the floating silk. He could not afford to ignore the most insignificant circumstances. With consummate skill, piece by piece he built up the story which was to deceive the poor mother, and to make him possessor of one of the largest private fortunes in England.

This was the tale he hit upon. He had been saved from the burning *Hydaspes* by a vessel bound for Rio. Ignorant of the death of Sir Richard, and prompted by the pride which was known to be a leading feature of his character, he had determined not to return until fortune should have bestowed upon him wealth at least equal to the inheritance from which he had been ousted. In Spanish America he had striven to accumulate that wealth in vain. As *vequero,* traveller, speculator, sailor, he had toiled for fourteen years, and had failed. Worn out and penitent, he had returned home to find a corner of English earth in which to lay his weary bones. The tale was plausible enough, and in the telling of it he was armed at all points. There was little fear that the navigator of the captured *Osprey*, the man who had lived in Chile and "cut out" cattle on the Carrum Plains, would prove lacking in knowledge of riding, seamanship, or Spanish customs. Moreover, he had determined upon a course of action which showed his knowledge of human nature.

The will under which Richard Devine inherited was dated in 1807, and had been made when the testator was in the first hopeful glow of paternity. By its terms Lady Devine was to receive a life interest of three thousand a year in her husband's property—which was placed in the hands of two trustees—until her eldest son died or attained the age of twenty-five years. When either of these events should occur, the property was to be realized, Lady Devine receiving a sum of a hundred thousand pounds, which, invested in Consols for her benefit, would, according to Sir Richard's prudent calculation exactly compensate for her loss of interest, the remainder going absolutely to the son, if living, to his children or next of kin if dead. The trustees appointed were Lady Devine's father, Colonel Wotton Wade, and Mr. Silas Quaid, of the firm of Purkiss and Quaid Thavies Inn, Sir Richard's solicitors. Colonel Wade, before his death had appointed his son, Mr. Francis Wade, to act in his stead. When Mr. Quaid died, the firm of Purkiss and Quaid (represented in the Quaid branch of it by a smart London-bred nephew) declined further responsibility; and, with the consent of Lady Devine, Francis Wade continued alone in his trust. Sir Richard's sister and her husband, Anthony Frere, of Bristol, were long ago dead, and, as we know, their representative, Maurice Frere, content at last in the lot that fortune had sent him, had given up all thought of meddling with his uncle's business. John Rex, therefore, in the person of the returned Richard, had but two persons to satisfy, his putative uncle, Mr. Francis Wade, and his putative mother, Lady Devine.

This he found to be the easiest task possible. Francis Wade was an invalid virtuoso, who detested business, and whose ambition was to be known as man of taste. The possessor of a small independent income, he had resided at North End ever since his father's death, and had made the place a miniature Strawberry Hill. When, at his sister's urgent wish, he assumed the sole responsibility of the estate, he put all the floating capital into 3 per cents., and was content to see the interest accumulate. Lady Devine had never recovered the shock of the circumstances attending Sir Richard's death and, clinging to the belief in her son's existence, regarded herself as the mere guardian of his interests, to be displaced at any moment by his sudden return. The retired pair lived thus together, and spent in charity and *bric-a-brac* about a fourth of their mutual income. By both of them the return of the wanderer was hailed with delight. To Lady Devine it meant the realization of a lifelong hope, become part of her nature. To Francis Wade it meant relief from a responsibility which his simplicity always secretly loathed, the responsibility of looking after another person's money.

"I shall not think of interfering with the arrangements which you have made, my dear uncle," said Mr. John Rex, on the first night of his reception. "It would be most ungrateful of me to do so. My wants are very few, and can easily be supplied. I will see your lawyers some day, and settle it."

"See them at once, Richard; see them at once. I am no man of business, you know, but I think you will find all right."

Richard, however, put off the visit from day to day. He desired to have as little to do with lawyers as possible. He had resolved upon his course of action. He would get money from his mother for immediate needs, and when that mother died he would assert his rights. "My rough life has unfitted me for drawing-rooms, dear mother," he said. "Do not let there be a display about my return. Give me a corner to smoke my pipe, and I am happy." Lady Devine, with a loving tender pity, for which John Rex could not altogether account, consented, and "Mr. Richard" soon came to be regarded as a martyr to circumstances, a man conscious of his own imperfections, and one whose imperfections were therefore lightly dwelt upon. So the returned prodigal had his own suite of rooms, his own servants, his own bank account, drank, smoked, and was merry.

For five or six months he thought himself in Paradise. Then he began to find his life insufferably weary. The burden of hypocrisy is very heavy to bear, and Rex was compelled perpetually to bear it. His mother demanded all his time. She hung upon his lips; she made him repeat fifty times the story of his wanderings. She was never tired of kissing him, of weeping over him, and of thanking him for the "sacrifice" he had made for her.

"We promised never to speak of it more, Richard," the poor lady said one day, "but if my lifelong love can make atonement for the wrong I have done you—"

"Hush, dearest mother," said John Rex, who did not in the least comprehend what it was all about. "Let us say no more."

Lady Devine wept quietly for a while, and then went away, leaving the man who pretended to be her son much bewildered and a little frightened. There was a secret which he had not fathomed between Lady Devine and her son. The mother did not again refer to it, and, gaining courage as the days went on, Rex grew bold enough to forget his fears.

In the first stages of his deception he had been timid and cautious. Then the soothing influence of comfort, respect, and security came upon him, and almost refined him. He began to feel as he had felt when Mr. Lionel Crofton was alive. The sensation of being ministered to by a loving woman, who kissed him night and morning, calling him "son"—of being regarded with admiration by rustics, with envy by respectable folk—of being deferred to in all things—was novel and pleasing. They were so good to him that he felt at times inclined to confess all, and leave his case in the hands of the folk he had injured. Yet—he thought—such a course would be absurd. It would result in no benefit to anyone, simply in misery to himself. The true Richard Devine was buried fathoms deep in the greedy ocean of convict-discipline, and the waves of innumerable punishments washed over him. John Rex flattered himself that he had usurped the name of one who was in fact no living man, and that, unless one should rise from the dead, Richard Devine could never return to accuse him. So flattering himself, he gradually became bolder, and by slow degrees suffered his true nature to appear. He was violent to the servants, cruel to dogs and horses, often wantonly coarse in speech, and brutally regardless of the feelings of others. Governed, like most women, solely by her feelings, Lady Devine had at first been prodigal of her affection to the man she believed to be her injured son. But his rash acts of selfishness, his habits of grossness and self-indulgence, gradually disgusted her. For some time she—poor woman—fought against this feeling, endeavouring to overcome her instincts of distaste, and arguing with herself that to permit a detestation of her unfortunate son to arise in her heart was almost criminal; but she was at length forced to succumb.

For the first year Mr. Richard conducted himself with great propriety, but as his circle of acquaintance and his confidence in himself increased, he now and then forgot the part he was playing. One day Mr. Richard went to pass the day with a sporting friend, only too proud to see at his table so wealthy and wonderful a man. Mr. Richard drank a good deal more than was good for him, and returned home in a condition of disgusting drunkenness. I say disgusting, because some folks have the art of getting drunk after a humorous fashion, that robs intoxication of half its grossness. For John Rex to be drunk was to be himself—coarse and cruel. Francis Wade was away, and Lady Devine had retired for the night, when the dogcart brought home "Mr. Richard". The virtuous butler-porter, who opened the door, received a blow in the chest and a demand for "Brandy!" The groom was cursed, and ordered to instant oblivion. Mr. Richard stumbled into the dining-room— veiled in dim light as a dining-room which was "sitting up" for its master ought to be—and ordered "more candles!" The candles were brought, after some delay, and Mr. Richard amused himself by spilling their meltings upon the carpet. "Let's have 'luminashon!" he cried; and climbing with muddy boots upon the costly chairs, scraping with his feet the polished table, attempted to fix the wax in the silver sconces, with which the antiquarian tastes of Mr. Francis Wade had adorned the room.

"You'll break the table, sir," said the servant.

"Damn the table!" said Rex. "Buy 'nother table. What's table t'you?"

"Oh, certainly, sir," replied the man.

"Oh, c'ert'nly! Why c'ert'nly? What do you know about it?"

"Oh, certainly not, sir," replied the man.

"If I had—stockwhip here—I'd make you—hie—skip! Whar's brandy?"

"Here, Mr. Richard."

"Have some! Good brandy! Send for servantsh and have dance. D'you dance, Tomkins?"

"No, Mr. Richard."

"Then you shall dance now, Tomkins. You'll dance upon nothing one day, Tomkins! Here! Halloo! Mary! Susan! Janet! William! Hey! Halloo!" And he began to shout and blaspheme.

"Don't you think it's time for bed, Mr. Richard?" one of the men ventured to suggest.

"No!" roared the ex-convict, emphatically, "I *don't*! I've gone to bed at daylight far too long. We'll have 'luminashon! I'm master here. Master everything. Richard 'Vine's my name. Isn't it, Tomkins, you villain?"

"Oh-h-h! Yes, Mr. Richard."

"Course it is, and make you know it too! I'm no painter-picture, crockery chap. I'm genelman! Genelman seen the world! Knows what's what. There ain't much I ain't fly to. Wait till the old woman's dead, Tomkins, and you shall see!" More swearing, and awful threats of what the inebriate would do when he was in possession. "Bring up some brandy!" Crash goes the bottle in the fire-place. "Light up the droring-rooms; we'll have dance! I'm drunk! What's that? If you'd gone through what I have, you'd be glad to be drunk. I look a fool"—this to his image in another glass. "I ain't though, or I wouldn't be here. Curse you, you grinning idiot"—crash goes his fist through the mirror—"don't grin at me. Play up there! Where's old woman? Fetch her out and let's dance!"

"Lady Devine has gone to bed, Mr. Richard," cried Tomkins, aghast, attempting to bar the passage to the upper regions.

"Then let's have her out o' bed," cried John Rex, plunging to the door.

Tomkins, attempting to restrain him, is instantly hurled into a cabinet of rare china, and the drunken brute essays the stairs. The other servants seize him. He curses and fights like a demon. Doors bang open, lights gleam, maids hover, horrified, asking if it's "fire?" and begging for it to be "put out". The whole house is in an uproar, in the midst of which Lady Devine appears, and looks down upon the scene. Rex catches sight of her; and bursts into blasphemy. She withdraws, strangely terrified; and the animal, torn, bloody, and blasphemous, is at last got into his own apartments, the groom, whose face had been seriously damaged in the encounter, bestowing a hearty kick on the prostrate carcase at parting.

The next morning Lady Devine declined to see her son, though he sent a special apology to her.

"I am afraid I was a little overcome by wine last night," said he to Tomkins.

"Well, you *was*, sir," said Tomkins.

"A very little wine makes me quite ill, Tomkins. Did I do anything very violent?"

"You *was* rather obstropolous, Mr. Richard."

"Here's a sovereign for you, Tomkins. Did I *say* anything?"

"You cussed a good deal, Mr. Richard. Most gents do when they've bin—hum—dining out, Mr. Richard."

"What a fool I am," thought John Rex, as he dressed. "I shall spoil everything if I don't take care." He was right. He was going the right way to spoil everything. However, for this bout he made amends—money soothed the servants' hall, and apologies and time won Lady Devine's forgiveness.

"I cannot yet conform to English habits, my dear mother," said Rex, "and feel at times out of place in your quiet home. I think that—if you can spare me a little money—I should like to travel."

Lady Devine—with a sense of relief for which she blamed herself—assented, and supplied with letters of credit, John Rex went to Paris.

Fairly started in the world of dissipation and excess, he began to grow reckless. When a young man, he had been singularly free from the vice of drunkenness; turning his sobriety—as he did all his virtues—to vicious account; but he had learnt to drink deep in the loneliness of the bush. Master of a large sum of money, he had intended to spend it as he would have spent it in his younger days. He had forgotten that since his death and burial the world had not grown younger. It was possible that Mr. Lionel Crofton might have discovered some of the old set of fools and knaves with whom he had once mixed. Many of them were alive and flourishing. Mr. Lemoine, for instance, was respectably married in his native island of Jersey, and had already threatened to disinherit a nephew who showed a tendency to dissipation.

But Mr. Lemoine would not care to recognize Mr. Lionel Crofton, the gambler and rake, in his proper person, and it was not expedient that his acquaintance should be made in the person of Richard Devine, lest by some unlucky chance he should recognize the cheat. Thus poor Lionel Crofton was compelled to lie still in his grave, and Mr. Richard Devine, trusting to a big beard and more burly figure to keep his secret, was compelled to begin his friendship with Mr. Lionel's whilom friends all over again. In Paris and London there were plenty of people ready to become hail-fellow-well-met with any gentleman possessing money. Mr. Richard Devine's history was whispered in many a boudoir and club-room. The history, however, was not always told in the same way. It was generally known that Lady Devine had a son, who, being supposed to be dead, had suddenly returned, to the confusion of his family. But the manner of his return was told in many ways.

In the first place, Mr. Francis Wade, well-known though he was, did not move in that brilliant circle which had lately received his nephew. There are in England many men of fortune, as large as that left by the old shipbuilder, who are positively unknown in that little world which is supposed to contain all the men worth knowing. Francis Wade was a man of mark in his own coterie. Among artists, *bric-a-brac* sellers, antiquarians, and men of letters he was known as a patron and man of taste. His bankers and his lawyers knew him to be of independent fortune, but as he neither mixed in politics, "went into society", betted, or speculated in merchandise, there were several large sections of the community who had never heard his name. Many respectable money-lenders would have required "further information" before they would discount his bills; and "clubmen" in general—save, perhaps, those ancient quidnuncs who know everybody, from Adam downwards—had but little acquaintance with him. The advent of Mr. Richard Devine—a coarse person of unlimited means—had therefore chief influence upon that sinister circle of male and female rogues who form the "half-world". They began to inquire concerning his antecedents, and, failing satisfactory information, to invent lies concerning him. It was generally believed that he was a black sheep, a man whose family kept him out of the way, but who was, in a pecuniary sense, "good" for a considerable sum.

Thus taken upon trust, Mr. Richard Devine mixed in the very best of bad society, and had no lack of agreeable friends to help him to spend money. So admirably did he spend it, that Francis Wade became at last alarmed at the frequent drafts, and urged his nephew to bring his affairs to a final settlement. Richard Devine—in Paris, Hamburg, or London, or elsewhere—could never be got to attack business, and Mr. Francis Wade grew more and more anxious. The poor gentleman positively became ill through the anxiety consequent upon his nephew's dissipations. "I wish, my dear Richard, that you would let me know what to do," he wrote. "I wish, my dear uncle, that you would do what you think best," was his nephew's reply. "Will you let Purkiss and Quaid look into the business?" said the badgered Francis.

"I hate lawyers," said Richard. "Do what you think right."

Mr. Wade began to repent of his too easy taking of matters in the beginning. Not that he had a suspicion of Rex, but that he had remembered that Dick was always a loose fish. The even current of the *dilettante's* life became disturbed. He grew pale and hollow-eyed. His digestion was impaired. He ceased to take the interest in china which the importance of that article demanded. In a word, he grew despondent as to his fitness for his mission in life. Lady Ellinor saw a change in her brother. He became morose, peevish, excitable. She went privately to the family doctor, who shrugged his shoulders. "There is no danger," said he, "if he is kept quiet; keep him quiet, and he will live for years; *but* his father died of heart disease, you know." Lady Ellinor, upon this, wrote a long letter to Mr. Richard, who was at Paris, repeated the doctor's opinions, and begged him to come over at once. Mr. Richard replied that some horse-racing matter of great importance occupied his attention, but that he would be at his rooms in Clarges Street (he had long ago established a town house) on the 14th, and would "go into matters". "I have lost a good deal of money lately, my dear mother," said Mr. Richard, "and the present will be a good opportunity to make a final settlement." The fact was that John Rex, now three years in undisturbed possession, considered that the moment had arrived for the execution of his *grand coup*—the carrying off at one swoop of the whole of the fortune he had gambled for.

CHAPTER III
EXTRACTED FROM THE DIARY
OF THE REV. JAMES NORTH

MAY 12th—Landed to-day at Norfolk Island, and have been introduced to my new abode, situated some eleven hundred miles from Sydney. A solitary rock in the tropical ocean, the island seems, indeed, a fit place of banishment. It is about seven miles long and four broad. The most remarkable natural object is, of course, the Norfolk Island pine, which rears its stately head a hundred feet above the surrounding forest. The appearance of the place is very wild and beautiful, bringing to my mind the description of the romantic islands of the Pacific, which old geographers dwell upon so fondly. Lemon, lime, and guava trees abound, also oranges, grapes, figs, bananas, peaches, pomegranates, and pine-apples. The climate just now is hot and muggy. The approach to Kingstown—as the barracks and huts are called—is properly difficult. A long low reef—probably originally a portion of the barren rocks of Nepean and Philip Islands, which rise east and west of the settlement—fronts the bay and obstructs the entrance of vessels. We were landed in boats through an opening in this reef, and our vessel stands on and off within signalling distance. The surf washes almost against the walls of the military roadway that leads to the barracks. The social aspect of the place fills me with horror. There seems neither discipline nor order. On our way to the Commandant's house we passed a low dilapidated building where men were grinding maize, and at the sight of us they commenced whistling, hooting, and shouting, using the most disgusting language. Three warders were near, but no attempt was made to check this unseemly exhibition.

May 14th.—I sit down to write with as much reluctance as though I were about to relate my experience of a journey through a sewer. First to the prisoners' barracks, which stand on an area of about three acres, surrounded by a lofty wall. A road runs between this wall and the sea. The barracks are three storeys high, and hold seven hundred and ninety men (let me remark here that there are more than two thousand men on the island). There are twenty-two wards in this place. Each ward runs the depth of the building, viz., eighteen feet, and in consequence is simply a funnel for hot or cold air to blow through. When the ward is filled, the men's heads lie under the windows. The largest ward contains a hundred men, the smallest fifteen. They sleep in hammocks, slung close to each other as on board ship, in two lines, with a passage down the centre. There is a wardsman to each ward. He is selected by the prisoners, and is generally a man of the worst character. He is supposed to keep order, but of course he never attempts to do so; indeed, as he is locked up in the ward every night from six o'clock in the evening until sunrise, *without light*, it is possible that he might get maltreated did he make himself obnoxious.

The barracks look upon the Barrack Square, which is filled with lounging prisoners. The windows of the hospital-ward also look upon Barrack Square, and the prisoners are in constant communication with the patients. The hospital is a low stone building, capable of containing about twenty men, and faces the beach. I placed my hands on the wall, and found it damp. An ulcerous prisoner said the dampness was owing to the heavy surf constantly rolling so close beneath the building. There are two gaols, the old and the new. The old gaol stands near the sea, close to the landing-place. Outside it, at the door, is the Gallows. I touched it as I passed in. This engine is the first thing which greets the eyes of a newly-arrived prisoner. The new gaol is barely completed, is of pentagonal shape, and has eighteen radiating cells of a pattern approved by some wiseacre in England, who thinks that to prevent a man from seeing his fellowmen is not the way to drive him mad. In the old gaol are twenty-four prisoners, all heavily ironed, awaiting trial by the visiting Commission, from Hobart Town. Some of these poor ruffians, having committed their offences just after the last sitting of the Commission, have already been in gaol upwards of eleven months!

At six o'clock we saw the men mustered. I read prayers before the muster, and was surprised to find that some of the prisoners attended, while some strolled about the yard, whistling, singing, and joking. The muster is a farce. The prisoners are not mustered outside and then marched to their wards, but they rush into the barracks indiscriminately, and place themselves dressed or undressed in their hammocks. A convict sub-overseer then calls out the names, and somebody replies. If an answer is returned to each name, all is considered right. The lights are taken away, and save for a few minutes at eight o'clock, when the good-conduct men are let in, the ruffians are left to their own devices until morning. Knowing what I know of the customs of the convicts, my heart sickens when I in imagination put myself in the place of a newly-transported man, plunged from six at night until daybreak into that foetid den of worse than wild beasts.

May 15th.—There is a place enclosed between high walls adjoining the convict barracks, called the Lumber Yard. This is where the prisoners mess. It is roofed on two sides, and contains tables and benches. Six hundred men can mess here perhaps, but as seven hundred are always driven into it, it follows that the weakest men are compelled to sit on the ground. A more disorderly sight than this yard at meal times I never beheld. The cook-houses are adjoining it, and the men bake their meal-bread there. Outside the cook-house door the firewood is piled, and fires are made in all directions on the ground, round which sit the prisoners, frying their rations of fresh pork, baking their hominy cakes, chatting, and even smoking.

The Lumber Yard is a sort of Alsatia, to which the hunted prisoner retires. I don't think the boldest constable on the island would venture into that place to pick out a man from the seven hundred. If he did go in I don't think he would come out again alive.

May 16th.—A sub-overseer, a man named Hankey, has been talking to me. He says that there are some forty of the oldest and worst prisoners who form what he calls the "Ring", and that the members of this Ring are bound by oath to support each other, and to avenge the punishment of any of their number. In proof of his assertions he instanced two cases of English prisoners who had refused to join in some crime, and had informed the Commandant of the proceedings of the Ring.

They were found in the morning strangled in their hammocks. An inquiry was held, but not a man out of the ninety in the ward would speak a word. I dread the task that is before me. How can I attempt to preach piety and morality to these men? How can I attempt even to save the less villainous?

May 17th.—Visited the wards to-day, and returned in despair. The condition of things is worse than I expected. It is not to be written. The newly-arrived English prisoners—and some of their histories are most touching—are insulted by the language and demeanour of the hardened miscreants who are the refuse of Port Arthur and Cockatoo Island. The vilest crimes are perpetrated as jests. These are creatures who openly defy authority, whose language and conduct is such as was never before seen or heard out of Bedlam. There are men who are known to have murdered their companions, and who boast of it. With these the English farm labourer, the riotous and ignorant mechanic, the victim of perjury or mistake, are indiscriminately herded. With them are mixed Chinamen from Hong Kong, the Aborigines of New Holland, West Indian blacks, Greeks, Caffres, and Malays, soldiers for desertion, idiots, madmen, pig-stealers, and pickpockets. The dreadful place seems set apart for all that is hideous and vile in our common nature. In its recklessness, its insubordination, its filth, and its despair, it realizes to my mind the popular notion of Hell.

May 21st.—Entered to-day officially upon my duties as Religious Instructor at the Settlement.

An occurrence took place this morning which shows the dangerous condition of the Ring. I accompanied Mr. Pounce to the Lumber Yard, and, on our entry, we observed a man in the crowd round the cook-house deliberately smoking. The Chief Constable of the Island—my old friend Troke, of Port Arthur—seeing that this exhibition attracted Pounce's notice, pointed out the man to an assistant. The assistant, Jacob Gimblett, advanced and desired the prisoner to surrender the pipe. The man plunged his hands into his pockets, and, with a gesture of the most profound contempt, walked away to that part of the mess-shed where the "Ring" congregate.

"Take the scoundrel to gaol!" cried Troke.

No one moved, but the man at the gate that leads through the carpenter's shop into the barracks, called to us to come out, saying that the prisoners would never suffer the man to be taken. Pounce, however, with more determination than I gave him credit for, kept his ground, and insisted that so flagrant a breach of discipline should not be suffered to pass unnoticed. Thus urged, Mr. Troke pushed through the crowd, and made for the spot whither the man had withdrawn himself.

The yard was buzzing like a disturbed hive, and I momentarily expected that a rush would be made upon us. In a few moments the prisoner appeared, attended by, rather than in the custody of, the Chief Constable of the island. He advanced to the unlucky assistant constable, who was standing close to me, and asked, "What have you ordered me to gaol for?" The man made some reply, advising him to go quietly, when the convict raised his fist and deliberately felled the man to the ground. "You had better retire, gentlemen," said Troke. "I see them getting out their knives."

We made for the gate, and the crowd closed in like a sea upon the two constables. I fully expected murder, but in a few moments Troke and Gimblett appeared, borne along by a mass of men, dusty, but unharmed, and having the convict between them. He sulkily raised a hand as he passed me, either to rectify the position of his straw hat, or to offer a tardy apology. A more wanton, unprovoked, and flagrant outrage than that of which this man was guilty I never witnessed. It is customary for "the old dogs", as the experienced convicts are called, to use the most opprobrious language to their officers, and to this a deaf ear is usually turned, but I never before saw a man wantonly strike a constable. I fancy that the act was done out of bravado. Troke informed me that the man's name is Rufus Dawes, and that he is the leader of the Ring, and considered the worst man on the island; that to secure him he (Troke) was obliged to use the language of expostulation; and that, but for the presence of an officer accredited by his Excellency, he dared not have acted as he had done.

This is the same man, then, whom I injured at Port Arthur. Seven years of "discipline" don't seem to have done him much good. His sentence is "life"—a lifetime in this place! Troke says that he was the terror of Port Arthur, and that they sent him here when a "weeding" of the prisoners was made. He has been here four years. Poor wretch!

May 24th.—After prayers, I saw Dawes. He was confined in the Old Gaol, and seven others were in the cell with him. He came out at my request, and stood leaning against the door-post. He was much changed from the man I remember. Seven years ago he was a stalwart, upright, *handsome* man. He has become a beetle-browed, sullen, slouching ruffian. His hair is grey, though he cannot be more than forty years of age, and his frame has lost that just proportion of parts which once made him almost graceful. His face has also grown like other convict faces—how hideously alike they all are!—and, save for his black eyes and a peculiar trick he had of compressing his lips, I should not have recognized him. How habitual sin and misery suffice to brutalize "the human face divine"! I said but little, for the other prisoners were listening, eager, as it appeared to me, to witness my discomfiture. It is evident that Rufus Dawes had been accustomed to meet the ministrations of my predecessors with insolence. I spoke to him for a few minutes, only saying how foolish it was to rebel against an authority superior in strength to himself. He did not answer, and the only emotion he evinced during the interview was when I reminded him that we had met before. He shrugged one shoulder, as if in pain or anger, and seemed about to speak, but, casting his eyes upon the group in the cell, relapsed into silence again. I must get speech with him alone. One can do nothing with a man if seven other devils worse than himself are locked up with him.

I sent for Hankey, and asked him about cells. He says that the gaol is crowded to suffocation. "Solitary confinement" is a mere name. There are six men, each sentenced to solitary confinement, in a cell together. The cell is called the "nunnery". It is small, and the six men were naked to the waist when I entered, the perspiration pouring in streams off their naked bodies! It is disgusting to write of such things.

June 26th.—Pounce has departed in the *Lady Franklin* for Hobart Town, and it is rumoured that we are to have a new Commandant. The *Lady Franklin* is commanded by an old man named Blunt, a *protege* of Frere's, and a fellow to whom I have taken one of my inexplicable and unreasoning dislikes.

Saw Rufus Dawes this morning. He continues sullen and morose. His papers are very bad. He is perpetually up for punishment. I am informed that he and a man named Eastwood, nicknamed "Jacky Jacky", glory in being the leaders of the Ring, and that they openly avow themselves weary of life. Can it be that the unmerited flogging which the poor creature got at Port Arthur has aided, with other sufferings, to bring him to this horrible state of mind? It is quite possible. Oh, James North, remember your own crime, and pray Heaven to let you redeem one soul at least, to plead for your own at the Judgment Seat.

June 30th.—I took a holiday this afternoon, and walked in the direction of Mount Pitt. The island lay at my feet like—as sings Mrs. Frere's favourite poet—"a summer isle of Eden lying in dark purple sphere of sea". Sophocles has the same idea in the *Philoctetes*, but I can't quote it. Note: I measured a pine twenty-three feet in circumference. I followed a little brook that runs from the hills, and winds through thick undergrowths of creeper and blossom, until it reaches a lovely valley surrounded by lofty trees, whose branches, linked together by the luxurious grape-vine, form an arching bower of verdure. Here stands the ruin of an old hut, formerly inhabited by the early settlers; lemons, figs, and guavas are thick; while amid the shrub and cane a large convolvulus is entwined, and stars the green with its purple and crimson flowers. I sat down here, and had a smoke. It seems that the former occupant of my rooms at the settlement read French; for in searching for a book to bring with me—I never walk without a book—I found and pocketed a volume of Balzac. It proved to be a portion of the *Vie Privee* series, and I stumbled upon a story called *La Fausse Maitresse*. With calm belief in the Paris of his imagination—where Marcas was a politician, Nucingen a banker, Gobseck a money-lender, and Vautrin a candidate for some such place as this—Balzac introduces me to a Pole by name Paz, who, loving the wife of his friend, devotes himself to watch over her happiness and her husband's interest. The husband gambles and is profligate. Paz informs the wife that the leanness which hazard and debauchery have caused to the domestic exchequer is due to *his* extravagance, the husband having lent him money. She does not believe, and Paz feigns an intrigue with a circus-rider in order to lull all suspicions. She says to her adored spouse, "Get rid of this extravagant friend! Away with him! He is a profligate, a gambler! A drunkard!" Paz finally departs, and when he has gone, the lady finds out the poor Pole's worth. The story does not end satisfactorily. Balzac was too great a master of his art for that. In real life the curtain never falls on a comfortably-finished drama. The play goes on eternally.

I have been thinking of the story all evening. A man who loves his friend's wife, and devotes his energies to increase her happiness by concealing from her her husband's follies! Surely none but Balzac would have hit upon such a notion. "A man who loves his friend's wife."—Asmodeus, I write no more! I have ceased to converse with thee for so long that I blush to confess all that I have in my heart.— I will *not* confess it, so that shall suffice.

CHAPTER IV

EXTRACTED FROM THE DIARY
OF THE REV. JAMES NORTH

AUGUST 24th.—There has been but one entry in my journal since the 30th June, that which records the advent of our new Commandant, who, as I expected, is Captain Maurice Frere.

So great have been the changes which have taken place that I scarcely know how to record them. Captain Frere has realized my worst anticipations. He is brutal, vindictive, and domineering. His knowledge of prisons and prisoners gives him an advantage over Burgess, otherwise he much resembles that murderous animal. He has but one thought—to keep the prisoners in subjection. So long as the island is quiet, he cares not whether the men live or die. "I was sent down here to keep order," said he to me, a few days after his arrival, "and by God, sir, I'll do it!"

He has done it, I must admit; but at a cost of a legacy of hatred to himself that he may some day regret to have earned. He has organized three parties of police. One patrols the fields, one is on guard at stores and public buildings, and the third is employed as a detective force. There are two hundred soldiers on the island. And the officer in charge, Captain McNab, has been induced by Frere to increase their duties in many ways. The cords of discipline are suddenly drawn tight. For the disorder which prevailed when I landed, Frere has substituted a sudden and excessive rigour. Any officer found giving the smallest piece of tobacco to a prisoner is liable to removal from the island. The tobacco which grows wild has been rooted up and destroyed lest the men should obtain a leaf of it. The privilege of having a pannikin of hot water when the gangs came in from field labour in the evening has been withdrawn. The shepherds, hut-keepers, and all other prisoners, whether at the stations of Fongridge or the Cascades (where the English convicts are stationed) are forbidden to keep a parrot or any other bird. The plaiting of straw hats during the prisoners' leisure hours is also prohibited. At the settlement where the "old hands" are located railed boundaries have been erected, beyond which no prisoner must pass unless to work. Two days ago Job Dodd, a negro, let his jacket fall over the boundary rails, crossed them to recover it, and was severely flogged. The floggings are hideously frequent. On flogging mornings I have seen the ground where the men stood at the triangles saturated with blood, as if a bucket of blood had been spilled on it, covering a space three feet in diameter, and running out in various directions, in little streams two or three feet long. At the same time, let me say, with that strict justice I force myself to mete out to those whom I dislike, that the island is in a condition of abject submission. There is not much chance of mutiny. The men go to their work without a murmur, and slink to their dormitories like whipped hounds to kennel. The gaols and solitary (!) cells are crowded with prisoners, and each day sees fresh sentences for fresh crimes. It is crime here to do anything but live.

The method by which Captain Frere has brought about this repose of desolation is characteristic of him. He sets every man as a spy upon his neighbour, awes the more daring into obedience by the display of a ruffianism more outrageous than their own, and, raising the worst scoundrels in the place to office, compels them to find "cases" for punishment. Perfidy is rewarded. It has been made part of a convict-policeman's duty to search a fellow-prisoner anywhere and at any time. This searching is often conducted in a wantonly rough and disgusting manner; and if resistance be offered, the man resisting can be knocked down by a blow from the searcher's bludgeon. Inquisitorial vigilance and indiscriminating harshness prevail everywhere, and the lives of hundreds of prisoners are reduced to a continual agony of terror and self-loathing.

"It is impossible, Captain Frere," said I one day, during the initiation of this system, "to think that these villains whom you have made constables will do their duty."

He replied, "They *must* do their duty. If they are indulgent to the prisoners, they know I shall flog 'em. If they do what I tell 'em, they'll make themselves so hated that they'd have their own father up to the triangles to save themselves being sent back to the ranks."

"You treat them then like slave-keepers of a wild beast den. They must flog the animals to avoid being flogged themselves."

"Ay," said he, with his coarse laugh, "and having once flogged 'em, they'd do anything rather than be put in the cage, don't you see!"

It is horrible to think of this sort of logic being used by a man who has a wife, and friends and enemies. It is the logic that the Keeper of the Tormented would use, I should think. I am sick unto death of the place. It makes me an unbeliever in the social charities. It takes out of penal science anything it may possess of nobility or worth. It is cruel, debasing, inhuman.

August 26th.—Saw Rufus Dawes again to-day. His usual bearing is ostentatiously rough and brutal. He has sunk to a depth of self-abasement in which he takes a delight in his degradation. This condition is one familiar to me.

He is working in the chain-gang to which Hankey was made sub-overseer. Blind Mooney, an ophthalmic prisoner, who was removed from the gang to hospital, told me that there was a plot to murder Hankey, but that Dawes, to whom he had shown some kindness, had prevented it. I saw Hankey and told him of this, asking him if he had been aware of the plot. He said "No," falling into a great tremble. "Major Pratt promised me a removal," said he. "I expected it would come to this."

I asked him why Dawes defended him; and after some trouble he told me, exacting from me a promise that I would not acquaint the Commandant. It seems that one morning last week, Hankey had gone up to Captain Frere's house with a return from Troke, and coming back through the garden had plucked a flower. Dawes had asked him for this flower, offering two days' rations for it. Hankey, who is not a bad-hearted man, gave him the sprig. "There were tears in his eyes as he took it," said he.

There must be some way to get at this man's heart, bad as he seems to be.

August 28th.—Hankey was murdered yesterday. He applied to be removed from the gaol-gang, but Frere refused. "I never let my men 'funk'," he said. "If they've threatened to murder you, I'll keep you there another month in spite of 'em."

Someone who overheard this reported it to the gang, and they set upon the unfortunate gaoler yesterday, and beat his brains out with their shovels. Troke says that the wretch who was foremost cried, "There's for you; and if your master don't take care, he'll get served the same one of these days!" The gang were employed at building a reef in the sea, and were working up to their armpits in water. Hankey fell into the surf, and never moved after the first blow. I saw the gang, and Dawes said—

"It was Frere's fault; he should have let the man go!"

"I am surprised you did not interfere," said I.

"I did all I could," was the man's answer. "What's a life more or less, *here?*"

This occurrence has spread consternation among the overseers, and they have addressed a "round robin" to the Commandant, praying to be relieved from their positions.

The way Frere has dealt with this petition is characteristic of him, and fills me at once with admiration and disgust. He came down with it in his hand to the gaol-gang, walked into the yard, shut the gate, and said, "I've just got this from my overseers. They say they're afraid you'll murder them as you murdered Hankey. Now, if you want to murder, murder *me*. Here I am. Step out, one of you." All this, said in a tone of the most galling contempt, did not move them. I saw a dozen pairs of eyes flash hatred, but the bull-dog courage of the man overawed them here, as, I am told, it had done in Sydney. It would have been easy to kill him then and there, and his death, I am told, is sworn among them; but no one raised a finger. The only man who moved was Rufus Dawes, and he checked himself instantly. Frere, with a recklessness of which I did not think him capable, stepped up to this terror of the prison, and ran his hands lightly down his sides, as is the custom with constables when "searching" a man. Dawes—who is of a fierce temper—turned crimson at this and, I thought, would have struck him, but he did not. Frere then—still unarmed and alone—proceeded to the man, saying, "Do you think of bolting again, Dawes? Have you made any more boats?"

"You Devil!" said the chained man, in a voice pregnant with such weight of unborn murder, that the gang winced.

"You'll find me one," said Frere, with a laugh; and, turning to me, continued, in the same jesting tone, "There's a penitent for you, Mr. North—try your hand on him."

I was speechless at his audacity, and must have shown my disgust in my face, for he coloured slightly, and as we were leaving the yard, he endeavoured to excuse himself, by saying that it was no use preaching to stones, and such doubly-dyed villains as this Dawes were past hope. "I know the ruffian of old," said he. "He came out in the ship from England with me, and tried to raise a mutiny on board. He was the man who nearly murdered my wife. He has never been out of irons—except then and when he escaped—for the last eighteen years; and as he's three life sentences, he's like to die in 'em."

A monstrous wretch and criminal, evidently, and yet I feel a strange sympathy with this outcast.

CHAPTER V

MR. RICHARD DEVINE SURPRISED

THE town house of Mr. Richard Devine was in Clarges Street. Not that the very modest mansion there situated was the only establishment of which Richard Devine was master. Mr. John Rex had expensive tastes. He neither shot nor hunted, so he had no capital invested in Scotch moors or Leicestershire hunting-boxes. But his stables were the wonder of London, he owned almost a racing village near Doncaster, kept a yacht at Cowes, and, in addition to a house in Paris, paid the rent of a villa at Brompton. He belonged to several clubs of the faster sort, and might have lived like a prince at any one of them had he been so minded; but a constant and haunting fear of discovery—which three years of unquestioned ease and unbridled riot had not dispelled—led him to prefer the privacy of his own house, where he could choose his own society. The house in Clarges Street was decorated in conformity with the tastes of its owner. The pictures were pictures of horses, the books were records of races, or novels purporting to describe sporting life. Mr. Francis Wade, waiting, on the morning of the 20th April, for the coming of his nephew, sighed as he thought of the cultured quiet of North End House.

Mr. Richard appeared in his dressing-gown. Three years of good living and hard drinking had deprived his figure of its athletic beauty. He was past forty years of age, and the sudden cessation from severe bodily toil to which in his active life as a convict and squatter he had been accustomed, had increased Rex's natural proneness to fat, and instead of being portly he had become gross. His cheeks were inflamed with the frequent application of hot and rebellious liquors to his blood. His hands were swollen, and not so steady as of yore. His whiskers were streaked with unhealthy grey. His eyes, bright and black as ever, lurked in a thicket of crow's feet. He had become prematurely bald—a sure sign of mental or bodily excess. He spoke with assumed heartiness, in a boisterous tone of affected ease.

"Ha, ha! My dear uncle, sit down. Delighted to see you. Have you breakfasted?—of course you have. *I* was up rather late last night. Quite sure you won't have anything. A glass of wine? No—then sit down and tell me all the news of Hampstead."

"Thank you, Richard," said the old gentleman, a little stiffly, "but I want some serious talk with you. What do you intend to do with the property? This indecision worries me. Either relieve me of my trust, or be guided by my advice."

"Well, the fact is," said Richard, with a very ugly look on his face, "the fact is—and you may as well know it at once—I am much pushed for money."

"Pushed for money!" cried Mr. Wade, in horror. "Why, Purkiss said the property was worth twenty thousand a year."

"So it might have been—five years ago—but my horse-racing, and betting, and other amusements, concerning which you need not too curiously inquire, have reduced its value considerably."

He spoke recklessly and roughly. It was evident that success had but developed his ruffianism. His "dandyism" was only comparative. The impulse of poverty and scheming which led him to affect the "gentleman" having been removed, the natural brutality of his nature showed itself quite freely. Mr. Francis Wade took a pinch of snuff with a sharp motion of distaste. "I do not want to hear of your debaucheries," he said; "our name has been sufficiently disgraced in my hearing."

"What is got over the devil's back goes under his belly," replied Mr. Richard, coarsely. "My old father got his money by dirtier ways than these in which I spend it. As villainous an old scoundrel and skinflint as ever poisoned a seaman, I'll go bail."

Mr. Francis rose. "You need not revile your father, Richard—he left you all."

"Ay, but by pure accident. He didn't mean it. If he hadn't died in the nick of time, that unhung murderous villain, Maurice Frere, would have come in for it. By the way," he added, with a change of tone, "do you ever hear anything of Maurice?"

"I have not heard for some years," said Mr. Wade. "He is something in the Convict Department at Sydney, I think."

"Is he?" said Mr. Richard, with a shiver. "Hope he'll stop there. Well, but about business. The fact is, that—that I am thinking of selling everything."

"Selling everything!"

"Yes. 'Pon my soul I am. The Hampstead place and all."

"Sell North End House!" cried poor Mr. Wade, in bewilderment. "You'd sell it? Why, the carvings by Grinling Gibbons are the finest in England."

"I can't help that," laughed Mr. Richard, ringing the bell. "I want cash, and cash I must have.—Breakfast, Smithers.—I'm going to travel."

Francis Wade was breathless with astonishment. Educated and reared as he had been, he would as soon have thought of proposing to sell St. Paul's Cathedral as to sell the casket which held his treasures of art—his coins, his coffee-cups, his pictures, and his "proofs before letters".

"Surely, Richard, you are not in earnest?" he gasped.

"I am, indeed."

"But—but who will buy it?"

"Plenty of people. I shall cut it up into building allotments. Besides, they are talking of a suburban line, with a terminus at St. John's Wood, which will cut the garden in half. You are quite sure you've breakfasted? Then pardon me."

"Richard, you are jesting with me! You will never let them do such a thing!"

"I'm thinking of a trip to America," said Mr. Richard, cracking an egg. "I am sick of Europe. After all, what is the good of a man like me pretending to belong to 'an old family', with 'a seat' and all that humbug? Money is the thing now, my dear uncle. Hard cash! That's the ticket for soup, you may depend."

"Then what do you propose doing, sir?"

"To buy my mother's life interest as provided, realize upon the property, and travel," said Mr. Richard, helping himself to potted grouse.

"You amaze me, Richard. You confound me. Of course you can do as you please. But so sudden a determination. The old house—vases—coins—pictures—scattered—I really—Well, it is your property, of course—and—and—I wish you a very good morning!"

"I mean to do as I please," soliloquized Rex, as he resumed his breakfast. "Let him sell his rubbish by auction, and go and live abroad, in Germany or Jerusalem if he likes, the farther the better for me. I'll sell the property and make myself scarce. A trip to America will benefit my health."

A knock at the door made him start.

"Come in! Curse it, how nervous I'm getting. What's that? Letters? Give them to me; and why the devil don't you put the brandy on the table, Smithers?"

He drank some of the spirit greedily, and then began to open his correspondence.

"Cussed brute," said Mr. Smithers, outside the door. "He couldn't use wuss langwidge if he was a dook, dam 'im!—Yessir," he added, suddenly, as a roar from his master recalled him.

"When did *this* come?" asked Mr. Richard, holding out a letter more than usually disfigured with stampings.

"Lars night, sir. It's bin to 'Amstead, sir, and come down directed with the h'others." The angry glare of the black eyes induced him to add, "I 'ope there's nothink wrong, sir."

"Nothing, you infernal ass and idiot," burst out Mr. Richard, white with rage, "except that I should have had this instantly. Can't you see it's marked urgent? Can you read? Can you spell? There, that will do. No lies. Get out!"

Left to himself again, Mr. Richard walked hurriedly up and down the chamber, wiped his forehead, drank a tumbler of brandy, and finally sat down and re-read the letter. It was short, but terribly to the purpose.

"THE GEORGE HOTEL, PLYMOUTH, 17*th April*, 1846.
    "MY DEAR JACK,—

    "I have found you out, you see. Never mind how just at present. I know all about your proceedings, and unless Mr. Richard Devine receives his "wife" with due propriety, he'll find himself in the custody of the police. Telegraph, dear, to Mrs. Richard Devine, at above address.

> "Yours as ever, Jack,
> "SARAH.
>
> "To Richard Devine, Esq.,
> "North End House,
> "Hampstead."

The blow was unexpected and severe. It was hard, in the very high tide and flush of assured success, to be thus plucked back into the old bondage. Despite the affectionate tone of the letter, he knew the woman with whom he had to deal. For some furious minutes he sat motionless, gazing at the letter. He did not speak—men seldom do under such circumstances—but his thoughts ran in this fashion: "Here is this cursed woman again! Just as I was congratulating myself on my freedom. How did she discover me? Small use asking that. What shall I do? I can do nothing. It is absurd to run away, for I shall be caught. Besides, I've no money. My account at Mastermann's is overdrawn two thousand pounds. If I bolt at all, I must bolt at once—within twenty-four hours. Rich as I am, I don't suppose I could raise more than five thousand pounds in that time. These things take a day or two, say forty-eight hours. In forty-eight hours I could raise twenty thousand pounds, but forty-eight hours is too long. Curse the woman! I know her! How in the fiend's name did she discover me? It's a bad job. However, she's not inclined to be gratuitously disagreeable. How lucky I never married again! I had better make terms and trust to fortune. After all, she's been a good friend to me.—Poor Sally!—I might have rotted on that infernal Eaglehawk Neck if it hadn't been for her. She is not a bad sort. Handsome woman, too. I may make it up with her. I shall have to sell off and go away after all.—It might be worse.—I dare say the property's worth three hundred thousand pounds. Not bad for a start in America. And I may get rid of her yet. Yes. I must give in.—Oh, curse her!—*(Ringing the bell)*—Smithers!" *(Smithers appears.)* "A telegraph form and a cab! Stay. Pack me a dressing-bag. I shall be away for a day or so. *(Sotto voce)*—I'd better see her myself.— *(Aloud)*—Bring me a Bradshaw! *(Sotto voce)*—Damn the woman."

CHAPTER VI

IN WHICH THE CHAPLAIN IS TAKEN ILL

THOUGH the house of the Commandant of Norfolk Island was comfortable and well furnished, and though, of necessity, all that was most hideous in the "discipline" of the place was hidden, the loathing with which Sylvia had approached the last and most dreaded abiding place of the elaborate convict system, under which it had been her misfortune to live, had not decreased. The sights and sounds of pain and punishment surrounded her. She could not look out of her windows without a shudder. She dreaded each evening when her husband returned, lest he should blurt out some new atrocity. She feared to ask him in the morning whither he was going, lest he should thrill her with the announcement of some fresh punishment.

"I wish, Maurice, we had never come here," said she, piteously, when he recounted to her the scene of the gaol-gang. "These unhappy men will do you some frightful injury one of these days."

"Stuff!" said her husband. "They've not the courage. I'd take the best man among them, and dare him to touch me."

"I cannot think how you like to witness so much misery and villainy. It is horrible to think of."

"Our tastes differ, my dear.—Jenkins! Confound you! Jenkins, I say." The convict-servant entered. "Where is the charge-book? I've told you always to have it ready for me. Why don't you do as you are told? You idle, lazy scoundrel! I suppose you were yarning in the cookhouse, or—"

"If you please, sir."

"Don't answer me, sir. Give me the book." Taking it and running his finger down the leaves, he commented on the list of offences to which he would be called upon in the morning to mete out judgment.

"*Meer-a-seek, having a pipe*—the rascally Hindoo scoundrel!—*Benjamin Pellett, having fat in his possession. Miles Byrne, not walking fast enough.*—We must enliven Mr. Byrne. *Thomas*

Twist, having a pipe and striking a light. W. Barnes, not in place at muster; says he was 'washing himself'—I'll wash him! *John Richards, missing muster and insolence. John Gateby, insolence and insubordination. James Hopkins, insolence and foul language. Rufus Dawes, gross insolence, refusing to work.*—Ah! we must look after you. You are a parson's man now, are you? I'll break your spirit, my man, or I'll—Sylvia!"

"Yes."

"Your friend Dawes is doing credit to his bringing up."

"What do you mean?"

"That infernal villain and reprobate, Dawes. He is fitting himself faster for—"

She interrupted him. "Maurice, I wish you would not use such language. You know I dislike it." She spoke coldly and sadly, as one who knows that remonstrance is vain, and is yet constrained to remonstrate.

"Oh, dear! My Lady Proper! can't bear to hear her husband swear. How refined we're getting!"

"There, I did not mean to annoy you," said she, wearily. "Don't let us quarrel, for goodness' sake."

He went away noisily, and she sat looking at the carpet wearily. A noise roused her. She looked up and saw North. Her face beamed instantly. "Ah! Mr. North, I did not expect you. What brings you here? You'll stay to dinner, of course." (She rang the bell without waiting for a reply.) "Mr. North dines here; place a chair for him. And have you brought me the book? I have been looking for it."

"Here it is," said North, producing a volume of 'Monte Cristo'. She seized the book with avidity, and, after running her eyes over the pages, turned inquiringly to the fly-leaf.

"It belongs to my predecessor," said North, as though in answer to her thought. "He seems to have been a great reader of French. I have found many French novels of his."

"I thought clergymen never read French novels," said Sylvia, with a smile.

"There are French novels and French novels," said North. "Stupid people confound the good with the bad. I remember a worthy friend of mine in Sydney who soundly abused me for reading 'Rabelais', and when I asked him if *he* had read it, he said that he would sooner cut his hand off than open it. Admirable judge of its merits!"

"But is this really good? Papa told me it was rubbish."

"It is a romance, but, in my opinion, a very fine one. The notion of the sailor being taught in prison by the priest, and sent back into the world an accomplished gentleman, to work out his vengeance, is superb."

"No, now—you are telling me," laughed she; and then, with feminine perversity, "Go on, what is the story?"

"Only that of an unjustly imprisoned man, who, escaping by a marvel, and becoming rich—as Dr. Johnson says, 'beyond the dreams of avarice'—devotes his life and fortune to revenge himself."

"And does he?"

"He does, upon all his enemies save one."

"And he—?"

"*She*—was the wife of his greatest enemy, and Dantes spared her because he loved her."

Sylvia turned away her head. "It seems interesting enough," said she, coldly.

There was an awkward silence for a moment, which each seemed afraid to break. North bit his lips, as though regretting what he had said. Mrs. Frere beat her foot on the floor, and at length, raising her eyes, and meeting those of the clergyman fixed upon her face, rose hurriedly, and went to meet her returning husband.

"Come to dinner, of course!" said Frere, who, though he disliked the clergyman, yet was glad of anybody who would help him to pass a cheerful evening.

"I came to bring Mrs. Frere a book."

"Ah! She reads too many books; she's always reading books. It is not a good thing to be always poring over print, is it, North? You have some influence with her; tell her so. Come, I am hungry."

He spoke with that affectation of jollity with which husbands of his calibre veil their bad temper.

Sylvia had her defensive armour on in a twinkling. "Of course, you two men will be against me. When did two men ever disagree upon the subject of wifely duties? However, I shall read in spite of you. Do you know, Mr. North, that when I married I made a special agreement with Captain Frere that I was not to be asked to sew on buttons for him?"

"Indeed!" said North, not understanding this change of humour.

"And she never has from that hour," said Frere, recovering his suavity at the sight of food. "I never have a shirt fit to put on. Upon my word, there are a dozen in the drawer now."

North perused his plate uncomfortably. A saying of omniscient Balzac occurred to him. "Le grand écueil est le ridicule," and his mind began to sound all sorts of philosophical depths, not of the most clerical character.

After dinner Maurice launched out into his usual topic—convict discipline. It was pleasant for him to get a listener; for his wife, cold and unsympathetic, tacitly declined to enter into his schemes for the subduing of the refractory villains. "You insisted on coming here," she would say. "I did not wish to come. I don't like to talk of these things. Let us talk of something else." When she adopted this method of procedure, he had no alternative but to submit, for he was afraid of her, after a fashion. In this ill-assorted match he was only apparently the master. He was a physical tyrant. For him, a creature had but to be weak to be an object of contempt; and his gross nature triumphed over the finer one of his wife. Love had long since died out of their life. The young, impulsive, delicate girl, who had given herself to him seven years before, had been changed into a weary, suffering woman. The wife is what her husband makes her, and his rude animalism had made her the nervous invalid she was. Instead of love, he had awakened in her a distaste which at times amounted to disgust. We have neither the skill nor the boldness of that profound philosopher whose autopsy of the human heart awoke North's contemplation, and we will not presume to set forth in bare English the story of this marriage of the Minotaur. Let it suffice to say that Sylvia liked her husband least when he loved her most. In this repulsion lay her power over him. When the animal and spiritual natures cross each other, the nobler triumphs in fact if not in appearance. Maurice Frere, though his wife obeyed him, knew that he was inferior to her, and was afraid of the statue he had created. She was ice, but it was the artificial ice that chemists make in the midst of a furnace. Her coldness was at once her strength and her weakness. When she chilled him, she commanded him.

Unwitting of the thoughts that possessed his guest, Frere chatted amicably. North said little, but drank a good deal. The wine, however, rendered him silent, instead of talkative. He drank that he might forget unpleasant memories, and drank without accomplishing his object. When the pair proceeded to the room where Mrs. Frere awaited them, Frere was boisterously good-humoured, North silently misanthropic.

"Sing something, Sylvia!" said Frere, with the ease of possession, as one who should say to a living musical-box, "Play something."

"Oh, Mr. North doesn't care for music, and I'm not inclined to sing. Singing seems out of place here."

"Nonsense," said Frere. "Why should it be more out of place here than anywhere else?"

"Mrs. Frere means that mirth is in a manner unsuited to these melancholy surroundings," said North, out of his keener sense.

"Melancholy surroundings!" cried Frere, staring in turn at the piano, the ottomans, and the looking-glass. "Well, the house isn't as good as the one in Sydney, but it's comfortable enough."

"You don't understand me, Maurice," said Sylvia. "This place is very gloomy to me. The thought of the unhappy men who are ironed and chained all about us makes me miserable."

"What stuff!" said Frere, now thoroughly roused. "The ruffians deserve all they get and more. Why should you make yourself wretched about them?"

"Poor men! How do we know the strength of their temptation, the bitterness of their repentance?"

"Evil-doers earn their punishment," says North, in a hard voice, and taking up a book suddenly. "They must learn to bear it. No repentance can undo their sin."

"But surely there is mercy for the worst of evil-doers," urged Sylvia, gently.

North seemed disinclined or unable to reply, and nodded only.

"Mercy!" cried Frere. "I am not here to be merciful; I am here to keep these scoundrels in order, and by the Lord that made me, I'll do it!"

"Maurice, do not talk like that. Think how slight an accident might have made any one of us like one of these men. What is the matter, Mr. North?"

Mr. North has suddenly turned pale.

"Nothing," returned the clergyman, gasping—"a sudden faintness!" The windows were thrown open, and the chaplain gradually recovered, as he did in Burgess's parlour, at Port Arthur, seven years ago. "I am liable to these attacks. A touch of heart disease, I think. I shall have to rest for a day or so."

"Ah, take a spell," said Frere; "you overwork yourself."

North, sitting, gasping and pale, smiles in a ghastly manner. "I—I will. If I do not appear for a week, Mrs. Frere, you will know the reason."

"A week! Surely it will not last so long as that!" exclaims Sylvia.

The ambiguous "it" appears to annoy him, for he flushes painfully, replying, "Sometimes longer. It is, a—um—uncertain," in a confused and shame-faced manner, and is luckily relieved by the entry of Jenkins.

"A message from Mr. Troke, sir."

"Troke! What's the matter now?"

"Dawes, sir, 's been violent and assaulted Mr. Troke. Mr. Troke said you'd left orders to be told at onst of the insubordination of prisoners."

"Quite right. Where is he?"

"In the cells, I think, sir. They had a hard fight to get him there, I am told, your honour."

"Had they? Give my compliments to Mr. Troke, and tell him that I shall have the pleasure of breaking Mr. Dawes's spirit to-morrow morning at nine sharp."

"Maurice," said Sylvia, who had been listening to the conversation in undisguised alarm, "do me a favour? Do not torment this man."

"What makes you take a fancy to *him*?" asks her husband, with sudden unnecessary fierceness.

"Because his is one of the names which have been from my childhood synonymous with suffering and torture, because whatever wrong he may have done, his life-long punishment must have in some degree atoned for it."

She spoke with an eager pity in her face that transfigured it. North, devouring her with his glance, saw tears in her eyes. "Does this look as if he had made atonement?" said Frere coarsely, slapping the letter.

"He is a bad man, I know, but—" she passed her hand over her forehead with the old troubled gesture—"he cannot have been always bad. I think I have heard some good of him somewhere."

"Nonsense," said Frere, rising decisively. "Your fancies mislead you. Let me hear you no more. The man is rebellious, and must be lashed back again to his duty. Come, North, we'll have a nip before you start."

"Mr. North, will not *you* plead for me?" suddenly cried poor Sylvia, her self-possession overthrown. "You have a heart to pity these suffering creatures."

But North, who seemed to have suddenly recalled his soul from some place where it had been wandering, draws himself aside, and with dry lips makes shift to say, "I cannot interfere with your husband, madam," and goes out almost rudely.

"You've made old North quite ill," said Frere, when he by-and-by returns, hoping by bluff ignoring of roughness on his own part to avoid reproach from his wife. "He drank half a bottle of brandy to steady his nerves before he went home, and swung out of the house like one possessed."

But Sylvia, occupied with her own thoughts, did not reply.

CHAPTER VII

BREAKING A MAN'S SPIRIT

THE insubordination of which Rufus Dawes had been guilty was, in this instance, insignificant. It was the custom of the newly-fledged constables of Captain Frere to enter the wards at night, armed with cutlasses, tramping about, and making a great noise. Mindful of the report of Pounce, they pulled the men roughly from their hammocks, examined their persons for concealed tobacco, and compelled them to open their mouths to see if any was inside. The men in Dawes's gang—to which Mr. Troke had an especial objection—were often searched more than once in a night, searched going to work, searched at meals, searched going to prayers, searched coming out, and this in the roughest manner. Their sleep broken, and what little self-respect they might yet presume to retain harried out of them, the objects of this incessant persecution were ready to turn upon and kill their tormentors.

The great aim of Troke was to catch Dawes tripping, but the leader of the "Ring" was far too wary. In vain had Troke, eager to sustain his reputation for sharpness, burst in upon the convict at all times and seasons. He had found nothing. In vain had he laid traps for him; in vain had he "planted" figs of tobacco, and attached long threads to them, waited in a bush hard by, until the pluck at the end of his line should give token that the fish had bitten. The experienced "old hand" was too acute for him. Filled with disgust and ambition, he determined upon an ingenious little trick. He was certain that Dawes possessed tobacco; the thing was to find it upon him. Now, Rufus Dawes, holding aloof, as was his custom, from the majority of his companions, had made one friend—if so mindless and battered an old wreck could be called a friend—Blind Mooney. Perhaps this oddly-assorted friendship was brought about by two causes—one, that Mooney was the only man on the island who knew more of the horrors of convictism than the leader of the Ring; the other, that Mooney was blind, and, to a moody, sullen man, subject to violent fits of passion and a constant suspicion of all his fellow-creatures, a blind companion was more congenial than a sharp-eyed one.

Mooney was one of the "First Fleeters". He had arrived in Sydney fifty-seven years before, in the year 1789, and when he was transported he was fourteen years old. He had been through the whole round of servitude, had worked as a bondsman, had married, and been "up country", had been again sentenced, and was a sort of dismal patriarch of Norfolk Island, having been there at its former settlement. He had no friends. His wife was long since dead, and he stated, without contradiction, that his master, having taken a fancy to her, had despatched the uncomplaisant husband to imprisonment. Such cases were not uncommon.

One of the many ways in which Rufus Dawes had obtained the affection of the old blind man was a gift of such fragments of tobacco as he had himself from time to time secured. Troke knew this; and on the evening in question hit upon an excellent plan. Admitting himself noiselessly into the boat-shed, where the gang slept, he crept close to the sleeping Dawes, and counterfeiting Mooney's mumbling utterance asked for "some tobacco". Rufus Dawes was but half awake, and on repeating his request, Troke felt something put into his hand. He grasped Dawes's arm, and struck a light. He had got his man this time. Dawes had conveyed to his fancied friend a piece of tobacco almost as big as the top joint of his little finger. One can understand the feelings of a man entrapped by such base means. Rufus Dawes no sooner saw the hated face of Warder Troke peering over his hammock, then he sprang out, and exerting to the utmost his powerful muscles, knocked Mr. Troke fairly off his legs into the arms of the incoming constables. A desperate struggle took place, at the end of which the convict, overpowered by numbers, was borne senseless to the cells, gagged, and chained to the ring-bolt on the bare flags. While in this condition he was savagely beaten by five or six constables.

To this maimed and manacled rebel was the Commandant ushered by Troke the next morning.

"Ha! ha! my man," said the Commandant. "Here you are again, you see. How do you like this sort of thing?"

Dawes, glaring, makes no answer.

"You shall have fifty lashes, my man," said Frere. "We'll see how you feel then!" The fifty were duly administered, and the Commandant called the next day. The rebel was still mute.

"Give him fifty more, Mr. Troke. We'll see what he's made of."

One hundred and twenty lashes were inflicted in the course of the morning, but still the sullen convict refused to speak. He was then treated to fourteen days' solitary confinement in one of the new cells. On being brought out and confronted with his tormentor, he merely laughed. For this he was sent back for another fourteen days; and still remaining obdurate, was flogged again, and got fourteen days more. Had the chaplain then visited him, he might have found him open to consolation, but the chaplain—so it was stated—was sick. When brought out at the conclusion of his third confinement, he was found to be in so exhausted a condition that the doctor ordered him to hospital. As soon as he was sufficiently recovered, Frere visited him, and finding his "spirit" not yet "broken", ordered that he should be put to grind maize. Dawes declined to work. So they chained his hand to one arm of the grindstone and placed another prisoner at the other arm. As the second prisoner turned, the hand of Dawes of course revolved.

"You're not such a pebble as folks seemed to think," grinned Frere, pointing to the turning wheel.

Upon which the indomitable poor devil straightened his sorely-tried muscles, and prevented the wheel from turning at all. Frere gave him fifty more lashes, and sent him the next day to grind cayenne pepper. This was a punishment more dreaded by the convicts than any other. The pungent dust filled their eyes and lungs, causing them the most excruciating torments. For a man with a raw back the work was one continued agony. In four days Rufus Dawes, emaciated, blistered, blinded, broke down.

"For God's sake, Captain Frere, kill me at once!" he said.

"No fear," said the other, rejoiced at this proof of his power. "You've given in; that's all I wanted. Troke, take him off to the hospital."

When he was in hospital, North visited him.

"I would have come to see you before," said the clergyman, "but I have been very ill."

In truth he looked so. He had had a fever, it seemed, and they had shaved his beard, and cropped his hair. Dawes could see that the haggard, wasted man had passed through some agony almost as great as his own. The next day Frere visited him, complimented him on his courage, and offered to make him a constable. Dawes turned his scarred back to his torturer, and resolutely declined to answer.

"I am afraid you have made an enemy of the Commandant," said North, the next day. "Why not accept his offer?"

Dawes cast on him a glance of quiet scorn. "And betray my mates? I'm not one of that sort."

The clergyman spoke to him of hope, of release, of repentance, and redemption. The prisoner laughed. "Who's to redeem me?" he said, expressing his thoughts in phraseology that to ordinary folks might seem blasphemous. "It would take a Christ to die again to save such as I." North spoke to him of immortality. "There is another life," said he. "Do not risk your chance of happiness in it. You have a future to live for, man."

"I hope not," said the victim of the "system". "I want to rest—to rest, and never to be disturbed again." His "spirit" was broken enough by this time. Yet he had resolution enough to refuse Frere's repeated offers. "I'll never 'jump' it," he said to North, "if they cut me in half first."

North pityingly implored the stubborn mind to have mercy on the lacerated body, but without effect. His own wayward heart gave him the key to read the cipher of this man's life. "A noble nature ruined," said he to himself. "What is the secret of his history?"

Dawes, on his part, seeing how different from other black coats was this priest—at once so ardent and so gloomy, so stern and so tender—began to speculate on the cause of his monitor's sunken cheeks, fiery eyes, and pre-occupied manner, to wonder what grief inspired those agonized prayers, those eloquent and daring supplications, which were daily poured out over his rude bed. So between these two—the priest and the sinner—was a sort of sympathetic bond.

One day this bond was drawn so close as to tug at both their heartstrings. The chaplain had a flower in his coat. Dawes eyed it with hungry looks, and, as the clergyman was about to quit the room, said, "Mr. North, will you give me that rosebud?" North paused irresolutely, and finally, as if after a struggle with himself, took it carefully from his button-hole, and placed it in the prisoner's brown, scarred hand. In another instant Dawes, believing himself alone, pressed the gift to his lips. North returned abruptly, and the eyes of the pair met. Dawes flushed crimson, but North turned white as death. Neither spoke, but each was drawn close to the other, since both had kissed the rosebud plucked by Sylvia's fingers.

CHAPTER VIII

EXTRACTED FROM THE DIARY
OF THE REV. JAMES NORTH

OCTOBER 21st.—I am safe for another six months if I am careful, for my last bout lasted longer than I expected. I suppose one of these days I shall have a paroxysm that will kill me. I shall not regret it.

I wonder if this familiar of mine—I begin to detest the expression—will accuse me of endeavouring to make a case for myself if I say that I believe my madness to be a disease? I do believe it. I honestly can no more help getting drunk than a lunatic can help screaming and gibbering. It would be different with me, perhaps, were I a contented man, happily married, with children about me, and family cares to distract me. But as I am—a lonely, gloomy being, debarred from love, devoured by spleen, and tortured with repressed desires—I become a living torment to myself. I think of happier men, with fair wives and clinging children, of men who are loved and who love, of Frere for instance—and a hideous wild beast seems to stir within me, a monster, whose cravings cannot be satisfied, can only be drowned in stupefying brandy.

Penitent and shattered, I vow to lead a new life; to forswear spirits, to drink nothing but water. Indeed, the sight and smell of brandy make me ill. All goes well for some weeks, when I grow nervous, discontented, moody. I smoke, and am soothed. But moderation is not to be thought of; little by little I increase the dose of tobacco. Five pipes a day become six or seven. Then I count up to ten and twelve, then drop to three or four, then mount to eleven at a leap; then lose count altogether. Much smoking excites the brain. I feel clear, bright, gay. My tongue is parched in the morning, however, and I use liquor to literally "moisten my clay". I drink wine or beer in moderation, and all goes well. My limbs regain their suppleness, my hands their coolness, my brain its placidity. I begin to feel that I have a will. I am confident, calm, and hopeful. To this condition succeeds one of the most frightful melancholy. I remain plunged, for an hour together, in a stupor of

despair. The earth, air, sea, all appear barren, colourless. Fife is a
burden. I long to sleep, and sleeping struggle to awake, because of
the awful dreams which flap about me in the darkness. At night
I cry, "Would to God it were morning!" In the morning, "Would
to God it were evening!" I loathe myself, and all around me. I am
nerveless, passionless, bowed down with a burden like the burden
of Saul. I know well what will restore me to life and ease—restore
me, but to cast me back again into a deeper fit of despair. I drink.
One glass—my blood is warmed, my heart leaps, my hand no longer
shakes. Three glasses—I rise with hope in my soul, the evil spirit
flies from me. I continue—pleasing images flock to my brain, the
fields break into flower, the birds into song, the sea gleams sapphire,
the warm heaven laughs. Great God! what man could withstand
a temptation like this?

By an effort, I shake off the desire to drink deeper, and fix my
thoughts on my duties, on my books, on the wretched prisoners. I
succeed perhaps for a time; but my blood, heated by the wine which
is at once my poison and my life, boils in my veins. I drink again,
and dream. I feel all the animal within me stirring. In the day my
thoughts wander to all monstrous imaginings. The most familiar
objects suggest to me loathsome thoughts. Obscene and filthy images
surround me. My nature seems changed. By day I feel myself a wolf
in sheep's clothing; a man possessed by a devil, who is ready at any
moment to break out and tear him to pieces. At night I become a
satyr. While in this torment I at once hate and fear myself. One
fair face is ever before me, gleaming through my hot dreams like a
flying moon in the sultry midnight of a tropic storm. I dare not trust
myself in the presence of those whom I love and respect, lest my wild
thoughts should find vent in wilder words. I lose my humanity. I am a
beast. Out of this depth there is but one way of escape. Downwards.
I must drench the monster I have awakened until he sleeps again. I
drink and become oblivious. In these last paroxysms there is nothing
for me but brandy. I shut myself up alone and pour down my gullet
huge draughts of spirit. It mounts to my brain. I am a man again!
and as I regain my manhood, I topple over—dead drunk.

But the awakening! Let me not paint it. The delirium, the fever, the self-loathing, the prostration, the despair. I view in the looking-glass a haggard face, with red eyes. I look down upon shaking hands, flaccid muscles, and shrunken limbs. I speculate if I shall ever be one of those grotesque and melancholy beings, with bleared eyes and running noses, swollen bellies and shrunken legs! Ugh!—it is too likely.

October 22nd.—Have spent the day with Mrs. Frere. She is evidently eager to leave the place—as eager as I am. Frere rejoices in his murderous power, and laughs at her expostulations. I suppose men get tired of their wives. In my present frame of mind I am at a loss to understand how a man could refuse a wife anything.

I do not think she can possibly care for him. I am not a selfish sentimentalist, as are the majority of seducers. I would take no woman away from a husband for mere liking. Yet I think there are cases in which a man *who loved* would be justified in making a woman happy at the risk of his own—soul, I suppose.

Making her happy! Ay, that's the point. Would she be happy? There are few men who can endure to be "cut", slighted, pointed at, and women suffer more than men in these regards. I, a grizzled man of forty, am not such an arrant ass as to suppose that a year of guilty delirium can compensate to a gently-nurtured woman for the loss of that social dignity which constitutes her best happiness. I am not such an idiot as to forget that there may come a time when the woman I love may cease to love *me,* and having no tie of self-respect, social position, or family duty, to bind her, may inflict upon her seducer that agony which he has taught her to inflict upon her husband. Apart from the question of the sin of breaking the seventh commandment, I doubt if the worst husband and the most unhappy home are not better, in this social condition of ours, than the most devoted lover. A strange subject this for a clergyman to speculate upon! If this diary should ever fall into the hands of a real God-fearing, honest booby, who never was tempted to sin by finding that at middle-age he loved the wife of another, how he would condemn me! And rightly, of course.

November 4th.—In one of the turnkey's rooms in the new gaol is to be seen an article of harness, which at first creates surprise to the mind of the beholder, who considers what animal of the brute creation exists of so diminutive a size as to admit of its use. On inquiry, it will be found to be a bridle, perfect in head-band, throat-lash, etc., for a human being. There is attached to this bridle a round piece of cross wood, of almost four inches in length, and one and a half in diameter. This again, is secured to a broad strap of leather to cross the mouth. In the wood there is a small hole, and, when used, the wood is inserted in the mouth, the small hole being the only breathing space. This being secured with the various straps and buckles, a more complete bridle could not be well imagined.

I was in the gaol last evening at eight o'clock. I had been to see Rufus Dawes, and returning, paused for a moment to speak to Hailey. Gimblett, who robbed Mr. Vane of two hundred pounds, was present, he was at that time a turnkey, holding a third-class pass, and in receipt of two shillings per diem. Everything was quite still. I could not help remarking how quiet the gaol was, when Gimblett said, "There's someone speaking. I know who that is." And forthwith took from its pegs one of the bridles just described, and a pair of handcuffs.

I followed him to one of the cells, which he opened, and therein was a man lying on his straw mat, undressed, and to all appearance fast asleep. Gimblett ordered him to get up and dress himself. He did so, and came into the yard, where Gimblett inserted the iron-wood gag in his mouth. The sound produced by his breathing through it (which appeared to be done with great difficulty) resembled a low, indistinct whistle. Gimblett led him to the lamp-post in the yard, and I saw that the victim of his wanton tyranny was the poor blind wretch Mooney. Gimblett placed him with his back against the lamp-post, and his arms being taken round, were secured by handcuffs round the post. I was told that the old man was to remain in this condition for three hours. I went at once to the Commandant. He invited me into his drawing-room—an invitation which I had the good sense to refuse—but refused to listen to any plea for mercy. "The old impostor is always making his blindness an excuse for disobedience," said he.—And this is *her* husband.

RUFUS Dawes hearing, when "on the chain" the next day, of the wanton torture of his friend, uttered no threat of vengeance, but groaned only. "I am not so strong as I was," said he, as if in apology for his lack of spirit. "They have unnerved me." And he looked sadly down at his gaunt frame and trembling hands.

"I can't stand it no longer," said Mooney, grimly. "I've spoken to Bland, and he's of my mind. You know what we resolved to do. Let's do it."

Rufus Dawes stared at the sightless orbs turned inquiringly to his own. The fingers of his hand, thrust into his bosom, felt a token which lay there. A shudder thrilled him. "No, no. Not now," he said.

"You're not afeard, man?" asked Mooney, stretching out his hand in the direction of the voice. "You're not going to shirk?" The other avoided the touch, and shrank away, still staring. "You ain't going to back out after you swore it, Dawes? You're not that sort. Dawes, speak, man!"

"Is Bland willing?" asked Dawes, looking round, as if to seek some method of escape from the glare of those unspeculative eyes.

"Ay, and ready. They flogged him again yesterday."

"Leave it till to-morrow," said Dawes, at length.

"No; let's have it over," urged the old man, with a strange eagerness. "I'm tired o' this."

Rufus Dawes cast a wistful glance towards the wall behind which lay the house of the Commandant. "Leave it till to-morrow," he repeated, with his hand still in his breast.

They had been so occupied in their conversation that neither had observed the approach of their common enemy. "What are you hiding there?" cried Frere, seizing Dawes by the wrist. "More tobacco, you dog?" The hand of the convict, thus suddenly plucked from his bosom, opened involuntarily, and a withered rose fell to the earth. Frere at once, indignant and astonished, picked it up. "Hallo! What the devil's this? You've not been robbing my garden for a nosegay, Jack?" The

Commandant was wont to call all convicts "Jack" in his moments of facetiousness. It was a little humorous way he had.

Rufus Dawes uttered one dismal cry, and then stood trembling and cowed. His companions, hearing the exclamation of rage and grief that burst from him, looked to see him snatch back the flower or perform some act of violence. Perhaps such was his intention, but he did not execute it. One would have thought that there was some charm about this rose so strangely cherished, for he stood gazing at it, as it twirled between Captain Frere's strong fingers, as though it fascinated him. "You're a pretty man to want a rose for your buttonhole! Are you going out with your sweetheart next Sunday, Mr. Dawes?" The gang laughed. "How did you get this?" Dawes was silent. "You'd better tell me." No answer. "Troke, let us see if we can't find Mr. Dawes's tongue. Pull off your shirt, my man. I expect that's the way to your heart—eh, boys?"

At this elegant allusion to the lash, the gang laughed again, and looked at each other astonished. It seemed possible that the leader of the Ring was going to turn milksop. Such, indeed, appeared to be the case, for Dawes, trembling and pale, cried, "Don't flog me again, sir! I picked it up in the yard. It fell out of your coat one day." Frere smiled with an inward satisfaction at the result of his spirit-breaking. The explanation was probably the correct one. He was in the habit of wearing flowers in his coat and it was impossible that the convict should have obtained one by any other means. Had it been a fig of tobacco now, the astute Commandant knew plenty of men who would have brought it into the prison. But who would risk a flogging for so useless a thing as a flower? "You'd better not pick up any more, Jack," he said. "We don't grow flowers for your amusement." And contemptuously flinging the rose over the wall, he strode away.

The gang, left to itself for a moment, bestowed their attention upon Dawes. Large tears were silently rolling down his face, and he stood staring at the wall as one in a dream. The gang curled their lips. One fellow, more charitable than the rest, tapped his forehead and winked. "He's going cranky," said this good-natured man, who could not understand what a sane prisoner had to do with flowers. Dawes recovered himself, and the contemptuous glances of his companions seemed to bring back the colour to his cheeks.

"We'll do it to-night," whispered he to Mooney, and Mooney smiled with pleasure.

Since the "tobacco trick", Mooney and Dawes had been placed in the new prison, together with a man named Bland, who had already twice failed to kill himself. When old Mooney, fresh from the torture of the gag-and-bridle, lamented his hard case, Bland proposed that the three should put in practice a scheme in which two at least must succeed. The scheme was a desperate one, and attempted only in the last extremity. It was the custom of the Ring, however, to swear each of its members to carry out to the best of his ability this last invention of the convict-disciplined mind should two other members crave his assistance.

The scheme—like all great ideas—was simplicity itself.

That evening, when the cell-door was securely locked, and the absence of a visiting gaoler might be counted upon for an hour at least, Bland produced a straw, and held it out to his companions. Dawes took it, and tearing it into unequal lengths, handed the fragments to Mooney.

"The longest is the one," said the blind man. "Come on, boys, and dip in the lucky-bag!"

It was evident that lots were to be drawn to determine to whom fortune would grant freedom. The men drew in silence, and then Bland and Dawes looked at each other. The prize had been left in the bag. Mooney—fortunate old fellow—retained the longest straw. Bland's hand shook as he compared notes with his companion. There was a moment's pause, during which the blank eyeballs of the blind man fiercely searched the gloom, as if in that awful moment they could penetrate it.

"I hold the shortest," said Dawes to Bland. "'Tis you that must do it."

"I'm glad of that," said Mooney.

Bland, seemingly terrified at the danger which fate had decreed that he should run, tore the fatal lot into fragments with an oath, and sat gnawing his knuckles in excess of abject terror. Mooney stretched himself out upon his plank-bed. "Come on, mate," he said. Bland extended a shaking hand, and caught Rufus Dawes by the sleeve.

"You have more nerve than I. You do it."

"No, no," said Dawes, almost as pale as his companion. "I've run my chance fairly. 'Twas your own proposal." The coward who, confident in his own luck, would seem to have fallen into the pit he had dug for others, sat rocking himself to and fro, holding his head in his hands.

"By Heaven, I can't do it," he whispered, lifting a white, wet face.

"What are you waiting for?" said fortunate Mooney. "Come on, I'm ready."

"I—I—thought you might like to—to—pray a bit," said Bland.

The notion seemed to sober the senses of the old man, exalted too fiercely by his good fortune.

"Ay!" he said. "Pray! A good thought!" and he knelt down; and shutting his blind eyes—'twas as though he was dazzled by some strong light—unseen by his comrades, moved his lips silently. The silence was at last broken by the footsteps of the warder in the corridor. Bland hailed it as a reprieve from whatever act of daring he dreaded. "We must wait until he goes," he whispered eagerly. "He might look in."

Dawes nodded, and Mooney, whose quick ear apprised him very exactly of the position of the approaching gaoler, rose from his knees radiant. The sour face of Gimblett appeared at the trap cell-door. "All right?" he asked, somewhat—so the three thought—less sourly than usual.

"All right," was the reply, and Mooney added, "Good-night, Mr. Gimblett."

"I wonder what is making the old man so cheerful," thought Gimblett, as he got into the next corridor.

The sound of his echoing footsteps had scarcely died away, when upon the ears of the two less fortunate casters of lots fell the dull sound of rending woollen. The lucky man was tearing a strip from his blanket. "I think this will do," said he, pulling it between his hands to test its strength. "I am an old man." It was possible that he debated concerning the descent of some abyss into which the strip of blanket was to lower him. "Here, Bland, catch hold. Where are ye?—don't be faint-hearted, man. It won't take ye long."

It was quite dark now in the cell, but as Bland advanced his face was like a white mask floating upon the darkness, it was so ghastly pale. Dawes pressed his lucky comrade's hand, and withdrew to the farthest corner. Bland and Mooney were for a few moments occupied with the rope—doubtless preparing for escape by means of it. The silence was broken only by the convulsive jangling of Bland's irons—he was shuddering violently. At last Mooney spoke again, in strangely soft and subdued tones.

"Dawes, lad, do you think there is a Heaven?"

"I know there is a Hell," said Dawes, without turning his face.

"Ay, and a Heaven, lad. I think I shall go there. You will, old chap, for you've been good to me—God bless you, you've been very good to me."

*

When Troke came in the morning he saw what had occurred at a glance, and hastened to remove the corpse of the strangled Mooney.

"We drew lots," said Rufus Dawes, pointing to Bland, who crouched in the corner farthest from his victim, "and it fell upon him to do it. I'm the witness."

"They'll hang you for all that," said Troke.

"I hope so," said Rufus Dawes. The scheme of escape hit upon by the convict intellect was simply this. Three men being together, lots were drawn to determine whom should be murdered. The drawer of the longest straw was the "lucky" man. He was killed. The drawer of the next longest straw was the murderer. He was hanged. The unlucky one was the witness. He had, of course, an excellent chance of being hung also, but his doom was not so certain, and he therefore looked upon himself as unfortunate.

CHAPTER X

A MEETING

JOHN Rex found the "George" disagreeably prepared for his august arrival. Obsequious waiters took his dressing-bag and overcoat, the landlord himself welcomed him at the door. Two naval gentlemen came out of the coffee-room to stare at him. "Have you any more luggage, Mr. Devine?" asked the landlord, as he flung open the door of the best drawing-room. It was awkwardly evident that his wife had no notion of suffering him to hide his borrowed light under a bushel.

A supper-table laid for two people gleamed bright from the cheeriest corner. A fire crackled beneath the marble mantelshelf. The latest evening paper lay upon a chair; and, brushing it carelessly with her costly dress, the woman he had so basely deserted came smiling to meet him.

"Well, Mr. Richard Devine," said she, "you did not expect to see me again, did you?"

Although, on his journey down, he had composed an elaborate speech wherewith to greet her, this unnatural civility dumbfounded him. "Sarah! I never meant to—"

"Hush, my dear Richard—it must be Richard now, I suppose. This is not the time for explanations. Besides, the waiter might hear you. Let us have some supper; you must be hungry, I am sure." He advanced to the table mechanically. "But how fat you are!" she continued. "Too good living, I suppose. You were not so fat at Port Ar— Oh, I forgot, my dear! Come and sit down. That's right. I have told them all that I am your wife, for whom you have sent. They regard me with some interest and respect in consequence. Don't spoil their good opinion of me."

He was about to utter an imprecation, but she stopped him by a glance. "No bad language, John, or I shall ring for a constable. Let us understand one another, my dear. You may be a very great man to other people, but to me you are merely my runaway husband—an escaped convict. If you don't eat your supper civilly, I shall send for the police."

"Sarah!" he burst out, "I never meant to desert you. Upon my word. It is all a mistake. Let me explain."

"There is no need for explanations yet, Jack—I mean Richard. Have your supper. Ah! I know what you want."

She poured out half a tumbler of brandy, and gave it to him. He took the glass from her hand, drank the contents, and then, as though warmed by the spirit, laughed. "What a woman you are, Sarah. I have been a great brute, I confess."

"You have been an ungrateful villain," said she, with sudden passion, "a hardened, selfish villain."

"But, Sarah—"

"Don't touch me!"

"'Pon my word, you are a fine creature, and I was a fool to leave you."

The compliment seemed to soothe her, for her tone changed somewhat. "It was a wicked, cruel act, Jack. You whom I saved from death—whom I nursed—whom I enriched. It was the act of a coward."

"I admit it. It was."

"You admit it. Have you no shame then? Have you no pity for me for what I have suffered all these years?"

"I don't suppose you cared much."

"Don't you? You never thought about me at all. I have cared this much, John Rex—bah! the door is shut close enough—that I have spent a fortune in hunting you down; and now I have found you, I will make you suffer in your turn."

He laughed again, but uneasily. "How did you discover me?"

With a readiness which showed that she had already prepared an answer to the question, she unlocked a writing-case, which was on the side table, and took from it a newspaper. "By one of those strange accidents which are the ruin of men like you. Among the papers sent to the overseer from his English friends was this one."

She held out an illustrated journal—a Sunday organ of sporting opinion—and pointed to a portrait engraved on the centre page. It represented a broad-shouldered, bearded man, dressed in the fashion affected by turfites and lovers of horse-flesh, standing beside a pedestal on which were piled a variety of racing cups and trophies. John Rex read underneath this work of art the name,

MR. RICHARD DEVINE
THE LEVIATHAN OF THE TURF

"And you recognized me?"

"The portrait was sufficiently like you to induce me to make inquiries, and when I found that Mr. Richard Devine had suddenly returned from a mysterious absence of fourteen years, I set to work in earnest. I have spent a deal of money, Jack, but I've got you!"

"You have been clever in finding me out; I give you credit for that."

"There is not a single act of your life, John Rex, that I do not know," she continued, with heat. "I have traced you from the day you stole out of my house until now. I know your continental trips, your journeyings here and there in search of a lost clue. I pieced together the puzzle, as you have done, and I know that, by some foul fortune, you have stolen the secret of a dead man to ruin an innocent and virtuous family."

"Hullo! hullo!" said John Rex. "Since when have *you* learnt to talk of virtue?"

"It is well to taunt, but you have got to the end of your tether now, Jack. I have communicated with the woman whose son's fortune you have stolen. I expect to hear from Lady Devine in a day or so."

"Well—and when you hear?"

"I shall give back the fortune at the price of her silence!"

"Ho! ho! Will you?"

"Yes; and if my husband does not come back and live with me quietly, I shall call the police."

John Rex sprang up. "Who will believe you, idiot?" he cried. "I'll have you sent to gaol as an impostor."

"You forget, my dear," she returned, playing coquettishly with her rings, and glancing sideways as she spoke, "that you have already acknowledged me as your wife before the landlord and the servants. It is too late for *that* sort of thing. Oh, my dear Jack, you think you are very clever, but I am as clever as you."

Smothering a curse, he sat down beside her. "Listen, Sarah. What is the use of fighting like a couple of children. I am rich—"

"So am I."

"Well, so much the better. We will join our riches together. I admit that I was a fool and a cur to leave you; but I played for a great stake. The name of Richard Devine was worth nearly half a million in money. It is mine. I won it. Share it with me! Sarah, you and I defied the world years ago. Don't let us quarrel now. I was ungrateful. Forget it. We know by this time that we are not either of us angels. We started in life together—do you remember, Sally, when I met you first?—determined to make money. We have succeeded. Why then set to work to destroy each other? You are handsomer than ever, I have not lost my wits. Is there any need for you to tell the world that I am a runaway convict, and that you are—well, no, of course there is no need. Kiss and be friends, Sarah. I would have escaped you if I could, I admit. You have found me out. I accept the position. You claim me as your husband. You say you are Mrs. Richard Devine. Very well, I admit it. You have all your life wanted to be a great lady. Now is your chance!"

Much as she had cause to hate him, well as she knew his treacherous and ungrateful character, little as she had reason to trust him, her strange and distempered affection for the scoundrel came upon her again with gathering strength. As she sat beside him, listening to the familiar tones of the voice she had learned to love, greedily drinking in the promise of a future fidelity which she was well aware was made but to be broken, her memory recalled the past days of trust and happiness, and her woman's fancy once more invested the selfish villain she had reclaimed with those attributes which had enchained her wilful and wayward affections. The unselfish devotion which had marked her conduct to the swindler and convict was, indeed, her one redeeming virtue; and perhaps she felt dimly—poor woman—that it were better for her to cling to that, if she lost all the world beside. Her wish for vengeance melted under the influence of these thoughts. The bitterness of despised love, the shame and anger of desertion, ingratitude, and betrayal, all vanished. The tears of a sweet forgiveness trembled in her eyes, the unreasoning love of her sex—faithful to nought but love, and faithful to love in death—shook in her voice. She took his coward hand and kissed it, pardoning all his baseness with the sole reproach, "Oh, John, John, you might have trusted me after all?"

John Rex had conquered, and he smiled as he embraced her. "I wish I had," said he; "it would have saved me many regrets; but never mind. Sit down; *now* we will have supper."

"Your preference has one drawback, Sarah," he said, when the meal was concluded, and the two sat down to consider their immediate course of action, "it doubles the chance of detection."

"How so?"

"People have accepted me without inquiry, but I am afraid not without dislike. Mr. Francis Wade, my uncle, never liked me; and I fear I have not played my cards well with Lady Devine. When they find I have a mysterious wife their dislike will become suspicion. Is it likely that I should have been married all these years and not have informed them?"

"Very unlikely," returned Sarah calmly, "and that is just the reason why you have not been married all these years. Really," she added, with a laugh, "the male intellect is very dull. You have already told ten thousand lies about this affair, and yet you don't see your way to tell one more."

"What do you mean?"

"Why, my dear Richard, you surely cannot have forgotten that you married me last year on the Continent? By the way, it was last year that you were there, was it not? I am the daughter of a poor clergyman of the Church of England; name—anything you please— and you met me—where shall we say? Baden, Aix, Brussels? Cross the Alps, if you like, dear, and say Rome."

John Rex put his hand to his head. "Of course—I am stupid," said he. "I have not been well lately. Too much brandy, I suppose."

"Well, we will alter all that," she returned with a laugh, which her anxious glance at him belied. "You are going to be domestic now, Jack—I mean Dick."

"Go on," said he impatiently. "What then?"

"Then, having settled these little preliminaries, you take me up to London and introduce me to your relatives and friends."

He started. "A bold game."

"Bold! Nonsense! The only safe one. People don't, as a rule, suspect unless one is mysterious. You *must* do it; I have arranged for your doing it. The waiters here all know me as your wife. There is not the least danger—unless, indeed, you are married already?" she added, with a quick and angry suspicion.

"You need not be alarmed. I was not such a fool as to marry another woman while *you* were alive—had I even seen one I would have cared to marry. But what of Lady Devine? You say you have told her."

"I have told her to communicate with Mrs. Carr, Post Office, Torquay, in order to hear something to her advantage. If you had been rebellious, John, the 'something' would have been a letter from me telling her who you really are. Now you have proved obedient, the 'something' will be a begging letter of a sort which she has already received hundreds, and which in all probability she will not even answer. What do you think of that, Mr. Richard Devine?"

"You deserve success, Sarah," said the old schemer, in genuine admiration. "By Jove, this is something like the old days, when we were Mr. and Mrs. Crofton."

"Or Mr. and Mrs. Skinner, eh, John?" she said, with as much tenderness in her voice as though she had been a virtuous matron recalling her honeymoon. "That was an unlucky name, wasn't it, dear? You should have taken my advice there." And immersed in recollection of their past rogueries, the worthy pair pensively smiled. Rex was the first to awake from that pleasant reverie.

"I will be guided by you, then," he said. "What next?"

"Next—for, as you say, my presence doubles the danger—we will contrive to withdraw quietly from England. The introduction to your mother over, and Mr. Francis disposed of, we will go to Hampstead, and live there for a while. During that time you must turn into cash as much property as you dare. We will then go abroad for the 'season'—and stop there. After a year or so on the Continent you can write to our agent to sell more property; and, finally, when we are regarded as permanent absentees—and three or four years will bring that about—we will get rid of everything, and slip over to America. Then you can endow a charity if you like, or build a church to the memory of the man you have displaced."

John Rex burst into a laugh. "An excellent plan. I like the idea of the charity—the Devine Hospital, eh?"

"By the way, how did you find out the particulars of this man's life. He was burned in the *Hydaspes*, wasn't he?"

"No," said Rex, with an air of pride. "He was transported in the *Malabar* under the name of Rufus Dawes. You remember him. It is a long story. The particulars weren't numerous, and if the old lady had been half sharp she would have bowled me out. But the fact was she *wanted* to find the fellow alive, and was willing to take a good deal on trust. I'll tell you all about it another time. I think I'll go to bed now; I'm tired, and my head aches as though it would split."

"Then it is decided that you follow my directions?"

"Yes."

She rose and placed her hand on the bell. "What are you going to do?" he said uneasily.

"*I* am going to do nothing. *You* are going to telegraph to your servants to have the house in London prepared for your wife, who will return with you the day after to-morrow."

John Rex stayed her hand with a sudden angry gesture. "This is all devilish fine," he said, "but suppose it fails?"

"That is your affair, John. You need not go on with this business at all, unless you like. I had rather you didn't."

"What the deuce am I to do, then?"

"I am not as rich as you are, but, with my station and so on, I am worth seven thousand a year. Come back to Australia with me, and let these poor people enjoy their own again. Ah, John, it is the best thing to do, believe me. We can afford to be honest now."

"A fine scheme!" cried he. "Give up half a million of money, and go back to Australia! You must be mad!"

"Then telegraph."

"But, my dear—"

"Hush, here's the waiter."

As he wrote, John Rex felt gloomily that, though he had succeeded in recalling her affection, that affection was as imperious as of yore.

CHAPTER XI

EXTRACTED FROM THE DIARY
OF THE REV. JAMES NORTH

DECEMBER 7th.—I have made up my mind to leave this place, to bury myself again in the bush, I suppose, and await extinction. I try to think that the reason for this determination is the frightful condition of misery existing among the prisoners; that because I am daily horrified and sickened by scenes of torture and infamy, I decide to go away; that, feeling myself powerless to save others, I wish to spare myself. But in this journal, in which I bind myself to write nothing but truth, I am forced to confess that these are *not* the reasons. I will write the reason plainly: "I covet my neighbour's wife." It does not look well thus written. It looks hideous. In my own breast I find numberless excuses for my passion. I said to myself, "My neighbour does not love his wife, and her unloved life is misery. She is forced to live in the frightful seclusion of this accursed island, and she is dying for want of companionship. She feels that I understand and appreciate her, that I could love her as she deserves, that I could render her happy. I feel that I have met the only woman who has power to touch my heart, to hold me back from the ruin into which I am about to plunge, to make me useful to my fellows—a man, and not a drunkard." Whispering these conclusions to myself, I am urged to brave public opinion, and make two lives happy. I say to myself, or rather my desires say to me—"What sin is there in this? Adultery? No; for a marriage without love is the coarsest of all adulteries. What tie binds a man and woman together—that formula of license pronounced by the priest, which the law has recognized as a 'legal bond'? Surely not this only, for marriage is but a partnership—a contract of mutual fidelity—and in all contracts the violation of the terms of the agreement by one of the contracting persons absolves the other. Mrs. Frere is then absolved, by her husband's act. I cannot but think so. But is she willing to risk the shame of divorce or legal offence? Perhaps. Is she fitted by temperament to bear such a burden of contumely as must needs fall upon her? Will she not feel disgust at the man who entrapped her into shame? Do not the comforts which surround her compensate for the lack of affections?" And so the torturing catechism continues, until I am driven mad with doubt, love, and despair.

Of course I am wrong; of course I outrage my character as a priest; of course I endanger—according to the creed I teach—my soul and hers. But priests, unluckily, have hearts and passions as well as other men. Thank God, as yet, I have never expressed my madness in words. What a fate is mine! When I am in her presence I am in torment; when I am absent from her my imagination pictures her surrounded by a thousand graces that are not hers, but belong to all the women of my dreams—to Helen, to Juliet, to Rosalind. Fools that we are of our own senses! When I think of her I blush; when I hear her name my heart leaps, and I grow pale. Love! What is the love of two pure souls, scarce conscious of the Paradise into which they have fallen, to this maddening delirium? I can understand the poison of Circe's cup; it is the sweet-torment of a forbidden love like mine! Away gross materialism, in which I have so long schooled myself! I, who laughed at passion as the outcome of temperament and easy living—I, who thought in my intellect, to sound all the depths and shoals of human feeling—I, who analysed my own soul—scoffed at my own yearnings for an immortality—am forced to deify the senseless power of my creed, and believe in God, that I may pray to Him. I know now why men reject the cold impersonality that reason tells us rules the world—it is because they love. To die, and be no more; to die, and rendered into dust, be blown about the earth; to die and leave our love defenceless and forlorn, till the bright soul that smiled to ours is smothered in the earth that made it! No! To love is life eternal. God, I believe in Thee! Aid me! Pity me! Sinful wretch that I am, to have denied Thee! See me on my knees before Thee! Pity me, or let me die!

December 9th.—I have been visiting the two condemned prisoners, Dawes and Bland, and praying with them. O Lord, let me save one soul that may plead with Thee for mine! Let me draw one being alive out of this pit! I weep—I weary Thee with my prayers, O Lord! Look down upon me. Grant me a sign. Thou didst it in old times to men who were not more fervent in their supplications than am I. So says Thy Book. Thy Book which I believe—which I believe. Grant me a sign—one little sign, O Lord!—I will not see her. I have sworn it. Thou knowest my grief—my agony—my despair. Thou knowest why I love her. Thou knowest how I strive to make her hate me. Is that not a sacrifice? I am so lonely—a lonely man, with but one creature that he loves—yet, what is mortal love to Thee? Cruel and implacable, Thou sittest in the heavens men have built for Thee, and scornest them! Will not all the burnings and slaughters of the saints appease Thee? Art Thou not sated with blood and tears, O God of vengeance, of wrath, and of despair! Kind Christ, pity me. *Thou* wilt—for Thou wast human! Blessed Saviour, at whose feet knelt the Magdalen! Divinity, who, most divine in Thy despair, called on Thy cruel God to save Thee—by the memory of that moment when Thou didst deem Thyself forsaken—forsake not me! Sweet Christ, have mercy on Thy sinful servant.

I can write no more. I will pray to Thee with my lips. I will shriek my supplications to Thee. I will call upon Thee so loud that all the world shall hear me, and wonder at Thy silence—unjust and unmerciful God!

December 14th.—What blasphemies are these which I have uttered in my despair? Horrible madness that has left me prostrate, to what heights of frenzy didst thou not drive my soul! Like him of old time, who wandered among the tombs, shrieking and tearing himself, I have been possessed by a devil. For a week I have been unconscious of aught save torture. I have gone about my daily duties as one who in his dreams repeats the accustomed action of the day, and knows it not. Men have looked at me strangely. They look at me strangely now. Can it be that my disease of drunkenness has become the disease of insanity? Am I mad, or do I but verge on madness? O Lord, whom in my agonies I have confessed, leave me my intellect—let me not become a drivelling spectacle for the curious to point at or to pity! At least, in mercy, spare me a little. Let not my punishment overtake me *here*. Let *her* memories of me be clouded with a sense of my rudeness or my brutality; let me for ever seem to her the ungrateful ruffian I strive to show myself—but let her not behold me—*that!*

CHAPTER XII

THE STRANGE BEHAVIOUR OF MR. NORTH

ON or about the 8th of December, Mrs. Frere noticed a sudden and unaccountable change in the manner of the chaplain. He came to her one afternoon, and, after talking for some time, in a vague and unconnected manner, about the miseries of the prison and the wretched condition of some of the prisoners, began to question her abruptly concerning Rufus Dawes.

"I do not wish to think of him," said she, with a shudder. "I have the strangest, the most horrible dreams about him. He is a bad man. He tried to murder me when a child, and had it not been for my husband, he would have done so. I have only seen him once since then—at Hobart Town, when he was taken."

"He sometimes speaks to me of you," said North, eyeing her. "He asked me once to give him a rose plucked in your garden."

Sylvia turned pale. "And you gave it him?"

"Yes, I gave it him. Why not?"

"It was valueless, of course, but still—to a convict?"

"You are not angry?"

"Oh, no! Why should I be angry?" she laughed constrainedly. "It was a strange fancy for the man to have, that's all."

"I suppose you would not give me another rose, if I asked you."

"Why not?" said she, turning away uneasily. "*You?* You are a gentleman."

"Not I—you don't know me."

"What do you mean?"

"I mean that it would be better for you if you had never seen me."

"Mr. North!" Terrified at the wild gleam in his eyes, she had risen hastily. "You are talking very strangely."

"Oh, don't be alarmed, madam. I am not *drunk!*"—he pronounced the word with a fierce energy. "I had better leave you. Indeed, I think the less we see of each other the better."

Deeply wounded and astonished at this extraordinary outburst, Sylvia allowed him to stride away without a word. She saw him pass through the garden and slam the little gate, but she did not see the agony on his face, or the passionate gesture with which—when out of eyeshot—he lamented the voluntary abasement of himself before her. She thought over his conduct with growing fear. It was not possible that he was intoxicated—such a vice was the last one of which she could have believed him guilty. It was more probable that some effects of the fever, which had recently confined him to his house, yet lingered. So she thought; and, thinking, was alarmed to realize of how much importance the well-being of this man was to her.

The next day he met her, and, bowing, passed swiftly. This pained her. Could she have offended him by some unlucky word? She made Maurice ask him to dinner, and, to her astonishment, he pleaded illness as an excuse for not coming. Her pride was hurt, and she sent him back his books and music. A curiosity that was unworthy of her compelled her to ask the servant who carried the parcel what the clergyman had said. "He said nothing—only laughed." Laughed! In scorn of her foolishness! His conduct was ungentlemanly and intemperate. She would forget, as speedily as possible, that such a being had ever existed. This resolution taken, she was unusually patient with her husband.

So a week passed, and Mr. North did not return. Unluckily for the poor wretch, the very self-sacrifice he had made brought about the precise condition of things which he was desirous to avoid. It is possible that, had the acquaintance between them continued on the same staid footing, it would have followed the lot of most acquaintanceships of the kind—other circumstances and other scenes might have wiped out the memory of all but common civilities between them, and Sylvia might never have discovered that she had for the chaplain any other feeling but that of esteem. But the very fact of the sudden wrenching away of her soul-companion, showed her how barren was the solitary life to which she had been fated. Her husband, she had long ago admitted, with bitter self-communings, was utterly unsuited to her. She could find in his society no enjoyment, and for the sympathy which she needed was compelled to turn elsewhere. She understood that his love for her had burnt itself out—she confessed, with intensity of self-degradation, that his apparent affection had been born of sensuality, and had perished in the fires it had itself kindled. Many women have, unhappily, made some such discovery as this, but for most women there is some distracting occupation. Had it been Sylvia's fate to live in the midst of fashion and society, she would have found relief in the conversation of the witty, or the homage of the distinguished. Had fortune cast her lot in a city, Mrs. Frere might have become one of those charming women who collect around their supper-tables whatever of male intellect is obtainable, and who find the husband admirably useful to open his own champagne bottles. The celebrated women who have stepped out of their domestic circles to enchant or astonish the world, have almost invariably been cursed with unhappy homes. But poor Sylvia was not destined to this fortune. Cast back upon herself, she found no surcease of pain in her own imaginings, and meeting with a man sufficiently her elder to encourage her to talk, and sufficiently clever to induce her to seek his society and his advice, she learnt, for the first time, to forget her own griefs; for the first time she suffered her nature to expand under the sun of a congenial influence. This sun, suddenly withdrawn, her soul, grown accustomed to the warmth and light, shivered at the gloom, and she looked about her in dismay at the dull and barren prospect of life which lay before her. In a word, she found that the society of North had become so far necessary to her that to be deprived of it was a grief—notwithstanding that her husband remained to console her.

After a week of such reflections, the barrenness of life grew insupportable to her, and one day she came to Maurice and begged to be sent back to Hobart Town. "I cannot live in this horrible island," she said. "I am getting ill. Let me go to my father for a few months, Maurice." Maurice consented. His wife *was* looking ill, and Major Vickers was an old man—a rich old man—who loved his only daughter. It was not undesirable that Mrs. Frere should visit her father; indeed, so little sympathy was there between the pair that, the first astonishment over, Maurice felt rather glad to get rid of her for a while. "You can go back in the *Lady Franklin* if you like, my dear," he said. "I expect her every day." At this decision—much to his surprise—she kissed him with more show of affection than she had manifested since the death of her child.

The news of the approaching departure became known, but still North did not make his appearance. Had it not been a step beneath the dignity of a woman, Mrs. Frere would have gone herself and asked him the meaning of his unaccountable rudeness, but there was just sufficient morbidity in the sympathy she had for him to restrain her from an act which a young girl—though not more innocent— would have dared without hesitation. Calling one day upon the wife of the surgeon, however, she met the chaplain face to face, and with the consummate art of acting which most women possess, rallied him upon his absence from her house. The behaviour of the poor devil, thus stabbed to the heart, was curious. He forgot gentlemanly behaviour and the respect due to a woman, flung one despairingly angry glance at her and abruptly retired. Sylvia flushed crimson, and endeavoured to excuse North on account of his recent illness. The surgeon's wife looked askance, and turned the conversation. The next time Sylvia bowed to this lady, she got a chilling salute in return that made her blood boil. "I wonder how I have offended Mrs. Field?" she asked Maurice. "She almost cut me to-day."

"Oh, the old cat!" returned Maurice. "What does it matter if she did?" However, a few days afterwards, it seemed that it did matter, for Maurice called upon Field and conversed seriously with him. The issue of the conversation being reported to Mrs. Frere, the lady wept indignant tears of wounded pride and shame. It appeared that North had watched her out of the house, returned, and related—in a "stumbling, hesitating way", Mrs. Field said— how he disliked Mrs. Frere, how he did not want to visit her, and how flighty and reprehensible such conduct was in a married woman of her rank and station. This act of baseness—or profound nobleness—achieved its purpose. Sylvia noticed the unhappy priest no more. Between the Commandant and the chaplain now arose a coolness, and Frere set himself, by various petty tyrannies, to disgust North, and compel him to a resignation of his office. The convict-gaolers speedily marked the difference in the treatment of the chaplain, and their demeanour changed. For respect was substituted insolence; for alacrity, sullenness; for prompt obedience, impertinent intrusion. The men whom North favoured were selected as special subjects for harshness, and for a prisoner to be seen talking to the clergyman was sufficient to ensure for him a series of tyrannies. The result of this was that North saw the souls he laboured to save slipping back into the gulf; beheld the men he had half won to love him meet him with averted faces; discovered that to show interest in a prisoner was to injure him, not to serve him. The unhappy man grew thinner and paler under this ingenious torment. He had deprived himself of that love which, guilty though it might be, was, nevertheless, the only true love he had known; and he found that, having won this victory, he had gained the hatred of all living creatures with whom he came in contact. The authority of the Commandant was so supreme that men lived but by the breath of his nostrils. To offend him was to perish and the man whom the Commandant hated must be hated also by all those who wished to exist in peace. There was but one being who was not to be turned from his allegiance—the convict murderer, Rufus Dawes, who awaited death. For many days he had remained mute, broken down beneath his weight of sorrow or of sullenness; but North, bereft of other love and sympathy, strove with that fighting soul, if haply he might win it back to peace. It seemed to the fancy of the priest—a fancy distempered, perhaps, by excess, or superhumanly exalted by mental agony—that this convict, over whom he had wept, was given to him as a hostage for his own salvation. "I must save him or perish," he said. "I must save him, though I redeem him with my own blood."

Frere, unable to comprehend the reason of the calmness with which the doomed felon met his taunts and torments, thought that he was shamming piety to gain some indulgence of meat and drink, and redoubled his severity. He ordered Dawes to be taken out to work just before the hour at which the chaplain was accustomed to visit him. He pretended that the man was "dangerous", and directed a gaoler to be present at all interviews, "lest the chaplain might be murdered". He issued an order that all civil officers should obey the challenges of convicts acting as watchmen; and North, coming to pray with his penitent, would be stopped ten times by grinning felons, who, putting their faces within a foot of his, would roar out, "Who goes there?" and burst out laughing at the reply. Under pretence of watching more carefully over the property of the chaplain, he directed that any convict, acting as constable, might at any time "search everywhere and anywhere" for property supposed to be in the possession of a prisoner. The chaplain's servant was a prisoner, of course; and North's drawers were ransacked twice in one week by Troke. North met these impertinences with unruffled brow, and Frere could in no way account for his obstinacy, until the arrival of the *Lady Franklin* explained the chaplain's apparent coolness. He had sent in his resignation two months before, and the saintly Meekin had been appointed in his stead. Frere, unable to attack the clergyman, and indignant at the manner in which he had been defeated, revenged himself upon Rufus Dawes.

THE method and manner of Frere's revenge became a subject of whispered conversation on the island. It was reported that North had been forbidden to visit the convict, but that he had refused to accept the prohibition, and by a threat of what he would do when the returning vessel had landed him in Hobart Town, had compelled the Commandant to withdraw his order. The Commandant, however, speedily discovered in Rufus Dawes signs of insubordination, and set to work again to reduce still further the "spirit" he had so ingeniously "broken". The unhappy convict was deprived of food, was kept awake at nights, was put to the hardest labour, was loaded with the heaviest irons. Troke, with devilish malice, suggested that, if the tortured wretch would decline to see the chaplain, some amelioration of his condition might be effected; but his suggestions were in vain. Fully believing that his death was certain, Dawes clung to North as the saviour of his agonized soul, and rejected all such insidious overtures. Enraged at this obstinacy, Frere sentenced his victim to the "spread eagle" and the "stretcher".

Now the rumour of the obduracy of this undaunted convict who had been recalled to her by the clergyman at their strange interview, had reached Sylvia's ears. She had heard gloomy hints of the punishments inflicted on him by her husband's order, and as—constantly revolving in her mind was that last conversation with the chaplain—she wondered at the prisoner's strange fancy for a flower, her brain began to thrill with those undefined and dreadful memories which had haunted her childhood. What was the link between her and this murderous villain? How came it that she felt at times so strange a sympathy for his fate, and that he—who had attempted her life—cherished so tender a remembrance of her as to beg for a flower which her hand had touched?

She questioned her husband concerning the convict's misdoings, but with the petulant brutality which he invariably displayed when the name of Rufus Dawes intruded itself into their conversation,

Maurice Frere harshly refused to satisfy her. This but raised her curiosity higher. She reflected how bitter he had always seemed against this man—she remembered how, in the garden at Hobart Town, the hunted wretch had caught her dress with words of assured confidence—she recollected the fragment of cloth he passionately flung from him, and which her affianced lover had contemptuously tossed into the stream. The name of "Dawes", detested as it had become to her, bore yet some strange association of comfort and hope. What secret lurked behind the twilight that had fallen upon her childish memories? Deprived of the advice of North—to whom, a few weeks back, she would have confided her misgivings—she resolved upon a project that, for her, was most distasteful. She would herself visit the gaol and judge how far the rumours of her husband's cruelty were worthy of credit.

One sultry afternoon, when the Commandant had gone on a visit of inspection, Troke, lounging at the door of the New Prison, beheld, with surprise, the figure of the Commandant's lady.

"What is it, mam?" he asked, scarcely able to believe his eyes.

"I want to see the prisoner Dawes."

Troke's jaw fell.

"See Dawes?" he repeated.

"Yes. Where is he?"

Troke was preparing a lie. The imperious voice, and the clear, steady gaze, confused him.

"He's here."

"Let me see him."

"He's—he's under punishment, mam."

"What do you mean? Are they flogging him?"

"No; but he's dangerous, mam. The Commandant—"

"Do you mean to open the door or not, Mr. Troke?"

Troke grew more confused. It was evident that he was most unwilling to open the door. "The Commandant has given strict orders—"

"Do you wish me to *complain* to the Commandant?" cries Sylvia, with a touch of her old spirit, and jumped hastily at the conclusion that the gaolers were, perhaps, torturing the convict for their own entertainment. "Open the door at once!—at once!"

Thus commanded, Troke, with a hasty growl of its "being no affair of his, and he hoped Mrs. Frere would tell the captain how it happened" flung open the door of a cell on the right hand of the doorway. It was so dark that, at first, Sylvia could distinguish nothing but the outline of a framework, with something stretched upon it that resembled a human body. Her first thought was that the man was dead, but this was not so—he groaned. Her eyes, accustoming themselves to the gloom, began to see what the "punishment" was. Upon the floor was placed an iron frame about six feet long, and two and a half feet wide, with round iron bars, placed transversely, about twelve inches apart. The man she came to seek was bound in a horizontal position upon this frame, with his neck projecting over the end of it. If he allowed his head to hang, the blood rushed to his brain, and suffocated him, while the effort to keep it raised strained every muscle to agony pitch. His face was purple, and he foamed at the mouth.

Sylvia uttered a cry. "This is no punishment; it's murder! Who ordered this?"

"The Commandant," said Troke sullenly.

"I don't believe it. Loose him!"

"I daren't, mam," said Troke.

"Loose him, I say! Hailey!—you, sir, there!" The noise had brought several warders to the spot. "Do you hear me? Do you know who I am? Loose him, I say!" In her eagerness and compassion she was on her knees by the side of the infernal machine, plucking at the ropes with her delicate fingers. "Wretches, you have cut his flesh! He is dying! Help! You have killed him!"

The prisoner, in fact, seeing this angel of mercy stooping over him, and hearing close to him the tones of a voice that for seven years he had heard but in his dreams, had fainted. Troke and Hailey, alarmed by her vehemence, dragged the stretcher out into the light, and hastily cut the lashings. Dawes rolled off like a log, and his head fell against Mrs. Frere. Troke roughly pulled him aside, and called for water. Sylvia, trembling with sympathy and pale with passion, turned upon the crew. "How long has he been like this?"

"An hour," said Troke.

"A lie!" said a stern voice at the door. "He has been there nine hours!"

"Wretches!" cried Sylvia, "you shall hear more of this. Oh, oh! I am sick!"—she felt for the wall—"I—I—" North watched her with agony on his face, but did not move. "I faint. I—"—she uttered a despairing cry that was not without a touch of anger. "Mr. North! do you not see? Oh! Take me home—take me home!" and she would have fallen across the body of the tortured prisoner had not North caught her in his arms.

Rufus Dawes, awaking from his stupor, saw, in the midst of a sunbeam which penetrated a window in the corridor, the woman who came to save his body supported by the priest who came to save his soul; and staggering to his knees, he stretched out his hands with a hoarse cry. Perhaps something in the action brought back to the dimmed remembrance of the Commandant's wife the image of a similar figure stretching forth its hands to a frightened child in the mysterious far-off time. She started, and pushing back her hair, bent a wistful, terrified gaze upon the face of the kneeling man, as though she would fain read there an explanation of the shadowy memory which haunted her. It is possible that she would have spoken, but North—thinking the excitement had produced one of those hysterical crises which were common to her—gently drew her, still gazing, back towards the gate. The convict's arms fell, and an undefinable presentiment of evil chilled him as he beheld the priest—emotion pallid in his cheeks—slowly draw the fair young creature from out the sunlight into the grim shadow of the heavy archway. For an instant the gloom swallowed them, and it seemed to Dawes that the strange wild man of God had in that instant become a man of Evil—blighting the brightness and the beauty of the innocence that clung to him. For an instant—and then they passed out of the prison archway into the free air of heaven—and the sunlight glowed golden on their faces.

"You are ill," said North. "You will faint. Why do you look so wildly?"

"What is it?" she whispered, more in answer to her own thoughts than to his question—"what is it that links me to that man?

What deed—what terror—what memory? I tremble with crowding thoughts, that die ere they can whisper to me. Oh, that prison!"

"Look up; we are in the sunshine."

She passed her hand across her brow, sighing heavily, as one awaking from a disturbed slumber—shuddered, and withdrew her arm from his. North interpreted the action correctly, and the blood rushed to his face. "Pardon me, you cannot walk alone; you will fall. I will leave you at the gate."

In truth she would have fallen had he not again assisted her. She turned upon him eyes whose reproachful sorrow had almost forced him to a confession, but he bowed his head and held silence. They reached the house, and he placed her tenderly in a chair. "Now you are safe, madam, I will leave you."

She burst into tears. "Why do you treat me thus, Mr. North? What have I done to make you hate me?"

"Hate you!" said North, with trembling lips. "Oh, no, I do not—do not *hate* you. I am rude in my speech, abrupt in my manner. You must forget it, and—and *me*."

A horse's feet crashed upon the gravel, and an instant after Maurice Frere burst into the room. Returning from the Cascades, he had met Troke, and learned the release of the prisoner. Furious at this usurpation of authority by his wife, his self-esteem wounded by the thought that she had witnessed his mean revenge upon the man he had so infamously wronged, and his natural brutality enhanced by brandy, he had made for the house at full gallop, determined to assert his authority. Blind with rage, he saw no one but his wife. "What the devil's this I hear? *You* have been meddling in my business! *You* release prisoners! *You*—"

"Captain Frere!" said North, stepping forward to assert the restraining presence of a stranger. Frere started, astonished at the intrusion of the chaplain. Here was another outrage of his dignity, another insult to his supreme authority. In its passion, his gross mind leapt to the worst conclusion.

"You here, too! What do you want here—with my wife! This is your *quarrel*, is it?" His eyes glanced wrathfully from one to the other; and he strode towards North. "You infernal hypocritical lying scoundrel, if it wasn't for your black coat, I'd—"

"Maurice!" cried Sylvia, in an agony of shame and terror, striving to place a restraining hand upon his arm. He turned upon her with so fiercely infamous a curse that North, pale with righteous rage, seemed prompted to strike the burly ruffian to the earth. For a moment, the two men faced each other, and then Frere, muttering threats of vengeance against each and all—convicts, gaolers, wife, and priest—flung the suppliant woman violently from him, and rushed from the room. She fell heavily against the wall, and as the chaplain raised her, he heard the hoof-strokes of the departing horse.

"Oh," cried Sylvia, covering her face with trembling hands, "let me leave this place!"

North, enfolding her in his arms, strove to soothe her with incoherent words of comfort. Dizzy with the blow she had received, she clung to him sobbing. Twice he tried to tear himself away, but had he loosed his hold she would have fallen. He could not hold her—bruised, suffering, and in tears—thus against his heart, and keep silence. In a torrent of agonized eloquence the story of his love burst from his lips. "Why should you be thus tortured?" he cried. "Heaven never willed you to be mated to that boor—you, whose life should be all sunshine. Leave him—leave him. He has cast you off. We have both suffered. Let us leave this dreadful place—this isthmus between earth and hell! I will give you happiness."

"I am going," she said faintly. "I have already arranged to go."

North trembled. "It was not of my seeking. Fate has willed it. We go together!"

They looked at each other—she felt the fever of his blood, she read his passion in his eyes, she comprehended the "hatred" he had affected for her, and, deadly pale, drew back the cold hand he held.

"Go!" she murmured. "If you love me, leave me—leave me! Do not see me or speak to me again—" her silence added the words she could not utter, "*till then*."

CHAPTER XIV

GETTING READY FOR SEA

MAURICE Frere's passion had spent itself in that last act of violence. He did not return to the prison, as he promised himself, but turned into the road that led to the Cascades. He repented him of his suspicions. There was nothing strange in the presence of the chaplain. Sylvia had always liked the man, and an apology for his conduct had doubtless removed her anger. To make a mountain out of a molehill was the act of an idiot. It was natural that she should release Dawes—women *were* so tender-hearted. A few well-chosen, calmly-uttered platitudes anent the necessity for the treatment that, to those unaccustomed to the desperate wickedness of convicts, must appear harsh, would have served his turn far better than bluster and abuse. Moreover, North was to sail in the *Lady Franklin,* and might put in execution his threats of official complaint, unless he was carefully dealt with. To put Dawes again to the torture would be to show to Troke and his friends that the "Commandant's wife" had acted without the "Commandant's authority", and that must not be shown. He would now return and patch up a peace. His wife would sail in the same vessel with North, and he would in a few days be left alone on the island to pursue his "discipline" unchecked. With this intent he returned to the prison, and gravely informed poor Troke that he was astonished at his barbarity. "Mrs. Frere, who most luckily had appointed to meet me this evening at the prison, tells me that the poor devil Dawes had been on the stretcher since seven o'clock this morning."

"You ordered it fust thing, yer honour," said Troke.

"Yes, you fool, but I didn't order you to keep the man there for nine hours, did I? Why, you scoundrel, you might have killed him!" Troke scratched his head in bewilderment. "Take his irons off, and put him in a separate cell in the old gaol. If a man *is* a murderer, that is no reason you should take the law into your own hands, is it? You'd better take care, Mr. Troke." On the way back he met the chaplain, who, seeing him, made for a by-path in curious haste.

"Halloo!" roared Frere. "Hi! Mr. North!" Mr. North paused, and the Commandant made at him abruptly. "Look here, sir, I was rude to you just now—devilish rude. Most ungentlemanly of me. I must apologize." North bowed, without speaking, and tried to pass.

"You must excuse my violence," Frere went on. "I'm bad-tempered, and I didn't like my wife interfering. Women, don't you know, don't see these things—don't understand these scoundrels." North again bowed. "Why, d—n it, how savage you look! Quite ghastly, bigod! I must have said most outrageous things. Forget and forgive, you know. Come home and have some dinner."

"I cannot enter your house again, sir," said North, in tones more agitated than the occasion would seem to warrant.

Frere shrugged his great shoulders with a clumsy affectation of good humour, and held out his hand. "Well, shake hands, parson. You'll have to take care of Mrs. Frere on the voyage, and we may as well make up our differences before you start. Shake hands."

"Let me pass, sir!" cried North, with heightened colour; and ignoring the proffered hand, strode savagely on.

"You've a d—d fine temper for a parson," said Frere to himself. "However, if you won't, you won't. Hang me if *I'll* ask you again." Nor, when he reached home, did he fare better in his efforts at reconciliation with his wife. Sylvia met him with the icy front of a woman whose pride has been wounded too deeply for tears.

"Say no more about it," she said. "I am going to my father. If you want to explain your conduct, explain it to him."

"Come, Sylvia," he urged; "I was a brute, I know. Forgive me."

"It is useless to ask me," she said; "I cannot. I have forgiven you so much during the last seven years."

He attempted to embrace her, but she withdrew herself loathingly from his arms. He swore a great oath at her, and, too obstinate to argue farther, sulked. Blunt, coming in about some ship matters, the pair drank rum. Sylvia went to her room and occupied herself with some minor details of clothes-packing (it is wonderful how women find relief from thoughts in household care), while North, poor fool, seeing from his window the light in hers, sat staring at it, alternately cursing and praying. In the meantime, the unconscious cause of all of this—Rufus Dawes—sat in his new cell, wondering at the chance which had procured him comfort, and blessing the fair hands that had brought it to him. He doubted not but that Sylvia had interceded with his tormentor, and by gentle pleading brought him ease. "God bless her," he murmured. "I have wronged her all these years. She did not know that I suffered." He waited anxiously for North to visit him, that he might have his belief confirmed. "I will get him to thank her for me," he thought. But North did not come for two whole days. No one came but his gaolers; and, gazing from his prison window upon the sea that almost washed its walls, he saw the schooner at anchor, mocking him with a liberty he could not achieve. On the third day, however, North came. His manner was constrained and abrupt. His eyes wandered uneasily, and he seemed burdened with thoughts which he dared not utter.

"I want you to thank her for me, Mr. North," said Dawes.

"Thank whom?"

"Mrs. Frere."

The unhappy priest shuddered at hearing the name.

"I do not think you owe any thanks to her. Your irons were removed by the Commandant's order."

"But by her persuasion. I feel sure of it. Ah, I was wrong to think she had forgotten me. Ask her for her forgiveness."

"Forgiveness!" said North, recalling the scene in the prison. "What have you done to need her forgiveness?"

"I doubted her," said Rufus Dawes. "I thought her ungrateful and treacherous. I thought she delivered me again into the bondage from whence I had escaped. I thought she had betrayed me—betrayed me to the villain whose base life I saved for her sweet sake."

"What do you mean?" asked North. "You never spoke to me of this."

"No, I had vowed to bury the knowledge of it in my own breast—it was too bitter to speak."

"Saved his life!"

"Ay, and hers! I made the boat that carried her to freedom. I held her in my arms, and took the bread from my own lips to feed her!"

"She cannot know this," said North in an undertone.

"She has forgotten it, perhaps, for she was but a child. But you will remind her, will you not? You will do me justice in her eyes before I die? You will get her forgiveness for me?"

North could not explain why such an interview as the convict desired was impossible, and so he promised.

"She is going away in the schooner," said he, concealing the fact of his own departure. "I will see her before she goes, and tell her."

"God bless you, sir," said poor Dawes. "Now pray with me"; and the wretched priest mechanically repeated one of the formulae his Church prescribes.

The next day he told his penitent that Mrs. Frere had forgiven him. This was a lie. He had not seen her; but what should a lie be to him now? Lies were needful in the tortuous path he had undertaken to tread. Yet the deceit he was forced to practise cost him many a pang. He had succumbed to his passion, and to win the love for which he yearned had voluntarily abandoned truth and honour; but standing thus alone with his sin, he despised and hated himself. To deaden remorse and drown reflection, he had recourse to brandy, and though the fierce excitement of his hopes and fears steeled him against the stupefying action of the liquor, he was rendered by it incapable of calm reflection. In certain nervous conditions our mere physical powers are proof against the action of alcohol, and though ten times more drunk than the toper, who, incoherently stammering, reels into the gutter, we can walk erect and talk with fluency. Indeed, in this artificial exaltation of the sensibilities, men often display a brilliant wit, and an acuteness of comprehension, calculated to delight their friends, and terrify their physicians. North had reached this condition of brain-drunkenness. In plain terms, he was trembling on the verge of madness.

The days passed swiftly, and Blunt's preparations for sea were completed. There were two stern cabins in the schooner, one of which was appropriated to Mrs. Frere, while the other was set apart for North. Maurice had not attempted to renew his overtures of friendship, and the chaplain had not spoken. Mindful of Sylvia's last words, he had resolved not to meet her until fairly embarked upon the voyage which he intended should link their fortunes together.

On the morning of the 19th December, Blunt declared himself ready to set sail, and in the afternoon the two passengers came on board.

Rufus Dawes, gazing from his window upon the schooner that lay outside the reef, thought nothing of the fact that, after the Commandant's boat had taken away the Commandant's wife another boat should put off with the chaplain. It was quite natural that Mr. North should desire to bid his friends farewell, and through the hot, still afternoon he watched for the returning boat, hoping that the chaplain would bring him some message from the woman whom he was never to see more on earth. The hours wore on, however, and no breath of wind ruffled the surface of the sea. The day was exceedingly close and sultry, heavy dun clouds hung on the horizon, and it seemed probable that unless a thunder-storm should clear the air before night, the calm would continue. Blunt, however, with a true sailor's obstinacy in regard to weather, swore there would be a breeze, and held to his purpose of sailing. The hot afternoon passed away in a sultry sunset, and it was not until the shades of evening had begun to fall that Rufus Dawes distinguished a boat detach itself from the sides of the schooner, and glide through the oily water to the jetty. The chaplain was returning, and in a few hours perhaps would be with him, to bring him the message of comfort for which his soul thirsted. He stretched out his unshackled limbs, and throwing himself upon his stretcher, fell to recalling the past—his boat-building, the news of his fortune, his love, and his self-sacrifice.

North, however, was not returning to bring to the prisoner a message of comfort, but he was returning on purpose to see him, nevertheless. The unhappy man, torn by remorse and passion, had resolved upon a course of action which seemed to him a penance for his crime of deceit. He determined to confess to Dawes that the message he had brought was wholly fictitious, that he himself loved the wife of the Commandant, and that with her he was about to leave the island for ever. "I am no hypocrite," he thought, in his exaltation. "If I choose to sin, I will sin boldly; and this poor wretch, who looks up to me as an angel, shall know me for my true self."

The notion of thus destroying his own fame in the eyes of the man whom he had taught to love him, was pleasant to his diseased imagination. It was the natural outcome of the morbid condition of mind into which he had drifted, and he provided for the complete execution of his scheme with cunning born of the mischief working in his brain. It was desirable that the fatal stroke should be dealt at the last possible instant; that he should suddenly unveil his own infamy, and then depart, never to be seen again. To this end he had invented an excuse for returning to the shore at the latest possible moment. He had purposely left in his room a dressing-bag—the sort of article one is likely to forget in the hurry of departure from one's house, and so certain to remember when the time comes to finally prepare for settling in another. He had ingeniously extracted from Blunt the fact that "he didn't expect a wind before dark, but wanted all ship-shape and aboard", and then, just as darkness fell, discovered that it was imperative for him to go ashore. Blunt cursed, but, if the chaplain insisted upon going, there was no help for it.

"There'll be a breeze in less than two hours," said he. "You've plenty of time, but if you're not back before the first puff, I'll sail without you, as sure as you're born." North assured him of his punctuality. "Don't wait for me, Captain, if I'm not here," said he with the lightness of tone which men use to mask anxiety. "I'd take him at his word, Blunt," said the Commandant, who was affably waiting to take final farewell of his wife. "Give way there, men," he shouted to the crew, "and wait at the jetty. If Mr. North misses his ship through your laziness, you'll pay for it." So the boat set off, North laughing uproariously at the thought of being late. Frere observed with some astonishment that the chaplain wrapped himself in a boat cloak that lay in the stern sheets. "Does the fellow want to smother himself in a night like this!" was his remark. The truth was that, though his hands and head were burning, North's teeth chattered with cold. Perhaps this was the reason why, when landed and out of eyeshot of the crew, he produced a pocket-flask of rum and eagerly drank. The spirit gave him courage for the ordeal to which he had condemned himself; and with steadied step, he reached the door of the old prison. To his surprise, Gimblett refused him admission!

"But I have come direct from the Commandant," said North.

"Got any order, sir?"

"Order! No."

"I can't let you in, your reverence," said Gimblett.

"I want to see the prisoner Dawes. I have a special message for him. I have come ashore on purpose."

"I am very sorry, sir—"

"The ship will sail in two hours, man, and I shall miss her," said North, indignant at being frustrated in his design. "Let me pass."

"Upon my honour, sir, I daren't," said Gimblett, who was not without his good points. " You know what authority is, sir."

North was in despair, but a bright thought struck him—a thought that, in his soberer moments, would never have entered his head—he would buy admission. He produced the rum flask from beneath the sheltering cloak. "Come, don't talk nonsense to me, Gimblett. You don't suppose I would come here *without* authority. Here, take a pull at this, and let me through." Gimblett's features relaxed into a smile. "Well, sir, I suppose it's all right, if you say so," said he. And clutching the rum bottle with one hand, he opened the door of Dawes's cell with the other.

North entered, and as the door closed behind him, the prisoner, who had been lying apparently asleep upon his bed, leapt up, and made as though to catch him by the throat.

Rufus Dawes had dreamt a dream. Alone, amid the gathering glooms, his fancy had recalled the past, and had peopled it with memories. He thought that he was once more upon the barren strand where he had first met with the sweet child he loved. He lived again his life of usefulness and honour. He saw himself working at the boat, embarking, and putting out to sea. The fair head of the innocent girl was again pillowed on his breast; her young lips again murmured words of affection in his greedy ear. Frere was beside him, watching him, as he had watched before. Once again the grey sea spread around him, barren of succour. Once again, in the wild, wet morning, he beheld the American brig bearing down upon them, and saw the bearded faces of the astonished crew. He saw Frere take the child in his arms and mount upon the deck; he heard the shout of delight that went up, and pressed again the welcoming hands which greeted the rescued castaways. The deck was crowded. All the folk he had ever known were there. He saw the white hair and stern features of Sir Richard Devine, and beside him stood, wringing her thin hands, his weeping mother. Then Frere strode forward, and after him John Rex, the convict, who, roughly elbowing through the crowd of prisoners and gaolers, would have reached the spot where stood Sir Richard Devine, but that the corpse of the murdered Lord Bellasis arose and thrust him back. How the hammers clattered in the shipbuilder's yard! Was it a coffin they were making? Not for Sylvia—surely not for her! The air grows heavy, lurid with flame, and black with smoke. The *Hydaspes* is on fire! Sylvia clings to her husband.

Base wretch, would you shake her off! Look up; the midnight heaven is glittering with stars; above the smoke the air breathes delicately! One step—another! Fix your eyes on mine—so—to my heart! Alas! she turns; he catches at her dress. What! It is a priest—a priest—who, smiling with infernal joy, would drag her to the flaming gulf that yawns for him. The dreamer leaps at the wretch's throat, and crying, "Villain, was it for *this* fate I saved her?"—and awakes to find himself struggling with the monster of his dream, the idol of his waking senses—"Mr. North."

North, paralysed no less by the suddenness of the attack than by the words with which it was accompanied, let fall his cloak, and stood trembling before the prophetic accusation of the man whose curses he had come to earn.

"I was dreaming," said Rufus Dawes. "A terrible dream! But it has passed now. The message—you have brought me a message, have you not? Why—what ails you? You are pale—your knees tremble. Did my violence—?"

North recovered himself with a great effort. "It is nothing. Let us talk, for my time is short. You have thought me a good man—one blessed of God, one consecrated to a holy service; a man honest, pure, and truthful. I have returned to tell you the truth. I am none of these things." Rufus Dawes sat staring, unable to comprehend this madness. "I told you that the woman you loved—for you *do* love her—sent you a message of forgiveness. I lied."

"What!"

"I never told her of your confession. I never mentioned your name to her."

"And she will go without knowing—Oh, Mr. North, what have you done?"

"Wrecked my own soul!" cried North, wildly, stung by the reproachful agony of the tone. "Do not cling to me. My task is done. You will hate me now. That is my wish—I merit it. Let me go, I say. I shall be too late."

"Too late! For what?" He looked at the cloak—through the open window came the voices of the men in the boat—the memory of the rose, of the scene in the prison, flashed across him, and he understood it all.

"Great Heaven, you go together!"

"Let me go," repeated North, in a hoarse voice.

Rufus Dawes stepped between him and the door. "No, madman, I will not let you go, to do this great wrong, to kill this innocent young soul, who—God help her—loves you!" North, confounded at this sudden reversal of their position towards each other, crouched bewildered against the wall. "I say you shall *not* go! You shall not destroy your own soul and hers! You love her! So do I! and my love is mightier than yours, for it shall save her!"

"In God's name—" cried the unhappy priest, striving to stop his ears. "Ay, in God's name! In the name of that God whom in my torments I had forgotten! In the name of that God whom you taught me to remember! That God who sent you to save me from despair, gives me strength to save you in my turn! Oh, Mr. North—my teacher—my friend—my brother—by the sweet hope of mercy which you preached to me, be merciful to this erring woman!"

North lifted agonized eyes. "But I love her! Love her, do you hear? What do you know of love?"

"Love!" cried Rufus Dawes, his pale face radiant. "Love! Oh, it is you who do not know it. Love is the sacrifice of self, the death of all desire that is not for another's good. Love is Godlike! *You* love?—no, no, your love is selfishness, and will end in shame! Listen, I will tell you the history of such a love as yours."

North, enthralled by the other's overmastering will, fell back trembling.

"I will tell you the secret of my life, the reason why I am here. Come closer."

*

CHAPTER XV

THE DISCOVERY

THE house in Clarges Street was duly placed at the disposal of Mrs. Richard Devine, who was installed in it, to the profound astonishment and disgust of Mr. Smithers and his fellow-servants. It now only remained that the lady should be formally recognized by Lady Devine. The rest of the ingenious programme would follow as a matter of course. John Rex was well aware of the position which, in his assumed personality, he occupied in society. He knew that by the world of servants, of waiters, of those to whom servants and waiters could babble; of such turfites and men-about-town as had reason to inquire concerning Mr. Richard's domestic affairs—no opinion could be expressed, save that "Devine's married somebody, I hear," with variations to the same effect. He knew well that the really great world, the Society, whose scandal would have been socially injurious, had long ceased to trouble itself with Mr. Richard Devine's doings in any particular. If it had been reported that the Leviathan of the Turf had married his washerwoman, Society would only have intimated that "it was just what might have been expected of him". To say the truth, however, Mr. Richard had rather hoped that—disgusted at his brutality—Lady Devine would have nothing more to do with him, and that the ordeal of presenting his wife would not be necessary. Lady Devine, however, had resolved on a different line of conduct. The intelligence concerning Mr. Richard Devine's threatened proceedings seemed to nerve her to the confession of the dislike which had been long growing in her mind; seemed even to aid the formation of those doubts, the shadows of which had now and then cast themselves upon her belief in the identity of the man who called himself her son. "His conduct is brutal," said she to her brother. "I cannot understand it."

"It is more than brutal; it is unnatural," returned Francis Wade, and stole a look at her. "Moreover, he is married."

"Married!" cried Lady Devine.

"So he says," continued the other, producing the letter sent to him by Rex at Sarah's dictation. "He writes to me stating that his wife, whom he married last year abroad, has come to England, and wishes us to receive her."

"I will *not* receive her!" cried Lady Devine, rising and pacing down the path.

"But that would be a declaration of war," said poor Francis, twisting an Italian onyx which adorned his irresolute hand. "I would not advise that."

Lady Devine stopped suddenly, with the gesture of one who has finally made a difficult and long-considered resolution. "Richard shall not sell this house," she said.

"But, my dear Ellinor," cried her brother, in some alarm at this unwonted decision, "I am afraid that you can't prevent him."

"*If* he is the man he says he is, I can," returned she, with effort.

Francis Wade gasped. "If he is the man! It is true—I have sometimes thought—Oh, Ellinor, can it be that we have been deceived?"

She came to him and leant upon him for support, as she had leant upon her son in the garden where they now stood, nineteen years ago. "I do not know, I am afraid to think. But between Richard and myself is a secret—a shameful secret, Frank, known to no other living person. If the man who threatens me does not know that secret, he is not my son. If he does know it—"

"Well, in Heaven's name, what then?"

"He knows that he has neither part nor lot in the fortune of the man who was my husband."

"Ellinor, you terrify me. What does this mean?"

"I will tell you if there be need to do so," said the unhappy lady. "But I cannot now. I never meant to speak of it again, even to him. Consider that it is hard to break a silence of nearly twenty years. Write to this man, and tell him that before I receive his wife, I wish to see him alone. No—do not let him come here until the truth be known. I will go to him."

It was with some trepidation that Mr. Richard, sitting with his wife on the afternoon of the 3rd May, 1846, awaited the arrival of his mother. He had been very nervous and unstrung for some days past, and the prospect of the coming interview was, for some reason he could not explain to himself, weighty with fears. "What does she want to come alone for? And what can she have to say?" he asked himself. "She cannot suspect anything after all these years, surely?" He endeavoured to reason with himself, but in vain; the knock at the door which announced the arrival of his pretended mother made his heart jump.

"I feel deuced shaky, Sarah," he said. "Let's have a nip of something."

"You've been nipping too much for the last five years, Dick." (She had quite schooled her tongue to the new name.) "Your 'shakiness' is the result of 'nipping', I'm afraid."

"Oh, don't preach; I am not in the humour for it."

"Help yourself, then. You are quite sure that you are ready with your story?"

The brandy revived him, and he rose with affected heartiness. "My dear mother, allow me to present to you—" He paused, for there was that in Lady Devine's face which confirmed his worst fears.

"I wish to speak to you alone," she said, ignoring with steady eyes the woman whom she had ostensibly come to see.

John Rex hesitated, but Sarah saw the danger, and hastened to confront it. "A wife should be a husband's best friend, madam. Your son married me of his own free will, and even his mother can have nothing to say to him which it is not my duty and privilege to hear. I am not a girl as you can see, and I can bear whatever news you bring."

Lady Devine bit her pale lips. She saw at once that the woman before her was not gently-born, but she felt also that she was a woman of higher mental calibre than herself. Prepared as she was for the worst, this sudden and open declaration of hostilities frightened her, as Sarah had calculated. She began to realize that if she was to prove equal to the task she had set herself, she must not waste her strength in skirmishing. Steadily refusing to look at Richard's wife, she addressed herself to Richard. "My brother will be here in half an hour," she said, as though the mention of his name would better her position in some way. "But I begged him to allow me to come first in order that I might speak to you privately."

"Well," said John Rex, "we are in private. What have you to say?"

"I want to tell you that I forbid you to carry out the plan you have for breaking up Sir Richard's property."

"Forbid me!" cried Rex, much relieved. "Why, I only want to do what my father's will enables me to do."

"Your father's will enables you to do nothing of the sort, and you know it." She spoke as though rehearsing a series of set-speeches, and Sarah watched her with growing alarm.

"Oh, nonsense!" cries John Rex, in sheer amazement. "I have a lawyer's opinion on it."

"Do you remember what took place at Hampstead this day nineteen years ago?"

"At Hampstead!" said Rex, grown suddenly pale. "This day nineteen years ago. No! What do you mean?"

"Do you not remember?" she continued, leaning forward eagerly, and speaking almost fiercely. "Do you not remember the reason why you left the house where you were born, and which you now wish to sell to strangers?"

John Rex stood dumbfounded, the blood suffusing his temples. He knew that among the secrets of the man whose inheritance he had stolen was one which he had never gained—the secret of that sacrifice to which Lady Devine had once referred—and he felt that this secret was to be revealed to crush him now.

Sarah, trembling also, but more with rage than terror, swept towards Lady Devine. "Speak out!" she said, "if you have anything to say! Of what do you accuse my husband?"

"Of imposture!" cried Lady Devine, all her outraged maternity nerving her to abash her enemy. "This man may be your husband, but he is not my son!"

Now that the worst was out, John Rex, choking with passion, felt all the devil within him rebelling against defeat. "You are mad," he said. "You have recognized me for three years, and now, because I want to claim that which is my own, you invent this lie. Take care how you provoke me. If I am not your son—you have recognized me as such. I stand upon the law and upon my rights."

Lady Devine turned swiftly, and with both hands to her bosom, confronted him.

"You shall have your rights! You shall have what the law allows you! Oh, how blind I have been all these years. Persist in your infamous imposture. Call yourself Richard Devine still, and I will tell the world the shameful secret which my son died to hide. *Be* Richard Devine! Richard Devine was a bastard, and the law allows him—nothing!"

There was no doubting the truth of her words. It was impossible that even a woman whose home had been desecrated, as hers had been, would invent a lie so self-condemning. Yet John Rex forced himself to appear to doubt, and his dry lips asked, "If then your husband was not the father of your son, who was?"

"My cousin, Armigell Esme Wade, Lord Bellasis," answered Lady Devine.

John Rex gasped for breath. His hand, tugging at his neck-cloth, rent away the linen that covered his choking throat. The whole horizon of his past was lit up by a lightning flash which stunned him. His brain, already enfeebled by excess, was unable to withstand this last shock. He staggered, and but for the cabinet against which he leant, would have fallen. The secret thoughts of his heart rose to his lips, and were uttered unconsciously. "Lord Bellasis! He was my father also, and—I killed him!"

A dreadful silence fell, and then Lady Devine, stretching out her hands towards the self-confessed murderer, with a sort of frightful respect, said in a whisper, in which horror and supplication were strangely mingled, "What did you do with my son? Did you kill *him* also?"

But John Rex, wagging his head from side to side, like a beast in the shambles that has received a mortal stroke, made no reply. Sarah Purfoy, awed as she was by the dramatic force of the situation, nevertheless remembered that Francis Wade might arrive at any moment, and saw her last opportunity for safety. She advanced and touched the mother on the shoulder.

"Your son is alive!"

"Where?"

"Will you promise not to hinder us leaving this house if I tell you?"

"Yes, yes."

"Will you promise to keep the confession which you have heard secret, until we have left England?"

"I promise anything. In God's name, woman, if you have a woman's heart, speak! Where is my son?"

Sarah Purfoy rose over the enemy who had defeated her, and said in level, deliberate accents, "They call him Rufus Dawes. He is a convict at Norfolk Island, transported for life for the murder which you have heard my husband confess to having committed—Ah!—"

Lady Devine had fainted.

CHAPTER XVI

FIFTEEN HOURS

SARAH flew to Rex. "Rouse yourself, John, for Heaven's sake. We have not a moment." John Rex passed his hand over his forehead wearily.

"I cannot think. I am broken down. I am ill. My brain seems dead."

Nervously watching the prostrate figure on the floor, she hurried on bonnet, cloak, and veil, and in a twinkling had him outside the house and into a cab.

"Thirty-nine, Lombard Street. Quick!"

"You won't give me up?" said Rex, turning dull eyes upon her.

"Give you up? No. But the police will be after us as soon as that woman can speak, and her brother summon his lawyer. I know what her promise is worth. We have only got about fifteen hours start."

"I can't go far, Sarah," said he; "I am sleepy and stupid."

She repressed the terrible fear that tugged at her heart, and strove to rally him.

"You've been drinking too much, John. Now sit still and be good, while I go and get some money for you."

She hurried into the bank, and her name secured her an interview with the manager at once.

"That's a rich woman," said one of the clerks to his friend. "A widow, too! Chance for you, Tom," returned the other; and, presently, from out the sacred presence came another clerk with a request for "a draft on Sydney for three thousand, less premium", and bearing a cheque signed "Sarah Carr" for £200, which he "took" in notes, and so returned again.

From the bank she was taken to Green's Shipping Office. "I want a cabin in the first ship for Sydney, please."

The shipping-clerk looked at a board. "The *Highflyer* goes in twelve days, madam, and there is one cabin vacant."

"I want to go at once—to-morrow or next day."

He smiled. "I am afraid that is impossible," said he. Just then one of the partners came out of his private room with a telegram in his hand, and beckoned the shipping-clerk. Sarah was about to depart for another office, when the clerk came hastily back.

"Just the thing for you, ma'am," said he. "We have got a telegram from a gentleman who has a first cabin in the *Dido*, to say that his wife has been taken ill, and he must give up his berth."

"When does the *Dido* sail?"

"To-morrow morning. She is at Plymouth, waiting for the mails. If you go down to-night by the mail-train which leaves at 9.30, you will be in plenty of time, and we will telegraph."

"I will take the cabin. How much?"

"One hundred and thirty pounds, madam," said he.

She produced her notes. "Pray count it yourself. We have been delayed in the same manner ourselves. My husband is a great invalid, but I was not so fortunate as to get someone to refund *us* our passage-money."

"What name did you say?" asked the clerk, counting. "Mr. and Mrs. Carr. Thank you," and he handed her the slip of paper.

"Thank *you*," said Sarah, with a bewitching smile, and swept down to her cab again. John Rex was gnawing his nails in sullen apathy. She displayed the passage-ticket. "You are saved. By the time Mr. Francis Wade gets his wits together, and his sister recovers her speech, we shall be past pursuit."

"To Sydney!" cries Rex angrily, looking at the warrant. "Why there of all places in God's earth?"

Sarah surveyed him with an expression of contempt. "Because *your* scheme has failed. Now this is mine. You have deserted me once; you will do so again in any other country. You are a murderer, a villain, and a coward, but you suit me. I save you, but I mean to keep you. I will bring you to Australia, where the first trooper will arrest you at my bidding as an escaped convict. If you don't like to come, stay behind. I don't care. I am rich. I have done no wrong. The law cannot touch me—Do you agree? Then tell the man to drive to Silver's in Cornhill for your outfit." Having housed him at last—all gloomy and despondent—in a quiet tavern near the railway station, she tried to get some information as to this last revealed crime.

"How came you to kill Lord Bellasis?" she asked him quietly.

"I had found out from my mother that I was his natural son, and one day riding home from a pigeon match I told him so. He taunted me—and I struck him. I did not mean to kill him, but he was an old man, and in my passion I struck hard. As he fell, I thought I saw a horseman among the trees, and I galloped off. My ill-luck began then, for the same night I was arrested at the coiner's."

"But I thought there was robbery," said she.

"Not by me. But, for God's sake, talk no more about it. I am sick—my brain is going round. I want to sleep."

"Be careful, please! Lift him gently!" said Mrs. Carr, as the boat ranged alongside the *Dido,* gaunt and grim, in the early dawn of a bleak May morning.

"What's the matter?" asked the officer of the watch, perceiving the bustle in the boat.

"Gentleman seems to have had a stroke," said a boatman.

It was so. There was no fear that John Rex would escape again from the woman he had deceived. The infernal genius of Sarah Purfoy had saved her lover at last—but saved him only that she might nurse him till he died—died ignorant even of her tenderness, a mere animal, lacking the intellect he had in his selfish wickedness abused.

CHAPTER XVII
THE REDEMPTION

*

—"THAT is my story. Let it plead with you to turn you from your purpose, and to save her. The punishment of sin falls not upon the sinner only. A deed once done lives in its consequence for ever, and this tragedy of shame and crime to which my felon's death is a fitting end, is but the outcome of a selfish sin like yours!"

It had grown dark in the prison, and as he ceased speaking, Rufus Dawes felt a trembling hand seize his own. It was that of the chaplain.

"Let me hold your hand!—Sir Richard Devine did not murder your father. He was murdered by a horseman who, riding with him, struck him and fled."

"Merciful God! How do you know this?"

"Because I saw the murder committed, because—don't let go my hand—I robbed the body."

"You!—"

"In my youth I was a gambler. Lord Bellasis won money from me, and to pay him I forged two bills of exchange. Unscrupulous and cruel, he threatened to expose me if I did not give him double the sum. Forgery was death in those days, and I strained every nerve to buy back the proofs of my folly. I succeeded. I was to meet Lord Bellasis near his own house at Hampstead on the night of which you speak, to pay the money and receive the bills. When I saw him fall I galloped up, but instead of pursuing his murderer I rifled his pocket-book of my forgeries. I was afraid to give evidence at the trial, or I might have saved you.—Ah! you have let go my hand!"

"God forgive you!" said Rufus Dawes, and then was silent.

"Speak!" cried North. "Speak, or you will make me mad. Reproach me! Spurn me! Spit upon me! You cannot think worse of me than I do myself." But the other, his head buried in his hands, did not answer, and with a wild gesture North staggered out of the cell.

Nearly an hour had passed since the chaplain had placed the rum flask in his hand, and Gimblett observed, with semi-drunken astonishment, that it was not yet empty. He had intended, in the first instance, to have taken but one sup in payment of his courtesy—for Gimblett was conscious of his own weakness in the matter of strong waters—but as he waited and waited, the one sup became two, and two three, and at length more than half the contents of the bottle had moistened his gullet, and maddened him for more. Gimblett was in a quandary. If he didn't finish the flask, he would be oppressed with an everlasting regret. If he did finish it he would be drunk; and to be drunk on duty was the one unpardonable sin. He looked across the darkness of the sea, to where the rising and falling light marked the schooner. The Commandant was a long way off! A faint breeze, which had—according to Blunt's prophecy—arisen with the night, brought up to him the voices of the boat's crew from the jetty below him. His friend Jack Mannix was coxswain of her. He would give Jack a drink. Leaving the gate, he advanced unsteadily to the edge of the embankment, and, putting his head over, called out to his friend. The breeze, however, which was momentarily freshening, carried his voice away; and Jack Mannix, hearing nothing, continued his conversation. Gimblett was just drunk enough to be virtuously indignant at this incivility, and seating himself on the edge of the bank, swallowed the remainder of the rum at a draught. The effect upon his enforcedly temperate stomach was very touching. He made one feeble attempt to get upon his legs, cast a reproachful glance at the rum bottle, essayed to drink out of its spirituous emptiness, and then, with a smile of reckless contentment, cursed the island and all its contents, and fell asleep.

North, coming out of the prison, did not notice the absence of the gaoler; indeed, he was not in a condition to notice anything. Bare-headed, without his cloak, with staring eyes and clenched hands, he rushed through the gates into the night as one who flies headlong from some fearful vision. It seemed that, absorbed in his own thoughts, he took no heed of his steps, for instead of taking the path which led to the sea, he kept along the more familiar one that led to his own cottage on the hill. "This man a convict!" he cried. "He is a hero—a martyr! What a life! Love! Yes, that is love indeed! Oh, James North, how base art thou in the eyes of God beside this despised outcast!" And so muttering, tearing his grey hair, and beating his throbbing temples with clenched hands, he reached his own room, and saw, by the light of the new-born moon, the dressing-bag and candle standing on the table as he had left them. They brought again to his mind the recollection of the task that was before him. He lighted the candle, and, taking the bag in his hand, cast one last look round the chamber which had witnessed his futile struggles against that baser part of himself which had at last triumphed. It was so. Fate had condemned him to sin, and he must now fulfil the doom he might once have averted. Already he fancied he could see the dim speck that was the schooner move slowly away from the prison shore. He must not linger; they would be waiting for him at the jetty. As he turned, the moonbeams—as yet unobscured by the rapidly gathering clouds—flung a silver streak across the sea, and across that streak North saw a boat pass. Was his distracted brain playing him false?—in the stern sat, wrapped in a cloak, the figure of a man! A fierce gust of wind drove the sea-rack over the moon, and the boat disappeared, as though swallowed up by the gathering storm. North staggered back as the truth struck him.

He remembered how he had said, "I will redeem him with my own blood!" Was it possible that a just Heaven had thus decided to allow the man whom a coward had condemned, to escape, and to punish the coward who remained? Oh, this man deserved freedom; he was honest, noble, truthful! How different from himself—a hateful self-lover, an unchaste priest, a drunkard. The looking-glass, in which the saintly face of Meekin was soon to be reflected, stood upon the table, and North, peering into it, with one hand mechanically thrust into the bag, started in insane rage at the pale face and bloodshot eyes he saw there. What a hateful wretch he had become! The last fatal impulse of insanity which seeks relief from its own hideous self came upon him, and his fingers closed convulsively upon the object they had been seeking.

"It is better so," he muttered, addressing, with fixed eyes, his own detested image. "I have examined you long enough. I have read your heart, and written out your secrets! You are but a shell—the shell that holds a corrupted and sinful heart. *He* shall live; *you* shall die!" The rapid motion of his arm overturned the candle, and all was dark.

Rufus Dawes, overpowered by the revelation so suddenly made to him, had remained for a few moments motionless in his cell, expecting to hear the heavy clang of the outer door, which should announce to him the departure of the chaplain. But he did not hear it, and it seemed to him that the air in the cell had grown suddenly cooler. He went to the door, and looked into the narrow corridor, expecting to see the scowling countenance of Gimblett. To his astonishment the door of the prison was wide open, and not a soul in sight. His first thought was of North. Had the story he had told, coupled with the entreaties he had lavished, sufficed to turn him from his purpose?

He looked around. The night was falling suddenly; the wind was mounting; from beyond the bar came the hoarse murmur of an angry sea. If the schooner was to sail that night, she had best get out into deep waters. Where was the chaplain? Pray Heaven the delay had been sufficient, and they had sailed without him. Yet they would be sure to meet. He advanced a few steps nearer, and looked about him. Was it possible that, in his madness, the chaplain had been about to commit some violence which had drawn the trusty Gimblett from his post? "Gr-r-r-r! Ouph!" The trusty Gimblett was lying at his feet—dead drunk!

"Hi! Hiho! Hillo there!" roared somebody from the jetty below. "Be that you, Muster Noarth? We ain't too much tiam, sur!"

From the uncurtained windows of the chaplain's house on the hill beamed the newly-lighted candle. They in the boat did not see it, but it brought to the prisoner a wild hope that made his heart bound. He ran back to the cell, clapped on North's wide-awake, and flinging the cloak hastily about him, came quickly down the steps. If the moon should shine out now!

"Jump in, sir," said unsuspecting Mannix, thinking only of the flogging he had been threatened with. "It'll be a dirty night,

this night! Put this over your knees, sir. Shove her off! Give way!"
And they were afloat. But one glimpse of moonlight fell upon the
slouched hat and cloaked figure, and the boat's crew, engaged in the
dangerous task of navigating the reef in the teeth of the rising gale,
paid no attention to the chaplain.

"By George, lads, we're but just in time!" cried Mannix; and
they laid alongside the schooner, black in blackness. "Up ye go, yer
honour, quick!" The wind had shifted, and was now off the shore.
Blunt, who had begun to repent of his obstinacy, but would not
confess it, thought the next best thing to riding out the gale was to get
out to open sea. "Damn the parson," he had said, in all heartiness;
"we can't wait all night for him. Heave ahead, Mr. Johnson!" And
so the anchor was atrip as Rufus Dawes ran up the side.

The Commandant, already pulling off in his own boat, roared
a coarse farewell. "Good-bye, North! It was touch and go with ye!"
adding, "Curse the fellow, he's too proud to answer!"

The chaplain indeed spoke to no one, and plunging down the
hatchway, made for the stern cabins. "Close shave, your reverence!"
said a respectful somebody, opening a door. It was; but the clergyman
did not say so. He double-locked the door, and hardly realizing the
danger he had escaped, flung himself on the bunk, panting. Over his
head he heard the rapid tramp of feet and the cheery

"Yo hi-oh! and a rumbelow!"

of the men at the capstan. He could smell the sea, and through
the open window of the cabin could distinguish the light in the
chaplain's house on the hill. The trampling ceased, the vessel began
to move slowly—the Commandant's boat appeared below him for
an instant, making her way back—the Lady Franklin had set sail.
With his eyes fixed on the tiny light, he strove to think what was
best to be done. It was hopeless to think that he could maintain
the imposture which, favoured by the darkness and confusion, he
had hitherto successfully attempted. He was certain to be detected
at Hobart Town, even if he could lie concealed during his long and
tedious voyage. That mattered little, however. He had saved Sylvia,
for North had been left behind. Poor North! As the thought of pity

came to him, the light he looked at was suddenly extinguished, and Rufus Dawes, compelled thereto as by an irresistible power, fell upon his knees and prayed for the pardon and happiness of the man who had redeemed him.

*

"That's a gun from the shore," said Partridge the mate, "and they're burning a red light. There's a prisoner escaped. Shall we lie-to?"

"Lie-to!" cried old Blunt, with a tremendous oath. "We'll have suthin' else to do. Look there!"

The sky to the northward was streaked with a belt of livid green colour, above which rose a mighty black cloud, whose shape was ever changing.

CHAPTER XVIII

THE CYCLONE

BLUNT, recognising the meteoric heralds of danger, had begun to regret his obstinacy. He saw that a hurricane was approaching.

Along the south coast of the Australian continent, though the usual westerly winds and gales of the highest latitudes prevail during the greater portion of the year, hurricanes are not infrequent. Gales commence at NW with a low barometer, increasing at W and SW, and gradually veering to the south. True cyclones occur at New Zealand. The log of the *Adelaide* for 29th February, 1870, describes one which travelled at the rate of ten miles an hour, and had all the veerings, calm centre, etc., of a true tropical hurricane. Now a cyclone occurring off the west coast of New Zealand would travel from the New Hebrides, where such storms are hideously frequent, and envelop Norfolk Island, passing directly across the track of vessels coming from South America to Sydney. It was one of these rotatory storms, an escaped tempest of the tropics, which threatened the *Lady Franklin*.

The ominous calm which had brooded over the island during the day had given place to a smart breeze from the north-east, and though the schooner had been sheltered at her anchorage under the lee of the island (the "harbour" looked nearly due south), when once fairly out to sea, Blunt saw it would be impossible to put back in the teeth of the gale. Haply, however, the full fury of the storm would not overtake them till they had gained sea-room.

Rufus Dawes, exhausted with the excitement through which he had passed, had slept for two or three hours, when he was awakened by the motion of the vessel going on the other tack. He rose to his feet, and found himself in complete darkness. Overhead was the noise of trampling feet, and he could distinguish the hoarse tones of Blunt bellowing orders. Astonished at the absence of the moonlight which had so lately silvered the sea, he flung open the cabin window and looked out. As we have said, the cabin allotted to North was one of the two stern cabins, and from it the convict had a full view of the approaching storm.

The sight was one of wild grandeur. The huge, black cloud which hung in the horizon had changed its shape. Instead of a curtain it was an arch. Beneath this vast and magnificent portal shone a dull phosphoric light. Across this livid space pale flashes of sheet-lightning passed noiselessly. Behind it was a dull and threatening murmur, made up of the grumbling of thunder, the falling of rain, and the roar of contending wind and water. The lights of the prison-island had disappeared, so rapid had been the progress of the schooner under the steady breeze, and the ocean stretched around, black and desolate. Gazing upon this gloomy expanse, Rufus Dawes observed a strange phenomenon—lightning appeared to burst upwards from the sullen bosom of the sea. At intervals, the darkly-rolling waves flashed fire, and streaks of flame shot upwards. The wind increased in violence, and the arch of light was fringed with rain. A dull, red glow hung around, like the reflection of a conflagration. Suddenly, a tremendous peal of thunder, accompanied by a terrific downfall of rain, rattled along the sky. The arch of light disappeared, as though some invisible hand had shut the slide of a giant lantern. A great wall of water rushed roaring over the level plain of the sea, and with an indescribable medley of sounds, in which tones of horror, triumph, and torture were blended, the cyclone swooped upon them.

Rufus Dawes comprehended that the elements had come to save or destroy him. In that awful instant the natural powers of the man rose equal to the occasion. In a few hours his fate would be decided, and it was necessary that he should take all precaution. One of two events seemed inevitable; he would either be drowned where he lay, or, should the vessel weather the storm, he would be forced upon the deck, and the desperate imposture he had attempted be discovered. For the moment despair overwhelmed him, and he contemplated the raging sea as though he would cast himself into it, and thus end his troubles. The tones of a woman's voice recalled him to himself. Cautiously unlocking the cabin door, he peered out. The cuddy was lighted by a swinging lamp which revealed Sylvia questioning one of the women concerning the storm. As Rufus Dawes looked, he saw her glance, with an air half of hope, half of fear, towards the door behind which he lurked, and he understood that she expected to see the chaplain. Locking the door, he proceeded hastily to dress himself in North's clothes. He would wait until his aid was absolutely required, and then rush out. In the darkness, Sylvia would mistake him for the priest. He could convey her to the boat—if recourse to the boats should be rendered necessary—and then take the hazard of his fortune. While she was in danger, his place was near by.

From the deck of the vessel the scene was appalling. The clouds had closed in. The arch of light had disappeared, and all was a dull, windy blackness. Gigantic seas seemed to mount in the horizon and sweep towards and upon them. It was as though the ship lay in the vortex of a whirlpool, so high on either side of her were piled the rough pyramidical masses of sea. Mighty gusts arose—claps of wind which seemed like strokes of thunder. A sail loosened from its tackling was torn away and blown out to sea, disappearing like a shred of white paper to leeward. The mercury in the barometer marked 29:50. Blunt, who had been at the rum bottle, swore great oaths that no soul on board would see another sun; and when Partridge rebuked him for blasphemy at such a moment, wept spirituous tears.

The howling of the wind was benumbing; the very fury of sound enfeebled while it terrified. The sailors, horror-stricken, crawled about the deck, clinging to anything they thought most secure. It was impossible to raise the head to look to windward. The eyelids were driven together, and the face stung by the swift and biting spray. Men breathed this atmosphere of salt and wind, and became sickened. Partridge felt that orders were useless—the man at his elbow could not have heard them. The vessel lay almost on her beam ends, with her helm up, stripped even of the sails which had been furled upon the yards. Mortal hands could do nothing for her.

By five o'clock in the morning the gale had reached its height. The heavens showered out rain and lightnings—rain which the wind blew away before it reached the ocean, lightnings which the ravenous and mountainous waves swallowed before they could pierce the gloom. The ship lay over on her side, held there by the madly rushing wind, which seemed to flatten down the sea, cutting off the top of the waves, and breaking them into fine white spray which covered the ocean like a thick cloud, as high as the topmast heads. Each gust seemed unsurpassable in intensity, but was succeeded, after a pause, that was not a lull but a gasp, by one of more frantic violence. The barometer stood at 27:82. The ship was a mere labouring, crazy wreck, that might sink at any moment. At half-past three o'clock the barometer had fallen to 27:62. Save when lighted by occasional flashes of sheet-lightning, which showed to the cowed wretches their awe-stricken faces, this tragedy of the elements was performed in a darkness which was almost palpable.

Suddenly the mercury rose to 29:90, and, with one awful shriek, the wind dropped to a calm. The *Lady Franklin* had reached the centre of the cyclone. Partridge, glancing to where the great body of drunken Blunt rolled helplessly lashed to the wheel, felt a strange selfish joy thrill him. If the ship survived the drunken captain would be dismissed, and he, Partridge, the gallant, would reign in his stead. The schooner, no longer steadied by the wind, was at the mercy of every sea. Volumes of water poured over her. Presently she heeled over, for, with a triumphant scream, the wind leapt on to her from a fresh quarter. Following its usual course, the storm returned upon its track. The hurricane was about to repeat itself from the north-west.

The sea, pouring down through the burst hatchway, tore the door of the cuddy from its hinges. Sylvia found herself surrounded by a wildly-surging torrent which threatened to overwhelm her. She shrieked aloud for aid, but her voice was inaudible even to herself. Clinging to the mast which penetrated the little cuddy, she fixed her eyes upon the door behind which she imagined North was, and whispered a last prayer for succour. The door opened, and from out the cabin came a figure clad in black. She looked up, and the light of the expiring lamp showed her a face that was not that of the man she hoped to see. Then a pair of dark eyes beaming ineffable love and pity were bent upon her, and a pair of dripping arms held her above the brine as she had once been held in the misty mysterious days that were gone.

In the terror of that moment the cloud which had so long oppressed her brain passed from it. The action of the strange man before her completed and explained the action of the convict chained to the Port Arthur coal-wagons, of the convict kneeling in the Norfolk Island torture-chamber. She remembered the terrible experience of Macquarie Harbour. She recalled the evening of the boat-building, when, swung into the air by stalwart arms, she had promised the rescuing prisoner to plead for him with her kindred. Regaining her memory thus, all the agony and shame of the man's long life of misery became at once apparent to her. She understood how her husband had deceived her, and with what base injustice and falsehood he had bought her young love. No question as to how this doubly-condemned prisoner had escaped from the hideous isle of punishment she had quitted occurred to her. She asked not—even in her thoughts—how it had been given to him to supplant the chaplain in his place on board the vessel. She only considered, in her sudden awakening, the story of his wrongs, remembered only his marvellous fortitude and love, knew only, in this last instant of her pure, ill-fated life, that as he had saved her once from starvation and death, so had he come again to save her from sin and from despair. Whoever has known a deadly peril will remember how swiftly thought then travelled back through scenes clean forgotten, and will understand how Sylvia's retrospective vision merged the past into the actual before her, how the shock of recovered memory subsided in the grateful utterance of other days—"Good Mr. Dawes!"

The eyes of the man and woman met in one long, wild gaze. Sylvia stretched out her white hands and smiled, and Richard Devine understood in his turn the story of the young girl's joyless life, and knew how she had been sacrificed.

In the great crisis of our life, when, brought face to face with annihilation, we are suspended gasping over the great emptiness of death, we become conscious that the Self which we think we knew so well has strange and unthought-of capacities. To describe a tempest of the elements is not easy, but to describe a tempest of the soul is impossible. Amid the fury of such a tempest, a thousand memories, each bearing in its breast the corpse of some dead deed whose influence haunts us yet, are driven like feathers before the blast, as unsubstantial and as unregarded. The mists which shroud our self—knowledge become transparent, and we are smitten with sudden lightning-like comprehension of our own misused power over our fate.

This much we feel and know, but who can coldly describe the hurricane which thus o'erwhelms him? As well ask the drowned mariner to tell of the marvels of mid-sea when the great deeps swallowed him and the darkness of death encompassed him round about. These two human beings felt that they had done with life. Together thus, alone in the very midst and presence of death, the distinctions of the world they were about to leave disappeared. Then vision grew clear. They felt as beings whose bodies had already perished, and as they clasped hands their freed souls, recognizing each the loveliness of the other, rushed tremblingly together.

Borne before the returning whirlwind, an immense wave, which glimmered in the darkness, spouted up and towered above the wreck. The wretches who yet clung to the deck looked shuddering up into the bellying greenness, and knew that the end was come.

EPILOGUE

AT day-dawn the morning after the storm, the rays of the rising sun fell upon an object which floated on the surface of the water not far from where the schooner had foundered.

This object was a portion of the mainmast head of the *Lady Franklin*, and entangled in the rigging were two corpses—a man and a woman. The arms of the man were clasped round the body of the woman, and her head lay on his breast. The Prison Island appeared but as a long low line on the distant horizon. The tempest was over. As the sun rose higher the air grew balmy, the ocean placid; and, golden in the rays of the new risen morning, the wreck and its burden drifted out to sea.

APPENDIX

BOOK I: CHAPTERS I, IV, V, VII

Report of the Commission of Inquiry into the state of the colony of New South Wales. Printed by order of the House of Commons, 1822.

"Two Voyages to New South Wales and Van Diemen's Land", by Thomas Reid (*Surgeon on board the* Neptune *and* Morley *transport ships*), Member of the Royal College of Surgeons in London, and Surgeon in the Royal Navy. London: Longman and Co., 1822.

"Narrative of a Visit to the Australian Colonies", by James Backhouse. London: Hamilton, Adams and Co., 1843.

Report of a Select Committee on Transportation. Printed by order of the House of Commons, 1838. (Evidence of Colonel Henry Breton.— Q.2,431–2,436.)

BOOK II: CHAPTERS I, II, III

Report of a Select Committee (*ut supra*), 1838. Evidence of John Barnes, Esq., pp.37–49. Also Appendix to above Report, I., No. 56, B.

"Tasmanian Journal of Natural Science", etc., vol. ii. *Account of Macquarie Harbour*, by T. G. Lempriere, Esq., A.D.C.G., pp.17, 107, 200. Tasmania: Henry Dowling. London: John Murray, 1846.

"Van Diemen's Land Anniversary and Hobart Town Almanac, 1831." *Account of Macquarie Harbour*, by James Ross, p. 262. Hobart Town: James Ross, 1832.

"Meliora", April, 1861—"Our Convict System": case of Charles Anderson, chained to a rock for two years in irons. See also "Our Convicts", p. 233, vol. i., Mary Carpenter. Longmans, 1864.

"Backhouse's Narrative" (*ut supra*), chapters iii, iv.

Files of *Hobart Town Courier*, 1827–8, more especially October 23 and December 7, 1827, and February 2, 1828.

CHAPTERS IV, VIII

Report of a Select Committee (*ut supra*), 1838, pp.353, 354, 355.

"Tasmanian Journal" (*ut supra*), vol. i.: *Account of Macquarie Harbour*, by T. G. Lempriere, Esq. (*ut supra*). *The seizure of the Cypress* (*sic.*), pp.366–7. *Escape of Morgan and Popjoy*, p. 369. *The seizure of the Frederick*, pp.371–375.

"Van Diemen's Land Annual", 1838: *Narrative of the Sufferings and Adventures of certain of Ten Convicts*, etc., pp. 1–11. Hobart Town: James Ross, 1838.

"Old Tales of a Young Country", by Marcus Clarke: *The Last of Macquarie Harbour*, pp.141–146. *The Seizure of the Cyprus*, pp.133–140. Melbourne: George Robertson, 1871.

BOOK III: CHAPTER II

Transportation: Copy of a communication upon the subject of Transportation addressed to Earl Grey by the Lord Bishop of Tasmania. Reprinted for private distribution to the heads of families only. Launceston: Henry Dowling, 1848.

Report of a Select Committee (*ut supra*), 1837. Evidence of Ernest Augustus Slade, Esq.—Q.870. *Ibidem*, 1838: Evidence of James Mudie, Esq.—Q.804–813.

CHAPTER IX

Backhouse's Narrative (*ut supra*): Appendix, lxxvi.

CHAPTER X

"Van Diemen's Land Annual", 1838 (*ut supra*), pp.12–33. *Old Tales*, etc, (*ut supra*), *The Last of Macquarie Harbour*, pp.147–156.

CHAPTER XV

Report of a Select Committee (*ut supra*), 1838: Evidence of E. A. Slade, Esq.—Q.1882–1892. *Ibidem*: Appendix No. ii., E.

CHAPTER XX

Report of a Select Committee (*ut supra*), 1837: Evidence of John Russell, Esq., Assist.-Surgeon 63rd Regiment.—Q.426–615. *Ibidem*: Evidence of Colonel Geo. Arthur—Q.4,510, 4,548.

"The Adventures of Martin Cash, the Bushranger." Hobart Town: J. L. Burke, 1870. pp.64–70.

"Van Dieman's Land Annual" (*ut supra*), 1829: Visit to Port Arthur. *Account of the Devil's Blow-Hole.*

CHAPTER XXVII

Report of a Select Committee (*ut supra*), 1832, Appendix I., No. 56 C. and D. Deposition of Alexander Pierce and official statements of trial and execution of Pierce and Cox for murder and cannibalism.

"The Bushrangers", by James Bonwick, Esq. Article—"Port Arthur."

BOOK IV: CHAPTERS III, IV

Sessional Papers printed by order of the House of Lords, 1847. Enclosure to No. XI. Extract of a paper by the Rev. T. B. Naylor. Enclosure 3 in No. XIV. Copy of Report (*dated Hobart Town, 20th June, 1846*) from Robert Pringle Stewart, Esq.: (*officer appointed by the Lieut.-Governor of Van Dieman's Land, to inspect the penal settlement of Norfolk Island*) to the Comptroller-General.

House of Lords Report of a Commission on the execution of Criminal Law, 1847, Evidence of the Lord Bishop of Tasmania—Q.4,795–4,904 and 5,085–5,130.

Despatch of His Excellency Sir William Denison to Secretary of State, 10th July, 1847.

Report of a Select Committee (*ut supra*), 1838: Evidence of the Very Rev. Wm. Ullathorne, D.D.—Q.150–318.

Report of House of Lords (*ut supra*), 1847: Evidence of Albert Charles Stonor, Esq., Crown Solicitor of New South Wales—Q.5,174–5,197. Also evidence of Rev. Wm. Wilson, D.D.—Q.5,545–5,568.

Correspondence relating to the dismissal of the Rev. T. Rogers from his chaplaincy at Norfolk Island; for private circulation. Launceston: Henry Dowling, 1846.

"Backhouse's Voyages" (*ut supra*).

CHAPTERS VII, VIII, IX, XII

Adventures of Martin Cash (*ut supra*), pp.133–141; Cases of George Armstrong, "Pine Tree Jack", and Alexander Campbell.

Punishment of the "gag" and "bridle". Correspondence relating to the Rev. T. Rogers (*ut supra*), pp.41–43.

Report of a Select Committee (*ut supra*), 1838: Evidence of the Very Rev. Wm. Ullathorne, D. D.—Q.267:—"As I mentioned the names of those men who were to die, they one after another, as their names were pronounced, dropped on their knees and thanked God that they were to be delivered from that horrible place, whilst the others remained standing mute, weeping. It was the most horrible scene I have ever witnessed."

Ibidem: Evidence of Colonel George Arthur.—Q.4,548.

Ibidem: Evidence of Sir Francis Forbes.—Q.1,119.

Ibidem: Q.1,335–1,343:—"...Two or three men murdered their fellow-prisoners, with the certainty of being detected and executed, apparently without malice and with very little excitement, stating that they knew that they should be hanged, but it was better than being where they were."

NOTES

I. p.42: crow—the "look-out man" of a burglar's gang.

II. p.133: ovalled—"to oval" is a term in use among convicts, and means to so bend the round ring of the ankle fetter that the heel can be drawn up through it.

III. p.349: beshdellamare—Bêche-de-la-mer.

Text Classics

textclassics.com.au